I0608914

THE SYNNER

GODFALL

BOOK THREE OF THE SYNNER SAGA

NOOBURAI

PUBLISHED BY DRAFT2DIGITAL

ALSO BY NOOBURAI

Creating *The Synner* universe, writing it out, editing, and self-publishing it for the world to see was once a distant dream, but know that it's here, I know that I wouldn't have made it here without a few people:

First and foremost: Mom. At the time of writing this, it's been *three and a half* years since you left the Realm, and while I know that death is not the end of all things, I can only hope to hold my head up high, knowing I've done you proud.

Second: My siblings. If it weren't for their support, encouragement, and presence during my childhood, I don't think I would have been able to accurately portray a sense of *family* that these characters have.

So, thanks for that, assholes. I love you all.

Third: Everyone else who's either read it, supported it, commented, or given their honest feedback. This kind of stuff has certainly helped me grow as an author, and we all know that a good author doesn't evolve or grow when placed inside of a bubble. Thank you.

Finally: The haters. I feed off your tears, jealousy, and whatever else you decide to throw at me, and will continue to stand by what I've been saying from the start:

Git gud... *fuckers.*

PREFACE

The Synner Saga initially began as a passion project born from my deep love for immersive storytelling. With *heavy* inspiration from series such as *The Witcher, Lord of the Rings, The Beginning After the End*, and *The Name of the Wind*, it grew, evolved, and over time, became a world that's very near and dear to my heart.

With that said, I must note that this *is* the second edition of this book. When I first published it in 2024, I found that there were a lot of mistakes and formatting errors I'd made, and while I apologize for those, they've taught me valuable lessons about producing content and having an increasingly scrutinous eye for detail.

Keep in mind that there are a total of *six books* in this series that are *planned*. That doesn't mean that there isn't room for one or two more, but I'll let you do what you will with that information.

I hope you enjoy the world I've built here, and look forward to hearing from anyone who reads it.

Sincerely,

Nooburai

DISCLAIMER

Many of the topics, verbal descriptions, and uses of language are NOT appropriate for children. If you have to ask whether your child should read this, the answer is *no*. In all honesty, if you've made it this far in the series, I shouldn't even have to tell you that, but here I am, beating a dead horse for the sake of those who haven't gotten that through their heads yet.

Seriously, do NOT let your children read this, unless you're one of those parents who doesn't give the slightest turtle shit. Just saying. That said, any and all characters are merely created to serve a purpose, and are not intended to depict my personal views or feelings toward anything that could be (somehow, probably through *extreme* extrapolation) connected to the real world. Again, this is a *fantasy series,* meaning any similarities to real people, living or otherwise, is purely coincidental.

CONTENTS

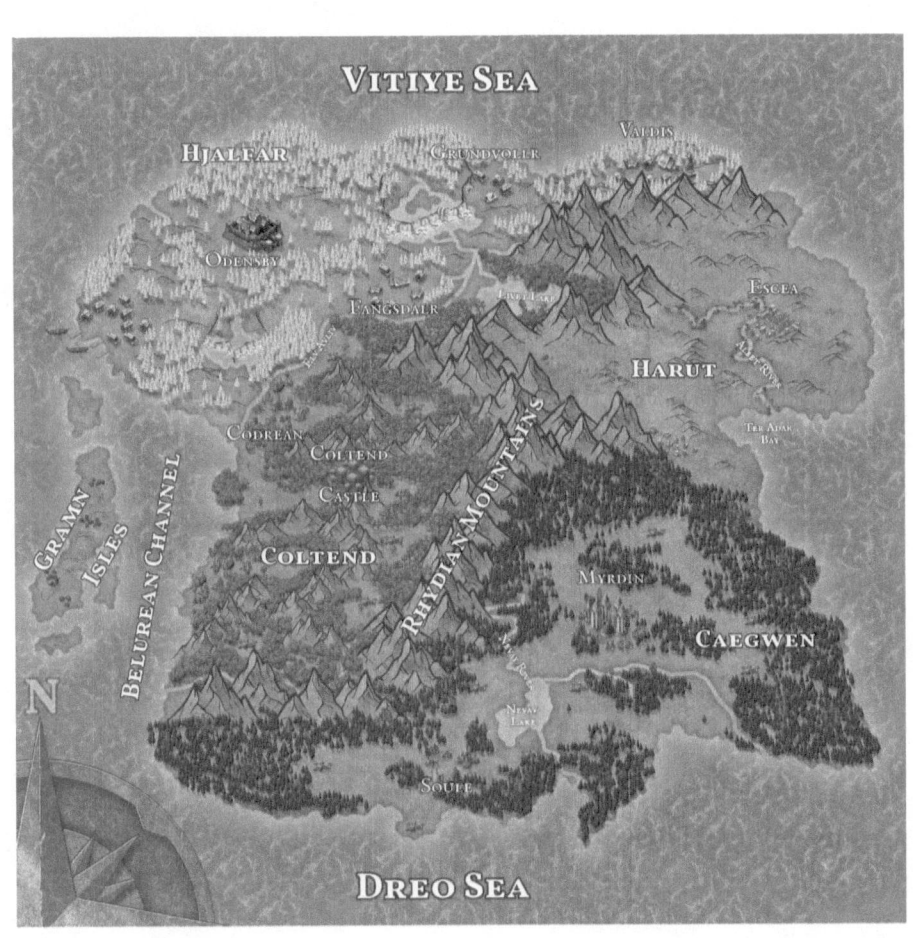

PROLOGUE
LEFT BEHIND

I heard my mother's voice grow increasingly distant, her features much less defined now than a moment ago. She walked through the main entrance to our house as my eyes began to blur and my heart began to pound.

"Where are you going? Why do you have to leave?" I shouted. Tears streamed down my face and snot fled from my nostrils as I called out after her. I couldn't have been much older than five when I saw my mother for the last time; her steel-colored hair was stuck close to her body from the rain as she walked out into the twilight.

There was no warning, no sign of anything being wrong, or of anyone at fault. I wept, but I didn't know for how long. It felt like an eternity, though, as I didn't know what would happen to me. The only thing I *knew* was that my life was about to change forever.

An older man with a scar on the left side of his face and silver hair walked in the door, but I didn't recognize him at all. For a few moments, he argued with my father, who was a plump piece of shit, though all I can recall is their stuttering silhouettes bouncing off the walls just as angrily as their tones of voice.

"That *monster* of a mother of his is finally leaving, and you think *you're* going to take care of him better than *I* will?" my father said, his jowls shaking just as much as the light bouncing off the wall.

"Absolutely. You've already sent his older brother to me out of spite for *her*, and yet you have the gall to believe that I'm going to believe you will take care of this child?" the scarred man asked with a twisted and angry face, but that wasn't what I was focused on.

As he glanced at me, his eyes glowed like twin suns against the dark of the room that the fireplace's light couldn't touch.

"W-well, yes," my father said, his voice beginning to tremble as the scarred man growled before speaking. "You've done enough already. You've gone against her will and done the unthinkable, and yet you expected her to forgive you for it?" the scarred man asked, his anger was evident and almost tangible in the thickened air.

I could feel a strange *pressure* emanating from him, like the world was itching to bend to his will. I wiped the tears from my eyes, trying to make sure it wasn't just the light of the fire being blurred in my vision, but it wasn't.

What is that glowing stuff? Is that fire? I thought, trying to understand what I was seeing.

Oh, how wrong I was.

The scarred man looked at me. He couldn't have been much older than my father, or at least, he didn't *look* like he was. There was, however, something with the way he carried himself that told me he was strong.

Extremely strong.

He was in the middle of saying something I either couldn't understand or chose to ignore; I don't remember which. I reached my hand out, and these odd hair-like strands of his aura that surrounded him came towards me. I felt it gathering in my palm and around my hand like a warmed glove.

He stopped mid-sentence and stared at me more intently. What-ever it was I was doing had certainly drawn his attention. I remember laughing as the warm cloud of golden... *whatever it was* began to move fluidly around my arm and chest.

Suddenly, it halted all movement, and a sharp pain riddled my body that started in my chest. I couldn't figure out what in the realms had just happened, but whatever it was, my father *clearly* took some delight in seeing me suffer.

I blinked and immediately saw a smoky arm materialize in front of me. It grabbed my father by the neck and pinned him against the wall, making sure his feet were off the ground.

"What the *fuck* did you do to him?" the scarred man growled through clenched teeth as spittle flecked my father's face. "I did the only reasonable thing *to do* to him," my father said through his tight-ened throat. He began to chuckle, though the sound wasn't clear and cheerful. Instead, it was more like a wet gurgling, as the large, smoky claw tightened even further.

With a heavy sigh, he tossed my father aside, slamming him into the wall. The scarred man walked over to me, and after having seen that display of power, I could only wonder what would come for me next.

"Hello there. You're Thoma, right?" he asked in a much warmer voice than he had used when he first arrived, wrinkling the scar on his face as he smiled. I could only nod out of fear of saying something that might anger him. "Gods above, he's done a real number on you, hasn't he?" he glanced over his shoulder to make sure my father was still unconscious.

"Yes," I said, the only words I could muster in my confusion. "*Yes* to *what*, exactly?" he asked, keeping the same, warm tone as if he'd somehow forgotten I was only a small child. "I-I'm Thoma," I said bashfully. He chuckled lightly and tousled my hair. "Yes. Of course, you are. So, can you do me a favor, young man?" he squinted his eyes as if he was going to challenge me somehow, or doubted my abilities to do whatever he was going to ask.

I nodded my head.

Just as I did, my father groaned in an apparent regaining of consciousness. The scarred man sent another fist of what I could only describe as hardened smoke, smashing my father's face into the ground without him even bothering to look, keeping the same, warm smile on his face.

"Like I was saying, I need you to do me a favor, Thoma," the scarred man said. He paused, almost as if he was choosing his words carefully, and I thought I almost saw his smile fade for a moment, but he recovered before any significant change was made. "I need you to grab some of your things and grab your best cloak," he said.

"But why do I have to go? Are we going after my mother?" I asked, but the man shook his head. "I'm sorry, but we can't go after her now. Things are... *complicated*, and she's going somewhere we can't follow right now. I'm sorry," he said dejectedly.

I sniffed back some snot as the tears began to well in my eyes again as his words set in.

The man seemed unsure of what to do, so he conjured a swirling sphere of light in front of me. It looked a lot like the fire dying down behind me, only far more controlled and compacted into a sphere not much larger than an apple.

"Do you know what this is?" he asked. "N-no. Is that like the shining stuff that I was playing with earlier?" I asked, almost reaching for it. "This... *stuff* is called *mana*," he said softly. He began to mold it into a few different but easily recognizable shapes.

"All things have mana in them, Thoma; you, me, your mother. Some of us even learn to control it with special abilities we can train and develop," he said, turning the sphere into an arrow-like shape which he quickly sent barrelling through the room.

It turned sharply and avoided all kinds of objects in the room, then came to a quick stop in his hand, where it turned back into a sphere. "*Ooh!* That was amazing! Can you teach me to do that?" I asked, rubbing my eyes to see more clearly, if he had decided to do more with it.

"I can, but remember that favor I asked you to do for me earlier?" he said, dispelling the mana and putting a hand on my shoulder. I nodded my head quickly. "Good. Grab your things. I'll deal with your father in the meantime," he said.

I raced upstairs and grabbed the items he asked for, failing to notice the note left on my pillow, and ran back downstairs. When I came down, I saw that my father was loosely tied to a chair. Not so tight that he couldn't have escaped on his own, though it was more to hold him upright than anything else. The scarred man had sat him down on a chair near a small table with an open bottle of wine on top of it.

"Ready to go?" he asked me from over his shoulder. "I'm ready," I said, still unsure what to call him or even who he was. He merely grunted a response and jabbed something into my father's leg. I could hear the drops of blood hitting the ground from where I stood. As the sound reached my ears, I noticed a letter attached to the cheese knife my father always used, which was now embedded in his upper thigh.

"Sorry about that," the man said softly, turning my head away. "Your mother made me promise I would do what I can to protect you, and this is my version of it," he continued. "Why couldn't she do it herself?" I asked, accidentally forcing him to struggle for words. "That's a difficult question that I can't answer right now, Thoma," he replied, looking down at the floor. "*Oh*... okay," I said, feeling my facial features slump slightly.

"Come on. We need to get going. I know it's dark and rainy outside, but we need to leave tonight," he said, ushering me out the door. Just before we stepped outside, he bent down and ensured that the small notch around the neck of my cloak was clasped correctly, then patted me twice on the shoulders.

He grabbed an iron cage with small panes of glass embedded into it from just outside the door. He opened one of the glass panels that had a small knob on it, and pushed a sphere of pure mana inside, and closed the door. The cage sealed shut with a sheen of blue, translucent mana, allowing the light to shine through cleanly.

"Where are we going?" I finally asked. I'd trusted the man until now, but that was more out of survival instincts than anything else. I didn't know much about him, but something felt familiar about him that I couldn't quite place. He helped me onto his horse, then mounted the beast behind me, making sure I was secure in the saddle before kicking his heels into the horse's sides.

"We're going to my home in the North-Western corner of Coltend," he replied, having to use a bit more of his voice since the rain had gotten worse. We rode silently for a few minutes while I tried to piece together everything that happened until this point. My chest was hurting a little bit, but I couldn't tell if that was from all the crying I'd done, or something else entirely.

"What's your name?" I finally asked. I'd spent the better part of an hour trying to figure out what it might be, but when nothing of the conversation that I recalled held the information I was looking for, I decided I *had* to ask that question myself. In response, the man chuckled and patted my shoulder again.

"You can call me *The Master of Codrean*," he said warmly.

CHAPTER I
THOMA FAYREN

Cold, piercing rain fell from the sky.

It was late in the afternoon, and I stood at the entrance to the stables of Codrean waiting for my older brother, Bernar, who had promised me a gift on the day I turned eighteen. After about an hour of waiting and shivering, he finally showed up. I felt a sense of relief as I watched him lead a large dark figure through the thick mud and horse shit that lined the path to the stables.

Bernar and I have an age difference of about five years, give or take a few months, but he is much stronger and taller than I am. Granted black hair like a raven's feathers, golden glowing eyes, and a generally athletic build, he also wore a pendant around his neck which he often kept tucked away.

The black leather jerkin, with hose and boots to match, was shrouded by a rain repellent cloak. The heavy downpour made it a little tricky to see whatever it was he had behind him, but as he approached, it became evident that it was, in fact, a giant horse.

I would be lying if I said I didn't immediately become ecstatic with the gift.

"Gods above and below, this thing is massive," I said, not bothering to hide the excitement in my voice. "Yes, he is! I figured it would probably be a good gift for your horse-caster certification today," he shrugged. "By the way, what kind of *psychotic turd* decides to do something like this on their birthday, huh?" he raised an eyebrow.

His voice sounded a lot like mine, if not a little higher in pitch, making it somewhat challenging to tell apart by just hearing our voices.

"Haha, well, about that..." I trailed off as I rubbed the back of my neck beneath my hood. "He cost me three months' worth of my salary, but I'm glad you like it," he patted the horse's neck, cutting me off slightly. "Go on then; get him saddled and get ready for your exam," he gestured dismissively.

I did as instructed and threw the saddle over its back. I did what I could for the leather bindings, but since my father had used this saddle for a long time before passing it down to Bernar, the holes and buckles were well worn and difficult to tighten.

Seeing as I was a little too short to get my foot in the stirrup, Bernar dragged a nearby shodding stool my way. I crawled up onto the horse's back with difficulty, as the size of the damned creature was much larger than the one I was previously used to.

This, in turn, also meant I struggled to get my right foot to the other side.

Bernar cackled while watching me fumble-fuck my way about the giant quadriped; infinite mocking was his prerogative as the older brother, after all. "I should have considered this as a possibility. It's true that you're a good sword-caster, but if Mom had seen you struggle like this, there is *no way* she would have let you try to become a horse-caster," he said between laughs.

I felt my mouth grimace as I squinted my green eyes. "*Oh*, just lay it on thicker, you derisive thundercunt. It's my first time trying to mount a horse this large. My old horse was much shorter than this one, and that's not even mentioning the fact that you put the stirrups a little too high," I replied with a sardonic sneer.

Bernar shook his head, still chuckling a little to himself. "That's because our *rotund* father had used this saddle for decades until it was passed down to me. I'm not sure how much you remember about him, but he cared *almost* as much for this saddle as his *own sons*," he replied with a tongue click. "Sounds about right," I chuckled, recalling the night I was brought to Codrean.

"After having kept it in storage for so long, I had forgotten about how sad a state it was in," he continued with a sigh. "I meant to get it repaired before giving you the horse, but I had already drained a lot of my savings," he shrugged. "It's still a mighty horse. I don't know how to repay you for it," I said with as much gratitude as possible.

"You can repay me by not fucking your exam up and making father, the shit nugget that he is, eat his words," Bernar snorted. "If worse goes to shit, at least you'll have a horse worthy of the gods themselves. Just, *uh*, make sure your spell doesn't backfire, okay? That would suck," he added with a wry grin. "Sure, sure," I waved dismissively.

A spell was the simplest form of magic we, the Synners, used primarily to augment our combat abilities. Sure, some druids and mages solely relied on their mana manipulation skills, but *we* were monster slayers to our cores.

However, unlike mages or druids, we gained improved mana-based abilities by consuming a plant known as Gwynnleaf. While this wasn't the only reason we could control mana, it certainly aided the process. We'd earned our moniker of *Synner* due to the Church of

Mideia branding us such, as we, according to *their cult-like views*, thought we opposed the natural order between gods and men.

It was laughable at best.

"And what if I do pass this certification? Do you think the Master will finally train me to become an all-caster?" I asked, openly displaying my hopes and dreams for the future. Bernar sat on the question briefly, placing a soaked glove on his chin.

"Well, you're still missing your spear and bow-casting certifications, and that's not to mention reaching the next stages of mana manipulation, so I can't say for sure," he lifted a finger for each point. "But, if he accepts you for all-caster training, I would suggest you dig deep and dedicate yourself to succeed," he tilted his head seriously.

"All-casters are rare enough as it is, and we Synners are likely to become a dying breed. There are even some in other nations that have become outcasts, living like nomads or bandits for hire because of their skills," he began, spreading his arms. "But why? What the hell could they possibly have done to get *that* title?" I raised an eyebrow.

This wasn't the first I'd heard of these *outcasts*, after all. There were several rumors among the other New Bloods and Juniors, like me, of Synners turning their backs and betraying their kinsmen over conflicting ideals or other such reasons. According to them, those rumors had reached the far corners of the Continent.

"Beats the *fuck* out of me, little brother," Bernar shrugged. "However, the Master told me that *we must always do our best to avoid following in their footsteps, because when all is said and done, we were created for ridding the world of evil; not adding to it*," he continued, giving his best impression of the Master.

I chuckled at the accuracy of his imitation, but I also knew the depth of what my brother meant from his history lessons over the years.

"In any case, let's begin," Bernar waved his hand. I nodded and stuck my heels into the horse's side. Hoof-fall like rolling thunder whipped up a splash of mud, and I could feel the strands of my hair flowing in the wind.

I held onto the reins as tight as I could, focusing on breathing in rhythm with the horse's gallop and relaxing my mind to focus on the challenge ahead.

Casting from a solid stance is relatively simple, but this is a whole new devil I'll have to manage, I thought.

I was closing the distance to the target quickly, and knew I had to begin gathering mana. The enchanted ring, which all junior Synners wore, served as a magical ward that helped to stave off, but not entirely block, the heat produced by the condensed mana just before casting a spell. I focused on the one I had to produce, and reviewed the training I'd had since I was only five years old.

First decide, transfer, then conduct, and finally, release! Never mix the order up or the spell won't work, the Master's words echoed in my head.

For whatever gods-forsaken reason, I decided it would be fun to try to impress my brother with a bolt of lightning that could be cast from my fingertips. The target was well within striking range for the spell's effect, and I took a deep breath before the channeling process.

This process required anyone who wished to use a spell to draw mana from the Ethereal; The invisible realm surrounded all things, both living and inanimate, which, to *my knowledge,* was the origin of mana itself. I began to focus intensely, while still trying to maintain my posture in the saddle.

I forcefully closed my eyes for an instant, using all of my willpower to divide my attention, sending my consciousness into the other realm. My eyes reopened as the familiar feeling of my dilating pupils covered the olive green irises and the whites of my eyes, *as my consciousness went from the Between into the immaterial world.*

The Ethereal was a realm of pure and plentiful power where bright, colorful shafts of light circled a glowing sphere of pure power in the sky. Stars of all sizes wheeled overhead and meshed with the shafts, releasing a blue and yellow flare whenever they merged.

I looked around and observed the ongoings above me as I did every time I drew mana from the realm. I never had any need to rush this process, as time was not something the realm took into consideration, the only one I knew of *to have such a characteristic.*

It was filled with life forms that roamed the vast forest of magnificent trees. A stone's throw away, the shimmering lake glistened and reflected the light produced from the sphere above it.

The river that flowed beside me constantly changed its shape and color, according to the stars that merged with the tendrils of power. I outstretched my right hand towards the sphere, spreading my fingers as wide as possible. The mana responded to my call and began to flow in tendrils towards my hand, warming the air around it wherever it went.

They wrapped around my fingers, and my connection to them began harnessing and transforming them into a nebula of raw mana. As I drew more from the sphere, it encased my body like a flowing, gaseous cocoon, which began to show itself in the Between.

Exerting my will on the mana in my mind, I quickly absorbed it into my body and mind, where it could be molded into the spells I'd already learned. I then condensed what I had gathered into my hand to cast the spell out in front of me.

The mana cloud surrounding my body suddenly condensed in the palm of my right hand, moving with the fluidity of a river as it rushed toward it. As it moved, it warmed what little armor I was wearing, making the hairs on my arm stand on end as it went.

The warmth gathered into an opaque indigo sphere that glowed brightly in the palm of my hand. The heat it generated grew rapidly and began seeping through the minor ward from the ring.

Time to cast. Otherwise, my ward will fail, and my hand will melt from the heat, I winced, feeling the heat begin to seep through my meager protection measures.

I found my target and whirled my arm the same way I'd practiced so often in the late-night hours. With the casting hand, I whirled my arm in a clockwise circle, followed by a pull-push motion, making quick work of the spell's release. The heat that threatened to burn through the ward went along with it. The best way I can describe it would be like quickly removing my hand from a campfire.

All of this happened in a fraction of a second as the bolt of indigo lightning shot out from the fingertips of my glove.

The mana-bolt, now traveling through the air, vaporized the raindrops near it as it flashed. The difference in temperature from the bolt and the air around it was so great that the resulting *boom kicked* up large clumps of mud as it careened towards the target.

Charred bits of the exploding target flew everywhere as it struck, with more than a few passing by a little too closely for comfort.

The unfortunate chicken pecking at the ground behind the target was, unsurprisingly, turned into little more than a pink feathery mist.

Bernar's jaw dropped as he looked on in astonishment. "*Haha*! I didn't think you had *that* in you, sneaky *little shit*," he shouted. I looked over my shoulder as I turned the horse. "Didn't you have some kind of wager with Roburn on whether I was going to fuck it up?" I scoffed with no small hint of sarcasm.

"N-no, why would I have that?" he chuckled nervously. "I was actually *hoping* you would be able to do it, though, as for the others..." he trailed off with a shrug.

Yeah, he definitely *had a bet with Roburn,* I shook my head.

I rode to my brother's side and dismounted with more grace than I'd had when I tried to mount the large horse. Bernar embraced me firmly and patted me on the back with matching force.

"Finest use of the *Kyr* spell I've seen in a while," he smiled brightly. "Well executed, but dangerous," his tone shifted, prompting me to raise an eyebrow. "Horses get spooked easily, and most horse-casters recommend using *quieter* spells while riding. Luckily for *you*, this one's well-trained to handle *surprises* like that," he continued.

"I see," I muttered pensively. "I just hope the Master will be surprised once he hears about this," I shrugged. "I don't doubt it, little brother," he smiled, tousling my hair. "I know *I* wasn't pulling these stunts at your age. Hell, he might even train you to be the best all-caster of *all of us*," he grinned. My eyes widened in surprise when I heard him say that. "You really think so?" I asked, hardly containing my excitement.

"Why wouldn't I? After all, he does sense that you have much more power than most other boys here," he shrugged nonchalantly.

"I really hope you're not just saying that to make me happy, brother. You know damn well I would do my best to be the best he's ever seen," I said with ironically little self-confidence.

My brother smiled and put a gloved hand atop my shoulder, tilting his head slightly and looking at me from beneath his dark eyebrows. "I'm sure you will be, and I'll help you in that endeavor wherever I can," he said warmly. "Does that mean you'll let me kick your ass during training?" I asked, making him laugh heartily.

"You're more than welcome to try, but I guarantee you won't land a blow if you don't pack on some muscle and learn a few new tricks. Your arrogance far outweighs your flagpole build as it is," he lightly punched my arm. "I might not have your strength, but I'm at least twice as fast as you," I grinned as I nursed my arm.

"Sure, sure," he waved his hand dismissively. "But what is speed when your legs are sore, arms are tired, breathing heavy, and all that after only 10 minutes of having it out with one of those damned-ugly creatures outside?" he asked, the smile slightly fading from his face.

"No, *shit bird*. You'll need both to survive out there. Being good with mana will only get you so far," Bernar said with a seriousness that I had never seen in him until that point.

I began to think about the reality of the world outside the fortress walls, which I had yet to explore.

He never did explain why I haven't been allowed to go on expeditions yet, has he? I thought, trying to remember any conversation we'd ever had about the topic.

"But, enough about that for now. We should head back to the dorms and celebrate your accomplishment today," Bernar flicked the back of his hand on my chest. "It's colder than a witch's tit out here, and pissing more than the sea goddess herself can muster," he grinned. "Yeah, and I've been standing out here waiting for you since lunchtime," I added, prompting him to roll his eyes at my sarcasm.

"We still have some time before supper, so we should change our clothes before the Master rips us *both* a new one," he continued. "I guess you're right," I agreed reluctantly because I loved the rain and cold. "I'm always right, *fuck-ass*," Bernar flicked me again.

"Not *always*..." I said, grinning slyly. "If you're going to mention that incident with the Dawn Nymph..." he trailed off, his arm rearing to punch my shoulder again. "I didn't say anything," I raised my hands placatingly. When we both started chuckling, I shook my head in disbelief as I recalled the story he'd told me. "Alright, let's get back inside. I've had enough rain for one day," he glanced upward.

I brought my new horse into the stall and removed the saddle. Thankfully, the treated leather didn't absorb much water, but I still struggled under its weight.

It truly is a beautiful horse. I wonder what I should call it, I thought as I closed the gate behind me, patting its neck before I left.

"I suppose we could try this again, or perhaps spar with each other tomorrow?" I asked expectantly. Bernar shrugged and displayed a one-sided smile "I suppose we could do *some* sparring tomorrow, but we'll have to deal with whatever the Master has planned first. I hear he wants to give us his version of a surprise test tomorrow," he replied.

I held a pensive expression for a few seconds, but quickly dismissed any ideas that came to mind. "You don't happen to know what that might be, do you?" I raised an eyebrow, hoping to get more information from him.

"I do, actually, but I'm not allowed to talk about anything coming from the Master that he doesn't clearly state himself," he groaned. "*Ah*, damn. I'd rather like a challenge," I said, blissfully unaware of the reality outside the fortress. "I'm sure you would," he grinned.

I had no idea just *how much* of a challenge we would *all* be facing in the coming weeks.

A half hour and a change of clothes later, we arrived at the mess hall. A long wooden house, with well-thatched roofing where two massive pillars supported the front of the roof above the main entrance, both engraved with tales of past Synners and their heroic actions. We walked under the tall doorway and were relieved at seeing the feast before us.

Typically, the food we would eat during our days at Codrean tasted little better than watered-down nasal mucus, which held all of the necessary nutritional value we needed. However, the feast that awaited us was certainly a surprise to be remembered for the next few months.

There were slaughtered pigs on the tables with apples in their mouths amid platters of deer and lamb haunches. There was more than enough vodka and ale to go around, and the Synners, seniors and juniors alike, were just going in for their second round when we walked in. The New Bloods, as we called the youngest members, weren't allowed to drink for obvious reasons.

Many of those sitting at the tables acknowledged our presence, since Bernar was one of the few there whom the Master had recognized at eighteen.

I never told him back then, but I'd always hoped to match it.

Since our daily training often consisted of various different types of exercises, sword and spell drills were modified to fit each Synner's style, while still honing the core basics. Some preferred more flashy styles, whereas others preferred the more *conservative* movement types.

Bernar was one of the few who had mastered four styles of blade-and-spell work, which led him to be recognized as a prodigy by the Master.

Although we would all spend hours each day, training, polishing and perfecting our techniques for our preferred weapon systems, we would also have to face the rigorous physical conditioning part of it all; league-long runs in minimal amounts of time, lifting and tossing tree trunks, and endless weapon swing repetitions to name a few.

This all had to be done in full gear so that there wouldn't be a difference in performance when the time came to fight. In turn, it made us formidable warriors who were nearly unmatched in our physical capabilities.

Usually, there was no such feast waiting for us at the end of a long training day. The habitual gruel we would eat sufficed to supply their bodies with nutrients. However, today was a day unlike the rest, as our eyes glistened at the sight of the feast before us.

We walked towards the long hearth running down the center of the barracks, which heated the general area to a fair temperature, and chose some empty seats that our comrades had saved for us.

"*Ah*! There you are," the Master, who now stood at the far end of the hearth, exclaimed. His voice rang across the mess hall like a tidal wave of sound. Everyone's hearts skipped a beat, and they sat still with eyes peeled, but the scariest part was that *no one* had seen him enter the hall.

He was not a man any of them would have liked to have annoyed or anything of the sort. Rumor had it that he had killed a Synner long ago for insubordination in the mess hall. At other times, he was known to beat future Synners, or new bloods as we called them, for being even a single minute late.

"I'm glad to see you're all enjoying yourselves, and you aren't wrong to do so," he said in a voice much warmer than most were used to. His audience was quiet and attentive, holding their breath as our white haired, glowing-eyed master spoke.

"I believe everyone present heard the sound of a single thunderbolt strike near our home this afternoon. I thought the thunder god would have brought more with him. Disappointing, really, given the amount of rainfall we've had today," his piercing gaze fell upon the two of us.

Oh, *fuck! We're dead,* I glanced at Bernar, who raised both his eyebrows and shifted his gaze away from me.

Surprisingly, the Master didn't dally on the subject, but a thin-lipped grin managed to escape the corner of his mouth, wrinkling the scar on his cheek. He waved his hand and decided moving on to what was most important was better.

"I digress. I expect you all know that at the end of every day, we have our briefing for the following day. Now, I know that many of you have more than obviously noticed that something is very different from any other day up until now," he leaned forward, interlocking his fingers.

Here it comes, I anxiously elbowed my brother's rib cage.

"We're having this lovely feast for one reason: tomorrow we're going on an expedition," he observed carefully as some of the younger Synners shifted in their seats. "I expect all of you to be looking sharp as ever at first light. We'll head southeast to Coltend Castle to participate in a war council," he said, making me wonder if *this* was the surprise test.

"We have received an invitation from King Truls himself to attend, but only a handful of representatives of our section will be present at the meeting. If you have any questions, now would be the *best and only* time to ask them. Otherwise keep your shit to yourselves," the Master glanced around the room for any raised hands.

A few of the young ones grew uneasy, some anxious to go on their first expedition, while others out of pure fear. There was no way of knowing what they might encounter on the road that could make some seniors shake in their hardened leather boots.

However, this *would* be my first time being so far from the fortress I called home.

I abruptly raised my hand, and in the same instant, the Master raised an eyebrow. "Yes? What is it, young Thoma?" his gaze snapped to me. "I've never been to Coltend, Master, and I was just wondering what sort of beasts or monsters we could encounter on our way there," I said with a slight tremble.

I know others have similar questions, but hopefully I can get enough out of him right now to help them out, I assured myself I hadn't just made a mistake.

The Master must have sensed that I was as nervous as a whore in church, and wrinkled the scar on his cheek once more. "I've only ever been there a few times myself, and I still don't know every monster or beast that lies on the path towards it," the Master replied nicer than usual, giving me a slight sense of relief.

"However, the one thing I *can* tell you is that if we do encounter any threats along the way, you'll need all the skills you've learned until now," he said with an air of caution.

"Does that mean there's a high chance of that happening, Master?" I asked the moment the last word left the Master's mouth. He looked at me with a warm stare I could only assume was a nostalgic one; eager to get into a battle and show my prowess as a Synner. He chuckled lightly through his nose in response to whatever he was thinking.

"I'm not saying it's not *unlikely*," he grinned. "In case any of you forgot, the creatures we have long since trained to deal with are rarely ever alone. I wouldn't count on there not being in a skirmish at some point along the way," he looked around the Hall.

"Just be prepared and remember your training. You'll do well enough from what I've heard, Thoma," he said, prompting everyone to stare or scowl at me.

Shit, now I've got another *target painted on my back,* I curled into myself, as even some of the seniors glared at me.

Thankfully, Bernar glared back at them, nearly making me laugh as I watched them buckle beneath his intense glare.

The reason for the glares was relatively simple. The Master rarely complimented anyone above the rank of New Blood, and while I couldn't read minds, their expressions showed the jealousy stirring within them.

"Thank you, Master. I'll do my best," I said with more excitement than I had initially intended. "I know you will," the Master said calmly, and sent a small chill down everyone's spine.

However, I froze solid.

"W-What do you think he meant by that?" I quietly asked Bernar after we'd left the mess hall as we headed back to the dorm that was in the main fortress of Codrean. "Fucked if I know," he shrugged. "The Master's been awfully strange these days and I'm not too anxious to find out what's been eating him," he sighed as I eyed him curiously.

That's because you already know, *don't you?* I raised an eyebrow, but he never noticed.

"Besides, it's not like he'd let us figure it out anyway, right? I mean, the bastard's creepy as hell, smart as can be, and meaner than my friend's ex-wife when she's on those days of the month," he chuckled, scratching the back of his head with a shit-eating grin across his face.

I smiled and felt a little calmer at the last comment, knowing it was aimed to cheer me up and remove the chill that still rolled down my spine from dinner.

"*Ah*, screw it," he blurted out. "At least we'll get to truly see what you're made of if we *do* face any creatures along the way," he said excitedly. "I'm sure that if you can prove yourself to the Master, then you'll soar up the ranks," he said confidently. "I sure hope so," I muttered, averting my gaze slightly.

"Well, we should get some sleep, little brother. Got a long day tomorrow, and not enough time to sleep or women to keep us company through the night," he sighed. "I have to review the spell I've created. It's best to always keep it fresh in mind," I shrugged.

"*Oh*, you practice *that thing* every night?" his eyebrows raised in surprise. "You were the one who taught me not to neglect practicing it," I scoffed. "I did, but not at the cost of *sleep*," Bernar sighed as we reached the entrance to the large, stone fortress.

"Just don't stay up too late, you mischievous little turd," he said, pushing the wooden door open and scuffing up my hair. "Alright, *alright*! I won't," I replied with a smile from ear to ear.

My brother tilted his head and raised an eyebrow, obviously expecting me to add something I'd forgotten. "*Okay*, I promise I won't," I groaned. "Better not," he scoffed. "Otherwise, I'll make you drink a bowl of goat's piss," he brought his finger to the tip of my nose.

Nooooo, thank you, I smiled nervously.

"Rest well, brother. Tomorrow's a big day... for both of us," he continued, patting me on the shoulder, and turned down one of the stone hallways that led towards his own quarters.

I proceeded down the opposing hallway, reaching one of the rooms where I found the others drunkenly snoring in their beds. I removed my clothes, avoiding a bucket of someone's piss along the way, and got into my sleeping attire.

I did my best to stay quiet as I tucked myself under the covers and lay awake, staring into the dark shadows of the thatched roof above me, and wondering what sort of things I might encounter the next day.

As my imagination ran freely, I pictured myself in the middle of a flat, grassy meadow at twilight to review my new spell, calculating how powerful it might be, and how much mana I would need to cast it.

Obviously, I knew of the dangers of casting an untested spell in battle, as they were frequently addressed during training. I just hoped that whatever happened the next day wouldn't force my hand to use it.

However, that answer would only come the next day when I'd depart on my very first expedition at first light.

CHAPTER 2
EVE OF THE EXPEDITION

Ugh, this sucks, I thought as I writhed beneath the covers of my bed.

I could still hear the pouring rain outside, but there was a distinct *drip* every few seconds, helping me keep track of time and the sleep I was no longer getting.

I closed my eyes again and held them shut for a few minutes before giving up and smacking the cold stone wall behind me with a balled fist. It had hundreds of individual scratchings, with names, dates, and carvings of all sorts that turned the plain granite wall into a grotesque canvas.

I'd even added some of my own over the years, though nowhere *near* as profane as some of the others.

Doesn't look like I'm going to be getting much sleep tonight anyway. I should probably use this time to review my spell, just in case, I thought.

Even though Bernar was originally the one to help me create this spell, it still demanded a dangerous amount of mana. I couldn't fault him for trying to teach me such a high-level spell, but the difference in abilities between us was *staggering*.

He is a fifth-stage all-caster, after all, I reminded myself.

I knew it would be devastating if used correctly, so I took the time to hone it as close to perfection as I could. I lay there, calculating and recalculating every movement to the single-digit degree, the amount of mana needed to condense the spell, how it would react with the ring's ward, and whether it would hold.

As time passed, I continued tossing and turning, probably more times than a dung-beetle would roll a turd-ball back to his home.

I absolutely hate *waiting to try this out. Although if I go out and test it now, the lack of sleep is going to kick my ass and I'm* sure *the Master will pick up on the mana because of it,* I sighed.

I decided against going outside and tugged on the woolen blanket I was using to keep warm in the cold night.

Gods above and below, it's fucking cold in here and this new blanket is itchier than I thought it was going to be. I can't seem to find a comfortable spot around my neck for it, I huffed, nearly giving up on the idea of sleep entirely.

The gray, cotton pajamas I wore to sleep *also* did little to stave off the cold, and what little hair I had on my limbs stood on end as gooseflesh riddled my skin, causing me to shiver.

Should I try that spell Roburn was using earlier this morning? It didn't seem to do any damage to his gear, so it should be fine, right? I asked myself as my teeth chattered.

Roburn was another one of the synners who had graduated some years before that fateful night. He often liked to show off his abilities with mana-cloaks and masterful sword-casting techniques. Although I had never tried to *cast* a mana cloak before, I *had read* about them in the dark hours of the night.

Fuck it. I'm too cold to give a damn right now. What's the worst that could happen? I shrugged as I peered through my memories to recall what it looked like.

My eyes darkened, coating my sclera in the black as I *stretched out my hand to draw from the sphere in the sky. I knew I only needed a little and used my will to control the flow from the spiraling rings of light above me, even though I wasn't fully attuned for just how much was actually needed.*

That was mistake number one.

The tendrils wrapped around the tip of my finger, down my arm, and onto the rest of my body, encapsulating me in a cloud of mana. I severed my connection to the realm, and my awareness of the world lurched as my consciousness returned.

I could still feel the swirling cloud of mana around me, warming the air around my entire body like the heat of a small hearth.

Hmm, not quite there yet, I thought, drawing the mana in closer.

In truth, I was unsure of exactly what I was doing, but whatever it was seemed to be working, so I thought it would be alright.

Mistake number two.

I condensed the mana lining my entire body, creating a small barrier between myself and the blanket. I stupidly flicked my index finger against my thumb, as though I were lighting a flint and tinder kit. The result, which I hadn't yet considered, sent sparks of mana from inside my palm towards the barrier.

Mistake number three.

As soon as the sparks touched the barrier, it began to burn like the coals at the end of a wood-fire's life. However, instead of dying out, it quickly gained copious amounts of heat in such a short period of time that I could feel the heat coming through my pajamas.

Ah, there it is! The Fuckening has begun, I thought, accepting my inevitable death.

The heat from the barrier rapidly set the blanket ablaze, forcing the protective coating to disappear about as quickly as it was formed.

Shit, it was too hot! I can't just lie here and die! I have to do something, I panicked, knowing I wouldn't withstand the heat for much longer.

My eyes darkened again as I *drew more mana* to shield myself from the ever-intensifying heat. It surrounded me once more and acted as a shield between myself and the blanket. I tried to swat out the newborn flame with my hand, but to no avail. The fire engulfed the blanket, and I threw it to the floor beside my bed.

Shit, shit, shit! That was too close for comfort, I thought *far* too soon.

The fire spread onto my bed, and I began to panic even more so than before, given the fact that I'd just lit something on fire at an hour when I should not even have been awake. The fire spread as I desperately searched for a way to extinguish it.

This is probably the second worst idea I've had today, I sighed as I got out of bed, moving toward a piss bucket I'd noticed next to one of the other boys' beds.

The smell quickly reached my nose as the bucket's contents sloshed around when I picked it up. In a fruitless, last-ditch effort, I threw the piss in the bucket onto the blanket now fully engulfed in mana flame.

Mistake number four.

The evaporated piss quickly filled the room, making my eyes and nose sting with the stench.

Congrats, dumbass! You've made matters worse! Well, if I can't stop the fire itself, I can at least prevent the others from dying in this hellish sauna, I coughed and mentally kicked myself for thinking that would work.

"Fire!" I shouted. After noticing my mistake, the three other young synners in the same dorm abruptly woke up and displayed little more than pure, unadulterated panic. The flame had now spread to the bases of their beds. The three were just as, maybe even *less,* experienced than I, prompting them to mimic my shout sporadically.

The fear in their eyes was real enough, for none of the three had ever seen a fire-based spell in such close proximity, as they would only begin to meddle in such matters the following year. The others desperately attempted to douse the flames with their blankets. However, since this was a mana flame, it quickly spread to their blankets and induced *more* panic.

Oooooh, this is bad. This is really *bad,* my eyes widened in realization of what I'd done. *Bernar's going to kill me, and there's no telling what the Master will do. You're a fool, Thoma Fayren. You could probably have a more intelligent conversation with a fucking rock than with me,* I felt my stomach churn, heavily influenced by the panicking trio.

The three boys were wailing, but I heard a distinctive command through their desperate cries. "Keep away from the door!" the voice shouted.

It was the Master.

We hurried and pressed our backs as hard as possible on the wall adjacent to the doorway, assuming the door would have swung open the other way, leaving us untouched.

Just how much mana is he pulling that even I can feel him drawing it through the door? I thought, feeling the hairs on my arms and neck standing up.

I sensed the rippling mana stop as quickly as it began, allowing a split second of pure silence. As the air became still and the pressure grew, it compressed our bodies like we were at the bottom of a lake. The pressure was released, and the resulting *boom* cracked the air around us. It bent the door inwards, releasing screws and nails from their positions, as a turquoise wave of mana smashed through the door, obliterating it.

Even though my ears rang, I was glad to see that my *accident* was fully extinguished.

As we recovered from the shockwave, we noticed all of our bedding had been redecorated in our room, like some scary story a parent would tell their child. Overturned bunk beds, mattresses, pillows and sheets were strewn about the room, and the palpable smell of evaporated piss didn't help the situation either.

We stumbled back from the doorway, looking back in awe. Honestly, I don't think any of us had ever seen such destruction inside the living quarters before, and I knew that whatever came next would *not* be a pleasant experience.

We coughed due to the pungent steam and smoke from the now-charred blankets, making our eyes tear up as a result. The Master's silhouette stood in the doorway, backlit by a wall lamp that caused it to flicker. Two pairs of yellow eyes glowed in the doorway's frame; one was his, while the other was *Bernar's*.

Doo-do-dooo, I'm dead. Long live the Dipshit, I played the fanfare in my head as soon as I felt his gaze on me.

As he stepped through the doorway, I saw the Master wearing a loose white shirt with laces around the chest and neck, with his sleeves rolled up to the middle of his forearm. His gray cotton pants were tailored perfectly to his height, preventing any material from dragging on the ground as he walked. He also wore leather-soled slippers that muffled the sound of his footsteps.

He moved forward, his hands clasped behind his back, holding his head high like a walking statue. We looked at him in fear, not knowing what came next. Bernar, his right-hand man, stepped in behind him with a noticeable amount of less grace and fluency than the Master, nearly knocking over a cup that had been on a bedside table nearby.

He wore the same style of clothes as the Master, though they were *a little* dirtier. The thick, smoky air was filled with the sounds of our heavy breathing and coughing. I caught my brother's eye, but he only sighed in response. The Master flinched his right eye at the sound behind him, but decided not to turn around.

"Boys," his voice rang out. "I understand the mischief youngsters find themselves in more often than not. However, I would like to know who attempted the Pyrus spell," his eyes quickly landed on *me*.

Ah, shit, I felt my pulse quicken, already knowing he'd traced the residual mana back to me.

The others gazed at each other, bug-eyed and shaking nervously. "It was me, Master," I sighed, accepting my fate. "I was the one who attempted the spell and lost control of it," I bowed, staring at the ground beneath me.

While I didn't see his expression, I heard the Master give a small grunt after shifting his weight to look at Bernar, who I knew would shake his head as subtly as he could. The Master said nothing, but turned and faced us again.

"That was very foolish of you, Thoma. However, I won't give you a lecture here. Follow me to my quarters," he commanded firmly. The moment the word quarters left his mouth, I knew I was in for it, shuddering at the thought. "Yes, Master," I quickly replied. As the Master turned on his toes, I looked over at the others who were just as shocked as I was.

This is it. This is how I'm going to die. Goodbye, gentlemen, I tried to transmit with a pained, thin-lipped smile, which earned me a few crisp salutes in response.

I looked at my brother, who showed mixed emotions of awe and shame. I stepped forward and followed the Master and my brother through the destroyed doorway, avoiding the small splinters in my path. The stone hallway was cold and barely lit, with large corner stones at every angle.

Wooden torches wrapped in cloth and liquified troll fat hung on the walls in iron sconces, dimly lighting the cold corridor. Due to our heel-toe walking technique, the sound of our footfall was nearly inaudible on the cold stone floor.

On a real mission, one could walk silently across almost any surface while moving quickly. Our leather-soled boots aided in silencing our steps. However, the thin slippers I wore out of bed didn't do much to keep the cold from the stone floors from reaching my feet.

As we walked, Bernar glanced back at me and sighed inwardly before seemingly returning to an unspoken conversation between him and the Master.

I know what I did was wrong, but why do I feel like I'm going to be executed over this? I felt my stomach turn in an unnatural way. *I think it's trying to send the remnants of dinner back the way they came, or perhaps toward the other end at this point,* I grimaced.

Either way, I just have to calm down. I'm sure things will work out... right? I thought, feeling guilty enough as it was, with my heart beginning to race as we climbed a flight of stairs.

Ah, yes. The executioner's chamber, I nodded as I saw the heavy cedar door that marked the entrance to the Master's study.

My mouth was dry and I could swallow nothing but a cotton ball of spit. The heavy door creaked open and I hesitated to go inside. Bernar, however, put a reassuring hand on my shoulder and led me into the room, following closely behind the Master.

As we crossed the threshold, I caught my brother's grin out of the corner of my eye. Torches immediately appeared to light themselves in a clockwise circle around the room, revealing the interior fantastically.

Did he use mana to light those? A bit dramatic, but still impressive to say the least, I wondered.

The room had eight walls, four of which had bookcases taller than the average man, all fully loaded with countless books and scrolls. Some were old, dusty, and covered in cobwebs, while others appeared to be newer, or at least more frequently used.

I noticed a green-banded book on the third shelf from the ground, near the border of the bookcase itself. Other weathered books surrounded it, yet it seemed to have been used recently. However, before I could draw any conclusions, Bernar gave me a light shove forward as we walked toward the furthest wall where the Master's desk was.

"Sit down, Thoma," the Master gestured to the wooden chair in front of me. I shot my older brother another questioning glance, but he simply nodded and urged me toward it.

The maple chair had been hand-carved in Hjalfar, far to the North, by an old boat maker who had given it to the Master as a token of his gratitude for slaying the Mother Ochelon of the town.

I stared at the detailed carvings, utterly befuddled by their accurate depiction of the creature.

The ochelons were tall, humanoid creatures, whose thick fur and skin helped keep it alive during the winter months in the Northern Countries. Their sharp claws were excellent for hunting, and they generally resided in deep caves near bodies of water. This posed potentially hazardous conditions for anyone who decided to settle near such a place.

I hesitantly sat down, analyzing the carvings as I ran my finger along them. They told the story of the battle between the Master and the Mother Ochelon in intricate detail. From stances to displaying movement, the carvings had almost appeared to come alive as I looked over them.

It was at that moment that I realized my feelings were mixed, and I couldn't decide whether it was awe or fear of the Master. After all, I had just followed the Master to his chamber to have what I knew to be more than a little midnight chat.

"I'm glad to see you like the chair, but do you remember how the Synners first came to be?" the Master asked calmly, snapping me out of my musing. "I vaguely remember the legend, but no specific details, Master," I slowly shook my head. "Then allow me to refresh your memory," he said with a chagrined smile.

"A little over one thousand years ago, when monsters first slipped through the cracks of the Underworld, the gods descended from the heavens. They came not as angelic beings, but as humble beggars to avoid unwanted attention," he began, folding his hands atop the desk.

"The six who descended found themselves close to a town near ruin, with only a few formidable warriors remaining after the monsters had razed it to the ground," his face shifted slightly.

He talks about it as if he were there, I noted, maintaining my outward attentiveness.

Bernar shuffled. "I had always heard it said that one of the monsters was so heavily encased in mana that it blew into little red chunks after an arrow had struck it," he interrupted, causing the Master to purse his lips and lift an eyebrow at him. His brow furrowed, and his irises instantly went from an intense yellow to a flaming orange, making Bernar flinch.

"Please do not interrupt me while I'm schooling a *young pup* who just so happens to be your younger brother," he sighed, relieving the sting with a small smile that caused the scar on his right cheek to wrinkle. "Forgive me, Master," Bernar instantly replied, bowing his head and stepping backwards.

"Now, where was I?" he asked no one in particular. "*Ah*, yes, the town. So, the gods found themselves at the ruined town, where the remaining survivors found them wandering outside the few standing wall stones. The leader of the warriors went out to meet them in the low grassy field just outside the town," he continued.

"The eldest of the beggars bowed as low as he could to the tall leather-clad warrior, and the man responded by picking him up off the ground. The beggar didn't quite seem to understand what had just happened, after all, what warrior would have a beggar stand as his equal?" he asked.

"Anyone with half a brain and heart would have done the same, I'd imagine," I shrugged as if stating the obvious. "That's where you're wrong, Thoma," he shook his head. "For this was no ordinary grunt you'd find on the battlefield. He was the Lord of Codrean and a *very* powerful mage," he said in an honorific tone.

My father was a supposed lord, but I don't know what became of him once I was recruited into the Synners, I avoided saying that part aloud.

I raised my eyebrows. "The *Lord of Codrean*, Master? I thought lords weren't supposed to do battle," I cocked my head. "As far as I know, they generally sit in their comfy castles and large rooms surrounded by whores and wine while the lowly soldiers get thrown into the shitstorm of a battlefield," I said bitterly, but his nod of agreement was a surprise to me.

"This lord, however, was well known for being able to see the true nature of people. While he didn't know *who* they were, he could tell they were no ordinary beggars the moment he saw the first bow lower than anyone before," he continued, leaning back in his chair a little. "Doesn't sound like much to me," I muttered.

Obviously, he'd heard my comment, but chose to say nothing. "In any case, he happily invited them for supper, making the first gasp in surprise given that food was notably scarce. The disguised gods agreed before he led them to the makeshift tents they'd constructed after the attack in preparation for the next," he continued.

"The following morning, the beggars decided to leave the small settlement but wanted to speak to the lord first. The first beggar revealed that they were, in fact, gods and that each one would bestow a single gift to him and five of his bravest warriors for his altruism. Taken aback by the gesture and revelation of their godhood, he immediately fell to his knees in reverence," he leaned forward once more.

"But what were the gifts, Master? I'm sure they must have been powerful artifacts," I felt my interest peak as I leaned forward. "Of course, they were," he chuckled softly.

Wait, he can laugh? I desperately tried to hide my surprise.

"To the Lord of Codrean, the leader gave the *Realmwalker Blade*, capable of cutting through the fabric of reality if the wielder infused mana into it," he began almost reverently.

"To the largest and strongest of them, the second goddess gave the *Fate-bearer Shield*. She had forged it from the bones of a great serpent, which negates all magic used against it. It could even use the negated spell's mana to heal the bearer and those around him," he continued.

"The third god gave the *Night-kissed Mantle* to the woman who had been an assassin for the Lord for over a decade. This mantle coated the user in mana, making them virtually undetectable," he grinned with the last word, but I couldn't figure out why.

"The fourth goddess approached the archer, and she granted him the *Nethersong Mask*, which allowed for a vast improvement in eye-sight, as well as produced an autonomous bestial claw made of pure mana for offensive or defensive purposes," his face contorted slightly this time. Still, like before, I couldn't figure out why.

"The fifth god took pity on the most severely wounded of them and, after healing his wounds, granted him the *Dreambinder Jerkin*.

It would allow the wearer to phase through any physical attack not infused with mana," he continued with a hint of jealousy.

"The sixth goddess noticed one of the warriors wielding dual-blades, and thus produced the *Benevolent Ring*, which could populate items placed within its storage spell at a moment's notice," he grinned, obviously hiding something. "Those all sound incredibly useful," I noted, getting a quick nod of agreement.

"Yes, they are. However, the leader of the gods decided to bestow a *second* gift, not just for the warriors but for everyone, producing a brightly glowing plant and instructions on how to correctly use it from a ring on his finger.

To say that I was *confused* would be an understatement.

"A *plant*, Master?" I asked, unsure of what I'd just heard. "Naturally, after hearing about these magnificent weapons and such, one must wonder what a plant has to do with all of this," he chuckled again, only adding to my confusion.

"A *plant*?" I asked again. "Y-yes," the Master replied curtly. "As unlikely as it seems, that plant helped make us what we are. Both gifts are *almost useless* individually, but if the instructions are followed carefully, drawing mana from the Ethereal is *much* less risky," he explained. "What do you mean by *risky*?" I cocked my head.

"It's not *impossible* for one to connect with the Ethereal without the plant's blessing, but it *does* speed up and simplify the process," he shrugged slightly. "But this gift is what sets us synners apart from other warriors, as we can train with mana from a young age as opposed to the decades of learning normally required," he continued in a more serious tone.

"While the ability *can be passed down* through direct bloodlines of those who have consumed the plant, you must never take this gift lightly. It was bestowed upon us by the gods to help us defend our homeland. Do you understand, Thoma?" he tilted his head downward to look at me from beneath a slightly furrowed brow.

"I do, Master," I swallowed dryly. "Good," he nodded before leaning back in his chair. "Now, I want you to listen to me very carefully," he said in a voice that made the hair on my arm stand up like a wooden palisade.

"I have two things in store for you, but only after we visit Coltend, as I would not have you do anything tonight. I would like to give you a choice," he almost grinned as he spoke. "A choice?" I asked weakly.

What the hell is that supposed to mean? I thought.

"I want you to know that I must either punish or test you for your insolence tonight. However, since this was more of an accident than a willful happening, I will tell you the two options," the Master said.

I felt more scared than I had ever been. The Master and Bernar, standing two paces behind my chair, sensed it but showed no sign of doing so.

"One is to spend a week in solitary confinement with only bread and water as sustenance, and the other is to hunt down the creature in the cave that lies just outside our fortress," he said methodically.

I still couldn't understand why a hunt was considered a form of punishment.

"So, which will it be?" the Master asked.

I looked to Bernar again for answers, but he simply shrugged and upturned his bottom lip. I thought for what seemed like an eternity, but eventually came to a decision. "I'll go with the creature, Master," I said with as much courage as I could muster.

"Are you sure? Do you even know what you'll be fighting?" Bernar urged. "Well, I've studied the bestiary a lot, and I don't think the Master would send me on a mission he didn't think I could accomplish," I shrugged.

The Master looked at me inquisitively, then nodded to my brother shortly after.

"Very well, then. Study what you have to take with you, be it knowledge, spells, or otherwise. You'll need your sword sharpened, your mind well-rested, and you shouldn't forget to be mindful of your surroundings," the Master said.

"I will, Master," I nodded firmly. "Good. Once we've returned from Coltend, Bernar will help you prepare for your first solo hunt. That is all I have for you tonight, Thoma. You may go now," he waved dismissively.

I swallowed another dry ball of spit before I rose and bowed, turning to leave his study as quickly as I dared without being rude. "*Oh, one last thing, Thoma,*" he called out, making me flinch.

I was wondering when the air was going to sour, I thought.

The color fled from my face as I turned back around to face the Master slowly as I could. "Find another blanket, and do try not to set *this one* alight," he said wryly. "I'll do my best to keep it from happening again, Master," I replied nervously. I walked out of the chamber and proceeded down the steps with Bernar just behind me.

I almost died, but why did he give me a choice? There's probably more to it than just a punishment, I thought, feeling a bead of sweat drip down my cheek.

"You got lucky, you lanky little shit," Bernar said, nudging me with his elbow. "Don't think I've ever seen anyone actually given a choice of punishment before tonight," he said pensively, though I could only shrug.

"Now don't get me wrong, I know just how frightening it is to go on your first hunt, *especially* if your first time is going in alone," he chuckled, likely reminded of his first time. "Most junior synners don't get to go on their first hunt alone since that's only allowed for seniors," he continued.

"I just don't understand why he'd even give me the option between solitary and a solo hunt. It simply doesn't add up," I shrugged again. "*Ah*, don't go getting your hose in a knot over it," he swatted the air. "I've been to solitary before, and believe me, that was anything but a pleasant experience," he cautioned, making me shudder at the thought.

"Worms and maggots are everywhere, and there's nothing but a pile of dirt that serves as a bed. The walls are covered in *scratchings* of past visitors, while the small confinement smells like years of accumulated piss and shit," he said, a wave of relief washing over me since I knew I wouldn't be going there.

"Well, at least now I know what I should expect to happen the next time I fuck up," I chuckled as Bernar joined in. "*Should* that ever happen, I'll be sure to leave you a nice *runny* present," he said with a wicked smile. "Besides, it's been a while since anyone's been sent to solitary, and by a while I mean a few days," he grinned.

"That still doesn't answer my question, though. Why would he bother giving me a choice?" I asked. "Beats the hell out of me," he replied with an indifferent shrug as we walked down the corridor towards the dormitory, seeing the remnants of destruction caused by the fire and the blast from the spell.

We both stared at it blankly for a moment before chuckling lightly at the ridiculousness of the whole situation.

"Seeing as things currently stand, or *don't* for that matter, I suppose you could sleep in my room for the night," Bernar suggested. "Guess I'll have to," I sighed. "What of Irun, Batch, and Edryd?" I asked, noticing they were nowhere to be found.

I was still concerned about my roommates whom I'd almost just killed in an accident, after all.

"I'm sure they're alright. They're tough little bastards; quite possibly tougher than *you*," he replied with a grin. I looked up at my brother and tilted my head. "Is that so, *big brother*? Do you remember when I pinned you to the ground for five seconds?" I prodded him with an elbow before heading down the hall to his room.

"I had passed the fuck out because I tripped on that stupid meditation stool of yours and hit my head on the floor," Bernar snapped back with a laugh while I scoffed. "My *stupid meditation stool* is what got me recognition for my casting abilities," I returned mockingly. "It helps me to think and focus better than ever," I explained, but Bernar only squinted his eyes and pursed his lips.

"*Uh-huh*," he squinted dubiously. "Whatever, let's get some sleep. It's already the second hour of the morn and we're to be up and out the gate at first light," Bernar suggested.

We walked softly and quickly, as though we were the shadows we left behind in the torchlight. We soon arrived at Bernar's dorm room, which wasn't unlike my own, though perhaps with less charring and fewer bits of the door lying across the floor.

I made a bed of fallen straw from my brother's bed and an old potato sack for a pillow. We bid each other goodnight and Bernar stretched out his hand to put out the bedside candle by absorbing the small flame into his hand. I saw it happen, and was anxious to try it.

I think I've had more than my fair share of fire for one night, I chuckled.

Soon after, I rolled onto my back into the same position I was in when all of this began, closed my eyes, and returned to the grassy field in my dreamscape once more.

CHAPTER 3
THE ROAD TO COLTEND CASTLE

Three and a half hours later, I was being shaken awake by my older brother.

With dark circles like a fighter's black eyes, and a drowsiness that could kill a moose, I rose out of my makeshift bed and began getting into harness. My brother, of course, needed far less sleep than I did, what with being a fifth stage and all, leaving him in much better shape than I was.

"You should have let me die," I groaned when I opened my burning eyes, getting a chuckle then a sudden light kick from my brother. "Hurry up or you'll be late," he chided. I lazily dismissed him with a wave before mustering the strength to escape my impromptu bed.

The black leather jerkin, hose, and boots I was attempting to put on hadn't thoroughly dried from my horse-casting certification from the day prior. This made them heavier than usual and, compounded by the lack of sleep, brought my regular pace to little faster than a child's crawl.

Bernar, on the other hand, had used the rain-proof cloak to stave off the rain, leaving most of his equipment unsoiled. He got into his jerkin and hose quickly, though his boots were still caked in mud and smelled of horse shit.

"You look like hell, little brother," he said. I, who was far too tired to give the slightest amount of a shit, lazily rolled my eyes in his direction, slowly turning my head and saying nothing in the process. "Never mind, I'll take that back. You look *worse*," he jeered.

"I feel worse than I look, to be honest. It's like my entire body has been encased in a heavy metal," I groaned as I bent over to get my foot into the boot. I moved at half speed that morning, and finding my equipment in what remained of the charred, piss-smelling dorm was easier said than done. I found my equipment chest under a large piece of the door, a stark reminder of my fuck-up the night before, and lifted the piece with some effort.

I opened the oaken chest and was relieved my equipment had not been reduced to ash. I began by pulling out my sword and belt and lacing them to my waist through loops in my hose. I buckled it tightly so it wouldn't jolt around as I walked, and patted it twice. He turned my back to the door and walked towards the opposite end of the room.

As I looked out of the charred window frame, I heard light footsteps coming from behind me at what sounded like a run.

Edryd, my best friend and one I had nearly killed the night before, stormed into the room, tripping over the bucket that still lay on the floor. He wasn't usually clumsy, but it seemed he was in too much of a rush to be cautious this time.

"Thoma!" Edryd cried out from down the hall. I lazily turned to face the boy standing in the doorway, excitement clearly showing on his face. He had deep, brown eyes that could pierce even steel, and dark brown hair tied behind his head in a short ponytail. He had a toned jawline and a slightly upturned nose, and the first few whiskers of his beard were beginning to sprout, which was widely respected for a boy of seventeen.

"Thoma," Edryd said again, panting in the doorway. "Hullo, Edryd," I returned. "What is it? Why are you in such a rush?" I asked, curious as to why he was so sweaty. "Don't you remember? We're about to head out towards Coltend, and our scouts have returned saying that they've seen a few monsters on the prowl about a league out on the road," he jittered with excitement and fear.

They've never come this close to home before, I thought.

"*Hm*, that is odd," I replied, lightly scrunching my cheek with the corner of my mouth. "In any case, it's a chance for us to show our skills! That is, of course, contingent on there being anything left for us to kill," he said with a smirk and a gleam in his eyes. "I know I might sound like a psychopath, but I can't wait to kill my first monster finally," Edryd began. "After all, it's what I've been training for for most of my life," he said, spreading his arms widely as he finished his sentence.

Come to think of it, he's never been on an expedition either, has he? I thought, recounting the number of them in recent years.

There hadn't been many, at least not around Codrean anyway.

"I don't blame you," I chuckled lightly. "I've been itching to try out a spell I created, but I haven't even tested it out of battle, yet," I lowered my head a little in dejection.

"*Oh*, I wouldn't worry too much about that," Ed waved a hand in front of him. "There's not a shadow of a doubt that you're the most adept caster of our age group," he shrugged. "Even if you're not the most physically strong," he added after a short pause. We both laughed at the final comment and stopped when we heard a blaring noise coming from outside.

The Dragon Horn, I recognized the sound.

It was carved from a dragon's tooth, and passed down through the generations to signal that it was time to leave. While it was felled by one of the first Synners, there haven't been many sightings of dragons since then, making the one we had especially rare.

We looked at each other, and we knew exactly what that meant. "Time to go. Do you have all of your stuff?" I asked, grabbing the last of my things and bundling them under my curled arm. He nodded his reply just before we both took up our gear and headed out the door, making our way down the hall that led to the outer courtyard.

The sun was just beginning to show the tip of its face over the distant Frellen Hills, the warmth from the few rays that slipped between the peaks greatly contrasted the cold of the previous night. The birds began to sing in the nearby oak and cedar trees, while the other creatures were slowly crawling out of their holes and dens to greet the sun as if it were a long-lost friend. The cold morning wind began to blow, gently swaying the trees in all directions.

I couldn't have imagined a more beautiful morning even if I'd dreamed about it for a hundred years, I thought, breathing the morning air deeply as I looked over the tops of the trees.

I shifted my gaze from the trees down into the courtyard where all the other synners, the Master included, had gathered; tightening harnesses, checking stirrups, feeding the horses their morning apples, and checking equipment against a list.

I walked over to my horse, Celer, which I had so adequately named due to his speed that had been proven the day before, and checked my saddle. I tied much of my equipment onto the left side of the saddle, ensuring the loop I'd made wouldn't hurt my mount in the long run.

Looks like you're ready to go, too, friend, I patted my horse's nape.

"Listen up!" Bernar yelled from atop a beam where the Master's horse was tied. The Master was sitting on his horse, idly fiddling with a chain around his neck, but as Bernar's words left his mouth, he suddenly jumped up and stood on his horse's saddle, getting a better view of the group of Synners.

He stood there for a few moments, without movement, waiting for everyone to quiet down. He did a headcount: twenty Synners with him, Bernar, and me included.

"As I am sure you remember, today we ride southeast towards Col-tend Castle, to answer King Truls' summons," he began. "I expect nothing less than exemplary behavior from all once we arrive at the castle, for they are not so lenient as I am over insolence," he said, glancing over at me.

If he's lenient, we're all fucked, I lifted my eyebrows in unison with Edryd, who was probably thinking the same thing since he stared back at me with widened eyes.

"I believe these summons to be for a trivial matter, which shall be dealt with quickly and thoroughly. Although I suspect we will stay within the castle walls for at least a day or two, perhaps longer depending on how things go," he announced, getting quiet whispers among the Synners before him.

They knew exactly what that meant, at least the older ones did.

"On this most beautiful morning, bear in mind that there are very real dangers out there as our scouts have already noted a handful of the ugly bastards a little way from here. Remember, one must always be watchful and attentive, understood?" he asked. "Yes, Master!" we roared. "Good. Now, mount up!" he shouted.

We got into our saddles immediately, starting from the left side, throwing our right legs over the horse and placing our feet in the other stirrup. After adjusting our seating and gathering their reins, we silently awaited the Master's signal.

My anxiety must have bled into Edryd's, since he was showing mild signs of either unease or excitement. Perhaps it was both, but I couldn't tell. They glanced over at each other with wide, nervous grins and nodded.

Let's show them we're ready, I thought with a grin.

The sword-casters, myself included, carried two swords: A bastard sword mainly used on horseback, and the other a longsword for ground combat. They clanged about on our backs and hips but were otherwise reasonably secure.

We all wore thick, leather jerkins, with thicker seams at the joints than there would typically be to lessen wear and tear. Our boots were mostly made from elk or bear skin, and the few, more experienced sword-casters had glick or ochelon-skin hoods and riding cloaks.

The younger, less experienced sword casters wore regular, weather-proof cloaks and were usually in the middle of the group, surrounded by the more experienced ones to avoid unnecessary losses.

Of course, Ed and I counted ourselves among their numbers.

The few bow-casters, who could infuse their arrows with mana drawn from the Ethereal, were on both sides in the middling ranks. Their unstrung bows hung from hooks and were tied down with a singular leather strip for easier access on the side of their saddles. Most of them wore woodland green cloaks, attached with many different kinds of brooches and hooks. Some more intricate than others, although it usually depended on the bow-caster's rank.

We went under the stone overpass and between the great wooden doors, facing southeast and moving at a steady trot. The Master was at the head of the group, closely followed by Bernar to his right, and Garett, the master bow-caster, to his left.

He was a quiet man of, what I could only guess to be, eighty winters. He didn't very much enjoy the company of others. Instead, he often spent his time in the woods, tracking deer instead of dealing with *blundering idiots* as he liked to call nearly everyone. He wore a griffin-hide cape, with its feathers still attached even after years of use, a griffin talon-skin jerkin, with boots and gauntlets to match.

The road the Master decided to take to leave was well worn. Over the years, it had been used to transport both supplies and Synners to their contract destinations, and within the few hundred years, it had proved to be ever more helpful than before, since the road was wide, flat, and held few rocks for wagon wheels to break upon.

Batch and Irun, my other roommates, were two horse-lengths in front of me, likely what sort of things they might discuss whenever they thought no one would be eavesdropping. Irun was about my age, while Batch... well, we didn't know much about him, but we guessed he was around our age.

At least according to how he acted, anyway.

"I'd wager they're talking about all the whoring they'll do once we get to Coltend Castle," Irun nodded to the three leaders of our group. "Shut up, you red-headed dolt," Batch snapped with a finger to his lips. "If one of them hears you, it'll mean *both of us* being discharged for spreading false accusations," he continued hushedly.

"Well, well, Batch, I'd have never taken you to be one who worries so much about that," Irun sneered sarcastically. "Just like *I'm* sure that you are truly too much of a *dumb-fuck* to understand why I *do care*," Batch retorted. "As much as I find the Synners to be little more than mercenaries with special abilities, it's the life I've decided to continue living. Not for gold, but glory, you goat-plowing turd," he said with a disgusted look on his face. "*Oi*, take that back!" Irun growled, prompting Ed to roll his eyes after overhearing their belligerent conversation.

"You two never know when to shut up, do you?" he spat. Batch looked over at Edryd on his left and shrugged. "What? Don't look at me," Batch shook his head, attempting to deflect Edryd's piercing gaze. "It's not my fault he has the brain of a field mouse and the mouth of one of them damned harpies," he said. "While you have shit for brains," Irun sneered with a scoff.

"What was that? I'm sorry, I couldn't hear you over the shit pouring out from between your teeth," Batch chuckled. "I have the best grades in timed logical reasoning, mind you. Besides, mocking someone's intelligence often means you have very little, yourself," he continued as though comparing grades might have helped his case.

"It's not that your grades don't mean anything, it's just that you really are an idiot who loves running his mouth," I grinned. We chuckled at the last comment, but Irun scoffed, white knuckling over the comment for the next few minutes, praying his beloved Isla wasn't listening.

In the end, knowing she *had heard it* wasn't a large stretch of the imagination.

I watched as Irun caught her gaze, blushed, and immediately fumed over our laughter. He had never really enjoyed being the ass-end of our jokes, but it's not like he didn't make any at our expense. In reality, he was a bit of a shit-head who didn't know how to laugh at himself, though that didn't make him any less our friend.

"Don't worry about them," Isla's voice came behind him. He turned to face her, *the woman of his dreams*, or so he called her. He felt warmth coming from her radiant, blue-eyed stare. He tried, and failed miserably, to shift his gaze away from her, but her golden hair flowed in the breeze in a dreamlike fashion. "I'll do my best," he flushed a bright shade of red as he nodded.

"I pray that you do," she returned with a warm, friendly smile that he embedded in his memory like an engraving in stone. He considered everything from his recent mishaps to his faults and this most recent attempt at trying to fit in with the other Synners, of which none had succeeded, and felt at a loss.

While I couldn't fully understand what was running through his mind, I felt empathetic toward him.

He must be ridiculing us in his head. Poor bastard never learned that it's not that we don't like him, he's just a bit out of touch, I thought, watching him click his tongue and shake his head in our direction.

I knew he wouldn't stay angry forever, for the image of Isla seemed to *nullify any feelings of anger or hatred* the more he thought about her, or so he would always tell us.

After our banter, I looked around excitedly, for I had never left Codrean's walls before on an expedition since becoming a Synner. Not to say that I hadn't left the fortress, but it wasn't as if we'd ever gone much further than a kilometer or two.

The only exception to this, of course, was my childhood.

Still, I was in awe to see so many different kinds of trees lining the road. Cedar, oak, elm, redwood, pine, spruce, and hickory were just a few of the trees I recognized from the books I'd read within the fortress walls.

Seeing these magnificent beings up close and personal is like nothing I've ever felt. It's almost as though I can feel them pulsating with the same mana we synners draw from the Ethereal, though on a much more tangible level, I thought as I gazed at my surroundings with my jaw just slightly agape.

The trees moved and swayed in the cold wind, like some ancient, freely-moving Dericoed of Caegwyn. The rain from the day before had washed away most of the fresher tracks along the road, though the deeper cart-wheel grooves could still be seen. Birds sang and flew overhead, aiming towards their nests in the canopy.

I never would have guessed it could be this peaceful out here, I thought as I breathed in the fresh air.

I finally decided to look ahead, and saw a significant fork in the road with a waypost standing between the two paths. "Take the right," Bernar shouted back to the company. The company pulled on the right side of their reins, and everyone flowed down the path as one body. I rode by the worn-down oak post, with deeply scratched markings in its planks pointing toward other distant cities.

The first board pointed to the North of its current position toward Elvsbyen, a town of tradesmen and fishermen who lived along the Elv Avliv River. The second board pointed towards our current destination, Coltend Castle, where the king had summoned us for an, as of yet, unknown reason.

I can't help but wonder what Coltend looks like; after all, I've only heard stories and tales of its grandeur. Some of Coltend's most outstanding leaders have also *come from there, from what I've read, and now that I'm finally on my way, I can't wait to see it for myself,* I felt an anxious smile grow at the thought.

We continued down the well-worn path for a few more kilometers, when Garett spotted something a few hundred meters down the road.

"Master," he began. "What is it, Garett?" the Master asked. "I count thirty or more glicks converging on a single wagon just ahead of us. We need to investigate the matter, as they have never been seen this close to our home," he stated.

The Master simply nodded. "Ill news, indeed. Take eight of the more experienced synners with you, and four of the lesser experienced; give them a chance to prove themselves," he said wryly, glancing back at me.

"Very well, Master," Garett replied, looking back at the nearest members and giving a silent command for them to fan out. "Edryd, Batch, Irun, and Thoma; you're with Roburn," Garett said plainly as if reading items off an itemized list.

We four looked at each other with a fair amount of surprise, before I began looking for my brother, praying he could give me some final advice about the dangers we were about to face. Bernar spun his horse around when he heard my name called out and rode back towards me.

"This is your chance, little brother. Don't fuck this up by trying out your spell just yet," he said quietly, reining his horse in beside mine. "Don't worry; I'm smart enough to know that *one should never use an untested spell in open combat*, unlike someone I've heard of," I finished my sentence with a grin. Bernar chortled and grinned back before riding over to the Master's side.

Edryd, Batch, and Irun were already becoming nervous, and some of their nervousness began to bleed onto me, too. Their palms and foreheads began to sweat, even in the cold of the early morning, and it was easy to see that things could go very wrong *very* quickly.

"We'll be fine," I said more to myself than to the others in my group. We looked at each other briefly, each seeking reassurance in the other, though there was not much to be found, since we were all just as scared. Irun turned to take what he thought might be his last look at Isla, and she returned his frightened stare with a warm, encouraging smile.

Must be nice, I thought, admittedly jealous that he had *someone* like that in his life.

"The rest of you lot back over there, with me," Garett pointed to the corner of the triangular formation. The eight synners who were equally split between bow and sword-casters nodded in agreement and kicked their spurs into their horses' sides. "Let's move," Garett ordered, and as soon as those words left his mouth, my heels found themselves in my horse's sides.

The thirteen of us rode off towards the downed cart at a gallop. I looked back at my older brother, who simply grinned and nodded as though he were encouraging me onward.

"We're in it now," Batch said, spurring his horse to catch up to mine. "Let's not put all that training to waste," he said, obviously trying to sound much braver than he was outwardly showing. "Did your training involve *running your mouth*? Or, maybe, you have

some kind of *master plan* that you could share with the others?"
Garett spat back towards him, to which Batch could only respond
with dejected silence.

"*Oh*, you don't? I thought not. Now shut the fuck up, and focus!"
Garett said, looking back at the rest of us, too. "Smooth," Irun said
under his breath with a smug look on his face, making me chuckle
even as nervous as I was.

"Listen up," Garett began. "We've a decent grouping of the ugly
bastards out there, so don't get too far ahead of yourselves," he began.
"Sword-casters, you shouldn't need to expend yourselves by using
spells. Use the techniques you should have drilled into your souls by
now, and you will survive. Remember your training and do not panic
no matter how bad things get," he shouted, but I knew his words
aimed at the four of us.

His words hit me like a bucket of cold water, as the realization
set in. The four of us had never been in an actual fight, and our
inexperience was evident enough in how we talked with each other.
Of course, he was right; we had no choice *but* to focus and follow our
training.

It was the only thing that was the likeliest to keep us alive, after all.

I glanced at Ed and the others momentarily, each of them meeting
my gaze with likely the same thoughts behind their eyes: this could
be our first battle of many, or our last.

No one said a word.

"Archers," Garett called out to the ones behind the sword-casters.
"Stay within bow-shot, and infuse if necessary. Otherwise, aim for
the gaps between their scales around their shoulders. That should

slow them down enough for one of the sword-casters to take it down fully," he barked.

They pulled back and spread out two to a side, while the rest of us organized ourselves to make a miniature boar's head formation. Garett pulled back towards the rear center to better view the battlefield, while one of the seniors took his place. The glicks were still approaching the downed cart, moving incredibly fast. The four of us rode in formation just behind the more experienced Synners.

As we got closer, I got my first look at one of the glicks in person. There was something to be said about seeing something like that in a drawing in a book versus seeing one in real life. Nothing in a book could ever have prepared me for the smells, sounds, or anything about their existence.

It was a humanoid creature, with olive green scales that ran from the top of its head to the base of its feet and down its back, forming an external spinal cord that ran from its hip up to the base of its neck, fanning out towards its arms and running down their lengths. Its mouth was primarily covered in needle-like teeth that dripped poison to aid digestion of its prey, and lined the inner part of its mouth.

Is there even an antidote for that? I tried to recall the lessons I'd had since childhood, but nothing came to mind as I drew nearer to the creatures.

Its strong leg and arm muscles underneath the scales made it a formidable enemy for any young Synner, I noted, and with those thoughts, I began feeling something I'd never truly felt before.

That feeling was *fear*.

It came over me like a blanket of ice being unrolled on my abdomen and flowed throughout my body. I could feel my hands shaking and heart beating faster, while my lungs were desperately trying to pump enough air to compensate for the thumping in my chest. As my palms began to sweat, I felt my leather gauntlet beginning to be soaked with sweat. Strands of my brown hair began to stick to my face under the force of the wind.

It was comforting to know that my swords were withstanding the sheer force of Celer's gallop. He kept his pace without missing a beat, his hooves thundering and shaking me as I forced myself to focus, though I was still nearly two hundred meters away from the creatures.

"Draw your swords and get ready!" Garett barked, knocking me out of my head and back into reality.

With my right hand, I drew my riding sword from over my shoulder, and assisted with my left to help it clear the sheath, wrapping the reins around the horn of my saddle. The blade gleamed in the morning sunlight and was sharp enough to shave. I tightly gripped the blackwood, wire, and leather-wrapped hilt as tightly as I could, ensuring it wouldn't slip out of my hand on the first strike.

Since the relatively short blade was primarily used on horseback, the well-designed hilt was a decent bit lighter than my longsword, making it easier to deal damage using only one arm. I shifted my grip slightly, realizing I hadn't adequately spaced my hand beneath the gently upward twisting guard. The pommel, which had my initials inscribed into it, swung beneath my wrist as the weight shifted into the correct position.

One hundred meters, I gauged briefly.

I looked over at Edryd and saw he was already getting into a good striking position, leaning forward with his sword's hilt at the height of his chest with the point aimed forward, and decided to get into the same position.

"Alright, boys, remember their weak spots: shoulder blades, armpits, backs of their legs, groin and under their chins," one of the older Synners said, as if he were sounding off items on a grocery list.

Roburn, I recognized the voice.

His charcoal black hair, shaved on the sides and with a long interwoven braid running down the unshaved part, had been his trademark for the past decade.

"Thanks for the advice," I nodded. "*Eh,* no need to thank me. I'm sure you'd do the same if our places were swapped," he grinned. I nodded sincerely and looked ahead towards my approaching foes.

Twenty meters, I felt my shoulders tighten as I began to search for my target, which proved more challenging given the others riding so close to me.

Remember to lean into the cut to prevent the bastard from getting back up, I heard the Master's instructions in my head again.

Ten meters, I felt my grip tighten even more than it already was.

I followed the muscle tension in my lower back and briefly shifted my weight back in the saddle for extra momentum. The sword in my right hand was beginning to rise up behind me, my arm now slightly bent and flexed, preparing itself for the impact to come.

Five meters, I thought, taking a deep breath before beginning my swing.

My target had approached just as I'd calculated it would. I knew the added momentum from the Celer's speed would add much more force to the blow, in comparison to simply swinging on the ground, and I banked heavily on this fact given my lack of physical strength.

Time seemed to slow as I leaned my head forward, my chest almost pressed against Celer's nape, and swung with all my might.

The sword cut through the air, finding its target. I grunted in exertion as the sword bit into the scales on the glick's forehead, splitting them wide open and releasing their sickly, green ichor. My sword, slicing through the scales, bone, and the underlying fleshy material that was the monster's brain, gave a sound akin to an egg being crushed, emerging on the other side lathered in thick, green blood.

I breathed heavily, feeling the copious amounts of adrenaline flowing through my veins. The glick had been my first kill as a Synner, and I knew, right then and there, that the fire born inside after that first kill hungered for more. I continued riding forward, and another two targets emerged, feeding the ravenous flames within.

I swung again at one target, then another, followed by a third, hearing the same egg-crushing sound from the strikes, while a fourth was crushed under Celer's hooves. Batch, Edryd, and Irun were also feeding their swords, and in the first few seconds of battle, the three had already killed at least seven glicks between them.

Roburn, not wanting to miss out on the killing, quickly dismounted with a leap and began his sword song, charging at his first target. Just before he swung, an arrow struck his target squarely between the eyes. The glick let out a ghastly squeal like a slaughtered pig, and Roburn glanced backwards to the general direction the arrow had come from.

He couldn't find who'd fired the arrow, but he could guess who it was.

I kept riding forward, slaughtering at least two more glicks before I was taken by surprise. A glick jumped from my left side and knocked me off my horse, taking me to the ground as it clawed at my armor.

"Shit," I grunted as my sword was knocked out of my hand, already feeling my shoulder beginning to throb with a dull pain. The glick scrambled to its feet after the fall and began to head towards me, regardless of whether I had fully recovered. It threw an overhead claw down to my right side, and I pirouetted out of the attack as gracefully as I could, given that I was still a little dazed from the fall.

I gathered my wits momentarily, and another strike came towards my gut. I jumped back on the balls of my feet and almost slipped due to the rain-soaked ground from the previous day. Even with the handicap, I barely managed to curve my body to avoid getting hit.

My riding sword had fallen out of my hand with the fall, and with the barrage of attacks, I could only focus on not getting struck while trying to find a small opening to draw my sword from my hip. The monster attacked again, this time trying to slam my head to the ground, which I was forced to side-step. With a bit of my momentum's help, I drew my longsword with a wire-wrapped handle and twisted guard.

I managed to distance myself a little from the monster. My guard was poised, with my sword held up at head height, my left hand gripping the pommel, and my right hand choked up on the hilt by the guard. My left leg was more extended than my right, which supported the bulk of my weight. I could feel my abdominal muscles tightening to keep myself steady through the pain from the fall, making me wince.

The monster stared intensely at my sword, then darted its slit-like pupils over to me, widening its already large eyes even further, getting a grin out of me. "Come at me," I said as threateningly as I could. The creature seemingly understood my words.

As the chaotic battle raged around us, it began to flick its scales together as if to challenge me and let the others know not to interrupt our duel.

I furrowed my brow, and the glick showed its horrid teeth in response. It came forward, with the same squealing sound he'd heard before, only much more vicious and hateful this time. I stood my ground and awaited the perfect moment to strike. It came at me like a rabid dog to fresh meat, sprinting as quickly as its legs could carry it.

When it was just outside of a typical strike's range, I pushed hard from my right leg, turning on the ball of my left foot, and jumped. The movement sent him into a spin, and the rest of my body followed suit. The sword, having lagged behind just a little, came down from my right side with the added force from the spin and struck the monster's collarbone, splitting its torso into two, uneven, bloodied chunks.

Green blood sprayed across my face and covered my jerkin in a light sheen of its filth. "Fuck, that stinks!" I exclaimed with a disgusted look on my face.

Garett, I noticed, had seen the attack happen, and I caught him grinning pridefully. From where I stood, I could see Roburn's sword singing a beautiful tune of slaughter and gore, while the archers kept back and provided cover fire for the lesser experienced Synners.

Their broad-head arrows and ash shafts with alternating goose wing-feathers performed flawlessly against the gaps in the glicks' hard scales. The wind made it a little more challenging to be as precise as usual, but they'd been trained for that over the years. Their arrows, shot from recurve riding bows, soared through the air and struck their marks with incredible precision, even with the morning breeze.

Meanwhile, Edryd's sword and horse were covered in glick blood, as he swung to cut yet another one down.

Looks like he's doing alright, but... Oh, shit! I thought, as I noticed a glick preparing to launch itself.

"Ed!" I tried to call out, but through the cacophony of battle, it fell on deaf ears. He was fighting voraciously when a glick knocked him off his horse in the same manner that I had been just a few minutes before. "Edryd!" I yelled again, much more desperately this time, and sprinted to help my best friend.

While he didn't have as bad a fall as mine, he was still visibly hurt from it, wincing in pain as he pressed the hilt of his sword up to his shoulder. A few neighboring glicks turned, watching him desperately trying to get back on his feet and grab his sword simultaneously, and began to charge him.

Damn it. He can't take them all on at once, I thought, and doing the only thing I could think of, I began running towards him with my sword in my right hand, flowing behind me in the air.

As I watched them begin their charge, I could feel a sense of dread creep in. Regardless of whether I'd tested it, I knew only one spell I could cast in time that would deal damage to the glicks around him.

My eyes turned into the obsidian ovals once more, as I *reached into the Ethereal, drawing mana from the world without time.* I felt the warmth flow from my fingertips, rolling over my whole body, and condensed the mana to my left hand as I ran. I held the sphere for a few seconds, anxiously waiting for the glicks to be in a closer bunch than they were at the moment.

They continued to charge towards him and, in doing so, unconsciously converged into a tight group. Ed, on the other hand, could only watch as his attackers approached, but the fire in his eyes told me he was calculating whether he could strike them all at once, even with his arm in the state it was.

Fear gripped me again; not for my sake, but for *his*.

I kept sprinting, my mud-caked boots getting heavier as I went, making it difficult to continue at the same pace I had been at only a few seconds prior. I saw the glicks approaching faster than I could get there, and knew I had no time left to get any closer. The jade sphere of mana had gotten so hot that my glove felt like it was catching fire.

Fuck it. I hope this works, I thought, drawing my left hand back over my shoulder like I was going to throw something.

"Duck!" I shouted, throwing my arm forward to release the spell a half-second later, the air vibrating and rippling around it.

The ball transformed into a whip-like tendril that moved incredibly fast towards my friend. Luckily, he both heard and saw I cast the spell out of the corner of his eye. Seeing the whip-like spell coming quickly, he ducked and rolled to his left as fast as he could to escape.

I flicked the whip, wrapping it around the oncoming glicks' torsos and groins. I followed it up with the same motion I had used on the *Pyrus* spell, flicking my index finger from the base of my thumb to the tip, and ignited my spell. The mana-flame traveled along the tendril and reached the intended targets, melting flesh and bone wherever the spell wrapped around them.

Their limbs flew away from their bodies after having been viciously severed by the spell. All four glicks fell to the ground in chunks of molten flesh and bubbling blood. I could tell Roburn saw the spectacle out of my peripheral vision, though he was too occupied with slaying the remaining glicks.

Shit, I used too much mana, I thought, my vision growing blurred and dark as the dull ache in my core returned strongly.

Another glick came my way, its screeching, ravenous mouth dripping with poison and hate, forcing me to weakly ready myself for the incoming strikes. Thankfully, Garett, watching the battle from a distance, decided it was time for the bow-casters to finish off the stragglers.

"Infuse!" I heard him bark, each bow-caster around him immediately following his order. Like any other Synner, they drew from the Ethereal; however, instead of condensing it to their bodies, they condensed their mana to the bows themselves.

"Aim!" he shouted again.

The mana coated the bow's curves and string, becoming denser at the grip and anchor point. Having nocked their arrows, the mana flowed into the arrow itself. With an index finger above, and the middle and ring fingers below the arrow's shaft, they were ready.

"Fire at will!" he called out. The arrows, now enhanced with mana, rapidly soared through the air without being tampered with by the wind.

The remaining glicks were few and far between, but the bow-casters' arrows found their marks. They rained down from above, and struck the glicks' heads, piercing their scales, bones, and flesh. The arrowheads came out on the other side, just between the bottom of their jaws and necks. As soon as the arrows struck, each one fell limp as a boned fish, and dropped to the ground with a squelching *thud*.

Just as I was about to strike, my attacker crumbled onto the bloodied ground after the arrow had struck its scaly head. It skidded a short way on the slick ground, coming to a halt just before my feet.

That was close, I breathed a heavy sigh of relief.

I looked around, watching the remaining monsters fall like haunches from a butcher's rack and slamming into the ground. Their green blood soaked their limp bodies and seeped into the ground beneath them. The stench of sour meat began to overwhelm and surround us. Most of us had kept our composure, except for Batch.

Poor bastard was the first of us to vomit up his breakfast in projectile form, but I'd be lying if I said I didn't come close once or twice myself.

The bow-casters on the hill's slope began to laugh at us poor bastards below, wallowing in our enemies' reek. At that point, I was barely phased by the smell now, since I'd already had it in my nostrils for the past few minutes, and I knew how to control my body well enough not to puke.

The taste of bile was enough for me to react by swallowing my morning oats back down from whence they came. I shook my head and immediately turned toward where Edryd lay motionless. "Edryd!" I shouted, desperate to find him unharmed after the spell had blown the creatures' limbs off into all directions, but Irun had already reached him and was kneeling by his side.

"He's wounded!" he shouted back, sending a chill down my spine as I rushed to their location. Ed was lying on the ground, unconscious, with a significant talon mark across his chest and shoulder that had been bleeding profusely.

"We need some help over here!" I called out while Irun was trying to make sure the wound wasn't as severe as it looked. Garett himself rode over and dismounted from his black stallion. He rushed over to us, kneeling at Edryd's side, and briefly looked between the flaps of the sliced jerkin.

"He'll live, but I need to close this wound if he's going to continue to *have* that option," his eyes glowed with an intense, amber color as he began to pour an intense amount of mana into the wound. "Open the flaps of the jerkin for me, Thoma," he ordered in a calm voice. I moved as quickly as I could to open them, coating my hands in my best friend's blood, thinking back on the severed limbs as they flew through the air.

Damn it, one of their claws must have gotten him, I thought, making sure I didn't avert my gaze from what was happening in front of me.

Garett placed both of his hands over the open, bloodied gash that was the young boy's chest and shoulder. He alternated his index and middle fingers to release the spell slowly. The wound began to sew itself shut, using the raw mana tendrils to pull the separated skin together and seal it shut. The heat from the spell was enough to sear the skin, giving it an even tighter seal.

The smell of burning flesh and blood filled the air around us, and I almost couldn't bear to see or *smell* it.

"There," Garett said with a sigh of relief. "The bleeding has stopped, but he'll have to be careful for the next few days. Wouldn't want that opening back up, now would we?" he looked at us, tilting his head slightly. "No, Master Garett. I'll see that he recovers properly," I replied solemnly. "Good. Make sure he gets put in one of the wagons. He won't be riding on horseback for a few days by the looks of things," Garett said. "Yes, Master Garett," I bowed, then quickly returned my eyes to Ed.

The rest of the convoy came down the hill and met up with us and the rest of the bloodied synners. When the Master arrived, he gazed out over the small amount of havoc the young ones and the bow-casters had wreaked, and smiled. Garett whispered something to him, then nodded in my direction. I figured he must have told him what happened briefly, but I couldn't hear it clearly enough to confirm that.

"A pity Edryd isn't awake at the moment," the Master looked down in what I thought was *worry*. "I'd have loved to congratulate him for his bravado in combat. Holding his ground to face at least three of these bastards at a time is nothing to sneer at," he said with pride.

"See to it he gets a comfortable spot on one of the wagons to recover," he said, looking at one of the nearest synners, who responded with a slight nod. "However, that's not even mentioning the spell that was cast as they were advancing," he said in a subtly praising tone while looking at me.

I looked down at my muddied and blood-soaked boots, humbled by the Master's second compliment in two days, but I knew this was no time to grin or smile. "Master," Garett began, "We best be on our way. We've at least twelve leagues ahead of us, and I for one would like to be there before nightfall," he said. "Very well," the Master relented, motioning for the others to gather near his position.

"Wait," someone cried out. It was an old farmer who crawled out from underneath a few sacks of potatoes. He had a long, unkempt beard with white hairs among black. He was mostly bald and had probably seen at least 60 winters, with a bright red nose and cheeks.

"Yer a' headin' out yonder-ways, ain't ye?" he pointed southeast. "Yes, my good sir," the Master began, giving the elderly man a once-over glance. "Though I would imagine that you're not here only to be attacked by these foul creatures," he continued.

"Aye, that be true," the farmer shook his head. "I was on my way to me farmstead when me wheel got stuck in this puddle o' mud. When I was a leapin' from me wagon, I saw the bastards a' comin' from about a league off to the East," he said, raising an index finger to point in the general direction of the morning sunlight.

"I see," the Master nodded, gazing off into the East. "I hid meself from them foul beasts, to avoid gettin' in the way of progress, if ye get me meanin'," the farmer said with a rapid succession of head bobbing movements. "Yes, I get your *meanin'*," he replied without mockery in his voice.

"What is your name?" he asked. "Jehn Boone, at yer service," the old man replied. "Very well, Jehn Boone," the Master began. "Safest of travels, and gods' speed to you and your oxen," he nodded. "*Oh,* thank ye, master, and thank the young-uns for savin' me wagon 'n' oxen," Jehn replied, smiling from ear to ear.

We gave a short, respectful bow and began to mount our horses, who were trained to return to us after a battle. Edryd was carried to the nearest wagon and placed on top of a sack of bedding materials by two bow-casters.

Bernar rode up next to me, grinning as he always did. "I told you never to use an untested spell in combat," he said, adjusting his ass in the saddle. "*Oh*, and I imagine I was supposed to let my best friend die a death worse than I can imagine," I replied with remorse seeping through my tone as I fought back the emotions of nearly having killed my best friend.

"No, not at all. But what's important here is that you pulled it off. So, I suppose now would be as good a time as any to give you the apology I owe you for having doubted your capabilities," he shrugged as my eyes widened.

I was puzzled to hear that, but nodded for lack of anything else to do.

"Thanks, I guess," I said solemnly. "*Bah*, don't thank me till we're at the castle and Edryd's awake," Bernar said. I nodded once again and mounted my horse.

The others reformed their original formation and waited for me to get into position. Once I was, the Master signaled to begin moving again, and we were off, heading southeast to Coltend Castle.

The place where everything I thought I knew about the world would begin to be tested.

CHAPTER 4
COLTEND CASTLE

After my first battle, we met up with the others and continued on our way. We kept a respectable pace throughout the afternoon until reaching the castle. As we went over the rolling hills, and beneath the tallest trees I'd ever seen, I rode alongside Edryd, who lay in the back of one of the carts on top of a few sheets of now blood-soaked linen.

I honestly should have thought about the possibility of that happening. I now know why they always warn us never to use an untested spell in battle. You're a fool, Thoma Fayren. Just like your father, I mentally kicked myself.

As if hearing my thoughts, Bernar pulled up next to me, carefully eyeing us both before speaking. "He'll be alright," he began to say after seeing the worried look on my face. "He's a strong boy. Well, stronger than you anyway, but then again, that's not hard to be now, is it?" he said, obviously trying to cheer me up in his usual way.

I slightly raised my eyebrows and grinned from the corner of my mouth. "You're an asshole," I scoffed, holding the same expression. "Like I said, I wouldn't worry about him. He'll heal in about two days," he nodded. "It was my fault," I said curtly, my line of sight moving from my brother to Celer's nape as my eyes began to water.

"I know I should've tested the spell before today, and now my friend has paid the price for my stupidity," I managed with an ever-growing lump in my throat. "You managed to save him from being outnumbered and killed. Nothing more, nothing less," Bernar said as if stating the obvious. "I'd be focusing more on that fact, if I were in your shoes," he shrugged with an upturned lip.

I looked back at my brother with stinging, bloodshot eyes as the tears began to well. I forced myself not to let one fall, but the lump in my throat made it difficult to speak. "Thanks," my voice cracked as I nodded. "*Eh*, you don't have to thank me, just do your best to focus on the *positive* side of things from here on, okay?" he reached to put a hand on my shoulder, shaking it to get me out of my own head.

I looked at him with no small amount of surprise. I hadn't expected him to be so mature about these kinds of things, but I wasn't about to complain. "I will," I finally nodded.

"Good. Glad we got that cleared up," Bernar said, patting me on the shoulder. "Do your best to clear your eyes and get that slime out of your nostrils. We're almost there," he finished and rode ahead to be at the Master's side again.

I did what I could regarding his suggestion, but the skin around my eyes would likely still be a bit red. We rode over the last hill, and at its peak, we saw it in the distance with its mountainous backdrop.

Coltend Castle.

I almost couldn't believe my eyes. Granted, they were still full of tears, making my vision a little blurry, but from what I could see, it was massive. I forced myself to blink a few times to clear up my eyesight, but I still struggled to believe what I saw.

The walls were well over forty meters high and made of solid granite slabs. On top of the walls stood guard posts made from the trees of the nearby forest, placed at regular intervals along the circumference of the wall.

The Western Gate stood tall and mighty at twenty meters tall, and was made of steel and cedar. It was a formidable obstacle for any invasion attempts or against almost any form of enemy, though I never really thought any army would've been dumb enough to try.

The palace, where the royal family resided, stood in the exact center of the circular wall. The towering structure rose far above the wall as it gleamed in the late afternoon sun, reflecting the last rays out towards the countryside.

It's like a lighthouse on land, I thought of the only comparison I could make.

"We're almost there," the Master called out. "Now pick your jaws up off the ground, and let's get a move on," he shouted back. Everyone put their heels to their horse's sides and trotted down the hillside. Irun and Batch rode up next to me, whose eyes were only now clear enough that I could lift my head and look around without embarrassment, and trotted alongside me. "Have you ever seen anything like that? 'Cause I sure as shit haven't," Batch began. "I have once or twice before being inducted into the Synners," Irun replied.

Batch and I looked at him curiously. It wasn't like Irun to share much about his past, but we both knew this was an opportunity to let him share it with us.

"My father was a trader. He and I would often travel together to deliver our village's goods as taxes to the king. My mother was a Synner, but after going on a few trips with my father, she decided that being a trader wasn't a life I should want or have," he began, but something didn't feel right.

"Your mother was a Synner?" I asked. "Yeah, she *was*," he said distantly, but I didn't want to prod much further. After a silent moment digging through what I could only imagine were difficult memories, he looked back at us.

"She was a very strong-willed Harutian, but after the accident, she just wasn't the same, nor were things at home," he shook his head, clearly leaving out the rest of his story. I looked to Batch, but he could only offer me a shrug and a shake of his head. "Well, after she passed, I was brought to live in Codrean by some old friend of hers, apparently," he sighed, glancing up at the afternoon clouds.

"All that to say that I'm proud to be able to follow in her footsteps, even if I'm nowhere near her level of skill," he chuckled to himself, shifting his gaze away.

"I'm sorry," I said after digesting his words. "I had no idea that was how you came to be in Codrean," I continued. "No, it's fine. Only the Master and maybe a handful of others know about that," he waved his hand. "Does Isla know? You might want to tell her before she asks to meet your parents," Batch leaned in. "Batch," I glowered, shaking my head. "W-What?" he raised an eyebrow. "No, I haven't told her yet. I don't think I'll ever get the chance to, either," he sighed. "But you like her, right?" I asked, to which he only nodded his head and blushed. "Well, then you've got to say *something*," I grinned wryly.

He paused, looking at me momentarily, then closed his eyes and chuckled. "If I'm being honest, I don't think I deserve her, but thanks," he smiled, letting a few moments of silence pass between us.

"If you ever need to talk… *the other stuff*, I'm always happy to lend an ear," I leaned in. "*Oh*, it's alright. It's been so long now that I don't remember much about her. I just want to have my own stories to tell," he painedly smiled.

"Well, we're about to reach Coltend Castle. What better place to make those stories of yours, right?" Batch punched Irun's shoulder, making him flinch slightly. "You're right. Let's try to make the best of our time here," he nodded.

Batch and Irun looked at each other and then back at me, who held an obvious and almost boastful grin on my face. "Be honest, Thoma; do you really think the Master, Master Garett, and your brother will allow us to meander about, spending our small amounts of pocket money on taverns and women?" Batch asked, already knowing the answer to his question.

It was a reasonably rhetorical question; however, I could only shrug in lieu of an immediate response.

"I think after what we pulled off this morning, we should be allowed a little time off the leash they keep us on," he said after a few moments' pause and with no small amount of sarcasm in his voice.

"I agree. While I've never had a woman, nor ale to go along with one for that matter, I think it's about time boys of our age learn about that, no?" I asked, my mind running rampant with what that might actually be like, and whether I even *could* do anything about it in the castle.

My inexperienced ass, of course, was wrong.

"Best not get too far ahead of yourself, young one," Garett said, forcing a ghostly expression on our collective faces. He had overheard the entire conversation and now knew what our late-night activities would be, should they be able to leave their rooms. He looked at us and pushed his bottom lip out a little.

"I'm merely *disappointed*, though not surprised. I suppose that's what I'd do, were I in your boots," he said with a face of someone who'd just thought of a good memory. "Just pray your asses are going to be allowed out after dark," he said, turning his head back towards the castle. We looked at each other, probably all wondering whether going out at night was even possible for us.

I can't put my finger on it, but I can feel there's more to him saying that than we think, I thought as I looked over at the trio of riders ahead of me.

We were approaching the castle's walls. It became evident just how massive the flags in the castle were. From where we were, I gathered it was almost a kilometer, and I could finally begin to see the details on the flags that flew above the massive gate.

The square flag of Coltend Castle had sewn on it the image of a griffin devouring a sun, while crushing the moon with its talons above an unfurled scroll with indecipherable words on it. To be honest, I had no idea what they meant, if anything at all, as they were still far too blurry for me to read them.

As the sun was just about to set on the distant horizon behind the hills we had ridden over earlier in the day, the entirety of the castle's face was illuminated by the golden rays.

"The size of these walls is starting to make my neck hurt from looking up at them," Irun said, rubbing his nape. Batch and I agreed with his statement, catching ourselves also rubbing our napes. About fifty meters from the gate, the guardsmen's faces were becoming increasingly detailed, but then again, so were ours.

"Keep your mouths shut unless you want flies getting in," Bernar grinned, speaking quietly over his shoulder. Batch and Irun chuckled, but followed his orders promptly. When we were about fifty meters from the gate, a voice called out through a steel hatch on a much smaller doorway built into it. It was heavily reinforced like the rest of the gate, so it wasn't a weak point, but that didn't mean it wasn't *invincible*.

When we got close enough, the hatch opened fully with a sharp crack. "Hallo, there!" the voice called out. It was a man's voice, and judging only by the sound, I knew the man to be reasonably large.

I thought guardsmen were meant to ask the age-old question of who we are, but it struck me as odd that he didn't ask our names. Not to mention, he had the weirdest way of saying *hello* I think I'd ever heard.

"Hello, there! I am the Master Synner of Codrean and am here for the council meeting. "*Oh*, then you're welcome, Master," the man on the other side replied cheerfully. "I presume you know why we're here," The Master said.

"Of course I know why. I already knew who you were even before I opened the hatch, Master," the man said. "I'd seen you from the top of the wall, and recognized your armor shortly after. Took me a while to pinpoint where it was from, but I got it right. You simply confirmed it," he chirped, closing the hatch.

I could hear orders being barked from behind the gate as its chains became taut, lifting the massive gate. The chains creaked and strained to lift the mighty gate, wrapping around a large drum winch tightly.

Batch, Irun, and I tried peering under the gate to see who could get the first glimpse, but Bernar whistled softly to get our attention, subtly shaking his head to prevent us from doing so. With no small amount of dejection, we settled back into our saddles.

Once the gate was fully raised, the man stepped out from behind the nearby pillar of the guardhouse. He was a huge man indeed, as I had guessed from the sound of his voice.

Well I'll be damned. He must be one of the descendants of the giant tribes in the North, I thought.

He stood at least a head taller than anyone present, had long fair hair, deep blue eyes, and a thick, well-kept beard that reached down to the medallion around his neck that told others of his station. His armor was plate metal, not leather like the Synners' uniforms, since his was made for being able to withstand blows that could crush a man without it. It was polished bright, and his red cape split in two lengths just above knee height. His left pauldron had the Griffin of Coltend's insignia.

That must mean he's left-hand dominant. It's difficult to fight against that, since their guards are all mirrored, I thought, noticing his greatsword hung from the right side of his hip.

The Master rode closer to him and looked him over, gauging his size. "Gods above," the Master said. "It's easy to forget how large members of your race are, though, in all my years, you're the first I've met who is *this* tall," he said astonishedly.

The man stood almost as tall as the Master on his horse and stared at him cheerfully, his flat face showing a significant smile. "What is your name, guardsman?" the Master asked. "Sir Magnar Thorsen, Master," the giant replied, handing him an apple.

Thorsen? Sounds like someone descended from the gods themselves, I thought, noting the suitable name for someone his size.

"Well, Sir Thorsen, I thank you for the welcome, but must bid you farewell, grateful for the hospitality as I am," the Master said respectfully, as he flipped the apple in the air. Thorsen gave a slight bow in response. "I take it you know your way to the palace, Master?" Thorsen sensed, his eyes darting across the Master's features and confident posture. "I do, indeed. Thank you for your concern," the Master replied.

As we moved through the massive gate, we passed by the giant, nearly a half-head taller than we were, even on horseback. He looked at us briefly, noting our equipment and any accolades we might have had, greeting us with a smile and a firm nod. We immediately felt we had no other option but to automatically respond by doing the same, though our smile was more nervous than anything else.

Bernar saw the exchange and chuckled. "Never seen such unruly boys put in their place so quickly by anyone other than the Master or Garett," he chirped. I knew I needed to say something witty in retort, but failed to think of anything in the moment. As soon as the last few of our group went under the gate, the large gate came down and was quickly locked into place.

Batch, Irun, and I looked around at the nearby houses, where a few doorways allowed inquisitive eyes through the cracks.

Coltend Castle had a social system in which the common folk and the upper class were drastically separated. The common folk had to plough and till the land surrounding the castle to make ends meet, while the rich simply sat back and paid next to nothing for the commoners' hard work.

The housing differential was so significant that the small wooden shacks or the poorly built brick and straw houses were but a stone's throw away from each other, which upset many of the rich. They would often complain about the filthiness of the poor, who could be seen throwing their buckets of piss and shit out of the window in the early mornings.

The younger children would attempt to see if they could hit a *Big Belly*, their term for a tax collector, with a clump of shit as they made their rounds.

According to what I'd heard, their aim was astonishingly good.

Along the main street, countless beggars leaned on the walls of the houses, begging for alms and donations to feed their empty bellies. Their cups and cracked wooden bowls were empty. "Even with all of the riches of Coltend, nothing means more to them than a person stooping down to place a single coin in their cups," Bernar said, noting the look I wore.

I guess the sour look on my face gave away everything else I was thinking in that moment.

"Don't think too hard about it. Feeling sorry for them won't do you much good in the long run," he shook his head. "But I can't help it," I retorted. "I feel as though one day I'll be able to help them, and the fact that I can't do anything about it right *now* makes me angry," I furrowed my brow.

"You've always had a good heart and attitude," Bernard chuckled. "Hold on to it while you still can. Seeing enough of the world, how it *truly* is, might change you," he began with a heavy sigh. "However, if you can hold on to that level of empathy, then you'll be the strongest of us all," he finished his sentence and smiled when he noticed I'd taken his words to heart.

"So, you're telling me you don't care about other people. Is that it?" I asked after a brief pause. I still care about a *few people*. You and the Master are two I can name off the top of my head, at least," he shrugged sarcastically. *Ah*, I see. It's a little cold-hearted, but I think I get it," I nodded.

I began to look around and observe the filth and grime on their faces, days of accumulated dirt under their fingernails during their days plowing and tilling fields could be seen from a few meters away. Even though their whispers couldn't be heard through the cacophony of the street, I guessed that they were commenting on our armor and general appearance.

After all, it had been nearly fifty years since they last saw so many of us in one spot.

The sound of our hooves resonated down the small alleys that ran perpendicular to the main street, and small children ran to the roadside to see what all the commotion was about. Pointing and staring were among the most common actions, while whispers and giggles were a close second from some older girls. Irun and Batch noted a few who seemed to be their own age. "Don't even think about it..." Garett said quietly toward the pair, destroying their hopes.

Bernar and I stifled a laugh when we saw their faces.

We continued down the street without speaking for the most part, but when we reached the general marketplace, it was teeming with busy shopkeepers, angry shoppers, and show animals being kept in place by their trainers. There was so much to look at that I finally decided to ride up to my brother's side, knowing my idiot self would get sidetracked and, consequently, lost.

"Do you think we'll be allowed to leave our quarters?" I asked, nudging Celer a little closer to speak quietly. "Not sure about you, but I'm definitely getting out of there," Bernar replied with a shit-eating grin.

The moment the last word had left his mouth, I noticed a red-haired prostitute, wearing little more than a corset and stockings, standing on the balcony of a two-story house laced with red ribbons. "And that's likely the place I'll be all night," he said, nodding in the building's general direction.

"You're sure you'll have the coin for an all-night expedition with every woman in that... *establishment*?" I asked, knowing my brother's nearly insatiable lust for women. "Believe me, little brother, as soon as I'm done with the first, the rest will give me a discount after they hear what I've done," he said confidently.

I could have sworn I heard Isla groan in disgust as soon as she understood what he meant, but I could only give her a tight-lipped, apologetic smile.

"Are you sure about that?" Roburn chimed in from my right side. "I've heard stories about the ones here," he said as if he had more knowledge than he cared to share. "I suppose you'd know all about them. You might even be *the cause* of a few," Bernard said with a wry smile. Roburn chuckled and turned to me with a sly smile on his face.

"You know, I would take you along with me, so I could show you the ones to avoid. For *educational purposes*, of course," he grinned. "*Of course*," I nodded firmly. "They've been known not to be clear of the, *uh*, *illnesses*," he said with a hush on the last word. My eyes opened widely with genuine concern.

"You mean they've got some kind of plague?" I asked hushedly. "More like a sort of *rot*, but sure, we'll go with that," my brother and Roburn simply laughed at some internal joke, refusing to elaborate any further.

We neared the main palace and were shocked at the sight of the gate. Two golden griffins facing each other loomed over the main entrance. Scarlet cloth hung from the top of the ivory-imbued gate, and intricate designs portraying the beasts crushing the moons on each door. The Master raised his hand, a signal to the gatekeeper, who looked out over the edge and called out to open the doorway.

Two guardsmen pulled on massive levers which, through ingenious mechanisms, made opening the gate easier than one would think. The giant doors swung open gracefully and without making much noise.

We were awestruck at the sight before us. Tall pine trees lined the sides of the road. Beneath the trees, a fence of interwoven roots had been formed, as though the trees themselves were connected. The street was made of smooth granite slabs, each carved and covered in resin to protect it from the elements. Seen from above, the pattern formed the Griffin of Coltend with its wings spread.

All of us, except for the Master, Garett, Roburn, and Bernar, of course, looked about in awe. Behind the fence, we saw fountains and a large open garden with fair maidens picking strawberries from the bushes. Their long, red dresses had their hems trimmed just enough not to drag along the floor.

Down the road a little way, the doors to the main palace could be seen, with a score of guardsmen on either side. Their gear looked a little less garnished than Thorsen's had been, but they were all equally well-equipped. Each man stood on a single step of the stairway that led into the main Palace. I looked at Batch, who shot me a look as if to tell me he wanted their armor, too.

I wholeheartedly agreed with him.

"Do you know what those two large flags are, Thoma?" Roburn asked, but I shook my head. Even with the lessons I'd had growing up, there was limited information on such boring stuff like flags. "Those are the flags of the Church of Mideia, and the Warrior's Guild," he began, pointing to each one in order. "The Church is a nasty bunch to deal with, but the Guild, if I'm being honest, isn't *anywhere near* as rough. They can at least hold a civil conversation without needing to spout some insults about us," he continued, catching himself from spitting on the ground.

So they just hate us regardless of everything we do for them? That's a bit unfair, I noted, already feeling a bitter taste in my mouth beginning to churn.

The stairway had a long carpet running down in a strip to the base, while the flags Roburn had mentioned earlier hung overhead. The Church showed its green colors and the image of a person reaching out for help to a serpent that hung between a sword and a staff in the shape of a cross. The Warrior's Guild, also known as the *Barracks,* hung their standard of an ox and a blade linked together by a chain on a blue background.

The remaining flags were those of the neighboring cities and villages that the castle would attend to, and each proudly showed their colors and markings. Some were somewhat obscure, others entirely offensive. Nevertheless, the castle had always wanted to prove that they were unified no matter what, so even the offensive flags were shown.

As we neared the main stairway, we finally got a closer look at the guards in their armor. "Magnificent work, isn't it?" Bernar asked, looking back at the three of us who nodded vigorously. "It really is extraordinary," I said, my eyes as wide as possible. "For them to be standing there like that for hours and hours on end in full gear is impressive. Either they're extremely well disciplined, or their armor must be lighter than it looks," I suggested.

"You have a point there, Thoma," Garett began. "Their armor is forged under the supervision of a master smith, who just so happens to be an elf," he said matter-of-factly. "An elf?" Batch asked, as though he hadn't quite heard it correctly.

Bernar raised an eyebrow at Garett, but said nothing as he chuckled quietly to himself.

"Yes," Garett said. "You see, they have special techniques for making armor light and strong. Not only that, but a single piece of armor might last you a lifetime, if you take care of it properly," he continued. "They're certainly not cheap. I'd wager a breastplate alone is about two thousand crescents," my brother chimed in with a bit of uncertainty.

Our collective jaws dropped. "T-two *thousand*?" Irun asked, his jaw slack and with eyes as wide as mine. "It's an investment Coltend is willing to make. After all, it is the central trading hub for all four countries," Garett said. "But we haven't seen anything that would suggest as much," Batch said curiously. "Not yet," Garett replied wryly.

We didn't understand what he meant by that, so we simply looked at each other and shrugged.

"Halt!" Garett shouted after he had seen the Master raise his hand. The whole party came to a complete stop and began to dismount. Our legs hurt from riding for the better part of the day, so it was quite a relief to stand on our own two feet again.

"All of you, listen up! Master's got a few words for you," Garett shouted again and everyone looked at the Master who was stepping forward. "I want you all to listen closely, as I will only say this once," he began with an air of caution as he looked at all of us.

"Since this is mostly directed toward the juniors, I will keep this short. Where we're about to enter is full of influential people and politicians from all four countries. They will be scattered around the palace, so mind who you talk to and how you talk to them," he glowered at us warningly, sending another shiver down our spines.

"As tempted as you may be to try and do something out of league simply because you think I won't be watching or hearing about it later, *don't*," he said, his intonation falling heavily on the last word.

I gulped a disappointed, dry ball of spit as the gloom also hung over Irun and Batch's heads.

"Not that I *expect you to*, but you've been warned," he said. Bernar grinned, trying to hide it from the others. "Don't forget that just because we're amidst other people, and important ones at that, never be caught off your guard. Do you understand?" he said sternly. "Yes, Master," everyone said in unison. He nodded, turned on his toes like he had the night before, and proceeded towards the stairway.

"You heard what he said?" Batch asked quietly. "Yeah, though I find it rather strange how they would simply all be here at once without something bigger going on," Irun replied.

I wonder what he's not telling us, I thought.

At the top of the stairway, they were met by a short man with graying, slicked back hair and a large stomach. He was clean shaven and wore Coltend's colors on his tightly-fitting doublet. "Welcome, Masters," he said, bowing low and straining the fabric around his waist.

I should probably shield my eyes before a button pops out, I winced.

"My name's Fulco, and I am honored to be the one tending to your needs on behalf of King Truls," he said cheerily as the wrinkles around his eyes scrunched up. "We're honored to have been invited," the Master replied. "Tell me, good man, where might our accommodations be?" he asked plaintively.

"Follow me, good sirs," Fulco replied with a motion, and they walked through the doorway. Once inside, I couldn't help but notice the tall, granite pillars that supported the great roof lathered in grandiose carvings and battles from past times. There were also *six* stained-glass windows that had depictions of the gods from the Master's story, one appearing in each window.

The red strip of carpet led down the hallway to the end of the large room. Benches were placed in rows facing the back of the room, where the king and queen would sit. The hall was far quieter than I had expected, at least for the time being, though I would be lying if I said I'd noticed it from the start. Like the others, I was too busy looking at all the details carved into the pillars and such.

Sorry you're missing out on this, Ed, I thought, wondering where he was carted off to.

"This way, please," Fulco called out and turned to the left wing of the room, where there was yet another stairway. We followed him up the stairs, and on the walls, we saw fine oil paintings of the old captains of the Royal Guard. Their standard wasn't on display outside, but it was obvious to tell who they were given their high-quality armor and majesticly posed paintings.

"I'm just going to assume he's taking us to the barracks portion of the palace," Irun said, hoping to sleep on a more comfortable bed for once. "Seems like that's where we'll all be sleeping," Batch replied. I was in too much awe to come up with any intelligible response.

"You will have all of the necessary items to take care of yourselves and your equipment, so shut up for now," Bernar whispered back. "Yeah, but sharing a room with the Master was not on my bucket list of things to do before I eat dirt," Batch muttered, getting a chuckle out of my brother.

"Here we are," Fulco said promptly, pushing open a door to a large room with numerous beds lined up beside the walls. Batch spotted a hallway that looked like it led to a bathing area, and nudged Irun excitedly.

"I shall summon the servants to take your..." he paused, glancing at my armor as I passed him that still had a few bloodstains from the battle earlier in the day. His eyes opened wide at the sight of me, and he quickly put his hand to his mouth.

This poor fucker didn't notice the smell before, either? I'm sorry, Fulco, but I've been wearing this all day, so suck it up, I mentally chuckled.

"My goodness, is that...?" he stammered. "Yes, it is, good sir," the Master cut him off, stepping in front of me. "We'd very much appreciate it if the servants could assist us in getting their garments all cleaned up by tomorrow," the Master said politely. "I-I-I assure you they'll be cleaned by then," Fulco said with a slight bit of disgust in his voice. "Thank you for your troubles," the Master said, smiling warmly as Fulco scurried off to find the servants.

Sorry about that, I winced at the Master who glanced at me over his shoulder.

The Master fully turned around and smiled. "He turned about as green as the blood on your armor, boys," he said. It was the first time anyone aside from Bernar or Garett had heard him say something with a hint of humor. We weren't entirely sure it had been meant as a joke, so we just nervously grinned. "Let's get cleaned up and get some food in our bellies," Bernar suggested to everyone, noticing the awkward exchange. "Yes, I'm aching to try their apple cobbler. I hear it's superb," the Master said before leading us inside.

There was a score of beds lined up along the walls, covered in freshly washed linen sheets. Comparing it to our beds in Codrean, this felt *far too luxurious* for us. Nevertheless, this was where Fulco had told us we would stay, and I knew I wasn't the only one giddy with excitement.

"Never would have taken you for having a sweet tooth, Master," a voice came behind us. We all turned towards it, only to find that it was a servant girl. Her hair was covered by a red head wrap, except for a single lock of black hair that hung from the brim down to her pale cheek. Her deep, green eyes flicking from one person to the next indicated that she felt like she had done something wrong.

After all, no one had seen or heard her come in.

Gods above, she's gorgeous! I thought, feeling my heart skip a beat or two.

"I'm sorry," she said, quickly bowing. "I had no intention to startle you. Especially not all dressed up like that in fancy armor," she said. "Not at all! It's alright," the Master said warmly, glancing at me over his shoulder again. I only noticed him doing so out of the corner of my eye, since I still hadn't taken my eyes off of her when she caught me staring at her.

I briefly blinked and shook myself out of my daze, trying to wake up from the trance her beauty had put me in.

"What is your name, child?" he asked calmly, making sure she felt comfortable around him. "My name is Meliss, Master," she said timidly. "Well, Meliss, would you do us all a favor and take our garments to have them cleaned? I'm sure Fulco has probably already instructed you to do so," he continued. "Yes, of course, Master, but they need to be off your bodies for me to wash them, Master," she said quietly.

They fucking need to be what *now?* I thought, feeling my face beginning to flush with color.

The Master smiled and turned with a malicious glare in his eye. "You heard the young lady. Strip," he said playfully and with an air of command that no one dared to defy.

Irun, Batch, and I looked at each other seeking counsel, but none of us knew what to do about this situation.

None of us youngsters had been in our undergarments in front of a lady before, let alone entirely naked, so most of the others were *also* apprehensive to be in that state. That's not to say that we didn't have female synners. We were merely separated when it came to bathing, changing clothes, and sleeping. Aside from those things, we did everything else together as equals.

"Except for the females who will change in the bathing area," the Master added quickly, gesturing for the women to go. "The rest of you can get started," he said. When we hesitated a little, his eyes flared with a bit of mana, adding to the intensity of his next word. "Now," the Master tilted his head, his voice filled with a rumble I'd never heard before as it permeated the room like a thunderclap.

Like the others around me, I flinched at the suddenly barked order. It felt strange to be forced to do this, but Meliss' expression hadn't shifted in the slightest.

Regardless, I did my best not to make eye contact.

Batch and Irun had miserable looks on their faces, while Meliss, on the other hand, was entirely unfazed; almost as if she felt almost nothing seeing us strip. It was, apparently, a common thing for maids and servants to wait on other people to undress so they could take their clothes. To her, it was nothing more than a few bloodstained people changing their attire.

First impressions are everything, right? How can she be so beautiful yet so unfazed by everyone naked in front of her? It seems cruel that someone would have to see so many different people in their birthday suits enough times to become numb like that, especially at her age, I thought while mentally admiring her beauty.

I quickly finished undressing, and I felt something I hadn't really felt in years: *exposed*. Thankfully, it wasn't just me, as some of the others did as well. The tell-tale sign of this was with the awkward manner in which they placed their jerkins, undershirts, and under-garments into the small trolley she brought.

When it was my turn to put my stuff in the trolley, she smiled at me. I froze on the inside as butterflies did somersaults in my stomach, but I tried to keep my arms and legs moving, making it look like this was my usual state of being. I caught her gaze as I let go of my blood-soaked jerkin, and she smiled at me, giving me a knowing nod.

Ah, fuck. I looked at her, after all, I thought, flushing with embarrassment.

I stepped away from the trolley without turning around, but she just kept staring at me. She couldn't have been much older than I was, yet we'd had this strange connection I'd never heard of before.

At least, that's what *I thought* we had.

"Well, then," the Master cleared his throat after noticing the exchange. "*Oh,*" Meliss said, breaking whatever thought ran through her mind. "Right away, Master," she grabbed the trolley handles and scurried out of the room. She almost ran into the door frame on her way out, and it was clear her mind was somewhere else entirely.

Bernar gave the Master a knowing look and laughed at me just as she turned the corner. "For someone as quiet as she was when she arrived, she was a bit clumsy on her way out," he began. "Although she didn't even have to say a fuckin' word, and she's got your prick all tied up in a knot," he elbowed me in the ribs.

"What, I can't think someone's beautiful?" I asked defiantly. "Of course you can. I'm just *doing you a favor* by telling you not to get hung up on her after only seeing her once, *little shit,*" Bernar said. I raised an eyebrow questioningly, mostly because I couldn't tell if he was joking, or if it was just my lack of experience getting the better of me. "There are *even more* beautiful women than her out there," he whispered, causing me to raise an eyebrow. "Just take my word for it," he patted me on the shoulder. "Alright, *alright!* I get it," I retorted somewhat reluctantly.

"Gentlemen," Fulco called out, relieved not to see bloodstained clothing everywhere as we all turned to face him. He walked through the doorway with two servants carrying bundles of clean, red linen undergarments. "These are for you after you bathe, and, if you so wish, you may keep them when you leave. We are as generous as we can be with our guests," he said with pride.

"Thank you," the Master said, grabbing one from the pile. The two servants began handing them out according to size. Comments on the softness and smoothness of the undergarments came *en masse*, and others could simply not fathom the quality of the material. "I will leave a servant for you just outside the door should you need any food or drink," Fulco gestured to the doorway.

"Thank you, dear Fulco. We've had a long journey, so for now, we shall all retire. Tomorrow is a big day, from what I hear," the Master said tiredly. "*Oh,* very much so, Master," Fulco said with excitement.

There it is again, I thought.

"I'll leave you to it," Fulco said as he bowed and walked out the door. "Let's get cleaned up and rest, shall we, lads?" Garett suggested, turning to face us. Everyone nodded at his command and headed off to the bathing area Batch had spotted previously. "But, what of Edryd, Master Garett?" I asked. "He's being taken care of. Quite possibly by that *young maiden* who was just here, I might add," Garett said.

Lucky bastard, I thought, relieved to hear my friend was probably in excellent hands.

The air outside might not have been as cold as it was at Codrean, but the stone walls made for excellent insulators from the sun's heat. After a quick shower, Bernar took the bed next to mine and plopped himself down, locking his fingers behind his head as he let out a heavy sigh. "Not going to try and light this bed on fire, too, are you?" he asked mockingly. "I'm pretty sure I've learned my lesson already. Thanks," I replied with a sarcastic grin. He gave me a thin-lipped smile, nodded, and turned onto his side.

First, the Master told us that important *figures were in the area, and then Fulco made it seem more grandiose than I initially thought. What's* really *going on?* I tried to piece it all together, but when nothing made sense, I closed my eyes and *returned to the endless dreamscape again.*

The following morning, I woke to the sound of a rooster off in the distance. I looked out from the window beside my bed and saw a large crowd gathering around the doorway by which we had entered the castle the previous evening.

The sun was just rising over the side of the high wall, and a few beams were entering the room, gently caressing some of the beds and stone tiles in their paths. I rubbed my eyes, trying to clear the need for sleep from them, and noticed a few around me were doing the same.

Garett walked in just as I mentally prepared myself to get out of bed. "Rise and shine, *daisies,*" he yelled with evident sarcasm, stirring some of the others who were still asleep. He was already in full harness. His jerkin smelled of lavender and looked almost as good as new. I scurried out of bed in a rush, only to find my jerkin cleaned and hanging at my bedside.

It's so clean. Almost as if there was never any blood on it, I thought as I also caught the lavender scent on my jerkin.

As I put my gear on, I kicked my brother, who had somehow slept through Garett's booming shout, to get out of bed. "I'm up, you daft little..." he didn't finish his sentence, instead, he threw a pillow at my face, hitting me square in the nose.

I caught the pillow mid-fall and swung back down at him, aiming for his head. "Then get out of bed already, you lazy *fuck-nugget,*" I said jokingly. He stuck his tongue out at me, and for a moment, I wondered whether *I* was the older brother.

Batch and Irun were having some trouble getting into their attire, but that was quickly remedied when Garett used a bit of his mana to pull down the top part of their jerkins, which had shrunk a little due to the cleaning.

Nice going, I subtly lifted my thumb to the two of them with a shit-eating grin.

After a few minutes of hustle and bustle, brushing and tying hair up, getting jerkins, boots, and hose on, everyone was ready and formed up. Batch, Irun, Roburn, Bernar, and I all stood at attention in the front row. The Master looked out over everyone and quickly checked to ensure none had weapons on them. "We're not allowed any weapons inside where we're about to go, so I'm just making sure no one was dumb enough to forget that," he said, almost as if reading all of our thoughts.

"We must go, gentlemen," Fulco said as he stopped in the doorway. "Right this way," he gestured, directing us out of the room and down the hall to the right. The Master went first, then Bernar, Garett, and the rest of us.

Fulco led us back down the same hallways and halls as we had come through the previous evening, and I still couldn't shake the awe. Every time we walked down a hall, I'd notice something different about it. A new painting, carving, or something of the like. It was all so new that it took me longer than expected to take it all in.

"What do you think all the commotion is about?" Batch asked with a bit of nervousness. "I wish I knew, but I guess that it's going to be important. Otherwise, we might not have needed to be here, let alone with so many important figures walking about," I replied.

I had already been thinking about that since looking out my window earlier that morning. Nevertheless, I had failed in getting the answers I wanted. Batch noted the worried look on my face, sighing quietly as he shook his head.

After a few short minutes of walking, Fulco stopped and turned on his heel. We weren't expecting a man of his stature to move so eloquently or quickly, so we ended up paying close attention to him without being instructed to. "Through this doorway, you will be in the presence of various leaders from all around the Continent," he said with a grandiose air.

I've never seen anyone from outside our country besides Mom, and I barely remember her as it is, I thought, feeling a sense of nervousness come over me.

Fulco turned his attention to the Master. "I'm certain your Synners will know how to behave themselves in the Council Room, Master," he said, looking for reassurance. "Of course, my good Fulco,. Although I will only take a handful with me," the Master confidently replied. "*Ah!* All is well, then. In that case, we may enter," Fulco breathed a sigh of relief.

He moved to the door and pulled on the lever that kept it locked. The lever clacked and thudded, and the door swung open, as my eyes opened wide. He stepped aside to the left and showed us into the Council Room. As we walked through the doorway, we saw leaders from all regions sitting around the most enormous meeting table on the Continent.

The four Lords of the Continent, King Truls Wishert of Coltend, King Mads Oden of Hjalfar, King Bashaa Ibn'Escya of Harut, and King Elhael Phrys of Caegwen, observed our entry as they stood near their respective seats.

The table's details could be seen from afar, and it portrayed carvings of past battles between monsters and men. The gold ring that lined the table's edge was covered in runes, ancient spells for calming and harmony, good judgment, understanding, respect, and industriousness. Its frame had been carved from a solid oak tree that had once been touched by the gods, and had grown taller and broader than any other of its species.

Numerous monster heads hung on the walls, some with horns, others with ghastly mouths agape, hanging from wooden frames with their mouths spread widely and menacingly. The stained glass windows were also present, with details of rivers and forests instead of battles to remind those present of what they were gathering for.

I walked cautiously behind my older brother, and my friends followed closely behind me. Everyone was wondering just what was going to happen at this apparent council meeting. Some guessed it was to discuss trade routes, while others thought it would be about farming goods.

No one was even *close*; not even a little.

"Ladies and gentlemen, please be seated," Fulco called out. The four kings sat down first at the vertices of the table. The others sat between them, mixed as they were; Harutians with Coltenders, Hjalfarians with Caegweni.

Well, this is unusual, I noted a large Hjalfarian sitting next to Batch, making his face sweat nervously.

I sat opposite King Elhael Phrys of Caegwen, who regarded me curiously for a moment, prompting me to bow as much as I could from my seated position, my brown hair falling in front of my eyes. He tilted his head, then shifted his gaze to someone else whom I didn't dare try to identify, and nodded his head to whoever it was.

"I know what you're thinking, but it helps maintain a sense of equality during the council," Garett whispered, noticing my raised eyebrow as I got up from the bow.

Once everyone had been seated, the rest of the warriors and councilors sat down. I sat next to my brother, while Garett sat next to the Master. Batch and Irun were split between a Harutian warrior, and both did their best to avoid cross communication.

Truls had his wife, Queen Leona of Maeredia, sit at his right. Her beauty was angelic, to say the least. She wore a red dress with her black hair tied up in a fanciful bun. Her pale, blue eyes and perfect complexion had, in some instances, led her to be mistaken for an elf of Caegwen, though it was always quickly proven otherwise due to the lack of pointed ears.

"Your Majesties, ladies, and gentlemen," Fulco began in a practiced voice. "Please take note of everything that will be said here today, for it may change the course of our history in this world. Feel free to ask questions, so long as they are relevant to what is being discussed. Otherwise, they will be ignored by the council," he continued. "As the primary host of this council, King Truls Wishert of Coltend will be the one to commence," Fulco finished, bowed, and stepped back.

Truls pushed back his chair and stood. His long, graying hair floated softly on his shoulders, while his beard was neatly trimmed for the occasion. He was not a small man, by any means, for his eating habits had caused him to be overweight. His red doublet was stretched tightly across his body, making his breathing labored even before he spoke.

His eyes were dark blue, and the bags under his eyes from countless drunken nights showed their weight. His aquiline nose had a significant bump in the middle, while the crown he wore had the pattern of the Griffin carved into it. He also wore a gold-plated necklace depicting his accolades and feats as a younger man.

"My fellow Kings, lords and ladies present," he began with a voice of rolling thunder. "I am certain most of us here know why I've called this council," he said. I looked over to Batch and Irun, each of us raising an eyebrow and shrugging quickly.

"These monsters have recently increased their assaults, emboldened by something we do not yet understand. Their numbers are also rapidly approaching undefendable levels, and we simply can no longer sit on our hands. This matter must be resolved before it wipes out our supply lines and mercantile routes," he glanced around the room, then lifted a hand, gesturing towards where I thought the Master was sitting.

"The Synners of the Continent have been doing their best to suppress their numbers in each country. However, no matter how many of those ugly bastards they slay, the bastards keep coming back," he said, and raised his voice a little at the last word.

"Our leading experts on the monster incursions, as well as the Synners of Codrean, believe we have found the answer to rid ourselves of these bastards once and for all," he said with an air of finality.

Ah, so that's what the secrecy was for, I thought.

"The Underworld has found a way to leak their monsters through portals that begin in their worlds and end in ours. Now, I know how that sounds. However, I beg you to let King Elhael Phrys of Caegwen explain it in greater detail, for he is far more knowledgeable in these matters than I," Truls sat back down in his chair while Elhael pushed his chair back.

He glanced at me again as he rose to his feet, then over to my brother and a handful of others as if to disguise the fact that he'd done so.

That's the second time he's looked at me. Is it just because I'm sitting across from him? I wondered.

He stood at least a head taller than anyone in the room, and his fair silver hair, straight as an arrow, hung down to his middle back. His nearly perfect complexion, lack of beard, and bright green eyes made him stand out amidst the others. His pointed ears were sharp, but they had a certain elegance that matched his other features perfectly.

"I thank you, King Truls, for the compliment," he began, his voice sounding like a river flowing softly through the air. Much less brutish than the one who had spoken before him. "Indeed, what King Truls has said is true. Unlike their original entry to this world - the cause of which we have yet to understand how or why it happened," he shook his head.

"My *scouts* have found such a portal in the forests of Caegwen. After observing it for three months, they noted that once every full moon, the portals open and these foul beasts pour out until the morning sun closes the portal," he continued.

"This is not exclusive to Caegwen, however, as there are portals in every country, we just happened to find *ours* first. We are still unsure why this is happening on such a consistent basis. However, we currently lack the manpower to make any attempts at closing them," he sighed.

"The only foreseeable way to close such breaches in our realm is through powerful spells, though other suggestions are more than welcome," he glanced around the room. "My mages are tirelessly working on ways to close those, as mentioned earlier; however, any recent attempt at closing them has failed drastically, resulting in the deaths of more than a few of my warriors," he said, with a drop of tone towards the end of his sentence, getting scattered gasps from around the room.

"Regrettable as their downfalls are, we must move on. I propose that my mages work with the others scattered around the Continent so that we can end these incursions," he said with conviction.

"I agree, Your Majesty," the Master said, raising a hand. "The more people we have working on how to close them, the sooner results will come. However, I must ask the following: How do the portals open, and are they two-way or one-way portals?" he asked. "We believe them to be *two-way*," Elhael shrugged. "However, none of my men thus far have dared to attempt to go into one," he said dejectedly.

"I believe we should mount a party of the bravest men and women, volunteers of course, to go in and at the very minimum see if *it is* a two-way portal," Prince Bashir of Harut said, raising his hand, causing Leona to turn her head towards him instantly.

He was the son of King Bashaa and a good-looking man overall. He was tanned, dark-haired, and had pale green eyes. His close-cut hair and beard showed he cared much for his appearance. His warrior past had given him a strong and able body to match, so it was no small wonder why she'd be interested in him.

"I don't entirely disagree with you, Prince Bashir," Elhael said. "However, I must ask you where you may find such valiant folk to pull that off," he said with curiosity. "We could always let Mideia handle it," a voice came away from the table.

My brother and I winced at the exact same time.

An old, hooded man stepped out from behind Truls' guardsmen and began walking toward the table. He was hooded, with the sign of the Church's sword and staff sewn into his robes. The hems were dirty, and the areas around his knees were well-worn out from kneeling often. His face was wrinkled as unfolded clothes, and his beard looked like a gray cloud. His eyes were pale and gray, yet he saw more than most.

"Mideia will save us. He has always been there for us in our times of need, and he will be with us now," the old man croaked with conviction. "Father Mourtis. How nice of you to join us," Truls said courteously. "Who is this man, and what is he doing in a war council if he is a priest?" King Bashaa asked angrily. "This is the high priest of the Church of Mideia," the Master answered, lacing his words with subtle sarcasm and malice.

"It's good to see you, too, *Master of Codrean*," Mourtis returned the greeting with equal venom in his tone, ignoring Bashaa's comment.

"That's all well and good, but what is he doing in a war council?" Bashaa asked once more, more angrily than before. "Essentially, my Lords, they want the eradication of all things deemed evil by their *god*," the Master said. "Unfortunately for the followers of Mideia, smiting evil hasn't exactly been on his to-do list of late," he grinned, getting a chuckle out of a few at the table.

Mourtis was white with rage. "How dare you blaspheme against the one true god who stands above the rest, you *non-believer*?" he belted at the top of his lungs. "*Non-believer*?" the Master asked calmly. "I know that there are many gods, I simply don't believe yours is the most powerful," he continued calmly.

Mourtis furrowed his brow. "Mark my words: He will smite you down with bolts from the sky, and brimstone from the deepest corners of the Underworld," he bellowed threateningly.

"Have you ever been to the *Underworld* before, *priest*?" the Master asked calmly, surprising the old man with the question. "N-no, I have not! Of course not! What a ridiculous notion!" he retorted. "*Ah*, I see. If you had, you would have known there is *no brimstone* there, and that it is also not *geometric* in shape, I might add," the Master's lips thinned.

"I don't know for sure how powerful Mideia is, or what bullshit you spue to your followers, but if you think he could strike me down, I'd love to see him *try*," he tilted his head with a malicious grin.

Oh shit! I thought we were trying to watch what we said, I felt the nervousness ripple through me and the others present.

Mourtis was taken aback, while the rest of us, Bernar and Roburn included, stifled our laughter at the prospect of the Master verbally demolishing this priest. His eyes burned with a fire no one had seen or even guessed the old man had, but it seemed like he took the Master's words seriously enough.

"Calm down, you two," Elhael interjected, his voice raised just enough to get their attention. "Bickering over such menial things is pointless right now. Let us focus on what we must do to rid ourselves of these beasts," he concluded, raising his eyebrows at the Master slightly as if to tell him to stop.

"He's right. It may be entertaining to the rest of us to watch the High Priest squirm, but King Elhael has a point, nevertheless," Bernar chimed in, giving the elven king a knowing nod which was returned in kind. Everyone calmed back down, and the sound of light laughter faded. Mourtis glared at the Master, who kept a straight face the whole time.

Just then, I felt a surge of mana flowing through the room, but I couldn't pinpoint it due to all of the other casters in the room. "I think we've got a problem here," I whispered, tapping Bernar's shoulder. "I felt it too," he began, leaning in closer. "But this is a war council, and there's not a single *turtle shit* I can do about it without starting an all out war over breaking tradition," he said while looking around the room.

The Master came close enough just now, didn't he? I guess I'll just have to watch for anything suspicious, I frowned.

Well, then," King Mads began in a grunty voice after clearing his throat. "We need options, and fighting like dogs over meat about what to do won't solve our problem. I agree with sending a party as King Bashaa had suggested before. However, how we will acquire such brave people might be more complicated than we think," he said, looking at everyone in the room inquisitively.

"Advertising a certain amount of gold per person willing to go might do the trick," Leona said, and everyone turned their attention towards her. Bashir's eyes opened wide, blatantly staring at her.

If his facial features could write words, they would have something regarding how beautiful she is strewn across them, I thought, noticing the man's apparent lack of lustful disguise.

"I agree with Her Majesty, though it will take no small amount to convince young men and women to take up a task they might not return from," Elhael said. "The proper amount for each willing person will be decided by whether they have family, and before the actual test takes place," Truls added.

"So we all agree on this happening, I take it?" Bashaa asked, gazing around the room briefly. "I believe so," Elhael replied. "All in favor say *aye*," Leona called out. A unanimous aye resounded from every man and woman present, and all looked towards Truls.

"Then, Your Majesties, lords and ladies present, I believe our council here is finished now. We will reconvene after lunch," Truls declared. "Kings Elhael, Bashaa, Mads, and I shall meet once again to discuss the economic viability for each country," he gestured across the table to them. The four nodded to each other and began to move away from the table. "All are now excused," Fulco called out and showed the leaders to the door.

As they were leaving the room, Mourtis stopped the Master and began speaking to him privately. I noted the High Priest's expression on his face during their conversation as it contorted into a mix of anger and resentment.

Damn it, I can't hear what they're saying. Although judging by how intense the High Priest seems, it almost looks like he's threatening the Master, I thought.

Just then, a servant came up to me and interrupted my thoughts. "Young master," the servant said. "Your friend is awake and is asking to see you and the others," he said excitedly. My eyes opened widely at the news, and I curtly nodded. "Thank you for the news! It's much appreciated," I said briefly, running off, taking Bernar, Irun, and Batch along with me.

Just before I left the council room, I saw Leona staring at Bashir, who tried to avoid staring back, but had a hard time keeping his eyes off of her. "Come, my sweet," Truls said, touching her shoulder, which caused a shiver to run down the length of her sleek body in what looked like disgust, but she began to walk alongside the king.

That was weird, I thought, but quickly dismissed that line of thinking, as I had a new focus in mind.

I ran into the nursery and almost knocked over a healer or two on the way in. I found his friend, though only one eye was open. "Thoma," he said weakly. "Edryd! You're...you're...," I didn't want to finish. "No, I'm not blind in one eye if that's what you wanted to say. It's just a bit hard to open it with all the clotted blood around it," he smiled weakly.

"I'm relieved to hear that," I said. "Well, it could have been much worse," Batch began. "You could have lost your prick," he said with a chuckle. Edryd wheezed heavily from the pain that was laughing, but he still had a smile on his face.

"So, tell me what happened after I blacked out," he said, his tone carrying genuine curiosity. The other boys and I began telling of the battle and council, while Bernar was warming up to a nearby nurse.

Surprising *no one*, she rejected him shortly after he began speaking.

She rejected him shortly after he began speaking.

After a few hours of talking about our experiences the previous day and on that day, we bid farewell and a speedy recovery to Edryd, and went to our dormitory. I sat down on a bench in the bathing area, going over the information and everything I had seen that day.

What the hell was that mana burst? I thought.

CHAPTER 5

VALDIS

F ar in the northern region of Hjalfar, where travelers are seldom seen, a citadel lay deep in the mountains.

A man dressed in a long, black robe meandered the vast halls of the long-forgotten citadel of Valdis. He eventually seated himself in a throne located in a large hall and made use of the armrests that had been built into it. His long, black robe draped over the edges, while the holes and tears near the hem gently kissed the floor. Around his neck hung a necklace with an eye carved into a small, round crystal.

As he sat, he stared straight ahead of him from under his hood, through the eye-slits in his mask, as a deep, purple glow shone through. He thought about the world outside his fortress, as it had been years since he had been in a town or castle with humans present.

As the memories returned, he sighed heavily, the breath that seeped through the mask he wore formed a small misty cloud in front of his face. His eyes glowed violet, *drawing from the Underworld,* as he poured the dark mana into the breath he released, forming a small talon which rotated in the air in front of him like it was on display.

After a few moments of inspection, he released the talon, the dark mana dispersing into the air around where it once was in a violet mist.

I grow tired of waiting for that idiot to return from the communication chamber. Perhaps I should remind him why he's still alive, he grinned maliciously, pleased with the thought.

He noticed there was a thin layer of mist that floated just above the stone floor, indicating that it was a much colder day than usual in the snow-ridden land. Even though he never felt the effects of the cold, it still prevented any overly curious travelers from reaching its location easily.

He stared above him into the high arches of the Great Hall that were bathed in violet light that reached the height of the citadel directly above his throne. It lit up the walls of bent horns made from an unknown metal, which hung the heads of various types of formidable creatures. Wyrms, ochelons, glicks, and many other types of such beast trophies were present.

These creatures were once heralded as the greatest in the Continent. Now, look at them. Reduced to nothing but trophies, staring into the abyss of an unforgiving world, praying nothing stares back at them; but I am, he thought.

Pouring mana into his mask, he formed a large, scarlet claw attached to his arm and raked it against one of the many trophies, its silent screams of agony were translated into those of shattering bones. The entire hall seemed to flex and bend with his mana as he did so, shifting the violet hue uncomfortably against the thick supporting pillars that lined the Great Hall.

Releasing his hold over the mana, he realized that there was the sound of faltering footsteps at the far end of the Hall, which he immediately recognized.

Ah, the prodigal idiot returns, he grinned.

The young man came up to the foot of the steps that led to the throne, ignoring the destroyed trophy nearby, and kneeled. "My lord, I bring news from Coltend," the young man said, visibly exhausted. "Catch your breath and be out with it," he sneered impatiently, sending a shiver down the man's spine.

Just as I thought, he's pissed, the man thought through clenched teeth.

Athar, the young man, breathed heavily for a few beats, his long dark hair rising and falling along with his broad shoulders.

"My lord, the kings of the Continent have decided to join forces to find a way to close the portals," he said nervously. "*Ah,* so that's why the council had been called," the Masked One realized. "Those idiots should have tried that centuries ago, when monsters first entered the realm and the *gods* still gave a damn about them," he sighed.

Well, at least I'm not the only one he thinks is an idiot, Athar mentally shrugged.

"King Truls still rules in Coltend, does he not?" the mage asked distractedly. "He does, my lord," Athar nodded. "*Ah,* I'm surprised that the arrogant *narcissist* has decided to take action for once," the Masked One raised his eyebrows beneath his mask. "I'm surprised *you're* surprised," Athar muttered. The Masked One didn't hear the comment, and if he did, he simply didn't care much for it.

"You have done well, for once," the mage rose from his throne, glaring at him imperiously. "Come with me, I'd like to show you something as a *reward*," he continued, his last word striking Athar as more cryptic than inviting. "M-Might I ask what it is you would like to show me, my lord?" he stammered.

"No," the Masked One snapped, making the young man flinch. "Simply follow me, and you will see," he said impatiently, dragging his long robe behind him as he walked past the still-kneeling man. Athar rose to his feet and scurried behind his master, carefully avoiding the trailing robe.

If I step on that, he's definitely going to kill me, Athar moved his foot away just in time to avoid doing just that.

"You know, you're the first non-beast I've ever shown this part of my tower," the Masked One said, making Athar both uncomfortable and curious. "I-I'm honored, my lord," he replied with an unseen nod. His master led him down a side hall to a large metal door with a ward over it. Undoing it quickly, the Masked One pushed it open to reveal a spiraling flight of stairs that radiated the violet light much more intensely than the halls above.

Athar gazed downwards to the bottom, and could only hope to think that whatever was there wasn't meant for him, for the sounds he could hear resonating through the unlit hallway were gut-wrenching. "Come," the Masked One said and began down the stairway, with Athar reluctantly following as closely as he dared.

I don't have much of a choice here. We all die someday, I suppose, but this is still better than stealing food off the streets, he shrugged.

Reaching the bottom of the violet stairway, the Masked One poured mana into yet another ward, this one spanning the large threshold that could easily fit a small house beneath it.

It wasn't there to prevent others from getting in; rather, it stopped whatever was behind it *from getting out.*

"You might have some difficulty passing through the ward otherwise, so I've reduced its potency momentarily," the Masked One noted over his shoulder as he easily passed through the threshold. "Thank you, my lord," Athar bowed. Given his master's consideration, Athar thought it would be easy to pass through. However, that wasn't the case as his nose quickly squished against his face.

Damn it, is he really that *much stronger than me?* Athar rubbed the bridge of his nose.

"*Oh,* I forgot to mention that you might want to put your *hand* through it first," his master said, trying to hide his evident annoyance.

That would have been nice to know, the young man thought, doing as instructed.

After forcing his way through the barrier with a grunt of exertion, he nearly stumbled as he struggled to pull his foot out from the ward's grasp. He felt a surge of pride ripple through him as he finished pulling the remainder of his leg out, however, the sudden release of the force caused him to fall flat on his ass.

His master sighed without looking behind him and continued walking as he shook his head.

As Athar got to his feet and dusted himself off, he took a look at his surroundings. His eyes opened wide at the sight of hundreds, perhaps even *thousands* of individual cages that lined the walls.

They're monsters; *all of them,* his breath halted when his mind finally comprehended what he was looking at.

Inside the cages, there was no shortage of magnificent and terrifying beasts. Some tried to break the bars to their cages to eat him whenever they walked past one, making him flinch at the sight of claws or tusks slammed into the thick bars. Growls, snorts, sneers, and maniacal cackles rippled throughout the cages as they passed them.

"They can't reach you from there, but I'd keep an eye on the addia over there," the Masked One said, pointing at a large, empty cage. The young man looked over at it, but failed to see anything. He decided to move a step closer to see if his eyes had betrayed him.

Was that a ripple I saw in the air? Or, maybe... his thoughts cut off as one of the creature's large tentacles seemingly appeared out of thin air to lash at him.

"*Oh,* fuck!" he stumbled with the force his master used to pull him away, landing on his back. "You really are an idiot. If I say *don't go there,* I fucking mean it," the Masked One growled above him. "U-Understood," Athar nodded quickly, getting a groan of annoyance from his master as he turned and continued down the long line of cages.

That was a bit too close for comfort, the Masked One thought with a mental sigh.

Athar quickly scurried up to his master, but kept an eye out for any more of those invisible bastards. As the cages began to descend in a spiral, he couldn't help but notice that the size of the cages only seemed to grow the further they descended. Most of these he had only heard of in legends or stories from merchants on the street, but seeing them in person filled him with both awe and fear.

Reaching the final cage, he strained his neck to look up at the creature within.

"Beautiful, isn't it?" the Masked One said. "Very much so, my lord, but what is it?" Athar asked, entirely unable to recognize the creature. It stood about sixty meters tall, with pale, white fur and a horn on its forehead.

It looks like an unholy cross between a unicorn and an ogre, but more threatening, he thought.

"It's known as a Royal Ochelon. There are very few of its kind remaining in *this* Realm, but I found this one meandering a little far from its den," his master replied simply. "It was injured when I found it; likely a territorial dispute, but I never confirmed it," he gestured to a large scar spanning across its muscular abdomen.

"You may be wondering why I've brought you here to see the horde beneath this place," he continued, glancing over toward his servant. Athar could only nod his head. "I've come to show you what true power *really* looks like," he said.

"My lord, this is an incredible beast, to be sure, though why you keep them in cages is beyond me," the young man began. "I have always assumed, being as powerful as you are, that you could control them, regardless of whether they're in a cage," he concluded.

"I can. Although the expenditure of mana is quite high. I'd rather keep them where I won't have to use it perpetually until I find another way of controlling them," the Masked One explained. "But that's beside the point," he began, shaking his head.

"I've also brought you here to see how well you would handle yourself amidst such creatures. Showing any signs of weakness is probably the quickest way to being eaten by them," he said, making Athar swallow dryly.

"It seems as though you are comfortable enough around them. However, your lack of experience is... *telling,*" the Masked One said. "I've had my fair share of experiences with beasts, although I should mention that an addia was not on that list, my lord," Athar explained.

"*Ah*. Well, you won't make the same mistake twice, will you?" the mage asked ironically. "Of course not, my lord," Athar shook his head quickly. "Good. That is the very least I expect from a *bastard* like you," his master said with disgust.

I wish I knew why he calls me that, Athar frowned slightly.

"My lord," he began after a short break in their conversation. "What is it?" his master asked. "I'm assuming you have some sort of plan to disrupt the destruction of the portals," Athar said matter-of-factly. "I do. However, there is one final thing I need to be sure of before I show you what that will be," he said and turned to stare his *idiot slave* in the eyes as he put a hand on his sternum.

"Stay still; I don't need you to do anything other than that," the Masked One said, as Athar gazed down at whatever it was his master was doing. Mana began to flare beneath his rib cage as his master's eyes flared, giving him a sense of unease he'd never felt before.

Ugh, it's like he's digging into my soul, Athar strained against the pressure.

His thoughts began to race, though it was not by his command, but the work of his master. Worrying that he might have suppressed a memory his master wouldn't like, he tried to follow his own thoughts, going over every memory, every emotion, every heartbreaking moment.

The mana sank deeper, digging into parts of himself that not even he knew he had, but before he could piece together what was happening, his master withdrew his hand and the mana along with it. "H-how?" he asked shakily, observing the swirling sphere of violet mana in his master's grip.

The young man's palms began to sweat, and with his knees buckling at the sheer pressure of having his soul dug into, he strained to stay on his feet. The mage glared at the sphere momentarily, as if confirming something unspoken. He looked at his servant and smiled wickedly beneath his mask.

So he was *right,* he thought, shifting his gaze back to his servant momentarily.

"I hope you're ready for what I'm about to show you, Athar. Your cooperation just now will be one of the keys to *our* success," the Masked One said cryptically, condensing the small sphere of mana into the palm of his hand.

That's the first time he's called me by my name. Then again, I don't think he ever asked for it. Did he only find out after digging through my soul? Athar considered with widened eyes.

"What do you want to show me, my lord?" he asked with an air of caution, still shaking from the spell. The Masked One didn't reply, but proceeded to undo the ward on the towering ochelon's cage. Just as the ward was dispelled, a rune made of mana appeared on the creature's head to control it.

"Follow me," the Masked One commanded. The creature exited the cage in a zombie-like state. "That means you too, Athar," he continued.

I should be astonished at his abilities, but after having felt him dig through my soul, I can only imagine what this creature is going through, he thought.

Just behind the cage was a door that led to an incredibly octagonal ring with runes inscribed along its circumference. Through the slits of his mask, his eyes glowed an even deeper violet, as the tendrils that once flowed from them were drawn into his eyes as *he reached into the Underworld.*

Though its use was not as widespread as that of the Ethereal realm, it still held its own power. A dark and devastating power, one granted to him from the Undergod, Volzuk.

He looked about him and saw the exact inverse of the Ethereal's spiral above him. The streaks of power were dark and nearly lifeless, except for occasional bolts of violet lightning that sewed their way through.

They moved about in a monochromatic dance, one streak weaving into the other, all heading towards an otherwise lifeless orb in the middle of the sky far above him. Dead trees riddled the ashen ground beneath his feet, making it feel like the very life had been drained from the Realm.

Dried bones of countless creatures lay intermittently between the fallen logs, while oozy smells stung his nostrils. With every step taken, the ashen dust engulfed his feet and ankles, while a river of murky water and blood was filled with dismembered remains.

It was a wonder anything could survive there at all.

Looking at the lifeless orb far above him, he reached his hand out to call the mana down. It voraciously followed his command, swarming and engulfing him much faster than mana from the Ethereal. In accordance with his will, he returned his consciousness to the Between and pushed the mana into his mask just like before.

This time, however, his mask began to glow and produce a claw of pure, scarlet mana, which surprised Athar.

This is different than his usual spells, I know that much for sure; but what the fuck is that? It must be the mask's power, he gathered, hoping he was right as the claw reared behind the mage like a viper ready to strike its prey.

"What do you plan to do with that, my lord?" he asked nervously. "This," the Masked one said, grinning beneath his mask. The claw rapidly lurched forward and buried itself in the royal ochelon's chest, but the creature didn't react. After a few seconds of astonishment, Athar felt a surge of mana and noticed the blood that had spilled onto the floor moving into the air where it became stationary.

Just then, a mist of mana began to seep from the creature's body, eventually bursting it into chunks of meat. The blood, sinew, and entrails were flung around the room by the explosion, as well as Athar's face and clothes.

He let out a yell of disgust and vomited his breakfast from earlier that morning. "What the actual fuck?" he asked, desperate for an answer other than *just for fun*. "Stop being so weak and look," the Masked One said, visibly disturbed by his servant's attitude. He was also covered in entrails and blood, but he had to maintain his focus on the task at hand.

Athar looked over at the claw that had impaled the beast and noticed a glowing, red orb in its grasp. "What... is that?" he asked, astounded at the sight before him. "This is a *core*," the Masked One said. "A core?" Athar asked incredulously.

"Yes, though it is more commonly referred to as a soul. You see, the core and the body are not one and the same. It is made of pure mana, while our bodies are not. It can be altered, broken, repaired, or even transformed into something else entirely," the Masked One explained.

Is that sadness or regret in his voice? Athar thought as he listened intently.

"However, some creatures have been known to have more than one core, making actions like this a bit more challenging, though those creatures are few and far between," he rotated the core to check for any damage. "I see, my lord. But what happens when you remove a core from a body?" Athar asked, regarding the core curiously.

"By removing the core, the rest of the body becomes practically useless unless its core is returned. If you destroy the body while removing its core, then it has nothing to command, thereby allowing one full control over it, provided you have the skill," the Masked One explained.

Athar was stunned. "So, what you're saying is that the core is what controls the body? Is it not the brain of the creature that does that?" he asked. "In essence, the brain performs the bodily functions needed for things like eating, speech, and movement. The core is what commands and *guides* the brain to perform those actions. A body cannot function without its core, but the core has its own properties that allow it to exist autonomously," the Masked One answered.

"I think I'm beginning to understand, my lord," Athar said, still trying to wrap his head around the concept. "But, what purpose does a core have without a body to make use of its commands?" he asked, prompting his master to chuckle maliciously. "Observe," he commanded.

He outstretched the hand holding what he had taken from the ochelon and absorbing its contents fully, causing his body to begin surging with a power Athar had never seen before.

I can't believe it. He's taking it all, Athar realized as the color began to drain from the core.

The mage's body began to grow larger and more beastlike, as his nails thickened and grew darker, while his muscles bulged beneath his cloak. As soon as the core was fully drained of power, he crushed its remains in his hand as the mana within the emptied shell dissipated into thin air.

"You see, Athar, there are various forms of magic and mana in this world, many of which I do not have the time nor patience to explain right now. Those fools in their castles think there is only the kind that the Synners have. However, I am going to show them what true power is as the herald of *my* master's second coming," he flexed his hand open and shut, testing his newfound strength.

He has a master? A second coming? Wait, when was the first? Athar wondered, genuinely confused by his master's words.

"I can tell you're confused," the Masked One said, tilting his head slightly. "I am indeed, my lord," he nodded quickly. "This is precisely why I needed you to see this. You're going to help me, as you are one of the catalysts needed for it to happen," the mage said with a dark tone.

Athar swallowed hard and nodded his head. "Is that what you were doing to me? You were looking at my memories," the young man said, finally understanding. "Originally, I did not think you would have much more involvement in this matter, but your past is going to play a vital role," the Masked One sighed.

"I was commanded, and now so are you. You don't have a choice anymore, Athar," the Masked One said, looking him dead in the eye. "If you did, I'm certain you wouldn't remain here in the north, serving someone you obviously loathe," he continued.

Athar could say nothing in return.

"I own you, as I have since the day you arrived here in Valdis. But, for now, we both serve a *much higher* purpose, and an even darker power," the Masked one said in an unusual tone. Athar felt a chill go up his spine as the hair on the back of his neck stood up.

"I understand, my lord," he said dejectedly. "I'm just glad you didn't do... whatever *that* was to me," he gestured to the entrails scattered across the floor. "I *still could*, if you make me angry enough," the Masked One growled. "However, there would be little benefit to me doing so, as you have no favorable attributes to acquire," he continued.

"What do you mean?" Athar shuddered, feeling both relief and fear. "I absorbed the ochelon's attributes by draining its core. While the changes are random, they still offer a fair gain in power or strength depending on the creature they come from," his master explained briefly.

If he didn't scare me before, hearing that *definitely did,* Athar blanched momentarily.

"Still, there is much work to do, and we must move on from here. I'm sure you've noticed by now that there is a summoning circle beneath our feet," the Masked One gestured around the large room. "The runes embedded within the rings can serve different purposes, but one of them is this," his eyes glowed brightly as he condensed a large amount of mana into his hand and slammed it into a ring beneath him.

The floor radiated violet light as the runes lit up sequentially. The center of the numerous rings glowed, as a handful of crystals materialized before them. "What the...?" Athar asked breathlessly, gauging the size of the summoned items.

"As I've said before, controlling these creatures one by one is difficult, and so I have devised a way to cut out my need for direct control. The royal ochelon's core, now infused with my own, will leave its mark on the mana I imbue. It takes some time to fully charge them, but it can be done passively - another benefit of using the circle with my mana signature," his master explained.

"But how do you know that will work, my lord?" Athar looked at him in astonishment. "*All creatures* must bow to something more powerful than they are. It is embedded in their instincts. By using the mana within these crystals to power the spell I cast on the horde, they will answer to me, and only me. Do you understand now?" the mage raised an eyebrow beneath his mask.

"I-I think so, my lord," Athar nodded slowly. "Good. Now, come; there is something *else* I want to show you," his master gestured for him to follow. They exited the large room and proceeded down a hall to their left. A doorway at the end of the hall led to yet another large room that appeared to be filled with nests and eggs from the creatures held within the citadel. Athar could hardly make out what he was seeing, given the dim lighting of the room.

His master noticed his strenuous attempt to see all that was before him, and infused his eyes with a bit of mana, allowing him to see more clearly in the dark, which widened with surprise at the sight before him.

The nests not only hit the ceiling, but they extended to the end of a hall that turned out to be nearly as large as a small farm. "By the gods both light and dark, what is this?" Athar asked. He could barely speak the words, as his thoughts began to run rampant. "This, Athar, is a breeding ground," the Masked One said. "A *what*, my lord?" Athar raised an eyebrow in confusion.

"The Undergod, and I have been working in tandem for many a century now, and he has given me new ways of bringing hordes of beasts into this realm," he explained. "So you mean to breed hordes of the beasts and unleash them on the countries?" Athar asked. "Precisely. This would throw those idiots in their castles for a loop when they realize the portals aren't the only way these creatures emerge," the Masked One said mockingly.

They ventured deeper into the hall, and Athar soon found himself wandering around, observing all the different kinds of nests and eggs that were present. Eventually, he stumbled upon one of the eggs that had fallen to the floor beside one of the larger nests.

What are you doing down here, little one? It looks rather... helpless, he reached for it in an almost dreamlike state.

"Step back," the Masked One commanded Athar who instinctively did just that. His eyes glowed once more as he outstretched his left hand. Mana could be seen gathering in the palm of his hand as he said a few words. Slowly and carefully, he encased the egg in mana, putting it back where it belonged.

Suddenly, the egg burst with mana-flame, blinding Athar, and scorched the nest in which it lay. Out of the smoke and burst of heat, they heard a grunt and a snort. Athar uncovered his now stinging eyes to see a small fire golem, covered in ash and flame staring up into their eyes.

"Magnificent creatures, aren't they?" the Masked One asked. "Once they are old enough, they have been known to breathe fire, although only a few recorded cases exist," he said with some disappointment. "I thought only wyrms were capable of that, my lord," Athar said while staring at the golem's features.

Its eyes were pure amber, and its body was a mixture of volcanic stone and flame. Within its mouth, burned a white flame hot enough to melt anything the golem would bite into.

Athar couldn't tear his eyes from it.

"Wyrms are the most common creatures to have that talent, but there are other beasts which just so happen to have that same gift," the Masked One explained. The golem lay down in its nest of ash and stone, and fell asleep during his explanation.

Aw, it's actually kind of cute when it's not trying to burn a hole into my eyes, Athar smiled awkwardly as he observed the sleeping creature.

"Come, we must let him grow to at least half his size before he is ready for battle," the mage said, leading him over to the next oversized nests across the way. He cast once more, only this time, a frigid wind flowed from the center, nearly freezing Athar's boots solid.

Within the thatch, there lay a small ice golem. White and light blue crystals formed its general complexion, while its eyes were as black as night. Athar looked at each golem with awe, since he had never seen one before, much less two different types in the same day.

"They will hold their own, and spawn new ones of their own ilk every eight weeks, for they do not need sustenance other than mana," the Masked One explained as Athar looked at the two, shaking his head to make sure he wasn't dreaming.

Huh, I guess I'm not after all, he felt a smile tug at the corner of his mouth.

After feeding the pair of golems some of his own mana, the Masked One turned toward his servant. "The time has come at last," he said ominously, interrupting Athar's focus on the pair of small creatures. His confused expression gave him away.

"We must speak with him," the Masked One said. "Him?" Athar asked, stepping away from the pair. "The Undergod," his master replied with an air of severity, causing Athar's stomach to somersault.

Well, that can't be good, he thought, following behind his master.

CHAPTER 6
THE RETURN TO CODREAN

A week had passed since the first day of the council, and most of us were fairly satisfied with our stay, having gone to the main market where all sorts of items, trinkets, and elixirs could be purchased at reasonable prices.

Ed finally recovered from his wounds and was able to walk, so we invited him to come with Batch and me the morning we were meant to leave. Irun and a few others had gone back to Codrean a day before to scout the roads ahead in case of another incident.

We roamed the market early in the morning while the stalls were still being set up, buying trinkets and other mementos we could bring on our journey home. In the meantime, the Master and the other synners were gathering their gear and packing their newly acquired items.

There wasn't much time left before we would have to ride back to our fortress, so most of the others were already grabbing their gear and packing their horses.

After about an hour or two of scouring the marketplace, we made our way back, but noticed everyone was nearly finished packing. "*Shiiiit*, we took too long. We should hurry," I said, urging my friends to break into a run to grab our belongings. Batch, after having gathered his own small amount of gear, helped Edryd with his while I got my own.

"*Oh*, I was beginning to wonder when you bastards would show face. Must have been a fun night out on the town," Bernar grinned sarcastically, having noticed us scurrying about. "How much longer before we set off?" I asked, ignoring the shit-eating grin on my older brother's face.

"Not much longer than you think, so hurry up," he replied. "It's not as if we knew we'd have to leave today," Edryd snapped back. "Yeah. Normally, we have at least a twelve-hour warning before we go anywhere," Batch chimed in. "We *did*, we just fucked up and should have kept a better track of the time we spent outside," I felt a tinge of embarrassment come over me as I could feel Bernar's head shake in disappointment behind me.

"Well, the Master has declared that we should leave as soon as possible, so I gave out orders for everyone to pack their shit up and get going immediately," Bernar shrugged. "We weren't told *that*," Edryd began, as we all looked to each other for confirmation. "I'm sure that's because we weren't even *here* in the first place," I said, not having any other answer.

"Where the hell were you guys, anyway?" Bernar asked. "We were at the market," I replied matter-of-factly. "*Riiiight*, the *market*. Of course. Prey tell, doing what, exactly?" my brother asked, completely unconvinced of my response.

"*Oh*, fuck off, will you? We bought trinkets and such for ourselves," I replied quickly, producing a small sackcloth bag and waving it in front of him. "Shouldn't you have done that yesterday?" he swatted the bag aside. "Ed's shoulder has only just gotten better, and we were not going there without him," I replied

"Now, if you'll excuse us, *big brother*, we've got to finish packing up our shit and get going before the Master verbally and morally destroys us," I continued. "Alright, *alright*. On your way, *young ones*," Bernar said through a small burst of laughter.

We quickly gathered the rest of our gear, which, once again, was hanging on their bedsides, cleaned and dried; just like the first morning they had been put there. I found a note pinned to my jerkin, and unfolded it to read the contents.

Remember me, please. Yours, M. I read, scratching my head to try to figure out who the hell this *M* person was.

The words had been messily scribbled on the small parchment, and I looked around to see if I could find whoever wrote it, but it was hopeless.

Was it the servant girl from the first night? Damn it, what was her name again? I rummaged through my memories, finding nothing.

I decided that I didn't have time to try to figure that out, so I scribbled my *own* note, folded it, and left it on my pillow, praying she would find it. I placed her note in my riding bag in a pocket where I was sure it wouldn't be wrinkled or torn.

The others finished gathering their things and I noticed no one else had gotten a note. I chuckled and grinned from ear to ear, thinking I, momentarily, was privileged.

We rushed downstairs to our horses and tied our bags to our saddles. We looked around for the Master, but he was nowhere to be seen. Garett was already mounted and called for attention.

"Listen up, you lot," he began as everyone turned to face him. "We're heading back to Codrean, and the Master has given me and Bernar explicit instructions to go ahead without him. He will catch up to us soon enough," he said. We all looked at one another, as this was both unprecedented and unusual behavior for the Master.

Something's not right, I thought, trying to piece together any semblance of reason I could.

"Let's move!" he called out. We spurred our horses and followed him out of the large gate before us. Just as we were about to cross the threshold, I thought it might be a good idea to get one last look at the palace itself. It was beautiful in its design, to be sure, but I quickly noticed something even *more beautiful* stood in one of the lower windows.

That's her! I thought, barely able to see her through the reflection of the glass.

She was, apparently, looking for me as well, as she held up the note I'd left her and waved it from side to side. Her hair was tied up in a strip of cloth that wrapped around her forehead and covered her ears, tying itself together at the back.

She found me amid the other riders and our eyes met.

I humbly nodded to the figure in the window. My eyesight was good, but I only noticed the tear running down the left side of her face a little too late. I felt I had no choice but to continue on ahead, not looking back another time lest my heart drop further. I couldn't figure out why she was crying; after all, she had only known me for about a week, but I was sure I wouldn't get an answer soon.

After riding for the better part of an hour, I could feel the sun's early rays begin to warm my back. The air was still a little chilly, and

I was more than happy to feel those rays welcoming me into their embrace.

However, just as I was about to get lost in a daydream of my muse, I heard hooves thumping in the distance, ones that didn't quite match the pace we were at. I glanced over my shoulder to see what it was, and sure enough, I saw a familiar figure coming towards us at nearly a full gallop.

The Master had finally caught up to our group.

"Well, well. I'd say it's about half past the time you were supposed to catch up to us," Garett was saying as the Master rode beside him. "My apologies, I had some rather unpleasant business to attend to back at the palace," the Master said, his eyes glowing like they would whenever he was angry.

Bernar noticed, and sent a nod back to me, even though I had already guessed as much.

"Well, aren't you glad that's over and done with," Garett said cheerfully. "I suppose I am. Although I doubt that that was the end of it," the Master grimaced, prompting Garett to raise an eyebrow, but shrugged soon after. "*Bah*. With all due respect, Master, fuck them sideways," he spat. "Tell me, since I'm sure you must know more than I do regarding them, what *respect* are they due?" the Master asked angrily.

"I meant with respect to you," Garett said calmly. "But to answer your question: Not even the amount a beetle can shit," he said. "Glad to hear we're on the same page," the Master said, finally calming down a little. Garett, who had known the master since he was a boy, knew his personality well enough to be the only one able to calm him down in times like these.

I wonder what happened back there, I thought after their brief exchange.

We rode on for a few more hours, eventually stopping for lunch beneath the shade of a few pine trees that lined the path. After washing down the dried meats and bread with a bit of ale, Fulco gracefully sent us off with.

When we were a few kilometers away from the main fortress, I felt something I'd never felt before, like a pebble scratching at my core. Shortly after, I spotted a silhouette against the nearly setting sun.

What's a raven doing out here? I wondered, calculating its trajectory, trying and failing to properly shield my eyes.

It wasn't that ravens were rare, by any means, but since they were normally used as rapid forms of written communication, they often required special permissions to leave their homes. Those, however, were usually easily identifiable with the leather pouches they carried.

I can't see if it was a messenger raven with the sun making my eyes water. It did come from the direction of the fortress, but it might just be nothing, I thought, shrugging it off as I rubbed my stinging eyes after staring almost straight into the sun.

About a kilometer outside of Codrean, Bernar and I both spotted a second raven flying overhead in the same direction as the last.

"Brother," I whispered, leaning forward in hopes that he could hear me. "I saw it. Was there one before it?" he asked, turning in his saddle to face me. "There was, but I had assumed it to be nothing more than a lone raven since I couldn't see it well enough with the sun beaming into my eyes," I replied.

"Shit," my brother muttered.

I didn't quite understand why he was so worried, bu I knew it had to be something serious if he was freaking out that much. I leaned in to see if I could hear what Bernar was telling the Master. The Master quickly snapped his head towards him and then back towards me with a glare.

What the fuck is happening right now? I thought, confused at the odd exchange.

The intensity of the glare surprised me. I *also* had no idea what was going on, making everything that much worse, thinking I had done something wrong. An unsettling feeling began to brew in my stomach as I watched the Master whisper back to Bernar, who nodded in agreement and slowed his horse, which shook its head from the pull on the reins.

"Little brother, I need to tell you a few things once we arrive. Do not let anyone else know where you are going after I do so, do you understand?" he asked with a seriousness that was not like him at all. "I do," I replied, still uncertain of the reason behind the request. "Good," he nodded and rode back up to the Master's side, continuing an inaudible discussion.

"I'm not entirely sure what just happened, but I'm going to assume it was nothing good," Edryd said, having kept an eye on the whole exchange. He had been riding next to me the whole way, after all.

During our return to Codrean, he and I had talked about my adventures in the castle and the run-in with the servant girl. It put Edryd's mind at ease to know that even though he had missed many things, he was still knowledgeable of them.

However, this was clearly something different altogether.

"Damn right about that, Ed," I replied. "I'm guessing you can't tell me much, if anything at all," Edryd said, almost rhetorically. "I don't even know enough to say anything about it. I'm just as confused as you are, if I'm being honest," I replied with an upturned lower lip and a shrug.

Ed simply nodded his head and looked onward. Batch was close behind and ended up overhearing most of our conversation. He looked at me for an answer, but when he received nothing but a confused shrug as a response, he shook his head and sighed.

We entered the main courtyard to Codrean, where the Master, Bernar, and Garett were clearly in a rush. "Feed and water our horses," the Master called out to one of the nearby servants, who rushed to finish the job as quickly as possible. He motioned to me subtly, prompting me to dismount and walk quickly after unlacing my pack from the saddle.

"Sorry about this, Ed, but would you mind taking Celer for me?" I asked. "You're gonna have to tell me what that was all about later," he said with a sly grin, taking my horse by the reins.

I caught up to the Master and the others just before entering the fortress. Down the cold stone corridors and up the stairs, the four of us went to the Master's office. I rued over the memories of the first time I'd been in the dimly lit room full of books, scrolls, and other strange objects.

I feel worse than I did that *night,* I realized as the door creaked open.

The Master seated himself in the carved, wooden chair and folded his hands together, steepling his fingers together on his chin. Bernar closed the door behind us and peered out of the eye-hole to ensure we didn't have any eavesdroppers.

"How much do we know about this raven, and where did it come from?" he asked bluntly. "I'm afraid there isn't much to tell, Master," Bernar replied, walking from the door. "Thoma told me there had been a second one before the one I saw, about half a league out from here," he continued. "Is that so?" the Master raised an eyebrow at me.

I quickly nodded in agreement, receiving a sigh from the Master in response. "Well, this isn't good news. There is one thing I would like to check on, and I think now would be as good a time as any," he said, pushing his fingers away from his chin and giving me a look I couldn't quite put my finger on.

"Thoma, you have not yet atoned for your mishap the other night, so I will have you take this task on yourself. Obviously, Bernar will instruct you on what you'll need to take with you on your investigation, but for the most part, you will do it alone," he said.

Shouldn't something this important be a job for someone more experienced? I thought, recalling the punishment I'd chosen and realizing now that the two were somehow connected.

"Hold on, I'm doing this alone? Shouldn't Bernar be coming with me if it's that important?" I asked, genuinely concerned at both the amount of trust the Master had in me and whether I'd be able to pull this off.

"Well, yes," the Master replied. "I know of your skills, young as you may be, so I entrust this task to you. The three of us have other matters to attend to, and you're the only other one we can trust right now," he said calmly.

I looked at my brother, who simply nodded reassuringly.

"As you command, Master," I said, looking back at the Master. "Good. Bernar, take him to the armory. Move as soft and quick as shadows, for this is of utmost importance and time is not on our side," the Master said.

"I'm sure there's more to you sending him off alone than you're telling us," Garett gave the Master a stare. "Of course there is," he admitted. "However, there are some things about him that need to be brought out, and this is a good opportunity to do so," he explained, glancing over at me with a wry smile.

"As far as I can tell, there's nothing particularly wrong with the boy," Garett said nonchalantly as if I weren't standing right in front of him. "I'm not saying I can *read minds*, but I have seen his progress. Given that he's Bernar's brother, I also know I can trust him to nearly the same degree you do," he gave me a knowing nod. "You *most certainly* can," the Master nodded.

I would be lying if I didn't feel a bit of pride surge within me.

"Don't forget to stay on your toes, lad," Garett called out just before closing the door behind us. I nodded and followed my brother down the stairs.

"Okay. Run that by me again," I said as we were walking down the corridors that led to the gear room. "Run *what* by you again?" he asked. "You know what I mean," I said, beginning to feel that ice-cold fear again.

"I'm supposed to explore the rumored cave on my own, and the only thing I have to go off is that those rumors are true about there being a massive creature inside? Not to mention the fact that I've only been in a real fight once. Is that right?" I asked, not knowing what to think or feel at that moment.

"If you remembered everything I said, why ask me to tell you again?" my brother asked. "*Oh*, I don't know. Maybe because I'm about ready to *shit my pants*, and then waddle about like some dwarf whose pants are too big for him? Also, what does *any of this* have to do with the ravens we saw earlier?" I threw my hands into the air.

"Don't worry, and speak less," my brother said comfortingly. "As small of a turd as you are, I'm sure you'll be just fine down there. Besides, it's not like you've never swung a sword before. Simply remember your training, and all will go well," he put his hand firmly on my shoulder.

Bastard ignored my other question, I thought, gulping dryly.

As soon as we arrived at the armory, I was astonished at the number of options before me.

Generally speaking, junior Synners were not allowed inside under normal circumstances. The main reason being that juniors seldom fought in battles, so all we had to do was learn to keep our training gear in proper order and hone our sword-casting; the basics for any Synner.

Only when we were on the cusp of becoming seniors would we choose our specialty and actually use it in expeditions.

My eyes sparkled as I gazed over the various weapon choices. Bows, swords, shields, axes, and spears were hanging on all four walls of the room.

I don't think I'd do well to choose a piece of equipment that I'm not familiar with, I thought, moving away from the walls without swords on them.

Most were too long or heavy for me, but my choices of long swords, bastard swords, and broadswords were palpable. I picked up a long sword and began swinging it around, testing its weight. Its black, wire-wrapped hilt fit nicely in my hand as I gripped it tightly.

The sword had a pommel shaped like a bear's head and a slightly upturned guard perfectly balancing it. It was a stunning piece of work, to say the least, and I knew it would last me a lifetime if properly taken care of. My eyes gleamed with joy and awe, nearly forgetting the reason we were there in the first place.

"Here, let me see that," Bernar said, stretching out his hand. After looking it over, I handed it to him, and he tested its weight and balance. "It's a good sword and, since I don't believe you'll be growing much taller, I think this is a good choice of weapon," he said.

He returned the sword to me just as I finished the last loop of the scabbard's strap around my belt. I slid the sword in smoothly, and a satisfying click halted the blade, making me smile like a toddler in a bakery full of sweets.

Bernar walked over to one of the racks, where different-sized wooden masks that only covered the top half of one's face were hanging. "Here, you'll need this," Bernar said, putting the tied leather loop around my neck. "What am I supposed to do with this?" I asked, curious about the eyeless mask.

"Just put it on," he said almost tiredly. I looked at the oddly shaped mask and covered my face, pulling the beaded knot at the back a little tighter to get a more snug fit.

"This is fine. I can't see a fucking thing out of this," I said, rather annoyed. "Give me a second, shit-bird," my brother shot back mercilessly. I sighed and shrugged, accepting my fate.

I could feel his mana surge *as he reached into the Ethereal to draw mana.* While I couldn't exactly see what he was doing, I could *feel* him rubbing his hands together with mana, then tracing his fingers across where my eyes would be.

He condensed his cloud into the mask, and I felt my jaw drop at the sight before me.

Within the dimly lit gear room, my visual senses were enhanced ten times over. The room itself was no longer a darkened cellar full of weapons beneath the fortress, but a glowing, living one. I could see my own breath move freely through the air, as though it had been lit aflame. The room appeared to be lit by the sun itself, and I could see even the smallest creature from across the room as though it were placed in front of me.

"*Haha!*" I said aloud through a bit of excited laughter. "See? I fucking told you to wait," he grinned and flicked my forehead. "You're right, you're right. I should have listened to you. I won't ever doubt you again," I said bashfully.

"It's alright," Bernar said. "Just remember that once they're taken off, the spell will no longer be active, and you'll have to re-cast, do you understand?" he tilted his head seriously. "Yep, got it! Wait, what was the spell again?" I asked through the smile on my face.

Obviously, I wasn't really paying attention.

"We'd better be on our way," Bernar said, ignoring my question. "The darker it gets, the more violent they become," he continued.

They? I wondered, following him out the door.

After leaving the armory and walking for twenty minutes, we reached a gate at the back of the main fortress covered in moss and other flora. Bernar pulled the lever on the door that led outside the wall, and we started down the overgrown path.

Every step I take feels as though my heart will jump out of my mouth and beat upon the floor, I thought nervously, as the reality of my situation was finally kicking in.

I held back the urge to hurl after the first few hundred meters. After about two kilometers, and a handful of urges to puke later, we came to a cave in the rocky formation at the base of the nearby mountains. The sun was setting behind the mountains and the air was becoming colder as we stopped at the entrance of the cave.

"Put your eyes on. It's gonna be dark in there," Bernar said. I nodded and put them on promptly as I waited for him to activate the mask again. A smile instantly grew on my face as the vision enhancement was drastically expounded upon now that we were outside.

"I don't think that will ever get old for me," I said through a slight chuckle. "I've been using it for years and it hasn't for me, yet," Bernar lied, since I knew his senses were *always* enhanced. "But enough talking. It's time to find out what that raven might have sent out, and I need to return to the Master quickly," he continued.

"But why *here* of all places? I mean, it could have come from anywhere in the castle, right?" I asked. Bernar sighed and shook his head. "There are... *items* in there that you will find to be of great value," he began, choosing his words carefully. "Can't you at least tell me what they are? Or even what they look like?" I asked, still just as confused as before.

"You'll find out once you've slain the bastards. Now, get in there and get some," he said, giving me a slight, encouraging shove. I nodded in response, but I couldn't help but wonder what was in there. Regardless, I drew my sword and passed beneath the entrance to the cave.

I don't fully understand why I'm supposed to do this on my own, much less why anyone hasn't slain whatever is in here already, but I've got to survive this. Survive. That's the key. Yeah, I should focus on that, I thought, trying my best to quell the unease in my stomach.

My footfall was silent on the soft moss that grew within the cave that stunk like a thousand dead bodies. My stomach threatened to reintroduce my lunch to the outside world, but I knew I had to press on.

Ugh, I don't know how I'll be able to draw a breath with this gods-forsaken stench driving itself up my nostrils. Push through, get it over with, and take a bath, I thought, shaking the smell out of my nose.

The *eyes* I was wearing made the cave look as bright as day; every little detail stood out clearly in the pitch-black cave. I walked as cautiously as possible, with my new favorite sword tightly grasped in my gloved hands. The air was thick and humid, while absolutely silent save for a sudden, deep rumbling ahead of me, trembling the ground beneath my feet.

Sounds like that came from behind those rocks over there, I thought.

I strafed around the corner of the rock formation that lay in front of me, and sure enough, there it was.

An ochelon? By the gods both light and dark, this thing is fucking massive, I exclaimed in the realm of my own thoughts.

The beast lay in a ditch with a pile of bones surrounding it. Its short, brown fur coated the majority of its body except for its massive claws, face, and lower half of its stomach. Its large, strong maw could bite a man in half without effort, with two tusks protruding from its lower jaw.

The large eyes, capable of seeing well in the dark, were covered by a gray, leathery skin that was much thicker than the average hide.

I breathed heavily, trying my best not to make any further noise. My adrenaline had already been coursing through my veins for some time, but now, it seemed like my heart was about to burst through my chest. I took a step back and felt a crunch under my foot. I quickly looked down to see what it was, and instantly regretted doing so.

Fuuuuuck, I mentally sighed, realizing I had crushed something's remains.

A chill went up my spine, and my heart beat even faster. The beast began to stir soon after the sound had reached its ears. I felt a wave of icy fear pass over me. The beast lazily began to wake up, grunting while its large muscles began to lift its body. I was frozen in a mixture of fear and adrenaline.

Fuck my life, I swallowed dryly.

The beast sniffed the air and snapped directly towards me. Its eyes were burning bright with anger and hatred, and it let off a grunt as it rose to its full height, towering at least four meters above me.

The beast roared loudly, almost piercing my eardrums, and swung its massive claw in my direction. My eyes opened wide, staring at the incoming blow, and I rolled backwards, just dodging the deadly swipe.

Remember your training. Always keep your eyes on the beast's center of mass, that way you can see where the blows are coming from, I recalled.

I got to my feet and bared my teeth. The beast recovered from its failed attempt to squish its newfound enemy. Its saliva dripped down to the ground, which made a splashing sound as it hit.

I looked up at it in despair, and began to strafe around the beast to at least make myself a little bit harder to hit. It swiped again, and I rolled back once more, feeling the wind of the blow rush by me.

How am I supposed to get in close enough to hit this thing? I thought, pushing air through my teeth.

The ochelon was beginning to get frustrated, and so it raised both hands and smashed the ground in front of it, trying to crush me as I adeptly stepped out of the way. The shockwave, however, could not be avoided and sent the ground I was stepping on up into the air, taking me along with it.

I rose up to about the same height as the monster and I swung at the beast's face, cutting a small gash in its cheek. The beast staggered back a few titanic steps and spread its arms in an attempt to swat me out of the air. I twisted in the air and narrowly escaped the blow, absorbing the fall by rolling.

The beast recovered from the blow and became enraged at the smell of its own blood. It curled over and got on all four claws, and began to charge. I rolled out of the way to the right, leaving my sword out perpendicular to me, cutting deeply into the beast's leg. It stumbled and I attacked its now wounded leg once more, cutting deep into flesh and sinew this time.

The beast stumbled briefly and tried to sweep me off my feet as it fell, but I jumped over the long arm that wanted me. I cut a few more times, only to further invoke the beast's rage. Within a split second, it turned and struck me with the opposite arm I had been expecting, digging deeply into my jerkin and back muscles.

The blow sent me flying across the cave, and I screamed in pain when I hit the cave's wall. I began to recover from smacking into the wall, feeling a sogginess that wasn't there before.

I was quickly losing blood.

Damn it, that doesn't make things any easier, I winced.

I recovered from the attack as best I could, blood streaming from my back and forehead. Just as I was turning to face my enemy, the beast was already sending another blow my way. I managed to leap out of the way and narrowly escaped a second just like it, not even a second after the first.

The beast spun around as quickly as lightning with its claw extended, and just missed my gut. I cut down with my sword and severed the beast's wrist at the joint. Blood sprayed all over me, and the beast roared with the pain of having lost a claw.

I was surprised it had done so much damage with so little effort, and smiled through the pain for the first time since I arrived.

I love this sword, but I need a damage boost to kill this bastard. Just cutting off a claw won't be enough to disable it, but I know what will, I thought.

My eyes went black as I *went into the world without time to gather mana. I drew from the sky,* wrapping the tendrils around my sword, and condensed the mana into it.

The beast, still in agonizing pain after the loss of its claw, roared uncontrollably. While it was was distracted, I flicked my finger, and ignited the condensed mana. The white flame lit up the cave naturally, making it harder for me to see with the eyes still doing their job.

Finally, an opening! I rushed in, escaping the incoming blow by the width of a hair.

I screamed and cut upwards into its gut with my flaming sword. The cut was deep enough to partially disembowel it, and the smell of seared flesh filled the air. It fell to its knees, leaning on its one remaining claw, grunting heavily in pain. I cut at the joint on its wrist, severing it from the body.

I breathed heavily, feeling the pain from the gash in my back, furrowing my brow and looking the beast in the eyes. "Your claws belong to me now, and so does your life. *Thank you for the fight,*" I said aloud, my voice filled with a power I hadn't felt before. The beast leaned on the bloodied stumps that replaced its claws and stared into my eyes, while its innards fled its body.

I looked it straight in the eyes and let out a warcry, driving the sword up under its gaping mouth. The flaming sword pierced the other side of its skull, and its eyes rolled back into its head. As I pulled the sword out, the beast fell to the ground, lying in a pool of its own blood.

"I did it! By the gods' shit, I did it!" I exclaimed, chuckling weakly as I did. I stepped away from the steaming body. My chuckle turned into a full-blown laugh, but was quickly interrupted by the sharp pain in my back from the blow I had received earlier. I was drenched in blood, and the taste of metal filled my mouth as I prepared for what came next.

I didn't care as much as I should have, since the adrenaline was still heavily influencing my pain receptors.

I felt another sharp pain in my back, and I *drew from the Ethereal* once more, condensing the mana to the opened wound. I flicked my finger once more, and the mana seared and sealed the wound. I fell to my knees, screaming from the immense pain that was the result of charring my own flesh.

That's gonna leave one hell of a scar, I thought.

After I stopped the bleeding, I began to get a better look at the cave, noticing details I hadn't come across during my battle.

There are so many bones on the ground, it's a wonder how this creature even finds this much food to eat. Wait, Bernar said the word bastards, *not* bastard, I thought, feeling a cold stone sink in my gut.

The harsh reality set in as I observed the body of the ochelon I had just slain. "It's a female…" I said more loudly than I had hoped to. The moment those words left my mouth, I noticed a pair of glowing, red eyes surrounded by dense fur glaring at me from the depths of one of the many outlets in the cave.

The male ochelon had arrived, and it made the female look like it was but a toddler in comparison. Its bright red fur stood out in the vision of my mask, giving a much more menacing feeling than the female ever could. Its claws and tusks were much, much larger than those of the female's, and I knew immediately that this would be a challenge.

"You've got to be shitting me…" I said, readying my sword once more. The enormous male towered over the lifeless body of his mate, and nudged it with the back of its massive claw. It glared at me so intensely, I thought I would collapse.

I can hardly stand as it is with the gash in my back, and now this guy shows up? He's at least twice her size, and I've just killed his wife. Damn it! No other choice but to use that spell at the start of the battle. This can't be a drawn-out fight or I won't survive it, I thought.

I drew again from the Ethereal, gathering as much mana as I knew I could handle and condensing it into my sword, desperately trying to control the sphere through the pain. I hoped to land a similar blow as I had to the female, as the mana-flame's intensity grew exponentially. I lifted the flaming sword and pointed it at the creature as I stared into its glowing eyes.

"Hey, you oversized abomination! Your life or mine. Let's do this," I challenged, knowing my odds of success were slim. The ochelon charged as though it understood the words, immediately launching an attack aimed at my head. I barely ducked under the blow, with the pain of my wound nearly rendering me unconscious. I struck upwards, aiming for the elbow joint, but the only thing my sword sliced was air.

An attack came from overhead with the intent to squash me, but with a quick pirouette, I dodged the attack and sliced again. I found my target, but it did minor damage even with the mana-imbued sword.

"Oh, come on!" I shouted, meeting the monster's eyes after realizing the lack of damage. The creature roared as it flicked me into the wall like an insect. My back slammed into it, the pain riddling my body as I gasped for air. I could hardly stand, and noticed the creature looking at the wound curiously.

"So it *does* hurt," I said aloud. The creature snarled, realizing that the mana-flame wasn't dissipating. I reflected on my first battle, and what my spell had done to those glicks.

If I can use that on this bastard, I might just stand a chance. Mana-based attacks seem to work on him, even if my sword skill doesn't deal a lot of damage, I thought as I watched it scream.

After observing the ochelon for a moment, I sheathed my blade and did my best to focus on what I was about to do.

Although it was something I'd never even dreamed of attempting before now.

Driven by necessity, I took one deep breath, as I drew once more from the Ethereal, gathering as much as I could in both hands. The creature, now moving towards me a little more cautiously, noticed what I was doing. "I don't know if this will work, but you're going to kill me if it doesn't, anyway," I spat out a wad of blood that had pooled in my cheek.

"Come and get me, you angry son of a bitch," I seethed.

The creature, showing more intelligence than I had anticipated, charged at me, moving much more quickly this time. I dove under the creature's hind legs, avoiding the blow from both claws, and was now behind it. I could feel my eyes begin to glow like my older brother's, though less refined, as I could also feel tendrils of mana licking at my temples.

I whipped both of my arms, releasing the mana I held in my hands and wrapping each of the beast's limbs in it. "Hold this for me," I said with that same power from before in my voice. I screamed as I pulled the tendrils away from the creature's body. The ochelon roared, and tried to fight against it, but as this was a battle against mana, there was little it could do but feel its limbs being torn from its body.

"Tell your wife I said *hi*!" I shouted in response.

A squelching sound could be heard beneath the loud roar that resonated throughout the cave, as the massive limbs were flung in opposing directions. The ochelon's massive body flopped to the ground, as its blood meshed with the previously formed pool. I could feel my eyes stop glowing, as the reality of my situation set back in.

"Fuck!" I shouted, realizing that for a few moments, the pain had subsided while I was casting the spell. I panted heavily, feeling the pain from every bruise, scratch, and cut growing more intensely by the minute.

I fell onto my knees, reveling in the silence after my victory. Even through the immense amount of pain, I chuckled. "Master sure knew what he was talking about. *Keep your sword sharp and wits about you,*" I said with my best imitation of the Master's voice. Through the cave's quiet, I heard footsteps rapidly approaching.

Please don't be another creature. Please don't be another creature, I thought.

I couldn't tell you how relieved I was to see my brother's form come into view from the entrance.

"I heard the roar come to an abrupt stop, and thought you had been squished," he said, seeing me on my knees. Since I had already lost a lot of blood with the wound on my back, I could only weakly smile at my older sibling.

"*Oh,* shit! Are you okay?" he asked, realizing I wasn't my usual self. "Do I look *okay?*" I replied weakly, but still maintained my smile. "With that attitude, I guess you're better than you look," my brother said warmly. "*Heh,* you should see the other guy," I pointed towards the pair of carcasses and multiple body parts strewn about the cave.

"What the fuck...?" he muttered breathlessly. "I knew they were ochelons, but I didn't think they were fully grown yet. How the hell did you...?" I heard him ask, but couldn't hear the rest because I lost consciousness, falling flat on my face.

A few minutes later, my eyes reopened, and I felt a calming warmth.

Did I die? I thought as I began to regain my focus.

I could feel him pushing mana into my body, reconstructing the shattered ribs and seared tissue on my back. The only way that I could describe the feeling would be comparing it to his fingers dipped in warm oil digging around in my rib cage. Not that *that* description makes it any easier to understand, but it was the best way I could describe it.

"How do you feel?" my brother asked, helping me sit upright. "A little better, but my back still feels like it's on fire," I said, moving my shoulder around. "Well, you did *sear* the wound shut. Good thinking, by the way. Just know it's going to leave one *fuck* of a scar," he smiled wryly. "I'd be surprised if it didn't," I grunted and groaned as he helped me get to my feet.

After allowing myself a moment to breathe, I realized how much darker the cave was without the *eyes* to help me. "Here," my brother handed me the mask, which I donned with a little difficulty. Shortly after, the cave became bright once more with the infusion of Bernar's mana.

Observing our surroundings briefly, I walked over to a curious object near where I had encountered the first ochelon. I moved in to get a closer look. "A torch? It seems to have been freshly lit, too. Maybe not even a month old," I said, picking it up to examine it more closely. "That's odd. No one other than the Master should have come through here recently," Bernar stated half to himself.

I wonder who the hell would have gotten past not one, but two of these titans, I thought.

I stepped over the dead ochelon's torn limb and moved towards where I had seen the female sleeping. Its lair was covered in old, gnawed bones from many meals. I suddenly felt a small rush of air sweep across my sweaty cheek.

A breeze? Better check that out, I motioned to my brother to follow me in the direction the breeze came from.

I moved into the deepened ground where the beasts had lain, and noticed a small crack in the rocks. "How good are you with earth manipulation?" Bernar asked, seeing what I had found. "I'm not as good as you, that's for sure. Care to do the honors?" I asked weakly.

Bernar snorted, but seemed glad to see me in better shape than when he first arrived. He gathered mana in his hand, pushing it forward into the cave's wall, then dragging it to the right. It pulled the crack open like a curtain, scattering dust and gravel as it moved. After the dust had cleared, we walked through the hole Bernar had made, looking around the revealed room.

Books? Scrolls? What in the world are they doing here in a place like this? I thought.

The walls of the inner chamber I had just stepped into were lined with books, and shelves as high as the ceiling lined the walls. A desk in the corner of the room had various notes strewn across it.

"Someone obviously left in a hurry. Either that, or this person is more disorganized than Batch," I scoffed. The two of us looked over the notes, analyzing the titles and what secrets they held in the ink. "These are probably the oddest names I think I've ever seen," I began.

"*Dissection* by a certain *Nexis Pelantyr.* I wonder who that is. Here it talks about uses for the plant the Master mentioned. Look, there's an incomplete copy of it, but it's not the same handwriting. Someone else was obviously in here, but what they copied is hard to tell. Judging by the handwriting itself, whoever did this must have been in a rush," I continued.

"I agree," Bernar said loosely, flipping through several pages. I glanced at the other notes, but found nothing of importance and decided to move over to the shelves.

"The *Effects of the Ethereal, Habits Of Trolls And Other Beasts, A Voyage To The Underworld, Wards And Other Defenses Against Dark Magic, How To Make Alcohol By Using Citrus And Mana*," I listed off the names aloud, hoping my brother would recognize any of them.

I'm probably still too young for that last one, but it's good to know that's possible, I chuckled quietly before taking another glance at the first book I'd read the name of.

Something inexplicable drew me toward it, like I instinctively knew it held many of the answers I was looking for. With a pained grunt as I pulled it from the shelf, I opened it and began to read. There wasn't much dust on it; a tell-tale sign that someone had either read it frequently or it was only *recently* placed there.

Either way, I knew something was wrong right away because after sifting through a handful of pages, I came to a small, but noticeable gap in the page numbering that was too great not to draw attention to.

Damn, just when it was getting good, too, I thought.

"Bernar, come look at this," I beckoned. He immediately recognized the book when I waved it in the air, but his eyes widened when he noticed the torn-out pages. "Well, that's not good. This book...

We need to inform the Master quickly," he said urgently. I took the book and left the cave through the main entrance.

There was still so much more to be seen there, but it's too dark to tarry any longer. I'll have to come back another day, I thought.

We set off at a slow trot rather than a walk as we returned to the fortress.

CHAPTER 7

QUEEN LEONA

A few days after the Synners had left, Meliss carried a tray to the queen's bedroom, where morning light was seeping through the curtains in front of the vast windows.

She set it on the bedside table to the right of the sleeping beauty. She did so carefully to avoid awakening the person still sound asleep in the oversized bed. Under the thick, red covers to her left lay Leona, the queen.

She slept on her back, and her fair black hair strewn across the goose-feather pillows made her face look like the night sky had swallowed it. Meliss double checked the tray to ensure it was filled with the best breakfast treats before stepping away from it.

Fresh bread from the bakery, toasted with a small cube of butter on the side, scrambled eggs, and a green apple were the order of the day. She returned to the small basket she had brought and picked up the small pot of tea.

I really hope she's up before her food and tea get cold, she thought as she gingerly poured some into the cup.

Just as she completed her thought, Fulco stepped through the door with a look of disappointment, startling her in the process. "Come now, Meliss. This is not a reasonable time at which Her Majesty should be sleeping," he said loudly. Meliss felt embarrassed that she had done something wrong, and looked down at the ground in silence.

"Your Majesty, it's almost lunchtime, and you still have guests here in the castle that you must attend to," Fulco grabbed her shoulder to shake her gently. When that didn't work, he sighed in frustration and moved toward the large curtains, pulling them aside with a jolt of force.

"*Agh*, I heard you the first time," Leona grunted, shielding her eyes from the bright sunlight. "Then, with all due respect, you should have shown a sign of life when I shook you," Fulco said with a mild sigh. "I'd rather not wake up and deal with those below," her eyes squinted and squished as she turned to bury her face away from the source of her distress.

Fulco, with another sigh, opened the second set of curtains on the far side of the room, removing her shield from the bright light entirely. "Alright! I admit defeat," she rolled onto her back, smacking her hands against the covers. Her eyes opened but a little, and her pupils shrank from the sun's intensity.

"I hope you're happy, Fulco, as it pains me to be woken in this manner," Leona said with a raspy grunt. Had she not been so beautiful, one might have assumed it was the voice of some disgruntled dwarf. "I wouldn't have to if you weren't trying to imitate a hibernating bear, Your Majesty," he answered wryly, watching her rub her eyes with her knuckles.

She sat on the edge of the bed for a few moments, staring at the food Meliss had brought her. She grabbed a slice of the toast and took a few bites out of it, but quickly put the remnants of the now violated bread back on the tray as she washed down the rest with the tea.

"Your Majesty, where are your *manners*?" Fulco asked, appalled at her demeanor. "I thought you said I was out of time, Fulco. Besides, where are the other rulers or members of the court?" she asked with a sneer just as abruptly, prompting him to shake his head.

"*Oh*, you don't see any here among us? So then tell me why I ought to act like a queen if I am in the confines of my bedroom, because I see no reason to do so," she said with an air of arrogance and frustration. Fulco scratched the back of his head and looked down at the floor.

Leona smiled, knowing she had won the small argument and continued eating breakfast.

"My dear Fulco," she began with a genuinely warm smile. "Please do me a favor and summon Clare so I may dress," she said. "Right away, Your Majesty," he bowed quickly and left the room, leaving Meliss in the same position she had been in since Fulco had called her out.

This is awkward, Meliss kept perfectly still hoping Leona wouldn't notice her presence.

"Has anyone ever told you that you would have beautiful children?" Leona asked as she wiped her mouth, setting the remains of her food down on a plate. "I beg your pardon, Your Majesty?" Meliss asked, startled by the question as her complexion went from a pale white to a bright red instantly.

"By the Graces, Meliss, there's no need to be so *embarrassed*," Leona said playfully, after staring at her body momentarily. "It was a simple question from one woman to another. Now, please, answer the question," she continued playfully. "I do not believe I've ever heard that before, Your Majesty," Meliss replied, getting a chuckle from Leona.

"Come now, you don't need to reply so *formally*," the queen said with a warm smile. "Imagine I'm just a regular person, difficult as that may be. As I have said before, there are no other lords or ladies present," she said in an attempt to make her feel more comfortable.

Meliss pondered the reason for this new form of treatment for a few moments, but found none. She looked back at her queen. "I don't think anyone has had the guts to tell me so, except for you," Meliss finally replied in an extremely thick accent.

"I beg your pardon? I barely understood what you said," Leona's eyes widened in surprise. "Your accent is *definitely* not one from the Continent. If I were to guess, I would say it is from the Gramm Isles," she concluded.

"And you'd be right," Meliss chuckled. "My family is from there, and they brought me here to the Continent as a wee babe. Pa died when I was about six winters old, and ever since I can remember, I've helped my Ma tidy up other people's houses," she shrugged.

"Work had been regularly scheduled for us and then, one day, we found ourselves cleaning Father Mourtis' house. That was the day Fulco found us. He admired our work and offered us positions here at the palace," she explained loosely. "And what an excellent job you have done so far," Leona said without sarcasm, giving her a grateful nod. "Thank you," Meliss' eyes widened, prompting her to quickly bow.

"You said your *Pa* died when you were only six, which makes you how old, now?" Leona asked. "I have eighteen winters behind me," Meliss replied brightly. "By the Graces, you don't look your age at all," Leona's jaw dropped. "You're much more of a woman than *I was* at your age," Leona said through a curt giggle.

The sound of footsteps resounded from the bottom of the stairway, and Leona heard them clear as a whistle. "That must be Clare, the heavy old goat that she is," she said, pursing her lips. "Listen, Meliss, it was really nice to get to know you a little, and I look forward to learning more about you," Leona said. "Thank you, my lady," Meliss replied with a curt bow.

Just as she was getting back up, Clare walked through the door with the queen's robes for the day. "Forgive me for taking so long, Your Majesty. Those stairs are always a challenge for me," Clare said with her chest rising and falling.

She was at least twice Meliss' height and weight, and had her light brown hair tied up in a bun. "I was having a discussion with Fulco regarding what you should wear today, but we could *not* come to a conclusion. So, I brought a few of my personal choices, much to his disapproval," she explained.

The sweat dripped down from her brow and rolled over her round cheeks, and the whites of her hazel eyes and button nose were red.

Ah, she's been drinking again, Leona sighed.

"I see," she took note of Clare's composure. "Well, it doesn't matter. Let's get this over with," she shook her head. "Yes, of course, Your Majesty," Clare replied promptly, laying her various options out on the bed before her. Leona regarded them carefully, then looked out the window to see what the weather was like, and reached for a blue dress.

"*Ah!* An excellent choice," Clare said excitedly, knowing it was the one Fulco had disliked the most. "Here, let me help you into it, Your Majesty," she walked over to Leona, who was observing her gait.

That's not the straightest of lines she's drawing on the floor with her feet, she thought.

When Clare got closer, Leona could clearly smell the alcohol in her breath, and soon found herself gasping for a drag of clean air. "Your Majesty, I need you to turn so I can unlace your gown," Clare said. "*Oh,* my apologies," Leona curtly said, trying not to let too much air escape from her lungs. "Is everything alright?" Clare asked after clearing her throat.

Her breath went straight into Leona's face and nearly made her gag with the smell. Thankfully, Leona's court training took over to help her maintain her composure.

I'm not sure I can hide the fact that my eyes are watering, though, Leona thought with a pained smile before answering the question.

"Y-Yes," she managed, turning around to do as Clare asked, blinking away the tears as best she could. Meliss, who was now directly in front of her tried to figure out what Leona was trying to tell her.

She drank eel vodka, Leona mouthed to her. *What? Shrank a sealed froth cat?* Meliss raised an eyebrow subtly in absolute confusion, causing Leona to shake her head in frustration.

No, no. She. Drank. Eel. Vodka, Leona mouthed the words slowly. Meliss's eyes widened when she finally understood. *Ah, Eel Vodka,* she nodded.

Leona snorted in a desperate attempt to stifle her laughter, but the subtle rising and falling of her shoulders made Clare's shaky hands falter momentarily. The tears that welled in her eyes with stinging disgust were quickly transformed into those of subdued laughter.

"Hold still, Your Majesty; I'm almost done," Clare stood up once more with a grunt, then tugged on Leona's shoulder to turn her back around. "There, all done," she said, and the waft of eel essence and vodka went back into Leona's eyes which teared up again as a result.

Meliss did her best to keep her own composure, but her face still scrunched in disgust as she, too, got a whiff of the vodka.

"Get that off of you while I get the dress," Clare stepped aside to grab it from the bedside. Leona followed the order and shrugged off the gown she had worn all night long. Her slim, proportionate body in combination with silky, smooth skin made it no surprise that she was frequently sought after by nearly every lord in the kingdom.

She did not bother hiding her breasts, after all, there was no one else in the room besides her two servants. The windows were too high for anyone to see into the room from the outside, so there was no risk of her nudity being exposed.

Clare came up behind her, swathed her in the blue dress, and tied up the laces. "Come, see how you look in the mirror," she pushed the mirror towards her.

Leona faced the mirror and smiled brightly. The dress followed the curves of her body as though it were a second skin she was wearing. The dip in the fabric near her breasts was a little more promiscuous than what she usually wore, but due to the warming weather, it seemed appropriate enough.

"You were right, Clare. This is a *beautiful* dress," Leona said, turning and twisting to watch how the dress flowed. "Thank you, Your Majesty," Clare smiled from ear to ear.

Leona was now fully awake, especially after the magic the eel vodka had worked on her eyes. "I'm sure my *husband* wouldn't want me to tarry any longer than I already have," she said dryly. "Of course not, Your Majesty," Clare agreed, watching Leona give her dress one final twirl in the mirror, and begin to walk towards the door, following behind her with Meliss.

A few moments later, she was in the throne room, where Truls was having a small debate with Elhael, Mads, and Bashir, who was there with his son Bashaa as they discussed something inaudible to her.

"*Ah*, and there she is!" Truls exclaimed, spreading his arms widely. The others near him turned around to see who he was talking about. Their eyes were so glued to her slim figure that they might as well have been like a dog to meat.

Pigs, Leona thought through an outwardly pleasant smile.

"Come, come! We were just talking about having a feast later on this evening, and we were wondering what sort of theme it should have," Truls reached out for his wife's hand. She didn't allow her hesitation to show, but took the king's hand and stood at his side.

"Well, I don't know about a theme, although I do know what I want to have for supper," Leona said in a practiced voice. "And what might that be, my *sweet*?" Truls asked, causing her to shudder slightly.

She looked at the other lords for a moment, but had slight difficulty taking her eyes off Bashaa. "*Zebura*," she said with eyes still fixed on him. He had bright green eyes, a gift from his mother, making them look like they glowed in the morning light that beamed through the upper windows.

"I'm not one to question her choice, however, I was expecting something much less *commonplace*," Mads shrugged. "I could always change my mind, King Mads," she replied, smiling gracefully.

"*Zeburas* are known to be eaten as a sign of peace between kingdoms. With this being the first time in nearly a century that our countries have been in unison over a common cause, I see no reason why we shouldn't indulge in it," she explained.

Mads let out a hearty laugh, prompting the other lords to join in. "A very *astute* observation. Does anyone disagree with Her Majesty?" he asked cheerfully. "No complaints here, Your Majesty," Bashaa smiled at her brightly, causing her to almost lose control over herself as he looked at her.

Not the time, she finally caught herself and gave a brief chuckle.

"Very well, then. I suggest we begin the preparations as it will take some time for my servants to prepare it," Truls cleared his throat, noticing the exchange. "Each of you has a long journey ahead come tomorrow, after all," his tone dropped subtly.

"Indeed," Elhael stepped in, getting the attention off the Harutian prince. "Although most of us may travel the same distance in opposite directions, the Rhydian Pass *is* a narrow and dangerous one at that," he continued.

"I can only imagine the perils that may lie along the way," Leona began. "I will send a prayer to the gods for your safekeeping on your journeys home," she put a hand across her chest and bowed. "Thank you, Your Majesty," Elhael and Bashir said in unison, although her eyes quickly snapped to the latter when she heard his voice.

By the Graces, it's difficult to be around him with him *present,* she mentally noted Truls standing to her left.

"Very well. I will have Fulco see to the preparations for the feast, while these fine gentlemen and I discuss a few final things before they all depart," Truls waved himself off as he turned away from the group.

"I will be with you in a few moments, as I would like to speak to Her Majesty for a brief moment," Bashir smiled at Leona, who could only nod a response. Truls shrugged indifferently before continuing to walk away. "We shall head towards the market. Join us when you can, my lord," he said over his shoulder as Elhael and Mads followed at his sides. Bashir bowed as he watched the others head off, already deep in conversation.

"I have a favor I'd like to ask of you, my lady," Bashaa turned to face her. "And what might that be, my lord?" she asked calmly, hiding her surprise as best she could as his son moved in closer.

"You see, my son was only able to arrive on the morning of the council, and, unfortunately, missed the tour we received of the castle given to us by Fulco. He has always wanted to come to Coltend to visit the magnificence of the great castle," Bashir began with a warm smile.

"You want me to give him a tour *myself*," Leona completed his request with a knowing nod. "Y-Yes, precisely," he grinned, returning the nod.

Be still, my heart. He saw right through me, and now the sly dog is trying to get me alone with his son. He's smarter than he looks, but I wonder what he's really after, she swallowed dryly.

"I would be delighted to give him a tour, my lord," she said, trying to maintain her composure.

"This is *wonderful* news! Allow me to give you my thanks for such an honor," Bashir said excitedly as he lightly clapped his hands. "There is no need for thanks," she said and smiled at him nervously. "*Oh*, but there *is*!" Bashaa said stubbornly, causing Leona to chuckle nervously, allowing her inner lack of composure to show a little. "If you insist," she bowed slightly, regaining her composure.

"Please, enjoy yourselves. We will meet you in the market when you're done," Bashir bowed before he left to catch up to the others, leaving them alone.

Well played, Bashir, she mentally scoffed.

"Shall we, then?" Bashaa asked in his thick accent and held out his arm for her to take. "Of course," Leona replied, feeling her heart skip a beat. She was as red as a tomato and quickly found that hiding her true feelings would be more of a struggle than initially thought after a few minutes of walking together in silence.

"Walking in silence when in such good company would be an absolute waste," he began as if reading her thoughts plastered on her cheeks in bright red paint. "It would, indeed," she replied charmingly.

"To be brutally blunt, and bluntly brutal, I simply have to ask: Why were you staring at me so fervently just now?" he asked. "By the Graces! You don't waste a second, do you? Frankly, I'm astonished as to why you'd want to know at all," she scoffed, feeling her composure whittling away.

"It is painfully obvious that I am the wife of the *great* King Truls. That fact alone should have steered your gaze away from me," she stated with little confidence in her own words. Bashaa tilted his head. "The *great* King Truls..." he repeated with similar derision in his tone but quickly chuckled with a shake of his head.

"Well, in my culture, it is common not to wait around to speak one's mind. It helps to avoid... *confusion*. Therefore, I am doing only what my culture and people have taught me. I apologize if that was inappropriate," he said apologetically.

I didn't know their culture was like that, she thought.

"In that case, it helps make your question make a little more sense," she said. "However, to answer your question just as brutally blunt, and bluntly brutal: I am very interested in you. You're a very handsome man. Your father has obviously picked up on that, which is why we're walking together per his little *ruse*," she said wryly.

"*Ah-hah!*" he exclaimed, showing off his bright smile. "You see, I had figured as much, though I wasn't sure. I thought it would be better to ask you as soon as I had the opportunity, although I will be leaving in a few days," he said.

"So, you *knew*. The whole time?" she squinted her eyes. "Yes, that is correct," he replied. "And did you and your father plan for us to be alone like this?" she asked, with a bit of indignation in her voice.

"Not exactly. I simply assumed there would be some form of tour for me, though I didn't account for the possibility of it being with the most *beautiful woman* I have ever seen," he replied, causing her to blush with his praise.

"My head might explode from all the compliments if you continue like this," her eyes widened as she put a loose hand to the open part of her chest, knowing he would look.

Because, *of course*, he did.

"I'd rather it didn't," he turned and looked deeply into her eyes. "For the world would suffer such a loss, that I do *not* honestly believe that it would ever recover," he said. "What makes you think that? You barely even know me," she retorted.

Keep your composure, woman! Leona shouted internally.

"I know a strong woman like a hound knows its prey," he replied with a sly grin.

And there it goes; my composure is floating away in the wind. Perhaps I should wave as it passes by, she thought, feeling her heart begin to race.

"Now that is interesting. Where did you learn that?" Leona asked, taking note of every word he would say next. "When your father has a *harem* of women at his disposal, and you are but a small child who does not know much about the opposite sex, you tend to learn a few things through observation or listening," he replied.

"Something few men are capable of, apparently," she said in compliance with his last phrase, getting a low chuckle from him. "A man must know how to do a few things if he is to succeed in life: how to battle, hunt, manage his property and money, and, of course, how to *treat a woman*," he lifted a finger for each thing listed as nervous butterflies flittered within her gut.

"These are all, with the exception of the last, things that require only a small degree of skill. People can be trained to do those things. However, knowing how to treat a woman not as an object, like most do in my culture, but as a person requires an entire shift in perspective," he continued, raising a knowing eyebrow at her.

"What sort of shift?" she asked plainly, reading his expression. Respect and privacy, rights, and confidence; these things are vital to give, as they are due, to an equal," he concluded smugly. "Color me impressed, Prince Bashaa. I'd never expect *that* from someone who grew up with a *harem* at his disposal," she said with an upturned lip.

"I aim to impress; particularly when my opponent is the *great* King Truls Wishert," he shrugged, making something shift in her mind as soon as the words left his mouth.

Immediately noticing the tall wooden doors that led to the wine cellar to her left, she quickly grabbed his hand and began to drag him in that direction. "Where are you ta-..." his words cut off as she put a finger to his lips. "*Shhh,* just shut up and follow me," she said hushedly, checking over her shoulder for anyone who might see them.

It was lit by two torches nearest to the doorway. On each pillar supporting the racks of enormous barrels of wine and other spirits, there was an unlit torch for each one. Meads, wines, vodkas, and ciders were neatly organized and labeled accordingly with stamps of ink or brands charred into the wood.

They stepped through the door, their eyes taking a short time to adjust to the room's torchlight.

"This way," she said, leading him between racks and shelves that held the countless wooden barrels. The sound of their footsteps was dampened by the barrels in the dark, chilled room.

She stopped herself by leaning up against one of the nearby barrels, staring at Bashaa. Her inviting eyes were straining to see him properly, but she managed. He said nothing, as he could feel her intent, and moved in to kiss her by putting one hand on her waist and the other on the lower half of her face.

While they were kissing, he undid the laces to her dress, following its movement down her body with his mouth to her waist. As he moved back up her body, she undid the sashes that held up his pants, hearing a buckle hit the floor.

She turned around, leaning against the barrel, and no sooner was his pelvis meeting her backside with his hands on her hips, but they were quickly interrupted by a noise coming from the far side of the cellar.

"What was that?" she whispered, using her hand to stop him momentarily. "I'm not sure," he replied, pausing his thrusting movement for a few heartbeats. "It's probably something small, judging by the sound of it," he continued after listening for a few seconds. "If you say so," she said, and they continued what they had started a few moments ago.

About half an hour later, they finished and had to put their clothes back on in the dim light. Bashaa fumbled with the laces, attempting to replicate the knots Clare had tied earlier.

"That will have to suffice," he said, tying a knot he often used on his horse's reins. "Pray no one notices the knot," he said with a shrug. "That's comforting," she replied sarcastically before peeking out of the cellar through the crack between the frame and the door, seeing not a single soul about them.

"We're clear," she whispered back to him as he followed her out, taking her arm as if nothing had happened. A few minutes of walking and awkward conversation later, they were back in the main throne room. The tables were already being set up for the feast later on that evening, but they did not find the other lords.

"Truls must still be in the Market," she concluded, breaking the silence between them when she noticed none of the royal guards were nearby. "We'd better hurry to them. Otherwise, suspicions might arise," Bashaa said, intensifying the pace of his gait. "I'm certain they already suspect enough," she muttered.

She was only a little shorter than Bashaa, but felt a degree of difficulty keeping up with him, especially in the clothes she was wearing.

"I really hope you have a plan to explain our elongated absence. After all, a tour of the castle couldn't have taken that long," Bashaa said nervously, making her squint at his obvious display of mistrust in her.

"Of course, I do. We go to the market, find them, and tell them that we had no idea where they were and that we spent the entire time looking for them. A *half-truth*, if you will," she lifted her arm with a palm facing upward suggestively. "Lead the way," he said with an assertive nod. "We both know where I'd lead you if I had a choice," she scoffed quietly through a thin-lipped grin that he matched.

They made their way down a few flights of steps that eventually led to the main market. They looked out over the hundreds of small tents and booths that were the organs of the market itself. The racket produced from countless shopkeepers and clients yelling at each other to haggle for better prices resounded across the enormous courtyard. The market had a wide variety of supplies such as meats, hides, fauna, flora, precious stones, and jewelry hung in tent-like stalls or sealed in glass cases.

"I think I might know where he may be," Leona said, looking out over the horde of people under the midday sun. She took him by the hand and walked into the crowd of people. Without guards to pave the way for her, she finally felt what it was like to be a regular person in her own skin.

Rubbing up against countless sweaty and grimy people, as well as breathing in the same air as maybe a hundred others, took a toll on her psychological health, but she pressed on.

"Through here," she called back to her companion, turning down the market's main street, where, at long last, there was a little room to breathe a drag of fresh air.

"I pray I never have to cozy up to a hide seller to get by again. The stench on that man," she wrinkled her nose, still feeling the man's sweat dripping down her cheek. "That is because you only just missed the butcher himself. I swear he smelled worse than a thousand carcasses left in the sun to rot," Bashaa added wryly as though it were a contest to see who had suffered the most, but she only laughed at the concept.

"We'd better keep moving," she regained her composure after adjusting her dress. "Agreed. They might cause a rabble, or *worse*, if they find out you're here without your guards," he cautioned.

They walked for about fifty more meters before finally finding the king himself, surrounded by the others, and a few animals they had chosen for the feast. They quickened their pace to reach them before being seen, but one of the guardsmen noticed them.

"*Ahah!* There you are, *my sweet*! Thank you, Thorsen," Truls said loudly as he turned to face them. "Yes, I am here, my lords. We have concluded our tour, and went looking for you," she gave a short curtsy.

"Our small journey led us here, though we were hard pressed to find you," she continued. "You could have simply asked one of the servants," he replied with a bit of distrust. "I could have, but where would the adventure be? I have never been in such a crowd as this one, nor do I think I ever will be again," she said with a chuckle.

"*Adventure*, you say? It was foolish and dangerous to do so; doubly so in the company of one who has yet to learn the truth of the world," Truls glared at him with a darkened tone. "Nevertheless, I am glad you are both here with us," his tone shifted back to normal.

"Thank you, my lord. I apologize for our tardiness, as Her Majesty's knowledge of the castle was *enthralling*," Bashaa returned with a low bow, but Truls subtly sneered at the man. Elhael, noticing the strange tension between them, decided it was time to step in.

"My lords, the day has grown quite hot and I do believe we need to prepare for the feast this evening," he said diplomatically, getting a low, frustrated rumble from Truls. "You're right. I don't want to show up smelling like I've just come off a battlefield," he sneered, then whistled for a nearby servant to take the animals they'd purchased back to the palace to be prepared.

"How long do you think that will take to prepare? I wager twenty thousand crescents for them to prepare it in four hours," Mads leaned in toward Elhael. "I wager *thirty* for them to do it in *three*," he responded with a grin. "Now, now. Bear in mind we have some of the best chefs on the Continent," Leona chuckled, overhearing their wager.

"I stand by what I wagered. A man never backs down on his word like that," Mads huffed and held out his hand. "Your loss," Elhael shrugged, though he hesitated to take the extended hand as it wasn't customary for elves to exchange physical contact.

Bahsaa and his father, however, were regarding Leona as she laughed heartily at the exchange. "Magnificent, isn't she?" Bashir asked his son in a whisper. "Hush, father. Truls might hear you. You know he can speak our language," Bashaa cautioned, but struggled to maintain his concentration as the memories of the cellar replayed in his head. "Like all the other ruling kings, we all must know each other's languages as though they were our own," he continued.

"However, his guards don't speak it, so we're free to comment on whatever we like as long as we keep it down," Bashir scoffed. "It is unwise to risk it anyway," his son retorted. "*Oh,* undo the calamity that is thine mammaries, Bashaa. You know as well as I do that she is a goddess amongst men and women of this world. Are you so dense that even mana would bend around you to not acknowledge her beauty?" he asked.

It's probably for the best that he doesn't know what we did, Bashaa thought, still feeling the sting of the insult that clearly shook him to his core.

"I understand, Father. I just do not wish to do so whilst in the presence of the king himself," he said in return. "Fearing things that may not come to be reality is folly, my son," his father said dismissively. "Take a gander at her while we're still here, and when we have departed, no one will know you have. It's what your mother would have wanted you to do," he continued.

"I'll consider it," Bashaa replied with a slight grin. His father smiled back and nodded, returning his posture to its regular state. He looked over at Elhael, who seemed not to have been paying attention, and was content at the fact.

As Truls and his entourage passed through the market, guards and merchants alike knelt before them and opened the way for them to walk freely.

"Your people love you, it seems," Elhael said, walking beside Truls and noting the kneeling citizens. "I couldn't give a turtle shit about them. They kneel for you and the others, not for me," Truls growled, shocking Elhael to hear him speak like that.

"I am saddened to hear that. May I ask why?" Elhael asked, hoping to glimpse the humanity a king was supposed to have, but Truls only shook his head. "I'm not sure *you* would understand," he said. "In my tongue, my name means *wise one*," Elhael said, raising a thin eyebrow. "Very well," Truls gave a relenting sigh.

"It began long ago, a few short days after my coronation. My father's passing was taken as a heavy blow by the society you see today. He was a just, fair king who was loyal to his subjects, and did everything in his power to ensure that his people would want to leave the place where they wanted for nothing," he began, glancing around at the kneeling merchants.

"Unfortunately, he fell ill with some dark sickness. Some say it was a curse, others say he was being poisoned, but I think he was *searching* for something," he said, with a dead stare aimed at the ground beneath a wicker basket to his left as a memory of his dying father flashed in his mind.

"I'm assuming you have your own theories," Elhael said, attempting to capture the king's divided attention. "Forgive me," Truls said, getting a nod from Elhael.

Memories of his father. I wonder if he somehow found out the truth, Elhael thought momentarily.

"Indeed, I do have a theory of my own, although I am not at liberty to share it with anyone other than myself. I pray you understand," Truls sighed. "I do, however, I must respect your privacy," Elhael said with a pained smile.

"At any rate, this benevolent lifestyle of his came to an end when his bookkeeper came to him with the large amount of debt he owed. There wasn't even enough gold in the *kingdom* to pay it off, though he felt something was off and began investigating the cause since this place has been a central trading hub for *centuries*," Truls shrugged.

No, that's not it. He's leaving something out intentionally, Elhael thought, but said nothing.

"With the massive debt, his reputation was tainted, and at just *seventeen*, the resolution of that debt was passed on to me. After investigating the cause for myself, I was *forced* to do everything I could to *get rid* of that debt, but my people grew to hate me for it. Gods, even my *own wife* hates me for how I've become," Truls scoffed and shook his head.

"I had no idea it got so bad," Elhael said in as comforting a tone as he could. "*Fuck* them. They can hate me all they want, but I know that *I saved* this country with everything I've had to do. Do you see *why* I know they're not bowing for me?" he spat, furrowing his brow. "I do, though I believe it's because they never knew *why* you did those things," Elhael put a hand to his sharp bare chin. "No, not even that would change a thing," he shook his head in dejection before they continued walking.

A few hours later, everyone reconvened at the vast banquet hall for the feast. The tables were set out as a large *T*, a custom handed down from generation to generation. At every feast, the tables were laid out in the form of the first letter of whatever the king's name was. The tablecloths had the castle's insignia sewn into each one; a daunting task, but the seamstresses around the castle were glad to have done the work.

They had been well remunerated for it, after all.

Along the long table of the joyous feast were trays of pheasant, venison, pork, lamb, and copious amounts of ale or vodka; far more than enough to satiate the entire *palace*. Jokes were made, food was thrown and stuck in beard hairs, as gravy, wine, ale and mead ran down chins.

All in all, the feast was in full swing, and all seemed to be going smoothly.

"This is a grand feast, if ever I've seen one, King Truls, and this venison is incredible! You must tell me what the secret is!" Mads had to bellow his sentence over the uproar below.

"Thank you for your kind words, King Mads. However, I regret to inform you that my chef is a magician when it comes to food. As everyone knows, a true magician never reveals his secrets. Sadly, not even to his own king." Truls raised a mug toward him, prompting Mads to pout momentarily. After a few moments, he raised his own drinking horn, blindly thinking it was in his direction.

Instead, it was raised toward the men's lavatory, where one of the palace's male servants had just stepped out. Seeing the horn raised in his direction, he winked at the king in response. Mads' eyes opened wide, and his face paled. He quickly proceeded to drown himself in the remaining alcohol in his drinking horn.

Elhael had seen it happen and burst into an almost uncontrollable fit of laughter. "Axes, arrows, spears, bears, and monsters; you have encountered all of these, and yet one wink from a man who does not share your sexual preference and you go white as a sheet of clean linen," he said between laughs.

Mads became mildly infuriated that someone other than he and the noble had noticed, mainly because it was the *overly observant* elf. "Now, now," Elhael said, raising a hand to try and calm Mads down. "We are never going to speak of this again," Mads said coldly, getting a quick nod from the elf, then a burst of laughter which infected Mads as well.

The male servant anxiously returned to the table designated for close servants of the palace, where Meliss, Clare, and a handful of others were seated. "*Oh*, hey! What's that on the f-floor?" Clare said, looking down at the stone floor.

"Behold! It's a *f-fuck* to give. I think you've lost it, Leland," she said cheerfully, jolting her head up. Leland looked at her in confusion. "He won't kill you over something so s-simple as that. It's a feast, and people have been, *hic*, drinking for a while," she continued, slurring her words.

"Fine, but if my body is found with a slit throat tomorrow morning, at least we'll know why" Leland said, flicking his dark hair over his eyes. "Calm yourself before you burst a vessel," Meliss threw in her two cents in a vain attempt to calm him down, passing him a full mug of ale. "Chug, you nervous wreck, chug!" she said with a smile.

He looked at her, then at the mug, which seemed to magically have appeared in his hand. He threw the contents of the mug down the back of his throat as fast as he could and shook his head. "There. Now do that a few more times and you're good to go," she said, still smiling as he nodded back to her gratefully.

"I don't blame you f-for doing what you did, *Leeeland-uh*," Clare began with a heavy hand on his not-so-muscular shoulder. "Hell, I'd have done the same if Prince Bashaa did that to me," she said. "You fancy him?" Meliss asked. "Of course! Have you s-seen his eyes, and the way he looks at you with them?" she asked playfully.

"They are marvelous, indeed. It's no wonder the lady he was with earlier couldn't resist him in the cellar," Leland said in agreement.

"And that's supposed to mean something to me?" Meliss asked. "Wait a minute," Clare said, reaching for a moment of clarity. "He was with the queen for the better half of the afternoon. You don't think...?" she stopped speaking halfway through, realizing Fulco, who was walking right behind her as she spoke, had suddenly frozen solid.

He sighed and said nothing, but his expression told the group everything they needed to know.

"Holy cocksneeze. I think he heard us," Clare said, trying to sober herself up. "We'd best be out of here," Leland urged. "No. We can't leave now. If we did that, we'd only paint bigger targets on our backs," Meliss said sternly. "Ok, then, *mastermind*; What the actual fuck are we supposed to do now?" Leland hissed as he shook with fear. "Nothing we can do besides acting as naturally as possible. Keep drinking," she replied.

The *Zebura* was brought out at the royal table, and Truls rose from his chair to whack the rim of his mug on the wooden table. The loud knocking sound immediately got everyone's attention.

"I'd like to propose a toast," he slurred his words a little and rocked back and forth as all eyes were on him. The three servants swallowed hard, concerned about their knowledge having leaked out to the last person it shouldn't have.

"On this most auspicious of evenings, I would like to have it known that I am glad to have such good and *loyal* company to share this with," he said. Everyone clapped and cheered unanimously.

He raised his hand to calm them.

"Tonight, we, the rulers of the countries of the Continent, have gathered here to celebrate peace amongst ourselves. That is not to say that we don't have the very real threat of the monsters lurking just outside our castles and citadels. However, we are celebrating something that has not happened since before my father's father was king. We are gathered here as friends, and brothers in arms to rid ourselves of those ugly bastards who take our husbands, our wives, and our children," he aimed his mug toward the end of the hall with another cheer.

"As an expression of this friendship, my lovely queen, Leona, suggested we partake in this *Zebura* to bring us *all together*, regardless of our cultural differences as we strive for peace," he gestured to the haunches before him, getting a thunderous applause as he did so.

Elhael pulled the servant who had brought the meal to them aside. "How long did it take to prepare *this*?" he asked quietly. "According to the master chef, it was *three* hours exactly," the servant replied. Elhael burst into laughter and pointed a finger at the color-flushed Mads.

"Told you, you drunken bastard! Now, pay up!" he exclaimed cheerfully. Mads sighed deeply and removed the coin purse from his side. "Take it," he mumbled just before the elven king snatched it out of his hands and tossed it in the air with a chuckle.

Truls cut the first slice of the dark, steaming flesh, then handed it to Leona, who sat immediately next to him and nodded deeply with gratitude. The next slice went to Bashir, who also nodded, and gave thanks in his native tongue.

Leona looked at him, wondering if he knew about what she and his son had done just a few short hours before meeting them in the market. He caught her eye, smiled, and nodded to her as well, but as he did so, she saw Bashaa, who sat just beyond him. He followed his father's example, and she felt a nervous stir in her belly.

"*Fuuuuuck*, he knows," Clare whispered after seeing the short exchange, prompting Meliss to glare at her to *shut up*. Clare noticed, immediately taking her eyes off the two and promptly gazing into her emptying mug.

In the meantime, Truls continued cutting the steaming meat before him, passing the slices down to both Mads and Elhael, who nodded and gave thanks. "To peace!" Truls called out, raising a slice of the flesh in one hand and a mug of ale in the other. "To peace!" the others in the hall returned, and the kings proceeded to bite into the *Zebura*'s meat.

Everyone cheered except for Leland, whom Fulco noted.

After the feast, the three left the hall and went their separate ways towards their dormitories. Meliss went into her room, only to find a folded nightgown on her bed with a note on it. "Thanks for being the best *lass* I've had the pleasure of meeting in a long time," the note said, and was signed with only the letter *L* at its base. She smiled, briefly forgetting about the possibility of her and her friends dying for having been overheard.

This fits as if she had it made for me, she giggled after putting it on and giving it a quick twirl.

The following morning, Fulco did his habitual rounds about the castle, ensuring everything was in order. After completing his checks on most areas of the palace, he found himself in the kitchen where a brunch was being prepared.

Smelling the fresh pastries and fruits being prepared and sliced, he smiled at the scent of it all. Washing the fruit to be prepared was none other than Leland, who could think of nothing other than the previous night.

Between the hangover and anxiety I feel, I don't know which one is worse, he thought.

"A late start today for all of us, I imagine," Fulco said, stopping beside him. The dark circles around Leland's eyes grew wide, and his heart began to race. "Lucky to have survived after last night's festivities, wouldn't you say?" he asked, getting a curt nod in response.

He didn't dare look his interrogator in the eye.

Fulco noticed that he was nearly unresponsive, save the nodding. "Might I have a word with you in private, Leland?" he asked quietly. Leland felt his heart stop for a moment, and broke into a cold sweat. He nodded again, and followed him to the large, nearly emptied pantry.

"I'm not going to mince my words and just be done with it," Fulco began. Leland managed to raise his head to look at Fulco, but could barely withstand his gaze. "Do you, or do you not confirm that Her Majesty had some form of physical... *interaction* with Bashaa during their little expedition yesterday afternoon?" Fulco asked sternly.

Leland's face paled even further than it already was. "Answer me," Fulco said calmly, but in a voice that chilled the very air around them. Leland looked for some form of escape around him, but found nothing. "Answer me, Leland, before I have to ask you a third time," he said in a threatening, sing-song voice.

He knows. Fuck, he knows, Leland thought.

"Alright, *alright!*" Leland finally broke down in tears. "I hadn't any clue he was with *her* before last night when the ladies and I were talking about the kings. I saw him entering the cellar yesterday, but I swear I didn't see who he was with," Leland said through bubbling spit. "Once I saw him enter the cellar, I figured he had gotten lost somehow. I went to investigate whether he was lost, and I heard *noises*," he nearly flinched as Fulco's brow furrowed.

"What noises?" he asked in a tone that belied his usual nature. "I-I don't know. Like he was having his way with someone down there. At first, I thought it was just a servant girl, but after Clare's comment, Meliss and I figured there was no other option than Her Majesty to be the one with him," he stammered.

"Clare and Meliss, correct?" Fulco asked, getting a quick nod in response. "Yes, b-but they have nothing to do with it, I swear on my life!" Leland stammered. "*Oh*?" Fulco raised an eyebrow. "She tried to shut us up before we had gone too far, but it was too late for that. We figured you had overheard it since you walked right past us," Leland explained.

"And you're *sure* you didn't tell anyone else about this?" the head servant asked coldly, getting another silent nod from Leland. "Very well, but if I find out you lied, I'll have you hung by your prick off the castle ramparts, is that understood?" Fulco leaned in closer, causing Leland to flinch and nod out of fear.

"Good. Clean yourself up and get the fuck out of here; you're making a mess," Fulco sighed and pulled a handkerchief from his doublet pocket and threw it at Leland as he darted out of the pantry, wiping the snot from his nostrils before starting to wash the fruit again.

Little did he or Fulco know that just outside the pantry door, someone had eavesdropped on their entire conversation. The rumor spread like wildfire around the palace, and within two days, the entire kingdom had heard what had happened. On the third day, yelling could be heard throughout the palace.

"Tell me the rumors aren't true, Fulco," Truls begged his servant. They were in his private study, surrounded by notes, books, scrolls, and lit candles. Though dawn was on the rise, it was still dark enough outside to know it was still a few hours away.

"I'm afraid so, Your Majesty. Leland, the manservant, had seen them walking about the palace without any guards present, and Clare had heard people making love in the cellars," he replied solemnly.

Truls' eyes were bloodshot and had dark circles around them. He paused, staring off into one of the dark corners of his study with dead eyes. "I will have his head on a spike. I will make his ancestors weep once they see how he enters the afterlife. In pieces," he said, his voice rumbled like a rockslide. "But what of the peace you so loudly proclaimed the other night, your majesty?" his servant asked, visibly shaken at his king's reaction.

"Imagine you were in my place, if you will, Fulco," Truls began. "You hold a council of peace, and yet there goes one of your so-called *allies* behind your back to *plough your wife*," he raised his voice at the last segment, glaring at the person standing before him. "I wish you would tell me exactly what the *fuck* that is supposed to do to a man," he said.

Fulco remained silent, casting his gaze towards the ground around his feet. "Tell me!" Truls bellowed. "I don't know, Your Yajesty. Really, I don't," Fulco finally spat out. "What I *do* know is that if you kill Bashaa, the peace treaty will be broken, and you will be fighting a war on two fronts, which has never worked for anyone in the past," he sighed.

"Then what the actual fuck am I supposed to do, since I am not allowed to gut the little *weasel-shit*?" he asked. "Talk to his father and have him punish his son, Your Majesty," Fulco said, leaning in and lowering his voice. "We both know of their customs regarding such matters," he continued, insinuating that whatever came as a result would *not* be a lovely sight to behold.

"You're a fool if you think a man like Bashir would punish his own son in such a way, Fulco," Truls said. "I believe he would, in fact, congratulate his son for having his way with my wife. After all, she has been and still is desired by all men who cross her path," he continued.

"*Almost all*, Your Majesty," Fulco gave him a knowing nod. "*Ah*, right. My apologies, Fulco," Truls nodded, realizing what his servant meant. "In any case, they have laws that are imposed that would not allow him any other way to avoid such a thing," Fulco replied.

Truls toyed with the idea of Bashir suffering at the hands of their laws; however, his imagination began drifting to the satisfaction it would give him to wring the life out of the *weasel-shit* himself. He looked back at Fulco and nodded in agreement.

"Very well, arrange a meeting with Bashir and his son in the main hall when daylight comes. *Oh*, and Fulco; Tell *no one* what we've discussed," Truls said gravely, getting an understanding nod before Fulco bowed and turned to walk out of the study, leaving Truls in his seat in the candlelit room.

Dawn came, and Truls sat atop his throne, while Leona still slept. The morning light shone through the stained glass windows, lighting the main hall's walls with various colors. His eyes burned due to sleep deprivation while leaning his chin heavily on his right arm.

Fulco swung open the mighty doors and passed through them, not even glancing at the guards who stood watch in full harness and in silence. "King Bashir, and Prince Bashaa of Harut, your Majesty," he announced, then quickly took his leave. Truls' eyes regained their burning hatred at Bashaa's name.

"King Truls," Bashir said in a loud and firm voice. "King Bashir," Truls replied, trying to hide the hatred in his voice. "I do not fully understand why only we two have been summoned, whereas my advisors and other council members remain asleep," Bashaa began nervously.

"That, my lord, is simply because I decided I didn't want them here. You see, this matter is between the three of us. *Oh*, excuse me, I meant the *four* of us; although, only *two* here know who the fourth one is," Truls glared at Bashaa maliciously, who shuddered when he noticed the glare was directed at him.

"My lord, you are speaking in riddles, and it is too early in the morning to try to decipher them," Bashaa said, rubbing his eyes. "Then, if your feeble little mind cannot solve them, why don't you ask your son?" Truls said sarcastically.

Bashaa's eyes opened wide, and he immediately looked about him for some kind of support. He had forgotten for a moment that it was only he and his father who had been summoned. "Go on; Tell him, *boy*," Truls said, impatience ruling his voice. "Tell me what?" Bashir looked at his son, who began to shake his head.

"He. Fucked. My. Wife," Truls rose from his throne, growling and accentuating his words with the sound of his heavy footfall. "M-My son would never do such a thing, my lord," Bashir protested, gesturing to his son with one arm. "Tell him, tell him how it is all a lie," he said nervously. Bashaa couldn't move; he simply stood there looking like a paralyzed half-wit.

"Tell him!" Bashir continued to try to coax him to speak.

"You've been *had*. I know the dirty little secret you and my wife have together," he said with his voice low as he moved toward them. "My lord," Bashaa began. "Don't you *dare* call me lord, you oozing prick sore," Truls yelled in the young man's face.

"This is a conversation where, according to your actions, *status* does not matter. You come in here, drink my wine, gorge yourself on my food, and have the nerve to plough *my wife*? You are not a prince nor hardly even a man. You are nothing but a worthless cur, and I would not be surprised if you had a shriveled worm for a prick. You have *defiled* my wife, *shamed* my kingdom, and both of these *right under my very nose*," he shouted, making the two men flinch.

"I would have you dragged through the streets by your balls for all that you've done, and I will ensure that you make it to the Under-world, even if it means dragging you there *myself*," he bawled in rage as spit flew from his mouth.

Truls reached back under his tunic to draw a large dagger and thrust it at lightning speed into Bashaa's neck, spewing blood onto his wrist and forearm. Bashir screamed in terror as his bleeding son fell to the ground.

Truls began to step over his writhing legs and knelt on top of his chest, as his eyes glared with hatred and his knuckles were white due to his grip on the dagger. He began to sever the dying man's head off and danced in the blood that spilled forth from it.

In absolute horror, Bashir turned and ran out of the door as quickly as he could, calling his men out to flee the castle as bile crept up his throat.

Fulco quickly re-entered the hall after hearing the scream, and immediately fainted at the sight of Truls dancing in blood, holding the head in one hand, with the dagger in the other. Truls looked about him and noticed his servant on the ground, feeling nothing but pure elation after slaying the *worthless cur*.

His guards hadn't moved an inch; after all, there was nothing they could have done to stop it from happening. He chuckled to himself, and his laughter increased to a fit of maniacal laughter until Leona rushed down the stairs to see what the scream was about.

Her face paled at the sight of him dancing in the pool of blood, chopping the corpse up into pieces and flinging them around the throne room like some kind of *macabre confetti*. She let out a blood-curdling scream, which prompted him to turn on her immediately. His face was spattered with blood, and the rest of him was now covered in it.

She held back bile as best as she could, and bolted back up the flight of stairs she had just come down. She ran through the hallways and finally found what she thought to be a sanctuary in the confines of her room, slamming the door and bolting it in fear of her husband.

"Where did you go, *my sweet*?" she flinched as she heard his voice come from behind the door. "Why did you run from me? Why did you *do this to me*?" his voice turned from sing-song to unbridled rage in the span of his two questions.

Bile rose in her throat as she pressed her back against it, hearing his heavy footfall *thud* against the stone steps. "Your Majesty!"

Thorsen's voice called out, giving her a small flame of hope. "*Ahhh,* Thorsen, my ever-loyal giant. Fetch Commander Gorm and tell him to go after Bashir. I will not allow that *fucking pox-ridden rat* to live another day if I can help it," Truls growled, reverberating the door Leona was leaning against.

"And what of the body?" Thorsen asked, his tone suggesting he was wildly uncomfortable with everything that was going on. "Bashir couldn't have gotten far. Put the pieces of his son on spikes along the exit of the Palace. Make sure that bastard *knows* the price he will pay when we find him," he replied, spit drooling from his mouth.

"A-As you wish, Your Majesty," the sound of his armor clanking, letting Leona know he'd rendered a salute and moved away.

No, please! Please come back, she held a hand to her mouth as tears streamed down her face.

"Now, where were we, *my sweet?*" Truls' voice came from just behind the door, sending a ruthless chill down Leona's spine as a cold stone of ice sank in her stomach.

Just outside the palace, Thorsen did as instructed, bundled up the pieces into the dead man's robe, and dragged the chunks outside. He ordered the guards to give him their spears, and they did so without question, save for the ones about what was left of the Harutian prince.

When he arrived at the front gate of the main palace, he unraveled the pieces, planted the spears in the ground, and skewered the body parts. The head faced outward with its lifeless, gaping expression portraying a silent scream. A few of the guards who had been posted just outside that gate had their breakfast coming out of the wrong hole in a flash.

Making his way back inside, he found Gorm already riding out with his war party to hunt down Bashaa and, possibly, his men. He nodded and continued on his way towards the palace.

What could have prompted him to carve the Harutian prince into so many pieces? I didn't see Leona, but I know I heard her scream, which is why I went there in the first place. Where could she be? Thorsen rubbed a blood-soaked glove on his thick beard pensively.

Back inside the palace, Truls slammed the handle of his dagger firmly against the heavy door to Leona's room. "I know you're in there, *my love*. I just want to talk," he used a lighter tone of voice, but all it did was make her shudder and press her back to the door even more firmly.

Tears continued to stream down her face as she held her mouth to keep from screaming. "Open this *fucking door*, Leona! You would be nothing without me and what I've done for your family, and you *know it*! I *own you*, and I command you to open up!" he shouted, his voice hardly muffled by the heavy door.

What do I do? She shuddered, looking around the room for any means of escaping her personal hell.

The small iron screws that held the bolt in place already strained under the repeated impact from his banging, coming increasingly looser after a few more kicks and bangs from the enraged king. Unfortunately, even the iron screws couldn't survive a full body-weight assault from the heavy man, giving way and knocking her to the floor as she received the impact.

Hurriedly, she got back to her feet and ran to the corner of the room. Her eyes were swollen and red from the tears that streamed, but they opened widely at the sight of Truls' blood-soaked visage and wolfish smile.

"*Ah*, there you are, *my dove*," he said in a disturbing tone. She could barely breathe at the sight of him. "You murdered him!" she said breathlessly, struggling to mouth the words racing in her mind.

"Yes, I did; Ridding the world of yet another *vermin* in the process," he replied. "How could you do this after saying what you said at the feast?" she asked. He paused for a moment, appearing to be deep in thought. "Because I wanted to," he replied.

"You see, my dove, a man does not defile another man's wife without paying for it one day or another. He *defiled* you, the rumor spread like wildfire, and now the whole kingdom thinks that I'm a fool, and that you are a *worthless whore*!" he shouted the last five words.

Leona was shocked, and her face contorted in disgust as her hatred for the man she had once married grew exponentially. "Prove me wrong," he said, noticing her countenance. "Tell me that you didn't let him have his way with you, and that I have just made one of the largest mistakes of my life," he said.

He'll kill me no matter what I tell him, she thought, accepting the possibility of her death.

"I won't prove you wrong," she said after a moment to allow her mouth to catch up to her thoughts. "What?" he asked, darkening his tone. "I won't prove you wrong, because it wasn't he who had his way with me. In fact, it was the other way around," she said.

"He tried to charm me with his worthless wit, but deep down all I wanted was a *good fuck* because you can't even *keep it up*. Not even when you force yourself on me as you have so many times in the past, you *prickless pig*," she spat, landing a wad of thick saliva on his face.

He flinched with the impact, but when the wolfish grin grew on his face again, he wiped it off with his bloodied thumb and licked it off. "You filthy *bitch!*" he shouted the last word, smacking her with the back of his hand across her face. She fell across the bed, but quickly scrambled away from him to the far side of the room where she kept her easel.

"I have given you everything in my kingdom, everything you have ever wanted, and this is how you repay me? By shoving some *wart-ridden* prick up your snatch? I will see you pay for what you've done as well," he said with fiery eyes, walking towards her. He smacked her again, this time sending her head straight into the corner of her easel, forcing her to blindly reach for it to keep her from going to the ground.

He smacked her across the face once more, forcing her to turn around, as he began to lift up her dress while she was too stunned to resist.

"Help!" she cried out as tears streamed down her face. Truls quickly covered her mouth, muffling her voice. "No one is going to save you now," he seethed in her ear while undoing his trousers.

"Not Bashaa, nor anyone else in this *fucking place*. You're in my kingdom. My rules are the only thing that apply here, and currently, my only rule is that I don't have any rules. I don't have to be careful of what I do to you, since you're nothing more than *my property*," he said in her ear through bared teeth.

She glanced down through her tears and saw a thick paintbrush on the easel before her. She bit into Truls' finger, and he reeled with the pain as blood poured from the bite.

"You fucking whore!" he lurched toward her, but before his blood-soaked hands could reach her throat, she grrabbed the paint-brush from the easel and drove it beneath his jaw with a grunt of exertion. His eyes widened in shock as he glared at her, but quickly rolled into the back of his head as she pushed it deeper, piercing his brain.

Blood ran down her hand and wrist just before she ripped it out and let his body slump to the ground in a pool of blood, wriggling and writhing like a beheaded serpent.

The king was dead, and her trembling hands slowly began to steady themselves as the realization of what she'd done took over.

"The nightmare... It's *finally* over," she whispered in a shaky voice as the tears streamed down her face, not borne from sadness, but relief. As she allowed the paintbrush to fall, the paint that had soaked the bristles flecked a handful of specks across her face from the impact, but she could hardly flinch.

The king's body finally ceased its writhing, and within the silence that followed, she heard armored footsteps coming from beyond the broken door. "Y-Your Majesty?" Thorsen's voice came from beyond the threshold. His eyes widened when he realized that it was not her lying on the ground, but the king.

"Are you alright?" he rushed in, putting his comparatively massive hands on both her shoulders, staring into her blank eyes. "I'm fine, Thorsen," she said in a dreamlike voice, prompting him to glance down at the body again, then back to her. "Are you sure, Your Majesty?" he regarded her seriously.

"I promise I'm fine, Thorsen. I just need a moment to catch my breath," she used her sleeve to wipe away a string of snot. "What happened here, Your Majesty?" he kept his voice low and steady. "I..." she cut herself off before tears welled in her eyes again. "I couldn't take it anymore, Thorsen. The abuse, the name-calling, the absolute tyranny over *my* body," she shook her head. "I can't say that I understand, but I'm glad you're alright," Thorsen said calmly.

The pair looked down at Truls' lifeless body for a moment in silence, before Leona pulled away from Thorsen's hand, reaching for the dagger still clutched tightly in her former abuser's grasp. With a grunt of effort, she tore it free from his fingers, nearly staggering back as it came free. "What are you doing, Your Majesty?" Thorsen regarded her curiously since he knew better than to try to stop her now.

"The people outside the palace will have heard about Bashir's son by now since *you* put his pieces out on display," her eyes fixed on the body beneath her. "I did as I was commanded, Your Majesty," Thorsen lowered his head.

"I know, and I don't blame you for that, nor will I ever, but right now, I need to send the *rest* of the kingdom a message," she said, her tone growing increasingly colder as she steeled herself for what came next.

Gripping the back of Truls' hair, she lifted his neck and began to saw off his head, just like he had to Bashaa. Realizing it would be much more effort than it was worth, she chose an alternate route. With a grunt of frustration, she grabbed the body by the beard and began to drag it along with her down the stairs, leaving a trail of smeared blood in her wake.

Her eyes were as cold as steel when she walked back into the throne room. There was already a crowd of people near the entrance who were trying to see over the guardsmen's shoulders, or beneath their raised arms. "Step aside," she panted heavily, her shoulders curled over and arms taut as she dragged the large man's body behind her.

The guardsmen, who turned to look, immediately followed her order with widened, worried eyes. She glanced over to her left, where Fulco was just now waking back up, but fainted again as soon as he saw the king's half-decapitated body being dragged into the room.

She dragged his body into the middle of the throne room and dropped it in front of the throne he coveted so much. The crowd poured in to see the commotion, some even slipping on Bashaa's clotted blood on the floor as they scrambled to get in close. "Your Majesty! What happened here? What happened to the King? Whose blood is this?" a barrage of voices shouted in question.

Leona held a blank, emotionless stare on her face and raised the dagger high into the air, still coated in Bashaa and Truls' blood.

"The King did this to himself," she shouted, silencing the crowd immediately. "He first killed Prince Bashaa, then tried to kill me. Unfortunately for him, he *failed* to kill the latter," she shouted over a wave of murmurs from the crowd.

"*I* am the ruler of this land and its people now. I am the one who will do her best to bring about a new age of prosperity, *true prosperity*," she said, letting the words hang to see if anyone would object.

No one did or even *felt* they could, for that matter.

"No objections? Good. Then let this new age for Coltend and its people begin!" she shouted, getting scattered cheers from the crowd as her words slowly sank in. As more and more voices called out to cheer her on, she glanced at Thorsen, who nodded to her thoughtfully, then turned to face the crowd.

A new age indeed, Your Majesty, he thought, sternly looking at the ever-growing cheers of the people before them.

Fulco regained consciousness, and after seeing the crowd of people chanting her name, he steeled himself to reach the steps to stand beside her. He did what he could to hold in his breakfast and avoid looking down at the lifeless body before him.

The people continued to cheer as more came in to discover what all the commotion was about, and those who did, joined in with the crowd. Leona looked out over the amassing servants and smiled.

"Your Majesty, I have been his advisor for over twenty years. If there is anything you need from me, you need only ask," he muttered into her ear. "I know, Fulco. Thank you for understanding," she continued to stare blankly ahead as her free hand balled into a fist.

My turn, she thought.

CHAPTER 8
THE UNDERGOD

The Masked One led his apprentice down the gloaming halls, where the meeting with the Undergod was to take place.

"May I ask you a question, my lord?" Athar began. "It would seem you already have, but yes," the Masked One retorted. "How is it that you first came into contact with the Undergod?" the young man asked skittishly. "As you will come to know over time, Athar, there are many things that happen to us that may drive us to some... *extreme* measures," the mage began.

"Some men choose easier paths, by simply making a deal with him or fate itself. Others, not unlike myself, choose to try and work together with him to achieve a greater goal. He is very impatient, capricious, and unforgiving, so you must mind your manners," he continued.

"You didn't answer my question, master," Athar said shyly after a moment's pause. "And you noticed, like anyone with half a brain would, might I add. Perhaps you're not an absolute waste of a core," the Masked One replied. "I will not answer that question for one of two reasons: the first is that it is sensitive information I am not about to disclose. The second is simply because I don't want to, so shut your trap, and follow me without saying a word until we reach our meeting point. Do you understand?" he asked with evident irritation.

Athar felt a chill go down his spine.

Shit. I can't do anything or say anything without the cheese falling off his bread. I knew I should have paid more attention to those books that kind merchant always tried to make me read, Athar sighed.

"Yes, my lord," he tried to hide the sigh he wanted to let out so badly. They continued walking down the dimly lit halls, passing countless other staircases that led to, as of yet, unknown places for the young man.

They finally reached the doorway to his private study, where he unlocked and swung the door open with a wisp of mana. Athar's eyes opened with genuine surprise as he crossed the threshold and began committing the details to memory.

A large octagon of salt is in the center of the floor, candles are on every point, a large crystal is in the very center of the drawing itself, and a desk is at its base. It looks like another summoning circle, but this time it's more complex, Athar thought as he tried to understand its purpose.

"And you would be right," the Masked One said, answering his thoughts. "How the...?" Athar said, astonished. The Masked One, uncharacteristically, chuckled. "I have always been able to read your thoughts, even the ones *never meant for me,*" he said, interrupting what Athar was about to say, making his stomach drop.

"*Oh,* come now. Did you *really* think I would take you in without being able to keep tabs on what goes through that puny mind of yours?" he asked over his shoulder. "There has never been anything you've been able to hide from me, Athar. I brought you here *because* I know *who* you are," he said.

Athar stood in silence, while his head hung low.

The mage stopped himself from grabbing an item off a nearby shelf and sighed, then turned to face his slave. "Don't worry; there's a reason I'm telling you this, after all," he said, prompting Athar to look back up in surprise. "If you think *I'm horrible* for doing so, the Undergod can and *will* do much worse to you if you offend him in any way," he shrugged slightly.

"I see, my lord," Athar frowned, feeling his stomach drop. "Good. Then you'll do well to keep quiet, and your thoughts to yourself," the mage turned back around.

How the hell am I supposed to do that if you're reading them all the time? Athar raised an eyebrow silently, making his master halt.

"Do yourself a favor: stop doing *that*, and you'll be fine," the mage sighed before gathering mana. A violet orb began to swirl into his palm, growing exponentially as the dark tendrils began to gather. "I request an audience," he said firmly, slamming his hand into an apex of the octagonal ring.

The runes on the ground glowed brightly with violet light as the rings of salt began to rotate and fit together, locking into place before giving off one final burst of light.

The entire room began to shake with a ferocity Athar had never felt before, and he was genuinely concerned that everything would start to crash and fall. There was a voluminous puff of smoke from where the crystal once was, and a mixture of horrid smells like rotting flesh and sulfur filled the air. Athar could barely breathe, whereas the Masked One was accustomed to such smells.

A disgruntled voice like thunder rolled out through the smoke and across the room, shaking all the books on the nearby shelves off their supports. "Why do you disturb me, mage?" the Undergod asked, his voice rolled like thunder within the study as a projection of his form began to rise from the ground.

His lengthy horns nearly scraped the ceiling, talons grew down nearly past his knees, and his overall figure was one of a mountain of rotting, twitching flesh. The skinless figure loomed over them like a troll to ants, gazing down upon these inferior beings. His eyes burned bright with violet fire, as flame-like tendrils that danced around him licked the base of his horns.

So that's the Undergod. I had no idea this is what he looked like, but it's like nothing I've ever seen, Athar gulped dryly, hoping his thoughts hadn't been heard.

Before the Masked One could answer his master's question, Volzuk's gaze pierced Athar's core. The long, fleshy tentacle-like goatee hung heavily from his chin, swaying with the movements of his head. "Who are *you* to judge my appearance?" he asked Athar, who could have been easily confused for a marble statue.

"My lord, please forgive my servant's ineptitude to keep his thoughts to himself. He hasn't been trained to do so yet, though I will correct that shortly," the Masked One stepped in front of Athar, glancing at him from over his shoulder. "You should have thought of that before bringing him here," Volzuk rumbled.

"My apologies, my lord, I'm sure he meant *no offense*," the mage bowed slightly, glancing at Athar from the corner of his eye. "I will allow it this time, but know there will *not* be a second. Now, why did you disturb me, mage?" the Undergod asked after weighing his servant's words.

"I have news from Coltend, Lord Volzuk," the Masked One replied. "What news?" Volzuk grunted, giving the mage a scrutinizing look. "The Kings of this realm have gathered and held a council that aims to summon volunteers to close the portals from your Realm into ours," the mage replied.

"Then they're just as foolish as ever. They have no idea what they're doing, and yet they believe they can stop me?" Volzuk scoffed. "Agreed, my lord, but with the elves getting involved..." the mage cut off as Volzuk leaned in. "I *do not care* about the elves, or anyone else in your Realm, mage. I have left the handling of the others to *you* for that purpose," he growled.

"Yes, and I'm to overthrow the ruling powers here to help prepare for your arrival by using the outcast Synners and the creatures you've brought here. I know that, my lord, but the elves have recently grown much more powerful," the mage raised his hands placatingly. "So far, everything has gone according to your plan, but I can foresee an issue with them not being as weak as you once thought," he continued.

"Mind your tone, *mage*. I know what you're trying to say, and if you think *that* will be enough to stop me, then you are sorely mistaken. Have I not already shown and given you powers far beyond their comprehension?" Volzuk asked with visible annoyance. "You have, my lord," the mage relented. "Then *why* are you concerning yourself with those pointy-eared weaklings?" the Undergod asked bluntly.

"I'm not, but I will *not* underestimate them, either, my lord," the mage replied, getting a sigh of frustration from the Undergod.

"I'm disappointed in you, *Masked One,*" he said sardonically. "I had hoped that you would differ from the others of your world, and show true strength and wisdom unlike the ones before you. Yet here you are, acting as foolish as you consider your servant to be," Volzuk said.

The mage's eyes flared with mana momentarily. "I have not come to grovel at your feet, nor do I want you to look down on me. I will uphold *my* end of the bargain if you hold up yours," he gritted his teeth beneath the mask. "You and I *both* know just how powerful the Synners can be, even with their dwindling numbers. I am *warning* you not to underestimate them, as they *can* pose a threat to our plans," he continued.

"A *threat*? To whom? To you, perhaps, but not to me. Their fortresses, armies, weapons, and spells mean nothing to me," Volzuk said angrily. "If they truly pose no threat, then why do you need my help?" the Masked One asked, knowing the risk of doing so. Athar, who had been trying to maintain his composure, nearly gagged at the Undergod's swelling power.

"Silence!" Volzuk shouted, losing his composure. "You dare to use that tone with me, you insolent *worm*?" he continued furiously. "I can just as easily strip your power from you, leaving you to rot like the flesh upon my body," he said, his voice vibrating both the mage and servant's bones.

Holy shit, I can't breathe, Athar dropped to his knees beneath the pressure of the Undergod's flaring mana.

Even as a projection, it was still enough to make even the Masked One flinch.

"You should already know what the gods of the Ethereal have done to me. There is not a moment more that I will waste discussing this.

Uphold your end of the bargain, and bring me what I asked for. If you fail me, you will suffer," Volzuk said frustratedly.

The Masked One sighed. "You seem to have forgotten who *I am*, my lord. It's true that you *are powerful*, but you're not all-powerful *yet*," he said in a dark tone, making the Undergod raise a lump of flesh where his eyebrow would have been.

"You could strip me of the power you have given me, but may I remind you that I had no small amount of power before pledging my allegiance. Now that I know the inner workings of the dark power you gave me so long ago, it would only be a matter of time before I could overthrow you," the Masked One replied.

"You dare threaten me?" the Undergod growled. "All I'm saying is that you should perhaps consider taking better care of your allies, my lord," the mage shrugged. "*Ah*, like you take care of your slave?" Volzuk sneered, shifting his gaze over to Athar, who was still sitting on his ankles and clutching his chest.

He leaned in toward him, prompting Athar to look upward at the towering, rotten figure before him. "I *know* who you are, and with every word your master speaks, it makes me wonder whether keeping you around will even be worth it in the end. Make no mistake, *Athar*, the insubordination you see from *him* is not something I will continue to tolerate," he growled, gesturing with a large finger to the Masked One.

How does he know? Was that pressure I felt from him looking into my core? Athar wondered, still clutching his chest.

"I-I understand, Great One," Athar struggled to get the words out. "You're not strong enough to maintain yourself in *both Realms*. Perhaps you should consider *that* before you make threats," the Masked

One tilted his head. "You wouldn't dare..." Volzuk snapped to him. "I might, but if our deal and unlikely partnership is to be upheld, it doesn't do well to threaten your *only allies*, does it?" the mage asked wryly.

"You grow bolder by the day, *mage*," Volzuk growled, realizing he was right. "I have to be if I'm going to do your *bidding*, my lord," the mage sneered. "It would seem you've grown almost *too* bold, mage, but to answer *your* question, Athar: Yes, it was. However, I will not spoil the *fun*," he gave what could easily have been mistaken for a crooked smile.

"Train him to use mana, mage. He will play a vital role in the coming days, and I would be remiss if he didn't have the strength to do my bidding as well," Volzuk commanded, making Athar's eyes grow wide in surprise.

I know you can hear me, lord, so why does he want me to train in mana manipulation? Athar asked, hoping it had only gone to his master.

"I can *also* hear you, boy, but if you were even *half* the man you think you are, then you will voice those questions aloud," Volzuk sneered, making him flinch. "O-Of course, Great One, but it's difficult to speak under this pressure," he gritted his teeth. "Do it anyway," the Undergod said without a hint of compassion.

With a grunt of exertion, Athar did his best to get to his feet. His knees trembled as he did so, but even the Masked One looked at him in surprise. "Why do you want me to learn to wield mana?" he asked in a similarly cold tone, sweat pouring from his brow.

Volzuk raised the fleshy portion above his eye again. "*Oh*, the boy *can* stand after all," he said with an air of surprise. "Think of it as a form of *security*, Athar. I need you for my plans, but like your master, I cannot afford to have you be *weak* if you're going to be a part of them. You *will* play a vital role, but that is all you need to know for now," he said cryptically.

"I understand, Great One," Athar nodded, still struggling to even move in Volzuk's presence. "Do *not* fail me," the Undergod said, snapping his fingers with a squelching sound as he undid the summoning spell.

The little shit is already taking after my example, the Masked One grinned.

As the Undergod vanished, the pressure in the room quickly released, making Athar stumble as his muscles faltered momentarily. "Damn it," he muttered, looking at his shaking hands. "It looks like you need to start your training right away," the mage began, his eyes fixed on Athar's trembling hands. "Come with me," he motioned before turning to leave the study.

"Where are we going, my lord?" Athar asked. "You'll see," his master replied coldly. Athar had difficulty keeping up with him, since his augmented height caused his stride to be much longer than Athar's. After what seemed to be an eternity of winding, dark halls, they had finally made it to the entrance of his master's study.

"Whoa," Athar said, his excitement showing clearly. The bookshelves lined the twenty-meter-high walls, packed so tightly a knife's blade could barely fit between them on some shelves.

"I want you to use the time you have here to study as much as possible. The books I've gathered here over the *centuries* will likely be of great help to you," the mage gestured to them.

"You want me to learn from these forbidden books, master?" he asked, recognizing a few of the titles. "Forbidden for *whom*? There is no such thing as *forbidden* if one has enough *power*. Like the Undergod suggested, however, you must prove yourself worthy of them," the mage gestured to the wall of shelves where he wanted him to begin his studies.

Athar noted the evident lack of ladders, though the shelves nearly reached the top of the high ceiling. "My lord, how can I reach the ones I cannot grasp with my arms?" Athar asked. "Find a way, although I suggest you start with *this one*," his master replied coldly, tossing him a heavy, leather-bound book that he almost let fall to the floor.

"*Spells For Those With Baseline Mana Manipulation Skills,* by Feranger Efer. Who the hell is that?" he asked in a hushed voice. "He was one of the pioneers of mana after its discovery. It's been a few millennia since then, but his methods are still used throughout the Continent to varying degrees. You would do well to read through that one first, then move on to learning spells," the Masked One said, already pulling another book out.

Athar felt a hint of happiness for the first time since he was brought there. "That was uncharacteristically *supportive* of you, my lord," he grinned, knowing the intrusive thought wouldn't be hidden anyway. "Uncharacteristic, you say?" the Masked One asked.

"Normally, you have some demeaning remarks to make, but I think this is the first time you have shown a side that is far more *humane* than I am used to, my lord," Athar explained. His master stood silently for a moment as if pondering how to respond to the comment.

"Athar, I have always sought power," the Masked One began, making Athar's ears perk up like a dog hearing the word *meat*. "And throughout my many, many years procuring it, I have often found that those who do not seek power, or get excited by the prospect of it, are useless to me. Until I looked into your core, I had assumed you to be weak-willed, skittish, and an idiot in my eyes. That perspective has now changed, though the Undergod's command also drives it," he continued.

"Do you think I have potential, my lord? To wield mana, I-I mean," he stammered. "You do, but it will certainly take its toll on you. I just hope you're up to the challenge," the Masked One answered after a moment of consideration.

"Y-you're going to mentor me, my lord?" Athar's eyes gleamed with excitement. "*Mentor* is a strong word. Think of it as more of a *push* in the right direction than anything else. There is only so much I can do for you, since you will eventually walk your own path," the Masked One concluded.

"Walk my *own path*," Athar repeated the words. "What do you mean by that, my lord?" he asked. "I have already said too much," his master replied. "Use this hall as you see fit. I will be expecting you to be here more often than not, as I will have a few glicks to bring some of your things down from your room that you will need," he continued, making Athar blink repeatedly in surprise.

I can't believe what I'm hearing. It's like he's turned into someone else entirely in the span of a day, he thought.

"I can still hear you, Athar," the Masked One noted before leaving him to his studies. The door shut behind him, and Athar gave himself a small chuckle as he rushed to open the first book his master had given him.

This is the author's signature. How long has this book been around? he thought as his eyes finally met the preface and began to read aloud.

"This book, incomplete as all good magic books should be, serves as a guideline to the one who desires to acquire a higher knowledge than that of his or her colleagues, or as a review for those who already have. All spells and incantations do not require a basic knowledge of mana to learn, as I aim to instruct those on how to draw from both *currently known* Realms properly. Though many believe that one must be a direct descendant of one who has imbibed the famed plant's formula, this is not so, as I will demonstrate in the first chapter," he read.

"He wasn't joking after all," he smiled with a light scoff.

"With that being so, it is important to acknowledge that the plant makes mana manipulation *easier*, more effective, and poses much less risk. Perhaps, the one who reads this guide might even match their abilities," his eyes opened wide with the last sentence.

"If the process of drawing mana is not done in the correct order, the risk of failure or death grows exponentially," he read, feeling a drop of sweat trickle down his cheek.

Death doesn't sound fun. I'd better pay attention to this part, he thought.

"First comes the *Silence*; not of the world around you, but the silence of one's thoughts. One must not think of anything other than the task to prevent those thoughts from interfering with one's ultimate goal. Long, deep breaths and a comfortable sitting position are advised for this portion," he continued, trying to imagine what that would feel like.

"Second comes the *Immolation of Consciousness*. The most difficult part of connecting to the other Realms lies here, for an untrained and unsilenced mind will cause one to lose grip of reality, driving one mad," his eyebrows raised quickly. "*Oh*, that sounds... *fun*," he grinned nervously.

"The *Immolation of Consciousness* requires one to detach their consciousness and actively send it to the other realms. While there are various levels, or *stages*, as the Synners call them, to this ability, it is still one of the parts of this process that holds the most risk. It is important to note that your physical body will be about as conscious as a potato is aware of its own existence, so be careful where and when you try this," he read, feeling his stomach sink a bit.

"The third step is the *Draw*. One must command and mold the mana to their will using their emitted consciousness. Condensed mana can get extremely hot, so it is customary for a mage at the initial level, or *stage*, to use a ward-ring. I have provided one such ring, which I have stored in a small pouch on the backside of this book," he read, immediately flipping the book over to remove the small, silver ring from its holder.

He regarded it curiously for a few moments and put it on his index finger. It sat a little loosely, but within the heartbeats that followed, it shrunk itself to fit his finger perfectly.

"*Hah!* I didn't think it would do *that*," he chuckled, turning his hand over to observe the ring before continuing to read.

"Now, assuming one hasn't lost control of their consciousness to their realm of choice and has successfully drawn mana, it is time to

Condense. You must command it into the locations you wish it to go, though it is much easier to do this with an idea already in mind. Those ideas, in essence, are known as *spells,*" his heart skipped a beat when he read the words.

I can't wait, he thought, immediately flipping to the next page.

"The first spell I will teach is called *Exar;* a simple blast of air and mana that will be a good basis to start training with. This spell will be released from the tips of your fingers and as potent as the caster's ability to command the mana," Athar read quickly, feeling his excitement begin to boil over within.

"After drawing the mana, you must command it to gather to your fingertips and quickly expel it once it has. Don't hold it for too long, otherwise one might burn through the ward. Now, find a quiet spot to practice this concept, and *do not* skip ahead if one hasn't completed this simple task. Remember the order: Silence, Immolation, Draw, Condense, and Cast," he finished, setting the book aside.

"This is absolutely insane," he chuckled quietly as he got into a good, meditative position in the center of the study with hour-candles around him to keep track of the time it took.

"Alright," Athar said aloud as though it would boost his courage. He closed his eyes and breathed in and out in a controlled manner. Thoughts of his life before coming here to serve the Masked One returned; running through the streets, stealing food from a handful of merchants, and getting scolded by the ones who caught him. He focused on removing them from his mind, though it took longer than expected.

Damn, this is difficult, he thought.

Peeking at the candles, he noticed that a few hours had passed, but he was slowly progressing. Eventually, he found what he'd been trying to attain: *Silence.*

It was a peace like he'd never known before, as every thought, memory, and emotion suddenly and abruptly stopped in his mind. He didn't dare to acknowledge it verbally or through his thoughts, but he knew he'd reached the first step.

The second, *Immolation*, became his next target, though he was still unsure of which realm to draw from.

Deepening his focus, he committed to sending his consciousness forth, *giving him an outside view of his body as the world lurched around him. Darkness came forth, and a flood of involuntary emotions swept him forward into a timeless space between two large spheres that presented themselves to him per his limited abilities.*

The first swirled with multiple tendrils of various colors that raced across a golden orb. The second held violet streaks of lightning-like mana that slowly spanned a lifeless, gray orb.

He reached for the one swirling with bright colors, but a swarm of dark tendrils overcame him and dragged him toward the gray orb. The timeless space between the orbs lurched around him, and his vision immediately clouded in violet and gray.

When his vision returned, he quickly found that he was surrounded by dead trees and oozy smells.

His consciousness had gone to the Underworld.

The dark, vast wasteland with the body-ridden bloodstream and dead trees lay around him. The smell almost knocked him off his feet, which weren't firmly planted. He could hear the sounds of numerous creatures in the distance, prompting him to quickly ensure nothing was coming his way. He was shaken to his core, but maintained his focus.

He looked up at the sphere in the sky, enveloped in the dark streams of mana, and thought back to the information from the book. "Draw," the word came into his mind, doing his best to follow the instructions smoothly and calmly.

It took a few seconds for him to command mana from the sphere, but when it came, it did so with a force he wasn't expecting, aggressively enshrouding his body.

"Condense," the word showed up in his head, and he forced his will to move the mana towards his hand. It wavered a moment, and flowed slowly. He had to focus as much as possible to move it even an inch along his body.

Finally, the dark sphere formed in his hand, and he could feel the warmth resonating from it on his face and upper forearm. He formed his hand according to the text and returned his consciousness the same way he had come, both spheres growing more distant as he moved back into the Real.

The force of the return was so great that it knocked him backwards, and he had to use his free hand to support his weight. The candles had gone out, as a slight waft of air was coming from the mana in his hand.

"I've done it," he said with a laugh, carefully glaring at the mutating sphere in his hand. He didn't want to accidentally lose control of what had taken him so long to accomplish.

He recomposed himself to his original position, keeping his eyes fixed on the sphere.

Cast, the word entered his mind as he outstretched his hand, expelling it from his fingertips with a large, arcing blast of violet mana and air.

It sent the handful of candles before him spinning into the air, eventually crashing into the bookshelf on the far side of the room. The pages beside him ruffled, flicking the book wide open before skidding across the floor.

"*Haha!* I can't believe it," he said breathlessly as he stared at his hand, clenching it into a fist. "Holy shit," he huffed, and began to laugh. It was the first time he had laughed that hard in what seemed an age, so much so that his stomach muscles began to cramp up.

After reeling with the sharp pain, he regained his composure, hoping his abdominal muscles wouldn't cramp up again.

He looked for the book which he'd left beside him, only to find it a little ways away. He scrambled over to it, suddenly realizing how physically taxing it had been on his body as he was quickly forced to crawl toward it on his belly.

"More," he said in an exhausted voice. "I think you've had enough for one evening, Athar," a voice came from behind him. The Masked One had been watching him the whole time from the doorway.

"It feels good, doesn't it? All of that power in the palm of your hand," his master said with a slight touch of pride cutting through his voice. "I can't believe it," Athar replied with a breathless, exhausted chuckle. "You should. I didn't expect you to get it on your first try, let alone cast such a powerful *Exar*. Now that I am certain you not only seek power, but embrace it, your status has certainly moved up with me," the Masked One said.

"But I feel so weak that I don't even think I can stand," Athar said, panting heavily. "Drawing from the Underworld has its perks, but also its disadvantages," the Masked One began. "You see, drawing from the Ethereal is easy as it's not as taxing, but it's not as powerful as the Underworld," he said.

Athar grunted as he drew the book closer to him. "Keep it and study it," the Masked One said, walking over to his servant. "Here, drink this," he threw a small flask. "What is it, my lord?" Athar asked. "Since you have only just begun, you will need something to keep your vitality up until you learn to absorb power from cores, like me," the Masked One replied.

"Is that another reason for absorbing a core? Like why you did what you did to that ochelon, my lord?" Athar asked. "Precisely. For now, however, it's best if you get some rest. We have more work to do tomorrow, and you have more studying to do while I'm unavailable," the Masked One said.

Athar opened the flask and smelled the contents, immediately contorting his face in disgust. "*Ugh*, it reeks of deathmold," he said through coughs. "It is. Well, a diluted version of it, anyway," his master replied.

Athar looked up at his master and nodded, putting the flask to his lips and knocking back the contents while holding his breath. He squinted and squirmed at the taste, coughing heavily when he finished.

"Welcome to *true power*, Athar," the Masked One said, grinning under his mask.

CHAPTER 9
THE MASTER

Following the battle with the pair of ochelons, Bernar and I went to the Master's study. The skin around my new scar was taut and still felt a little odd under my shirt, but I decided to ignore it as best I could.

Well, this will take some getting used to, but it's fine. I've got something the others, aside from Edryd, don't have: The first of many battle scars, I thought, wincing as I tried to move my shoulder, but the pain riddling my entire body was still too fresh for me to walk comfortably.

"How are you feeling?" Bernar asked. "I should be okay to have this conversation with the Master, but I might not wake up in time for training tomorrow," I chuckled weakly.

"I'm not expecting you to show up, but we have to tell the Master what we found before *either of us* can get any rest," my brother said regretfully. "*Fuuuuck.* Well, don't mind me if I pass out during the meeting," I groaned before we walked through the doorway that led to the study, quickly realizing the Master wasn't there.

I wonder if he has a copy, I subtly looked over the books on the shelves.

Bernar must have seen what I was doing and joined me in my search, hoping to find a copy of the one they had found in the study in the beast's lair. "*Dissection*," I muttered repeatedly, running my fingers along the spines of a score of books.

Just as I was doing so, there was a knock on the door that surprised me enough to quickly remove my hand from the row.

"May I enter my study?" the Master asked. I was startled by the knock, but Bernar had seen him coming and pulled away from the shelf long before he entered. "I'm sorry, Master. I was only looking for..." I trailed off, noticing something in his hands.

"For *this*?" he raised an eyebrow, holding a green book. I looked back at the shelf and noticed it was missing from right where I was about to look. "Y-Yes, but how did you...?" I trailed off as he raised a hand. "I know why you've come, Thoma, and plenty of others like what you found in the cave," the Master cut me off with a smirk.

"We both have a lot of questions, Master. Though he probably has more than I do," Bernar said, trying to take the load off of me since he noticed I was nervously fidgeting.

We have to push him to tell us. Otherwise, I don't know when the next time I'll get the chance to ask will be, I thought.

"I hope I have *some* of the answers you're looking for. However, you must ask the *right* questions," the Master said, motioning to the chair. Bernar helped me sit back in the chair with the carvings, as the Master sat with perfect posture in his chair, his hands folded on his lap.

"So tell me about what you found," he began in a warm, yet cautious tone. "With all due respect, Master, you already know what I found," I chuckled weakly. "I do, but I want to hear it from you and how *you* remember it," he smirked, forcing me to blink as I tried to collect my memories about the place.

"It was well hidden just behind where the beast had made its lair. There was a wall of rocks that could not have been formed naturally, so Bernar and I investigated. We found a study that seemed like no one had been there for many years, and everything was covered in dust. All except for the main desk, where some hand-written papers were strewn across the top of it," I explained, hoping I had remembered everything correctly.

"And what exactly was written on the pages?" he asked, nodding to confirm everything before was correct. I was fiddling with my fingers as I tried to find the right words. "Whoever was in there was trying to copy something from a book by a certain *Nexis Pelantyr* called *Dissection*," I replied, watching for any reaction from him.

"*Ah*, yes. This one I have here," the Master replied, tapping the book on his desk without any change in his features or voice. "The one I saw was old, and a few pages had been torn out, Master. Almost as if they were trying to solve a riddle with the book as their guide," I shook my head, but he didn't look as surprised as I thought he'd be.

Does he already suspect something or someone? I thought momentarily, getting a strange look from Bernar that I couldn't read.

"A *riddle*, you say? I was wondering how long it would take, after all, it is only a matter of time before it begins," the Master said ominously, making me look at my brother in utter confusion. "What do you mean *begins*, master?" I asked.

"You're a smart boy, Thoma; I'm sure you've conjured up some form of hypothesis as to why that book was out of place with its pages torn out," he unfolded his hands. I thought about what the Master was trying to get at, but I knew I didn't have enough information, so I decided to push my luck.

"From what I saw, the book contained information about the plant that the gods had given our kind centuries ago," I began, lowering my tone just enough to let him know I was prying for information. "*Oh? Tell me more*," he raised an eyebrow.

"I believe someone is trying to uncover its secrets; ones that weren't meant to see the light of day again, Master," I finally replied after a long pause.

I was shocked to see a grim smile spread on his face.

"*That* is what I meant by *begins*, Thoma. Can you guess what was on those pages?" he asked, though I could only shake my head in response. "Do you believe they got what they came for?" he prodded again. "No, Master. At least, I'm not sure," I shifted my gaze away from him and shrugged.

The Master raised an eyebrow and tilted his head. "Why do you think that is?" he asked. "I don't know, Master," I replied. The Master looked at Bernar, and Bernar nodded in agreement as if they had spoken telepathically. "Thoma, I think it's about time I shared something with you," the Master said.

Does Bernar already know this? He didn't mention his name, I thought.

"There are *forces* that were once great powers that helped us rule this Realm. Elven scholars were the first to interact with them and have researched the cause of their existence for a long time. There is, however, some disagreement among the scholars as to what happened to a lot of the information we once had," he continued solemnly.

"Some say that these powers are the gods themselves, while others claim that they are what helps to maintain the balance between

Realms," he explained. "I'm confused, Master. What does this have to do with what was in the book?" I asked.

"There was a time when we had the answers as well, but over a *millennium* ago, all that vital knowledge was stripped from us. Every book, every scroll, and every memory regarding much of what happened during that time," the Master began, opening his own copy of the book.

"Even *this one* has had those pages torn from it. Look," he said, turning it towards me. "But why would anyone, or *anything*, want that knowledge gone? Wouldn't the progress we'd made back then have benefitted this world?" I asked, genuinely confused as I stared at the remnants of the pages left behind, but the Master shook his head.

"Whatever the contents of those particular pages were, they have been lost to time. However, one of the elven scholars had a divination. It was a gift from the gods, warning him that a war would be waged and that the weavings of fate would determine the fate of not just our world, but of *all Realms*. Unfortunately, much of the information on the source of that prophecy was lost," he explained.

I could feel a weight on my chest, the words hitting me like an ochelon's claw.

"I see," I sighed, trying to maintain my composure.

There's something else behind all of this, but I don't have the knowledge or the resources to determine what that is. If not even the Master has full knowledge of that time period, then who would? I thought.

"Those ravens we saw earlier on our way home; what was that all about?" I decided to shift the focus of the conversation. "The only times ravens leave from the direction of this fortress is when something is being sent somewhere. The approving authority for any transmittal of information has to go through me, and me alone," the Master said gravely.

I pensively stared out the window of his study, watching as the twilight sky settled in more deeply.

"So, whatever it was that raven was carrying..." I began, but didn't finish, already knowing what his answer would be. "Precisely. While the contents of the torn pages have been lost to time, there is still much information in that cave that has been safeguarded for generations," he nodded. "Then, if the beasts were there to protect it, why were they so aggressive? Was that entire fight for *nothing*?" I raised an eyebrow.

"No, not entirely. When a creature is charmed, it should only ever answer to one master or those it determines are trusted. If that charm is *broken* and replaced with another, then there is a chance that it could turn on everyone near it, disregarding the old charm entirely," he explained.

"You used me as a test subject?" I chuckled in disbelief. "I wouldn't put it that way, but I suppose that's one way of looking at it," he shrugged. "If you hadn't gone there to kill them, then whatever *new charm* they had on them would likely be used to transmit information to their new master at the earliest opportunity. I needed to ensure they wouldn't get much more than they likely already had," he continued, prompting me to regard him curiously.

I guess that explains why they were so hasty to try and kill me, I thought, recalling how swift the female ochelon was to attack me.

"I had also not forgotten about your punishment for setting a mana flame loose in your room, and figured this was a prime opportunity to use your skills. Well, that, and I wanted to see whether you could unlock the *second stage* of mana manipulation," the Master said with a sly grin as my eyes widened in surprise.

"You gambled on whether I could do that mid-fight?" I asked in disbelief. "You're still alive, so I take it you fared well enough against such foes," he said, glancing at Bernar, who nodded in agreement. "Well, aside from the scar on my back, my head feeling like it was crushed, and my shoulders burning like hot iron, yes, Master," I replied with a squint as I tested the skin on my back. "The first of many, Thoma," the Master said with a shallow smile.

I looked about the room pensively, digesting the information I just received. It wasn't often that I got a chance like this to ask such existential questions, and after having heard his real reason for sending me to that sanguine menagerie, I knew I had to keep seeking answers.

"Something troubles you?" he dipped his head, noticing my composure. He'd startled me with his question, so I took a moment to formulate what I wanted to say carefully. "Yes, Master. I can't help but wonder why all of this is happening now. Why couldn't this have begun when I was at least a little older, or more capable of handling whatever comes our way?" I shook my head and averted my gaze.

Bernar raised his hand to the master, as if stopping him from answering that statement. "Little brother, I know you better than anyone," he began, surprising me to hear his voice.

"Within the cave, there is only one way in, and one way out. Many things in life have many different ways of being achieved, but when it comes to challenges or difficult times, it is much like that cave; one way in, and one way out. Sometimes, the only way out is through," he said, his voice laced with a severity I'd rarely seen in him.

"The Master and I have both seen our fair share of difficult times, many of which *neither* of us would like to relive. You are just now facing your own challenges, and we will be here to help guide you through those times and become *much stronger*, as painful as those experiences may be," he concluded, lightly flicking my brand new scar and making me wince.

"I know you're trying to help, but it still hurts, *asshole*," I sucked air through my teeth. "Of course it does, *shit-bird*. It's a reminder that you will, eventually, learn through pain and hard times to push through anything that comes your way," Bernar said playfully.

The Master observed the two of us and smiled lightly. "You two remind me of a story from a long time ago," he chuckled. Both Bernar and I stared at him with utter confusion when we heard his light tone of voice.

He almost sounded a hundred years younger just then, I thought as I looked to Bernar to see if he'd heard it, too.

His shrugged response either feigned ignorance or he genuinely didn't know the answer either.

"It was a long time ago, before even my predecessor became the master of Codrean. Would you like to hear it?" he asked us. "Of course, Master," I nodded.

"A long time ago, there were twins named Taegin and Ardrin. They had a close relationship with each other, just like I see in you two," he gestured to us. "Both of them were inducted into the Synners at a very young age, but Ardrin was more unruly than his sibling. So unruly, in fact, that the master at the time had a hard time keeping him under control," he continued as we listened attentively.

"On the day they would turn fourteen, Taegin wanted to surprise his brother, even while knowing his brother hated them. It wasn't much; nothing more than a few stolen cakes from the pantry and mugs of ale. Not everything went as planned, however, as Ardrin was nowhere to be found. Taegin, worrying about his surprise being ruined, went out to search for his brother," he continued, nearly losing himself in thought for a moment.

"He eventually found his brother being beaten down by a handful of his seniors. Ardrin cast a flame cloak in self-defense, but lost control of it and ended up accidentally killing his attackers, leaving no remains behind," his tone dropped as I felt myself blink a few times in surprise.

"Well, that got dark," Bernar chimed in. "Well, it was an unfortunate accident, for sure. Ardrin feared what their master would do to him if the accident were reported, so he decided to leave of his own accord. Taegin, of course, tried to stop him, but nothing seemed to work as Ardrin left anyway. Taegin searched for him for years, but his brother left no trace behind anywhere he went," the Master shook his head.

"How does this relate to Bernar and I? I don't suppose Ardrin was ever found, was he?" I asked, genuinely confused. "*Heh*, all I'm saying is that you two should never let go of the bond you have. However, to answer your question, he wasn't, at least not to *my* knowledge. It's been long enough now that he might have died of old age for all I know," he shrugged.

"*Ah*, fair enough. But how do *you* know this story?" I asked, not bothering to hide my suspicion. "*Oh*, I knew them quite well, actually," he said, sitting back in his chair.

"His brother told me the story countless times. He wanted redemption for not escaping the fortress and going after his brother when it happened, but found none as he took his own life about six months later," he continued. "I'm sorry to hear that," I said solemnly.

How old is he anyway? That must have been well over a hundred years ago if we've never heard about it. No, wait, maybe he's intentionally leaving something out, I furrowed my brow as I tried to piece it together.

The Master looked at me curiously, as if he knew what I was thinking. "You thought *I* was Taegin, didn't you?" he asked, catching me off guard. After a moment of trying to find words to say, I decided that a single nod would suffice. "Sorry to disappoint you, but he's been dead for a long time now," he shook his head.

I had nothing left to say; no words of empathy or condolences as my theory came crashing to the ground.

"Either way, I thank you for coming to me with your findings. I won't keep you any longer; it's getting late, and you've had quite the eventful day," he said with a smile, gently placing his palms down on the table. "If you find any more information regarding who invaded the study, come to either Bernar or me directly. Is that understood?" he asked. "Yes, Master," I replied with a nod. I winced as I struggled to rise from my seat, but Bernar came to my aid.

"I think it best if you check in with Garett tomorrow, Thoma," the Master said, noting my struggle. "I'll have him tending to you these next few days, and I'm sure he'd *love* to hear about how you got that scar," he grinned wryly. I nodded again and walked out of the room. Just before I left, I looked back to thank him for the story, but he was staring distantly at the out-of-place book on the shelf across the room.

The following day, after lunch, the dull clang of training swords could be heard clashing throughout the training yard. I had just finished Garett's healing session, who was *very happy* to hear about my fight the previous day, and decided to follow the sounds to their point of origin.

"*Ouch!* That hurts," Edryd shouted, rubbing his shoulder. "*Oh,* calm down, you *wuss,*" Bernar chuckled. "It could have been much worse," I said while walking into the training yard. "I know, but the asshole did it on purpose!" Ed pointed a finger at my brother, who merely shrugged. "I'm glad to see you're alright. Bernar told me about your fight with the ochelons. How the *fuck* did you manage to kill not one, but *two* of them?" Ed raised an eyebrow.

"Honestly, I'm not sure either," I chuckled nervously. "I'm just surprised you're already back to training," he regarded me curiously. "You can thank Master Garett for that. His healing skills are certainly top-notch," I shrugged. "A shame *this asshole* couldn't heal you," Ed chuckled, then quickly flinched as Bernar smacked up upside the head.

"Hey!" Ed shouted, trying to land a return blow on my brother, hitting nothing but air. "You missed. Is your shoulder really still that bad?" I asked with a tinge of guilt. "Not really, but your brother keeps testing it like it was never damaged in the first place. He even went so far as to challenge me to an *arm wrestling match,*" Ed sighed. "Did you win?" I asked my brother sarcastically.

"I was just testing it to make sure it wasn't still fucked, but *duh*," he shrugged. "There are better ways to test that," I chuckled and shook my head. "Like what?" Edryd asked.

I could've sworn I saw my brother's eyes twinkle like a star in the night sky for a brief moment as I rolled my shoulder to warm it up a little.

"You, versus Bernar and I," I said maliciously. "*Oh*, no. Fuck that with the might of a wyrm," Edryd crossed his arms. "I think it's a great idea! Never really had the chance to see you in a two-ver-sus-one," Bernar jeered. "You two are gonna gang up on me, now?" Edryd asked, panic showing clearly on his face.

"We'll be nice, don't worry," I grinned at my brother. Edryd sighed and shook his head. "I hate you both," he said, making Bernar and me chuckle. "*Oh*, come on! It'll be fun!" Bernar said. Edryd wasn't happy about the way he had said that at all.

"This is gonna hurt, isn't it?" Ed sighed, adjusting his grip on his sword. "Probably. Provided you don't fuck up," I said, getting a chuckle from Bernar as he readied himself.

"Begin!" Bernar called out, immediately starting a charge towards Edryd. Bernar struck from above, but Ed parried it by sliding the incoming sword off of his and away from his body. I attacked from the left side and forced him out of position, only for him to block another from Bernar, who was waiting for him.

I struck again from above, but Edryd blocked it, throwing his weight against me as I pirouetted out of the way. Bernar stuck again, this time aiming for his legs. He blocked most of it, but the tip struck the base of his calf, throwing him off balance.

Edryd regained his stance, recovering from the blow with a grunt of pain. "It didn't draw blood, so don't be a turd about it," Bernar sneered. Edryd grinned and lunged at him, but he deflected the blow. I attacked immediately afterwards from behind, but he twisted his sword behind his back with the force from the deflection to stop my incoming blow.

I feinted an attack, then twisted out of the way of Bernar's that I knew was coming in behind me, aimed directly at Edryd's hurt shoulder. Ed grunted with the blow, but kneed Bernar in the stomach, and spun around, attacking me with a twisting leap. "That's my move, fucker!" Bernar shouted playfully. "I'm borrowing it," Edryd replied through a wry smile.

Bernar grinned and moved in for what would be a blow to end the fight, but I got there first, repeatedly attacking Edryd in a quick succession of blows. He had a hard time keeping up with them, but managed to find a gap amidst the barrage and swirled to trip me.

I hit the ground hard and was immediately winded, feeling the sting of the fresh scar racing across my back while Bernar was coming in for his turn. Edryd blocked the blows and tried to counter attack, but Bernar saw it coming.

He *had* baited him into that move, after all.

He grabbed Edryd's sword arm and kicked his legs, throwing him to the floor. "*Fuuuuck*," he coughed, losing his breath from the impact with a wheezing grunt. "*Eh*, you're okay," Bernar reached down to help him to his feet.

"Not bad for someone who's just come out of the ward," he said as I got to my feet. "Could've been better. I still feel the injury is limiting my movement a little," I shrugged, rolling my shoulders forward then back with a grunt. "On that note, I'm surprised you moved as well as you did with your own wounds being so fresh, Thoma," Edryd replied, dusting himself off.

"*Oh*, I was in pain the whole time, but I couldn't allow you to show me up *that* easily," I replied with a pained chuckle. "In the future, keep an eye out for open spaces like that one I had to trip you," Bernar mentioned, helping me dust my backside off. "I will," Edryd replied with a nod.

"Well, guys, it's been fun, but I have to go," Bernar said. "Kick your ass some other day," Edryd said. "You wish! Cocky little shit," Bernar muttered as he tousled his hair. I smiled as I walked over to Edryd and put a hand on his good shoulder. "I'm sorry about that, by the way," I said, gesturing to the other.

"*Eh,* don't worry about it. It's still better than being mauled to death by those fucking *bugs*," he shrugged. Flashes of the scene rushed into my mind like a white-water river.

"I guess," I shrugged. "In any case, I'm sorry. I had never actually tested my spell before using it back then," I said solemnly. "*Ah,* so *that's* what that was," he replied as if a puzzle piece had finally fallen into place. "Yeah. I know we're never supposed to use untested spells in battle, but it was all I could do from where I was at the time," I replied.

"Well," Edryd began, putting his hand on my shoulder. "If it's of any consolation, I'm still alive, so *thanks*," he said warmly.

I smiled, truly relieved to hear that.

"Good to have you back, bud," I gave him a hug. "Don't go all soft on me," Edryd said with a chuckle, patting my fresh scar. I grunted as pain shot across my back, immediately pulling away from him. We stared at each other, then burst out laughing for a short while before walking back to the main fortress.

"You know you're going to have to teach me that, right?" he said as he punched my shoulder. "I don't know if I can do it well enough to teach, but I'll try," I replied. "How long did it take you to come up with something like that?" he asked. "Three months," I replied, scratching the back of my head.

"*Three months*? Holy shit," his eyes widened. "I haven't given it a name yet. As one who has lived to tell the tale, why don't *you* name it?" I suggested. "How about *Whip of Doom*, or *Chaos Bind*?" he asked almost before I could finish my sentence.

I just looked at him and laughed, genuinely surprised at the speed with which he answered.

"*Whip of Doom* sounds a little foreboding, don't you think?" I asked through a light chuckle. "Nope. Sounds about right to me," he grinned. "I've seen it first hand, and I have to say it's pretty *dooming* to anyone or anything that gets in its way," he shrugged. "*Whip of Doom* it is, then," I laughed.

We continued walking for a short time, when Edryd heard something. "*Oh*, it's just a raven," he waved dismissively. I looked for it, and saw it flying southeast. "Shit," I muttered, my eyes opening widely as the realization hit me.

Please, let me be wrong, I thought, seeing the pouch on the fowl's chest.

"What? It's just a raven, Thoma," he shook his head, not understanding the look on my face. "Not just any raven; a *carrier* raven. Follow me," I said, sprinting towards the fortress. "What the...?" he trailed off and rushed after me.

We went through the fortress doors and straight up to the Master's study, where Bernar, Garett, and the Master had just begun holding council. I burst through the door and saw all six eyes snap toward me, staring at me curiously.

"Master, forgive my intrusion, but was it you?" I asked between breaths. "Calm down and tell me what the matter is. Was *what* me?" the Master replied. There was no surprise written on his features, but his tone suggested he knew I was about to say something that didn't bode well for anyone.

"Another raven; headed southeast," I urged. The Master's eyes opened widely. "I thought we'd found him already," Garett muttered in disbelief. "Apparently not," Bernar replied.

The Master remained still, looking straight into my eyes. He broke my gaze and walked about the study. "Come in and shut the door. You too, Edryd," he gestured to us. Edryd looked at me, though all I could respond with was a terse nod as I shut the door behind us.

"What I say here, *stays here*, understood, boys?" he asked. We both nodded quickly, but remained silent. The Master cast a spell on the door, blocking all sound from potentially being leaked through the wood and spaces in the door frame.

"To make sure we're all on the same page, here: It seems we might have a traitor in our midst," he began. Edryd looked at me with questioning eyes. "I know the hearts and minds of everyone in this room, but I must ask you, Thoma: do you trust Edryd?" he asked seriously.

"He was the one who spotted it first, Master. It couldn't have been him," I nodded, getting one in response to show understanding of my words before he continued. "Edryd, you might not be aware of this, but the fact remains that someone has been sending out unreviewed messages to someone outside the fortress," he said, the air of severity hanging heavily in his tone.

"Who would do that?" Edryd replied, immediately understanding the gravity of the Master's words as his face paled. "It could always be someone sending a love letter," Garett shrugged.

"Not likely. The day of our return, Thoma saw two ravens flying that way, one just before we had crossed into our land, and the other before entering the fortress. Which most likely means that someone was trying to keep track of our location, and judging by the frequency, someone not too far away from here," the Master said.

Ed and I glanced at each other briefly.

"There are only farmers and their families living near enough for something like that. Even if it were one of them, what business would they have in knowing our position?" Bernar chimed in. "Farmers sell their goods at the marketplace in Coltend at least once a week," Garett added.

"Precisely, but therein lies the problem: The three ravens," the Master nodded. "The chances of the first two being a farmer are pretty high, but this one was too close to be anything of the sort. Thoma, where did you see it come from?" he asked.

"I didn't see it initially, Master. Edryd had pointed it out for me only *after* I heard its call," I jutted my thumb toward him. I could tell he was starting to get nervous while standing right beside me.

"Fine, but where did you see it come from?" Bernar stepped forward.

If he gives the wrong location, it might spell death for a simple farmer, I thought.

"I saw it come from the northwest corner of the fortress, Master," Ed replied nervously, prompting the Master's eyes to widen. "Our fears have been confirmed, then," he said grimly. "The study?" Bernar asked, getting a nod from the Master before he looked at the four of us with him with a piercing gaze.

"It's one of our own," he said gravely.

"The northwestern corner of this fortress is where the study lies. Now that Thoma has killed the beasts and cleared the way for the traitor, it only confirms what I have been thinking these last few months. However, that's not to say I've merely been sitting idly by and not taken any precautions," he continued, giving me a knowing nod.

I finally understood.

He sent me there because he trusted me not to give away the secrets he was trying to keep inside, I thought.

"But Master, those pages on the table held nothing of value. At the very least, none that I could see. What else was hidden away in there?" I asked, both concerned and confused. "The location of the Gwynnleaf," the Master replied seriously.

Bernar and Garett knew what this meant, but Ed and I glanced at each other, entirely befuddled.

"How could we have been so *careless*?" Garett asked aloud. "We weren't entirely careless. They could have been after just about any other piece of knowledge there. However, the precautions I took were to charm the ochelons and cast a spell that jumbled the words in all of the books except the one you found, Thoma," the Master gave me a nod as he concluded.

Why the hell would he leave the most important information un-scrambled? I thought.

"But why that book alone, Master?" Edryd asked, feeling just as confused as I was. "Because the only way for us to confirm it was one of our own was to make sure that the information being sought after was the only thing left of value. This puts us in a better position to defend it and know exactly what they're after. As to *why* they're after it, I do not know," the Master replied.

"So, you decided to bait them by having me slay the monsters, and leave the information within reach to confirm your suspicion?" I asked, trying to make sure he understood it correctly. "Yes. It was a gamble on multiple fronts. I knew you were capable of it, and it was a true test of trust; the kind I have with everyone in this room. Including you, Edryd," he gave him a nod.

"Me, Master? But what have I done to deserve that level of trust?" Edryd asked, genuinely unaware of why that was so. "You're Thoma's best friend, and if he trusts you, then I am inclined to trust you too," he grinned, making Edryd blush and shuffle his feet. "Thank you, Master," he said with a hand on his chest, leaning into a grateful bow.

"I know your parents to be great Synners, and that you have the same fire in your heart as your mother did when I trained her all those years ago," the Master said with a slight smile. Ed's eyes widened and filled with tears. After all, he had never heard the Master say much of *anything* regarding his mother. "Thank you, Master," he choked.

The Master gave him a thin smile, then turned to look at the rest of us. "Since this has confirmed our suspicions, we are now tasked with figuring out who it is. I have a plan, but it will require *all of our* efforts," he leaned forward, folding his fingers together as we listened intently.

"Garett, you will watch the bow-casters, while Bernar will keep an eye on the seniors. But as for you two..." he trailed off, staring at Edryd and I intensely. "You will have the most vital roles, so pay close attention," he said, making both of us swallow dryly.

I'm not sure I like where this is going, I felt a bead of sweat trailing down my cheek.

"Bernar, Garett, and I are the masters during training, which means that the traitor is highly unlikely to say anything or do any-thing revealing around us. Seeing as no one else knows you're aware of our little plan, you are to be our eyes and ears within the barracks, understand?" the Master asked, looking us keenly.

"Yes, Master," we both said at the same time. "Keep an eye out for anything unusual, like the others and I will do. However, pay *even closer attention* to your circle of friends," he cautioned. "But, Master, why must we focus on our friends so much?" Edryd asked skittishly. "I will tell you why, but I want you to try to figure it out before I finish," the Master replied.

"You are very closely knit in your friendships, and I know you care a great deal for them. However, as it currently stands, the likelihood of someone outside your circle accidentally spilling something that may or may not be revealing is extremely low. Before we left for Coltend, do you remember I had commented on Thoma's use of the *Kyr* spell?" the Master asked.

"I do, though what relevance it has escapes me, Master," he shrugged. "Everyone there knew I was talking about him. He is Bernar's brother, my right-hand man before even Master Garett. Not to mention his recent *frequent* visits to my study..." the Master said, letting his words hang a little in hopes that Ed would begin to piece it together.

"So, the traitor, or *traitors*, will think that Thoma knows more than he should and make them more likely to slip up," Ed nodded his understanding. "Well done," the Master grinned. "That will be all for now, gentlemen. Everyone knows their job, and it is essential that *none* of what has been said here ever gets out. If it does, we will have to start over," he continued.

Ed and I recognized that our part was over when the Master lowered the barrier on the door. We bowed respectfully before leaving with Garret and Bernar to return to training.

At the base of the stairway, we all went our separate ways and returned to finish the remainder of our training for the day. Swords, bows, and hand-to-hand combat drills were being conducted across the training grounds, but Ed and I struggled to maintain focus.

Bernar took over for the seniors, overseeing their training and began teaching them new movesets and combinations to test out on each other. Grappling, disarming, tripping, and guard weaknesses were all addressed during the remaining four and a half hours.

Near the end of our training session, we heard a call from atop the fortress walls. "Someone is coming," the bow-caster who stood guard called out. "Hold," Bernar called out to his trainees and headed towards the main gate. When he arrived, he opened the hatch through the main doorway to find a hooded figure on a white horse.

"I bring news from Coltend and Caegwen," the hooded figure said in a near angelic voice. Bernar instantly recognized the voice and grinned. "Open the gates," he called out. The mighty wooden gate was opened, drawing everyone's attention as he rode a short way into the training yard with Bernar following closely behind.

The hooded figure dismounted his large horse and stood nearly a head taller than everyone present, including Bernar. He drew back his hood to show a perfectly carved face, with bright yellow eyes. His face was bereft of any facial hair, and his jawline was perfectly symmetrical to the rest of his features. Small hooped earrings of gold and silver intertwined hung from his pointed ears.

Bernar was seemingly the only one who knew the elf.

"Bernar, why are you grinning at me like that?" the elf raised an eyebrow. "Anwill *Taffy*, you old bat! It's good to see you again," Bernar said just before wrapping him in a tight hug.

The little I knew of elven culture reminded me that elves were not usually *fond* of physical contact when greeting each other. Instead, they often placed one hand across their chest and bowed, but the look on his face was *priceless* when my brother squeezed him tightly.

Don't laugh. Don't laugh, I snorted.

"It's *Taaff*, Bernar, though I *do* recall you always having issues with elven names. I must admit, it's good to see you, too," the Anwill said with an uncomfortable smirk as he pulled away. "You're not wrong. It took me *years* to learn your name, let alone all the others," my brother waved dismissively. "What are you doing here? Shouldn't you be locked away in a library somewhere?" Bernar asked sarcastically.

"You're still as much a thorn in my side as ever, but no; not this time. I'm here as an emissary for King Elhael," Anwill sighed. I could only stare at the strange interaction taking place in awe.

I knew Bernar had gone to train with the elves when he was a few years younger than me, but I had no idea he was still so close with them.

I wonder if that's *why the king was staring at me during the council,* I thought momentarily before utterly freezing when I noticed the elf was giving me the same, strange look as if he'd read my thoughts.

He exchanged a glance with my brother, then chuckled lightly as he shook his head. "Where is the Master?" he finally asked after a moment's pause. "*Oh,* he's probably still in his study. Follow me," Bernar nodded toward the door, prompting Anwill to look up at the fortress.

"A *thousand years* later and this place remains very much the same," Anwill muttered idly as he glanced around. "It's good to be back, after so long. Do you remember I once told you that the first of us trained here?" he asked. "You mean you *wouldn't shut up* about it, but yes, I do," Bernar rolled his eyes with a chuckle.

"It's not *my* fault I always felt like I had to repeat myself with you," Anwill grinned. "Fair enough. Welcome home, then. I'll lead you to him," Bernar smiled brightly as he scratched the back of his head.

What in the ever-living fuck *just happened?* I thought.

CHAPTER 10
THE RHYDIAN PASS

After the murder of his son, King Bashir rode his horse to near-absolute exhaustion as it foamed at the bit, and snorted heavily.

I've just spent the last two days at a gallop, and I don't think my arse or the horse can take much more, he thought.

He observed the path behind him, desperately searching for anyone who might be following him. The sun had begun to set, and he could just barely see a glint of the Coltend's tower reflecting the setting sun's rays. He had ridden as fast as he could from Coltend Castle, over the Lucent River, to reach the base of the Rhydian Mountains.

I know this horse well, but its hooves are covered in dried blood from riding over countless twigs and rocks in the road. I don't know how much longer it will survive without food and rest, he thought.

He promptly decided to make his small camp near a stream that ran down the mountainside. His small fire did little to ward off the cold air from the peaks, and the sheep-hide bed only maintained its warmth on the cold floor. The horse lay next to him, taking the blunt force of the wind while Bashir nibbled on a field mouse he had killed and tried to roast over his small flame. It was still partially raw, and he struggled with every bite.

"You've done well," he said to his horse, patting it on the neck after taking another bite of his questionable meal. He had stolen it from one of the men who had gone with him to the council, who had been waiting for him outside the palace walls.

"I know you cannot speak, and yet I feel as though I must know your name," he said, still stroking its massive nape. The horse shook his head slightly. He was pensive for a few moments. "I shall call you 'Hatal'. Do you want to know what it means?" he asked, breaking his silence.

The horse didn't reply, obviously.

"*Ah*, right. Well, I shall tell you anyway. It means *hero* in my language. Your strength saved me from what could have been a most horrible death. I thank you," he said with another pat. Hatal leaned his head over his rider's shoulder. "We make a great pair, you and I. Once we arrive in Harut, I will ensure you are fed an entire bowl of lush red apples. How does that sound, huh?" he said, stroking Hatal's long hair.

The horse snorted heavily, rubbing the side of his face against Bashir's. "Heh, you're a good horse," he said with a smile. "Let us rest now. We have only one final stretch before we're home. You're powerful, Hatal, and I know you and I will make it," he said comfortingly. He leaned back on the horse and curled up to keep himself warm.

I wonder what Bashaa would say if he could see me now, he thought.

Thoughts about the journey ahead began to flood his mind, but he pushed them aside as memories of his son began to flood his consciousness. Bashaa had been his pride and joy, the brightest of his sons. The others had died from an unknown disease after a feast, though Bashir and his son had been absent that fateful evening. When he returned, he found three of his sons in the morgue, covered in white linen.

"Do you know the pain of *loss*, Hatal?" he asked. The horse, once more verbally unresponsive, perked his ears up. "I don't suppose horses feel remorse or heartbreak, do you? Not that I would know what goes through your minds. But as it currently stands, I have no more sons. No heirs to continue my line, and no joys left in this world. I witnessed that monster slash my last remaining son's neck, and defile his corpse," he growled.

"As for my other sons, I just wish I could go back in time and be, at the very least, present for their final moments. I..." he choked, tears welling up in his eyes. "I have failed, Hatal," he began, struggling through tears. "I have failed as a King, as a husband, and as a father. Just look at me, now," he gestured his arms at his own body.

"I am nothing. An empty shell of my former self. A shadow and a thought of what once contained joy, laughter, and pride in myself and my sons. Now, I am here pouring my soul out to a fucking horse, all while fleeing for my life." Hatal, not understanding exactly what was said, but feeling the emotion behind his words, gently leaned his massive head on Bashir's shoulder, moving him to tears.

My dearest Bashaa, how I miss you. I feel as if a part of my soul has been torn from me. You were the last heir to the Ibn'Escea line, and even if I do have another child, I doubt they could live up to your reputation. You have joined the spirits of your brothers and forefathers, but your memory will live on with me. I will make Truls suffer greatly for what he has done to you, my son, he thought.

Hatal quivered, feeling the anger, frustration, and hatred growing. Bashir, considering numerous ways to torture Truls potentially, emitted a dark energy around him. Being sensitive to such things, the horse gently nudged his master as if to break the train of horrific thoughts.

Bashir snapped out of his attitude and noticed Hatal's face had come awfully close to his own. "Wh-what? I can't want revenge for what that piece of shit did to my son?" he asked. Hatal, without budging so much as a hair's width, snorted. The man seemed to understand what the horse meant and sighed.

"Even without words, you amaze me with your insight. Yes, yes, I will set that aside for now. We do have a long day ahead of us tomorrow, and the Pass will be no easy trip," he stated. He gave Hatal another pat and turned over to try to get some rest.

Morning came, and the tip of Coltend Castle could still be seen off in the distance, shining brightly with the morning sun beaming off its highest peak. Hatal was already awake, and prodded his master with his nostrils flaring in his face, making him wriggle in response to the nudge.

"I'm awake, I'm awake," he said, petting the horse's nostrils and chin. He put out his fire with his piss, and scattered the soaked ashes as best he could to not leave any trail to be followed. He rolled his small bed back up and mounted it to the side of the saddle, looking over his shoulder to see if anyone had caught up to him.

"We must go, Hatal," he said, getting his foot in the stirrup and throwing his leg over to the other side. He clicked his tongue, and they were off. The Rhydian pass was about two kilometers up a steep, winding trail. It was primarily used by merchants who sought to sell their goods in the Coltend markets, though not all made it through without trouble.

About halfway up the trail, he heard a sound coming from behind him. He stopped his horse and looked back to try and see what it was. Captain Gorm rode up the steep slope with about forty or more men following closely behind, as far as Bashir could tell. "There he is! After him!" Gorm's eyes widened as he shouted. "Shit," Bashir said, and dug his heels into Hatal's sides.

Neither he nor the party of men behind him could go very quickly up the steep slope, and the other, fresher horses were beginning to catch up to him. His heart raced, and his first thoughts were that he was going to die, without telling his people what had happened. He had assumed that his men, whom he had left behind in his flight, were already dead.

I must press on for their sakes. I need my country to know what happened to my son, he gritted his teeth as he dug his heels into Hatal's sides.

Hatal was breathing more and more heavily, desperately trying to keep up his pace. His eyes were wide, and Bashir knew he wouldn't last much longer at this pace. The riders got closer and closer to him, and they were within bowshot of him now. "Hurry, Hatal! We must make it over this ridge," he yelled, digging his heels in again.

The ridge he saw was that of the peak of the pass, which, if one were to stop, had quite a fantastic view of Caegwen to the southeast and Harut to the northeast. "Come on!" he yelled once more. Hatal gave it everything he had, and finally made it over the ridge. The riders weren't too far behind. "Hyah!" Bashir shouted, urging his horse to pick up the pace on the flat ground. "We're almost there, Hatal. Keep going," he said, patting his horse's nape.

The Rhydian Pass was known for being confusing for those who did not know the way. The harsh weather of the mountains had destroyed all the wooden signposts ever placed there, so traders resorted to carving signs into the rocks themselves. Bashir knew this and looked for the carvings at the beginning of every road.

"This way!" he said aloud, and turned his horse to follow the marker in the right direction, just managing to turn the corner in time to avoid being seen by Gorm and his riders.

The hunting party made it over the ridge, only a few short moments after Bashir had already disappeared. "Damn it. Where the *fuck* did he go?" Gorm yelled aloud, hoping one of his men had seen a trace of him. They looked about them for any signs of tracks, but found none in the well-used pathway's solid dirt. "Find him!" he barked.

The men dismounted to get a closer look at the ground. The merchant's tracks were embedded deep into the ground, and most were still fresh from the last caravan that had passed there the previous day.

"Nothing here, Captain," one of the guardsmen shouted. "Nor here, Captain," another chimed in. Gorm looked about him, hoping to find even a horseshoe mark out of place. He heard a rustling in the bushes nearby and turned to find out what it was. He dismounted and walked over to the origin of the sound, drawing his sword.

I have you now, you piece of shit, he thought.

He stepped as quietly as he could, and when he was close enough to where he thought nothing could escape, he saw the tip of an arrow sticking out from behind one of the bushes. "Ambush!" he called out, backing away. All of the men heard his cry and drew their swords immediately. They formed a circle with their backs to one another's, and watched as the figures began to sprout out of the bush.

The figures were none other than elven bandits, clad in dark green. Their tunics and boots were mud-stained, and most had holes in them. Each one had a curved blade and a knife lashed to their leather belts by a dark brown sash. Hardened by the elements, their hands and forearms had scars that could be seen through the holes in their gear.

"Bandits!" Gorm barked to prepare his men as they waited for an almost inevitable attack. "Some may call us that, whereas I would rather call my people and I *opportunists*," one of the elves replied to the remark. He was standing on a tall rock at the side of the pass. "Thieves. Bandits. Good-for-nothing degenerates; All of these are quite derogatory terms for free folk who have been cast out of their homes and seek a living elsewhere," he continued. "You mean making a living from other people's hard work," Gorm spat.

"That's one way of putting it, sure. Most of them have plenty more than they need, anyway. Their greed becomes their downfall," the elf shrugged. "However, we do not *steal* from everyone who comes through here. We tend to leave those who are visibly inferior to the other merchants alone; after all, we know what it is like to be in their shoes," he continued.

"A thief with *morals*; never thought I would see the day," Gorm scoffed. "Live as long as I have, and you will come to find that stranger things have happened. There is nothing wrong with having morals, as the dichotomy of good and evil is all but a matter of *perspective*," the elf said, scrutinizing the man.

"What is your name?" the elf asked. "I am the captain of the guard of Coltend Castle," Gorm replied. "And I am not as dumb as you presume me to be. Now, answer my question: what is your name?" the elf retorted, his patience growing thin.

"Gorm," the captain replied. "Are you sure it's just *Gorm*? No other fancy titles or family name?" the elf asked with a slight hint of sarcasm. "Just *Gorm*," he replied. "Well then, *Captain Gorm*, my name is Gwili Gwynn, and it would seem we have at least one thing in common," he smiled wryly.

"Let me guess: both of our names begin with the letter *G*? How adorable," Grom said with as much sarcasm as he could muster. "Well, that's probably *one* thing we have in common, but no. We're both commanders of bands of warriors, though mine are certainly *confused* at what you're doing here with yours," Gwili chuckled.

"We seek a lone rider who passed this way a few moments before you *interrupted* us," Gorm answered. "*We* interrupted *you*? *You're* the ones who aren't very good at tracking. Otherwise, you might have already found your prey," Gwili laughed.

"You *dare* mock the captain?" one of the guardsmen shouted. "*Oh*, but I do dare. I have you and your *bed warmers* surrounded, although you can only see me and the few who stand beneath me," Gwili replied.

"Shut the fuck up, Carl," Gorm snarled at his *avid* defender.

"I'm *sure* there's a way we can be reasonable about this whole situation, Gwili," he said. "Is there, really?" the elf asked with obvious sarcasm. "Yes, I believe so. You see, we have no business with you and your troops. All we seek is the rider who came through here," Gorm replied. "*Forty-some-odd* men after *one* man? Sounds a little unreasonable if you don't mind me saying so," Gwili replied, raising a thin, blonde eyebrow.

"I know how it looks, but the man we are after has done something terrible against my king," Gorm sighed. "Well, indeed he must have, if so many of you are after him. I would have liked to have gained that sort of recognition," Gwili said with a chuckle.

Gorm was becoming increasingly frustrated with the elf. "Can't we simply go on our way, and be done with this?" he asked. Gwili digested the question carefully. "I'm afraid not," he replied, causing Gorm to furrow his brow.

"You see, I know who the lone rider was and where he was headed. There was a reason I didn't stop him," Gwili answered. "And what reason might that be?" Gorm asked, clearly irritated. "The Rhydian Pass is used by merchants from all four countries. Each and every one of them knows *we live* here, and if they refuse to leave us tribute, be it money or food, we will take it by force," Gwili began, making the captain increasingly annoyed at his long-winded explanation.

That rat *will be long gone by the time he's done,* Gorm huffed in frustration.

"However, if a lone rider passes through here, then he is not to be touched by me nor any of my men. As you are no mere merchants and have excellent gear that my men and I would rather take for *ourselves*, it's only logical that we exert our rights here. Of course, we won't kill you, provided you don't resist. You'll be naked, but alive, at least," Gwili said sardonically.

"You *fucking bastard*," Carl spat angrily. "I've been called *much* worse by lesser men than you, *Carl*," Gwili shrugged, but noticed the soldier was already drawing his weapon and stepping forward.

"Carl, no!" Gorm reached for any piece of armor he could to stop the man, but it was too late. Gwili lifted a single finger, and an arrow soared through the cold mountain air, striking Carl right between the eyes. His body instantly slumped to the floor in a heap as blood gurgled in his mouth.

"Damn it, Carl," Gorm growled, staring back up at the elf.

"Why does no one ever listen to me? I said you would leave here *alive*, and yet this dipshit decides to challenge me without knowing where my other men are?" Gwili sighed. "Alright, I concede, Gwili. We will give you our..." he stopped when he felt a rumble in the ground beneath his feet and knew it couldn't be an earthquake.

Gwili felt it, too, and immediately looked to the northern side of the Pass, where he knew the creature would be coming from. "By the gods both light and dark, *ice troll!*" Gwili shouted, his eyes opening wide as the large figure approached them. Gorm turned in the direction he saw the elf facing, and felt a sinking feeling churn in his gut.

What the fuck...? He thought, nearly paralyzed by fear.

The troll was at least five meters tall, with white ice crystals in its tough hide. Its teeth were massive, with two tusks sticking out - each about as thick as a man's thigh, sticking out from the base of its enormous jaw. Its hands and feet were stocky and could quickly turn a full-grown horse into jelly with a single blow.

"Formation!" Gorm shouted, prompting the rest of his men to look in the same direction he was as the beast came at a running pace. The creature's growl shook Gorm to his core, for in all of his years of experience, he had never actually seen one before. "Steady! Don't shit through your teeth, men!" he called out.

Fifty meters.

"Focus! Aim for his eyes and ankles!" Gorm said. The troll was headed straight for them. "Fire!" Gwili called out to those under his command as they revealed themselves from behind neighboring rocks. The arrows soared and were aimed mainly at its large head, though the crystals deflected most.

Some of Gorm's men had struck the soft parts of the thick hide on its lower thighs, while most simply were also deflected by the crystals. It grunted from the pain of the arrows that found the spaces between its spotty armor, but kept its pace.

Fifteen meters.

"Ready your swords!" Gorm called out.

Five meters.

The monster had arrived, and brought unbridled death along with it. It swung its strong arms down from behind, as it smashed through the thin line of soldiers. Gorm, luckily, was between its legs, and cut at its left ankle while ducking beneath them, catching a slight glance at the waste the beast lay to his men.

Tough fucker, aren't you? he thought.

He recovered from his strike, only to find a bloodied, limb-ridden fist swiping backwards to get him. He rolled out of the way and watched a few of his men trying to stab at the beast's now exposed gut. It swatted the few men away like little blood-filled mosquitoes, turning them into little more than a macabre mist.

Gwili was still on his rock, watching what would have been a large amount of good armor going to waste due to the troll. He nocked an arrow in his bow and didn't pull until the beast had turned around.

He saw his target, which was surprisingly small for such a large beast. He drew his arrow to his cheek and released.

Unfortunately, the troll had seen him preparing for it, and breathed out a cloud of freezing air, stopping the arrow in its flight. "Damn it," he said aloud. He moved to another rock and tried again to avoid being seen. He drew his arrow to his cheek and released it to find its mark. The broadhead arrow sank deeply into the black orb that was the troll's eye, causing it to swing wildly around it in confusion and pain.

The roar set some of Gorm's men even more on edge, as they all recognized it to be its death throes as it tried to pull the arrow from its eye.

It managed to, but it pulled its eye out as a result, forcing a stream of blood to stream down the hideous creature's face. Gorm took the opportunity this created to get behind the creature and begin hacking away at the soft tissue just behind its knees, forcing it to kneel.

It swatted away a few more men with its free hand, but the remaining men cut deep into the beast's stomach between the thick crystal plating, to eviscerate it. The blue-blooded entrails leaked out on top of the men, covering them like a pig in a mud puddle. The ice troll's large, now *empty* corpse fell, making the ground tremble.

Gorm was panting hard, and looked about him at the havoc it had wreaked on his party. The morning sun reflected off the armor and blood strewn across the pass. More than half were dead, and the remainder of them were either puking off in the distance, or covered in the blue entrails. He had gotten some of it on his arm and proceeded to wipe it off with his red cape.

"I think that went well," Gwili said from atop his new rock. "*Well?* What the fuck do you mean it *went well?* Half of my men are dead, while the others are scarred for life!" Gorm shouted. "Look on the bright side: at least only *half of them* are dead," Gwili replied far too cheerfully.

Gorm spat in response. "If you and the rest of your *pox-ridden bastards* hadn't held us up for so long, none of this would have happened," he snarled. "You say that as if all elves are omniscient. I had no idea such an *incredible* beast was to come this way. If I had, I would have hid you, and stripped you naked only after the creature had passed," Gwili shrugged.

"That's comforting," Gorm said sarcastically. He looked about him once more at the devastation before him. "Men, grab the ranks off your fallen comrades' armor. We must take them back to their families," he commanded stoically. Gwili, visibly impressed at his resolve, commanded his men to watch along the other pathways.

The remaining soldiers began looking for recognizable pieces of their friends. Some of them had lost their best friends, while others, perhaps, had lost a brother. Tears welled in their eyes as they picked up the shreds of blood-soaked armor.

Meanwhile, Bashir had ridden down the other side of the Pass and reached the small town that resided at its base. It wasn't very large, but he was confident they had what he needed. "We made it, my friend! We're safe," he said to Hatal, who neighed in response as though he were happy to see a town. He rode towards the small town, and a few of the townsfolk had seen him from a ways off.

He dismounted when he got close enough to the nearest stable, and felt his inner thighs burn after having ridden for so long. He drew a cloth across his face to avoid being recognized and grabbed the horse by the bit, walking it to the nearest stable.

The tiny houses were well thatched, telling him it was a decently prosperous place. Located at the foot of the mountain, where most of the trade from Harut had to pass through, it was no wonder this little town had been so well-developed.

"I must speak with the owner," Bashir said, handing the stable boy the reins. "He's right over there, sir. Give me a moment and I will lead you to him," the boy said, tying the reins to the nearest post, which was already equipped with food and water. "Follow me, sir," he said, walking briskly towards the stable's main doors.

The stable boy led him straight to the owner's house, which was a little down the cobblestone street. "Thank you, boy," Bashir said, handing him a few small coins worth at least double what the boy had earned all month. "Thank you kindly, sir!" the boy exclaimed with joy-filled eyes. The boy ran off to get back to work, while Bashir knocked on the wooden door.

"Who might you be?" a voice called out from behind a steel latch. "I wish to speak to the owner of the stables, where I have had my horse tended to," Bashir replied.

I can't let them know who I am. If those men on the hill find my tracks and trace me here, at least these people won't know who I am, he considered.

"He's busy at the moment," the voice replied. "Tell him it's urgent," Bashir said impatiently. The voice sighed behind the door, and a latch was drawn back as the door opened, revealing a large man with a full beard that had scraps of food still stuck in it from breakfast. The man was at least a head taller than Bashir, possibly weighing twice as much. His light colored tunic had a few stains on it, and it was clear that this man cared little for his appearance.

"What is it, then?" the large man asked, irritated that someone had interrupted his peaceful morning. "I know you have a raven cage here, and I want to send a message. In addition, I would like to pay to stable my horse in one of your stalls," Bashir produced a handful of gold coins, making the man a bit more amiable than before.

"It's a shame you both look *and* smell like a dead horse," the man glinted, hoping he could get more from his uninvited guest. Bashir sighed and immediately pulled the cloth that covered his face. "Y-Your Majesty," the large man blanched. "*Shhh!* No one is supposed to know I'm here, so keep your fucking voice down," Bashir rushed to put a hand to the man's filthy mouth.

With a silent nod, the man agreed.

"In any other situation, I might have had your head for such disrespect," Bashir said threateningly. "I'm sorry, Your Ma-... *sir*," the man said, clearing his throat. Bashir had to stop him from bowing again. "Stop calling me that and fetch me parchment, a quill, and ink. Move!" he hissed. "I-I always leave a stack of parchment there by the cage, but I'll fetch the quill," the man said, and ran off to get it before he made his visitor even more disgruntled.

He returned a few moments later with a stained goose feather and a small inkwell, and handed the contents to Bashir. "Here you are," the man said. "Finally," Bashir sighed, quickly grabbing the items from the man's hands, and began writing.

Prepare to march on Coltend Castle. King Truls has murdered my son, and I will have revenge. King Bashir Ibn'Escea, he wrote on the parchment.

He signed the message with wax and used his ring to imprint his signet. He folded it up and stuck it into the small leather pouch that would latch onto the raven's chest. "The Harutian Palace," he whispered, holding the raven close to his mouth. The raven cawed in response to the command before he threw it into the air and watched it as it headed toward his home.

"What was that for, if I may ask?" the man shifted uncomfortably. "War," Bashir replied with a malicious smirk on his face. The man's eyes opened wide. "I thought the council taking place was to be of peace," the man said in a half-questioning voice. "What is your name?" Bashir asked. "Ahkmed Al'Talik," the man replied.

"Well, Ahkmed, if you allow me to hide here in your home, not that you have much else of a choice, I will tell you why I will have war," Bashir stated. "You can have my room. I'll take the guest room," Ahkmed nodded, gesturing for Bashir to follow him up the stairs and to the disaster that awaited him.

Bottles, plates, bowls, and other items lay across the floor. They looked as if they had been there for the past few days, and the whole room reeked of spilled wine and rotting food. The once-beautiful, handmade carpets on the floor had intricate geometric designs, which would have been a wonder to look at in their original states and *not* covered in filth.

This is the best he has to offer? It might be better than the guest room if the man offered me to take it, Bashir wrinkled his nose.

"It will have to do," he said with a sigh. "Forgive me, *sir*, but I have not quite been myself these past few months," Ahkmed said gloomily. Bashir turned to face the man and saw that something was troubling him. "What would drive a man to live in these conditions?"

he asked, noting the man's solemn expression, which began to well with tears.

"It's my wife, my lord," he choked. "She became increasingly ill, and no physician could figure out the problem. That started about six months back, and she died of a fever about a week ago," he sniffled, trying to hold back a flood of tears.

Shit, Bashir thought, realizing he'd accidentally been rude to the man.

"I... I have not yet recovered from her loss. She was everything to me. She fed me, clothed me when needed, and helped me set up everything I own. She was my lover and my best friend all in one. In her eyes, there wasn't a circumstance in the whole world that would tear us apart. I-I wasn't always a rich man, but I married into her family for more than *just that*. She was nothing short of an *angel*, and now with her loss..." he couldn't finish his sentence.

Bashir sighed through his nostrils and put a hand on Ahkmed's shoulder in solidarity. "I'm so sorry, my friend. Not just for your loss, but for the way I treated you," he shook his head. "It's alright, *sir*, you didn't know; there's no way you could have," Ahkmed sniffled again, wiping some snot on the back of his sleeve.

"I'm no *angel*, but had I known, I would have acted differently," Bashir said, his guilt nearly overwhelming him. Ahkmed suddenly fell to the ground in an uncontrollable fit of tears.

"I will see to it that your establishment wants for *nothing* once I return to the palace," he said comfortingly. "Y-you would do that for me?" Ahkmed asked, tears streaming down his prominent cheeks and into his thick beard. Bashir nodded and consoled the crying man for a while.

A few moments later, Ahkmed's crying had stopped, and he picked himself up off the floor. "I'll get this cleaned up for you. It's the very least I could do," he said, beginning to stack a handful of dirty bowls. Seeing this, Bashir started to grab a few of the bottles off the floor. "Wh-what are you doing? This is my mess, and my responsibility, *sir*," Ahkmed said, trying to stop him.

"And as your *king*, I must help my people, so I will help you clean up, anyway, and you will not say another word about it," Bashir said firmly. The man smiled, wiping away more tears that threatened to fall, as they began picking up the old bowls of food and empty bottles off the floor.

Meanwhile, the raven flew as fast as its wings would carry it towards the palace, making it to its destination by nightfall. One of the guardsmen who stood watch at the palace's raven cage room heard the incoming bird cawing a short way away. He turned to watch the carrier land and pant heavily on the roost provided for it. He walked over to the perch and saw the pouch on its chest, unlacing its bindings and removing the contents.

His eyes widened as he noticed the king's seal on the letter and immediately rushed down the tower stairs to bring it to his captain.

The palace was a beautiful place, with intricate tapestries and carvings so beautiful that they could easily be identified as the works of a master artisan. The nearly seamless stone floor was beige and cool to the touch, and each one had a pattern painted on it. The perfectly aligned pillars and walls supporting the palace made for excellent ventilation in the summer and insulation in the winter.

The guardsman sprinted down the staircase from the raven tower, through the vast halls to his destination, arriving there without being short of breath. "Sir," he said much more loudly than he had intended before rendering a proper greeting. "What is it?" the Harutian captain replied, relatively annoyed to be bothered at that hour of the night.

He was covered in a two-layer tunic that was slightly open at the neck. It protected slashing, but very little against stabbing movements, but lightweight armor came at that cost. His beige and brown sashes were wrapped around his waist, tying the large scimitar to the right side of his body. He had one red sash tied around his right arm, showing his rank.

"We've received a message from His Majesty," the guardsman said. "Give it here," the captain's eyes widened as he reached for the letter. The guardsman handed the small parchment to him, and he read its contents. After a few heartbeats, his eyes flared with a fiery anger. "Our king wants a war. Ready the men, we ride at dawn for Coltend and honor," he said, looking at the other two men he had been holding council with before being interrupted.

"But, sir, King Bashir has ridden there for a peace council. I don't understand why we would ride there in full gear ready for war," the guard cocked his head, causing the captain to fume. "The reason for that is that the king of Coltend has murdered Prince Bashaa," he snapped. "It's written here, and in the unmistakable hand of King Bashir," he brought the parchment over, tapping it firmly to ensure the guard looked at it.

"Read it yourself, and if you don't believe our king, then you have no place in our ranks. Would you want to stay put and suffer the consequences once he arrives, or would you rather obey the orders as you have been taught to do?" the captain growled. The man knew the consequences of disobeying a direct order, especially from the highest command. "Of course, sir," the guard rendered a crisp salute.

"We ride for the Rhydian Pass, and Coltend at dawn. For our King, our country, and our honor as warriors," the captain said sternly. He pulled a scroll from the shelf behind him and read it over to ensure it was the correct order before stamping the blue wax with the ring on his finger.

His insignia clearly showed in its imprint. He waited for it to dry completely and handed it over to one of the other men in the room. "You know what to do," he said. The guard saluted and proceeded out of the room.

The order was given out, and all the men were assembled by dawn. Horses had been fed, and swords sharpened. Three thousand men left the Harutian capital of Escea, riding for honor.

And to war.

CHAPTER II

ATHAR

"I feel... strange," Athar said, looking at his hands. He was still in the library, where he had just discovered his newfound powers.

"You will feel like that for a while. At least until you gain mastery over yourself," the Masked One replied. Athar rubbed his temples. "I feel like I've been run over by a merchant's fully loaded carriage. Does it always feel like this, or does it get better with time, my lord?" he asked.

I remember feeling like that, too. How long has it been since? his master thought.

"It will get better with time. After all, that was your first time having your consciousness separated from your body. It's only natural that you would feel backlash from it the first few times," he explained. Athar noted his master's composure, but decided not to say anything as he glanced around the room.

"These books, my lord," Athar began cautiously. "What about them?" his master asked. "There are so many of them, but I think I am beginning to see, or feel, I still don't know which, tendrils of mana coming from more than a few of them, my lord," Athar tried to stand, though his legs nearly gave way.

"I would much rather you figure out why they are like that on your own, for I have important matters to attend to. Right now, I cannot and will not give you all of the answers, as that would only stunt your growth as a mage," the Masked One said dismissively, but noticed Athar's dour expression.

"Besides, I prefer a more *practical* approach to learning mana manipulation. A little bit of challenge is good for your growth, and right now, you need to grow as quickly as you can," his master continued.

"So, you came to watch me struggle, my lord?" Athar half-scoffed. "In truth, I had rather hoped you *wouldn't*, but doing this for the first time with almost *no* oversight would have been a mistake on my part," the Masked One replied.

Awh, it almost sounded like he cared *for a moment,* Athar thought, immediately regretting it when his master turned to glare at him.

"Make sure you don't destroy anything. I won't even *begin* to tell you what I will do if you so much as *crack* a candelabra," he growled. Athar nodded, feeling a chill go down his spine again, and swallowed to clear his throat. When no sudden reprimand other than the chill came, Athar risked a grin behind the Masked One's back as he left the study.

He eventually reached the spawning chamber, where the countless nests and high shelves teemed with various newborn creatures. Above them was a high, transparent walkway suspended in the air by mana-infused crystals. A dark figure stood waiting for him, whose silhouette could only be described as grotesque and misshapen.

The Masked One's eyes glowed as he channeled mana towards his feet. He began to levitate up to the walkway and landed on it like a feather having fallen to the ground.

"I assume all goes well with the spawn," he said to the figure. "Indeed, my lord, it does," it replied in more of a gurgle than a normal voice; the sharp, protruding teeth making him difficult to understand. "Do you remember your first day here in the Between, Karak?" the Masked One asked.

Karak nodded and turned to face his lord. His dark, glossy eyes and grotesque features could barely be seen in the chamber's gloom. "I do, my lord. I remember first casting my eyes upon my new reality after being drawn out from my home in the Underworld," Karak began. "This world is much less *dead* than where I come from, with plenty of fresh bones to gnaw," the creature gurgled.

"Tell me, Karak, do you know why I have left you in charge of the ones who lie below us?" the Masked One asked as he began to walk along the translucent pathway. "No, my lord. I always assumed it's because you knew I could kill anything that tried to go against your wishes," Karak shrugged his sharp shoulders.

"While that is partially true, the reality of why I chose you is slightly different. It is because I know that if there is one I can trust within my small circle of allies, it is you," the mage replied. "I am honored to be called your *ally* and not your *slave*, my lord," the creature bowed, its figure distorting the darkness around it.

The mage nodded with a grunt and continued walking. "I'm sure you know this, but Athar has begun his mana manipulation training," he said. "I do, my lord, but what do you want *me* to do about it?" Karak asked expectantly. "Not at the moment, but I do want you to keep a closer eye on him than I can while I am away," the mage sighed.

"Do you worry that his heritage might sway his allegiance?" Karak asked. "I'm already certain that it will, at least to *some* extent. It is merely a matter of time before *he* tries to make his move," the Masked One grimaced beneath his mask.

"However, if the legends are to be believed and he becomes what I think he might, I must ask you to end him by whatever means necessary," he continued, getting a curious growl from Karak in response. "My lord, requiring the services of a daemon such as myself is both an honor and a privilege, but what of *his* plans?" the daemon asked.

"At this point, I can do little to stop them. All we have to do is follow his orders as best we can," the mage sighed. "A shame that not even one as powerful as you can break away from *that*, my lord. However, I *am grateful* that you've brought me here to escape whatever *he* has planned," Karak bowed, causing a long string of saliva to droop toward the floor.

The mage halted momentarily as if stunned by the daemon's words. "Go keep an eye on Athar. Report your findings back to me whenever he ends a training session. Is that understood?" he asked without turning to face the creature. "As you wish, my lord," Karak bowed again before leaving quickly.

The Masked One's eyes glowed again as he let himself down from the walkway. *He will not fail me, of course. However, Athar's newfound powers will grow exponentially. Now that I know he's not as much of an idiot as I had initially thought, he might prove a formidable ally, or end up complicating and disrupting my plans,* he thought on his way to his citadel's version of a ravenry.

As he passed, the violet gloom that lined the dark hallways and walls fluctuated. Once he arrived, he looked around to ensure nothing had changed since he was last there. Everything appeared to be in order and in its proper place.

I'm glad Athar's never wandered this far, he thought, idly picking up one of the many quills on the sizeable metallic desk.

As he pushed dark mana into the air, a score of quills and scrolls floated about the room, aligning themselves in preparation to receive dictation. "Begin," he said aloud, and the feathers scribbled the words that left his mind. He drew even more power and condensed it to his right hand.

The black, swirling sphere in his hand was then cast upon the floor, spawning featherless, winged beasts with sharp talons and pale eyes. "Stop," he commanded, forcing the quills to float back to their original places while the scrolls folded themselves and went into their respective pouches.

He lifted them with tendrils of violet mana and strapped them onto his winged creatures. "Fly now, to the outcast, the hated, the disdained, and most vile of Synners. We have work to do," he commanded. The creatures squawked in reply, their sharp beaks opening widely to let out a deafening cry. Their featherless wings spread wide, flying from the opened window before them, leaving only one behind.

"This one is for the Castle. Take extra care not to make yourself seen by anyone other than *him*," the Masked One said. The creature flew off through the window and turned in the opposite direction from the others. "So it begins," he sighed, watching the creatures soar into the moonlit night.

Meanwhile, Athar was still in the study practicing his control over the *Inar* and *Exar* spells he had learned. Through every spell cast, he sought to remove the books from their proper places, draw them to him, and place them back in their original locations.

I've been at this for hours and still don't know how much I'm progressing. At least, I can't tell, he thought.

There were more than a dozen books strewn across the floor around him. He breathed deeply, trying to recover some of his fatigue.

The headache has lessened a little bit, but my master said that it would take time to get used to it. If I can absorb myself in this newfound world of mana manipulation, I'm sure my master will be pleased, he thought, glancing at his flexing hand with a satisfied grin.

He followed the instructions in the book a handful of times before losing control on the last attempt. He let out an exhausted sigh, but smiled brightly when he noticed the hour-candles had gone down a complete eight markers.

This is more taxing than I thought it would be. I might not like him as a person, but gods above and below, the master is strong. Also, this deathmold solution is still just as unbearable as it was the first time, he thought as he sipped from the vial again, coughing as soon as it left his lips.

I've read through Farengir's book at least twice, but something is missing. Either that, or I haven't figured out this power's real potential. Wait, what's this about a Kyr *spell,* he thought, flipping through several book pages in his hand, hoping to find an answer.

He observed the diagrams that described the correct motions and quantities of mana required to perform it.

This looks like something I might be able to do, but I'll only try it once since I'm not sure how much more I can take. How long has it been since my master was here? Athar thought, noticing daylight was coming through the small openings far above him.

Alright, last one, he chuckled softly.

Silence, Immolation, Draw, and Return, he reviewed the words in his mind, just before the silence took over.

He reopened his eyes to feel them blacken in the familiar way they had been the last few hours. As he focused, *his consciousness was dragged toward the dark sphere again, only this time, he heard an indistinguishable voice coming from the sphere of light now behind him. His eyes briefly flicked to the bright one as it flared up like a flash of sunlight through the window of a dark room, causing him to lose focus and accidentally* return to his physical body, and he sighed.

"Fuck," he said aloud.

Just as he did, he heard a dripping sound coming from behind him. He could barely move, much less be able to turn and catch whatever it was that had made that sound.

I've never heard this place drip before. It's not even raining outside as far as I can tell, he thought, reaching for the vial, and took another swig of the disgusting solution.

"*Ugh,*" he shuddered as his face contorted itself. After a few seconds, his vitality returned, and he proceeded to stand.

Shit, I forgot to put away the books, he thought. He stacked them up and placed them on the same shelf where he had taken the first one.

Just before leaving the study, he glanced behind him and chuckled softly. "I'll see you tomorrow," he muttered to no one in particular. He remembered the dripping sound and tried to relocate where it had come from. He observed the ground nearest to the main entrance, but found nothing.

Hmm, it doesn't seem like anything's here after all. Maybe I'm just tired, he thought as he quickly scoured the library for any signs of liquid, but found none.

No, there's no way that was just my imagination. I know *I heard a dripping sound coming from somewhere around here, but there doesn't seem to be anything, or* anyone, *around,* he thought as he strode down the gloomy hall back to his quarters.

He opened his curtains briefly to confirm what time it *really* was, only to find himself blinded by the morning sun. His eyes shut and stung immediately, shielding themselves from the blinding light.

It's just like the sphere of light in the Between, with the exception of that weird voice. I guess I was in there for longer than I realized, he thought.

He closed his shutters with his eyes reduced to small slits on his face, and relaxed once the light had been removed from the room. He recovered from his short-lived ordeal and took the flask out of his pocket, placing it on his bedside table. He sat down on his bed, staring at the flask for a moment, eventually tucking himself under his blanket.

He lay awake for a few minutes, reviewing everything he had learned. He tried to contain his excitement for what the next day might hold. He closed his eyes, thoughts running wild, and decided to quiet them with the techniques he had learned earlier so he could sleep.

Meanwhile, the featherless creatures made their way to their destinations, avoiding being seen at all costs. They hid themselves from prying eyes during daylight, using terrain features as cover while they moved to their destinations. The first arrived just after midnight in northern Hjalfar, where a group of outcast Synners resided.

A hooded figure left his house after noticing a winged creature's silhouette blocking his view of the full moon. He followed its general direction a short distance outside the main town. He found the beast perched on a low-lying branch of an oak tree, with its wings folded like a large bird of prey.

Once he had gotten close enough to see the creature, the hooded figure was startled at its sight. Its dark skin glistened and its pale eyes reflected the moonlight, making it look like something out of his worst nightmares.

"What are you?" he asked quietly. The creature responded with a quiet snort and turned, showing him the leather pouch. The man cautiously stepped forward, after all, he had been trained to trust no beast he would ever encounter. After realizing the creature meant him no harm, he reached out and opened the pouch, removing its contents.

The time has come for those of you who read this message to take back what was once taken from you: your positions of power, your dignity, your families, and your loved ones. Join me and take it all back, cutting down all those who oppose you. Slay the leaders without mercy and bring their reigns to an end, his eyes widened in surprise at what he was reading.

"Could it be?" he muttered before continuing to read.

Only after doing so will you answer to no man and be free to rule your country as you see fit. Take back what is rightfully yours. Take back your homes. Revive your stagnant and wasted lives, and allow yourselves to live again. Join me, and I will help you regain what you lost. I am the

Masked One, and I have spoken, he concluded, quickly folding the note.

Why is he acting now? Something must have changed. I need to warn the others, he thought.

"I will answer the call," he replied, stuffing the note into a pocket. The creature snorted once more and flew off from whence it came. He ran back to the small town and began calling out the names of his friends and allies. They opened their doors to see him, standing in the middle of the housing district, with a scroll in his hand and arms spread wide.

"By the gods both light and dark, why must you call us out at this time of night?" one of the women asked. "Anders, you'd better have a good reason for waking us up at this hour," the woman called out. "I have received something that might aid us in our fight," Anders said aloud.

"And I suppose it's from that note you've got in your hand," the woman said. "Unni, I know you've always doubted me, but this time I'm asking you to trust me," Anders sighed as Unni spat in response to the comment. "Why should we? I mean, every raid you have ever led us on has gotten us shit for progress," she stepped forward and spread her arms.

"I know that it's been nearly ten years since we've been considered *outcasts*, and that those multiple attempts at revenge have gotten us almost nowhere. This time, however, *he's* making his move. There is hope, *real hope*, this time we'll succeed. I need your support now, more than ever, Unni. Please," Anders grabbed her shoulders gently.

She regarded him curiously, then shook her head with a shrug. "Fine, but if this fails, it's on *you*," she sighed, making him smile as he turned to address the others peeking out from behind cracks in their doors.

"My friends, I'm not going to ask you to take what I have to say lightly, but I have new insight that has given *me* hope for our futures. The Masked One has called upon us to take back our homes, our land, and be reunited with our families," he began, noticing a handful of the others in the small village were starting to step out into the cold.

"I understand that there have been many times where I have led us astray in the past, but *this time*, we have *his* support. Join me, and help me take back our homes, our lives! Let's get it all back!" he shouted, turning to look at those who had come forth. "How can you trust that secluded mage after all he's done?" an older man asked, making Anders shrug.

"I don't think you want to stay here any longer than I do," he began, getting nods of agreement from a handful of others. "All I'm saying is that, with his support, we can finally return to our homes!" he continued. "How do you know for *sure* that he was the one who sent it and that it's not some trap?" the older man asked. "Unni, please," Anders handed her the note.

She raised an eyebrow but took it anyway, rebuilding the cracked wax seal on the folded edge. "*Fy faen i helvete,*" she muttered in disbelief, looking back at him with a grin. "Anders speaks the truth," she shouted, holding it up for all to see. More mutters of agreement were scattered among the growing crowd, but Anders noticed one of the younger members gathering his courage to speak.

"Fuck dying of old age. I want to go *home*!" he shouted. "Let's take it back! Let's take it *all* back!" another middle-aged woman shouted, garnering nods of support from those around her. "Then we've made our choice. Prepare what you'll need to take, because tomorrow night, we're taking Odensby back for ourselves!" Anders flicked his arm out, gesturing for the others to return to their homes promptly. Cheers erupted from the small crowd before quickly scattering to return to their homes to do as instructed and get some rest. "I hope you know what you're doing," Unni muttered to him. "I do; I promise," he smiled, patting her shoulder.

The other creatures also reached their destinations, and each recipient around the continent responded accordingly. However, the lone creature that had departed last from Valdis finally reached its destination. Still, since Coltend was such a populated country, it only traveled under the cover of night. The difficulty of this only increased when it arrived at the well-guarded Coltend Castle.

A hooded figure was in the aviary that night, awaiting a response from his master, when finally, the creature arrived through the main window. He went to the beast and removed the parchment from the pouch.

I've set the pieces in motion. Do not disappoint me, the hooded figure read. "I will not disappoint you, my lord," the figure said to the creature. It screeched quietly before flying off to deliver the reply as its wings glistened in the moonlight.

So, the time has finally come, has it? He will likely be here soon. I must prepare the way for his arrival, the figure thought as he watched the creature soaring into the night sky.

Meanwhile, in Valdis, a few days had passed since Athar had first begun his training. He'd been making decent progress, though the dark circles beneath his eyes signified his dedication to this new ability. He sat upright against the wall on his bed, with a stack of books neatly organized on the small table beside it.

It's been nearly four days, and I've nearly finished Efer's book. Although, I still haven't figured out where the fuck that dripping *sound is coming from,* he thought as he flipped through to the far end of the book in his hand.

After reading a few pages, he realized he couldn't focus on anything properly, as another *dripping* noise came from just outside his door. He desperately tried to shun the thought from his mind, quieting it. After many hours of trying and failing, he finally got out of bed. He put on his clothes and grabbed a candle from his bedside table, aimlessly walking down the halls to see if the dripping would come after him.

What if it's a monster on the loose? I don't know if my master would appreciate me accidentally killing one of his beasts, even though I'm not sure I even could, he thought, listening for the sound again.

His palms began to sweat, adrenaline coursed through his veins, and his heart rate rapidly increased. He immediately became more aware of his surroundings as he walked without a distinct direction to follow, and after a few minutes, he heard it again.

Drip.

Fuck me, there it is, again! Alright, calm down and keep moving forward. Don't look back right now. Wait for an opportunity, he continued walking, pretending not to notice the sound that had reached his ears.

The library. That's where I'll face it, he thought, turning down the halls he had come to know over the past few years, and began making his way towards his now-favorite room in the whole citadel.

Drip.

He walked into the library and knelt in the center, as though he were about to practice even though he had already spent most of the day doing so. He pulled out the flask of deathmold solution and set it to his left, pretending he didn't just hear it again. He began to cycle through a handful of exercises to give whatever creature was following him a false sense of security.

Steady. Just keep doing what you're doing. Let it come in closer, he took a deep breath as violet mana swirled into his hand.

Drip. Drip.

Just a little more, you bastard, he thought, continuing to condense his spell.

Drip. Drip. Drip.

With the third droplet hitting the ground, he quickly turned to face whatever it was and released as powerful an *Exar* as he could, as a burst of mana tore through the air towards his target. The shadowy figure lept to another part of the study, prompting him to fire off another blast, but it dodged those as well, leaving craters behind where its claws had dug into the thick, metallic walls.

"Damn you!" Athar shouted, firing off another blast before taking a swig from the vial the Masked One had left him. With a grunt of exertion and blackened eyes, he *drew more mana from the Underworld,* letting it swirl into a large nebula that coated his entire forearm. "I've got you now, you piece of shit!" he shouted, extending his fingers outward to cast a *Kyr* spell.

The bolt of violet lightning shot out from his fingertips, making the hair on his arms and head stand on end. It soared through the air to its target, tearing through it as it went with a *crackling boom.*

It reached its target and struck it in the shoulder, causing it to fall to the ground.

Desperately, Athar rushed toward the creature, its gaping maw releasing a gut-wrenching screech as it writhed in pain. It noticed he was coming and quickly got to its clawed feet to defend itself, but it was too late. Athar grabbed it by a fold in its scale-like flesh and slammed his forehead into the bridge of its nose. It hardly flinched from the pain, but he did it again, this time snapping a handful of teeth and drawing more black blood from it.

"What the fuck do you want from me?" Athar shouted before headbutting it again, knocking its head back. Karak snarled and glared at him, but knew he wasn't there to kill his master's pet. "I was sent here to *watch* you, Athar," the daemon raised clawed hands, hoping it would stop the next headbutt from landing.

Athar halted and glared at the creature in disbelief. "You sure he didn't send you here to kill me, you *slimy fuck*? Then why the *hell* were you just sneaking around like that? Answer me!" he jostled the creature.

"He's concerned about your progress and told me to watch you closely. He's also worried that your allegiance might waiver if you grow into your fullest potential," Karak gurgled, but Athar could only shake his head in disbelief. "After over *two decades*, that bastard still doubts my allegiance? Even after everything I've had to go through?" he seethed.

"His concern is real enough, it would seem," Karak snickered just before being thrown to the ground. "Take me to him," Athar glared at the creature. "He's busy right now. He's preparing to make his move under the Great One's command," Karak spat, a few broken teeth clattering on the ground in front of him, coated in black blood.

Athar squatted before the daemon, causing it to scurry backward in fear. "Do I look like I'm the mood to give a shit, daemon? Take me to him, *now*. Otherwise, I'll headbutt you again and again until your teeth are coming out of your asshole," he said coldly. Karak glared at him for a moment, but eventually relented. "Fine, I'll take you to him, but don't expect a warm welcome," the daemon sighed as he returned to his feet.

Karak led him down the halls to find the Masked One in the room where he first encountered the addia and the ochelon. "My lord," Athar called out, trying to hide most of his anger. The Masked One was standing in front of yet another ochelon's cage, much smaller than the royal ochelon whose soul he had absorbed before. He appeared to be talking to it, in its language of grunts and snorts.

"I know why you're here, Athar, and I hope you will understand why I think the way I do," he said without turning around, following the sound of Athar's footsteps as he approached.

"After all these years, you still doubt my allegiance to you? How could you? I've given you everything I had to give. My service, time, life. All of it! Even though you know I hate how you've treated me, I still haven't betrayed you, and I won't, either!" Athar shouted.

"Not *yet*," the Masked One said curtly, his eyes flaring mildly. "What the hell do you mean by that, *my lord*?" he seethed. The mage stopped what he was doing, waving the creatures before him off to the side as he turned around. "I have taken you in, fed and clothed you, given you a *home*, and yet you still don't understand how much *I've* had to sacrifice for you to be here. Do you even know *why* I sent

Karak to watch you?" he stepped forward, his eyes shining brightly with violet mana as a dark aura enveloped him.

Athar stepped away, his eyes widening in fear of whatever came next.

"Do you have *any* idea what trouble it's been to rid the knowledge of your existence from the world, or what I've had to do to get to this point?" the mage snarled. "N-No, my lord," Athar stammered. "Of course, because I only tell you what you *need* to know, but I guess now is as good a time as any to put you in your fucking *place, Athar Wishert*," the mage's dark aura flared.

Wishert? Like Truls Wishert of Coltend? No, it's impossible, Athar considered, as a sinking feeling writhed in his stomach.

"*Oh*, no, no, no. It's not only *possible,* but a *fact.* Your bloodline, your *heritage*, is that of kings. I've done everything in my power to prevent you from being discovered and, consequently, killed. *You,* however, chose to be an ungrateful little shit and *dare to question* my putting Karak to watch you closely while you grew into your newfound abilities," the Masked One continued walking forward.

"But why? What's the big deal if I'm a bastard?" Athar asked, summoning what little courage he had. "I didn't fully understand it myself until just before I found you, but your bloodline, your *true heritage*, is dangerous. Far more dangerous than anything I would challenge on my own," the mage averted his gaze, lowering his tone.

"I might now know a much fuller extent of your past, but there are still things *even I* cannot tell you for now. For that reason, you had to be placed under a careful eye. One that was, apparently, not careful enough," he continued, glaring at Karak while Athar's features were riddled with confusion.

"There is no use in fighting back now, Athar. There is still much for you to learn and do, but I do not have the time to argue with an insolent child who needs careful observation," he continued.

He's right, I won't fight back, but I need to stand my ground if I'm going to learn more about my past, he thought, conjuring a small barrier of mana to scramble his thoughts while mustering his courage to speak.

"I cannot and will not do anything against you, my lord. I might hate how you treated me for all those years, but you have given me knowledge and opened my eyes to mana. I can't betray you for that debt, even if I wanted to," his tone firm and as confident as he could manage under the aura's pressure.

The Masked One tilted his head in curiosity and regarded him curiously. "Do you *swear* to that?" he asked calmly, prompting Athar to swallow dryly. "I-I do, my lord. The only thing I will ask for is the power to uphold that vow," he dropped to a knee. The mage reduced the aura of violet mana and held out a hand toward him.

"I'm glad you were able to recognize that I'm not putting you under observation out of hatred, but trying to protect you, instead," he said, helping Athar to his feet. Athar's eyes opened widely in surprise to hear the words coming from his cold-hearted master. "What do you mean *protect me*? From what, exactly, my lord?" he raised an eyebrow.

"The very thing I found hidden within your core," the Masked One said with a darkened tone.

CHAPTER 12
THE ELVEN EMISSARY

E dryd looked at me, then Anwill, then back to me with wide eyes.

"I don't suppose you know how your brother knows the elf?" he asked, staring at the friendly exchange between Bernar and Anwill. I could only shake my head and shrug. "If I had to guess, they met when my brother went to Caegwen for training a few years ago," I shrugged again.

It's still weird that he's on such friendly terms with someone so high-ranking, I thought, recalling that Anwill was here directly under King Elhael's command, still observing their friendly exchanges.

"What's this all about? Wait, who even *is that*?" Batch interrupted my thoughts as he walked toward us. "I heard the call that someone was here, but I had no idea it would be an elf. Do you know who he is?" he raised an eyebrow. "He's here as an emissary, but I've never heard of one who was a fifth stage," I shrugged.

"Your brother's a fifth stage, right?" he asked. "Yeah, but what does that have to do with anything?" I raised an eyebrow. "Well, maybe *he* was the one who helped him get there," Batch suggested.

I hadn't really thought about *how* he managed to do it at such a young age. After all, he was only in Caegwen for a handful of years, but I never considered just how fast he'd actually reached it.

The bastard never told me how long it took him, did he? I thought with a chuckle.

"It's possible, but there's still a lot we don't know yet. He's only just arrived, and so far, we have *way* more questions than we do answers," I said in response to Batch's suggestion. "Well, there is an elf here in Codrean, so I dare say that something smells, and it's not the smell of roses," Batch said.

We watched Bernar and Anwill walk towards the main fortress, conversing over something I couldn't overhear. The two went fully out of earshot, and I turned over to my friends, who were also just as puzzled as I was.

"Also, I just realized I haven't seen you in a few days. Where the hell have you been?" I lightly punched Batch's shoulder. "*Hey!* It's not *my* fault. Bernar has me training some new moves with Irun, and it's been quite, *uh*, painful," Batch chuckled, scratching the back of his head.

"It's alright. Hell, if I had to be put through Bernar's training, I think my arms would be turned into pudding. *Oh!* Wait, they *are*," Edryd said with a chuckle, rolling his injured shoulder. "On the bright side, at least you'd have emergency food readily available," Batch said sarcastically. "You know, I sometimes wonder if you're not a few marbles short of a full bag," Edryd replied with a disgusted look on his face.

"Disregarding that fucked up mental image, I've actually been able to get back to training," he continued. "That's true, and we still kicked your sorry ass. No mercy for arms made of pudding," I said with a shrug. "See? I knew I should've kicked you in the balls when I had the chance," he snapped immediately, causing the three of us to burst into a fit of laughter.

"*Ah*, it's good to be back. As much as I hate to admit it, I actually missed you fuckers. A few more days and I would have had to beg you two to swing by and watch me kick Irun's ass," Batch sighed. "*Oh*? I always thought he was the better of you two," I grinned. "*Oh*, don't get me wrong, he's still a damned-good swordsman; but with a little help from Bernar, I've finally managed to beat him more than once," Batch said pridefully.

"Well, well! I think we should have a sparring session sometime to see who's the best of us. *Pudding arms* and all. Speaking of *shit-for-brains*, where is he?" I asked, looking around to see if I could find the fourth member of our little fellowship. "I've only just noticed something," Edryd began, leaving us confused. "Well, I mean, he could be off training, but Irun hasn't been seen in some time by anyone other than you, Batch," Edryd said.

"He tends to run off to study his mistakes after each training session, or so he says. He hasn't really done much else other than that," Batch shrugged.

I looked at Edryd with a raised eyebrow that Batch noticed. "I'm not even going to ask what that was about, but let's get back to the matter of the elf," he said nonchalantly. "Right. Let's examine what we know," I began, preparing my hand to lift each finger as I listed the things we knew.

"He rode all the way from Caegwen to speak to the Master. Bernar has known him for a long time. We've only been back about a week or so since leaving the palace where King Elhael was with members of his council. I didn't see him, but he must have been somewhere near the castle, as it would have taken a much longer time to get here. Am I missing anything?" I asked.

"Well, there was that situation with the ravens, where the Master freaked out for some reason. Maybe they were meant for him?" Batch added. "True, which was rather odd, I mean, it's just a raven or two," Edryd chimed in.

He feigned his ignorance quite well, I thought, releasing a breath I didn't know I was holding.

"Well, a raven could mean a number of things," Batch began. "It could've been someone from the nearby farm, or something similar to that, at least," he said.

I was surprised, to say the least, and gave Ed a quick glance.

That's the same conclusion we had reached before the Master told us of the possibility of a traitor, I thought.

"True. For all we know, it could have just been that. However, it still doesn't explain how quickly he arrived, nor what the actual fuck that elf is doing here, though," I replied. "Well, we won't figure out much if we're just standing around," Edryd said with a wry, suggestive tone, causing Batch and I to raise our eyebrows in surprise.

"You're saying we should *eavesdrop* on their conversation? You know the Master can practically see through walls, right?" Batch asked. "I know he can, but I can't think of another way *we* can find out why he's here," Ed shrugged. "So what do you propose, Batch?" I asked, making him grin with obvious malicious intent. "Well, he likes drinking, doesn't he? Maybe we could bribe him with extra rations or something," Ed replied in Batch's stead.

"Do you really think he's going to accept that as a worthy trade?" I sighed, watching his face immediately sink in dejection. "I just want him to spill the beans on what they talked about," he said, finally understanding what I meant.

"Well, well, well. There goes Ed's innocence. Never thought I'd hear that bribery was on the table coming from you," Batch said with genuine surprise. "I'm not saying he would accept the bribe, but if he did..." Ed trailed off with a shrug.

I looked at him and nodded. "It would be very helpful to understand the situation. However, all we can do now is wait for them to be done," I concluded, patting Edryd's non-injured shoulder twice.

Just as I said that, Bernar was shutting the door behind him and subtly gestured for me to follow him. It took me a second to understand what it was he wanted from me, but after he repeated the gesture, I finally understood.

"Ed," I whispered out of the corner of my mouth as I subtly flicked my head in the direction of the door. "Go on, I'll catch up with you later," he shot back quickly. "Hey, Batch, I've got a question," he said, trying to distract our mutual friend.

I followed my brother's direction and made my way to the Master's study. As I cracked the door open, I saw that he was leaning on his desk, looking over a few scrolls with the others. He heard my footsteps coming up the stairs, and looked in my direction before any other of the visitors had even noticed I was there.

"Greetings, Thoma. Nice of you to join us," the Master said, glancing up from the unraveled map before him. "Greetings, Master," I said shyly as I closed the door behind me. "Please, sit. We're about to start," he gestured toward a small wooden stool in the corner of the room.

Time for the adults to talk, right? I thought as I gingerly made my way to the stool.

"It's good to see you again, Anwill. I'd be lying if I said I was expecting you to visit us," he said, extending a hand toward the elf who clasped it firmly. "Indeed. I came as quickly as I could, when I heard the news," Anwill replied.

I thought they didn't like physical contact. Maybe it's only for a select few? I thought with a grin aimed at my brother.

"You couldn't have come all the way from Caegwen simply to give me news," the Master said conclusively. "No, truly I have not. However, I must attend to the matter at hand with haste, as time is of the essence," Anwill replied. "Please, take a seat," the Master motioned to the chair with the carvings.

"Master, I bring news of Coltend and something that will be of great interest to you. However, I must speak of Coltend first. A few days ago, Truls brutally murdered the young Harutian prince Bashaa over the accusation of having intercourse with his wife, Queen Leona," he began.

"*Oh,* shit," Bernar and I said in unison from the back of the room. "Indeed. However, after the murder, Bashir fled, and Truls sent a small party out to hunt him down. The very same day, Truls died at the hands of the very person whose honor he was trying to protect, or so his servants say," Anwill shook his head, letting his words hang for a moment.

"As it stands, she is the one ruling over her subjects at Coltend Castle. While Bashir's state and location are currently unknown, we know he made his way towards the Rhydian pass, which would be the logical choice. After all, it's the shortest and most direct road to take back to his home," he said. "He's always been a good rider, so I'm sure he made it," the Master said, digesting the new information.

"Well, so we think. However, I must now speak of Caegwen, where situations have arisen that may prove to be worth your while," Anwill said. "Another queen murdered her husband?" Bernar asked jokingly.

"If only it were that simple," the elf scoffed and shook his head. "*Master*, as you well know, the monsters only come out of their portals from the Underworld every full moon. However, three days ago, a portal opened during the daytime; an unprecedented event in and of itself," the elf said, leaning forward.

Wait, did he intentionally not use the Master's real name? It sounded like his tongue almost slipped. But that's not important, what's this about the portals? I shook my head, trying to organize my thoughts.

"During the day? That's not good. Not good at all," the Master said with a slight frown. "Truly. The Commander of the Myrdinian Synners, whom you know *quite well*, has managed to organize enough troops to hold shifts over the locations and slay the few that passed through the portal. Although the last one that opened was far too close to our capital for comfort," Anwill said with his head aimed at the floor.

"They are growing bolder by the day, or so it seems," he began once more after a brief pause. "King Elhael and Queen Aurae, as well as myself and others of the elven council, believe the Undergod to be attempting to make a move of some sort. As things currently stand, we still do not know what he's after," he said with a hint of anger in his voice.

"Your Synners," the Master began, rubbing his scar lightly. "What about them?" Anwill asked. "They didn't notice anything strange about the portal, did they? The Commander didn't put anything out regarding its composition?" the Master raised an eyebrow. "The reports said it was emitting dark tendrils of power that faced towards the North, but I fail to see how that is relevant," Anwill said.

The Master looked at his visitor with questioning eyes. "If you don't mind me asking, but how old are you exactly?" he asked. "Eight-hundred and eighty," Anwill replied with a curious look on his face. "*Ah*, so it was *well* before your time, then," the Master sighed.

Well before his time? How old is the Master anyway? I thought, caught entirely off-guard by the strange reveal.

"Excuse me, but what does this have to do with the portal?" Anwill asked, genuinely confused. "About fifty years before you were born, a citadel was discovered in the far northern regions of Hjalfar. They called it Valdis, which is derived from their language meaning the dead goddess," the Master began to explain.

Valdis? That's not a Hjalfarian name, is it? I thought, genuinely confused.

"The citadel was named as such, given the fact that all who attempted to explore it in the years that followed never returned. The fact that the tendrils were facing in its general direction could have something to do with the reason why it appeared in the first place," he continued calmly.

"You're suggesting that the Undergod is somehow connected to this Valdis place, Master?" Bernar asked. "Exactly," he replied with a slight nod. "I believe something is beginning to stir there, and it is anything but *friendly*," he continued.

"I *know* what lives there, and it would seem he's growing more powerful every day. It would stand to reason if there were a connection to the Underworld," Anwill said ominously. "You do?" the Master asked with urgent curiosity. "Indeed, Master. It's..." Anwill cut himself off the moment shattering glass came from the nearby window. All of us turned to look at Bernar as he picked up the stone that promptly rolled across the floor.

Portal. Monsters, I managed to read, my eyes opening widely as I snagged a glance at the scratchings on the stone.

Bernar quickly looked out the window to see Edryd and Batch pointing towards the south. His eyes widened when he noticed what they were pointing at. "What is it?" the Master asked. "You couldn't have come at a better time, Anwill, as it's been a while since we fought side by side. Guess what just showed up at our doorstep?" Bernar said incredulously.

The Master's eyes opened wide, as did everyone else's.

"Sound the alarm and be ready for battle. Have you got a sword with you?" the Master asked the elf as he rose from his seat. "What kind of Synner would I be if I didn't?" he replied with a grin. "Good. Be ready to use it. Thoma, you're coming with us, now!" the Master commanded, to which Anwill and I replied with a unified nod.

"Sound the alarm!" Bernar shouted out of the broken window to Ed. As I quickly looked out of the window, I could tell he was startled by my brother's mana-enhanced command and quickly sprinted over to the bell, signaling the alarm. There were still synners honing their skill in the training ground who heard the call as we raced down the stairs to the courtyard.

"What's this all about?" a senior asked his training partner, running toward the sound of the commotion. "Sounds like we've got trouble. Gear up, boys!" I heard Roburn shout to the others. "We've got a real fight coming our way! Time to put all that training to some good fucking use! Now, move unless you want to become a glick's suppository!" he shouted, and everyone scrambled to switch out training swords for real ones.

After a few precious minutes, each one had our battle-ready equipment secured to our jerkins. We quickly mounted our respective horses, when I noticed Irun running up, still fumble-fucking his gear as he moved towards us.

"I heard the alarm ringing, but what's the situation?" Irun asked. "We're under attack," I said. "A portal not too far south of here is spewing glicks out faster than I can piss. Where the hell were you?" I snarled.

"I was studying and didn't hear the bell until about a minute after it had begun ringing," Irun replied. "Well, get a move on. Things are about to get ugly," Batch said, prompting Irun to nod and mount his horse that Batch had fetched beforehand.

The Master turned his horse to face us as the gate opened behind him. "Our enemies are at our gates, and we must not let them breach our defenses. All of you have trained your entire lives for moments such as this one, and I expect all of you to know exactly what you're doing out there. Protect this fortress, no matter the cost. Is that clear?" he shouted, getting a clear roar in response.

"We ride!" he shouted as the gates swung open.

The thunderous sound of our hooves echoed throughout the courtyard, hardly muffling the battle cries that came from the others. We galloped out of the fortress, and immediately turned south, riding directly towards the growing horde of monsters.

I knew the monsters were considerably disorganized and always used their numbers to overpower an enemy. However, *this* was different, somehow. The portals made sense for rapid means of transportation, but why they weren't all immediately killing each other was something I couldn't figure out.

I'm sure the Master is thinking the same thing, I thought, noticing his look of resolve.

Within the next few minutes, we were getting close enough to our new targets. "Formation!" Garett shouted, prompting us to form three boar's heads and maintain our speed. The formation was triangular in shape, hollow in the middle, and served as a wedge whenever there was a line that needed to be broken.

Three hundred meters, I calculated, adjusting my position to be just behind the apex of the boar's head.

The southern wind began to blow, and the stench of the oncoming horde of glicks and daemons became palpable, prompting a few of the less-experienced to almost greet their late lunches.

"Gods above and below, they smell awful," Irun said to Batch who rode by his side in our boar's head, making Batch take a deep breath through his nose. "*Ugh!* It's like a thousand pieces of rotten bacon put under the sun," he tried to expunge the stench from his nostrils. "Or an ochelon's ass," Irun grinned, trying to take his mind off the stench. "Not helping. There might be one there for all we know. So, focus!" I snapped.

Two hundred meters, I thought, starting to see the horde in more detail.

I could finally see the large portal clearly; a violet swirl of mana, with dark tendrils of power facing the northeast poured out the horrid creatures. The monsters screamed and gurgled their war-cries which echoed throughout the small valley just south of the fortress.

What the hell is that? I thought momentarily, noticing a creature I'd never seen before.

It was the first time I'd ever laid eyes on a daemon outside of a textbook. Its disfigured body and blackened, rotting skin almost made the glicks look like something straight out of a child's bedtime story.

"Swords," the Master shouted from the center of the second formation, a short command which we all followed promptly. "Bow-casters, fan out and support them," Garett barked, the rear part of the formation pulled back, supporting the others as commanded.

I could feel the copious amounts of mana they infused into their bows even from where I was. I quickly turned my head to see their bows beginning to glow with mana in accordance to the elements they wanted to use.

"Loose!" I heard Garett call out just before a rain of arrows bathed the front row of creatures in death. They screamed and writhed in pain, flopping to the black and green blood began to soak the ground beneath them.

Fifty meters. Just like before, lean in and... I swung, feeling the edge of my blade bite into the scaly flesh of a glick's shoulder.

The pungent green blood sprayed my cheek, but I didn't even have time to flinch as I was forced to prepare for another strike. I kept moving forward, hacking away at anything that was within striking range, hitting more than a few targets as I did so.

The boar's head was successful, wreaking havoc on everything in its path. Heads flew and blood sprayed up in the air as our swords sang a beautiful song of war.

My sword-hand was now covered in the obnoxious green blood, but I pressed on, slaying more than a dozen on my first pass. Edryd, too, was having his blade sink into the screeching monsters. "Take that, you ugly fucks! This is payback for last time," he shouted as his sword sank into a glick's mouth and came out the backside of its head.

The boar's heads finally broke with the swarming creatures, and it soon became every man for himself. Roburn was riding into one of the thicker clusters of daemons when suddenly, one of the horrid creatures jumped and knocked him off his horse. He fell to the ground with a *thud*, and was soon swarmed by the very ones whose blood he had already spilled so much of.

"Roburn!" Edryd called out and hacked his way over toward him.

Shit, did I just watch him die? I thought, watching them pile on top of where he landed, as my stomach turned.

Just as I was thinking that, a large explosion of mana was released from the newly formed mound of daemons and glicks, setting all of them alight. They squealed and attempted to swat out the mana-flames that began to consume their flesh.

Roburn, whose braided hair was now coated in his own blood and the monsters', stood up and cast the *Pyrus* spell. The flame cloak surrounded him, keeping the unburned monsters at bay briefly while he seared his wounds shut.

Ed rode towards him and dismounted his horse quickly when he arrived. "I've got your back," he said, cutting down a few daemons in his path. "Thanks. Just don't get yourself killed," Roburn replied, glaring behind him with glowing eyes. Both stood side by side, severing limbs and removing heads from shoulders.

I was still on my horse, but I too was nearly knocked off the same way I had been in my first battle. This time, however, I saw it coming and quickly dismounted off the back of my horse, who proceeded to crush a few creatures to make its escape, and rolled to my feet. In the same moment, I severed my attacker's head at the jaw, sending a spray of blood into the air.

A few more glicks came rushing towards me, and I got into my guard again. Chaos reigned about me, but it seemed the whole world was shut out at that moment, leaving only me and the monsters in my immediate vicinity.

Three daemons to the right and two glicks to the left, I thought, calculating which one would try to reach me first.

The first glick jumped at me, aiming a sharp claw for my head. I ducked under the blow and struck its gut, spilling entrails on the ground beneath it. Two daemons came from opposite directions, sprinting towards me.

Shit, they're quicker than the glicks, I thought.

I saw the first claw being raised, and knew that would be the first one to strike. I grazed the blow off my sword and took off its head, using my momentum to its fullest advantage. The other was now within striking range, and its claw found its target, cutting into the flesh on my left arm.

I barely even felt it through my armor and adrenaline, and severed the claw, the next claw that came for me. I swept its legs with a kick, causing the creature to fall on its back. With my eyes darkened, I *drew mana from the Ethereal* and sent an Exar blast downward, crushing the daemon's skull.

"Three down," I said, glaring at the remaining creatures in front of me. The glick fluttered its scales, and the daemon produced a horrifying, knocking and scraping sound by smashing its teeth together in protest of my bravado.

"You're dying first," I muttered, readying my sword for my attack. I pushed off my left leg, dashing quickly towards it. I brought my sword down, making a diagonal cut that split the creature in two, spilling more blood and entrails onto the ground. Seeing the other's attack out of the corner of my eye, I twisted my body quickly, jabbing my mana-infused sword into the final monster's eye socket, causing its head to burst into flames.

I watched as it hit the ground with a wet and crackling *thud*. I was breathing pretty heavily, but took a moment to survey my surroundings to get a better sense of what was going on.

We're winning! That's a powerful spell if ever I've seen one, I thought as a flash of bright green sent glicks and daemons flying into the air, immediately rushing over to its origin.

Anwill was busy exploding glick after glick, while the Master and Bernar had infused their swords with mana. Their swords glowed a vibrant orange and cut through the oncoming creatures like a hot knife to butter. Anwill continued casting in conjunction with the cuts made by his sword, turning any target into little more than a mist of bones and bloodied entrails.

I watched them for a moment, ensuring that no other creatures were around me first. Suddenly, I heard and *felt* loud roars coming from the direction of the portal. "Ochelons!" Irun called out over the screeches and screams of battle, prompting me to look in his direction.

Bernar, Anwill, the Master, and I cut down the remaining enemies around us and cast our eyes upon the lumbering beasts. Four of them could be seen exiting the portal that closed behind them, their eyes glowing red and claws spread wide, ready to strike.

"That's more like it. Ready for round two, *shit-bird*?" Bernar grinned at me. Anwill turned toward us, listening intently to our conversation, as if something had piqued his interest. "More like round *three*, fuck-ass. Lead me to the slaughter," I said, nodding with determination, not wanting to show my absolute exhaustion at that point.

Anwill scoffed and chuckled in amusement, but never voiced his reason for doing so.

However, the Master could tell I was already tired from fighting, but he knew that if I stopped right then and there, it would be no different than giving my neck to an executioner. "Go, now!" he commanded after a curt nod of acknowledgement of my resolve.

The four of us ran towards Irun and the ochelons. Edryd and Roburn had bested the creatures around them, and they converged on the ochelons as well. The roars were deafening and sent chills down everyone's spines, save the Master and Anwill, who had many more years of experience in fighting them.

"Thoma, Edryd, Roburn, Irun. You four take the male on the right. Bernar, Anwill, and I will take the other three on the left," the Master ordered. "Yes, Master," we replied as we spread ourselves out, leaving the remaining chaos behind us to the others. The ochelons noticed us charging them and roared their challenges, rippling the air between us.

I felt the Master's mana surge as his eyes glowed even more brightly to cast a massive globe of fire at his target to draw its attention. Anwill and Bernar did the same to their targets, and led them away from the four of us as the spells seared their fur.

"*Ah*, it's been a long time," the Master said with a smile, watching the annoyed beast approach him. He got in his guard, the *Vom Tach*, and held his longsword with both hands just above his forehead.

For whatever gods-forsaken reason, he just stood there, *waiting*.

The others and I circled around our own challenger, closing in around it. The ochelon swung its muscular arms, though each blow was dodged quite easily as it couldn't pick a single one of us to focus on.

Why is he just standing there waiting? I thought, dodging a claw that aimed to crush me into the ground, then immediately turned to swing at the others.

As I looked at the Master and Anwill, I turned back around just in time to see another blow coming straight for me, forcing me to move out of the way and cut off one of its fingers with a single cut.

Meanwhile, the Master was still standing his ground, while Anwill and Bernar were already engaging their enemies, combining spells and sword strikes to weaken the ochelon's tough hides. The Master focused on his enemy, who now came at a charge ready to strike.

He watched the large claw as it rose into the air with his peripheral vision, keeping his eyes fixated on its center of mass. The beast swung down from its right side, and the Master simply stepped out of the way, removing its wrist from its arm with one swift cut. The ochelon roared in pain and swung again at about waist height. He rolled backward and was quickly on his feet, keeping his eyes fixed on the beast.

It tried to slam the ground where he just was, and he stepped out of the way of the stump that tried to crush him in quick succession. He dashed forward, cutting the tendon at the ankle, forcing the beast to stumble in front of him.

His speed is hard to follow. I can hardly even tell what he's doing when he attacks, but I feel like he's still holding back, I thought, dodging another attack that cracked the ground beneath me.

He rushed forward once more, stabbing a vital organ. The beast roared and swung again with its claw in an attempt to swat him like a fly. The Master leapt over the attack, severing its wrist in the process. "Two bloodied stumps and a strong bite are all you've got left," I heard him say, already back on his feet.

The beast roared and tried to squash him with both of its stumps. The Master dodged the blows and jabbed his sword into its face, piercing an eye. The beast roared again and swung blindly, desperate to find its target. He dodged the attacks and went around the beast to strike at the remaining tendon above its heel.

It fell with a roar to the ground, unable to get back up, swinging one last time to reach its mark of empty air. The Master had rolled out of the way and was now in front of it, raising his sword, and turning it on its point.

He struck downward, pinning the beast's head to the earth below. It gurgled blood, as his eyes glowed more intensely, pushing mana into the creature's head with such force that it caused it to explode, leaving nothing but a puddle of blood where its head once was.

Holy fuck! I exclaimed, repositioning myself behind the creature as Ed and Roburn struck the ochelon's tendon behind its knee.

Anwill was finishing off his enemy with a stab to the gut and a burst of mana, leaving a hole the diameter of a wine barrel in its chest. Bernar, on the other hand, had managed to get on top of his ochelon and sliced into its nape. It fell to the ground with a resounding thud, twitching for a few moments as he stepped down from the creature, getting a nod of disappointment from Anwill.

"I thought you would have killed yours more quickly," he sighed. "*Nah*, I wanted to show off a little for my little brother. Who knows? Maybe it'll give him an idea for *his* target," Bernar chuckled with a swift swing to get the blood off his sword. "Should we help them?" Anwill asked with what I thought was genuine concern. "Nope. Let them work as a team. I want to see how they do," Bernar shook his head as the two of them, along with the Master, approached us.

Ed and Roburn were dodging swats from the large claws aimed at them, while Irun and I tried to get close enough to cut its legs at the same time. The beast saw a flicker of sunlight off of Irun's sword and swung its claw, which met its mark, sending Irun into the air for a few moments.

"Irun!" I called out, watching him land in a heap a few meters away, almost entirely unconscious.

Shit. That could've been me. It's too tall to try and strike its chest. I've got to bring it down to our level and make it an even fight, I thought, remembering my own battle just a few days prior.

I dodged another swat aimed for me with a roll, and got in close enough to hack at the flesh behind its knee, causing it to roar in pain and drop to a knee. "Aim for his eyes!" I yelled at Edryd, feeling a slight sting of pain from the scar on my back after the roll.

Edryd's eyes *went black* as he cast a fireball aimed at the beast's face, doing little to no damage. "Use your sword!" Roburn shouted. Edryd understood the command, and through the plume of smoke, he thrust his sword, just barely reaching its target.

Roburn, sliding under the hunched-over creature, sliced into its gut. "Damn it, too shallow," he grunted. As the beast reared from the attack, it slammed the ground just beside me, sending me flying high into the air. As I reached the apex of my impromptu avian mimicry above the beast, I saw its bare nape and aimed for it.

I have to land this strike. If I can just cut its nape, that will be enough, but how can I deal that much damage to it? I thought.

I brought my sword up just above my forehead, my *sclera blackening for a moment* as I did so. However, I could feel a familiar warmth streaming from my eyes toward my temples as my eyes began to glow intensely, leaking a mana trail behind me as I fell.

I gripped my sword with all my might and infused it with mana, striking its nape as I fell, using whatever momentum from my weight and rotational velocity I could muster. My sword, severing the head from the large body, continued into the ground, leaving an explosion of blood, dirt, and mana in its wake.

"Holy leather-donut of the Kingdom of Assecheeks, that was amazing!" Edryd exclaimed, as the beast's corpse fell to the floor, rumbling the ground beneath it. "Thanks," I said weakly, reaching for his hand to help me to my feet. I looked over at Bernar and the Master, who were smiling from where they stood, visibly impressed by what they had just witnessed.

Anwill, however, blanched as if a memory had just appeared in the forefront of his mind.

"We've got to help Irun," I said, catching my breath. The three of us rushed over to where he had landed, but he was nowhere to be seen. "Where the hell did he go?" Edryd asked. "I saw him land right here," I said with no small amount of confusion in my voice.

"I'm over here," a voice came from a pile of dead creatures. "Irun," I said, rushing over to him. "I'm fine, thanks for asking," Irun grinned, but I grimaced. "I thought he had crushed your ribcage," I said, looking him up and down. "He did, which is why I didn't return to help you," Irun grunted as he shifted uncomfortably.

"I stayed here casting what spells I could to patch them up, while you three took it down," he continued. "Well, at least you're not dead," Roburn said, slowly walking over to the three of us, prompting Irun to chuckle lightly, but instantly regretted it. "Right now, I kind of wish I were," he groaned.

"You've all done well," the Master said, after looking around and noticing the battle was nearly over. "Not as well as you, Master," I replied, hearing the bowcasters strike down stragglers as they attempted to flee. "Well, what were you expecting me to do? Let it have at me and then take it down all beaten and broken?" he asked with a grin.

Was that a joke about my fight in the cave? I thought with a curt chuckle.

"Of course not, Master. I've just never seen you *actually* fight. Actually, now that I think about it, I've *never* seen *anyone* fight the way you did," I replied. "Of course, you haven't. If you had, I wouldn't be the master at Codrean, would I be, Thoma?" he gave me a wry grin, making me flush with embarrassment. "Although I did see you do something quite impressive yourself, did I not?" he asked, tilting his head a little.

The fuck? He was impressed? I thought, feeling my face flush with even more color as I nodded my head.

The Master smiled and turned to Irun. "Can you walk?" he asked. "I can, Master, though it feels like I've been run through by a tree trunk," Irun wheezed as Roburn and Ed helped him to his feet. "And you, Roburn? You seem pretty tattered and torn," the Master continued. "I can still walk, though this gash in my forehead will leave a handsome scar," Roburn replied, gesturing at the wound he was searing shut with mana.

"Very well, then. You two ride back to the fortress with the other wounded," the Master gestured to Irun and Roburn, who nodded, and walked past him, whistling for their horses. Irun mounted with some of Ed's and my help and was off with Roburn following close behind.

"He's a strong boy. Well, stronger than he looks, anyway," I heard Anwill mutter behind me. "Remind you of anyone?" the Master asked wryly. "Unfortunately, yes. He's a little odd, no doubt, but definitely a strong boy," Anwill said as he watched Irun and Roburn ride off, while the Master turned to face the two of us who remained.

I could hardly contain my embarrassment, but tried my best anyway.

"As I've said before, you've all done well. You and the others worked as a team without having pulled an every man for himself situation. Well, at least until you pulled that little *aerial stunt* of yours," he said lightly. "I didn't feel like I had a choice, Master," I defended myself.

"Choice or not, that was extremely dangerous, Thoma. You could have been turned into little more than a bloodied chunk if you had missed," Anwill stepped forward, spreading his arms. "Still, it got the job done, and I must congratulate you for your courage, and for effectively using the second stage of mana in mid-combat," he continued with a relenting sigh.

"Thank you, Anwill, but that was not the first time I've managed to use it," I replied sheepishly. "*Oh*? When was the first?" he asked with a small amount of curiosity and worry in his tone that caused my brother to chuckle lightly.

"During my fight with the pair of ochelons, which I believe you've heard about from my brother," I grinned wryly. " But like this battle, I felt I was out of options and somehow... *unlocked* it? I'm not sure how else to describe it," I explained, unsure of my own words.

The Master looked at Anwill with the same look he gave my brother whenever they seemed to communicate wordlessly. The elf gave him a nod and took a step forward. "That's because the second stage is normally unlocked through extenuating circumstances, but it can also be controlled through one's intent," Anwill explained.

I looked at him, even more confused than before. "If you ever find yourself in Caegwen, I would love to teach you more about the various stages, young one, or at least point you in the right direction until *someone else* decides they want to take over," he said cheerfully.

He knows how to unlock the other stages? Is that how Bernar knows him? Who is this someone else *he's talking about?* I felt the thoughts rush through my mind, but quickly realized I was still mid-conversation. "I would love to receive your instruction, Anwill," I said with a bow. "That's Master Anwill to you, shit-bird," Bernar retorted.

"*Waaait*, what the fu-...?" I began, more confused than ever, but was immediately cut off by Anwill's waving hand. "*Oh*, shut it, Bernar. He's your brother, and seeing as how I'm no longer the master of the Sionaer Synners, there's no reason for him to call me that. In addition, he already *has* his Master," he said playfully. "Neither of those reasons makes a whole lot of sense to me, but if you say so," Bernar shrugged.

The Master observed Garett and his archers removing life from the bodies of the remaining creatures and sighed with relief when he realized all was going well. "That finishing blow you did," he began, turning to Anwill. "What about it, *Master*?" Anwill struggled with the name again.

"I assume they didn't teach you that at Sionaer," the Master said. "They did not, Master," Anwill replied. "That I learned from a young Synner a few centuries ago. I never got his first name, only that I was supposed to call him *Pelantyr*," he continued, making the Master's eyes flare momentarily. "You're *sure* that's the name he used?" he asked curiously.

"Y-Yes. He was young, probably no older than about seventeen at the time," Anwill replied awkwardly as the Master was taken aback.

"You'll have to tell me about that later," the Master said, trying to hide the shift in his features. "Of course," Anwill bowed.

There's something Anwill knows that the Master doesn't? I wonder why the name Pelantyr had such an effect on him. He showed no sign of anything the time I asked him about it, I thought.

"We still have much to discuss," Anwill continued while Bernar was making his way over to our small group on his horse, bringing Celer along with him.

"That was one hell of a flashy kill, *shitstain*," Bernar said, dismounting his horse, handing me the reins to my own. "So was yours, but I had help," I said, gesturing to Edryd. "All I really did was blind him. Thoma did all the slicing and dicing, not to mention the other damage Roburn and Irun dealt," he shrugged.

"Well, you helped nevertheless," Bernar said with a smile. "*Eh*, It was the least I could do," Ed shrugged again, making my brother chuckle. "Master, the monsters have been slain, and we'd best be off to the fortress," Bernar said, turning to the Master who nodded and immediately signaled for the others to return. Ed whistled for his horse, hoping it hadn't met some horrible fate, but luckily, it quickly appeared from the neighboring treeline.

However, some of the other Synners or their horses had fallen in battle, and as a result, most had to walk home after having given their horses to aid the wounded.

The sun was already setting as we began our short trip back to the fortress, and it stung my eyes as its final rays beamed from behind the distant mountains.

"Anwill," the Master began. "You would like me to continue telling you about the young Synner, wouldn't you?" Anwill replied as if already knowing what he was going to ask. "If it's not too much trouble," he replied briefly.

"It is not, after all, it's the *other* reason why I've come all this way to Codrean; one I did not wish to disclose with the others present," Anwill said, getting a nod of understanding from the Master.

I later heard from Bernar that they spoke through the night until the early hours of the morning, going through a few bottles of ale, as well as a few kettles of tea.

Later that night, I lay awake in bed, reviewing the information presented throughout the day. There was almost too much to process, and I decided that while sacrificing sleep was never a good thing, it was necessary after everything.

This isn't going to end well, is it? I thought as my mind began to race.

CHAPTER 13
OF KINGS AND OUTCASTS

The Harutian army marched toward the Rhydian Pass, on their way to begin their war with Coltend.

The raven they received from their king was enough to set them on the warpath. Their dedication to him was absolute, and knowing that their king was potentially in danger only fed their anger and hatred into even further depths. It drove them over the harsh terrain of Harut, and with every step, they knew that their fates were drawing nearer.

The commander of Bashir's guard, General Ari Vest, rode at the vanguard of the three-thousand-strong army, gazing out upon the landscape in search of potential threats. Granted, it wasn't the *full* army, but it was all they could muster at a moment's notice. His armor, decorated with a bright, yellow sash, not only stated his position, but also the degree of his accomplishments in service to the king.

These vast, barren wastelands of sand and small shrubberies make up more than half of the Harutian landscape, and though we have learned to survive in such harsh conditions over the generations, they always pose a very real threat. If it weren't for these compasses, we'd certainly be lost, he thought, noticing a small sandstorm rolling in from the marching army.

"General Vest," Colonel Khaleed Messir, Ari's second in command, said, trotting up beside him. He, too, was clad in the same light armor with a red sash, riding a large brown stallion. "How much do we know about our king's predicament, sir?" the man asked.

"Unfortunately not much, Khaleed," Ari replied. "All the information about his current status is that which he wrote in his message," he continued. Khaleed grimaced. "For all we know, he could be dead by now. Pray to the gods that he isn't," Ari said grimly.

"I do not believe he would die so easily, sir. "He might have made it to the town at the foot of the mountain pass. I've brought his armor just in case we meet him there," Khaleed gestured to the tightly packed satchel on the side of his horse. "I pray that you are correct in your beliefs, Khaleed," Ari sighed.

"If the worst-case scenario becomes our new reality, what shall we do?" Khaleed leaned in to speak quietly. "We have only our duty that needs to be done: honor our king and his fallen son as best we can," Ari replied gravely.

"That will be no small task. It might very well mean our deaths," Khaleed sighed. "True. However, the fact remains that our duty calls us to do what we have sworn so many years ago. We must fight with honor and courage, and bring down the ones responsible in any way we can," Ari said with determination. Khaleed nodded his agreement and held a distant stare as he digested his commander's words.

They continued riding for the remainder of the day, reaching the town at the base of the pass by nightfall. The moonlit town was as quiet as a graveyard. Everyone was fast asleep when they arrived, readying themselves for the following day's work.

Ari, Khaleed, and twenty others rode into the small town, while most of the army camped on the outskirts. He looked for the stables and hoped at least one person would be awake to tend to their horses.

He rode up to the quiet, dimly lit stables, and a horse was frightfully awoken from its sleep by the sound of his horse's hooves. He quickly dismounted his horse and ran over to calm the to it, bringing his hand up to its nape and patting it gently. The horse responded by lowering its head into Ari's chest. "There, there, my beauty," he said softly, holding the large head.

"You are a fine horse, indeed, but you are not one from Coltend nor Caegwen," he said as the realization slowly dawned on him. He opened the stall door and checked its hind leg to find the Harutian's brand on its hide.

"You're one of ours," he said softly, squatting to get a closer look. "Khaleed, come here, quickly!" he hissed as loud as current conditions would allow him. Khaleed dismounted his horse and walked over to his captain. "What is it, sir?" he asked. "Look," Ari said, gesturing towards the brand.

"It *is* one of ours," Khaleed said with genuine surprise. "My guess is that our king managed to escape and is somewhere here in this town. We must find him immediately," Ari concluded as the pair quickly left the stable to find the stablehand.

He found him a few moments later, fast asleep in a bale of hay. "Boy, wake up," he said quietly, shaking the boy. The boy jumped at being woken up in such a manner. "W-Who are you?" he asked, rubbing his eyes. "I am General Ari Vast of King Bashir of Harut's personal guard," he replied softly. "Bashir," the boy muttered, recognizing the name overheard in a conversation with his master.

"Yes, that's his name. Do you know where he is?" Ari asked. "He's here, sir?" the boy asked. "He must be. Otherwise, there wouldn't be a horse with the brand of the Palace Guard on its hind leg," Ari said, pointing to the horse he had just examined. The boy rose and walked over to examine the horse himself.

"The rider wore a sash that covered his face and didn't give me a name, sir, but I *have* heard it before," the boy said, recalling the events of a few days prior. "Where did he go?" Ari asked. "He said that he wanted to speak with the owner of the stables, so I led him to my master, sir," the boy gestured toward the largest house.

"Can you take me there?" Ari asked with an air of urgency. "My master will be sleeping, and he doesn't appreciate being woken in the middle of the evening," the boy replied nervously. "Well, he might not like it, but he's going to have to answer me, regardless," he sneered. "Alright, sir, but don't say I didn't warn you," the stablehand said begrudgingly.

He led Ari and Khaleed down the same roads he had taken Bashir just a few days before, and came to the same wooden door. "Thank you," Ari said, handing the boy a few coins for his troubles, who nodded with a smile and went back to the stables to tend to the new batch of horses.

Ari knocked on the door, but there was no response. He tried again, and still, no response. "Shit," he said quietly. "Perhaps a stone to the window might help," Khaleed said maliciously, picking a fist-sized one up from the ground. "I'm not here to destroy anyone's property," Ari gave a disappointed sigh.

"I'm just saying we *could*; It's an option," Khaleed retorted with a shrug. "Fine, but pick a smaller one, at least. That one could take out a wild boar," Ari caved. "Probably wouldn't do *shit* to your mother, though... sir," Khaleed added playfully as his commander scoffed and shook his head.

Khaleed took a few steps back to get a better angle on his target window. He threw the stone, and it ricocheted off the window, falling back into his hands, but there was no response. He threw it again, only to be met with the same lack of response.

"We're getting nowhere with this. Let me try," Ari said, picking up a larger rock than Khaleed's. Just as the stone left his hand at a reasonable velocity, the shutters opened and the stone hit the figure that replaced them. A grunt of pain and a string of muffled curses resounded from the shadows in the window.

"I think you hit him," Khaleed chuckled nervously. "Like I knew the shutters would open at that *exact* moment," Ari shrugged and shook his head. "Who's the belligerent fuck who keeps throwing rocks at my window and disturbing my sleep?" a voice said from the shadows of the moonlight. "General Ari Vest of Bashir's personal guard," he replied.

"Ari?" the voice asked excitedly. "Your Majesty? Is that you?" he asked with equal excitement. "By the gods, it is Ari! *Haha!* I will be right with you," Bashir's figure vanished, and the shutters closed as quickly as they opened.

A few moments later, the wooden door opened, showing a blood-ied figure lit by torchlight. "I humbly apologize for striking you with a stone, Your Majesty," Ari said with a low bow, realizing it had hit him squarely in the nose. "That was one way to wake one up without strong tea. Nevertheless, I have never been so happy to see a familiar face," Bashir wiped away the tiny amount of blood still dripping from the base of his curved nose. "Forgive me, Your Majesty," Ari said humbly.

"It's quite alright. Better a stone to the nose than a sword to the back like those bastards up on the Pass. It's good to see you, my friend," Bashir said, patting Ari on the shoulder with a smile.

As he rose from his bow, Bashir, surprisingly, hugged Ari. "I thought we might have arrived too late," Ari said, astounded by the display of gratitude. "Apparently, I'm a hard man to kill," Bashir grinned.

Bashir explained the situation to his general as best as he could remember it, making both Ari and Khaleed shudder when they heard what Truls did to Bashaa. "By Yarathea, how *dare* he?" Ari seethed. "He's a madman; one that will pay dearly for killing and defiling him to such an extent," Bashir's brow was tightly knit in anger.

"I mourn the loss of Prince Bashaa, Your Majesty. He was always good to us, and carried himself well amongst the soldiers," Ari said solemnly. "You have had quite the adventure, Your Majesty. How is your physical state?" Khaleed stepped forward.

"Aside from the recent encounter with Mother Earth's emissary, I am well. It truly was a harrowing adventure to get here, however, one that I do not wish to repeat anytime soon," he shook his head. "We have brought your armor, as we were sure you might want it," Khaleed said, pointing to the stables where his horse was. "You have done well, both of you," Bashir nodded approvingly.

"Thank you, but what of the men who chased you, Your Majesty? What became of them?" Ari asked after a moment's pause. "I would imagine they're still being held captive by the elves who live there, but I don't know whether they're still alive at this point," Bashir said as he glanced toward the pass.

"*Ah*, I see those *pointy-eared* bastards are good for something after all. Well, tomorrow we'll see what became of them, Your Majesty," Ari sighed with relief. "Yes, you have ridden hard and far, you must get some rest for tomorrow," Bashir said, patting Ari's shoulder again. "I will wake the stables' owner and tell him you have come to my aid. He will allow you to stay there as long as you need," he continued, leading the others inside the large house.

Meanwhile, in Hjalfar, Anders, Unni, and the others had ridden for nearly two days with little food, and even less rest. When they were a few kilometers from their destination, they dismounted and gathered the required gear for their mission.

"Take only what you'll need, as this should be quick," Anders whispered to the others as they tied their horses to nearby trees, leaving a few guards to ensure their safety.

They moved through the trees from cover to cover, doing their best to avoid being seen or heard by anyone save the moon, stars, and other creatures who ruled the night. They arrived at Odensby with a few hours to spare before dawn, and details of the world around them could begin to be seen.

The massive castle stood proudly at the edge of a short cliff within the city's walls, making a forced entry much more difficult with its limited avenues of approach.

"This is it," Unni said to Anders, who stood next to her, hidden in the treeline that surrounded the city walls. "Archers, listen up," Anders said quietly. Take out the guards who stand watch on the eastern wall. You five over there," he pointed to a group of swordsmen clad in furs and swords.

"Follow me up the wall to ensure the alarm doesn't get rung. We're going to take out anyone who stands in our way, understand?" he asked. "Yes, sir," the men replied in unison.

Generally speaking, the outcasts and bandits don't need a leader in their day-to-day lives, but when it comes to a fight, they will always choose the one with the most battle experience to be the leader. Tonight is Anders' turn, Unni thought with a proud smile.

"Unni, you and your team will follow us North along the wall while we clear the ramparts. Only climb up once the all-clear signal is given. The rest of you will follow behind them, got it?" he asked again. "Yes, sir," Unni replied in unison with the others.

"Let's do this," he hissed, waiting for the archers to get into position.

The archers strung their bows and nocked the first arrows to them. Anders looked around to make sure everyone was ready, and under the moon's light, he gave the signal to attack. The archers crept quietly through the tall grass between them and the high walls. They hid behind trees, finding the best angles to kill the few guardsmen quickly and quietly as they approached.

As they infused their bows with a *Stil* spell to silence their arrows and bowstrings, they each drew their arrows to their cheeks and waited for Anders' signal. He dropped his hand swiftly, and the arrows soared, cutting through the air and the thin cloth around the guardsmen's necks silently.

The guards collapsed simultaneously, each choking on their own blood as they tried to call for help. "Move in!" Anders hissed to those around him before sprinting out of the treeline to the base of the high wall, preparing their grappling hooks with a *Stil* spell.

At his command, they launched their hooks to grab the thick stone edges of the wall and began to climb. As they crept over the wall and finished off any guardsmen still alive after the initial barrage of arrows, they drew their daggers and approached the guardhouse silently.

Silence these bastards, he signaled to those nearest to it.

They followed his command quickly, severing the arteries and trachea of the unsuspecting guardsmen. As the last guard fell, he signaled for Unni and her team to scale the walls. "How far north do you want us to go?" she whispered as she took his hand to help her over the remainder of the wall.

"We will continue to clear out the western side of the walls. Take your team and head along the walls until you reach the rooftops closest to Mads' tower. Once you arrive, drop your hooks down to help us scale up to you," Anders said. "You're going to use the windows to your advantage, aren't you?" Unni asked wryly, getting a grin from him in return.

"I will go in through the window to his quarters, and I'll gut him in his sleep. In the meantime, I'll need you to clear the level below us. Keep watch for any of the other guardsmen who might get curious and silence them as needed," he said quietly. "Sounds like a plan," Unni replied. "Let's go," Anders nodded, removing the hooks from the walls the rest had finished climbing over.

Each team ran along the walls, taking care to avoid being seen by any who may lurk below. Anders and his men continued to clear out the Western ramparts, as Unni and her team reached their target destination with little resistance.

"We can cut across the rooftops over here. Follow me," he whispered to his men, noticing Unni's signal to move in. No sooner were they off, jumping from rooftop to rooftop. Luckily for them, the roofs were not made of thatch but granite, the main source of income for Hjalfar.

The nearby mines made it possible for all of the houses within the city to be made almost entirely of stone. The narrow, cobblestone streets below were bereft of any living thing aside from a few rats here and there, as the entirety of Odensby was sound asleep.

Things are going smoothly. Almost too *smoothly. I feel like something's off,* Anders thought as he reached the secondary wall, which guarded the main tower of the palace.

Granted, it wasn't as *vast* as Coltend's, though it was built to last against almost any assault.

Unfortunately, Anders noticed that a handful of guards were still keeping watch on the inner wall, forcing him to halt his team and hide in the shadows.

Damn it. She should have cleared those out already, he thought before noticing her silhouette lurking on the rooftop above them.

She signaled her team to take them out in unison. The poor bastards, drinking ale around an impromptu fire they had made to keep warm, never saw the blades that struck them down. Unni dropped the hooks off the side of the wall, aiding Anders and his team as they scaled them.

"We can't have any more surprises like that," he said, helping the last man behind him. "That wasn't my fault," Unni said quietly.

"You're the one who spent all those years here, you should have been the one to remember that," she sneered. "This must have been built after I left," Anders retorted, looking around him briefly.

"Well, let's hope the only surprise left will be for Mads when he shits himself seeing you. But how the fuck do we get in there? The windows are barred shut," Unni said, analyzing the situation. "Do you still have those hooks?" he asked. "Do you have shit for brains? Yes, of course, I still have them," Unni sneered.

"If we can make it to the outer portion of the tower that faces the edge of the cliff, we should be able to get in just fine," Anders whispered to her, gesturing to an unguarded section of the tower. "You're saying they didn't fortify the windows over there?" Unni asked. "Never have. That's the last place any normal person would suspect an attack to come from," he said, patting her on the shoulder.

She blushed, but Anders didn't notice in the shadows.

"Ladies first," he said with a barely visible smile. She nodded, and had one of the women with her infuse her bow and fire a grappling hook. It landed quietly and they soon began to scale the tower, taking note which windows were the stealthiest entry points, and the positions of the guardsmen that roamed the floors.

Luckily for us, the dipshit left his window open, Anders noticed the shimmering glass gently reflecting the candle light from within Mads' room.

"This is gonna be tougher than we thought with all those guards around," Unni whispered after reaching the top. "Can't turn back now. Remember, we'll go directly into Mads' room, while your team breaches the floor below and clears the guards as quietly as you can," Anders returned.

"You should go to Mads alone," Unni shook her head, facing her leader. "What?" he raised an eyebrow. "I know how much he has taken from you. Your position. Your home. Your family," she said, shaking her head. "How much do you *actually* know about me, Unni?" Anders asked, his unfounded suspicion growing more solidified.

"Now's not the time to discuss that. Right now, you must exact your revenge on everything he has done to you. You have the *only* right to do so," she whispered, putting a hand on his shoulder as he let the words sink in. After a moment's pause, he let out a quick sigh and rubbed his watering eyes as he nodded.

They grabbed the hooked ropes and began to descend to their respective entry points, waiting for Anders' signal to begin the final portion of their assault.

Three. Two. One. Go! Anders signaled nonverbally, prompting the others to push off the wall and swing into the tower, landing inside silently.

Anders, who had gone directly into Mads' room, steadied himself and observed his surroundings. He noticed paintings of the old queen of Hjalfar, as well as the king's sons, hung up on the walls. Furs were strewn across the floor, one of which he had landed on, and hunting trophies also hung upon the walls.

The small, seldom-used desk in the corner had a few bits of parchment with indiscernible scribblings on them. It was uncommon for any royal family member to write anything in their own hand, but he couldn't afford to pay it any more attention than he already had.

The large bed at the back of the room held a single, snoring, extremely dangerous person.

Meanwhile, Unni and three others had entered the floor just below where Mads lay, quickly and quietly dispatching the guards that roamed the floor. "Let's go, we have more guards to kill," she signaled quietly to the small group.

I hope he's alright, she thought, briefly glancing at the stairs that led to the royal bedroom.

Anders crept up on the sleeping king, his blade gleaming in the light of the single candle that dimly lit the room.

My heart feels like it's about to leap out of my throat. I can hardly hear his breathing pattern. I need to slow my heartbeat, he thought, adjusting his grip on his blade and taking a slow, controlled breath.

There are two things a person feels when they are going to kill. The first is a strong kick in the gut of adrenaline, making one's pupils enlarge and muscles twitch rapidly. The second is the realization of sending another's soul into the afterlife, be it an animal, monster, or another *human*.

The problem is that, sometimes, the second part doesn't come until long after the deed is done, which is where most mistakes are made, Anders thought, recalling his old master's lessons as he continued to quietly creep across the room, his grip tightening around his blade that nearly hummed with hunger for its next kill.

Unni, still downstairs, removed her blade from the last guardsman whose blood now made the floor slick and shiny, watching the stairs for any unwelcome guests. She motioned for the others to cross the hall and get into position in case of an attack, as she proceeded upstairs to the front door to Mads' room.

She silently opened the door, seeing the murderous, hateful look on Anders' face, and the blissful ignorance of the sleeping king.

Anders! It's time to finish this, Unni gestured, waving her hand to catch his attention. Anders snapped out of his small trance, blinking rapidly as he watched her repeat the gesture.

Mads stirred a little under his covers, and Anders nearly became one with the bear-fur carpet beneath him. A few silent and tense heartbeats later, Anders stood at the side of the bed, observing every detail of Mads' face.

He still looks the same as he did all those years ago, he thought, steadying his hand that was shaking with almost uncontrollable rage.

He put his blade to Mads' throat, and covered his mouth with his free hand, startling the sleeping king as he emitted muffled calls for help in vain. "*Shh,*" Anders hushed the man, his eyes downcast as if imperiously looking at an insect. "*No one is coming to save you now. Isn't that what you told my wife and child all those years ago?*" he seethed, cocking his head to the side. Mads' eyes opened wide, as he recognized the one with the cold blade to his bare throat.

"*Ah,* so you do remember me. I can see it in your eyes, but do you remember what you did? Do you remember the things that not even the most *loving* of the gods could ever forgive you for? Because I do, and like them, I'm not here to offer you forgiveness," Anders seethed, adding a bit more pressure to the blade.

The king's eyes widened as he tried to scramble out of his predicament, causing the blade to draw a line of blood across his neck.

"You took everything from me. You murdered my wife, my child, and the one unborn. You stomped on her stomach while she lay with a knife in her throat, and our child's head in her hands on the ground in front of you," Anders growled, holding down one of the flailing arms with a knee.

"Your guards held me as I watched it all happen. You laughed as you spat in her face and pissed into her gaping mouth, calling her a *worthless whore* as you did so. You chained me up, beat me to little more than a bloody mound of living flesh, and cut off two of the fingers of the hand that now holds a blade to your throat," he seethed, glaring at the trembling man.

Tears welled in his eyes and ran down his cheeks into his beard. "You deserve a much more painful punishment than death, but unfortunately, I don't have the time or the patience to work that all out. I've already spent over *ten years* dreaming of this day that I never thought would come," he said, causing Mads to squirm as Anders struggled to keep his hand over his enemy's mouth.

"You will not see the light of day, and you will become the plaything of the Undergod. There, you shall suffer for all eternity, and I will finally be at peace knowing that I have put you there," Anders quickly, pushing his face in close to make sure he could see every fragment of life leave Mads' eyes.

Surprisingly, Mads raised a hand to show that he wanted to speak. "You really think you're in a position to negotiate?" Anders sneered, but Mads shook his head to tell Anders he only wanted to say something before the end. "One scream, or anything louder than a whisper, and I'll do the same thing you did to my wife while you're still alive," he seethed.

Mads nodded and gingerly pried the hand away from his mouth. "I know an apology won't save me now," Mads said, his voice trembling and breaking. "You're right about *that*," Anders seethed, still holding the blade to his throat.

"I know what I have done, and I know that I must atone for it. I always knew that it wasn't you who had failed to guard my wife and children during their pilgrimage; but the one responsible for that failure fled after they were attacked on Hviten Path, never to be found," Mads explained shakily.

"Y-You knew it wasn't me?" Anders asked, his whole world falling apart with the words he was hearing. "I did," Mads replied solemnly, causing Anders to blink away tears that streamed down his face. "Why?" Anders growled, gripping his victim's shirt and pulling him up towards his face.

"Why did you have my family suffer for the fault of another? Why did you have to pull the rug out from under *my world*? Why did you have to make me beg for death every day since then?" Anders asked angrily.

Mads was silent.

"Answer me, you slimy weasel shit," Anders commanded. "Alright, alright," Mads conceded, raising his hands placatingly. "My councilmen told me that an example needed to be made to ensure that no other man under my command would ever betray their honor and allegiance to Hjalfar again," he began.

"What?" Anders asked, incredulous at what he was hearing. "It's true. I chose you, the one man I knew that everyone knew I trusted above almost all others aside from my wife. I wanted it to be known that no matter one's station or status, one was never above their honor and duty," Mads said regretfully.

"So you chose me? A man who, until that time, had never wavered in his loyalty and had earned his way to his status through pure effort? A man whose life had *such value* to you?" Anders asked, growing increasingly enraged. "Yes," Mads replied in a shaky voice. Anders' face was wet with tears.

"You dragged me through the deepest depths of the Underworld simply to prove a point. Gods above and below. No, no, no... I don't care about your sob story. Knowing what I know now, I almost wish *I had been* the one who murdered your family, you *mangy fuck*! I have never, and *will never* forgive you for what you did to me," Anders growled as drool fled from his gritted teeth.

"I know," Mads replied, looking up at him with a placid, accepting look in his eyes.

"Do it. Take what is rightfully yours, I have no qualms or arguments remaining that could ever hope to spare me. However, before I leave this world, I must ask you one final favor," he continued. "And why should I hear anything more of what you have to say?" Anders said coldly as Mads looked deeply into his eyes, seeing nothing but the embodiment of the purest hatred.

"Because if there's one thing I've learned in all my years, it is this: the council of others is, more often than not, in the benefit of their own ambitions. So choose your allies carefully. Remember that," Mads nodded. "I already have," Anders replied in the same, cold tone. "Not carefully enough," Mads retorted.

"What...?" Anders asked, confused by his words, but before the king could answer, a hand forced the blade into his throat. "Unni!" Anders raised his voice as he stared at her in confusion. "You were taking too long. We have to go," she urged, noting one of her teammates standing in the doorway.

His blade sank deeply into Mads' throat as blood flowed from the wound, drenching the pillow beneath it. He watched the life ebb from the eyes that stared at him for a moment and removed his knife, taking a deep breath.

"Anders," Unni whispered from the doorway, but he turned to face her with bloodshot eyes. She finally noticed the toll it had taken on him and rushed over to him, taking him in her arms, where he sobbed for a few moments.

"It's over," she said softly. The words felt like a warm bath coming over him as he looked into her eyes. "Thank you for everything, Unni," he said between sniffles. "I couldn't have done this without you," he grabbed her hand.

"I know,, but we must go now, the other guards will be taking their shifts any minute now, and when they find the dead bodies, it will not end well for us," she hushed urgently as he nodded.

"Let's go home," she said, helping him to his feet. "Wait," he held up a hand as he walked over to the desk and grabbed a quill and some parchment. "What are you doing?" she hissed. "Setting an example," he leaned over and began to write.

I, Anders Karlsson, ex-Synner of Odensby and all her glory, have slain the king for dishonorable deeds he has done in the past against myself and other innocent people whom I held dear. Let this be an example to all of those who wish to hunt me down, for this shall be your end should you find me. Soon, I will return to this place when I am ready to rule, and if a single hint of disrespect is shown to me, or any of my comrades, I will kill you myself, he wrote in shaky handwriting before using his blade to pin it to the dead man's chest.

Daylight was on the horizon, and the outcasts observed the guards entering the main palace to take their shifts from the walls where their hooks were prepared for their escape. "One day, we shall return to finish the job; to rule Odensby," Anders said, looking out over the city.

"One day, we'll finish taking it back for ourselves, and regain the lives we once had," he said, turning to Unni. She smiled, grabbed the rope, and began her descent, while he took one last look over the dimly lit city.

And that day will come soon. Wait, what's that dust cloud doing on top of the Rhydian Mountains? That can't be good, he thought before grabbing the hooked rope and descending the wall.

Daybreak arrived and Bashir awoke to the sound of a rooster just outside the window of Ahkmed's home. He rubbed his eyes when he got out of his bed, put on the armor that had been laid out for him the previous evening, and proceeded downstairs to meet with Ari, who was already gathering the others to prepare to march over the Rhydian Pass.

"Good morning, Your Majesty," Ari bowed when Bashir approached, his arms clasped behind his back. "A beautiful day for revenge, isn't it?" he replied idly, observing the red tinge in the morning sky. "A bloody sky in the morning bodes well for those who ride on the path to glory and honor," Ari said with a smile.

"That must be something you warriors say amongst yourselves, for I have never heard of such a thing," Bashir chuckled. "Perhaps, but that doesn't make it any less true, Your Majesty. Although many of our soldiers have probably forgotten all about it, since it's been over a *decade* since our last battle," Ari scoffed lightly.

"I see. Well, that is not always a bad thing, is it? Many families have been spared the loss of loved ones, I'm sure," Bashir said, patting Ari on his shoulder. "Indeed they have, Your Majesty. Bring our king his horse!" Ari shouted behind him, while Bashir gazed out over the three thousand battle-ready men under the red sky.

"You were right, Ari. I had forgotten how a large army can make a man tremble excitedly," he said breathlessly. "Unfortunately, this was all I could summon on such short notice, but I'm glad they still make you feel that way, Your Majesty," Ari joined him to look out over the army.

One of the soldiers brought Bashir's horse, with a fine, leather saddle, and a white and violet sash tied to its side. "Your horse, Your Majesty," the soldier bowed, handing the reins to Bashir. "Where is Hatal? The one that brought me here, where is he?" he asked, looking around the general to see if he was still in the stables. "You do not want *your* horse?" Ari asked, genuinely confused.

"Hatal might be tired from the harrowing journey here, but he's a hero nonetheless. Do I need to repeat myself, or have you simply forgotten the value of a hero?" Bashir raised an eyebrow, prompting Ari to quickly follow his order without further question.

Moments later, Hatal was brought out from the stables, his new saddle fit perfectly. Bashir noticed the horse trotted happily, as if giddy with excitement.

I've always wondered whether they felt emotions as we do. I guess that answers my question, he thought, smiling as he watched Hatal stamp his feet on the ground happily.

"He looks like one of the horses from the tales of old, my lord," Ari said, smiling as he watched the horse's trot. "He really is a fine horse indeed," Bashir replied, taking the reins from the soldier who walked him, patting Hatal's strong neck.

He placed his foot in the stirrup and swung his right leg over to the other side. After adjusting his riding position, he looked out over the sea of men who did the same as he did. "Men, we ride to Coltend! May our forefathers bear witness!" he shouted, and there was a roar in response.

Bashir stuck his heels into Hatal's sides and led his men to the foot of the Rhydian mountains. On the way up the trail, he recalled the flight he had made, and could swear he saw a few of Hatal's large hoof prints in the dirt beneath him.

I fled for my life in fear of being hunted down and slaughtered like my son. Now I am no longer the hunted, but the hunter, he thought.

The sun was now stronger on their backs than it had been when they began their march as they reached the top of the Pass. "This sun will be to our advantage. It will blind them, making them easy targets for our archers, avoiding the bloodshed of our own men, Your Majesty," he continued.

"Do not forget about the elven rebels, Ari. They might not be as welcoming as we hope they are," Bashir cautioned, getting a nod of understanding from the general. They reached the top of the Pass and turned the corner only to find a small camp placed in the middle of the way, a short distance from the body of an ice troll, with a foul stench ruling the air.

Bashir and Ari cast their eyes on the beast, and noticed the pile of stripped bodies - some of them missing limbs, while others were little more than mounds of rotting flesh. "That ice troll must have been the cause of that," Bashir said to Ari, who was still observing the ice troll's dead body. "The elves must be watching the encampment. It would be best not to get too close, Your Majesty," Ari said as Bashir dismounted his horse and walked over to the troll's body.

He noticed the point of an arrow sticking out of the beast's skull. He broke it off from its shaft and wiped the rotting brain matter off of it. "It's of elvish make," he said, showing it to Ari, who looked around him, hoping to see one of them. "In the name of King Bashir Ibn'Escea of Harut, come forth," Ari shouted.

A man from the camp came out from one of the small tents pitched on the far end of the pass. "That's him," Bashir said, pointing to Gorm, still in full gear. "Have you returned to die like a dog to its vomit?" Gorm shouted.

"Do not speak to the king in that tone," Ari shouted back. Gorm turned his head to Ari, who was still on his horse. "And who might you be to command me in that tone of voice? His personal, pox-ridden bitch? You don't scare me, boy," Gorm retorted angrily.

"I am Ari Vast, Commanding General of the Harutian Royal Guard, loyal servant of our great king," Ari replied. "Well, that's a fancy name and title for little more than a *boot-licker*," Gorm shouted back. "How dare you?" Ari snarled.

"Ari, until we have a location on the elves, do not attack, understand?" Bashir said quietly, making Ari sigh deeply. "Very well, but he will pay for what he said," he said, glaring at Gorm. "All in good time," Bashir replied.

"Gorm, was it?" he turned to face the captain. "That's the name I was given at birth, so yes," Gorm replied. "Gorm of what, might I ask?" he smiled, trying to maintain a semblance of diplomacy. "Just *Gorm*," the man replied curtly. "Such disrespect for a king. Did your parents not educate you at all? Gods, for all I know, your name was probably written in the remains of a *cocksneeze* that dripped off your mother's face," Ari shouted, growing increasingly enraged at the man's disrespect for his king.

Gorm furrowed his brow and bared his teeth like he was ready for a good fight.

"Silence, Ari! Compose yourself," Bashir snapped, making the man flinch. Ari was about to protest, but he waved him off as he began to walk toward the Coltendian captain, who responded by doing the same.

"There are elves all around us," Bashir gestured to the rocks that lined the Pass. "I know. They ambushed us just after we had arrived at the top of the Pass, and killed a few of my men. Then came that monstrosity you see lying before you, lifeless and numb to all things save decay," Gorm replied as Bashir looked down at the ice troll, admiring its crystalline armor.

"I see. Where are the elves, exactly?" he asked solemnly. "Everywhere and nowhere you try to find them," Gorm said. "That's not very helpful," Bashir replied. "Their leader, Gwili, has taken it upon himself to make us his prisoners, and so we're here awaiting our inevitable, slow deaths," Gorm said gravely. "Or perhaps something worse," Bashir replied.

He knew what the elves were capable of, and knew exactly what happened to many unsuspecting travelers who crossed their paths. Bashir looked up at the rock where Gwili once stood.

"Perhaps up there, I shall get a better view of what lies around us," he said. "That's where he stood, so I guess it's a decent spot," Gorm shrugged and uncouthly spat as Bashir passed and climbed the large rock.

He was a little short of breath when he reached its peak, but noted upon a trail that he had never seen before. He looked carefully, trying to see if he could find any shapes or colors that did not occur naturally.

His eyes caught the tip of a curved shape with a string tied tautly to it.

"Gwili! I know you and your men are here, so step forth and let us decide what is to be done," he shouted. There was rustling amongst the small bushes that lay about, and one by one, the elves began to appear. Bashir descended from his vantage point and made his way to the center of the pass.

"Not so well hidden after all," Gorm said with a grin. "Shut your trap," Gwili said, punching Gorm in the face. Gorm put a finger to his nose and saw that the blow caused blood to run out of his nostrils. "*Heh*, didn't know you had it in you to beat an unarmed prisoner, you pointy-eared *cuckold*," he spat the blood that ran down the back of his throat.

"Gentlemen," Bashir said, holding his hands up in an attempt to prevent a violent breakout. "We stand here atop the pass on this magnificent morning, let us converse first before we trade blows," he said calmly. "Talk *then* hit? What kind of stupid tactic is that?" Gwili spread his arms as he scoffed.

"Politics," Bashir replied with a grin. "Now, the situation, from what I gather, is as follows: Gorm wants my head for he wishes to regain his queen's honor, while you, Gwili, wish for their goods and armor, and I simply want to pass through to avenge my murdered son," he began. "*Wow*, your powers of deduction are truly superb,

King Dipshit," Gorm said with a bow in jest which Bashir shrugged off.

"Now, this can go one of three ways: The first being we all kill each other until the last man, although I find it rather hard to believe that only a few men can take on the army I have behind me," he gestured behind him, making Gorm's eyes grow wide.

"The second is that my army and I pass through, while the elves deal with their prisoners in any way they see fit," he continued. "And what of my honor as a knight?" Gorm asked with a snarl as he stepped forward, making Ari nearly draw his blade.

"I care greatly about one's honor, and if you had only shut your mouth, you would hear the third way we could play this out," Bashir snapped, silencing the captain.

This son of a bitch, Gorm spat.

"For the third and final option, I propose a duel between Captain Gorm and General Ari; seeing as how he is so willing to disembowel you," Bashir said, gesturing to Ari, who breathed heavily. "Should my man win, the elves may do what they like with you and the remainder of your hunting party. Should you win, we would then strip you of your armor, giving it to the ever-so-patient elves, and take you as our temporary prisoners back to Coltend, where you belong," he continued.

"And then what? You're going to kill us anyway," Gorm said angrily. "I find it hard to believe you have already forgotten that I care greatly for one's honor," Bashir shook his head. "We would not kill you. Well, at least not immediately, anyway. You would have the chance to rearm and recover from your ordeal, gather your men and face us on the battlefield that is to be your great city," he continued, spreading his arms wide.

"A fine way for a *knight of honor* to die, don't you agree?" he continued. Gwili remained silent, pleased that two of the three options spelled success for him, while Gorm mentally went over the possibilities for a moment. After a small amount of thought, he finally looked back at Bashir.

"I accept the duel between myself and General Piss-ass," Gorm said with an evil-looking grin aimed at Ari. "Excellent! Ready yourselves, men!" Bashir raised his arms.

Gwili whistled a bird call, and an elf brought Gorm's longsword, handing it to him, immediately feeling comfort in having it again. Ari drew his large scimitar with intricate details carved into the pommel and ivory handle. He pulled the tie that held his shield and grabbed it firmly, as they approached each other carefully.

"Let the duel begin!" Bashir commanded loudly.

CHAPTER 14

DISSONANCE

On the night of the raid in Odensby, a raven landed on its designated perch in the tallest tower of the citadel in Valdis.

Its caw echoed through the ravenry as the Masked One approached it to remove the contents from its pouch. He looked into its dark eyes briefly, subduing its natural tendency to bite anything that came too close. It clacked its beak a few times before turning toward him, enabling him to remove the contents from the pouch.

After removing the contents from the pouch, he gently ran his fingers over the top of the raven's head, making it tilt back as he scratched just behind its hidden ear.

Everything is going to plan, my lord. We will commence our attack tonight and prepare for your arrival, he read, immediately disintegrating it with mana.

"You have traveled far and brought me good news, dark one. Here's a gift for your troubles," he said, producing a small treat from his pocket, which it graciously took. He gave it a few more pats before turning to leave the ravenry.

"Karak," he called out once he reached the bottom of the stairs that led to the vast array of creature nests. "Yes, my lord?" Karak asked after dropping from the platform behind him, leaving a small trail of drool drops in his wake as he landed. "Have you received word from the outcasts?" the mage asked, walking between the main row of the breeding ground.

"I have, my lord. According to our informant, they're launching their assault on Odensby tonight," Karak replied with an unseen bow. "Good. What of our Harutian allies? Have they sent anything since their last communication?" the mage asked, idly feeding one of the younger creatures. "They have not, my lord. The Harutians have been quiet for some time, though I suspect they're still in the final stages of preparation," Karak said.

"Are you sure about that?" the Masked One turned toward the daemon. "Not entirely, my lord. After the incident with Bashaa, our informant suggested that they may be preparing to retaliate," Karak replied with a bow, causing the mage to sigh in frustration. "Those damned fools. I can't believe I once considered them to be a valuable asset," he shook his head and turned back to what he was doing.

"Even if they retaliate in full and manage to reach the castle, it will be quite a challenge to fully break Coltend's defenses, my lord. Their walls are thick, their steel strong, and their guards are well-trained. Can they really accomplish what you've asked of them?" Karak asked, genuinely concerned, but his master did not turn to face him.

"I don't believe that Coltend will give itself up so easily, no. They will likely lose many people during their portion of the fight, but I will break any and all who remain," the Masked One replied. "With the horde we have created, it should not be too difficult to accomplish our portion of the task," he continued, turning to inspect one of the infant ice trolls briefly.

"I do, however, share your concerns for *that woman*. After all, she has only aligned herself with us out of fear, as one should in the face of overwhelming power, just like that old man," he sneered at the thought as Karak chuckled maliciously.

"Did you not give him a small portion of your power, my lord?" the daemon asked. "I did, though how well he uses it is entirely up to him. In any case, it is often good to make even the crudest tools feel useful. Even if he *does fail*, it will not hinder us too greatly," the Masked One said confidently.

"The crystals to control the horde are also complete, and the strength we hold in numbers alone will be able to overwhelm the capital entirely," the Masked one said proudly as they began to walk toward the summoning circle. As they passed the cages, a handful of creatures grew restless with their presence, forcing him to send out a burst of mana to establish his dominance over them.

"Your horde has grown strong, my lord; they will serve their purpose well, it seems," Karak noted, nearly choking from the weight of the mana in the air. "We can only hope so, Karak. At this point, there are still too many outside factors to consider that we cannot afford to fully ignore," the mage replied, pushing open the large door to the summoning room, revealing a vast quantity of different-sized crystals that hummed with violet mana.

"Speaking of outside factors, there are a few things I've been forced to take into consideration, which is why I'll need your help to subdue the creatures while I implant the crystals into them," the Masked One said, drawing a handful to him with tendrils of mana and holding them aloft before the daemon.

"Y-You would have *me* assist you with this, my lord? It is an honor," Karak said with audible surprise before putting a claw across his chest and bowing. "While I *could* do it on my own, it would be much more efficient to have a second set of hands that can control the creatures while Athar is busy training," the mage began, closely analyzing one of the crystals.

"Besides, we have over *ten thousand* to work on, and I fear the toll it would take on him would be too great for him to handle," he continued, satisfied with the crystal's quality and gathering even more before returning to the cages just outside.

Karak followed closely behind, and with a massive pulse of his master's mana that reached every creature's core, they began to implant the smaller crystals into the foreheads of those still within the cages. They worked through the night until just before dawn at a speed that would have made Athar dizzy had he been there to see it.

"What of the Ochelons, my lord? What are we going to do with them?" Karak gestured to the massive creatures in their cage a few meters from their position. "Those will serve as the crystal bearers. They'll be the ones to pull the massive crystals imbued with my mana that will control the others. This way, I won't have to exhaust myself by trying to control each one individually," the Masked One replied with a satisfied grin beneath his mask.

"An excellent plan, my lord," Karak nodded understandingly. "Indeed. Come, I will require your assistance for these as well, since these ones tend to dislike being subjugated," the mage said as he walked over to the front of the first large cage.

The ochelon stood on its hind legs and snarled as he got closer. The Masked One grinned beneath his mask as his eyes glowed intensely and a large tendril of mana brought it to its knees. Karak quickly entered the cage with a crystal in hand and leaped high into the air, landing atop the creature's broad shoulders.

With a single claw, he made a deep incision into the creature's forehead, spilling blood into the thick fur that surrounded it. He buried the crystal just beneath the surface of its skin, causing the creature to roar in pain and try to swipe at him with a large claw.

The Masked One countered the blow with his mana, holding the tree trunk-sized arms in place with a grunt of exertion. Karak finished his work with the crystal and quickly leaped off the creature, landing deftly on the ground and scurrying out of the cage.

Pushing his mana into the crystal, the mage watched as a thin sheen of violet mana quickly spread and dissipated across the ochelon's body. "That's one, my lord," Karak said, observing the ochelon as the Masked One's spell took control of its body with a satisfied, toothy grin.

After the better part of an hour, they'd completed their task, but even the Masked One felt the mental exhaustion beginning to take over. He drank a vial of the deathmold solution, turning his face away from Karak as he did so.

"Why do you hide your face, my lord?" the daemon asked curiously. "Karak, as much as I trust you, I will not discuss that. Not now; not ever," the mage sighed. "As you wish, my lord," he bowed, but was immediately surprised when a vial of the solution appeared before him.

"Drink that. It's from your *homeland*, after all," the mage said as the daemon regarded the vial with widened eyes. "Thank you, my lord," Karak said humbly, bowing a little deeper before he drank the contents, accidentally spilling some out of the corners of his wide mouth. He wiped the spilled liquid off with his forearm and handed the vial back to his master, which he placed into a pocket of his cloak.

"*Ah,* the taste of death itself. I'd almost forgotten what it was like," Karak said, licking the remaining fluid off his forearm.

How long did that take? Four, maybe five hours? Dawn must be approaching soon, the mage thought.

"We must prepare to leave," the Masked One said urgently. "Take a crystal to aid you and gather the ones from the cages downstairs," he commanded. "Even the addia, my lord?" Karak asked. "Yes. I know you hate their kind, but it will play a vital role in the coming days," his master said sternly.

I'd rather not do this, but if that's what my savior wishes... the daemon's thoughts trailed off as he accepted his fate.

"Very well, my lord," Karak said dejectedly. He knew just how dangerous they were, and took a crystal with him as he went downstairs to the large cages. He released the creatures within and held the crystal high into the air. One by one, he noticed that even the largest of ochelons succumbed to his will, and was pleased that it had worked as his master said it would.

Finally, he walked over to the addia's cage. "I know you're in there, so come on out," he said. He looked down at the crystal, still emitting the dark glow. He pointed it at the cage, breaking the addia's camouflage just enough for it to become visible.

Its dark brown skin dimly reflected the chamber's light, while its glowing eyes were fixated on the crystal. Karak unlocked the cage and stepped back. The addia followed him as he walked back, as did the other beasts he had already unleashed.

Even though I am a powerful daemon and *using the crystal to control it, these creatures are not to be underestimated,* Karak thought, keeping his eyes fixed on the addia, as it could still very well be unpredictable.

The two long tentacles that protruded out of the sides of its face were draped atop its long body. Its legs were muscular and shiny like the rest of it. Its paws with their retractable claws made it a truly terrifying beast to gaze upon. "You will follow me. All of you," Karak said in a commanding voice, getting a collection of grunts, growls, and gurgles from the creatures in response before they followed him out of the fortress.

Meanwhile, Athar was outside preparing the large griffin for his master's arrival. "There, there. He'll be here soon," he stroked its neck feathers gently, ensuring to stay clear of its beak entirely. The elder griffin, whose black feathers and beak shimmered in the twilight, was led by the reins to the massive courtyard just outside the main tower.

The Masked One approached him, with a few pairs of ochelons dragging massive crystals behind them to assist with the mass-broadcasting of the spell. "Your mount is ready, my lord, though he did seem a little disgruntled that *I* was the one who woke him," Athar said, handing the reins to his master.

"Griffins are extremely attached to their masters, so that doesn't surprise me in the least," the mage said with what Athar might have confused for a chuckle. "That makes sense. I was a little hesitant to try to lead it here when I woke it up because it gave me a distrusting glare," he chuckled nervously.

"How did you even come across such a magnificent beast like this?" Athar asked, giving the griffin a final pat and then bowing to it in respect. "I saved him from an addia's den nearly three centuries ago," the Masked One said nonchalantly.

"Addias *eat* griffins?" Athar's jaw dropped. "Not always, but if a young giffin lands in the wrong location, it's not unlike an addia to hunt down anything that strays too close to its den," he shrugged just before mounting the creature.

"Have you given it a name?" Athar asked after a moment's pause. "His name is *Onyxe*, but I wasn't the one who gave it to him; he gave me his name as a gesture of trust," the mage replied, as the griffin ruffled its feathers in response to hearing its name. "*Onyxe*," Athar said in a dreamlike state with a warm smile on his face as the griffin looked at him with a single eye and nodded.

Can it understand human speech? Athar's eyes widened for a moment before he returned the nod.

A moment later, he heard the horde making their way from the dungeons over the long bridge that led to the citadel. Karak was at the head of the formation with a pair of royal ochelons dragging a massive crystal behind them. The aura surrounding it and the chains caused it to levitate a meter off the ground as they walked, preventing any damage from reaching it.

"My lord, am I going with you to Coltend?" Athar asked. "No. You must remain here and assist Karak in ensuring that no careless adventurer enters, as well as continue your studies," the Masked One commanded. "Very well, my lord. I wish you success in your mission," he said formally and bowed, returning to the citadel.

The mage looked ahead, giving Onyxe a gentle pat on its neck. "Are you ready, old friend?" he whispered, getting an excited screech in response. As he watched, the horde halted behind them at Karak's command. The daemon quickly sped to his side, nearly startling the large, black griffin.

"They await your command, my lord," Karak said, handing him the crystal he'd used to lead them there. "Keep an eye on Athar while I'm gone. We'll be back in a few days if all goes as it should," the Masked One said, taking the crystal from the daemon's claws and placing it into a socket in the saddle in front of him. "As you wish, my lord," Karak bowed and disappeared from sight.

The socketed crystal pulsed with mana and enveloped Onyxe in a thin sheen of violet mana before dissipating, getting an uncomfortable shudder from the creature beneath him.

I probably should have warned him that was going to happen, he thought as he pulled back on the reins to turn and face the horde.

"We will go through the mountains to the Rhydian Pass to Coltend Castle. You will not falter, yield, or surrender until our task is complete!" the Masked One commanded, his voice emanating mana that resonated with the crystals embedded into the creatures, causing them to glow.

There was a unified roar from them, each one emitting their own form of a war cry or challenge, rippling the air along the length of the bridge.

"To war!" the Masked One shouted, turning Onyxe around and prompting him to beat his enormous wings, lifting them high into the air with a single move. Athar looked behind him and could feel nothing short of awe at how well his master's plan was working as they followed him out of the large gate at the end of the bridge.

Meanwhile, in Coltend, Leona lay fast asleep and was suddenly woken by the sound of screams and swords clashing. She got out of bed, half dazed, and put on a thick robe, tying its drawstrings around her thin waist. Screams and cries for help could be heard coming from beyond her door, but she couldn't identify the cause from where she was.

She quickly rushed to unbolt her door and opened it, the cries growing louder and louder as she proceeded down the cold stone steps. She cautiously peered out from around the corner of the stairway leading to the throne room and gasped at what she saw.

Bloodied bodies glistened in the torchlight of the vast hall before her. She did all she could not to unleash a projectile stream of bile at the mere sight of them.

By the Graces, what the hell happened here? Are we under attack? she asked herself.

She took another look at the large hall and found hooded figures, clad in black robes, running about and chasing the servants down the other hallways and out the doors. Their screams pierced her ears, and she felt a wave of fear for her own life come over her.

Suddenly, out of the left side of the large hall, a small girl burst into the hall at a full run, and came in Leona's direction.

Meliss! Thank the Graces, she's still alive, she thought, watching her run as fast as she could, dodging a hooded figure or two along the way.

When she was about to enter the stairway that led to the royal bedroom, Leona stepped out and grabbed her, pulling her close. "Leo-!" Meliss began to say, but was cut short by the hand muffling her mouth. "*Shh*, it's alright. I've got you," Leona said as comfortingly as she could while trying to hide her own fear, and be strong for both their sakes.

"Thank the gods you're alive! What happened here?" she asked, hoping for an answer that she did not already suspect. Meliss took a moment to catch her breath, but was still shaking with fear in her eyes. "I-I was finishing up some of the dishes in the kitchen when I heard a clunking sound coming from the hallway. When I approached the door to see what was happening, all I could see were the hooded people stabbing one of the guardsmen repeatedly," she said in a hushed voice, her voice trembling as she spoke.

"By the Graces, who would do such a thing?" Leona asked. "I-I don't know. They seem to have come out of nowhere. O-Or maybe they were already inside the palace? I-I don't know," Meliss stammered and shook her head.

There was no warning, so it was likely the latter, Leona thought momentarily while Meliss gulped down a breath.

"The only thing I do know is that they wanted to kill me, too. I ran away from them as quickly as I could, but no matter where I went, there were always more of them," she explained with tears streaming down her cheeks.

Shit, that means that whoever's responsible for this attack must have known the guardsmen's locations and shift patterns, Leona thought.

The hooded figures in the main hall were landing finishing blows on their prey, coating the ground in a sheen of blood. They finished off the last servant in their group and began to search for more targets. They caught a glimpse of Leona trying to hide from them, and began to walk towards the two women with a malicious cackle.

Here they come, she thought, putting herself in front of Meliss.

"I'll handle this," she said quietly, pushing her gently to the side as she cried and clutched Leona's robes tightly. The figures gathered and continued walking towards the pair, whispering words that either of the women couldn't decipher.

Leona, taking the initiative, stepped out from her hiding spot. "I will not ask you who you are, since you do not wish to be known, and asking you would be pointless. The only thing I'll demand from you as your *Queen* is that you tell me *why*," she said loudly.

I can still hear people screaming in the distance. This will not end soon, will it? she thought.

The figures stopped as though she had touched a nerve, but continued to approach her, starting to form a line and trap the two. "Why do you slay innocent people who have been nothing but loyal to Coltend and its people?" she asked, growing increasingly enraged when they said nothing.

"You cowardly, spineless, and maidenless *cunts*! Answer my questions or I will have your *balls* dragged through miles of broken glass, just for me to cut them off and feed them to your mothers!" she shouted as spit flew from her mouth.

Meliss looked out from underneath Leona's arm and saw the hooded figures continue to approach the two of them, unfazed by her words. Out of the back of the large hall came a hunched, hooded figure.

It moved slowly, like an old man just getting out of bed on a cold morning. It stopped when it had reached a point where the other figures stood midway between it and the queen.

"*Oh*, Leona. Empty threats in the face of death make you look weak. It is unbecoming of you," the decrepit figure said from under his large hood. "You ask us why we do this, and yet *fail* to see the obvious," the figure continued, grinning maliciously. "Enlighten me, then," Leona furrowed her brow as she held Meliss back.

The hooded figure let out a slow, self-satisfied chuckle before raising his arms. "Very well. There comes a time when all things must come to an end. You, me, the others around us here, citizens, civilizations, and lifestyles; they *all* end. Your time of reign, short as it may have been, has run its course, for a new power will rise in your stead," the voice said.

"If my kingdom and I are to be usurped in such a manner, I would at least like to know who *you* are. I care not about the rest," Leona said. The hunched figure halted, cocked his head, then began to emit another raspy chuckle laced with malice. He pulled back his hood to reveal his true wrinkled face with gray eyes.

"Why, if it isn't Father *fucking* Mourtis; the sack-less, predatory, *un-palatable* bastard himself. Progenitor of the Church of Mideia, and lover of *little boys*," Leona spat uncouthly as she finished. "My, my! What *unladylike* behavior," Mourtis clicked his tongue, the malicious grin persisting on his face.

"I have no reason to behave like a *lady* in front of someone as disgusting as you," she sneered, getting a slight shift in his expression as a result. "How could you do this? The Church and your faith should not allow you to take the lives of these innocent people," she growled.

"*Innocent? Faith?* What the fuck could you possibly know about either of those two things?" Mourtis gritted his teeth. "You, who so readily lay with another man other than your husband, betrayed your loyalty to him and the others around you? No, no. You don't have the *right* to speak to me about innocence. Your lack of it also happened to get Prince Bashaa killed, or have you already forgotten that?" he spat, making Leona's eyes flare angrily.

"How *dare* you...?" she furrowed her brow and clenched her fist tightly to where her nails began to draw blood. "If you truly believed in the goodness of others and followed your faith, then you would not have committed such a heinous act. Not only did you betray your beliefs, but you also betrayed your country," he continued.

"Preaching your beliefs as you slaughter the innocent; you're just a hypocrite, after all," she scoffed. "I may be a hypocrite in your eyes, but this entire *continent* will soon pay for its transgressions, just as you will pay for yours," he snarled. "What?" she asked coldly.

"You see, Leona, neither you *nor* this continent know anything of faith or innocence. After all, how *could you* when you don't understand what's coming?" Mourtis asked, prompting her to gesture around the room. "And I suppose *this* is your display of your so-called *faith*?" she asked in disbelief.

"In a sense, yes. The *faith* you know and once held dear is but a plague on this world; a perfectly rotten mechanism to control the masses through ignorance and fear. That faith demands tithes and prayers to a higher power that couldn't give *two shits* about them nor how that faith is executed. However, *my faith* lies in what comes after this wretched world has suffered for its actions," Mourtis grinned, his tone laced with malice.

"What the hell are you talking about?" Leona asked with a confused look. "Do you believe Mideia will be the one to bring perdition? If you saw what I've seen, and beheld the true power that lurks beneath the surface, you wouldn't be so quick to judge *me* for my actions," he spread his arms.

"*That's* your justification for being so quick to deal out death and judgment? By the Graces, you really are insane," she shook her head. "It was something I was loath to accept at first, as I truly believed Mideia would be the one to descend upon this Realm. Unfortunately for *you,* and everyone else who fails to see the wretchedness of this world, Mideia is not the herald of change I've long since awaited," Mourtis shrugged.

"No, Leona. The new age that *he* will bring about will change the face of this Continent *forever*, bathing it in death to *cleanse* this world and strike at the one who abandoned us," he continued, taking a step forward.

"So, that's it, then? You say that I don't know about faith or innocence, and yet here you are, casting yours aside so easily, and for what? Are you so anxious to lick your *new master's* boot when he could so easily do to *you* what you claim Mideia has done?" Leona scoffed, causing his grin to shift into an angry snarl.

"After all this time, you still don't understand. If Mideia were truly *all-powerful* as I thought he was, then how could he allow such horrible things to take place in this Realm? How could he allow so much to be wrong with the world and yet still have those who would blindly follow him?" Mourtis seethed, clenching his fists tightly.

"No, Leona. Over the years, I've learned that faith in Mideia is misplaced, and I've used my position to its fullest advantage. Faith in Mideia is *bought* and *paid for* through ignorance, fear, money, and power. Lots of it, to be precise, and I have no issues wiping away the culmination of evils spawned within these walls, of which *you* are counted among them," he sneered, gesturing for his men to resume closing in around her.

Leona scoffed and shook her head in disbelief. "You've become nothing more than a *pawn*; a fraud who has lived a bountiful life taking people's money and pleas for help when you don't even believe in it *yourself*," she spat.

"A *special artifact* here, a baseless blessing or compliment there, and the people will lose all self-respect over it, believing they've been blessed to have encountered, felt, or heard such a thing that gives them only a temporary relief from their reality. After what you've done with the Harutian prince, can you truly say *you're any different*?" his malicious smile returned, making her blanche for a moment.

You bastard, she thought with clenched fists.

"From what children learn in schools to the reasons behind outbreaks in war, we have fed this Continent controlled information to ensure they stay *in line*. People are *incredibly* gullible and will pay *any* price to feel even an iota of the relief you felt when you murdered your husband. Unfortunately, enough is enough. I've done *my* part in trying to help fix this rotten world, but over the years, I've grown tired of trying," he sighed as he shook his head.

Leona was stunned, entirely unable to find any words to say, but did her best to keep stalling for time in hopes more guards would arrive.

"So, what now? You're just going to kill me and parade my body throughout the city in proclamation of ridding this world of someone you view as evil?" she asked with a feigned lack of fear.

Get ready to run, she motioned to Meliss with a hand behind her back.

"*Ah*, I've always *loved* how people fear the unknown. The Masked One has commanded that we eradicate all who could potentially stand against him. This, according to his will, includes *you*," Mourtis sneered.

"The *Masked One*? Your doing all this while putting your faith in a fucking *children's story*? You're just a sick, evil bastard," she scoffed, carefully gauging the others who were now just a few meters from her position.

"*Oh*, no, no, no, Leona. He's very much real, and he *is coming*. Evil is also just a matter of perspective, after all. What I may deem evil, you could deem worthy of praise, and vice versa," he shrugged.

"We all have our perspectives in life, and while that doesn't mean that all perspectives are correct, or can coexist in the same space, the one with the most *power* wins. Killing your subjects is but a means to an end in the grand scheme of things," he began to chuckle, eventually throwing his head back hysterically.

"Says the dog who's dug himself into a hole he can't crawl out of. I hope you die a horrible death, priest," she spat, immediately turning to take Meliss' hand and sprint up the stairs back to her bedroom. "Get them! Bring me their heads!" Mourtis shouted with hysterical laughter.

Three of the hooded figures chased after them as Leona's and Meliss' hearts were beating louder and harder than a battle drum. "In here," Leona said, pulling the girl with her as she entered the royal chambers. Just as one of the hooded figures reached for her, she turned and slammed the wooden door, crushing the hand caught between it and the doorframe.

Noticing the door was still ajar, she forcefully kicked it with all her might and severed the hand in two, spraying blood and bits of broken bone into the air between them as she immediately reached to bolt the door shut.

Meliss stood by and blankly stared at the half of the hand still inside the room gathering blood beneath it. Leona went to her easel and grabbed a thin paintbrush, sticking it into a small hole in the wall behind the curtains near the window. "Meliss, come quickly," she whispered, knocking her out of her daze. "What's that for?" Meliss asked, doing as she was told. "*Shh*, they're still outside," Leona put a finger to her lips and silently gestured to the door.

Meliss nodded and watched with curious eyes as Leona pushed on the stone wall near the window where she'd inserted the paintbrush into the hole. "What the...? I never would have guessed *that* was there," she whispered with genuine surprise.

"That's because only the royal family is ever told about it. Now, come on. We need to find help," Leona whispered with a wry grin before grabbing the young girl's wrist and leading her down the passage.

They moved as quickly as they could in the pitch black of the passage, and they used more of their sense of touch than their eyesight to find their way, coming to a solid wall a few moments later. "This is it," Leona said quietly. "Once we leave here, we must find Thorsen, do you remember him?" she asked. Meliss nodded in the dark, and then realized it was pointless. "Got it," Meliss said quietly. Leona patted her shoulder and pushed against the solid wall.

The stones moved, and the moonlight shone through the cracks it created. They arrived just outside the palace, where other hooded figures could be seen, scouring the streets for anyone they deemed unworthy of their revolt. Alarm bells could be heard in the distance, and a cacophony of screams and pleas for help ruled the night air.

"Quickly now," Leona said, pulling Meliss along behind her. They hid behind a small shack on a nearly empty street, and waited for one of the hooded figures to pass. They held their breath as he walked past them, only a meter's width away without noticing their presence. He continued down the street, and in the moonlight, Leona saw that their course was clear.

"To Thorsen's house," she said. She led Meliss down the narrow streets from house to house, down to the commoners' part of town, where the giant's house was. They ran to the door, and Leona knocked vigorously. "*Hallo*?" a strong voice came from behind the door. "Thorsen, it's Leona, I must speak with you," she answered as loudly as she dared.

The bolts were immediately undone, as the giant stood in the tall doorway, nearly matching its breadth. "What are you doing here at this hour of the night, Your Majesty?" Thorsen asked with visible confusion. "They've taken over, and killed most of my staff," Leona said shakily, as the stress of the whole situation began to take its toll.

"Who's done *what*?" Thorsen asked, his eyes flaring with concern. "The Church killed my people, and I think they're coming through here next. Please, help us," Leona replied desperately, looking over her shoulder to make sure none had followed them.

"You mean the bunch of pious, spineless *whoresons*, Your Majesty?" he asked almost in disbelief. "Well, if they didn't have spines before, they seem to have grown them quite quickly," Leona replied. "Come in and shut the door. Quickly," he stepped aside before checking for any potential eavesdroppers.

The two women entered the large house, which was decorated with swords and trophies from past hunts. They briefly looked around and found a large stool that accommodated both of them.

They appeared to be only children compared to the size of the stool.

"They would've killed us too, had it not been for her quick thinking," Meliss said with a panicked tone, prompting Thorsen to look at the desperation in their eyes, immediately knowing they wouldn't be lying about a situation like this. "I see. Give me a moment to gather my things. I'll help you get out of here," he nodded to the pair before stepping away.

He returned a few moments later, with a leather jerkin and a greatsword on his belt. "We must hurry if we're to make it out of here before dawn comes. With any luck, we'll slip by unnoticed. I can hear the contingency plan bells, which most likely means that more than a few people have escaped this horror. We should avoid joining them at all costs," he said, making the other two nod simultaneously.

He quickly snuffed the candles and carefully unlatched the bolts to the large door, peering out of the small crack he made when he pulled it open. "It's clear, but not for long, I assume," he said quietly.

He motioned for the two to follow him, and as soon as he did, a hooded figure appeared in front of them. He motioned for them to be silent, as he crept up behind the figure, snapped its neck, and lowered the limp body slowly. Meliss put a hand to her mouth to keep from screaming, while Leona put a hand around her shoulder.

Come, he mouthed, gesturing for them to stay close.

The two followed him to the Western Gate, where there were a few more hooded figures standing guard. He peeked a single eye out from behind the corner of a wall, and counted as many as he could. "It would seem as though some of the guards themselves were allied to the Church," he whispered, turning to face the two.

"By the Graces," Leona whispered, putting a hand to her mouth. Thorsen counted the figures he could see again to confirm his initial number. "We're not getting out of this without a bit of a fight," Thorsen said, handing the two women twin daggers he had strapped to his belt.

Meliss felt the weight of the large, gleaming dagger and looked up at Thorsen. "I've never killed a man before," she said quietly. "Let's hope you don't *have to*," Thorsen said, squatting down to her height. "If it comes to it, where it's your life or your enemy's, you stick the pointy end of it into their gut or throat, pull it out, and rush to my side, alright?" he asked calmly and concisely as Meliss' eyes filled with tears. She forced herself to nod quickly, regretfully understanding the consequences if she didn't do as he said.

"Let's move," he whispered. The three came out of the shadows, and Thorsen drew his sword. The figures outnumbered them three to one, and he immediately knew they'd put up a bit of a fight.

He lowered his sword to his left side, letting it trail behind him just above the floor, allowing his first target to become overconfident.

Leona and Meliss slowed their pace to be out of the way of the imminent strike, spacing themselves from the giant. One of the hooded figures tapped another who stood next to him, and a grin could be seen beneath their hoods. Thorsen's eyes were fixed between their centers of mass, using his peripheral vision to track their strikes when they came.

And they came *swiftly*.

The first figure tried to strike from above, hoping to hit the giant's chest and slash his jerkin, but Thorsen swung his sword in a flash of moonlit movement. The sword looked like a waning blood moon as blood arced through the air, severing the arm from its previous owner.

The second attacked from Thorsen's side, hoping to get in close enough to strike as his target recovered, but Thorsen was too smart. He quickly spun on his toes and hacked the second target in half. Blood sprayed from the severed body, landing on the women's faces standing a few meters away.

Two down; seven to go, he thought, already preparing for the next attack as his sword and face were coated in blood.

The other figures had been watching from a distance and realized that he was *not* to be toyed with. One of them ran off, and the giant knew he would be back with something to try to attack him from a distance.

I have about a minute before he comes back, he thought, planning his next attacks.

Thorsen charged the other six men, parrying attacks and severing limbs from bodies, and heads from shoulders, as blood soaked him and the ground around him. "There's still one left," he warned the other two as the last enemy fell. "Let's get out of here before he calls reinforcements," Leona reached for Meliss' hand without looking, but immediately felt a resistant tug on her arm.

Her eyes opened wide in surprise when she realized it was a hooded figure that had a knife to Meliss' throat, pulling her hair as he dragged her away. "Meliss!" she shouted, grasping at air as the thin forearm left her grip.

Thorsen immediately turned to try to kill the hooded figure, but it drew the knife closer to Meliss' throat, putting tension on the skin around her artery. "Make a move and she dies, big man!" the hooded figure grinned maliciously. Thorsen saw she still had the dagger in her hand, and that her attacker hadn't noticed it.

This bastard could end her life at any given moment. I can't close the distance quickly enough, even with my skills, he thought.

"Alright, calm down. There's no need to harm the girl," Thorsen raised his hands. "Shut up, giant," the figure said through gritted teeth as Meliss looked at him with a wide-eyed stare, fear clearly showing on her face.

"What do you want with the girl?" Thorsen asked, trying to buy some time. "The *fuck* does it matter to you? Maybe I just want to have some *fun* with her; maybe I just want to *kill* her. Who knows?" the figure said, smelling Meliss' hair. "You detestable *pervert*!" Leona called out.

The figure chuckled maliciously, putting his face closer to his prey. "I might have enjoyed this more if you two weren't here, but I guess this will have to do," the figure said, licking her temple.

Thorsen looked at Meliss, who could only close her eyes in disgust. "Meliss, it's going to be okay," he nodded calmly. "*Oh-ho-ho*, I don't think it will be; not for her, anyway," the figure said, eyeing the giant.

"Meliss, look at *me*," Thorsen gestured with two fingers to his eyes. She watched the giant as he nodded, briefly looking down at the dagger she still held, and subtly shook her head. He nodded again, and she took a deep breath, before her hair twisted in her attacker's hands. With a grunt of exertion, she stuck the blade deep into his upper gut, then cut downwards as she pulled the sodden blade out, spilling his entrails onto the floor.

"*Ack*, you bitch! You sly, dirty little *whore!*" he shouted, pressing a hand to his opened gut. Two other hooded figures nearby heard the scream and rushed to his aid. Meliss ran over to Thorsen and Leona, and they were out the door, running for their lives to the north. One of the figures opened the door and had a bow in his hand with an arrow nocked in place.

He drew the arrow to his cheek and loosed. The arrow whizzed through the air and struck Leona in the shoulder. She fell to the ground, screaming in pain. "Get up, Leona!" Thorsen urged, not bothering to use her title as he helped her to his feet.

He saw the bowman preparing another arrow, and placed himself between Leona and the arrow. Thorsen's eyes glowed with golden mana as the bowman drew back the second arrow. The arrow, now soaring through the air, was met by a concussive blast of air from the giant's fingertips, shattering the arrow mid-flight.

"What the hell? There aren't supposed to be any Synners here!" the hooded bowman shouted. "Too bad, because I'm here. I might know a rock with more intelligence than you, and I'll make sure you get to meet him *two meters deep*," Thorsen grinned, his eyes still glowing as he forced mana into his legs and dashed forward.

He caught the bowman by surprise at his speed, and decapitated him with a single blow. The strike was so clean that not even *blood* remained where it cut through the bowman's neck.

By the Graces, he's a Synner? Leona thought in absolute awe of his combat prowess as she watched him dash in to cut the other cleanly in half down the center of his body.

The two halves fell to the floor with a wet *thud*, spilling blood and other pungent smells on the ground and into the air. Thorsen quickly glanced around to make sure no others were present, and quickly swung his sword to get any remaining blood off.

"We're not going to make it far if I don't do this," he turned to face them with his eyes still glowing, as golden tendrils of mana licked his temples beneath the moonlight. "I apologize in advance," he nodded, confusing the two women profusely.

Within the time it took them to blink, he dashed forward, scooped the two of them into his arms, and carried them away. After another *Exar* blast, the door that marked their escape quickly became little more than shards, clearing the way for him to continue moving.

An hour passed, and the trio found themselves in the safety of the nearby forest, where Thorsen was sure that no normal man would dare follow them there. He set Meliss down first, then Leona with added care. "It's not so bad, Your Majesty," he said, observing the shaft in her upper right shoulder.

"I might puke," Leona replied with a groan. "Wouldn't be surprised if you did. Here, bite this," he replied with a half-hearted shrug as he handed her his leather glove. "Just get it over with," she said between grunts of pain. "Don't move," he said, pulling the shaft from her shoulder.

She screamed in pain, muffled by the glove, but he quickly put his hand over the bleeding wound, and his eyes glowed once more, *drawing mana from the Ethereal.* He condensed a small amount of it to his hand, searing the wound shut and only leaving a small scar behind.

"There, almost as though it never happened, Your Majesty," he said, trying to cheer her up, as Meliss watched the whole thing happen with wide eyes.

She had never seen a synner in action before.

"How does it look?" Leona asked her. "To be honest, it doesn't look too awful," Meliss said, looking at the new scar more closely. Leona nodded and tried to move her shoulder. The knot in her gut from the pain was still there, but the actual pain in her shoulder was dramatically lessened.

"Help me up," Leona said. Thorsen picked her up slowly and set her down on her feet, before she looked at the giant who had just saved her life. "You're a Synner," she said, finally understanding what had just occurred. "I am. Or at least I *was* until a few years ago, when I joined the Warriors' Guild, Your Majesty," he said with a frown.

"You must have had a really good reason to leave," Leona said, trying to better understand her savior. "I did, but it wasn't exactly my choice," he paused momentarily, remembering the course of events. "Grundvollr was attacked by a powerful mage, leaving little more than a tenth of us alive. We who survived knew we could never go back, and King Mads had refused to give us aid," he began, averting his gaze.

"By the Graces, that's horrible!" Leona said with her hands to her mouth. "It was. We were outcasts, even though we had all spent countless years defending Hjalfar. Mads had deemed us dishonored and useless by the fact that we were unable to take down the mage. As a result, we were banished from our own lands," Thorsen explained, but doing so took a visible toll on him and his usually cheerful demeanor.

"We never even so much as caught wind of such a terrible situation," Leona put a hand on his shoulder gently. "I'd be surprised if you had heard of it. No one outside of the surviving Synners and Mads knew about it," he chuckled weakly.

"He tried long and hard to keep our failure taboo for years. After having the rug pulled out from under our worlds, we knew we could no longer be Synners, and tried to live a normal life instead. Some of the others simply couldn't bear the fact that they took their own lives, or became bandits and outlaws. Myself and one other are the last living true Synners of Grundvollr, Your Majesty," he lowered his head with a shake.

"I am truly sorry such a fate befell you, my dear Thorsen. I can assure you that if I am ever in power again, be it in Coltend or anywhere else, I will ensure that you are given the highest quality of living possible," she said warmly.

"Thank you, Your Majesty," he bowed. "You needn't call me that any longer, for I am *no one's queen* anymore," Leona said with slight dejection. "You will always be *my queen*, Your Majesty," Thorsen said with a warm smile, which she returned as he looked up at the sky through the canopy.

Dawn was on the horizon.

"We must go," he said, quickly checking his gear. "Where can we go where they won't find us?" Leona asked. "North," he replied. "North?" Leona asked. "Yes, to Fangsdalr, just to the east of where Grundvollr once was," he replied with a grin. "What's over there?" Meliss asked.

"Do you recall how I said that there was one other true Synner who survived the attack? Well, he has done what Mads would not dare to dream of," Thorsen replied. "And that is...?" Leona asked.

"He built a hidden Synner school, Your Majesty," he said with a smile.

CHAPTER 15

CODREAN

After the battle for Codrean, we gathered our wounded and regrouped at the fortress.

The wounded were tended to by Bernar and Garett, as well as a few other of the senior synners. Any of our number that died during the assault were burned in a pyre to avoid the spread of disease that rotting corpses caused.

It was always a tough, but honorable way to say goodbye.

Meanwhile, I went over to speak with the Master, still covered in the Ochelon's blood from the battle. I found the Master in his study, accompanied by the Anwill. The two were discussing something I couldn't quite overhear.

"Master," I interrupted, knocking on the door. "*Ah*, if it isn't the ochelon slayer himself. What can I help you with?" he asked, acknowledging my presence. "Might I have a word with you?" I asked. "Of course," the Master replied. The elf remained stationary. "I assume the subject of our imminent conversation is to be held in private," the Master said, noticing the awkward stare I'd given Anwill.

"No, Master. The only privacy here would be considering *that* topic. However, if you trust him like Bernar, then Anwill may stay. After all, he might have information that could be useful," I gave Anwill a respectful half-bow. "I would trust him with my life, Thoma, so there is no need to worry. Please, sit," he motioned to the chair nearest to the desk.

"Master, Anwill. What I am about to say here is not out of conjecture, but out of my observations I've gathered during my time here," I began. "I understand," the Master said reassuringly. I paused and gathered my thoughts.

Ah, I wish it didn't have to be this way, but here we go, I thought.

"I've heard Batch mention that Irun has been scurrying off to study after their training sessions, although I don't believe that. Not one bit," I began. "What do you mean?" the Master asked, leaning forward intently.

"Well, you see, Master, Irun has never been one to study much of anything. He's *naturally* intelligent when it comes to books and academic studies. I know this because we have shared quarters during our time here together, and I've never once seen him reading so much as a book before bed," I explained. The Master tilted his head. "Is that so?" he asked, to which I could only nod my head solemnly.

The Master looked over at Anwill, who was visibly disturbed by the news, then back at me inquisitively, but it felt like he'd just probed my mind. "I can already guess what you are proposing, but I want to hear your reasoning for such a thing," he gestured for me to continue.

"I don't propose we do anything yet, as we have no concrete evidence. However, I *do* think we should try to keep a closer eye on him," I said hesitantly, trying to choose my next words carefully. "Given current events, and everything that has happened since our return from the council at Coltend, I have begun to see a pattern," I continued. "Forgive me for interrupting, but what *exactly* has happened since you returned?" Anwill asked, trying to grasp the situation.

"To make a long story short, we have seen ravens leaving from the direction of the fortress, as well as another which flew just before the attack," the Master said. "And you believe this to be the work of one of your own?" Anwill asked. "Yes," both the Master and I replied simultaneously.

"These are dark times, indeed," Anwill began, but paused to think for a moment. "I believe you may have a point, young Thoma. While on my way here, I heard rumors about creatures stirring far to the North. Even along our borders in Caegwen, plenty of portals bring these bastards to our world, though none have spawned so close to our school. This is a bit of a reach, but perhaps those ravens being sent out were to update someone to keep an eye on all of you?" Anwill asked with a raised eyebrow.

You've got to be shitting me. They haven't had any spawn that close? And why would anyone want to keep tabs on us? What the hell is going on? I thought as I processed Anwill's words.

"The problem is: What if I'm right and he really is a traitor? I don't want to sit here thinking that someone I've basically grown up with could do such a thing," I said, my voice shaking a little near the end. "I mean, I don't think I could beat him in a fight if it came to that," I continued with uncertainty in my voice.

"You've unlocked the second stage of mana manipulation, taken down *three* ochelons, as well as a few dozen glicks and daemons; I think you'd manage," the Master said with a grin. I felt a sigh of relief wash over me, but knew I still had a long way to go.

"Thank you, Master, but I can't seem to control the second stage fully just yet," I said, momentarily shifting my gaze away from him. "Your time will come, Thoma. However, Anwill and I must discuss our next moves. You're welcome to stay, if you want to," the Master suggested with as warm a smile as he could muster.

Like hell I'm about to miss an opportunity like this, I thought.

"If it's not too much of an inconvenience, Master. Since the incident with Edryd and the injury I caused him, I've learned the value of situational awareness, and would like to gain as much as I can," I replied. Surprisingly, he gave me a look as if he understood what was going through my head while the probing feeling returned once more, but I said nothing.

"There should never be any shame in seeking more information or bettering yourself. After all, pursuing knowledge is not a gift granted to all. Some taste wisdom once and chase it their entire lives, while others enjoy the taste of rocks and windows," Anwill said with a light chuckle at the end.

Oh, he's definitely *spent a lot of time with Bernar,* I chuckled, then followed the Master's instructions for me to sit on a nearby stool.

The Master returned to the map that was spread out on the desk. "As we were saying earlier, these attacks are becoming more frequent. It's not just near the school, either. Just a few days ago, another report was made of an attack near Coltend Castle. If these attacks are going to continue and progressively get worse, we will require reinforcements," he stated, giving Anwill a worried look.

"I agree. However, Caegwen is much too far away, and we have troubles of our own with some of the outcast Synners in our own country, let alone the creatures on our borders," Anwill said grimly.

I took in the words, though they sat like spoiled milk in my stomach. It made me realize two things: that outcasts in other countries were starting to cause trouble, and that they were *much* closer to Anwill's home than they could ever be to Codrean.

But why now? I mean, he's right that if we go to Caegwen we'd only end up wasting time. Not to mention the incidental damage to their reinforcements. Wait a minute... my thoughts trailed as an idea sparked in my head.

I got up from my stool and walked over to the table where the map was, looking at it carefully. Both Anwill and the Master regarded me curiously with a raised eyebrow as I leaned over the map.

"What if we went to Hjalfar?" I asked shyly, forcing them to share a wordless glance. "I mean, we're practically a stone's throw away from the nearest Synner school once we cross the border. As far as we know, we haven't heard of any large-scale attacks happening there. If I'm right, we might find our reinforcements there," I said, pointing to the general location on the map.

"He's got a point, Master," Anwill said after measuring the distance and surprisingly agreeing with me. "Indeed he does. However, we haven't had news from them in nearly *forty years*. While not hearing news of other schools is not unheard of, to go such a lengthy period of time without anything is cause for concern," the Master said grimly.

I observed the map again, noting the distance between them and Odensby. "What if we went and asked the king?" I suggested, prompting the Master to look at the map again. "It's almost the same distance, not to mention the king might offer us some help, Master.

He seemed friendly enough the last time we saw him," I said, hoping for a positive answer from him.

"*Hmm*, we could always send a raven up there, too," the Master said, stroking his chin. "True, but you know how ravenries can be; sometimes it will be a week or two before they even see the message, let alone have a proper answer on short notice," Anwill said with a shrug. "It's worth a shot, at the very least," I chimed in.

"The issue here is what would become of Codrean," the Master said, letting his words hang. "I'm not saying we should go in full force to Odensby. We would have to leave a few of us behind to stand guard. How many are we in total, Master?" I asked. "Just over two-hundred, after the battle," he replied with a lowered tone.

"If we were to leave here with a small party of about *twenty*, that would allow us to move quickly, while conserving plenty of resources and people to hold the fortress while we're gone," I said after a short pause.

"You have got a good head on your shoulders, young Thoma," Anwill noted approvingly. "I agree with him," he said to the Master, who immediately rose from his seat and began pacing his study. "While we know that Irun has a higher potential for being the traitor than most, that still doesn't confirm he's the one to blame," the Master began, pausing near the window that overlooked the training yard.

"If the traitor remains among us, we risk any and all information getting into the wrong hands. If this person, or these *people*, are capable of charming an ochelon, we have to assume that they could also break any mana wards I put up to prevent them from gathering the information stored in this very room," he continued.

"So we're taking everyone with us? Abandoning the fortress?" I asked, feeling my stomach drop. "It may be our only option, but I must consider it. I'm sure we are *all* exhausted after the battle, and we all could do with some rest," he said, sitting back down on his chair.

"We shall continue this discussion tomorrow. *Oh*, and I would very much appreciate it if you were present for that decision, Thoma," he nodded, making me blink a few times in confusion.

Is he finally starting to trust me as much as he does Bernar? I wondered.

"At first light, Master? I'll be there," I tried to hide the exhaustion and excitement in my voice. "Don't be late," he nodded with a grin. "And so will I," Anwill cut in a smile. "I'm sure that you must have more pressing matters to attend to back in Caegwen," the Master said. "Nonsense. This is the most fun I've had in nearly a century. Plus, before I left, I put *you-know-who* in charge of not just Myrdin's, but *Caegwen's* defenses," he said with a wry grin, getting a soft nasal chuckle from the Master.

Aaaand I'm kept out of the loop... again, I mentally sighed.

"Very well, then," the Master said with a nod. "Thoma, head down to the infirmary to notify your brother and Master Garett," he said. I nodded and headed out the door. The stairs that led from the Master's study to the infirmary seemed longer than they had ever been, but I nearly missed the turn I needed to take as I was lost in thought.

I can't imagine the Hjalfarian school falling so easily, he thought to myself. I mean, if only about a hundred of us could take on such a horde, the Hjalfarian school must have been under a heavy attack

indeed. Either that, or something truly powerful overcame their forces.
They were one of the oldest schools on the Continent, and had some of the
most experienced Synners. It just doesn't make sense. Think, you fool,
think, I furrowed my brow and tapped a pair of fingers to my temple,
trying to piece the facts together.

Continuing down the halls, I realized that nothing was as it had
been before. The walls seemed older and darker than they had looked
just a few weeks ago. I felt the weight of the battle finally weighing
down on me and my body.

Damn it, I feel like I'm carrying my brother on my shoulders after
having trained all day, I thought.I reviewed what had happened in
the battle, thinking about what I could have done better or more
efficiently. I'd gambled with my life with that final attack, after all.

Won't be doing that again any time soon, I thought with an awkward chuckle.

Walking down the final flight of steps that would ultimately lead
me to my destination, the smell of blood and sweat began to fill the
air. I stepped through the doorway and saw beds filled with wounded
Synners. I had never had much contact with most of them, since
most of the wounded were not in my immediate circle of friends, so
I began looking for the ones I did.

I found Garett kneeling by one of the beds, tending to a wounded
sinner whose chest had a ghastly cut in it. "Master Garett," I said
quietly. "In a minute," Garett said, holding up a hand. I observed
the wound being given the same treatment I had received from my
brother.

I don't miss that feeling of wounds being seared shut with mana. It feels like a small horde of maggots on fire burrowing through your skin, I shuddered briefly.

He finished searing the wound shut with mana and gently touched the woman's shoulder. "You'll live, lass," he said comfortingly. "Thank you, Master Garett," the woman replied weakly. "No need to thank me; just doing my job. Go on, get some rest," Garett replied with a warm smile.

He rose from his kneeling position and turned to face me. "Be quick about it. I have others that need tending to," he grunted. "The Master has called for you in his office at first light, Master Garett," I said quietly. Garett knew that couldn't be a good thing. "Anyone else invited?" he asked. "You, me, Bernar, and Anwill, Master Garett," I replied. "*Anwill?* The elf?" he raised an eyebrow.

Unfortunately, I was *even more* puzzled than he was.

"Y-Yes, Master Garett," I replied. He sighed and shook his head. "I don't usually trust elves. They're too old for their own good, and it creeps the living shit out of me. If the Master wants him to be there, I have no choice but to suck it up, I guess," he said with a sigh. "I'll be there, don't worry," he replied with a firm nod before moving on to his next patient.

I nodded and made my way over to my brother, who was tending to Irun's wounds.

A broken rib or two was never as severe as an open wound, unless of course they had punctured a lung, I thought.

"You got lucky," I overheard my brother say. "Lucky?" Irun wheezed. "The ochelon's claw could have impaled you. Would you rather it had?" Bernar asked with a shrug. "I think anything else at this point would be more comfortable than barely being able to breathe," Irun replied, getting an instant flick on the forehead from my brother.

"So you would take *death* over a bit of discomfort? You seem fine to me if your shitting that much from your mouth," I chuckled, approaching the side of the bed. "*Oh*, munch on a prick, will you?" Irun said with no small amount of sarcastic spice in his voice. He coughed and wheezed for a moment while I just shrugged my shoulders.

"As funny as that was, I don't think it's a good idea to cause more damage than you've already got," Bernar said with a grin. "Hurry up and fix me, then," Irun said impatiently. "Careful, now. Getting fixed in some places means having *itchy* and *scratchy* sawed off with a dull knife," I said, not bothering to hide the shit-eating grin on my face.

Bernar snorted with laughter and almost lost focus on what he was doing. "He's got a point. Careful what you wish for," he said, desperately trying not to lose focus as he continued sending mana towards Irun's wounds.

"Your parents must have been something special for you two to be able to make jokes at a time like this," Irun groaned. "Thanks, it's the trauma," I winked. "Shut up and lie still," Bernar spat, flicking his middle finger on Irun's forehead again. "*Oi,* can you *not* flick me for five fucking seconds?" Irun exclaimed, but after my brother glared, he gave in and put his head back on the pillow.

"There, all done. However, I wouldn't recommend taking us on just yet. You'll need a good night of rest before it heals completely," Bernar said, arresting the mana's flow after a few moments. Irun wriggled around, feeling almost no pain in his ribcage. "Thank you," he begrudgingly said. "Next time, don't be such a whiny piglet,"

Bernar chuckled and patted him lightly on the shoulder before stepping away.

"I think he was just glad you didn't flick him again," I muttered, getting a chortle from my brother. "He's a bit of an ungrateful little shit, isn't he?" he asked, jutting his thumb over his shoulder. "Yeah, he can be a real pain in the ass, but he means well, I think," I put a finger to my chin pensively as we passed a handful of other bedridden Synners.

"I know you came here for more than just to check on Irun," he began, leaning in a little. "The Master has summoned us to his study at first light," I replied quietly. "Any idea what for?" he asked with a curious stare. "All I can really say here is that he did. He also didn't want people trying to spread rumors," I said, raising my eyebrows.

"Got it. I won't pry, then," he replied quietly. "Let's go outside. We need to talk. That *ingrate* back over there was the last one for me for the night," he tilted his head in Irun's general direction. I nodded, and we promptly left the infirmary.

Under the dim light of the stars and the rising moon, not a soul to be seen about us, we walked towards the training grounds. "What did you want to talk about?" I asked after we had walked a short distance away from the main fortress. "I brought you here to ask you something," Bernar said.

This can't be good, I thought.

"Well, go on, then. Spit it out," I said with a mild anxiety creeping in. "I know you have very few memories of Mom, and many horrible ones about Father, but I have to ask you whether she had mentioned anything about our grandparents to you," Bernar said. "The *fuck* did this come from?" I spread my arms, expecting something entirely different, though I didn't know what that *something* even was.

"Just answer the damn question," Bernar said playfully. "Well, I know father's parents died a long time ago, leaving him a small fortune and a bit of land, being the son of a nobleman and all," I began. "What about Mom?" he asked, glancing at the starry sky.

I thought back as far as I could, struggling to unearth specific memories I thought had long since been forgotten. "I don't really remember her saying much about our grandparents," I admitted, furrowing my brow in frustration.

"Strange, don't you think?" he asked. "What do you mean?" I raised an eyebrow. "Neither of us remembers much of anything about her side of the family, only that she comes from a long line of Synners," Bernar replied. "Alright, what are you getting at?" I asked. "Don't you find it odd how little we *actually* know about our family?" Bernar asked.

I could only look at him with pure bewilderment written on my face. "Why would I find it weird? Mom wasn't the most open of people, was she? And Father, being the *shithead* he is, isn't exactly the most approachable person, either. The only things I can remember are that, and how she looked on the day she left," I said, venom dripping from my words as the memory resurfaced clearly.

"I hardly even remember what she looked like, come to think of it," I frowned, realizing my image of my mother was now blurred and askew from what I thought it should've been. "Well, I remember a *little more* than you. She was strong-willed; an unequivocally un-tameable force of nature, and she was an all-caster," he said, finally turning to face me. "She was?" I asked curiously, feeling a pride for her I didn't know I had. "One of the best," he smiled warmly.

"Father always hated her for being a Synner, and as a result, he broke off their marriage a few years after you were born, ridding her from his life and ours all in one fell swoop. Just before she left, she begged him to watch over us. At first, he didn't agree to it all, but with a bit of mana, she managed to convince him. He hated us so much because we always reminded him of her. Apparently, that was enough for him to do some pretty horrible shit to us *both*," he sighed and shook his head.

"Holy shit, I had no idea," I said, taken aback. "Holy shit on a *holy altar*," Bernar added with a weak chuckle. "So that's why he never really talked about her, nor her side of the family. It also explains why he's a piece of shit, but maybe he was already like that before she left," I concluded.

"Exactly. Another reason we don't know much about her lineage is that the two of us rarely ever saw her, and whenever we would, father would always be there to interrupt," he continued. "Because, *of course,* he was..." I said, looking away from my brother into the distance.

"Well, it can't be helped now, I guess. Either way, I'm glad to see you're *also* growing closer to the Master," he began with a shrug. "What do you mean by that?" I asked, tilting my head. "Over the last decade or so, the Master and I have grown close, and I can see he's beginning to trust you as he does me. To me, at least, he's like the father *neither* of us ever had," he continued, reflecting on the past few years.

Something's not adding up, I looked at him curiously.

"Does it have anything to do with you knowing Anwill?" I asked bluntly. "It does, but that, as well as a few other things, will have to be a story for another time," he replied tousling my hair so the front of it covered my eyes. "Can't even get answers out of my own, damned brother. *Sheesh*," I said disappointedly.

Just as Bernar was opening his mouth to speak, a figure appeared in the doorway behind us. "Bernar, Thoma," the figure called out. "Yes, Master Garett?" I asked, immediately recognizing his grouchy voice. "Lights out," he gestured for us to move inside. "Right away, Master Garett," I replied with a wave.

I looked at my brother, hoping he would reveal the answer to the questions I'd asked, but he simply shook his head. "We'll discuss this some other time. Otherwise, that geezer will have us for a midnight snack," he chuckled as we walked back to the fortress. My mind was racing, scrambling to find an answer to my questions.

I'll be sure to take him up on this conversation again when this is all over, I thought.

Each of us went our own way to our quarters, and I lay belly up on my bed, staring at the thatched roof above me. I glanced at the scratched names on the wall beside my bed, listening to my room-mates' soft snoring.

It must be nice to not have racing thoughts during the late hours of the night, I thought with an envious sigh.

I rolled over on my side and pulled the blanket up to my neck to help stave off the cold air the stone walls held. I closed my eyes, placing myself back *in the open field. I cast a few spells, each different from the other, and slowly but surely, my world went dark as I stepped into the dreamworld.*

Unfortunately, I awoke a little after dawn with a startle.

Shiiiit, he's going to kill me if I'm late! I thought, staring out of my window, then rushing to get what little clothes I could on before bolting out of the room. I arrived with only a few minutes to spare.

At least, I thought I had.

Phew, that was a close one! I thought as I knocked on the door. It opened slowly, only for me to come face to face with none other than the Master himself. "*Ah*, there you are. Glad you could make it," he said calmly.

Yep, he's going to kill me, I thought, accepting my fate.

"Good morning, Master. I apologize for my tardiness," I said with a bow. The Master noted my composure with a quick glance. I wasn't entirely out of breath, but sprinting like I did first thing in the morning was anything but enjoyable. "It's alright. We were about to start. Now that we're all here, let us begin," he said to the others, closing the door behind me. Anwill, Garett, Bernar, and I all sat in the chairs provided for us.

"Gentlemen, we are at an impasse," the Master began as he watched all of us give him our undivided attention. "The attack on us here at Codrean has led me to believe that there may be yet another coming soon, and with most of our men and women wounded, and not fully battle-ready, we have no other option but to seek out reinforcements in case of future engagements," he said plaintively as the rest of us exchanged wordless glances.

"As the situation currently stands, we are too far from Caegwen and Harut to request reinforcements, for they would have to travel over the Rhydian Pass just to get here, all the while having their issues to attend to. Our only remaining option is to travel North to

Hjalfar and request help from King Mads," the Master said, a tone of uncertainty lingered in his voice.

"The way there is anything but easy, and it may take us a few days to get there, but that is the least of our worries. The information in the fortress is of the highest importance, and it has never been left entirely alone," he sighed, making the rest of us nod in agreement.

"Two hundred of us in total have always given us the advantage of being able to leave a few behind. However, given the risk of them being overrun and slaughtered by more of those creatures, this call is tougher than any we have faced before," the Master said with a frown.

Just then, a raven flew through the open window with a small pouch attached. The Master removed the contents from the pouch, reading them swiftly.

His face grew pale.

The others watched him stride back and forth behind his desk. We waited patiently for him to say something, but after what felt like an eternity, nothing was said. "What is it, Master? What happened?" Bernar asked. The Master, reeling from the news, slumped in his chair.

"There has been an attack on Coltend Castle. It seems as though after the death of King Truls, the Church has decided to take it for themselves. There were some survivors, though exactly who's fallen during that attack is unknown," he said gravely. "The queen is dead?" Bernar asked. "I'm afraid so, but there is no confirmation in the letter," the Master replied with a sunken head.

I hope you're alive, Meliss, I thought fearfully, suddenly recalling her name from our first meeting.

Everyone looked at each other, wondering what our next move should be. However, for a few moments, no one spoke, leaving the air heavy and grim.

"The game has changed, and the decisions are as follows: We either entirely abandon the fortress and take everyone with us northeast to Hjalfar to seek reinforcements and help take back the castle, or we risk leaving a few behind, the traitor possibly being among them," he said.

"What of the information?" I asked. "We'll just have to take the most essential items with us. We'll have to seal away the rest, but how well that will hold up is a risk we'll just have to take," he replied gravely.

We all looked at each other, hoping one of us would answer the problematic situation presented. "I have summoned you all here to aid me in this decision," the Master began again after a short pause. "We shall hold a vote, myself not included, for it would be an uneven number. All in favor of leaving the fortress with a few, hopefully trustworthy, Synners left behind, raise your hand," he said.

Nobody did.

"Well, that was simple," Anwill said rather lightly. "Very well, then. I will take the most valuable books here, locked up in a chest and placed on a wagon directly behind me," the Master said. "What about the wounded? They will still need a few days to recover fully," Garett pointed out. "They will ride in the center of our convoy on all other available carriages. We must *avoid combat* as much as possible," the Master answered.

"The traitor will probably try to send a raven," Anwill cautioned. "As disturbing as that thought may be, at least there will be enough people around to see who it is. Are we all in agreement on this?" the Master asked.

Each looked at the other, ensuring we were on the same page. "We are, Master," Garett replied with a nod. "Then gather our supplies. We will ride to Hjalfar at first light tomorrow," the Master said.

I felt my stomach turn in a direction I didn't even know was possible.

CHAPTER 16
THE DUEL

Gorm and Ari's duel began under the bright sun of the early morning upon the Rhydian Pass.

As the two men circled each other, Gorm was already beginning to feel the weight of his sword grow lighter in his hands with the adrenaline that coursed through his veins. His pupils were dilated, and his heart pounded like a horse's hooves on a dirt road. Ari, too, was beginning to feel the same way, as he knew he had the support of his king and the army behind him.

I cannot afford to lose here. This situation might make life for my family harder if I fail to uphold the strength and honor bestowed upon me. I can tell he's a formidable warrior who knows what he's doing. His defense is air-tight with an astounding presence of mind and murderous intent weighing on my shoulders like an extra set of armor, he thought.

Gorm, on the other hand, single-mindedly thought only of his desire to kill his opponent. He continued to watch his opponent, whose face was locked in a state of pure hatred for him, but as he was observing his footsteps, he noticed a slight insecurity in Ari's footsteps.

Heh, he's scared shitless, Gorm thought.

Just as he finished the thought, Ari quickly dashed towards him, who stood his ground like a boulder stuck in the ground. Gorm judged the distance between himself and his attacker, and adjusted his guard to match his opponent's attack.

The sword's pommel was at waist height, while the point of the sword was tilted slightly forward. His legs were firmly planted on the ground at a comfortable width as he awaited the incoming blow.

Ari shouted loudly as he struck from above, his mighty blow carrying his full force behind it. Gorm raised his sword, deflecting the scimitar off to the side, and immediately stepped in towards his attacker to hit him in the nose with his large, wheel-shaped pommel. The blow drew blood from Ari's nose, who saw it as a wake-up call, forcing him to dodge an incoming slash.

That was foolish. I thought he would have moved differently, Ari thought.

He struck again from below, and Gorm easily deflected it, pirouetting out of the way of the following blow that just missed his shoulder to counter with one of his own, which Ari was forced to use his shield to block. Gorm raised an eyebrow and sneered as Ari attacked repeatedly, but the blows either glanced off Gorm's sword or hit nothing but air.

"Fight me like a man, you coward!" Ari shouted. "I will not fight an arrogant child as a man, because I would utterly *destroy* you. Right now, all I want to do is *enjoy* this kill," Gorm replied menacingly. "You can puff out your chest all you want, but it will not save your life. I will not be killed so easily," Ari said angrily.

"Maybe not, but it will make for one hell of a show. Watching you struggle against someone much older than you is also incredibly amusing to me and my men," Gorm replied. "*Struggle*?" Ari questioned. "You have tried to strike me again and again, and yet you still haven't been able to land a meaningful blow," Gorm snickered.

That bastard, Ari thought.

Ari angrily charged at him once more, striking quickly, desperately trying to find an opening, but Gorm's sword flowed through the air, parrying strikes as it went.

Time to teach the pup a lesson, he thought as he moved from defense to offense.

After dodging another overhead blow, he countered with a strike aimed at Ari's gut, shoulder, and leg in rapid succession. Ari deflected the majority of the blows with skills he hadn't previously shown, but Gorm decided to thrust, aiming at Ari's neck. He barely managed to redirect the tip of Gorm's sword, scratching his armored shoulder.

Oh? Maybe he's not so bad after all, Gorm thought, aiming another barrage of strikes to wear his opponent down.

Gorm noticed Ari's focus begin to improve, demonstrating his true skills as the duel raged on. He attempted a side cut aimed for Ari's liver, but the blow was deflected, and he responded with an elbow to the face, drawing blood from Gorm's nose. "Now we're even," Ari said. "Sure, but this is just going to make me enjoy killing you even more," Gorm snorted the blood that ran down the back of his throat, and spat it in Ari's direction.

He was pissed.

It was Gorm's turn to dash in for yet another blow, only to be deflected by the gleaming scimitar. Ari responded with a strike coming from the left, which Gorm could barely deflect in time. Ari began a rapid succession of strikes from the left, and Gorm realized he had found Ari's weakness.

Ari aimed a blow for Gorm's head, but he ducked out of the sword's path, taking a few steps back, and swiftly avoiding another one aimed for his gut. "You fight well, for a child," Gorm said with a malicious chuckle. "You're not so bad yourself, old man," Ari retorted with a grin.

"It's just a shame you're going to die today, even being as skilled as you are," he said mournfully. "Is that pity I hear in your voice?" Gorm asked. "It is indeed. I have never met anyone who could match my blade so well," Ari responded with a shrug.

"As much as I hate to admit it, you're much better than you let off at the beginning of the fight. Did you need to warm up a bit? Was that why you allowed me to strike your nose?" Gorm asked, genuinely curious.

"I struck in anger, as I had underestimated you. However, I recognize your skills and acknowledge you as a true warrior. I still think it's a shame you will have to die, as you would have made a great addition to our forces," Ari admitted. "That would never happen," Gorm quickly spat. "I could never work with *your kind*," he continued, disgusted at the thought of working under Harutian leaders.

"I take great offense in that comment, so I will fight you with everything I have," Ari responded grimly, entering his guard. "And I will repay your offer by dancing in your blood," Gorm responded maliciously.

Behind the duel that was taking place, one of the riders from Bashir's army spotted a moving object coming from the northern trail.

He turned his head away from the ongoing duel to see if it wasn't simply his mind playing a trick on him. The object moved again, and he dismounted to investigate.

He drew his scimitar and cautiously went over to the large boulder, where he had seen the object move. Just as he got close, a glick darted out from behind the boulder nearest to him and aimed a claw at his face. The blow scraped across the base of his jaw, missing his jugular by a hair's breadth as he stepped back.

"Glick!" he shouted, stepping out of the way of the next blow and landing one of his own, severing the creature's head. Pungent blood soaked the dirt as he panted and looked up, only to find a horde of others coming down the northern trail.

"By Yarathea, it's a horde! We're under attack!" he shouted, racing back to the others as quickly as his legs could carry him, prompting the others to stare at him. They followed the direction his hand was pointing in, and saw a larger number of glicks than the man had previously seen. "We're under attack!" the man shouted again, waving in the horde's general direction, hoping to get the others' attention.

Gorm and Ari were still dueling when Bashir noticed the commotion behind them. "My lord, an army of glicks approaches from the North," the man said, nearly out of breath. Bashir's eyes opened wide. "Stop the duel," he shouted. Gorm and Ari froze mid-blow and looked at Bashir.

"He must die, Your Majesty," Ari snarled. "We have a larger problem than his *death* right now, Ari," Bashir said angrily. "Glicks are coming from the northern trail, and we will need all the help we can get," he continued. "You have an army behind you; why should you worry about whether or not we continue?" Gorm asked through gritted teeth.

"I have brought no Synners with me, and these men are not exactly trained to fight these bastards. Set your differences aside for now, and when the battle ends, you may get back to killing each other. Right now, we need to fight them as one," Bashir regarded the two men carefully, observing their body language. "I will have your head when this is over," Ari said begrudgingly, looking at Gorm. "You're welcome to try and take it, *pup*," Gorm replied.

"Gorm, gather your remaining men, and stand with us," Bashir said. "Not like I have much of a choice. Men, to arms!" Gorm shouted. The elves guarding them from the nearby bushes slipped back, out of sight.

"Cowards!" one of Gorm's men shouted at them, noticing the elves' flight. "It's no use. They don't get involved with human affairs unless there's something in it for them other than death or imprisonment," one of the other men said.

"Get in formation," Bashir called out to his riders. Hearing the order, they made a line with their horses that faced the oncoming horde. Foot soldiers made their way up the pass, rallying behind the horsemen. "Wait for them to funnel together near that boulder," Ari shouted, pointing with his sword as the ground began shaking with the horde approaching them.

The horde's screams and screeches grew progressively louder, and some of the soldiers began to shake with fear. "Stand together, and we might win this," Ari commanded. Bashir caught a single glance of the glicks and made his way to the top of the rock where Gwili once stood. Meanwhile, Ari steadied himself and noticed Gorm was standing beside him.

"Not the most ideal of places, I know, but I'd rather be next to a good swordsman than one who has soiled himself," Gorm said with a shrug. "That's a fair point, but why take your enemy's side after saying you'd never work under Harutian command? A bit hypocritical, don't you think?" Ari asked with a scoff.

"Better the one you know will try to kill you, than the one you think might do it by accident. It's not that I don't trust my men, but I'd rather have a clean cut across my throat than get mauled by these nasty looking fuckers," Gorm said plaintively. "*Eh*, good point," Ari replied.

The glicks were nearing the boulder, and the horses became uneasy. "Steady, men!" Ari called out while Gorm gripped his sword tightly, lowering it to be almost parallel with his hind leg. The glicks passed the boulder in an unorganized fashion, causing a congestion in their flow. The few who made it past the congestion were staggering about like chickens without their heads.

"Now!" he shouted, pushing off the balls of his feet. The riders charged the group and took off with swords drawn. Gorm and his men went after them, with a group of Harutian soldiers coming along with his remaining men. The horsemen met the glicks, and the pungent, green blood began to flow. The screeches let off by the glicks having their limbs severed by the riders were near-deafening in the narrow section of the pass.

The congestion of glicks nearest to the boulder only allowed a few to pass through at a time, but they were so large in number that it was an unending stream of them. Gorm and the other soldiers cut down the stragglers missed by the riders, and all seemed to be going well, when suddenly, the glicks began to collectively tear the riders from their saddles.

"It's like these bastards are being told to do this shit! What the hell is wrong with them?" Gorm said his thoughts aloud as he sliced into a creature's neck. "No idea," Ari shouted back, swinging his scimitar upward while deflecting a claw with his shield.

One of the glicks grabbed Ari from behind, trying to wrestle him to the ground. He threw his head back, knocking a few of the glick's rotting teeth back into its mouth. The glick released its grip on him, reeling in pain, and he quickly turned to finish it off with his sword.

Gorm saw the riders falling quickly, and called for reinforcements. He saw the glicks taking down the horses, beginning to eat them while they were still alive and kicking. He felt pity for them, but there was nothing he could do to save them now.

The battle raged on for the better part of an hour. Glicks took down many of the inexperienced soldiers, but fell to the ones who actually knew what they were doing. Gorm and his men were bloodied, beaten, and getting tired.

They never stop coming, do they? Gorm asked himself.

Ari ran over to him, killing a few glicks on his way. "Seems as though we might die today after all," Ari said, severing a glick's head. "A pity that I won't be the one to kill you," Gorm said, thrusting his sword into another's neck. "Likewise," Ari replied with a grin as they stood back to back, dealing with the creatures as they came.

The other soldiers were starting to learn the glicks' attack patterns, and more than a few of them were becoming adept at slaying the beasts. Off in the distance, a deep, rumbling roar came from behind the boulders. "That can't be good," Ari said. "Not one bit," Gorm replied, slaying the last monster in front of him.

The ground began to tremble even more than it had before, and the two men looked out over the small river of glicks and corpses. "Fuck me, not more of them," Gorm said. "More of what?" Ari asked. "Trolls," Gorm snarled, making Ari's eyes open wide when he finally saw them.

"Yarathea, be with us," he muttered breathlessly, observing the lumbering creatures approach. "Retreat!" he called back. The soldiers began to move away from the boulder as the ground shook beneath their feet. The glicks began to pour in, as the trolls forced their way through the pile of the smaller creatures. "Get back, you idiots," Gorm shouted to his men and the Harutians around them.

They had almost fully retreated to the shelf in the pass when one of the trolls smashed through the boulder, releasing a stream of glicks and daemons. "Up to our necks in shit now. Run!" Gorm shouted, realizing that the horde was no longer being funneled.

The trolls smashed through the rocks and began to charge in behind the glicks. They covered more ground in less time than the glicks, and began crushing soldiers into little more than bloodied mounds of flesh. Screams of terror and fear resounded from the army, while some had dropped their weapons in fear.

There was little that could save them, after all.

The trolls took care of the soldiers above, as the glicks began to overpower them with their numbers, making their way down the pass and killing all who stood before them. Bashir was still up on his rock, watching the slaughter ensue. His eyes welled with tears for his fallen men, and he knew then that this may be their end.

"It could be worse," Gwili said from behind him. "How could it be worse?" Bashir asked, feeling distraught at the thought of his men dying and his revenge on Truls failing. "My men have been squashed into bloodied pulps by the ice and fire trolls, while the glicks are overpowering the others like ants to sugar," he continued.

"You have not lived as long as I have, so you'd better believe me when I say that it can always be worse," he said grimly. The two watched the slaughter continue, listening to the screams of the men and women beneath them being trampled and mauled. A fire troll spat molten rock over a group of soldiers, who melted away instantly.

"No!" Bashir exclaimed, watching his men smolder, the smoke from their burned bodies reaching his nostrils and causing his breakfast to pour out from between his teeth.

"Why do you not give us aid?" he growled to the elf. "Even if I had had my men place every arrow with the precision we elves are famous for, it wouldn't even have made a dent in this large of a force," Gwili explained. "So you will abandon us?" Bashir asked, desperately looking at Gwili with bloodshot eyes.

"It's nothing personal. Just know that I hope you die well," Gwili said grimly. He crept back down the boulder and was off into the bushes, leaving Bashir alone atop the boulder.

Bashir turned away from the fleeing elf to observe the battle. Many had fallen, and he could see his army on the uphill slope of the trail being overrun by glicks. "This is it, this is the force that will bring about the world's end," he said quietly. He watched the battle for another moment, listening to the sounds of his men fighting to their deaths.

He turned away and slumped behind the top of the boulder, placing his hands on his head.

I have sent my men on a suicide mission out of anger for Bashaa, bringing more death and destruction upon my kingdom, he thought as the battle raged on behind him.

My dearest Bashaa, I have failed to avenge your death, but I know that by the end of this day, we shall be together in the afterlife. I pray that you will welcome me with open arms, regardless of my failure as a father and broken promise to always keep you safe, he gritted his teeth, and gripped his sword tightly as he made his way down the rock.

He dropped off the edge of the rock and peered out from behind the corner, seeing the death and devastation the horde was leaving in its wake. "By Yarathea," he muttered, pushing his back against the wall to take a few deep breaths.

If there's no way out for any of us, then I have no choice but to accept my fate and pray that my son looks upon me proudly, as that is one of the only things a father could ever wish for from his children, he closed his eyes and sighed.

"Here and now, I will honor him, my forefathers, and my country. Let my sword sing with death and carry me onward into the afterlife," he muttered, tears beginning to stream down his face as he accepted his fate.

He stepped out from behind the corner of the rock, spreading his arms wide and roaring in a challenge that would have sent fear into the Undergod's heart.

To my wife, I hope you find solace in knowing that I died well, he gritted his teeth and prepared for the incoming attacks.

A few of the glicks saw him and began to charge towards him. He cut them down, one by one, removing limbs from bodies, and releasing a river of green blood that flowed around his feet. He continued screaming loudly, hacking down the horrid creatures, not even watching their limp bodies fall. He was keen on killing as many as possible in the time he had left.

To my sons, whom I will soon meet, I pray that you welcome me with open arms, embracing me in death as you did in life, he thought, slicing through the head of another.

The glicks began to circle around him as he looked into their grim faces. They snarled and squealed at him, some flicking their scales in challenge. "I will make you wish you had never been brought into this world," he growled threateningly. The glicks flicked their scales in unison, and he knew that his next breath might be his last.

Just as they were about to attack, a loud, eagle-like screech overhead prompted the glicks to look up, and they backed away from him, looking up at the figure in the sky. They no longer flicked their scales and stood down from their challenges at the sound of the screech.

Why aren't they coming at me? Do they have a master? Has he come here, to this place? Damn it, I can't see a thing with the sun in my eyes, he thought, looking up in the direction the screech came from.

The sun was now at its highest peak, and Bashir could only make out the silhouette of a winged creature in the sky. The beat of its wings created a strong breeze along the Pass, though there wasn't much dust being kicked up due to the blood-soaked ground.

As he flinched with the wind's increasing strength, he noticed many of the creatures had somehow been forced to stand still, as the crystals on their foreheads glowed with a more intense violet light.

Gorm watched the glicks around himself and Ari back away. "Was it the griffin that made them do that?" he asked his unlikely partner. "Not the griffin," Ari responded in shock, those being the only words he could say as he looked up.

The griffin perched itself on the highest peak in the pass, looking down on the mass of corpses. Gorm looked up at it, noticing a dark figure on its back that was holding one of the glowing crystals as it stepped off the griffin's back.

"It's him," Ari said breathlessly. "*Him*?" Gorm asked out of the corner of his mouth. "There were stories of one who resided in a dark citadel in the North. He must be the one who brought these monsters here," Ari continued, prompting Gorm to look up, though he could only just see the figure and the crystal.

"How are you so sure?" he asked. "Because glicks and trolls don't simply decide to work together of their own volition. It's not in their nature to do so. You, of all people, should know that, by now," Ari said, not bothering to hide the venom in his words. "I do," Gorm said, remembering his many years and everything he had learned during his time in the Guild.

The figure looked about at the devastation below. Bodies of both monsters and men strewn across the pass, motionless in the sodden earth. He raised the crystal and pushed a large amount of mana out from it, covering that section of the pass in a large dome of violet mana.

"You have fought hard and well," the rumbling voice said, his voice sounding like it was right next to each of the ones below. "I have seen your valor, and have proven yourselves worthy warriors," he spread his arms wide, making the rest of the warriors look toward him.

"I now offer you a choice: Join me, and we shall take over the four countries of the Continent together. In addition, your loved ones and families will be spared. Otherwise, you will die where you stand. Honorable, but foolish nonetheless," he said, glaring down at them imperiously.

"Who are *you* to ask us such a question?" Gorm asked with a snarl. "I am the one known as the Masked One. I am but a herald of my master and his power. If you think I hold great power, then that means you know nothing of what power truly is," he grinned beneath his mask, putting a hand across his chest and bowing.

"Again, I will ask: Will you ally yourselves with me and my horde, or will you suffer the consequences of your choices based on ignorance and folly?" the Masked One asked.

He commands these beasts through his own power alone, and his master is more powerful than he is? What could a handful of men do against such a force? Bashir thought as he looked at him.

Gorm and Ari now walked over to Bashir and stood by his side. "Should we believe him?" Ari asked as Bashir looked at the pair, unsure of what to say. "I don't like this one bit. All the years I've spent in the Guild have taught me never to trust one whose promises sound too good to be true. By Mideia, I'd sooner trust *Ari* than I would that mage," Gorm sighed, allowing his words to sink in. "We're dead men, either way, Gorm," Bashir began with a shake of his head.

"Our lives have long since revolved around cheating death in each and every moment. However, it would seem today Death itself has finally caught us red-handed. Our wives, our children, even us; we all come to the same fate in the end," he continued, turning to face them with a serious glare.

"It doesn't matter if we thought ourselves to be good men in life; all that matters is what we choose to do in the present. The past cannot be changed, that much is certain, but right now... Right now, we have a choice to make. Do we abandon our values, our honor, and our countries we've held so dearly, or do we uphold our honor and fight to the death?" he shifted his gaze between the pair of unlikely brothers in arms.

He walked over to the two bloodied warriors and put a hand on either of their shoulders. "We may have different opinions, beliefs, and other such matters. However, I must thank you two for being able to see past that, and work together as best you could," he nodded seriously, as Gorm's eyes widened.

"You have shown me that there is yet *hope* for this world, and that someday we may be able to work together in harmony once more," Bashir said, tears welling in his eyes.

"Gorm, I know you want to kill me, and I know Ari wishes to kill you. But I must ask the two of you to stand with me, in one final stand against this evil," Bashir bowed his head, confusing the two of them momentarily.

Gorm let the words stew for a moment before he gave a relenting sigh. "I'm going to regret this, aren't I? Well, I suppose if we're about to eat dirt, might as well do it the same way we came into this world; kicking, screaming, and covered in blood," he grinned. "So, you *do* have honor," Ari scoffed. "I might be an asshole, but I'm still a warrior," Gorm shrugged.

"One filled with honor to fight for what you believe in and the honor you uphold for your country, not only your inherently selfish desire to kill me. I praise you for that, Gorm," Ari said with a nod.

"I will see you in the afterlife, Ari. I hope that we can finish this duel when we get there," Gorm said, growing a slight grin on his face. "I'm sure we will," Ari responded in a surprisingly kind tone.

The three of them looked up at the Masked One on his rock. "We will not bow to you, your power, or your promises," Bashir shouted up at him. "Fools," the Masked one said, keeping the dark sphere around them and commanding the remaining army to converge on them. The three drew their swords and charged together headlong into the fray.

The Masked One watched as they cut down the first few monsters that came at them. The large force soon overcame the three, and their bodies could not be seen amidst the chaos. He undid the dark sphere, not even bothering to watch the warriors' deaths, and placed the crystal in its socket on the saddle.

He mounted the griffin, the large wings kicking around small rocks beneath him as it took to the sky once more, the horde below following him down the far end of the pass toward Coltend Castle.

Bloodshed, destruction, and death were the only things they left in their wake as they went.

Once the Pass finally cleared, an unrecognizably bloodied man had managed to escape the massive horde, stumbling his way down the mountain. He went to the nearest town, where he procured the owner of what he recognized to be a horse stable.

"Somebody help!" the stablehand cried out, noticing the man was covered in slash-like cuts, blood pouring profusely from them. "Please, you must help him! He's going to die!" the boy shouted as he ran to the front door of a two-story house. "By the gods, boy, what happened?" Ahkmed asked urgently, swinging the front door open.

"Sir, you have to help him! Look at him!" the boy cried out, pointing towards the newcomer.

Ahkmed looked at the man, noticing his bloodied state. "Shit. Boy, fetch a pail of clean water and some rags and bandages. Move quickly!" he commanded, rushing towards the man, who was too injured to stand any longer, and collapsed into the stable owner's arms.

"Hey! Hang in there! If you can speak, tell me your name and what happened," he said to the wounded man. "A horde of... creatures a-and... a dark mage... going to Coltend. Send... raven... to warn... Synners..." the man said weakly, coughing up some blood. "I will send the raven as soon as I get your wounds treated," Ahkmed nodded.

Nearly two hours had passed since the man had arrived at the town, and he was only just now finished being treated. After Ahkmed completed the man's treatment, he wrote the letter, even though his Common wasn't very legible.

"Sir, I have completed the letter, but I need your name to go along with it," he said gently. The man, covered in bloodied bandages, could hardly turn his head to look at Ahkmed.

"My name... is Gorm," he wheezed.

CHAPTER 17
THE JOURNEY NORTH

As the moon set in preparation for the morning sun on the distant horizon, there was already movement within the fortress. I gathered my gear from my room and checked every piece to make sure it was in proper working order.

I was still wearing the clothes I had put on just before going to sleep, and in the cold before the light of day, I shivered at their touch. The others in my quarters did the same as they checked their loadouts.

Sword is sharp, my jerkin and boots are clean, too. I think that's about it for here, I thought, putting my gear on, and lacing my sword and scabbard to my leather belt.

"Got everything there, Ed?" I asked. Edryd scratched the few whiskers that grew on his chin. "I think something's missing," he said curiously. "What makes you think that?" I asked. "Well, you see, all of my equipment's here, but my pendant isn't," Edryd said.

"Not sure I've ever noticed you had one," I said, thinking back as far as he could. "Well, it's fucking gone," Edryd said frustratedly, rummaging through his belongings one more time.

"I'll help you look for it," I said, joining my friend in pursuing the pendant. "*Uh,* wait," I thinned my lips. Edryd looked at him. "What?" he asked flatly. "I have no idea what it looks like," I shrugged, causing him to sigh and shake his head. "Seriously? After over *twelve years* of knowing me, you still don't know what it looks like?" he stepped forward to raise an eyebrow directly in front of my face.

"You never showed me what it looked like," I shrugged again. "F-Fair enough," he stammered, realizing I was right. "It's my family's crest," he began. "It was a gift from my Mom to my brother, who wore it during his time as a Synner. After he died, my mother found it in a small box under his bed. Not sure what it was doing there, as he never took it off, but that's where she found it," Edryd said grimly.

"I'm sorry," I said, lowering my head. "You've got nothing to be sorry about. He died bravely, or so they tell me," he said distantly. "*Oh*, I don't doubt that. I just can't imagine what it would be like to lose someone that close," I replied, trying my best to be sympathetic.

"I would doubt it, if I were you," Edryd began with a shrug. "What do you mean?" I asked. "Well, you see, he wasn't exactly the bravest of Synners nor the most adept at casting spells. Mom used to say I reminded her a lot of him when he was younger," he continued. "Was that supposed to be a compliment?" I scoffed. "Not sure, honestly," Edryd replied with a light chuckle.

"All I know is that I looked up to him, regardless of what my mother or friends thought. He might have had his difficulties with spells and courage in a fight, but he still did his job nonetheless," he said, looking as if he was recalling a few memories from his childhood.

"If it's of any comfort, you're not complete *shit* at casting spells, and you're pretty good with a sword. I think your brother would be proud of you," I said, trying to cheer my friend up. "You've only ever seen me cast during training. I have a hard time remembering that we have that power during a fight, so I simply stick to what I know," he replied with an upturned lip, raising his hands to shoulder height as he shrugged. "Well, we could practice that one of these days. Might do us *both* some good," I grinned.

Edryd shook his head. "I fear that this journey may very well spell the end for some of us," he began.

I know he's got good instincts, but for him to say something that dark is new, I thought.

"What do you mean?" I asked, hearing the tone in my friend's voice. "This whole thing of going to Hjalfar to fetch reinforcements is just...*weird*," he replied uncomfortably. "Well, we did just suffer a massive attack on the fortress, and the knowledge held here in the wrong hands would probably be a bad time for everyone," I said.

"I know. Trust me, I've been thinking the same thing," he replied, glancing over his shoulder to the doorway, then immediately turned back to me. "Ed, are you okay?" I asked, taking a step forward. Just as he opened his mouth to say something, his face paled, and his words were interrupted by Irun, who stood in the doorway.

"Need any help?" Irun asked plaintively, sending a chill down Ed's spine. "*Uh*, sure," he replied, trying to hide his nervousness. "What exactly are you looking for?" Irun asked. "My pendant," Ed stammered, prompting Irun to pull an object out of his pocket. "This thing?" he asked, holding a small pendant of a metallic hawk's beak that dangled loosely before Ed's widened eyes.

"You fucking *snitch*!" he snapped, quickly pulling it out of Irun's hands, who just looked at him in confusion. "*Whoa*, I didn't steal *shit*. I found it outside on the training yard's floor about a day or two ago. A *thank you* would be nice, you know," Irun raised his hands placatingly.

Ed looked at him curiously, then gave a relenting sigh. "Sorry. It's just very precious to me, and I thought you'd stolen it for whatever reason," he said, but I could tell that wasn't the *only* reason he'd said that.

"By the way, why do you even wear that old thing?" Irun tilted his head. "It was my brother's from a long time ago. He died when I was about five years old," Edryd replied, examining the pendant for any damage. Irun didn't say anything in return, but gave a slight sigh and lowered his head.

I stood silently, observing the exchange between the two.

"Well, it's back in your hands, and that's all that matters now," I said calmly, stepping in between the two. "Hope it never leaves them again," Edryd said, putting the pendant around his neck. "At least now I know whose crest that is. If it ever goes missing again, I'll bring it straight back to you," he continued, a small, sardonic grin showing on his face.

"Sure," Edryd shot back coldly, causing Irun to raise an eyebrow at the remark, but said nothing. Shortly after the awkward exchange, we left the room with our gear and headed toward the stables, where Batch was already prepping his horse.

"Early as ever. Did you even get any sleep?" Irun asked as Batch finished tying the last parcel to his saddle. "Nope. Better to be ready early than to rush to get things done," he replied. "Good point, but how slow do you have to be not to get any sleep?" Irun asked jokingly. "It's not that I didn't want to sleep, it's that I couldn't, you dim-witted *chuckle-fuck*," Batch snapped back mercilessly. "*Oh-hoo,* someone's extra spicy today," I said in jest, obviously fanning the flames.

Irun was anything but happy about Batch's retort, as he had nothing to return it with, or at least that's what it looked like. "Alright, Batch, you've made your point. Let the *dim-witted chuckle-fuck* get his stuff ready without taking his head off," Ed managed between laughs as he patted Irun on the shoulder.

We each walked over to our horses, tying supply bags to our saddles. The bags were mostly filled with apples, dried meats, and a few portions of mixed dried fruits and nuts. After loading our horses, we walked them out to the central courtyard, where a few other synners were already gathered. Garett was speaking with a couple of bow-casters, while Bernar was talking to Roburn.

"Decided to come along?" Roburn asked us. "Not like we had a choice," Irun shrugged, making him chuckle. "Nothing like a good ride with cheery companions, *eh*, Bernar?" Roburn said, driving his elbow into my brother's ribcage with a laugh.

"At least your little brother has decided to come along willingly," Roburn said. "Waking up before dawn to go towards Hjalfar, on a road I barely know anything about, with glicks and other horrible creatures potentially lying in wait; I'd hardly call it willingly," I replied with a slight chuckle. "In truth, I'm somewhat glad you're coming with us," he began, surprising me and the others.

"After that showmanship you put on during the most recent battle, I'd say you're more than ready for this trip," he said with a smile out of the corner of his mouth. I looked to my brother, hoping what I had just heard wasn't in jest, which he confirmed with a simple nod.

"I just hope he doesn't send anyone else to the *infirmary* this time," Edryd said playfully with a shrug. "Agreed. That spell you cast on our way to Coltend was extremely risky. You might have missed and hit Ed with it," Irun said, making me sigh and look to Bernar. He raised an eyebrow at me, while I looked at him with an expression that almost looked like I was asking to choke-slam the shithead.

For whatever reason, he decided to have the patience of a *monk* that morning and merely shook his head.

Fiiiine, I mentally sighed, rolling my eyes.

"I made my choice, Irun, and possibly saved his life in the process," I said coldly as he looked at me with a raised eyebrow. "You're not planning on doing that around *me*, are you?" he asked with a slightly worried look. "You're a bit of an asshole; I might consider it," I replied with a shrug, making Batch and Ed chuckle, while Irun scoffed and pulled his horse away, leaving the group.

"In his defense, he has been studying a lot, trying to prove himself worthy of going after a senior-level certification," Batch began. "Have you become his protector?" Roburn asked. "N-No, I'm just saying that he's got a lot on his mind. Maybe that's why he's being such a *flaccid* prick," he continued, making Bernar laugh aloud, followed by the others.

"Fuck him, I don't care. He's got no right to take his stress out on us, and I'd rather see him gone along with it if that's how he's going to act around people he's been with most of his life," I spat. Bernar looked at me and knew I meant it. "Not much you can do about that now," Roburn said as I watched Irun lead his horse away.

He's changed over the last few months. Too much, I thought, observing him carefully.

The Master walked down the steps from his study, with a small parchment in his hand. His gear was always in near-perfect condition, and his sword was tightly laced to his belt as he stepped into the courtyard. One of the stable boys awaited him with the reins in his hand. Daylight rose, and the morning mist could be seen over the distant hills in the background.

The Master walked past the other Synners gathered in the stone courtyard. He nodded to a few that he had come to know well over the years but maintained his pace. He reached his horse, taking the reins from the stable boy who looked into his glowing yellow eyes as he did.

"It is unlikely that we will return anytime soon. In the meantime, I want you to go home to your family, as you should be with your loved ones in these trying times," the Master said quietly as he handed the stable boy a bag of coins that was likely ten times the boy's salary.

"M-master, this is too much!" the stablehand exclaimed. "It's not just for you, silly. It's for your family, too," he said, scruffing up the boy's hair, but his expression sank.

"But... I don't have a family to go home to, Master," the boy's head lowered, making the Master raise an eyebrow and squat down to his level. "Since I've started working here, you have been the family I never had. Some have even allowed me to practice swordplay, and I have done my best to learn what I can to show my gratitude," he continued, sniffling quietly.

The Master was visibly touched by this display and placed a hand on the boy's shoulder. "Well, if you've no family to go to, would you like to come *with us*? You can ride with one of the carts, and I'm sure we could use your help with taking care of the horses," he said gently.

The boy was ecstatic with the Master's words. "You mean that, Master?" he asked with a glisten in his eyes that wasn't there before. "I do. Go and gather your things. We're leaving in a few minutes. Hurry, now," the Master said, giving the command gently. "I won't let you down, Master!" the boy said, happily sprinting off to gather his few belongings.

Well, that takes me back, I thought, feeling a solemn smile come across my face, watching as the same happened to the Master.

His smile faded quickly when he turned to look at me, as if he'd remembered that night as well. I gave him a knowing nod, and a much smaller grin appeared in the corner of his mouth, gently wrinkling his scar.

After ensuring all the others were prepared to leave, the Master mounted his horse, looking out over the crowd. He could feel the words he was about to say weigh heavily in his heart.

"I despise being the bearer of bad news, but I have received messages this evening that a large force of glicks, trolls, and other foul creatures has defeated a Harutian army destined for Coltend," he said to us, getting a few shocked gasps and murmurs from us as we all looked at each other, likely wondering whether or not this was going to be a suicide mission.

Another one? I felt my eyes widen.

"Not only that, but King Truls has been murdered, and now the Church has forcibly taken command of Coltend Castle. Therefore, our goals are now twofold: To protect Coltend from the oncoming horde and restore order to this country's capital. Perhaps a few of you will not like the idea, or maybe even decide to flee before the battle of our time, but believe me when I say there is more at stake than simply saving a city," he continued gravely.

A few more murmurs rose from those in front of him, but none dared voice it any louder than that.

"As it stands, we must ride to Hjalfar to seek help, since the Rhydian Pass has been overrun with beasts, denying help from Harut or Caegwen. I must know who will stand with me, and their fellow synners to save our country and possibly others from this dreadful fate," the Master continued. A few New Bloods shifted in their saddles, glancing at one another to see who would be the first to decline the challenge.

"I will not consider you as outcasts if you decide to leave now, but know that the odds of us all coming home are slim at best," he said, giving the crowd one more chance.

No one moved.

"Very well, then. We ride to Hjalfar," he said, the great wooden doors opening to the empty road ahead of them. The Master was the first to exit the fortress, followed closely by Bernar, Anwill, and Garett. I was ahead of the others in hopes of staying as close to my brother and the Master as I could. Hooves echoed across the courtyard, taking over the quiet of the first light of day.

"It might be a hopeless cause. I might be leading them to their *deaths*," the Master told Garett just loudly enough for me to hear. "Perhaps, but not for all of us. This may look like our final stand, but I am sure we will succeed in protecting this Continent to the extent of our abilities," he replied with a firm nod.

I admire your optimism," the Master replied, staring down the road for potential threats. "So do I," Bernar said, pulling his horse up next to the master bow-caster. "I mean, this might not be the *brightest* idea we've ever had, but it's our only hope of not being completely overrun and having it stolen from us," he continued.

"Which is exactly why we must not fail. I just hope the traitor will not pose so much of a threat to where it jeopardizes our mission," the Master said quietly. "We'll soon know who it is," Garett said. "Once again, your optimism is outstanding," the Master returned.

After deciding it was probably best to give up on eavesdropping any further due to the thunderous sound of hooves, I glanced over toward the sunrise. As we turned down the northern path, I felt the first beams of sunlight warm my face.

A blood-sky on the morning of a long journey is usually not *a good sign,* I thought as I observed the sky fade from a dark blue into a bright mix of orange and red.

I closed my eyes, taking the warm rays that warmed my cheek as a sign.

The night is always coldest before the dawn, or so I've heard. Every-thing will happen in the time and way it's meant to, but even with all my training and close brushes with death so far, I don't think anything could have prepared me for this feeling, I thought, taking in a deep breath through my nose.

I watched the sky begin to disappear behind the ever-thickening trees. Birds sang in the high canopy of the woods, completely oblivious to the ones below them and our fate-deciding quest. I listened to their early morning songs, breathing in the woodland air deeply. I filled my mind with their songs, and my lungs with air to calm myself down.

Not much else to do right now, after all. I just pray the gods will look down on us favorably, just like the Lord of Codrean all those years ago. If not, well, at least we tried, I mentally shrugged.

While I was lost in thought, Ed rode beside me and punched me lightly in the shoulder. "Morning, sunshine," he said brightly, obviously trying to get me out of my own head. "Yeah, it sure is," I chuckled, briefly looking behind me at the others, who were likely thinking the same things I was.

"I never would have thought it would come to this," he began with a heavy sigh, as a small cloud of steam rose from his mouth. "I had always thought I would die on a hunt far away from here," he said grimly. "You won't die," I said firmly. "You can't promise that," he scoffed. "You're right, I can't. Never have; never will, either. But you're my best friend, and I've known you long enough to know that no matter what happens to either of us, our memories will live on in the other," I smiled weakly.

"When did *you* get all philosophical?" he raised an eyebrow and blinked a few times in utter confusion. "Just now, dipshit," I chuckled. "Well, that's comforting, I suppose," he said with a false smile. "Don't get all emotional before the battle, you pair of *saggy tits*," Bernar interrupted.

"It fucks with your head, and that is not something you want to happen. We haven't even reached Hjalfar yet, and you're already thinking about your deaths?" he asked with a hint of disappointment. "It's not like that isn't possible," Ed shrugged. "It better *not* be. I don't want you to wet your hose again before you even draw your sword," Bernar said wryly. "That wasn't even me!" Ed replied louder than he intended. "*Sure* it wasn't," Bernar grinned. "Shut up, you two," Garett spat back, making the two of them flinch.

I looked at my brother with an upturned lip and raised eyebrows. "Not a word," he scowled at me, pointing his index finger between my eyes. "I didn't say anything," I replied smugly, causing him to squint his eyes and return to the Master's side.

"What is it between your brother and the Master, anyway? I mean, I know they both have the same glowing yellow eyes, but what's that got to do with playing favorites?" Batch asked, finally joining in on the conversation.

"Couldn't tell you even if I tried," I replied. "You don't have the same eyes as your brother, and yet the Master still seems to take you closer under his wing than the rest of us," Irun added. "Look, I don't know a *damn thing* about the Master and his choice of favorites, alright?" I shot back.

"*Ooooh*, kitty's got claws. Should I be scared?" he said mockingly. "They'll tear you from taint to throat, if you push me far enough," I retorted with a slight scoff. "*Oh*, you *wish* you could take me in a proper fight," Irun said, obviously trying to provoke me further.

I did my best to mimic my brother's *monk-like* attitude and not allow him to push me further.

I'd be lying if I said I didn't come close to *snapping*, though.

We continued on our journey, down the beaten path towards the borders of Hjalfar. We came to a choke in the river, which was teeming with aquatic lifeforms; trout, salmon, frogs, and other such animals could be seen just beneath the surface of the crystalline water. The horses and wagons had no difficulty wading through the gentle current as everyone crossed safely to the other side.

"We have just crossed into Hjalfar," Garett told the four of us behind him as we observed our surroundings. "This land is full of dangers, many more so than Coltend, so be on your guard," he continued.

We began to look more closely as the landscape changed from various trees into a pine forest. Birds and other beasts could be heard in the distant reaches of the forest, far away from the road we were on, when something stirred in the distance. Garett picked up on them through the trees and immediately moved towards the Master. "Master, we're not alone," he said quietly, nodding in the figures' general direction, allowing him to find them after looking into the indicated location. "Let's go," the Master said, turning his horse towards them.

Bernar signaled for me to follow along, while Garett halted the others. The three of us rode through the trees, leaping over rotting logs and low-lying bushes in our path. The figures saw us coming and rushed to find cover. The Master reached where the three figures once stood and looked around, finding little more than a few footprints in the disturbed mossy floor.

"We mean you no harm if you mean none to us," the Master called out.

No answer came.

Suddenly, a large man appeared from behind one of the larger pine trees. "Hallo, Master," the man said. "Thorsen!" the Master said astonishedly. "Where are the other two who were with you?" he asked. Leona and Meliss emerged from behind a nearby shrubbery, dirtied and cold.

"Your Majesty, young lady, are you alright?" the Master bowed from his saddle. "Not so *majestic* now, am I, master Synner? I am just a woman with little left but her life," she said, returning the bow. Bernar looked at her with wide eyes, remembering her beauty from the first time he saw her at the council.

What's the fucking queen doing here? Holy shit, is that who I think it is? She's alive! I hope she's not hurt, I thought, realizing Meliss was hiding herself behind Thorsen's large figure.

"You have no horses with you? How have you come so far from Coltend?" the Master asked the giant. "We failed to find any during our escape, Master, so I carried these two until I was sure we would be safe. Coltend has suffered a great treachery, Master," Thorsen said, shaking his head and glancing down at his filthy armor riddled with specks of moss, dirt, and dried blood.

"We're aware of the situation, but we only have minimal details," Bernar stated. "The Church decided that we were unholy and unfit to rule over Coltend, and so they took matters into their own hands by slaying nearly every innocent person who had failed to escape, or supported the royal family within the palace walls. I fear they may have taken over the *entire capital* by now," Leona sighed heavily.

"I didn't know priests knew how to fight like warriors," Bernar said incredulously. "Neither did I. They must have paid off most of the Guild to turn a blind eye to ensure their success in taking over the city," she said grimly. "I can think of more than a few who would readily accept such a deal, but it's just as likely they *joined in*," Thorsen added. "This is ill news, indeed. I pray you can tell me how it all began," the Master said.

"I was fast asleep in my quarters when the sound of screams echoed up from the hall to my ears," Leona began shakily. "I went downstairs to investigate the cause of the screams, and found the majority of my staff strewn across the floor, with the symbol of the Church engraved in their foreheads, and their throats slit from ear to ear," she said with difficulty, swallowing a lump in her throat.

"I found Meliss fleeing from a few of the murderers, and we managed to reach Thorsen, for he was the only one I could think of at the time who may have been able to help us. He gave us each a dagger, but we approached the nearest gate, where we encountered some resistance. He fought bravely, and healed the wound that an arrow had made when it struck my shoulder," she explained, causing our eyes to widen in surprise.

"He healed it? How?" Bernar asked, visibly intrigued. "With *mana*. He is one of the last Synners of Grundvollr to have survived the attack that didn't turn to banditry," she explained.

Well, I'll be... I thought, shocked at the news, but I quickly found that the Master was nowhere near as surprised as I was.

"You mentioned Grundvollr was attacked? When did this happen, and how the hell didn't we hear about this?" he asked in a tone I'd never heard him use before.

"King Mads had declared that its fall should remain a secret, one that remained so for over forty years. He considered anyone who had survived the attack to be a failure and a disappointment, hunting and branding them outcasts as a result," Thorsen began with a heavy sigh.

"What?" Bernar tilted his head angrily.

"Only I and one other remained true to our lives as synners for a time after, though he and I later went our separate ways," Thorsen said, averting his gaze. "By the gods, I am sorry to hear that," the Master said, lowering his head with a slight shake. "As am I for having lived through it," Thorsen replied as the Master was clearly lost in thought.

"If Grundvollr has fallen, why are you heading North? We were going under the assumption Grundvollr was still active, but why are *you* going that way?" he asked. "You see, Master, the fact that Grundvollr had fallen had stopped me from pursuing a Synner's life after a while, but it didn't stop the other one who had survived. He's hidden *here*, in the southern part of Hjalfar, far away from Mads' reach, and built a hidden synner school," Thorsen said, prompting my brother and the Master to glance at each other momentarily.

"Where is the school?" the Master asked. "Well, I'd be more than happy to show you, Master, but we have come a long way, and I fear the ladies might not hold out much longer at the pace we have maintained so far," Thorsen looked at their tattered appearances. "I will have horses brought for both of you. Can you ride?" the Master asked Meliss. "I can, Master, though not very well," she admitted. "Well, we're not moving very quickly, so I think you'll be alright," Bernar added with a warm smile.

However, I could only nod to her subtly since I couldn't get a word out, to which she blushed.

"Thank you. Both of you," Leona replied, giving them a warm smile. No amount of grime could hide her beauty, even as dirty as she was, and I could have sworn I saw my brother blush, but he turned away before I could confirm it.

"Bernar, take Leona with you back to the others. *Oh*, and Thoma," he said, finally acknowledging my presence. "Yes, Master?" I asked sheepishly. "You'll take *Meliss* with you. We'll get them some food and horses with the others," The Master said with a wolfish grin.

Fuuuuuuuuck, I thought as I realized what he was doing.

"I don't believe your horse will carry the *two of us,* Master. I can hold my own," Thorsen said with a toothy grin, judging the horse's size. It was a war horse, but Thorsen knew it would break under their combined weight. "*Oh,* good. I'm glad you caught that," the Master chuckled.

My heart nearly stopped beating entirely when I noticed *she* was walking toward me.

This can't be happening, he thought. I mean, I'm glad to see her, and more than happy to have her ride with me, but I'm a nervous wreck. Think I'd rather face an ochelon again than try to maintain my composure right now, I thought, feeling my pulse begin to quicken.

She stretched out her hand with a warm smile as I was helping her up to ride behind me. She wrapped her hands around my waist and squeezed lightly.

He's got that shit-eating grin of his again, I thought as I noticed my brother staring at me.

My heart raced and palms began to sweat, as my body felt like it was about to implode. "You're not about to spit your morning meal, are you?" Meliss asked me playfully. "N-no, I'm alright," I replied nervously. Bernar helped Leona get behind him in the saddle. While I couldn't read his mind, I knew a nervous look on my brother's face when I saw it.

That's not to say mine was any better, to be fair.

The Master rode at a slow trot, with Thorsen jogging briskly beside him. Meanwhile, Bernar kept Leona in place, placing a hand over her thin arms around his waist. We soon reached the others, where Garett had stopped the small army, and I saw the look on Ed and Batch's faces when they noticed who I had behind me.

Gods, not them, *too,* I blushed immediately.

Bernar helped Leona to the ground, where she was greeted by Garett and another synner who offered her water and food. I helped Meliss dismount my horse, with a bit of help from Bernar, and she thanked him warmly. Just before turning to accept a meal offered to her, she gave me as warm a smile as she could muster.

I did my best to return it, but my nervousness nearly got the better of me.

Leona maintained her graceful composure, dirty, hungry, and disheveled as she was, while she drank the water offered to her. "Here you are, Your Majesty," Garett said with a bow. "You needn't call me that any longer, for Coltend has fallen to our enemies and I am its queen no more," she said. I'd heard their brief exchange, but I couldn't take my eyes off Meliss, whose sole purpose in that moment was to ingest the food offered to her. She ate and drank her fill, and life returned to her quickly.

I tried to avert my eyes, but failed miserably when she caught me looking at her and gave me a shy smile like she was embarrassed to eat. I returned the smile, and did my best to encourage her to eat her fill without saying a word.

You are a fucking fool, Thoma Fayren, I thought.

"As I did not know of the hidden school, I'd like to ask you its precise location, now that we're in a more secure area," the Master said to Thorsen quietly. "It is in Fangsdalr, Master. Only about a day's ride from here," Thorsen replied with a mouthful of bread. "A *hidden school*? We'd best be on our way, then. Time is of the essence, after all," Garett said, not fully understanding why their destination was about to change. "Get horses for the lady and Thorsen, we must ride at once," the Master shouted.

Two extra horses were brought out for Leona and Thorsen, who immediately got into their saddles. "Meliss, you can ride with Thoma again," the Master said, with a grin just large enough to wrinkle the scar on his cheek. "Of course, Master," she replied kindly, making my face flush with blood so quickly that if she had seen it in that state, she might have agreed with my earlier thought about exploding.

Batch and Ed, of course, held shit-eating grins on their faces.

"We ride to Fangsdalr," the Master called out, turning his horse. Thorsen rode beside him, and they held an inaudible conversation. Bernar rode just beside us and next to Leona in silence, with a look that clearly showed he was trying not to make a fool of himself.

His eyes darted at her periodically as he noted her perfect riding form. The hems of her dirtied robes were draped over the sides and gently flowed in the wind. "I've never known a queen to ride with such ease," Bernar began, stumbling over his own words like a nervous child.

It made me giddy to see my once-confident brother shaking in his boots over a woman, just like my inexperienced ass.

"Thank you, though I'm not as adept as you Synners are," she replied warmly, immediately making him blush. She giggled lightly and smiled shyly back. "There's no need to blush. This is just a normal conversation," Leona said comfortingly. "I'm sorry, Your Majesty. I don't know why I am, truth be told," he said shyly.

Leona looked at him as if she knew he was around her age, but with far less experience in dealing with people who didn't carry a sword, or who weren't whores. She looked at his freshly-shaved face and black hair with an intent I couldn't read, but I was sure his glowing eyes added to her interest.

The audacity, I thought with a smile and a shake of my head.

"You already know my name, and yet I didn't catch yours earlier," Leona said inquisitively. "Bernar Fayren from Kinth, Your Majesty," he answered. Leona was puzzled. "I don't believe I have ever heard of Kinth before," she said, putting a finger to her small chin pensively.

"*Oh*, it's a small village *somewhere* on the map. Don't believe it holds much to be well known, Your Majesty," Bernar said dismissively. "Well, *you're* from there, so it at least held something of value," Leona said cheerfully. I was sure Bernar's heart skipped a beat or two, and after a slight pause, the two chuckled quietly.

"Not really. I mean, I'm certainly better with a sword and mana manipulation than most, but still not good enough to beat the Master in training, Your Majesty," he said with as much humility as he could muster, causing her to regard him curiously for a few heartbeats. "*How* good?" she asked playfully. "If I were there at the palace during the time of the attack, I would have turned the stone into *glass* just to save you," he blushed without meaning to.

Her eyes widened in surprise for a moment, but she must have assumed he was joking when she started to giggle, prompting him to do the same. After a few moments, she turned and looked back at *me* with her pale blue eyes, making even *my* heart skip a beat.

Alright, Bernar. I get it now, I mentally chuckled.

"Meliss, the girl here with me, is from the Gramm Isles," Leona began, trying to continue the conversation. "I think you two might have something in common, for until I met her, I had only ever heard rumors about the place," she said. "Well, I just hope she and my brother get along well enough. After all, they are riding together," Bernar said, using his head to gesture in our direction.

Leona looked beyond him and straight into my eyes again. With a quick, darting glance, she realized whose arms were wrapped around my waist, forcing me to blush even worse than I already had.

"He's redder than a maple leaf in autumn! What is his name?" she asked in a playful tone. "*Shit bird*, Your Majesty" Bernar said with obvious sarcasm, to which she snorted heavily, immediately putting a hand to her mouth to keep from bursting out with laughter.

I'm going to kill him, I held a chagrined smile as she looked back at me.

"I'm only kidding. His name's Thoma. He's just turned eighteen, and the horse he's riding is the one I gave him as a gift," he explained. "You two get along well, I assume," Leona said factually. "We do. Almost *too* well, at that. He's not as strong as I was when I was his age, about five years back, but he's got a good head on his shoulders, and a strong will; hard things to find in one person these days," he upturned his lip and shrugged lightly.

"Am I included in that select group of people?" Leona asked playfully. "I believe you to be *far beyond* that, Your Majesty," Bernar said with as low a bow as he could manage on horseback.

"You don't have to continue calling me that if you don't want to. I am no longer the queen of Coltend, and as it currently stands, I am simply a woman with the will to continue living, even if my old life of servants and banquets has ended abruptly," she said with a slight frown.

Bernar and I clearly understood what she meant.

"As sorry as I am to hear about your situation, I'm glad I don't have to call you by your full title. I've always hated them, after all," he chuckled, making her jaw drop in surprise. "That was *quick*," she said, lightly hitting his shoulder. "*Hey!* You were the one who wanted to be treated normally," he chuckled, lightly rubbing his shoulder.

I knew she hadn't even given him so much as a red mark on his skin, but I let him have that feigned moment of injury.

She's made it clear that she didn't want to be treated as royalty, but as a person. A human being. I can't imagine what life must have been like for her until now, I thought as I watched them continue their playful banter for a few moments.

"I never got your name," Meliss whispered, viciously reminding me that her arms were still around my waist.

Oookay, it's happening. Uh, think, you dumb bastard, think! Okay, we can do this! At least try to act naturally, I thought.

"Thoma," I replied after swallowing dryly. "Name suits you," Meliss said in her thick accent. "You're Meliss, right?" I asked, unable to think of anything better to say. "How'd you know?" she asked with a hint of sarcasm. "I remember you from the first time you showed up to take our armor back in the room at Coltend Castle," I grinned.

"True. I remember you had to strip down to your birthday suit," she chuckled, making me instantly regret reminding her of that fateful day. "Well, that's *one* way to meet someone for the first time," I said with a smile. "I'm sure there are worse ways," she said playfully. "Your accent... you're not from the Continent, are you?" I asked bashfully, unable to place its origin with my limited world knowledge.

"No, I came to the Continent about a year after my father died. My mother got us a job at the Castle a little while after we had arrived. I've been there ever since I was a wee child. The Castle, Leona, and the other servants there have given me *so much* to be thankful for that I feel like I could never repay them for their kindness to me," she said, her tone dropping melancholically, as her arms squeezed me a little more.

If only I could look at her, I thought, putting my hand on hers without realizing it.

I looked down at the tiny hands that fidgeted beneath mine. "Is something wrong?" I asked. "It might be a little much to say right now," she said hesitantly. "You've likely been through a lot already, so don't feel bad about getting it off your chest," I said as comfortingly as possible, feeling her take a small, shuddering breath.

"It's alright. I *have* to get it off my chest at *some point*," she said, balling her tiny hand into a fist. "I killed a man who wanted to kill me just before we fled the castle, and I don't know how to deal with it," she said shakily.

I could almost *hear* the tears running down her cheeks.

For a moment, I thought about what she said. I'd never killed another *human* before, only monsters, so while I could relate to what she was going through, it wasn't by much. "Well, what I'm about to say might not be of any consolation, but I hope it helps put things into perspective," I began, feeling her crying lessen momentarily.

"I've been training all my life to kill monsters. Terrifying creatures who wished nothing more than to see me dead on the floor, even though I have done nothing to them to bring that upon myself. However, until a few weeks ago, I had never actually killed *anything*," I paused, doing my best to choose my following words carefully.

"I had to kill them to protect myself and the others around me, and the bloodshed I've seen has since stuck with me. The man you killed was no different from the *monsters* I've had to kill. He wanted to see you dead, to destroy an *innocent life*, making him no different than any monster out there. You did what you had to do to survive, and you *should not* feel sorry for ridding the world of such an evil person," I said calmly.

Meliss sobbed behind me and tightened her grip around my waist. "Thank you," she said softly between her sobs. I looked down at the tiny hands and more intently placed one of mine on hers. They responded by gripping my calloused ones tightly, hearing her sob just a little harder.

"I don't know what to say to make you feel better. The most I can say is that you did the right thing, at the right moment. If you hadn't, you wouldn't be here, and I wouldn't have seen you again. *That* would have been an immense tragedy," I said, hoping my words were as reassuring as I thought they were. Her sobbing slowed down a little, as though my words had *actually* worked their intended magic.

"I'm glad to be here, and I'm even happier that I'm here with you," she said quietly, turning her face to lean her cheek on my back. "Me, too," I smiled, but said nothing else, hoping not to ruin the moment as we rode on in silence.

I watched the conversation between my brother and the queen, which seemed to be going quite smoothly, and I wished I could do the same with the one riding with me at some point.

I wonder if I'll ever be as happy as those two seem to be with each other, I thought idly.

I looked up at the canopy, seeing the sun's rays scattered throughout our surroundings. I could hear birds calling their mates off in the distant ceiling of branches above me, and wildlife on the ground shuffled the leaves around the trees, scurrying to find their breakfast of beetles and other such grubs to munch on. A weak breeze cut through the dense forest, making everything seem much more peaceful than it really was.

This place makes me want to believe that there is no evil looming just around every corner. It's almost as if this were an entire world that has been separated and secluded from centuries of destruction by those damn monsters, I thought, taking in as many little details as possible.

The Master still spoke with Thorsen ahead of him, and I strained my hearing to listen to what they were discussing. "Master, do you think he'll be ready?" he asked. "He's stronger than he looks. He may not look like it physically, but that boy has a willpower I don't think I've seen in a long time," the Master replied with a supportive nod from Anwill, who'd ridden silently the entire time.

"I pray you're right, Master," Thorsen said. "As do I," the Master said pensively.

What was that all about? I thought, confused by their conversation.

I knew they were talking about me, but what they meant precisely was far beyond my comprehension of the short conversation.

We rode until dusk and stopped along the side of the road where we made camp beneath the trees. The rising moon's light cast little light through the canopy beneath it. The silver rays licked the ground they could find through the canopy, while our centralized campfire filled the remaining dark spaces around us.

Meliss and I were separated for that night, having been given a tent for her and Leona to share until better lodging could be acquired. They didn't complain, but I knew it couldn't have been easy on them. Nevertheless, we slept blissfully, as the forest that teemed with life around us also slept.

Just before dawn, we geared up for another day of riding down the beaten paths towards Fangsdalr. Meliss appeared from her tent, as a few seniors helped her and Leona pack their things. She seemed to have recovered from her minor breakdown the previous day, and greeted me with a warm smile.

She could melt ice with that smile, I thought, feeling the winged creatures in my stomach doing consecutive backflips.

"Good morning," she said brightly. "It's much better now that I've seen you smiling," I replied warmly. I saw Meliss feel the blood rush to her face, as her eyes widened and she turned her face away momentarily. "Ready to go?" I asked, trying not to call her out on her reddened features. She didn't verbally reply, only giving me a curt nod, before taking my extended hand to help her onto Celer's back.

She sat behind me as she had the day before, making me a little nervous. However, I do remember that I could almost feel the warmth from her smile as she wrapped her arms around my waist again. It brought a subtle smile to my face that, unfortunately for me, was spotted by my brother and Leona.

They, too, had just finished packing up and were mounting their respective horses. He smiled at Leona, who blushed *ever so slightly*, prompting a quiet, subtle chuckle from him.

Role reversal since yesterday? Huh, who would've thought? I almost said aloud, but bit my tongue not to ruin their little moment.

Within a few moments, the entire group was off, heading north-east down the path, with the Master at the helm. Batch and Irun had stuck together for most of the journey, avoiding Ed's and my attempts to get them to join the conversation. My best guess was that the presence of both Leona and Meliss made them uncomfortable, but I had no real way of being sure.

We rode for a few more hours, observing the terrain change from grassy and forested plains to steep hills and mountains off in the distance. As we crossed the bridge built long ago over the Elv Avliv, everyone watched as the strong current flowed quickly beneath. The water was perfectly clear with all forms of aquatic life, both in the water and on the banks, taking in the early morning rays of sunlight.

"I've heard tales of great, winged creatures that live deep in the mountains," Meliss said idly as she observed the world around her. "You mean to say that there are wyrms and wyverns living in this portion of the Continent?" Ed asked, having finally mustered the courage to get near us. "Well, I didn't say *that*, specifically, but I've heard it said that one of the greatest ones of... whatever those names were, fell from a ball of flame from the sky," she said. "I'm no expert in wyvern births, but I'm not sure that's how that happens," he scratched his cheek.

"Let's just hope none decide to drop in on us during our time here," I said playfully. "Don't know what we would do if one did," Edryd. "Fight it with our fists? Hell of a way to go, if you ask me," I said sarcastically. Meliss and Edryd chuckled at the thought, terrifying as it was. "What's it like being a Synner?" she asked.

"Well, you wake up in the morning, eat some unidentifiable goop that looks like something that came out of a troll's nostrils, then practice your sword fighting and casting abilities for most of the day," I replied, keeping it as short as I could. "Then you fall asleep, hoping that the few bruises on your hands will heal the next day, only to find out your roommate has lit the room on fire with a mana-flame, and stupidly used a *piss-filled* bucket to try and douse it," Edryd chimed in.

"That happened *once*, Ed! For fuck's sake, I'm never living that down, am I?" I asked, my cheeks flushed with color. Meliss was giggling at the thought of the situation. "Once was enough to traumatize me for *life*, so thanks for that!" Ed continued mockingly. "But it's true. I always hope my bruises will heal the next day, and I tend to get a *lot* of them," he continued, gingerly rubbing his knuckles.

"Only time that ever happened to you was when you failed to pay attention, *dipshit*," Bernar said, butting in on our conversation. "Have you ever gotten hit in that way since I told you that?" he asked. "Not as often as I used to, I suppose," Edryd shook his head. "*Heh*, guess I'm not a horrible teacher after all," Bernar said with a chuckle as Leona slowed her horse to ride beside us.

"I don't know much about mana," Meliss said shyly. "Well, it's not *that* hard to understand. All you have to know is that there are other realms outside of the one we currently live in, and each one holds its own power. Right now, we can only tap into two of them, one light, the *Ethereal*, and one dark. However, we generally avoid the dark one," he tried to keep his explanation simple, but the look of utter confusion on her face told the rest of us it *hadn't* been simple.

"What happens if you use *dark mana*?" she asked, and as soon as she did, I noticed the Master slightly turn his head toward us.

"Well, you could become what's known as an *outcast*. Generally speaking, dark mana users only wield it for nefarious purposes. In the words of the Master, *one must always strive to do good unto others. Unless, of course, that bastard has done something worthy of your wrath. Lean not into the temptation of the Underworld's power, but instead, rely on your own judgment, lest you find yourself counted among the most vile of the world,*" he said in a near-perfect imitation, making the rest of us chuckle.

I think I was the only one who noticed the Master's subtle grin, but I don't know for sure.

The four of us continued to talk about our day to day lives, and Meliss shared what little experience she had had during her time as a servant to the queen. Bernar, of course, was particularly interested in that part, but did his best to hide it. Leona was deep in conversation with Thorsen, who'd also slowed his horse to join us, and smiled after learning all she had done for the young girl.

It still took Ed, Batch, and I some time to get used to the fact that she treated us like regular people, as we'd always believed royalty to be just a bunch of snub-nosed asshats with assholes for mouths, but we did our best.

As it turned out, she was more like a *goddess* than royalty, at least that's how my brother saw her, anyway.

The sun began to set, and the rocks and trees around us reflected the bright orange rays, making everything look like it was coated in a thin sheet of gold. We could see the Elv Avliv beneath them shimmering in the golden sunlight, flowing as swiftly and surely as ever.

"I never thought I would live to see a sight like that. In all of my years going from room to room, servants or guards trailing closely behind me, an adventure such as this was something I thought could only ever happen in books," she said blissfully. "I think I speak for everyone, *especially* my brother, when I say that we're honored to be able to show you this, even if it's not in the most perfect of conditions," I said, mustering any and all formal training I'd had during our week or so at the palace.

Leona looked at the others, who nodded in agreement, and smiled warmly. "It makes me glad to be in the company of such honorable and fine people," she replied, her pale-blue eyes aimed right into mine. I blushed as I felt Meliss pull closer than before.

I could get used to this, I thought, rubbing my thumb against her forearm gently.

"We've arrived," the Master called out. Anwill, who had been silent the whole way, breathed a sigh of relief, likely contemplating what needed to be done, among other matters like mortality and the fragility of life itself. "About damn time," he said to Bernar who laughed a little. "An *old man* like you must hate traveling this far in one go," he said with a grin. "*Elf*, and that's bullshit. I rather like traveling, it's just that I hate not knowing where I'm going," he said with a shrug. "Can't say I disagree with you," Bernar grinned.

The Master rode ahead with Thorsen and Garett to the top of the path, looking out over a few wooden houses and a small solid stone fortress. A single man stood atop the wooden palisade, wearing a black leather jerkin with green scales sewn into it. His white, shoulder-length hair flowed in the breeze, and his glowing yellow eyes watched the oncoming party.

"Master Pyle Rumia," the Master called out. "The Master of Codrean," Pyle shouted back. "What brings you here to my humble abode?" he asked with his arms spread wide. "We have traveled long and hard to find you. Thorsen has told us of Grundvollr's demise, and so we have come to you seeking aid," the Master replied.

"Magnar Thorsen is with you?" Pyle asked. "Hallo, my old friend," Thorsen shouted in his thick accent with a wave. "It *is* you! It has been too long," Pyle laughed heartily. "Indeed, it has been! It's good to see you're alive and well, friend!" Thorsen shouted up at him. "Please, come in!" Pyle shouted, motioning for the gates to the wooden palisade to be opened.

We rode inside, noticing many more houses inside than outside than they could have imagined. Pyle came down from the top of the palisade to greet us. Thorsen was the first one off his horse and ran over to greet him. They were about the same height, and to the shorter synners, it seemed that two gods were greeting each other.

"You've put on some weight," Pyle said, patting Thorsen's broad shoulders and giving him a once-over glance. "Being in Coltend's Guild will do that to you. Master, this is the one I spoke of," Thorsen said, watching the Master dismount his horse. "We've met before, but possibly long before you were born, Thorsen. It's good to see you again," the Master said, greeting Pyle with a firm handshake. "I thought that after that incident with the Ochelon by the river, you would never have come back," Pyle said with a raised eyebrow.

"I have always meant to return, not only to visit Hjalfar, but to thank you as well," the Master said. "Bullshit. I knew you'd find a use for what I had taught you, and it seems you have," he said, looking into Bernar's eyes. "Indeed I have," the Master said, looking over at Bernar, who dismounted and approached the three.

"An honor to meet you, Pyle," he said, stretching out his hand. "Likewise," Pyle replied, taking it and giving a nearly bone-crushing handshake. "So, down to business. What sort of aid do you seek?" he asked. "Well, we have traveled a long way to get here, so I think a place to rest and feed our horses will suffice for now," the Master began. "*Ah*, yes. My apologies, it's been a long time since we've had *any* visitors who came on friendly pretenses," Pyle said.

He put two fingers in his mouth and let off an ear-piercing whistle. A group of stable boys came rushing out of the nearby stables. The stablehand from Codrean rushed up from the cart he was riding in as well, and after getting their instructions, they immediately got to work. As they did so, the three, including Anwill and Garett, walked together, discussing a few things just out of earshot of the others.

"He didn't even introduce me," Leona said, somewhat discouraged. "I don't think the Master would want it to be known that you are here, lest someone spread the news that you're still alive," I replied hushedly. "I suppose you're right. I hadn't considered that news to have possibly traveled so far, so fast," Leona frowned, but quickly shifted into a smile when Bernar returned after a few moments.

"I'm to show you to your quarters," he smiled, gesturing to us. "What of the others?" Leona asked. "According to Pyle, they will be more than adequately cared for. Come, quickly," he said, taking Leona's hand, catching Ed and me by surprise, though Meliss was unfazed entirely by the gesture. We followed him down the main street, where everyone openly carried a sword, living peaceful lives.

There were no beggars nor any apparent signs of poverty within the palisade.

"This place reminds me a lot of Codrean, ironically enough," Edryd said, observing his surroundings. "Everyone carries a sword, and yet there doesn't seem to be any sign of violence here," Meliss added. "It's a lot like how we are at Codrean. We all understand that a real disagreement would likely lead to someone's death, which is why we speak the way we do to each other. Ironically enough, releasing constant tension through snide remarks and foul language staves off physical violence quite a bit," I explained, to which she and Leona nodded understandingly.

We followed Bernar into Pyle's house, where the others, Anwill included, were seated around a large wooden table cut from an ancient cedar tree. The size of the table made me think that it had been made from more than one tree, but I later found out I was wrong.

"Come, sit, for we have much to discuss," Pyle gestured towards the vacant chairs, each of which had their own distinct carvings of ancient and heroic feats performed by Synners of old.

The Master has one of these in his study, I thought back to the chair in Codrean.

"Ladies and gentlemen," Pyle began. "It has been a long time since I have had any visitors aside from traders and merchants, or other nefarious folk, so please forgive any inadequacies that you may find," he said. "I would like to first speak to Leona, who, even though she has been unlawfully removed from her throne, still remains a queen to all of us," he said with a smile. "I am truly flattered," she said with a bow of her head.

"The others in this town do not know who you are, which is why I made no ceremony when I saw you, but I knew exactly who you were; the main reason I have decided to speak with you in a more private setting," Pyle said.

"Told you," I whispered to Leona, who sat beside me.

"Keeping that in mind, I am more than certain that there are people here who would gladly sell you out to your attackers for a measly coin purse, but I will not allow that to happen," Pyle continued. "The Master has also informed me that a large force of monsters has just gone through the Rhydian Pass, making their way West, and possibly, to Coltend. We have discussed all possibilities, and I've already agreed to the terms the Master and Anwill have presented. Hopefully, with yours and Thorsen's help, we will find a way to take back what is rightfully yours," he said cheerfully.

"But first, I would have you and Meliss tell your story, as I would like to hear how this all came to be so I can better understand what we're getting ourselves into," he continued, gesturing for her to begin her explanation. "Thank you, Master Pyle," she replied with another bow.

Over the next hour or so, Leona and Meliss explained everything that had transpired over the past week. Thorsen added a few of his own points and mentioned their tactics in hopes of clarifying things for the group.

After hearing the complete story, Pyle sighed heavily and nodded with grave understanding. "Thank you for sharing that, your majesty. It must have been a harrowing experience, but I'm glad you made it out alive," he said, lowering his head in reverence. "We couldn't have done it without Thorsen, though," Leona replied.

"I know. He's one of the most trustworthy people I've had the honor of meeting. Speaking of which: Edryd, as I understand it, you are Thoma's best friend, but unfortunately, I must speak with him in private," he said with a thin-lipped expression. "That's alright, Master Pyle. I'll take my leave," Ed replied. "We'll retire to our chambers as well. It's been a long journey, and I would *very much* like a bath," Leona chimed in, getting a warm smile from Pyle.

"I'm sure you would, your majesty," Pyle said understandingly. Edryd excused himself with a bow as he rose from his chair, leading Meliss and Leona out and closing the door behind them.

Out of the frying pan, I thought, feeling the anxiety begin to stir in my chest.

"Thoma, the others in this room already know what I am going to tell you, so there is no need for them to leave," Pyle began. "Well, I'm already nervous, but that's a little comforting to hear, Master Pyle," I said. "There is no need to be nervous. I only want to ask you a simple question," he said. "And what might that be, Master Pyle?" I asked, trying to take his advice.

"I know that you are a smart boy, not much older than I was when I was first told that my abilities could be enhanced even further than what I thought possible. I'm sure you have spotted a few similarities between me, your brother, and the Master," Pyle said calmly. "You three having glowing eyes is the answer, I suppose," I replied, to which he nodded. "So, you must know, by now, that it is because we have unlocked deeper stages of mana manipulation. But what if I told you that this could be unlocked for you, as well?" Pyle asked.

"How, Master Pyle?" I looked at him and tilted my head. "Over the many years that Synners have been in existence, we have always had a few who sought out to *enhance* their abilities. Most failed because they did not understand what they were trying to do, while only a few succeeded. The Master is proof of one of the many tests done in the past," he explained.

"There are *five stages* of mana manipulation, as you know, though the *sixth* is currently unobtainable by humans," he continued. "Wait, there's one more? Why did we not learn about this when we began our training?" I asked. "That's because that level of mana manipulation would put one at the level of one of the many gods," Pyle frowned.

That's news to me. I wonder why that kind of information was hidden. He's probably debating whether it was a good idea to tell me that, I thought as I looked at the Master who was vacantly staring off into the distance.

"While I am not as expertly trained in teaching mana manipulation as someone like Anwill or his people may be, I am offering to help you reach the next stage. According to your brother, you've already reached the second stage, but do not have it completely under your control just yet," Pyle stated, his eyes staring at me intensely.

I took a moment to understand what he was trying to tell me, and considered his offer as carefully as possible. I knew there was a chance I wouldn't come out of it in one piece, but that was a risk I was more than willing to take if I was going to catch up to Bernar.

I looked to him and then to the Master, who both watched me curiously. I took a deep breath to calm myself down before I answered. "I gladly accept your offer," I bowed my head respectfully. "By the gods, Bernar, he hardly even hesitated!" Pyle exclaimed with a hearty laugh. "You should have seen him take on not one, but two ochelons," Bernar snickered, making Pyle's eyes open wide. "At the same time?" he asked excitedly, leaning forward in his seat toward him.

Bernar shrugged in response, pursing his bottom lip a little. "This little monster. Well, I suppose that concludes my business with you for today, although I would love to begin as soon as possible," Pyle said with a shake of his head and a dismissive wave. "Thank you, Master Pyle. I expect to hear from you soon," I replied, bowing again. "And so you shall, Thoma," Pyle grinned, however, Anwill regarded me with a curious look I couldn't place.

"Is something the matter, Anwill?" I asked without trying to sound disrespectful. "No, nothing's wrong. I was just considering the ramifications of bringing you to Caegwen for when you're ready to cross into the next stages," he smiled, though it was obvious to me that he wanted at least *some kind* of answer.

"You were the one who trained my brother, correct?" I asked, but his eyes shifted away from me momentarily to the Master, who exchanged a wordless glance. "I was there for his third and fourth stage training, yes," he said, causing me to raise an eyebrow.

He's hiding something, I thought, but didn't say anything.

"Then I would be honored to be under your tutelage," I bowed with a smile, which he promptly returned. "When this is all over, I'll be waiting," he said as I turned to leave the room. Bernar also decided it was a good enough time for him to leave and followed me out of the room.

"I know what you're thinking, bird-brain," he said quietly, thrusting his elbow into my ribcage as soon as I shut the door. "*Ow!* What the h-...?" I started, but he raised a hand to stop me. "Those were two difficult decisions you just had to make, and now you're wondering whether you'll even be able to make it through their training," he said as if he'd read my ungathered thoughts.

How the fuck does he know all that? I wondered in the heartbeat that followed.

"There are things I wish I could tell you right now, but unfortunately, I'm under strict orders from the Master not to," he continued. "You think it would have influenced my choice," I said briefly, understanding his meaning. "I don't think it would've, to be honest, although you would be more surprised than you could ever imagine," Bernar said with a grin.

What does he mean by that? I thought, holding a curious stare.

"Alright, what is it, bird-brain?" Bernar asked with a sigh. "Were you the one who recommended me for second-stage training?" I asked. Bernar thought about the question for a moment. "One day you'll understand that it is more than simply more power, to quote Master Pyle. Not like I knew that before accepting my own second and later stage training, but I have come to understand it in the last few years," he continued.

"You dodged my question, you fuck," I said with a slight grin. "Of course I did, twit," Bernar spat back. "Did you *really* think I would answer that? No, no. The reasoning for your being chosen had little to do with me. If that helps you piece it together," Bernar scoffed.

"Can't beat that argument," I sighed, looking at the ground away from him. "No, you can't. However, the others will come more easily if you can fully unlock the second stage. I know you've dabbled in it already, but *fully* locking it in is another story entirely," Bernar explained. I nodded, receiving a heavy pat on the shoulder. "Now go find Meliss, and get some, little bastard," Bernar said with a grin from ear to ear. "How did you...?" I felt my jaw drop to the floor. "Leona mentioned that Meliss likes you to me this morning," Bernar interrupted.

"Sh-she told you that?" I asked, my eyes widened to their utmost limits. "She did, but if you're not there with her, I don't know how much longer that liking will last," he shrugged, pushing me in the general direction of where she would be staying. "Run, dipshit, run," he said with a chuckle.

I was forced to take a second or two to process it all and nearly stumbled when I turned around to go find Meliss.

I can't believe it, Thoma thought. She... likes me? I mean, I'm definitely not the most handsome guy around, so why me? Fuck it, I guess I'll just have to find out, I thought as I felt an anxious smile creep onto my face.

I went to where I thought they would be and knocked on the thick wooden door. "Meliss? Leona?" I asked from the door, hearing a slight shuffling behind it come to a halt. I stepped back, realizing I was too close to the door, and wondered if I'd gone to the right room or had interrupted something else entirely.

After a few moments without a response, I turned to walk away from it but halted when I heard a bolt unlatch. I turned to find Meliss' eyes, peeping out of the tiny crack in the doorway. "*Oh,* it's you," she said quietly, excitement barely hidden in her voice.

I was puzzled.

"Who else would it be?" I asked. "Edryd was here a few moments before you knocked. He was looking for you," she said quietly. "Ed knew I was speaking with the others in Pyle's house, so why would he come here looking for me?" I raised an eyebrow. Just then, the two of us were interrupted by none other than Edryd himself. "*Ah*, there you are! So, what did they want with you?" he asked as he came down the hall.

You have terrible timing, I thought, wondering if Meliss was about to close the door on me.

"The Master told Pyle about that situation we had over in Co-drean. He wanted to see if I knew more about *you-know-who*," I lied. "What did you tell him?" Edryd asked. "The truth, that we still don't know who it is, and that we still have to be careful," I replied with a shrug. "Well, with any luck, he'll be able to help us with that," Edryd said. He looked at the crack in the doorway and found the pair of eyes watching the exchange.

It's about damn time, I mentally chuckled.

"Oh, I'm sorry. I-I didn't know..." he paused for a moment. "It's alright, Ed," I said with a smile. "I'll, *uh*, I'll be going, then," he stepped away, but the sly bastard gave me a wink and a childish grin that could hardly be out of the corner of his mouth. "Asshole," I muttered with a grin and a shake of my head.

I looked back at Meliss, who watched our brief exchange. "Well? Are you coming in or what?" she said quietly. I didn't really know what to say. Obviously, I wanted to go inside, but I was so inexperienced that I could only nod briefly and cautiously enter the room.

You're acting like an idiot, cut it out, I thought as I crossed the threshold.

The room was well furnished, with a few bear-hide rugs scattered throughout, a wooden closet, and a desk with a few bright candles on it that flickered as she shut the door behind me. "Listen, Thoma,

I don't want to be too forward, but no one invites someone of the opposite sex to their room late at night for just a chat," she said, closing the door behind her, and bolting the latch.

"*Oh*, yeah. I knew that," I lied. I had no idea what I was doing, but I did my best to play along as if I did. "*Oh*, alright. Well, I think you should know that this isn't my first time doing something like this. Granted, it has been a while, but I'm not new to this," she said as she walked toward me from the door with an almost embarrassed look in her eye

"I appreciate the honesty, and almost wish I could say the same," I said, knowing anything else I thought of saying would either be a lie or reveal how shocked I *actually was*. "You've never been with a woman?" she asked.

No way to escape that one, I mentally sighed.

"Never really got the chance. My days, up until recently, have been spent mostly in Codrean, where the female synners there are more focused on their training, rather than messing up the sheets with someone. However, I *do* have a question," I said shyly, prompting her to tilt her head to the side. "Why me?" I asked bluntly.

She took a moment to think about it, but shook her head as if she didn't really understand why, either. "I guess I just felt like you weren't like the others who've tried to eat me with their eyes this whole time we've been riding together," she said with a half-shrug, pushing the corner of her mouth into her cheek. "*Oh*, I, *uh*, didn't know that," I scratched the back of my head, causing her to giggle, prompting me to do the same lightly.

"Well, come on then," she nodded her head toward the bed near the back of the room. She began taking off her nightgown, slipping her shoulder laces off as she went, and stepping out of it as she walked like it were some sort of practiced dance. Naturally, I didn't know how to react, and felt that the only thing I really could do was stare at the ground.

"Nothing to be afraid of. I'm not going to bite you... *hard*, that is," she said calmly.

I could've sworn I heard the sly grin beginning to grow on her face.

I finally looked up at her, noticing she stood before me wearing nothing more than her skin. She motioned for me to come towards her, and as if I were in some sort of trance, I did so. Before motioning to the bed, she helped me undo the laces and straps to remove my jerkin, hose, and boots.

I sat down upon the soft, goose-feather mattress, and sank deeply into it when I did. She approached me, spreading her legs to envelop mine, and kissed my forehead, pressing her chest into my face. She kissed down my face, and I soon felt her soft, supple lips lock with mine.

"Lie back," she said sweetly, pulling her head back a little as she pushed her hand against my chest. I slowly fell backwards, gazing into her deep, green eyes as she followed me onto the mattress. She kissed me again, but this time, she moved away from my lips. She kissed her way to the backside of my jaw, down the side of my neck, and down my torso towards my hips.

Ah, so that's what that feels like, I thought.

Sparing further, and more *personal* details, we were at it for more than half the night. At the end of it all, Meliss lay on my bare chest as I watched her head rise and fall gently in time with my breathing. "You weren't bad for a first timer. How was it for you?" she asked quietly yet playfully as she looked at me with her dark green eyes. "You're incredible," I replied honestly, making her chuckle at my reply, but her smile faded faster than I'd thought it would.

"Thoma," she began, almost curling into a fetal position when she said my name. "What is it? Is something wrong? Please tell me I didn't accidentally bite you somewhere I shouldn't have," I said, trying to lighten her mood, pulling her closer. "I don't want to lose you," she said softly as I stroked her black hair that had more than a few strands strewn across my shoulder.

"I know this coming fight can't be avoided, but if there were a way..." she trailed off as I sealed her lips with mine. "There's nothing more to be done. We're on a mission to get yours and Leona's home back, and that's exactly what we're going to do," I continued. I could see tears begin to well in her eyes, as she tucked her face into my chest.

"But I don't want you to die, not when I've *just* found someone who doesn't treat me like I'm a piece of meat. I don't know how you fight, or how well the others around you will protect you, but I'm scared I'm going to lose you. I finally find a person that's not a complete menace to the female gender, and he immediately has to go to war? I- I'm scared, Thoma. I'm terrified that even if the rest of the synners succeed, you won't be there at the finish line," she said, tears streaming down her face.

What the actual fuck *am I supposed to say to that?* I wondered.

It was a common worry we *all* faced; from New Bloods to master Synners. Regardless of its nature, going into any battle was danger-ous, but it was a risk we were all willing to take. I'd grown used to the fact that I might die at any given moment, but what I didn't realize was just *how badly* that would affect someone on the outside of our world.

My stomach turned with a guilt that *shouldn't* have belonged to me.

"I won't die, or at the very least I'll do my best to take as many of those bastards with me on the way out," I said softly as her small hand moved to the side of my face. "Can you promise me that?" she asked, gazing into my eyes.

I looked into hers and pondered her question for a moment. "There is no way to know when either of us will die. All we can do is pray the gods don't let that happen sooner than it's supposed to," I said. "Then I'll pray to the gods to spare us *both*, and not have us suffer the loss of the other," she said softly as I kissed her forehead.

"But even so, I know I'm your first, making it a little more difficult for you to understand certain aspects of relationships. You have to understand that even though I've been with other people, forced upon or not, you're the first one I've met that I think I could *truly* care for," she said, moving her head back onto my chest.

I'd never thought I'd hear those words come out of someone's mouth, so to say that I was shocked would be a blatant disservice to how I felt in that moment.

"I'll admit, it's a little difficult for me to understand what you're going through, but I promise that I will do my best not to let you down, or *uh*, you know, become *past tense*," I said jokingly, trying to make the situation seem a little less heavy. "I know it's in your nature to make jokes in dark times, but for *fuck's sake*!" she managed a chuckle.

"Hey, look at that! You laughed a little. Mission complete!" I said with a bright smile. "G'night, Thoma," she whispered, smiling a little as she said it. "Good night, Meliss," I replied, kissing the top of her head as she snuggled closer. She was soon fast asleep, as our little adventure had drawn more out of her than it did from him.

I won't let that happen to either of us. Fate may be a fickle bitch, but I promise I'll come back to you, even if the gods disapprove of my methods, I thought, my mind already galloping over the infinite possibilities as I tried to get some sleep.

Dawn eventually came, and Meliss had barely moved from her previous position the whole night. I was just waking up, though, only now realizing what had happened the previous evening. I gingerly tried to take my numbed arm out from under her head, but failed miserably as she woke up with my movement.

"Is there something wrong?" she groaned in a raspy morning voice. "Nothing could possibly be wrong in this situation," I said, feeling my arm crackle with what felt like a *Kyr* spell. "It's just that I always wake at, or before dawn; old habits. Well, that and my arm doesn't feel like it belongs to me anymore," I said in jest. "*Oh*, right," she said softly, lifting her head just enough for me to get my arm out from underneath her.

"The Master may be looking for me," I began. "Leona knows you're with me. If anything, she can tell him where you are," she said, her voice raspy and sleepy. Not a minute passed before there was a knock on the door. "I've got to go," I said with a light-hearted shrug. "I know," she replied, frowning slightly. I was out of bed in a flash, putting on my jerkin and boots as quickly as my sleepy limbs would allow.

There was another knock on the door. "Coming," I replied, getting my last boot on. As soon as it was on, I rushed over to her side and kissed her on the forehead. "One for good luck," I said. She pulled my head close and kissed my lips. "*Two's* always better, but go now or you'll be late," she grinned and shooed me away before I rushed over to the door and undid the bolts, only to find my brother with his shit-eating grin.

"Someone popped their cherry," he said cheerfully. "Shut up, she might hear you," I replied. I couldn't hide that I also had a smile from ear to ear and probably the strong scent of whatever had happened the previous night. "Hope she didn't break your hip," Bernar said, patting me on the shoulder.

"That's none of your business," I replied defensively. "*Whoa*, touchy, are we?" Bernar said, the grin still showing on his face. "I just don't want her to hear you," I said quietly. "*Oh*, alright," he conceded with a roll of his eyes, moving away from the door.

"The Master wants to see us. Not sure what he wants, but if he's only summoned the two of us, it must be serious," he continued. "Let's go, then," I replied. I closed the door behind me, getting one final look at Meliss, who was still in bed. I smiled, but felt that leaving her in that state might make me out to be an asshole in her eyes.

Wish I could stay there forever, I thought as I closed the wooden door, following my brother over to Pyle's house.

The Master was waiting for us, along with Anwill, Pyle, Thorsen, and Garett, who sat in the same positions as the previous day. "*Ah*, there you are. Glad you could join us. Please, sit," the Master gestured with a knowing smile. My face flushed as I bowed to him and the others, then slowly made my way to the chair provided for me.

"As I was just telling the others, we must move sooner than we thought," Pyle said to help me understand the current topic of conversation. "Friends of mine from the country have sent me ravens saying that the large force of monsters has been making their way to Coltend, destroying every town in their path. I have already notified the ones who have volunteered to help us, and we ought to be off within the next hour or so," he continued gravely.

"How many do we have?" Bernar asked. "Counting the ones we've come with: A little over five-hundred," the Master said grimly. "So it's a suicide mission," Bernar noted sardonically. "Not exactly," the Master replied as Leona walked in from a hidden corner of the room, holding a scroll.

"Leona has laid out the city's plans for us; drawn entirely from memory," the Master said, prompting Bernar and I to look at each other in pure befuddlement. "I've drawn these up to help us make a better plan, since trying to summon the Coltendian Army from across the country would waste what precious time we have," she began, unfurling the scroll on the table.

"Not many people know this, but Coltend was once an *elven* city, one built on a large portion of its remains," she gestured to the outskirts to show just how much larger the city used to be, causing Anwill to widen his eyes. "I know that place. Legend tells us elves that it was once home to the Arwydus, the *Formidable Ones* in our native tongue," he said, looking at the map carefully, recognizing many of the same stylistic architecture from his homeland.

"I believe a passage there leads to one of the few Portal Stones. If we can muster enough mana, which I have nearly no doubt we will be able to do, we may yet be able to summon reinforcements from

Caegwen," she pointed to a spot some distance from the castle walls before glancing at the others.

"How would that even be possible?" Garett asked. "You humans have only a glimpse of what you can do with the other realms," Anwill began proudly but not in a disrespectful way. "If one of you were to volunteer to help me until all of the reinforcements were through, I will gladly show you how it can be done," he continued.

Each one in the room looked at the other, wondering who would be the first to raise their hand. "Roburn might be able to help you with that," the Master suggested. "Roburn? That self-centered glick-herder?" Garett asked.

"He may *appear* self-centered, but he is a formidable all-caster," he continued. "Seems as though we have little choice on the matter," Garett said. "I will begin his training at once, while the rest of you conjure up the plan," Anwill said, excusing himself from the room.

"I think the real question here, for someone with little or no knowledge of the last few hundred years, is: Why Coltend of all places?" I asked as I looked at the map. The others looked at each other and nodded. "It is where a large quantity of Gwynnleaf is kept on the continent," Pyle nodded.

I swallowed the information like a dry tuft of fur.

"Right, I get that, but monsters don't randomly team up to go somewhere. There must be someone leading them who knows it's there," I concluded. "The *Masked One*," Pyle replied gravely, making the others in the room visibly uncomfortable with mentioning that title.

"What in the *fuck* is a *Masked One*?" I raised an eyebrow. "Not what, but *who*. A long time ago, and far to the north of here, a dark power began to rise in a place known to us as Valdis. Thorsen and I are the only two here who have seen his power first hand," Pyle began.

"He was the one who attacked Grundvollr, slaying all in his path, and stealing our precious books of knowledge, as I'm sure you know every synner school has a copy of them. We initially thought it was simply a random act of violence against the Synners, though we only later discovered his true purpose," he continued, sighing as the memories came to the forefront of his mind.

"Thorsen and I traced him there, only to find a dark citadel infused with mana from the Underworld. King Mads kept the failure of Grundvollr hidden from the rest of the world, and expelled us from our own country, striking the attack from our country's history as well," he explained.

I pondered what I'd just heard for a moment. "If he knows that the source is there and is bringing an army to get it, why didn't he do this before?" I asked. "He wasn't strong enough to take on an entire city until now," Pyle answered.

No, that can't be right. He took down all of Grundvollr; a place filled to the brim with Synners. So why now? I thought.

"Alright, suppose we manage to make it to the Portal Stone and activate it. What then?" Bernar asked. "There are various openings placed around the city that would allow us to get in, hopefully without being noticed," Leona spoke as she pointed at a few points on the map. "Once inside, a small group will create a distraction outside the walls, while another will head directly towards the palace to thwart any attempt to open the passage to the source. The rest of us will keep the beasts at bay," the Master added.

"So much death," Anwill said quietly. "If we must die to protect the rest of the Continent, and possibly the *Continent* from such a fate, then it is a sacrifice I know we are more than willing to make. However, with a proper battle plan, I believe we will suffer minimal losses," the Master said with a nod.

"Even the best battle plans go to shit after the first sword is drawn," Anwill said. "I know, which is why we shall devise a secondary plan should the battle not go our way. So, shall we begin?" he asked.

The others, myself included, nodded in agreement, and we began preparing accordingly. A few hours of planning went by, and Leona brought some food in, surprising nearly everyone equally.

She knows how to cook, too? I smiled as I graciously accepted the plate, watching my brother's expression sour when she handed me mine first.

It immediately shifted back into a smile when she sat near him, nearly shoulder to shoulder, and continued their intermittent input on the plans being formed. A few more hours had passed, and the plan was finally coming together. All that was really left was the execution.

"All in favor, then?" the Master asked. "Aye," we replied in unison. "Very well, then. We'll ride just before dawn tomorrow. Anwill, find Roburn and teach him what you need to. Get some rest, everyone. We're going to need it," he nodded.

Each one went to their respective lodgings, while I returned to Meliss, who had cleaned the entire house before I arrived.

"You didn't have to do all of that, you know. But still, thank you," I said warmly with a bashful smile. "You're welcome, but I was bored," she shrugged. I walked over to her, pulling her in close by the small of her back and kissing her. "We're heading off to Coltend tomorrow at dawn," I said, my tone growing slightly heavier than intended, but she nodded, understanding what I meant.

"Will you ride with me again?" I asked, moving a few loose strands of hair behind her small ear as my eyes darted to each of her own. "'*Til the horse cannae carry us*," she replied, smiling while undoing the clasps that held my jerkin shut. I could've sworn I heard Bernar chuckle from just behind our door, though it sounded like he moved on towards Leona's room.

He'll never let me live that one down, will he? I mentally chuckled.

"Bernar," I began. "Yes, bird-brain?" Bernar asked. "Were you the one who recommended me for second stage training?" I asked. Bernar thought about the question for a moment. "One day you'll understand that it is more than simply *more power*, to quote Master Pyle," Bernar began. "Not like I knew that before accepting my own second and later stage training, but I have come to learn it in the last few years," he continued.

"You dodged my question, you fuck," I said with a small grin.

"Of course I did, twit," Bernar spat back. "Did you really think I would answer that? No, no. The reasoning for you being chosen had little to do with me, if that helps your *birdbrain* piece it together," Bernar said.

"Can't beat that argument," I said, looking at the ground away from him. "No, you can't. However, I will say this: If you can fully unlock the second stage, the others will come more easily. I know you've dabbled in it already, but fully locking it in is another story entirely," Bernar explained.

I nodded, receiving a heavy pat on the shoulder. "Now go find Meliss, and get some, little bastard," Bernar said with a grin from ear to ear. "How did you...?" I began. "Leona mentioned that Meliss likes you to me this morning," Bernar interrupted.

My eyes opened wide. "Sh-she told you that?" I asked. "She did, but if you're not there with her, I don't know how much longer that *liking* of hers will last," Bernar said. "Run, dipshit, run," he said with a chuckle as he pushed his younger brother down the hall. I took a second or two to process all of that, and nearly stumbled when I turned around to go find Meliss.

I can't believe it, Thoma thought. *She... likes me? I mean, I'm definitely not the most handsome guy around, so why me?* I asked myself.

"Fuck it," he said quietly, and ran off to find her. He went straight to where he thought Leona might be, and knocked on the thick, wooden door. I heard some shuffling going on inside, but no answer came. "Leona? Meliss?" I asked at the door.

The shuffling stopped.

I took a step back, wondering if they really were the ones behind the door, or if I had just interrupted something else entirely.

Still no answer.

I turned around to leave, when I heard the bolt being undone. I turned around to find Meliss' eyes, peeping out of the small crack in the doorway. "*Oh,* it's you," she said quietly, excitement barely hidden in her voice.

I was puzzled.

"Who else would it be?" I asked. "Edryd was here a few moments before you knocked. He was looking for you," she said quietly. "He knew I was speaking with the others in Pyle's house, why would he come *here* looking for me?" I asked.

The two of us were interrupted by none other than Edryd himself. "*Ah*, there you are," he said from a short distance away. "So? What did they want?" Edryd asked, walking up to my side.

"The Master told Pyle about that situation we had over in Codrean. He wanted to see if I knew more about you-know-who," I lied. "What did you tell him?" Edryd asked. "The truth - that we still don't know who it is, and that we still have to be careful," I replied.

"Well, with any luck he'll be able to help us with that," Edryd said. He looked at the crack in the doorway, and found the pair of eyes watching the exchange.

"*Oh*, I'm sorry," he stammered. "I didn't know..." he paused for a moment. "It's alright, Ed," I said with a smile. "I'll, *uh*... I'll be going, then," he said, stepping away from us.

The sly bastard gave me a wink and a childish grin that could hardly be out of the corner of his mouth.

"Asshole," I said to myself with a small chuckle.

I looked back at Meliss, who watched the two's brief exchange. "Well?" She began. "Are you coming in or what?" she said quietly. I didn't really know what to say. Obviously, I wanted to go inside, but I was so incredibly inexperienced that all I could do was nod briefly, and cautiously enter the room.

You're acting like an idiot, cut it out, I thought.

"Listen, Thoma," she began, closing the door behind her, and bolting the latch. "This isn't my first time doing something like this, not by a long shot. Granted, it *has* been a while, but I'm not new to this," she said.

To say that I hadn't expected as much would've been a lie, but for her to come right out and say it almost sent me for a loop.

"Wish I could say the same," I muttered under my breath, trying my best to hide my surprise at her candor with an embarrassed smile. "You've never been with a woman?" she asked.

No way to escape that one, I thought.

"Never really got the chance," I began. "My days, up until recently, have been spent mostly in Codrean; where the female synners there are more focused on their training, rather than messing up the sheets with someone," I said shyly.

Meliss noticed I was genuinely embarrassed by my own lack of experience. "Sorry. I didn't realize..." she said quietly. "It's alright," I said lightly. "No way you could've known that, right?" I said, trying to conjure a smile.

She nodded her head and, surprisingly, turned around, walking over to her bed, which was in the other half of the room. She began taking off her nightgown, slipping the shoulders off as she went; stepping out of it as she walked like it were some sort of practiced dance.

Naturally, I didn't know how to react, and felt that the only thing I really could do was stare at the ground. "Nothing to be afraid of. I'm not going to bite you... *hard*, that is," she said calmly.

I could've sworn I heard the sly grin beginning to grow on her face.

I finally looked up at her, noticing she stood before me wearing nothing more than her skin. She motioned for me to come towards her, and as if I were in some sort of trance, I did so. She helped me undo the laces and removed my jerkin, hose, and boots before motioning to the bed.

I sat down upon the soft, goose-feather mattress, and sunk deeply into it when I did. She approached me, spreading her legs to envelop mine, and kissed my forehead, pressing her chest into my face. She kissed down the side of my face, and I soon felt her soft, supple lips lock with mine.

"Lie back," she said sweetly, pulling her head back a little as she was pushing her hand against my chest. I slowly fell backwards, gazing into her deep, green eyes as she followed me down onto the mattress. She kissed me again, but this time, began to move away from my lips. She kissed her way to the backside of my jaw, down the side of my neck and all the way down my torso towards my hips.

Ah, so that's what that feels like, I thought.

Sparing further, and more personal, details, we were at it for more than half the night. At the end of it all, Meliss lay on my bare chest as I watched her head rising and falling gently in time with my breathing.

"You weren't bad for a first timer," she said playfully, turning her head to look into my eyes. "How was it for you?" she asked quietly. "Best I think I'll ever have," I replied honestly. She chuckled at my reply, but it faded more quickly than I'd thought it would.

"Thoma," she began. "What is it?" I asked calmly. "I don't want to lose you," she said softly as I stroked her black hair that had more than a few strands strewn across my shoulder.

"I know this fight that's coming is something that can't be avoided, but if there were a way..." she trailed off. I sealed her lips with mine. "There's nothing more to be done," I began softly. "We're on a mission to get yours and Leona's home back, and that's exactly what we're going to do," I continued.

Tears began to well up in her eyes, as she tucked her face into my chest.

"But I don't want you to die. I don't know how you fight, or how well the others around you will protect you, but I'm scared I'm going to lose you. I finally find a person that's not a complete menace to the female gender, and he immediately has to go to war? I... I'm scared, Thoma. I'm terrified that even if the rest of the synners succeed, that you won't be there at the finish line," she said, tears streaming down her face.

I know she's scared, but what am I supposed to say? I'm not immortal, and, to be honest, I'm probably more scared than she is, I thought, weighing her words heavily on my heart.

"I won't die, or at the very least I'll do my best to take as many of those bastards with me on the way out," I said softly. Meliss' small hand moved to the side of my face. "Can you promise me that?" she asked, gazing into my eyes.

I looked into hers, and pondered her question for a moment. "There is no way to know when either of us will die," I began. "All we can do is pray the gods don't let that happen sooner than it's supposed to," he said. "Then I'll pray to the gods to spare us both, and not have us suffer such a fate," she nodded her head with determination.

"I know I'm your first, and that makes this a little more difficult for you to comprehend certain things regarding relationships. You have to understand that even though I've been with other people, forced upon or not, you're the first one I've truly cared for," she said, moving her head back down onto my chest.

I'd never thought I'd hear those words come out of someone's mouth, so to say that I was shocked would be a blatant disservice to how I felt in that moment.

"It's true that it's a little difficult for me to understand what you're going through, but I promise that I will do my best to not let you down, or *uh*... you know, become *past tense*," I said jokingly, trying to make the situation seem a little less heavy. "I know it's in your nature to make jokes in dark times, but for fuck's sake..." she managed a chuckle.

"Hey, you laughed a little. Mission complete!" I said with a bright smile. "G'night, Thoma," she whispered, smiling a little as she said it. "Good night, Meliss," I replied, kissing the top of her forehead as she snuggled up more closely to me. She was soon fast asleep, as our little *adventure* had drawn more out of her than it did from him.

I won't let that happen to either of us, I thought.

Naturally, my mind began to race as it went over all of the possibilities.

I've decided that Fate was a cold-hearted bitch, that only took advantage of mere mortals for her own personal enjoyment. I promise I'll come back to you, Meliss, even if the gods themselves do not forgive my methods of getting there, I mentally asserted.

After coming to terms with that, I slept, *going back onto the plains, where he could train, and be free from all mortal worries.*

Dawn came, and Meliss had barely moved from her previous position the whole night. I was just waking up, though, only now realizing what had happened the previous evening. I gingerly tried to take my numbed arm out from under her head, but failed miserably as she woke up with my movement.

"Is there something wrong?" she asked. "Nothing could possibly be wrong in this situation," I replied. "It's just that I always wake at, or before dawn - old habits. Well, that and my arm doesn't feel like it belongs to me anymore," I said in jest. "*Ah*, right," she said softly, lifting her head just enough for me to get my arm out from underneath her.

"The Master may be looking for me," I began. "Leona knows you're with me. If anything, she can tell him where you are," she said, her voice was raspy and sleepy.

Not a minute passed before there was a knock on the door. "I've got to go," I said with a light-hearted shrug. "I know," she replied, frowning slightly. I was out of the bed in a flash - putting on my jerkin and boots as quickly as my sleepy limbs would allow.

There was another knock on the door. "Coming," I replied, getting my last boot on. As soon as it was on, I rushed over to her side, and gave her a kiss on the forehead. "One for good luck," I said. She pulled my head close, and kissed my lips. "Two's always better," she winked. "Go. You'll be late!" she smiled.

I rushed over to the door and undid the bolts, only to find my brother standing there with a smile from ear to ear.

"Someone popped their cherry," he said cheerfully. "Shut up, she might hear you," I replied. I couldn't hide the fact that I also had a smile from ear to ear, and probably the strong scent of whatever happened the previous night. "Hope she broke you in well enough," Bernar said, patting me on the shoulder.

"That's none of your business," I replied defensively. "*Whoa*, touchy, are we?" Bernar said, the grin still showing on his face. "I just don't want her to hear you," I said quietly. "*Oh*, right," my brother said, moving away from the door.

"The Master wants to see us," he began. "Not sure what he wants, but if he's only summoned the two of us, it must be serious," he continued. "Let's go, then," I replied. I closed the door behind me, getting one final look at Meliss, who was still in bed. I smiled, but felt that leaving her in that state might make me out to be an asshole in her eyes.

Wish I could stay there forever, I thought as he closed the wooden door, following my brother over to Pyle's house.

The Master was there waiting for us, along with Pyle, Thorsen and Garett, who sat in the same positions as they had the previous day. "Please, sit," the Master gestured.

"As I was telling the others, we must move sooner than we thought," Pyle began. "Friends of mine from the country have sent me ravens saying that the large force of monsters has been making their way to Coltend, destroying every town along the way. I have already notified the ones who have volunteered to help us, and we ought to be off within the next hour or so," he said.

"How many do we have," Bernar asked. "Counting the ones we've come with: A little over five-hundred," the Master said grimly. "So it's a suicide mission," Bernar said sardonically. "Not exactly," the Master replied. Leona walked in from a hidden corner of the room, holding a scroll in her hand. "Leona has laid out the plans of the city for us - drawn from memory," the Master said.

Bernar and I looked at each other in astonishment.

"Being that the army of Coltend would take far too long to send word to, assemble, and march to the castle, that option is one we do not have at the moment. However, that's not to say that all hope is lost, as deep beneath the city lies a network of sewers," Leona began.

"Coltend was originally an elven city, and a large portion of the city has been built upon the remains," she said, placing the map on the table, spreading it out as far as the parchment would reach.

"I know that place," Anwill began. "Legend tells us elves that it was the home of the Arwydus - the Formidable Ones in our native tongue," he said. He looked at the map carefully, recognizing a lot of the same stylistic architecture from his homeland.

"I believe there is a passage there that leads to one of the few Portal Stones," Leona said. "If we can muster enough mana, which I have nearly no doubt we will be able to do, we may yet be able to summon reinforcements from Caegwen," she said.

The others looked at her in surprise. "Your majesty," Garett began. "It would take an immense amount of mana to even open the portal, and so far as I know, we have but one full-mage among us," he said. Anwill looked over the diagrams of the inner workings of the underground passages. "I can draw an immense amount of mana, but to be able to hold it open, I would need someone to aid me in the Ethereal," he said.

"How would that even be possible?" Garett asked. "You humans have only but a glimpse of what you can do in the other realms," Anwill began. "If one of you were to volunteer to help me until all of the reinforcements were through, I will more than gladly show you how it can be done," he said.

Each one in the room looked at each other, wondering who would be the first to raise their hand. "Roburn might be able to help you with that," the Master said. "Roburn? That self-centered glick-herder?" Garett asked.

"Yes," the Master replied. "He may appear to be self-centered, but he is a formidable all-caster," he continued. "Seems as though we have little choice on the matter," Garett said. "I will begin his training at once, while the rest of you conjure up the plan," Anwill said, excusing himself from the room.

I looked over the map. "I think the real question here, for someone who has little or no knowledge of the last few hundred years, is: Why Coltend of all places?" I asked. The others looked at each other, and nodded. "It is where the Plant resides here on the continent," Pyle replied.

I swallowed the information like a dry tuft of fur. "Right, I get that, but monsters don't randomly team up to go somewhere," I said. "There must be someone leading them who knows it's there," he concluded. "The Masked One," Pyle replied.

I displayed a look of confusion and utter bewilderment to everyone in the room

"Who the fuck is *The Masked One*?" I asked with a raised eyebrow.

They sure had a lot of creativity with that name, I thought, not bothering to voice my sarcastic comment aloud.

"A long time ago, and far to the north of here, a dark power began to rise in a place called Valdis. Thorsen and I are the only two here who have seen his power first hand," Pyle began.

"He was the one who attacked Grundvollr, slaying all in his path, and stealing our precious books of knowledge, as I'm sure you know every synner school has a copy of them. We initially thought it was simply a random act of violence against the synners, though only later discovered his true purpose. Thorsen and I traced him back to Valdis - a dark citadel that more than obviously was infused with mana from the Underworld. King Mads kept the failure of Grundvollr hidden from the rest of the world, and expelled us from our own country, striking the attack from our country's history as well," he explained.

I pondered what I'd just heard for a moment. "If he knows that the source is there and is bringing an army along with him to get it, why didn't he do this before?" I asked. "He wasn't strong enough to take on an entire city, until now," Pyle answered.

Seems like we're in some deep shit, Thoma thought.

"Alright, suppose we manage to make it to the Portal Stone and activate it, what then?" Bernar asked. "There are various openings placed around the city that would allow us to get in, hopefully without being noticed," Leona pointed at a few points on the map.

"Once inside, a small group will create a distraction outside the walls, while another will head directly towards the palace to thwart any attempt to open the passage to the source. The rest of us will keep the beasts at bay," the Master said.

"So much death," Anwill said quietly. "If we must die to protect the rest of the Continent - and possibly the world - from such a fate, then it is a sacrifice I know all of us here are more than willing to make," the Master said. "However, with a proper battle plan, I believe we will suffer minimal losses," he continued.

"Even the best battle plans go to shit after the first sword is drawn," Anwill said. "I know that, which is why we shall devise a secondary plan should the battle not go our way" the Master replied.

"So, shall we begin?" he asked. The others, myself included, nodded in agreement and we began making preparations accordingly. A few hours of planning went by, and some food was brought in by Leona.

She knows how to cook, too? I thought, smiling as she brought my brother and I some food.

She sat next to my brother, nearly shoulder to shoulder, and continued their intermittent input on the plans being formed. A few more hours had passed, and the plan was finally coming together, and all that was really left was the execution thereof.

"All in favor, then?" the Master asked. "Aye," we replied in unison. "Very well, then. We'll ride just before dawn tomorrow. Anwill, find Roburn and teach him what you need to," the Master said. "Get some rest, gentlemen. We're going to need it," he said.

Each one went to their respective lodgings, while I returned to Meliss, who had cleaned the entire house before I arrived.

"You didn't have to do all of that, you know. But still, thank you," I said warmly with a bashful smile on my face. "You're welcome, but I was bored," she replied with a curt shrug. I walked over to her, pulling her in close by the small of her back and kissed her. "We're heading off to Coltend tomorrow at dawn," I said, my tone growing a little heavier than I had intended. Meliss nodded, understanding what I meant.

"Will you ride with me again?" I asked, moving a few, loose strands of hair behind her small ear as my eyes darted to each of her own. "'Til the horse cannae carry us," she replied with a smile, undoing the clasps that held my jerkin shut.

I could've sworn I heard Bernar chuckle from just behind our door, though it sounded like he moved on towards Leona's room.

CHAPTER 18

MOURTIS

Smoke rose from the East, as the towns along the road to the Rhydian Pass lay razed from the massive horde being driven across the open plains and hillsides.

The glicks, daemons, and other creatures massacred all who stood in their path, while the fire trolls set the houses aflame. Townsfolk slept silently, motionless in pools of their blood and shit. Creatures gnawed on the remains that the horde left behind, leaving little more than piles of bones and tattered clothes lying about.

The Masked One left destruction in his wake as he went to Coltend Castle, which was now in sight. The palace gleamed in the sunlight as it always did, though what lay within was less than the cheerful place it once was. He gazed over the griffin's mighty neck, observing the devastating force beneath him.

This will end quickly, he thought.

A few hours later, he reached the eastern gate and was met by a few hooded figures who stood watch atop the high walls. He bid Oryxe to fly up to the same height as the top of the wall, and watched the figures shuffle uncomfortably in the presence of their visitor. Their cloaks fluttered in the wind produced by the massive wings.

"Mourtis is expecting me," he said, his voice enhanced by mana so he could be heard clearly. "The city has already been taken, so what business do you have here?" one of the hooded men shouted. "You have no idea who I am, do you? This all came to fruition by my hand, planning, and will. Now, where is Mourtis?" the Masked One spat back. The two men began to tremble at the realization that he was the true orchestrator of the chaos beneath them.

"He's inside, but he told us not to let anyone through," the other hooded figure said shakily. "You insolent filth, I own you and everyone inside. Now, be good, little foot soldiers and open the fucking gates!" he ordered. The hooded man flinched at the command's brusqueness and authoritarian tone. "Y-yes, my lord," he said.

The man barked the order down to the ones beneath him, who speedily opened the gates. The Masked One landed his great beast, dismounting soon after as the horde gathered behind him. He peered inside the opening gates and saw no living soul besides the hooded figures. No bustling of merchants; no stable boys chasing horses back into their stables.

The once-mighty capital of Codrean had fallen and was now little more than a husk of its former self, a dead city.

"*Ah*, it's good to be back," he exhaled after breathing deeply the smell of death and decay in the air, speaking to no one in particular. "Thank you, Oryxe. You may return to Valdis at your own discretion," he gave the great beast a short bow. The griffin quickly nodded its head and screeched loudly as it beat its wings, soaring quickly into the air.

The Masked One passed between the gates and spread his arms wide, letting off a disturbing cackle. The hooded figures, slowly approaching the inner rampart's barrier, began to tremble more than they ever thought possible. He looked up and noticed they were glaring at him from above, but quickly hid themselves from his gaze.

He grinned under his mask, and his eyes glowed their bright violet once more, as *mana flowed from the dark sphere in the sky,* enveloping him instantly. He condensed the raw mana to both his hands and outstretched them to pull the two above him. Dark tendrils of violet mana flew out like a shipmaster's whip, latching themselves onto the hooded figures and tearing them from the ground.

The two were suspended in midair for what they felt was an eternity. The Masked One lowered his hands, maintaining the spell without the need to keep his hands in the air. "Mourtis should have told you by now that I am not one to be trifled with, so why are you acting like children?" he asked, glaring at the two hooded figures who squirmed, feeling their bonds tighten around them.

"I will not have this kind of insubordination from anyone, especially not lowly foot soldiers such as yourselves. I hope you don't have families waiting for you somewhere, because this example I am about to make of you will *not* be painless," he said with utter darkness in his voice. The bonds were tightening and beginning to tear into flesh. "Please, my lord, forgive us!" one of the men shouted.

"*Forgive* you?" the Masked one asked, tilting his head to the side a little. "A parent might forgive their child for acting brashly, but as I am neither your father nor an admirable person, I never forgive," he said in a low voice, tightening the bonds even more.

The two men screamed until their eyes burst from their sockets and their tongues exploded. They gurgled their blood for a moment as they smashed into the stone floor. He quickly turned to face the hooded figures nearby, who'd gathered to see what the commotion was about. After witnessing their friends' harrowing deaths with pale faces and horrific expressions, they immediately fled in terror.

"I think that will suffice," he muttered with a hint of satisfaction, moving deeper into the city. The other figures who hadn't fled in terror left with their heads bowed low. He walked down the street, observing what had once been a bustling city, which now smelled of death and decay.

His enlarged figure cast a long shadow onto the ground beneath him that extended over the ruins as he made his way to the palace, though not a soul was to be seen along the way. Only a handful of scavenger birds and rats nibbled on the lifeless corpses still in the shadows of their homes.

He passed them without a care.

A short while later, he reached the palace steps. Another figure stepped out from behind the wall and greeted him properly, along with six others, all clad in the same dark robes as the one in front. The leader held a wooden staff with the mark of Mideia etched into it. The leader leaned heavily on it as he slowly made his way forward.

"My lord, I have done all that you have requested, and it is an honor to meet you in the flesh," Mourtis bowed briefly, then looked at the Masked One from beneath his hood, who met his gaze. "Where is the queen?" the mage asked flatly. "She managed to flee our little coup; however, one of my men struck her in the shoulder with an arrow. She will likely not survive much longer if infections take hold of the wound, my lord," he said, bowing his head low quickly.

"I ordered her *not* to be harmed. Do your men enjoy not following orders and suffering punishment?" the Masked One asked in a low voice as he stepped forward. "Two of your men have already had a taste of how I deal with insubordination, although neither of them will be willing to disclose that information, unless you have a necromancer among you," he said.

"The fact that she was harmed was none of my doing directly, my lord," Mourtis felt a cold chill run down his spine. "I ordered my men to leave none alive in the palace, except for the queen. She should have been captured alive and remained unblemished. It would seem as though my men are dumber than I thought," he said with a sneer directed at the others.

"The culprit will be dealt with when we find him, I guarantee it, my lord," he said with a short bow. However, the Masked One didn't say anything in return and walked past the crooked old man and the others who followed him. The dark master pushed mana into the crystal he'd taken from the socket in his saddle, and commanded the beasts to pour in from the gate, slaying the remaining hooded figures as they found them throughout the city.

"My lord! You can't do this! I told you I would find the ones responsible for her injury!" Mourtis shouted after hearing screams coming from the direction of the gate. "Your stupidity and carelessness regarding my orders will not be tolerated. I recall giving explicit orders, and now, the queen is gone. As a result of your men's insolence, the only holder of the key to get me what I came for is now gone, wounded, and will probably die sooner than I can find her," the Masked One snarled, making Mourtis blanche with fear.

"I don't care about your men in the slightest. I only needed them to extricate the ones who might have stood in my way," the Masked One said, producing a scarlet claw as he slaughtered half of the hooded figures surrounding Mourtis with a single swipe. "Now that I've made my point, show me to the throne room," he ordered. Mourtis caught up to his new master as quickly as he could, while the ones who followed him ensured none of the creatures would disturb them.

They Masked One pushed open the door to the palace with a large blast of mana. He moved much quicker than Mourtis, who was struggling to keep pace, but a few moments later, he reached the main hall with a trail of dust and frightened men behind him.

He looked around the large, silent hall, observing everything. He noted the stained glass windows, which allowed the morning light to enter, barely lighting the hall, the thick pillars catching a few of the sun's rays. He walked down the hall on the carpet from the thrones to the main entrance, just a short distance from him. Dried blood and the smell of death ruled the air about them, forcing Mourtis to hold his breath at regular intervals to keep from vomiting.

The Masked One continued down the foul-smelling hall and went to the throne. He glanced over its intricate craftsmanship, noting every detail etched into it, while noticing the cushioned seat held a slight indentation from when Truls sat there.

Heavy bastard, he thought, quickly turning around to look in Mourtis' general direction, as he sank into the chair.

He placed both of his hands upon the armrests provided and leaned back. "I have waited for this day for a long time. You see, Mourtis, I also have my orders to follow like you. However, my agreement with the Undergod only requires me to retrieve him a certain something. He never specified how, when, or what I should do to get it," he began, causing Mourtis to feel a sinking feeling in his gut.

"May I ask what the point of you saying this is, my lord?" he asked sheepishly. "Autonomy is a fickle thing," the Masked One began. "On the one hand, you can do whatever you want, within reasonable expectations. On the other hand, you are given enough rope to hang yourself with. I gave you as much autonomy to do my bidding as the aforementioned agreement with the Undergod would allow. You, however, have taken your fair share of rope and tied yourself a fancy noose, *priest*," he said darkly.

"My lord, I don't understand what you mean by that. Surely you don't believe that *I* wanted the queen to run away?" Mourtis lied. "What?" his master replied curtly.

"I tried to get her to comply with your wishes. I tried to make her see that she is sinful, and that she should repent in hopes of offering up the key of her own free will to aid your success. I would never want to betray the trust you have given me," Mourtis lied again.

That's probably why she ran. No one likes being preached to by a hypocrite, the mage mentally sighed.

"*Oh*? And what of the men were you in command of?" he said, rising from his seat, walking towards the crooked man. "What are you saying, my lord? Do you think I ordered them to *kill her*?" Mourtis asked, taking a few steps backwards and spreading his free arm.

"Your little invasion would not have been possible without *my* help. If it weren't for me bribing the Guild to join our cause, you would have had an entire *city* full of guards and civilians trying to go against you," he raised his voice, making the Masked One halt momentarily.

"Do you honestly believe I wouldn't have killed them all *anyway*?" he began walking forward, causing Mourtis to backstep. "My invasion would have happened with or without your help. The only reason I had to invade was to ensure that no force could hinder what I came here to do. As if your mind were as crooked as your body, the queen and her key would still be here if you had only done what I told you," the Masked One barked.

"She must have fled through an unknown passage," Mourtis began. "None other than the royal families know everything there is to know about the palace," he said shakily as the Masked one continued walking towards him. "That is why you had your minions try to gather all the information they could on the palace, was it not?" he asked.

Mourtis tried to speak, but no words came out of his juttering mouth.

"Why, then, did I give you the runestone to use during the council meeting to provide me with information? Why were you in that room in the first place? Do you remember that? Can you answer me? Do you even know?" the mage asked, accentuating each step with a question.

"Decisions, Mourtis, to abuse the blindness of human perception; something I have long since tried to overcome in my pursuit of knowledge. You keep making these excuses, trying to cover for your subordinates, but you *also* fail just as miserably. The only thing you have done is kill a few useless people, and allow the one thing I *actually* needed from this gods-forsaken continent to escape. However, as a result of your failures, your *men* will pay the price," the Masked One said, his tone growing increasingly heavy, shocking Mourtis to his core.

"You... *tyrant*!" Mourtis shouted angrily. "You have treated me as little more than the scum beneath your boots for decades, and I have never wavered in my loyalty to you! I should have trusted my gut. I have always known, deep down, that you were a little more than the monster others make you out to be. You will never find what you seek without my help," he seethed.

"We'll see about that, *priest.* You have lined your pockets well enough with the coins stolen from those who gave their *all* to your church. Your men will die, but *you* will be banished from this country altogether. After all, I doubt you'd make it very far," the mage growled, flaring his mana.

Mourtis was taken aback, but quickly gathered what little composure he could under the weight of the mage's aura. "I-I will take what I own and leave this place, praying I never have to deal with the likes of you again in my remaining years," he managed. "*Years*? You don't have *seconds* if you keep talking," the Masked One flared his mana again.

Mourtis grimaced at him and spat on the ground, turning on his heel before descending a passage that led to his quarters. The Masked One watched the slow man's figure disappear into the hallway, followed by his remaining men.

It's a shame he is such a shriveled weasel. Decades ago, he was much more valuable as an asset. I should have taken the information and killed him after all, he thought, angry at his decision to let the maggot live yet another day.

He turned to the throne and began to reexamine its details. The armrests had been well worn over the generations of kings who had sat there. Wear and tear on the carpeting near where the king's feet would typically be was more than visible. He moved over to the queen's throne, her scent still strong enough to reach his nostrils as he ran his hand along the throne, hoping to find anything out of place.

His eyes flared a little brighter than usual as he got on his hands and knees to see what was beneath the thrones, if anything. He noticed a small lump in the carpeting directly beneath the king's throne.

"Interesting," he said to himself.

His eyes glowed as he drew again from the Underworld, casting the thrones against the wall with a mana blast. The carpet didn't budge in the slightest. He could clearly see the small lump in the carpeting and stepped away from it onto the stone floor. He tore the carpet from its lashings to the stone ground, tearing its bindings. Countless years of accumulated dust rose in the air about him, making things difficult to see.

There you are, he thought with a satisfied grin as the dust began to settle. He stepped on the small stone that was out of place, and the stone floor in front of the stairs to the thrones began to open, releasing more dust and an earthquake-like rumbling in the ground. The paintings and hunting trophies on the walls fell to the ground with a large crash, but he continued to watch the stones move apart.

A stone stairway became visible behind the throne, covered in dust. He looked at them, wondering where they would lead him. He stood at the top of the stairway and took the first step, kicking up a small cloud of dust as his foot landed.

This must be where they've kept it all these years, he chuckled with satisfaction.

His robes dragged across the steps behind him, leaving a cloud in his wake as he continued down the steps, until all light from the hall above him had vanished, making the passage as black as a moonless night. Through his mask, he could smell the air becoming dirtier and denser.

For this to be so well hidden, I must be on the right path, he thought.

A few moments later, the stairs ended, and his steps echoed in what he thought to be a large hall. His eyes didn't need a torchlight to see in the dark, and what lay before him was not what he had expected.

Books. Countless books. Leading nearly as far as his eyes could see, on numerous shelves. Every outlawed book and tome ever to be recorded or written during the time of the Continent, covered in ages worth of dust. Surprisingly enough, they were all very well preserved, due to the lack of fresh air reaching the large chamber. He looked at the motionless gargoyle sentries placed at the end of every shelf and felt his brow furrow in anger.

No, this can't be right. The information I got from Mourtis never mentioned a library, gargoyles, or anything else that seems to be here. Where the hell is it? It must be here, somewhere, he thought, pulling out books and collapsing shelves in a fit of rage.

After a few of the massive shelves collapsed, he grunted in frustration and returned up the steps, pushing the stone to reseal the library as it once was. He searched his memories fervently, though when he found nothing, he made a tight fist, drawing a few drops of blood from where his elongated nails sank into the skin.

I will find it even if it takes me all of eternity. I will *have it,* he breathed heavily, expelling a blast of mana that spread across the throne room, shattering the glass and anything hung on the walls.

The door at the far end of the hall fell victim to the blast, as it was also obliterated into a thousand wooden shards that soared through the air at the front of the palace. With a sigh, he sat back down on the throne, listening to the sound of his horde killing the remaining hooded figures in the distance.

I wonder if he will have anything of use for me when he arrives. It shouldn't be much longer, but I can't afford to wait much longer, since the Undergod has already grown impatient enough, he thought, resting his chin on his folded hands.

Just then, a small group of hooded men stormed through one of the doors to the right of the hall, desperate to find safety from the monsters just outside. He smiled wickedly at them, realizing they may serve another purpose.

"We're doomed," one of the figures said, not noticing the Masked One at the other end of the hall. "They'll find us anywhere we run," he continued. "If you don't shut your fucking gob, they will for sure," one of the others replied. "Osgar, I'm afraid Alf may be right," one of the others said. "Don't *Osgar* me, Wingar," Osgar began.

He was the largest of the three, and his voice carried heavily across the hall. "Alf, do us all a favor and put yourself out of your impending misery," he sighed, putting his hand on Alf's shoulder.

The Masked One rose from his seated position. "You three," his voice rang out, startling the three hooded men with his thunderous voice. "Who are you?" Wingar asked. "I suppose I could be considered the newest lord of Coltend, even though that is not really the title I wanted in the first place," the Masked One replied.

"The beasts..." Alf began, his voice carried weakly. "Are of my doing," he interrupted. "So it was *you* who brought those horrid creatures here?" Osgar asked. "I did, and I see they are doing my bidding well," the Masked One said.

The three looked at each other with worried expressions. "If we side with him, maybe he will let us live," Wingar whispered. "Why should we side with the one who *brought* this destruction to begin with?" Osgar asked. "That's just it. It's *because* he's in control of them, and right now, we're running out of options," Wingar replied. Osgar shrugged, but said nothing.

"If you truly are the new lord of Coltend and have brought these beasts with you, then the three of us here pledge our allegiance to you, great one," Wingar said with a low bow, motioning for the others to do the same. "You are members of the Church. What makes you so sure that I will simply take you in?" the mage asked, tilting his head.

Wingar looked at his robes and saw that he bore the sign of the Sword and Staff sewn into them. "We *were* members of the church, but not avid ones, lord," he said. "And what would cause that?" the Masked One asked, watching as Wingar knelt and paused momentarily, recalling the events that had led up to that point.

"Osgar, my blood brother, Alf, and I had seen what Father Mourtis was doing to the poor and hated him for it, but even more for what he had done to us over the years. We were raised in the poorer communities that were once here, and knew that the only way to make any kind of living was to join the Guild or the Church. We took part in prayers and such, yes, but neither of us is religious in any sort of way, lord," Wingar explained.

"Mourtis took us in, and from a very young age, he molested us until we were each strong enough to be able to resist him. One day, he gathered the three of us and told us that if we didn't let him have his way with us, he would cast us out, back into the streets to live like beggars. The three of us swallowed the harsh reality presented to us, and so we were forced into service until the day either we or he died, whichever came first, lord," he said with nods of agreement from the others.

The Masked One listened attentively to the story being told. "So you are no friends of Mourtis, that much is certain. However, what makes you think I will be a better master than he was?" he asked. "Our chances of survival are stretched thin as it is, and we never wanted to take part in his treachery, great one. He must be your enemy if he is not here with you. As the old saying goes, the enemy of *my* enemy is my ally," Wingar said, making the mage grin beneath his mask as if music had just reached his ears.

If they hate him, they might aid me in unveiling Mourtis' secrets, he thought, carefully regarding them.

"Very well, then, I shall take you in on one condition," he said. "Whatever you ask, lord," Wingar replied. "If I sense even the slightest bit of deviation of loyalty coming from any of you, I will see to it that you are fed to the monsters outside alive," the Masked One said threateningly. Wingar looked over at his brother, who simply shrugged. "Not like we have much of a choice now, brother," Osgar whispered,

"We will be your servants, lord," Wingar said, bowing again, prompting the others to follow suit as the Masked One tilted his head imperiously. "Very well. Your first task as my new servants is to uncover Mourtis' journals and any other documents that contain information about the palace itself," he commanded. "As you command, lord," Wingar replied with another bow.

The Masked One motioned for them to leave him, and within a few seconds, they disappeared to Mourtis' quarters. Up the steps they went, through the hallways of stone, making their way to their harasser's quarters. They entered the room, finding books and scrolls strewn about it.

The bed was messy, and countless wax stubs from previously burned candles were atop the nightstand. The smell was a palpable mixture of cinnamon and other unidentifiable herbs, smoking on a small tray in the corner of the room.

"I've always hated cinnamon," Osgar said. "Well, he's gone, and we have a task that we must complete unless we want to be fed to the beasts," Wingar put a hand on his shoulder. "I never agreed to be with you two," Alf began, but Wingar immediately turned to snap at him.

"I've just saved our lives and bought us precious time to figure out what to do next. So shut the fuck up, and help me look for his journals," Wingar spat back. Alf shook his head and reluctantly began rummaging through the scrolls and books on the floor. Wingar and his brother took to the bookshelves with more books than they could count.

"Look at this," Osgar said, pulling a brown covered book from the shelf. "*A Guide to Young Boys*, written by none other than the old, disgusting fuck himself," he said angrily. "We'll come back later and burn everything in here. I hate him just as much as you do, but for now, we must put our hatred for that shriveled cocksneeze behind us," Wingar nodded and continued his search.

The three went through the numerous iterations of books and began to think they would die to the monsters after all. Suddenly, Alf gasped as he looked under the bed.

"I think I've found something," he said to the others, who were no sooner on their hands and knees, looking under the bed with him. "These must be the ones he left behind," Osgar said, taking one of the books and bringing it into the light of the small window. "I think we've found our *salvation*, boys," he said, silently reading the first page, prompting Wingar to move beside him.

"Look here. It tells of how he first came into contact with someone called the *Masked One*. That must be who we encountered down-stairs," Osgar pointed near the top of the page, as Wingar did his best to read the handwriting. "Well, go on. Read it aloud for the rest of us," Alf said uncomfortably.

I'm not sure I really want to know what's in there, but if it means getting out of here alive, so be it, he thought, moving beside Wingar.

"Year one of my service to the Church: It is probably not the best of ideas to make a deal with a devil from the Underworld, but I have no choice. Mideia has not allowed me to escape the clutches of evil itself, and I am beginning to fear for my life," Osgar began to read, making Wingar's eyes open wide as he listened attentively.

"I met the one in the mask along the road of my pilgrimage to the *Hallowed Tree*, where he offered me a chance to improve my life infinitely. *Oh,* how I long to have had the wisdom to continue on my path simply. The one in the mask told me of a greater power than that of Mideia himself, and though I doubted him at first, I realized that there are many *mysteries* to our world that we have yet to discover. Of course, I wasn't *entirely* devoted to the idea, but my *heart* told me I should accept the offer," Osgar read, glancing momentarily at the others who urged him on.

"He asked me for my undivided loyalty to him and to aid him in his quest for *knowledge*. Over the past three months or so, he has *harassed* me for information on a source of power known only as *The Plant*, though I know nothing about it," he continued, raising an eyebrow.

"Here, I found a few more years. It looks like he's taken all the others except these; like he *wants* someone to know his story," Alf interrupted, handing two volumes to Wingar. "Read this one," Wingar said after giving it a quick glance, handing it over to his brother.

"Year twenty-seven: I have forsaken the idea of Mideia and his *goodwill* towards all men, for it is now clear to me that it is *the last thing* he wants for us. The *Masked One*, who, after all these years, has never said his real name, has allowed me to become the leader of the Church. I know that refusing it could mean the end of me, though I will have to cheat and murder my way to get there, only to give *him* information on *The Plant*," his eyes widened as he read the last sentence.

"So that perverted bastard *really did* murder his way to the top. I've always wondered how a sick *fuck* like him could reach that position," Alf scoffed. "There's still more," Wingar handed him another volume.

"Year forty: I can feel myself getting older each day, and yet even with all of my riches, stolen from blind believers, I can see nothing but *sorrow and misery* coming to the world. The Masked One has continued to search for *The Plant* itself, taking matters into his own hands. He must believe that my service to him all these years has been for naught. He has begun recruiting spies from all regions and classes of the world, including outcast Synners, desperately hoping for some information on its location. Even if I *do* find it here, I don't believe he will be willing to share its supposed power," Osgar read, closing the book and setting it aside.

"So the old fuck *wasn't* fully on board with the idea after all, and merely followed orders *out of fear*? That still doesn't explain his speech to Leona the night we took over. Maybe that was all a bluff?" Wingar asked the others. "It seems like it, but even if it was a bluff, it doesn't change what he *commanded us* to do or the fact that we *followed* his orders," Osgar sighed heavily as the others also felt the same wave of guilt come over them.

"Here's the last one," Wingar said, handing it to him with a nod.

"Year sixty-nine: I've discovered its location, but at a great price. He has forced me to reveal its location, but in the process, my suspicions of him having contacted a powerful force known only as *The Under-god* have been confirmed. I haven't told him *everything* I've found, and know I don't have much time. His plans have been set in motion, and he is coming for it. Although he will likely have wasted his time, as all the plants appear *long-since dead*," Osgar read the ominous words.

The final words hit everyone in the room as hard as a blacksmith strikes the steel on his anvil. They knew what Mourtis had meant when he wrote the final words of his journal. They were engraved in their memories, and the three looked at each other desperately. "What have I done?" Wingar asked himself weakly.

"There was no way we could have known any of this before, and you did what you thought was right, brother," Osgar put a hand on his shoulder. "I might have just sentenced the three of us to a painful death," Wingar said grimly, shaking his head. "We would have died anyway. We've been fucked since the beginning of our lives, both figuratively and literally. I suppose there's no point in trying to escape fate," Osgar sighed.

Wingar looked out the window to the distant, green hills covered in a dense forest and scratched his well-shaven chin. "What do we do, then?" he asked. "We survive for as long as we can. Think we've gotten the hang of it over the past few years," Osgar replied, but Alf didn't seem as enthusiastic, releasing a heavy sigh.

Wingar looked at his younger brother and agreed with him for once. He nodded, and they put the journals back in their place, returning to the hall where the Masked One sat on his newly forged throne borne from mana.

"Well?" he asked, subtly sending tendrils of mana out toward them. "We have found nothing, lord. The old man must have taken any information on it with him when he left," Wingar said, kneeling before him. The Masked One grunted in response. "Go to the libraries, or the Church itself. Search everywhere you can. The creatures outside will not bother you so long as you do my bidding," he commanded. "As you wish, lord," Wingar replied with a bow.

What was that strange feeling in my head just now? Was he reading my thoughts? Wingar thought.

The three of them walked outside to head towards the Church, and encountered several glicks gnawing on the bones of fallen guardsmen and servants just outside the palace itself. Alf vomited at the sight, but the monsters paid him no heed and continued about their disgusting business. Alf wiped the remaining fluids off his mouth with the sleeve of his robe, which smelled horribly during their search.

Meanwhile, the Masked One remained inside, thinking about what he'd seen in Wingar's mind. He rubbed his knuckles, considering every aspect of what he saw. Some of it was muddled, but one thing was present amid the cacophony of Wingar's thoughts that he knew for sure.

It's down there, isn't it? Those fools had better bring me some more information on it, he thought, rising from his throne and dispelling it immediately to look at the stone floor again.

CHAPTER 19
TO FATE AND COLTEND

I once again found myself unable to rest at the thought of the coming battle, causing me to toss and turn, even with Meliss at my side.

I should have been asleep a long time ago. Having her here, by my side and sleeping soundly, should have put me at ease, but I guess there's not much else to do but wear myself out a little more, I thought with an internal sigh.

I kissed Meliss softly on the forehead, and watched a small smile grow on her face, as she turned to squish her face into the pillow. I put on my boots and stepped outside.

Walking a little down the quiet streets, I observed the homes built in the surrounding area while looking for a good spot to train in. There wasn't much that reminded me of a Synner school; instead, it looked more like a secluded town than anything else.

Meandering for a few more minutes eventually led me to one of the training grounds used by the Fangsdalr synners. Marks of previous training battles and torn earth riddled the ground before me, and I could tell that whatever training took place here over the years, those fights were fearsome to say the least.

This is perfect, I thought, feeling a smile beginning to grow.

I closed my eyes, moving my arms in fluid-like motions, trying to focus my mind and body to be one. My eyes darkened as I began to *pull from the Ethereal. Mana raced from the sphere in the sky a little faster than usual*, enveloping me entirely. The dark left my eyes as I realized my body was coated in mana.

"Close, but not quite right," a voice said from behind me. I turned to face the voice's owner, only to find Pyle and the Master standing a few dozen meters away. I dismissed the mana quickly and bowed promptly. "I apologize for using the training grounds without permission, masters," I said humbly.

"*Oh*, don't worry about that. We *both* knew you wouldn't be able to sleep, so we devised a plan to help you. Although I will admit, I wasn't expecting it to have taken you this long to get here," he said with a light chuckle, forcing me to blush slightly as I gauged the words to be of a friendly origin, not a reprimanding one. "Will you help me, then?" I asked, bowing my head once more. "Why do you want to reach the second stage so badly?" the Master asked.

How the fuck do I answer that? I thought, frozen in place.

After a moment's silence, I finally raised my head. "Masters, I'm sure you both already know what I am about to say. However, I know that you only want me to voice the suspicions you already have," I began, hardening my will. "Go on, then," Pyle said, walking toward me.

"I know that the people I have cared about for so long can handle themselves in the fight to come. However, Fate herself has decided to weave a golden thread into the tapestry of my life, as I'm sure neither of you has failed to notice," I said, a slight grin on my face. "We've both noticed and *heard it*, yes," the Master sighed lightly, prompting me to blush harder than I ever thought possible.

Can I curl into a ball and die now? Thanks, I thought, scratching the back of my head as I let out an embarrassed giggle.

"R-respectfully, masters, there is little more I want to do in this world than make her as happy as possible. Not only that, but I want to make sure that I can keep myself and her safe in the face of the challenges to come," I blurted out, prompting them both to look at each other and laugh heartily.

"My, my, Thoma! I knew you were a smart boy, but to hear you so *ensnared* by a woman's charms... I might have expected that from your *brother*, but from you? Now that's going to make watching you grow up that much more fun!" the Master said, surprising me with the levity in his tone.

Maybe this is how he really *is? Why does he remind me so much of Bernar right now?* I thought with a raised eyebrow.

"It's true, Master. I just..." I trailed off with a shrug, cutting my retort shorter than I would have liked. "You're worried about losing her, aren't you?" the Master asked as if he'd read my thoughts. "I do, Master," I said after a moment of consideration. The Master looked at Pyle once again. "Very well. He's all yours, Pyle," he gestured toward me. "W-wait! Does that mean you're going to teach me the second stage right now?" I asked, surprised at what was happening.

"That's what you wanted, right?" the Master said, turning back slightly to get one last look at me, whose eyes began to shine brightly.

Pyle, on the other hand, grinned maliciously.

Uh-oh. What have I done? I thought.

Pyle moved from where he stood to my side in the time it took me to blink and held my shoulder, still keeping the malicious grin from before. "Before we begin, I have to ask: How high is your pain tolerance?" he asked. I shuddered at the words, sweat beading down my face since I was still reeling from how fast he'd moved.

"D-decently high?" I said, unsure of my own words. "Good. Since we don't have time to ease you into it, and given that you've already dabbled in it, we can speed this along by brute-forcing our way through the training," he replied with the same grin.

Brute forcing? Oh, fuck me, I thought, beginning to fear for my life.

"Don't worry, I won't push you so hard that you'll die, but it's going to hurt nonetheless, since we're out of time. I've only ever gotten to train two Synners like this, and that was well over a hundred years ago. I'm looking forward to seeing what you can do," he said, grinning even more wolfishly.

"First, I want to see how quickly you can cast an Exar spell," he said, pulling his own mana as he stepped back. "What?" I asked, but as soon as the words left my mouth, Pyle released his Exar spell, flinging me across the training ground. "Don't worry about your injuries; I'll heal them later. Now, try again," Pyle said, gesturing with his hands. "Try what again?" I asked, dusting myself off. "To counter my spell with your own Exar," he stated plaintively as he prepared another one.

What's the point of that? I wondered, doing my best to brace for the incoming blast.

I *drew just enough mana* to nullify most of its effects as I coated my body in mana, but it still felt like Celer had just kicked me in the gut. "Come at me," he said, spreading his arms widely in defiance.

"So that's how it's going to be. Alright then," I grinned, finally understanding what he was trying to do.

About two hours passed, and I was covered in sweat and out of breath. Pyle, on the other hand, barely showed any signs of fatigue. "H-How is that even possible?" I asked, desperately catching my breath. "Do you remember what you were doing just before we interrupted you? I said you had the right idea, but not quite," he said, sighing slightly. "What the hell does that even mean?" I asked, wiping the sweat from my brow.

"Bernar, Anwill, and even the Master have said you could reach the second stage mid-combat. Why do you think that is?" Pyle asked. I thought momentarily, recalling the events they were present for. "It was because I was in a *life-or-death* situation, I suppose. I don't understand *how* I did it, but it just sort of... *happened*," I shrugged.

"Do you remember how you felt in those situations? What was your body going through? What sensations do you remember?" he asked. "I felt like my whole body was *on fire*, but that was just due to adrenaline, wasn't it?" I replied after a few moments.

"Almost, but not quite. In reality, the part of your consciousness you would normally send to the Ethereal became *suppressed*, meaning you subconsciously imbued your *muscles and bones* with mana and continued circulating it throughout your body instead of coating yourself in it," he replied with a nod.

"I did?" I asked, genuinely confused, looking down at my hands. "I said you had the *right idea* before but weren't quite there, yet. Try doing what you did initially, but instead of wrapping the outside of your body, try focusing the mana into your muscles and bones. Only do a little to start; we don't want you to tear your body apart from the inside, do we?" Pyle asked wryly.

My eyes opened wide in surprise, but I understood what he meant. "I'll do my best," I replied. "Try it now. I'll watch over you and make sure you don't implode," Pyle gave me a reassuring nod.

I closed my eyes and *reached into the Ethereal, but as the tendrils began to wrap around my body, I focused my will, forcing it* into *me this time.*

My consciousness returned to my body, and I could feel the mana coursing through my veins and muscles as a burst of mana kicked up dust around me. My eyes, now glowing, had a slight mana-leakage that caused a steam-like trail of golden mana to lick at my temples like the top of a small fire.

"H-holy shit!" I chuckled, flexing my hand. "You really got it on your first try? It seems Bernar was right to call you a *monster*," Pyle said, equally surprised with an inquisitive look.

Is he trying to figure out whether I'm human? I thought idly.

I looked at my hands and arms, then to him, noticing the mana flowing inside *his* body as well. "I can see your mana, too! *Oh*, even my voice is different!" I exclaimed. "Of course you can. Your entire body has been enhanced because you properly infused the mana into your muscles," he chuckled with a shrug.

"Your vision, your sense of smell; everything is heightened, though not to its maximum potential yet. I'm still surprised you got it on the first try. Normally, that would have taken a few weeks to figure out," Pyle said, still observing me carefully to ensure I wasn't overdoing it.

I began looking at my surroundings and noticed that the trees had veins of green mana, whereas the earth beneath my feet had veins of brown mana flowing through it. The sky had wisps of light green mana flowing through it. "I've seen these colors before. That sphere of mana we pull from in the Ethereal..." I trailed off.

"Precisely. The only difference is that in the Real, they are all separated into what that mana belongs to. However, they all coexist and intertwine in the Ethereal, which is one of the reasons why it comes in individual tendrils when we draw from it," he explained.

"Now, do me a favor, Thoma," he began. "What do you need me to do, Master Pyle?" I asked, enjoying the sound of my altered voice. "Try moving to the other side of the training yard as quickly as possible. If you get it on your first try, I might need to *have a word* with your Master once we're done here," he said, trying to hide his excitement.

I took a few seconds to gauge the distance between myself and the other end of the yard. I bent over slightly and made sure my footing was sound. My eyes glowed more intensely just before pushing off the ground as a small explosion of dirt and wind trailed behind me. Within a second, I was already at the other end, where I skidded to a halt. "Holy shit!" I exclaimed, breathing heavily.

I've never moved that fast in my life! I thought.

"No... *fucking*... way," I heard Pyle say, his jaw dropping to the floor like a counterweight was pulling it down.

"Well, what do you think?" I asked, turning to face him as I steadied my breathing. "I think, Thoma, that you have the makings of one of the greatest Synners of our time," he said, chuckling and shaking his head.

I could feel the honesty in his voice, and acknowledged it with a bow. "Thank you, Master Pyle," I said humbly. "Of course! However, this is only the beginning. Now that you have learned to harness it, having mastery over it is another story entirely. Although with your skills, I don't see that taking you very long," he grinned.

"One step at a time, as over-exerting myself right now would probably be a bad idea. Well, more than I already have, anyway," I said, feeling the bruises begin to form all over my body. "You'll be fine. I'll heal you up and send you to bed. It's already much later than I had anticipated, but I'm sure we'll be fine tomorrow," he chirped. "You say that, but I feel like I'm still going to be sore tomorrow," I said, shrugging my shoulders.

For once, I was right.

As the sun rose over Fangsdalr a few hours later, we gathered our things to prepare for our journey to Coltend. Meliss either didn't notice or care that I'd left, but she *did* show some slight concern for my physical state, as the bags under my eyes were about as large as the ones I had tied to my saddle.

I was right about being sore. Gods above and below, I haven't felt this since the early days of learning to ride a horse, I thought.

The promised days of rest in Fangsdalr would have been a much-needed revitalization of expended energies; however, fate had decided otherwise for all of us. I looked around at the trees as we rode beneath them. The lack of sleep had caused me to become mildly delusional, and the calling of birds and other such creatures nearly sent me into a trance.

Each branch seemed to mesh into the other, and the small bursts of sunlight did little to help my mental state. The chatter of the other Synners around me added to the cacophony that was my mind at the time, jumbling my thoughts into an ever-entangling web I couldn't seem to escape.

Meliss noticed I wasn't doing all too well, and held me tightly. "Thoma," she said in my ear, noticing my head was bobbing in time with Celer's stride. I blinked, startled by the words in my ears. "*Oh, I'm sorry,*" I said, trying to hide my surprise. "Are you alright?" she asked softly. "Could I roll over and die right now? Probably, but with everything that has happened over the past few days, it has *really* taken it out of me, I think," I yawned, rubbing my eyes to try and keep my sleepiness at bay.

"I know the feeling well. When I was just a wee child, I'd often help my mother with her daily duties. It was exhausting, so I understand how you feel right now," she said reminiscently. "I don't mean any offense here, but have you *always* been a servant?" I asked, causing her to chuckle.

"None taken. Ma and I often took charge of cleaning the houses," she said, puffing up a strand of hair that had fallen near her eyes. "It was a slow life, but we were happy doing what we did," she continued. I chewed her words for a moment, trying to connect her lowly life and becoming a servant to the queen herself.

"Nope. It's not making sense to me," I muttered through the fogginess of my thoughts. "What's not?" she asked plainly. "I can't figure out how you became a royal servant," I said, trying to think through the brain fog. "Well, Fulco saw one of the jobs we'd done, and thought we were worthy of working at the Palace. Sadly, Ma couldn't handle the workload she was given as she got older and died about three winters back," her tone dropped as she put her chin on my shoulder momentarily.

"I'm so sorry. I-I didn't know…" I trailed off. "It's alright. Nothing much to be done about it now, anyway," she sighed lightly, leaving a silence between us that I didn't want to be the cause of. "Not very talkative today, are we?" Bernar injected himself into said silence, for which I was very grateful.

"*Oh*, we were just talking about the past, and I think I struck a nerve I didn't intend to," I said grimly.

"I'm alright, I promise," Meliss said comfortingly, rubbing my arm. "See? She's stronger than she looks," Bernar said with a warm smile aimed at her, who returned it. "Sometimes, you have to take the good with the bad, and right now, I think you're in a pretty *decent spot*," he said, glancing at the tiny hand rubbing my arm. "Yeah, but what about the rest of them?" I nodded behind me, causing him to look back and sigh.

"You know that our mission may either make us heroes or force history to forget us, right?" Bernar asked me. "I do. Although I will do everything I can to be the former until my last breath," I continued, gazing off into the distance.

I realized I hadn't voiced those thoughts aloud before, but I knew they came from the bottom of my heart as Bernar looked at me and seemingly knew what I meant. "I know you can handle yourself in battle, *little shit*, but Meliss can't. Speaking of which, I intend to keep you by my side with Leona. With any luck, we won't be too bothered by any creature that comes along," he said. "That makes me glad to hear that," Meliss said warmly.

There was a short silence as we digested our short conversation.

"So, you and Leona, *huh*? Quite the woman you've gotten your-self," I began, breaking the silence. "Shut up, *child of the ass*," Bernar grinned, punching me in the shoulder. "*Hey!*" I exclaimed while laughing, making Meliss laugh at our exchange. "I've always wished I had a brother. I think we would've been the same way," she said with a smile.

"No, you don't. He's an asshole," I jutted my thumb at him. "And you're a *shit bird*," Bernar added, making Meliss laugh again. "Wait, why are *you* laughing at that?" I asked with genuine confusion. "Apparently, that's how he introduced you to Leona when we first started riding with you," she giggled.

I stared at him with a chagrined smile.

"W-What?" he shrugged. "I might just tell Leona about the Dawn Nymph. You know, an *accidental slip of the tongue* or something," I turned my head and put a finger on my chin. "You wouldn't dare…" he seethed. "*Oh-ho,* I would and you know it," I grinned, knowing I had him in the palm of my hand.

Meliss, of course, was confused as shit the whole time.

"Anyway, getting back on the *other* topic, I don't know that you would like to have a brother like us," Bernar said, trying his best to divert away from *that* conversation. "Why's that?" she asked bluntly. "You're a *lady*," he said with a smile. "And that has something to do with it? You have female Synners, do you not?" she said, pursing her lips thoughtfully.

"We do, but they're all brutes in their own rights. Oftentimes, they're even more aggressive than the boys. Also, why every one of them assumes they can *kick my ass* is beyond me," Bernar said, rolling his eyes, making us all laugh. As the three of us laughed, Leona glanced back at the laughter's origin.

She saw Bernar's smile, and I could tell she felt something stirring in her stomach. She smiled when she saw us getting along well with Meliss, and probably felt a happiness she hadn't felt in a long time, and slowed her horse to join us.

"I hope I'm not intruding on whatever fun you're having," she said, riding beside my brother. "Never," I said with a tired smile. "You bring joy and light to even the darkest of places, and I pray, for my *brother's sake*, that you continue to do so, Your Majesty," I said, glancing at him, who was trying to subtly motion for me to stop. Leona laughed when she noticed the exchange. "So, you know, then?" she asked bluntly.

"I might be a *shit bird*, but I'm not an idiot, Your Majesty," I said wryly, getting a small scoff from her as she looked at Bernar. "I didn't say anything, he figured it out alone," he shrugged. "And do you approve of what you say you know?" she asked, genuinely seeking my approval. "If what I believe I know to be true, then you have my blessing," I said warmly.

Leona smiled and nodded slowly.

"When we make camp, I'd like to speak to you alone, if possible, Thoma," she said. "Have I done something wrong?" I asked, already fearing the worst. "No, no. Nothing like that. I just want to have a conversation without *anyone* influencing your answers," she gave Bernar a short glance. "I see. In that case, I look forward to our meeting, Your Majesty," I said, bowing as much as I could without dehorsing Meliss.

Leona looked at me curiously and sighed, though I couldn't tell of what I'd said or my lack of grace. "You needn't call me *that* any longer. You are now my friend, and since I am no longer queen of

Coltend, nor am I in the presence of other officials, there is no need for such formalities," she said with a smile. "*Oh*, thank fuck. I wasn't sure how much longer I could keep that up with how tired I am, and I've always hated titles," I groaned.

I could tell my response caught her completely by surprise because her pale blue eyes widened to their limits. "Well, that was quick, just like your brother," she chuckled. "*Eh*, I don't know how you manage to upkeep formalities around those *bureaucratic fuck sticks* for hours on end," I shrugged. "Well, you get used to it. If not, you become an *unladylike figure* in their eyes, which, as a queen, is *not* something you want to be seen as being," she said, her face contorting from its bright smile into a pained one.

Being unladylike in her position would probably create enmity among some of the officials, perhaps even leading some to question her capabilities as a ruler, I thought.

"Can't say I disagree with you, even with my limited experience in political matters," I sighed. "Fair enough, but let's talk about the more pleasant things in life," Leona said invitingly. The four of us rode on, telling jokes, stories, and adventures we had had in our pasts. Meliss had very little to say, since she had been a servant girl nearly all of her life, but she enjoyed the tales of Bernar's drunken acts and my bravado to try and contain my older brother.

Leona shared a few of her own, which surprised all of us, since no one suspected her of being capable of such things. She took little pride in her adventures, but was happy to finally share a few of them with people who didn't seem to worship or judge her every word.

We rode onward until the sun began to set to our right, transforming the land and trees about them into a golden-red river of windblown grass and trees. "Still not as impressive as the Elv Avliv at this time of day," Bernar said. "That place was truly spectacular, was it not?" Leona asked with a bright smile. "It really was," he replied warmly, and I was glad to see them getting along as well as they did.

Meanwhile, Anwill and Roburn had been conversing the whole journey together, discussing what they needed to do in unison to open the Portal Stone that lay in the network of sewers beneath the city. The Master spotted movement in the distance and raised his hand, signaling a halt to the others who followed him. "Is that who I think it is?" Garett asked. "The one and only," the Master replied quietly.

"We have already seen you, Jehn," the Master called out. "No point in hiding anymore," he continued. The old farmer slowly moved out from behind the large oak that he had hidden behind. "Forgive me, Master. Been a while since I've seen any come o'er them hills," he said, pointing in the general direction. The Master glanced over at Garett, who simply shrugged.

"Who did you think we were, my good man?" he asked. "I dunno. Bandits, mayhaps," Boone replied with a shrug. The Master looked around him, realizing just how far this man had come from his farmstead. "I take it you're out on a stroll?" the Master asked. "Nay, truth be told I *were* lookin' for ye, Master," Boone replied. "Looking for me? What for?" he raised an eyebrow.

"Well, the reason be as follows: After ye'd saved me from them damned *abominations*, I made my way to the market in Coltend. There, the vendor I were to sell me goods to asked me why some were fouled. I told him the tale, I did, and he were taken aback. He sent a letter off to the palace with a messenger of sorts, and no sooner was I summoned to meet with a man they called *Father Mourtis*. He questioned my house's where'bouts, an' I told him my farm lies about half a day's ride from yer fortress on the border of Kinth," Boone said, gesturing in the general location of his farm.

I looked at Bernar briefly, but he didn't seem to know anything about it either.

"He then asked me to spy on ye for a pretty amount of crescents, an' that I were to report to him an' none else. I agreed, I did, for my family an' I needed the coin at the time, an' yet, I'm sorry for nay havin' told ye," Boone said with his head low.

The Master looked around to see if anyone within earshot stirred at the information being said rather loudly. "I understand, Boone, I do. However, I must ask you how you sent the reports," he asked. "Why, even with the good Father's payments, I don't have the coin to use ravens, so I sent me son once every couple'a days to deliver the messages," Boone replied as though his reply should have been obvious.

"It's not him," Garett whispered. "But he did send messages nonetheless,' the Master replied. "So what do we do?" Garett asked. The Master paused momentarily, then looked at Boone, who was becoming a little nervous. "You are but a simple farmer, who needed the coin; that much I can understand. However, I must ask you never to send reports to Father Mourtis or *anyone else* who wishes to know of our whereabouts. Do you understand?" the Master asked.

"*Oh*, not me, Master! Me hands an' mouth are sealed shut like a bear trap," Boone shook his head, motioning to his mouth. "I hope so, for *all* our sakes," he nodded, causing Boone to pause momentarily, looking down at the ground around him.

"Master, there be one last thing I wish to tell ye," he began. "What might that be?" the Master asked. "Well, ye see, Master, during me last visit to the Market last week, I overheard a conversation between two hooded men who spake of a terrible thing comin' thataways," Boone replied, making the Master squint his eyes slightly.

"What sort of *terrible thing*?" he asked. "I dunno for certain, but sounded to me like some dark mage, or something o' the likes, were to be makin' its way there soon," Boone replied. The Master looked at Garett, whose eyes were wide open and eyebrows raised. "Did they happen to mention when this dark mage would be there?" the Master asked.

"The way they'd put it, sounded to me like it were to be sometime this week, Master," Boone replied solemnly. "That's not good at all, then. My good man, I must ask that you stay as far away from Coltend as possible until we return. *If* we return, that is," the Master cautioned. "An' me produce, Master?" Boone asked with tears almost welling in his eyes.

Leona, who had been paying attention to the whole conversation, rode up to him and dismounted. As soon as she did so, she pulled off one of her silver rings with an emerald embedded within. "Here, this should be enough to buy a year's worth of supplies," she said, grabbing his hand and upturning his palm to place her gift. His eyes widened in surprise, as more tears began to well in his eyes.

"T-This be *far too much*, good lady," he said, trying to give the ring back, but she took his calloused, dirty hand in hers and closed it around the ring. "The information you gave us is worth far more than that trinket. Consider it a form of *thanks* from all of us," she said with a smile. Boone tore his eyes from the emerald, only to find two more eyes as blue as the sky beaming back at him with a warm smile thrown in.

"Thank ye, lady," Boone said with his most humble bow. "I think you'd best be heading home, my good man," the Master said. "An' ye'd be right. The dark brings dark things, unless of course ye be one of those dark things creeping 'bout like some sort of *wraith* or *shade-walker*," he said. "We can when needed," The Master said with a grin, raising his hand and motioning for us to move forward.

We continued down the path, while Boone went to his farmstead, content at the priceless gift he had just received. Anwill rode up to the Master's side, trotting alongside him briefly. "That piece of information may prove to be more useful than we thought. With the passageways beneath the city, we may be able to infiltrate it and avoid many losses as a result," he said.

"That still doesn't guarantee that he hasn't already thought about that possibility, should anyone muster the courage to attack him. Chances are there will be more than a few sentries placed beneath the tunnels, by his doing or not," the Master replied grimly.

"Leona said that Coltend was an old Elven city, right?" Anwill asked. "If I recall correctly, she did," he replied. "Not many people outside the Elven Elders know about the old cities. Maybe, just *maybe*, whoever this *dark one* is doesn't know about them either," Anwill explained. "Even with that element of surprise, it might not be enough to retake the city completely," the Master sighed.

"That's why we're bringing five hundred of us, right?" Anwill asked with a sly grin. "I have always admired your optimism, my old friend," he said with a nasal chuckle. "I try to be as often as possible. I pray the gods will give us the knowledge to win this next trial," Anwill said, staring off into the distance. "And *I pray* the gods hear you," Garett chimed in.

We rode a bit longer as the twilight sky began to overtake the flame-colored sky, eventually stopping to set up camp before the final leg of our journey. The others made fires and camps, while Bernar and I helped Leona and Meliss set up a pair of tents. Bernar helped Leona set up her tent, since her lack of experience was only solidified by her collapsing tent, eliciting a friendly chuckle from both of us.

Meliss and I, on the other hand, made a single tent by conjoining the ones we each had, making it doubly spacious in the process.

Night came as quickly as it ever did, and a few of us, Batch, Edryd, and Irun included, sat around a small fire we had started, telling tales of the days of old. Meliss and I slipped away after a little while, and were content to have some time to ourselves, away from peering eyes. However, it was short-lived, as we heard someone approaching.

"Thoma, are you in there?" Leona's voice came from outside the tent.

Shit, I completely forgot about that, I thought.

"I'll be out in a moment," I said, kissing Meliss and proceeding out of the tent as she fell back in the furs and wrapped herself. "I suppose you've already forgotten that I wanted to speak with you," Leona began, noting the belt to my trousers being undone with a raised eyebrow, prompting me to look down and quickly tie it.

"Sorry," I blushed. "It's alright. I've seen *uglier* and *smaller* things dangling between the legs of men with much higher social standings than you," she said with a slight giggle. I instantly felt a bit more comfortable, but I would be lying if I said I didn't feel embarrassed.

She was still *royalty*, after all.

"Come with me," she said, taking me by the hand. Bernar watched the two of us from a distance, wondering what we might need to say without him present. He shrugged and joined the others around the campfire, grabbing a mug of ale from one of the younger ones. "You can't handle much more than that, you're too young," I heard him say as he did so.

Leona led me a short distance from the camp and gazed up at the stars. "Beautiful, aren't they?" she asked. I looked up, and just as I did, one of them streaked across the dark sky, as the moon had not yet risen. "They really are, but I assume you want to talk to me about more important matters than the stars," I said shyly, causing her to chuckle lightly. "Way to point out the *ochelon* in the room," she said warmly.

"The first thing I need to speak to you about, I believe to be the most obvious," she began. "My brother, you mean to say," I filled in for her, getting a nod in response. "He is a good man, from what I've seen, and I pray that our little... *relationship* doesn't affect you negatively," she said, making me chuckle lightly.

"*Oh*, my dearest Leona, if only you knew your *worth* to him and the world around you, you wouldn't even dare say something like that. Besides, after everything he and I have been through, I think having you by his side might make him an even greater person than I already know him to be," I said warmly, watching her eyes widen in surprise.

"Are you sure you were never trained in politics?" she asked playfully, but I could only shake my head. "No, but I'm just being honest," I shrugged. She smiled warmly, then looked back up at the stars again, lost in thought. "With a compliment like that, it's no small wonder why Meliss likes you the way she does," she said idly. "I try,"

I shrugged. "You are an amazing boy of... wait, how old are you, again?" she asked. "I just turned eighteen," I replied. "*Ah*, right," Leona nodded, recalling what Bernar had told her earlier.

"Being the remarkable man he is, and the inquisitive boy that you are, has made you both invaluable to me; something I never would have expected to happen so quickly," she said pensively, causing me to smile. "I pray that when this is all over, I will be able to grant both of you gifts worthy of a king," she said, but I shook my head and raised my hands in refusal in the dim light of the distant fire. "There is no need for that whatsoever," I said lightly.

"By the Graces, Thoma! I *will give you* the treatment you deserve," she said somewhat firmly. "*Stubborn* just like my brother. No wonder you two get along so well," I chuckled, patting her hand lightly. "Well, since I've lost this battle, I guess that means I can't turn you down," I shrugged. "I'm glad to hear that," Leona said, playfully nudging my arm with her elbow.

Leona looked back at the camp, probably listening to Bernar's laughter drown out the others'.

"There is, of course, one *other thing* I wanted to talk to you about. I haven't told anyone else, not even Bernar, though I suspect he and the Master may already know," she began, but I could only swallow dryly. I knew that whatever came next was paramount, and I listened attentively.

"The castle is taken, this we know, but there is one thing that the invader probably hasn't figured out yet, though I suspect he will soon enough. *The Plant*, or *Gwynnleaf* as you Synners call it, lies there in Coltend, buried underneath layers of stone. Over the years that the castle has existed, it has shifted its position under every king's rule.

Under Truls' rule, however, he moved it to a library beneath the main hall, where it was to be hidden in plain sight," she said.

What? No, that can't be right, I blinked a few times to make sure I wasn't dreaming.

"How is it possible to hide something like that in plain sight?" I asked, genuinely dumbfounded. "There is no sunlight down there that could reach it, not to mention the lack of airflow. As it needs no sunlight or water to survive, we have been able to hide it from prying eyes by *faking* its death," she sighed, as if it brought a bad memory to the forefront of her mind.

"We have always managed this by painting the plants with *mana-suppressant* paste, making it *look* dead. This paste can only be removed during the preparation, so it is highly unlikely that anyone outside the preparers has seen its full glory," she explained.

"So you're telling me that even if the invader found the library, they would believe the plants are dead?" I asked. "Precisely. Now, the purpose for us doing so is that the library beneath the palace is so vast, and has so many different routes to take, that it would be nearly impossible to find one that would let off a significant amount of mana to be found by a mage or otherwise," she explained.

I chewed on the information for a moment and considered all possible scenarios that may or may not become a reality.

"This may have come as a surprise to you, but the fact that it has been there, under so many people's noses for so many years has made it our best-kept secret," Leona continued, as I digested the information presented. "What if someone else knew its location besides the royal family and the Synner masters?" I asked, cautiously looking over to the fire to ensure no one could hear us.

"Then we would all be in much graver danger than we already are," Leona said grimly. "Then we must not let him have it," I said, furrowing my brow. "Listen, I might not be as powerful as my brother, but I promise I'll do whatever I can, if you and Meliss let me," I said sternly, but my bravado only made her chuckle.

"You've got a good heart, Thoma; for that, you have my respect and permission to do so. You are brave, kind, and selfless when it comes to matters larger than yourself," she said warmly, then wrapped her arms around me in a tight hug. I froze momentarily, but returned the hug briefly and, admittedly, awkwardly. We sat there for a few moments before she pulled away.

"Come on, let's get some food, drink, and rest for tomorrow," she suggested, taking me by the hand and leading me back to the campfire.

Bernar, you're one lucky bastard, I thought with a smile, letting her lead the way.

Within a few minutes, we were back in our tents with our respective lovers, Leona with Bernar, and I with Meliss. Naturally, there wasn't much sleep to be had in the dark hours of the night, but we still managed to get just enough sleep to where we felt rested the following morning.

The Master was the first to wake aside from myself and perhaps a handful of others. According to what Bernar told me, he'd had his first dream that night in many years, and I knew it must have been some kind of premonition, because it struck me as odd that the Master didn't dream often.

But then again, have I ever seen him sleep? I thought back.

As I stepped out of my tent, I noticed a stillness in the air, a quiet before the battle that hung over the camp. I knew instinctively that today would be a difficult battle for everyone. I walked to the crest of the small hill nearby and looked out toward the dawning sky. It was beautiful that morning, but I heard a slight rustling nearby that surprised me.

The Master? What's he doing here? I thought, realizing he'd made the same decision I had.

"Master," Garett began. "I know," he replied, turning to face the one who had disturbed him. "Wake the others who are still asleep. It's time to go," he said. Garett nodded, then went over to the other tents, leaving the Master to his thoughts again.

A few others were slowly getting up, readying their gear and horses as Garett woke them up. I watched as he looked at them, nodding to each one as he passed. He knew our thoughts, as they were likely similar to his own; we were about to ride into the challenge of our lifetimes.

I walked back inside the tent just as Meliss was putting on her gear. It was a gift from Master Pyle, after all, since he thought it might be a good idea to give her and Leona at least a little bit of protection. I noticed that she was having a little bit of a hard time getting used to the buckles and straps that accompanied it.

"Here, let me show you," I chuckled, reaching for the first buckle. Once it's through, you've got to place the prong through the little hole after pulling it to a comfortable tightness," I said, pulling on the leather strap. The movement caused her to jolt a little, and she was clearly surprised at just how close a fit the jerkin was.

"Heavy thing, isn't it?" she asked. "It *is* if you've never worn one before. Over time, though, it becomes much easier to wear and move in. Chances are very good that it will save your life if anything tries to get too close," I shrugged, but I noticed a frown grow on her porcelain features.

"Do you think it'll come to that?" she asked, but I shook my head and held her face. "Not if you stay by me, and if I'm not around, stay as close to either Garett or Bernar; you and Leona both, understand?" I said, looking into her eyes. She looked back into mine and nodded her response. "We'll be alright," I said, embracing her tightly.

"Thoma," Bernar called from outside the tent. "Time for us to go," I whispered to Meliss. "On our way," I answered the call. Our tent was packed away within a few minutes before we joined the others. Meliss saw Leona in the same attire as herself, and was instantly comforted that she wasn't the only one who had received the light armor.

"It fits you well, just as I thought," Pyle said cheerfully, approaching Meliss. "Thank you, Master Pyle," she replied with a bow. He walked over to her and grabbed the jerkin, briefly shaking and tugging on it to see if it would come loose. "A fine job on the lacings," he said, glancing at me.

"I had help from Thoma," she said shyly. "*Oh*, I know that," Pyle said cheerfully as he could. He reached for a leather-wrapped bundle and handed it to her. "Here, take this. It's dangerous to go unarmed," he said with a smile.

Meliss unwrapped the leather package and found a large knife in a leather sheath with intricate details and the sign of the Fangsdalr

Synners near the mouth. She reached for the carved wooden handle and drew the blade from its sheath.

It had a curved tip with a false bevel along the spine near the tip, and a long edge. "Thorsen mentioned that you know how it works," he said. "Have to stick the pointy end in," she said with a weak smile, getting a nod from him in return. "Just know that it's not just the point of a blade that will save you. The edge will put in plenty of work if you use it in the right spot," he put a hand on her small shoulder. She nodded and went with us to meet with the Master and the others.

I faced her as I put the leather belt through the loops provided by the sheath, sliding it over to her left side. "Pat it once or twice so you know exactly where it is every so often," I said. She did so immediately. "More weight," she frowned. "*Grams make kilos*. Or, do *ounces make pounds*? I never remember the proper saying, but it's still true nonetheless," I grinned, knowing she could handle it.

"Mount up," the call came from behind us. "Ready?" I asked, but she had no words, so she nodded in reply. I walked over to my horse and checked my equipment one last time before putting the ball of my foot into the stirrup, throwing my remaining leg over to the other side.

I was glad to have gotten used to the height of the stirrups by that point.

I took Meliss' hand and helped her up onto Celer's back. "My most honorable Synners and ladies present," the Master began to say a short distance away from the others. "Today's the day we reach Coltend, where a hoard of countless creatures awaits us, each eager to kill and devour our bodies. Fear may come over us, but I ask you to enter with the will to fight that fear and push through it like a plough to a field. Not having fear is impossible, but having the courage and strength to overcome fear *is* possible!" he shouted loudly enough for all of us to hear.

I could feel her arms tighten around my waist as a roar of support came from everyone present. "We have done this time and time again, but this time, we fight not just for Coltend and its people, but the *Continent*. Let's win this fight and get home alive!" he shouted, getting another roar in response.

Here we go, I thought, gently rubbing my hand against the tiny one at my waist as I looked to Batch, Irun, and Ed, who all gave me nods to show they were ready.

"To war!" he shouted, kicking his heels into his horse's sides, prompting the five hundred others to do the same. We all knew what we were getting into, and it forced us to harden our wills and calm our minds as much as possible.

However, off in the distance, a winged figure with burning eyes watched us as we rode toward the castle. It soared through the air as it made its way towards its owner.

CHAPTER 20
THE LIBRARY

Wingar shook uncontrollably on the chapel floor, while Osgar and Alf tried to calm him down.

"Wingar, talk to me! What happened?" Osgar asked, trying to understand his brother's mental state. "We're doomed, and it's my fault. He knows. He knows I lied," he replied shakily. Osgar squatted down next to his brother. "How can you be so sure?" he asked. Wingar looked at him in despair. "I could feel it. I felt his rage the moment the words left my mouth while that strange feeling rummaged through my mind," Wingar replied, clutching his chest.

"What do you mean you could *feel it*?" Osgar asked as Wingar blankly stared at him, shaking his head like a nervous twitch. "I don't know how or why, but it was almost as if I could feel his will boring into my mind, looking for something. I did what I could to hide my thoughts, but the way he sounded just before we left..." he said shakily.

"Honestly, that could have just been because you were *nervous* in his presence," Alf suggested, but Wingar turned and glared at his friend quickly. "I know what I felt, and had you felt it as I did, you would've shat yourself the moment the feeling came," he said angrily, but Osgar put a finger to his lips. "Shh, wouldn't want him to hear that, would you?" he asked hushedly.

Wingar fell to his side and curled up into a fetal position, where he sobbed uncontrollably. "I'm sorry. I... I don't know what we should do," he said between the hiccups that resulted from his weeping. Osgar looked over at Alf, who simply shrugged with an upturned lip. "None of us do. For now, all we can do is play along with the lie that we know nothing about what he wants. At this point, we are still uncertain *what that is* and what Mourtis meant by saying *he is coming for it*," Osgar said.

For once, the tables had turned: Osgar was now the reasonable one, while Wingar had taken Alf's place as the one to fret.

Wingar's sobbing slowed a little as he regained his composure. "You're right, brother. We have no other choice," he said, wiping away a wad of snot. "We must find out what he wants, and how we can still find a way to uphold our end of the bargain," he continued. Osgar helped him to his feet, while Alf brought him some water from the nearby jug, which he snatched quickly and took a few gulps of old water that had sat in the same container for far too long. He spat out most of the bitter-tasting liquid and instantly regretted having swallowed some before tasting it.

"Tastes like old socks," he said, spitting a few more times. "Well, if it got you out of your tantrum, then I suppose it was for the best," Alf said. Wingar looked at him angrily, but decided it was best they stuck together rather than get at each other's throats. Wingar wiped his mouth with his sleeve and looked around at the empty chapel.

The benches that faced them were empty, and the whole room smelled of old incense and spilled wine.

I remember this place, Wingar thought, recalling a speech Mourtis had once given there, spitting the remainder of saliva in his mouth at the sign of Mideia before heading down the steps.

"Where are you going?" Osgar asked. "To find something that will help us out of the shit-hole I got us into," he replied without turning around. The two were soon behind him as they went to the second floor, where the scribes made copies of the books Mourtis had commissioned to be translated into the common language.

A few benches were lined along a lengthy table, where stubs of old candle wax had melted, wrapping themselves around their supports, and inkwells lay spilled and dried upon the dense wood.

"Look for anything regarding the history of Coltend, and read through the table of contents. With any luck, we'll find something somewhat useful," Wingar ordered as they began to scour the scrolls and leather-bound books upon the shelves and table.

Most of the books on the shelves were covered in dust - countless years without a single hand touching them had left them looking like they had been lost in time. Osgar went straight to the table and began to read the first few lines of the works in progress. He went from page to page, all around the table, while the other two were scouring the titles of the books. "Nothing here," he said to the others, causing Wingar's stomach to turn.

If we don't find anything here, we're really *in for it,* Wingar thought.

"Keep looking," he urged, but Osgar shook his head and resumed his search. "There must be something in here," Alf said. Wingar heard it, but said nothing, continuing his search through the titles. After about an hour of searching, Alf sighed, prompting the others to look at him. "There's nothing here either," he said, spreading his arms. Wingar bit his lower lip in frustration, but continued his search alongside Osgar anyway.

"Wait a minute," he said after a few moments. "What?" Osgar asked. "A book about Coltend wouldn't *need* to be translated," Wingar began. "Why would anyone want to translate a book about the castle's secrets? So that potential enemies would know of every nook and cranny? Knowing the deepest secrets wouldn't make sense for anyone besides the royal family. Still, there must be information about them somewhere in case death takes the royal family before they could pass on the information," he explained.

Osgar looked at Alf, and then at his brother. At the same time, they realized where the book might be. "I think we ought to pay a visit to Mourtis' room again," Osgar said, looking to the others, then gesturing for them to follow him. They rushed down the wooden steps that creaked under their rapid movements. They exited the chapel doors, leaving them wide open, and sprinted back to the palace.

The Masked One heard their footsteps as they came through the previously obliterated doorway and rose from his throne. "So?" he asked. "We believe we may have found something, but we need *more time*, lord," Wingar replied after breathing deeply. The Masked One grunted. "*Time* is the one thing that is never on *anyone's side*. Get me what I need, and be quick about it," he commanded. Wingar bowed, and the three were soon off again, sprinting up the stairs to Mourtis' quarters.

The cinnamon smell filled their lungs and nostrils, and Wingar spat. "I'll never get over that *stench*," he said. "We've got bigger fish to fry than worrying about the stench," Osgar said, to which Wingar nodded, and they began their search. He noted the journals still by the window, and shuddered, remembering the feeling that had come over him just a few short hours ago. He shook his head and moved towards the back of the room, where there was a small, wooden nightstand with a drawer.

Wingar opened the drawer to the nightstand, creaking and whining as it opened. "What do you think is in here?" his brother asked. "I'm not sure, but if it hasn't been opened in a long time, then that could mean there's something inside he never wanted anyone to see," Wingar noted, observing the drawer cautiously.

The small drawer, now fully opened, contained only a single, black book. The pair looked at each other while Alf still rummaged through the other books in the background. Wingar flipped through a few of the pages, his eyes opening wide.

"This book *isn't* translated at all," he began. "What does it say?" Osgar asked, trying to get a better look at the pages for himself. "It's hard to say, as this is in a much older version of Coltendian than we now know. If I'm reading it correctly, it says there's a... *library*?" he said the last word, questioning his own translation. "A *library*? That can't be right," Osgar said, furrowing his brow and moving in closer.

Wingar shook his head and pointed to the first few lines on the page he was reading. "I think it is right, though. Look, there are more and more indications that it *is* a library. It talks about books and other such valuable things to the kingdom that are not often shared with the public," he traced his finger along the lines he read.

"Do you think that's where whatever he's looking for is?" Osgar asked, hoping for a better answer than the one he had in his mind. "Only one way to find out," he replied with a heavy sigh.

The three returned to the main hall, where the Masked One observed their cautious approach. "Lord, we've found this book inside Father Mourtis' study," Wingar began, prompting the mage to tilt his head, and rip the book out of Wingar's hands with a tendril of mana, sending it flying through the air. The book landed in his hands, and he opened it to read the first page. His eyes burned even more than they usually did.

"Where did you find this?" he asked angrily. Wingar felt his stomach do a flip. "We missed it the first time we went up to Mourtis' quarters, lord. It was in his room all along," he replied as calmly as he could manage. The Masked One's eyes dimmed, and he inhaled deeply. "You have done well, my servants," he smiled wickedly beneath his mask.

"It's all thanks to his quick thinking, lord," Osgar nudged his brother and raised an eyebrow. "We have done as you requested and held up our end of the bargain. Are we now free to go and live out the rest of our lives in peace, away from these creatures, lord?" Wingar asked humbly.

The Masked One thought for a moment. "If you wish to live the *impoverished* life of the common folk, then by all means, you are free. However, if that's not what you want for your lives anymore, I will offer you *power* in exchange for your *service*," he said in a calmer tone than they were expecting, given the recent display of anger. Wingar looked at the others, hoping to see how they would reply to such an offer.

"I'm tired of always worrying about things. I'm tired of being anxious, and most of all, I'm tired of this *world*. If what you say is true, then I will join you, lord," Alf stepped forward, walking over to the man in the mask and knelt on one knee. The Masked One didn't move forward, but simply outstretched his hand. "Will you follow in your friend's footsteps?" he asked.

Wingar looked at his brother, who began to itch at the rough beard patches on his slim face, and shook his head subtly.

"I can't believe you're considering it," he hissed quietly, but instead of agreeing with his brother, Osgar shrugged. "I can't believe you're *not*. Is avoiding a life of powerlessness and poverty a bad thing now? I don't want to be either of those anymore," he replied. "In exchange for your *soul*, brother? Please, reconsider his offer," Wingar said desperately. "My *soul* was taken and destroyed long ago by that creepy old fuck, brother," Osgar replied gravely, looking at the Masked One, who was observing the exchange and tapping his index finger on his knee.

There's no way my life with him *will be worse than it was before,* Osgar thought, stepping away from his brother.

Wingar reached out and grabbed him by the crook of his elbow. "Brother, no," he shook his head, but Osgar's decision was already made. He tore his arm away from his brother's grasp, glaring at him with widened eyes. "It's no use anymore, brother. I-I'm sorry, but I won't go back to living like *that*," he gave a brief gesture toward his brother's attire.

Fine, have it your way, then, Wingar thought as his brow furrowed.

The mage raised an eyebrow beneath his mask in curiosity as he stared at the last of the trio, whose fist began to clench. "What about you, then? Will you join me, or risk your chances outside?" he asked, regarding Wingar intently. "I for one will not sell my soul; what little there is *left*," he replied sternly as tears began to well in his eyes, blurring his vision. "I will not!" he shouted as spit flew from his lips.

"You are free to go, but this chance will never present itself to you again," the mage said, gesturing for him to leave. The threat was clear as the sun is at its highest point. "I pray to the gods both light and dark that we never meet again," Wingar spat before turning around and proceeding out of the palace, never looking back.

His choice, his end. Does that idiot honestly believe the mage will keep him around after this assault? What an insane idea, Wingar thought angrily as he crossed the threshold of the shattered door.

The Masked One looked down upon his two new followers. "You two were smart to join me," he said, glaring at them imperiously as they knelt before him. His eyes glowed violet once more, as tendrils of mana wrapped themselves around the two men, solidifying into a thick, dark violet armor that increased their height and general build. The eye sockets of their horned helmets began to glow as they each flexed their hands and rotated their shoulders to gauge how it felt.

"This armor shall give you the strength of ten men, so long as you remain in my service," he said as the final tendrils were absorbed into their armor. "You are no longer Alf and Osgar, but *Dakzul* and *Kimzul* instead. From now on, this will be how you introduce yourselves to anyone you come into contact with. Do you understand?" he asked, glancing between the two. "We do, lord," they said in unison, bowing their heads.

Masked One raised his right arm. "Rise, my servants," he commanded, forcing them to obey and stand before him. They had gained a meter in height each and could feel the armor's power surrounding them.

The Masked One could feel their awe through the armor and grinned beneath his mask. "This book you've brought me has a value no man can place on it. Consider this armor as a token of my gratitude," he began, but was interrupted by a dark, featherless figure that flew through the shattered windows above them, landing only a few meters away.

"Master, a force of Synners from the north is making their way here," the creature panted in a raspy, unnatural voice. The Masked One's eyes flared a little. "*Synners*, you say? Now that *is* interesting. I will send the signal for the creatures to prepare for battle," he said with a dismissive wave. "As you wish, master," the creature replied, flapping its leathery wings and flying out the window from which it initially arrived.

Dakzul and Kimzul glanced at each other. Neither of them really knew how to fight, and with a small army of professional monster slayers on the way, it was surely a cause for concern.

Wait, we weren't prepared to fight in a battle. When did this come into play? Kimzul shuddered a little.

He felt the same way as Wingar had just a few hours earlier and immediately understood his brother's concern. The Masked One, reading his thoughts, didn't react, since he knew they weren't ready. Unfortunately for the two newcomers, he showed no signs of caring in the slightest, making them exchange yet another glance.

The mage opened the book again, reading it more carefully, though still with immense speed. He went over to press the small stone that would open the passage behind the throne, but instead of pushing it once, he did it *three times* and slid it forward. Dakzul and Kimzul watched as the stones they had just stood on moved apart.

"Gentlemen, we have our mission to complete first, and we must do so before they arrive," he said. "What exactly are we looking for, great one?" Dakzul said, noticing his voice was now distorted. "One of the greatest gifts given to us by the gods over a thousand years ago: the Gwynnleaf," the Masked One replied over his shoulder.

The great stones continued their rumble, moving away from each other and revealing the stairway beneath them. He began to read the book once more while he led the other two down the steps and into the darkened library. His two servants were in awe at the vastness of it all and had difficulty understanding the information their eyes received.

The Masked One turned countless pages, nearly completing the book before descending the first flight of stairs. He noticed there were only gargoyles and tall shelves of books around him. "Gentlemen, welcome to the Library of Coltend," he said, a tone of grandeur ruling his voice.

Wingar was right; it was *a library, but this looks different from any library I've seen,* Kimzul thought.

"According to this book, the Gwynnleaf *is* located within this library, though it required me to insert a different pattern of presses into the stone to reveal the passages leading to it. We must find it before the Synners arrive, so split up and report back to me when you do," he commanded. "Yes, lord," they replied in unison, quickly

The three were off, down the vast halls leading to different library sections. "It's going to be like finding a needle in a haystack," Kimzul said with a distorted voice that echoed throughout the halls. "Only this needle is extremely powerful, important, and probably worth infinitely more than our lives," Dakzul replied. "Don't worry. We will find it, even if you two cannot keep your mouths shut," the Masked One snapped, his voice echoing throughout the chamber.

They went on silently, as the Masked One searched for even the slightest hint of mana, finding nothing. They turned down several different halls when Kimzul noticed a strange vase. "Lord, I think I found something," he began. The Masked One appeared before him in a flash of movement, nearly causing Kimzul to stumble with the amount of mana exuded.

He should have been a few halls over. How the hell did he do that so quickly? Kimzul flinched.

"What is it?" the Masked One asked impatiently.. "I've sensed a small draft of cooler air coming from this direction. There's also an empty vase here," he said, gesturing to the object in the dark. The mage regarded it curiously, bending over to inspect it more closely as he did so. "You might be on to something, after all," he grunted, leading the way down the nearest hallway.

The hallway led them into a confusing labyrinth of more shelves and countless books that gathered dust from ages past. At the end of the maze stood a large, iron door in their path.

This has to be it, the Masked One thought.

He drew immense quantities of mana from the Underworld and placed his palm on the door. He pulled his left hand back and cast an *Exar* spell, bending the door inwards and folding it in two. A rush of cold air filled the hallway, and the large room revealed before them was deathly silent. The Masked One frowned as he stepped through, feeling not even the slightest *tinge* of mana. He looked around and saw a field of what appeared to be dead, leafy structures, each in its own pot.

It can't be that the ignorant bastards allowed these Gwynnleaves to die, he thought with a disappointed sigh as he reached for the book again, desperately searching for any information regarding their appearance.

The structure of these plants matches the diagrams depicted in the book, but it also says that it's supposed to be glowing and resonating mana. Even so, there's no way it could have died; it was a gift from the gods themselves, he thought.

He walked over to the plant nearest to him, examining it closely as he plucked one of the leaves and instantly felt a slight tinge of mana. "There you are," he grinned wickedly, looking at the small stub the plucked leaf had left in its stem.

His two servants looked at each other, as neither could feel nor see what their master had seen. "What is it, lord?" Dakzul asked.

"We've done it," he said in a dark tone as he turned to face them. "I must contact the Undergod and tell him of our findings. He will know what to do next," he continued, examining the plucked leaf, causing the others to shiver at the name. He stuck the leaf into the pouch inside his cloak and walked past them. "Come, for you shall meet my master," he said, gesturing for them to follow.

They did as ordered, though the wordless glance shared between them openly displayed their anxiety about the whole situation. Within the hour, they were back in the vast throne room that felt void of life. A featherless creature flew in from the front door and perched itself on the Masked One's arm, where he used dark tendrils of mana to read its thoughts.

They're moving much more quickly than I thought. No matter, the horde outside will suffice to prevent their entry, he thought.

"You have done well, but continue to monitor *his* position," he spoke softly to the creature. The pair of servants didn't fully catch what he said, and shrugged at each other. The Masked One turned to them, gazing into their helmets. "Stand back, and do not speak unless spoken to," he said gravely. "Yes, lord," his servants replied.

He walked to the center of the great hall and *drew mana from the Underworld*. He collapsed a pair of violet spheres in his hands and slammed his palm on the ground, forming a massive summoning circle which he continued to pour mana into as its glow intensified.

Within moments, a prominent, horned, skinless figure rose from the blast and growled in annoyance. The smell of sulfur and rotting flesh quickly filled the air around them, as the pair of servants flinched away from the blast, even though it did them no harm.

Gods above and below, that is a foul stench, Dakzul thought.

"Why do you disturb me once more, *worm*?" Volzuk's voice trembled the hall around him as the Masked One bowed. The two behind him quickly followed suit, but it was more out of *fear* than reverence. "My lord, I have sought this audience with you for I bring news," the Masked One said humbly. "Have you finally completed the task I've given you, mage?" the Undergod asked, glaring at him from beneath a furrowed, fleshy brow.

"Indeed, I have, my lord. However, there is one small issue I will have to handle here before I can give you what you asked for," the Masked one explained, presenting the torn leaf. Volzuk reeled slightly at the sight, making the Masked One observe his countenance more closely. "What issue?" Volzuk asked impatiently.

"I have just received news that a group of Synners from the north is on the way here as we speak. Their numbers are not great, by any means, but it *is* a thorn in the side of our plans," he stated dismissively. The Undergod stroked the stringy flesh around his mouth and chin. "You once told me you eliminated the Synners in the north. Are you now telling me that the ones from Codrean are posing trouble?" the large figure asked.

The Masked One drew in a deep breath, knowing what sort of retaliation he might face, and exhaled heavily. "My lord, I *did* eliminate them; all of them. I made sure not to leave a single one of them alive. The Synners from Codrean, even never having posed much of a threat to us until now, have somehow found allies in the north. I am still unsure who these allies are, but according to my informants, five hundred are on the way here now. Again, it is not a vast number, but each one is likely well trained, my lord," he explained. "We will be ready for them," the Masked One said with a bow.

"I hope you are, mage. I sense much will come to pass that might *hinder* your judgment. End this quickly, and bring me what I require. I do not need to tell you what will happen should you fail," the skinless figure said menacingly. "I understand, my lord," the Masked One replied before Volzuk sank back into the ground, bringing the dark cloud of mana with him.

"Holy shit," Kimzul said quietly after watching the Undergod disappear. "You did well to keep that to yourself until he left. Otherwise, he might have killed you where you stood," the Masked One said. "So he's real, utterly terrifying to look upon, and smells like a thousand rotting corpses. Wonderful," Dakzul muttered to Kimzul, who merely shook his head.

"I would advise against mocking him. He is more powerful than any other on this continent, let alone the *realm*," the Masked One began, suddenly remembering the Undergod's recoil upon seeing the leaf itself.

Was that a flinch of his in surprise or disgust? It's too hard to tell right now, but I'll have my answer soon enough, he thought back.

He quickly snapped out of his thoughts, realizing he hadn't finished warning the other two. "Should you meet him again, know that he hears and *knows* all that happens in this realm. Speaking of happenings in this realm, we must prepare for battle. If I'm right, they'll attack at *dawn*," he said, gazing out of the shattered window to gauge the sun's position.

The pair glanced at each other with worried looks. "O-Of course, lord, but we were *not* trained for battle," Kimzul said with a nod of agreement from Dakzul. "Are you doubting the power I've just given you?" the mage snarled, causing them to flinch momentarily. "N-No, lord, it's just that we do not know how to fight," Dakzul added.

"I already *know* that. The armor should protect against most of their attacks *and* give you the strength to take down a few. When in doubt, use your fists. That said, I *highly* recommend you *not* underestimate them. Is that understood?" the Masked One asked, getting their nods in response. "Good, then you'll do just fine at dawn," he said, turning away from them. "How do you know they'll attack at dawn?" Kimzul asked.

"Most battles are won in the twilight hours of *dawn* and *dusk*, as it's when one's guard is most frequently lowered," he explained briefly with a shrug. "But enough of that. We have other matters to attend to, which *will* require careful planning. Synners are the ultimate swordsmen and strategists, so we must ensure that nothing escapes us while we plan our defense," he continued.

"Yes, great one," the two replied in unison.

CHAPTER 21
THE PORTAL STONE

Bernar idly toyed with the pendant around his neck as he rode beside me. It was clear that he was deep in thought, but exactly what was going through his mind was something I could neither read nor assume he would even tell me.

Every once in a while, he'd look at me with a slightly worried expression on his face. To be fair, it wasn't really like him to be worried about much of anything. This whole situation, however, was clearly different, as now we both had people close to us to worry about on top of everything else.

I wonder if anything else has got him so deep in thought. Did the Master tell him something that he wasn't ready for? I wondered since I couldn't remember the last time I'd seen him like that.

The forest around us grew thinner, and the wildlife that resided within the forest became increasingly sparse, almost as if they sensed what was coming. I heard a twig snap and glanced around nervously, almost waiting for something to jump out and attack us. When I found the creature to blame for it, I breathed a heavy sigh of relief to know that it was only a small rabbit.

"What's on your mind?" Bernar asked, having pushed aside whatever thoughts he was dwelling on. "*Oh*, it's nothing really. I'm just a bit *nervous*, I guess," I lied with a shrug.

I was actually thinking about how I might actually end up fucking dying during the fight that was coming, but I didn't want Meliss to hear me voice those thoughts after having promised her I wouldn't die.

Bernar glanced at me, weighing his words as if he were reading my mind. "Remember what I told you the first day we entered Coltend? *Don't think too much about it.* It's the mental equivalent of kicking yourself in the balls, and overthinking stuff like that will do you no good at the end of the day," he said, but I felt my mouth grimace in response to his words. "Well, I know that, brother. It's just... I can't help it. I've never been in such a decisive battle before," I said with a heavy sigh.

Meliss had lifted her head off my back to better hear our conversation, but nestled her forehead into the middle of my shoulder blades.

"All battles are decisive, *shit bird*. They can be fought with weapons, emotions, or even against your own mind," Bernar began. "Even though it may not look like it, the outcome of even the smallest fight can change the course of Fate itself. I don't know if you know this, yet, but everyone is constantly fighting battles we know nothing of," he said, glancing at Meliss briefly.

"However, it's never a good thing to simply bottle them up. It's good to have people you can *trust* around you, and even better, let those who care about you know that you're struggling with something. You might receive help from the most *unexpected* of places," he said, glancing over at Leona, who gave him a kind smile.

I hadn't expected such a mature view to come out of my brother's mouth, but I knew, deep down, that he was *right*.

I took comfort in that thought and could feel Meliss' arms tighten a little around my waist. "You'll be alright," she said in a low, sweet voice. "I hope you're right," I replied, rubbing her hand that was across my lap. "Leona knows her way about the castle. She'll know what to do and where to go. Trust her like she trusts you and your brother," she said comfortingly. "I'll trust her. I promise," I said, rubbing her hand with my own as I thought about what she said briefly.

I gazed off into the distant horizon, where just behind one of the hills, I could see the Palace's peak begin to grow. The early afternoon sun gleamed off the top, reminding me of the lighthouse analogy. I chuckled at the thought of it, as thinking back to a time when things were much simpler and easier brought me at least a little comfort. Deep down, however, I knew that it might be the last time I would get to see such a magnificent sight if things went wrong.

I didn't bother voicing my thoughts and continued riding with the others in silence. However, I noticed Bernar watched as Leona rode by the Master's side, holding a conversation just out of the larger group's earshot. "He must have found it by now," I overheard him say gravely. "If he *has*, we'll have to move quickly to make sure he doesn't get away with it," Leona began in a hushed voice. "He is more powerful than you think. He is ruthless, cunning, wiser, and possibly more powerful than I could ever have hoped to be," he continued as Leona gave him a strange, confused look.

"From the little I've learned about you, it's unlike you to use such a defeatist tone. I might not know much of *anything* regarding how to do battle, or strategize for a small army, but I *do know* that if you go into this fight without the will to win it, then you *will* fail," Leona chided him, reminding me of the Master whenever he was trying to teach us a lesson.

He held a chagrined smile for a brief moment, almost as if she had just reminded him of one of those lessons. "Thank you, Leona. Your wisdom is always welcome, and I apologize for not being quite myself at the moment," he gave her a shallow nod.

"You have nothing to apologize for. I'm sure that even though you've been through hundreds of battles, you are *still human*, one who worries for the men and women under your command. It's only natural that you would have doubts before such a decisive moment," she smiled warmly, catching him by surprise at her level of understanding.

"You're absolutely right. We have to focus on what's ahead of us, and do our best to get the outcome we're looking for," he nodded, then returned the warm smile. "However, I wish I shared in your optimism, as achieving that outcome will be no simple task," he said, furrowing his brow a little, causing her to reach out and touch his shoulder lightly. "Trusting in the abilities of those under you; *that's* how we're going to win," she smiled again.

I never would have guessed she'd *be the one to calm him down*, I thought, watching as the Master nodded with another grin, and I could tell Bernar was more than proud of her.

We were nearing the great stone walls of the castle when Leona nodded her head to the Master, who signaled us to turn off the path and head deep into the woods.

This must be the way to the passage under the city, I thought.

As we followed behind the Master, we did not say a word to each other. We all knew just how bad it would be if we were discovered sooner than we had hoped, but as the trees seemed to cower away from the malignant presence within the castle walls, I felt a sinking feeling in my gut that I couldn't ignore entirely. It was as though the wild *knew* our purpose, making our unbeaten path smoother and pulling its roots away from the edges. When we reached a small, disheveled shack a few kilometers away from the walls, the Master signaled a halt.

He dismounted with Leona and Thorsen at his side, following her towards the small, unassuming wooden door that could've been broken with a strong gust of wind. "This is the entrance," I heard her say as they approached the weather-beaten shack. The thatching on the roof was rotten, and the beams that supported the small, wooden house seemed to creak as they neared it.

"Wait here," the Master said, holding up a hand and signaling for my brother and I to come closer. We dismounted quickly and were soon at his side, along with Thorsen, Pyle, and Anwill. "Bernar, get the door," the Master ordered quietly. Bernar nodded his reply and proceeded to the left side of it, drawing the seax from his hip as quietly as he could and holding it at waist height, prepared to stab anything behind the door.

As the door squeaked open, I held my breath as Bernar took the first few steps into the shack. A few moments of utter silence, and a voice came from within. "It's clear," his voice hissed from inside. The Master and Leona were the first inside, followed by Anwill, Thorsen, Pyle, and me closely behind.

"Over there," Leona said, pointing to a small rug covered in years of mold and moss. Bernar quickly tore it from its resting place to find a hidden, wooden door that appeared to lead to an underground passage. He grabbed the iron ring attached to it and pulled the trap door open. I could hear air rush into the exposed hole, though it quickly expelled a foul stench, causing the others and I to immediately scrunch our faces.

Bernar flared his nostrils and spat, shaking his head as he tried to get rid of the smell. "I think we've found it," he wheezed, rubbing his nostrils with his forearm as Anwill approached and gazed downward into the hole. "This must be it. There are markings on the walls inside of elven make," he said, gesturing toward one of the only visible walls in the dark, to which the Master nodded his understanding. On the other hand, Pyle and I went outside and signaled for the others to dismount, tying their horses to the nearest tree.

I helped Meliss hop off first before leading Celer to the closest tree I could find, tying a quick half-hitch around its trunk. Edryd did the same and walked over to join us. "Guess this is it," he said, patting me on the shoulder. "Watch your ass down there. I don't want to be forced to use my *Whip of Doom* anywhere near you again," I said more lightly than the situation deemed appropriate. "You say that like I haven't learned my lesson," Edryd replied, punching me in the shoulder.

Irun and Batch came up to us after having secured their horses. "I say we hold a competition of who slays the most," Batch said with a slight air of arrogance. "I agree. After all, we still don't fully know who's the better sword-caster of us four," Irun said with a wry grin, but I could only shrug.

I knew he was a good sword-caster, but my arrogance immediately assumed either Batch or I could beat him; maybe even Edryd, if he actually gave enough of a shit to *try* hard enough. "I think it's the *difficulty* of the kill, not the *quantity* that matters," I chuckled as I checked Meliss' gear to make sure nothing had come loose. "*Sure it is,*" Irun scoffed, knowing all too well that I'd already killed *three* ochelons.

"*Oh,* quit being such a wet hose," Batch threw his arm around Irun. "If Thoma's going to be stuck at the Master's side, then you and *I* can have that match together. What do you say?" he asked, putting his face right beside Irun's. "We could do that. I swear I'll win, though," Irun grinned as he tore away from Batch's arm.

"Remember what I told you about staying near to Leona and the other masters," I whispered as we made our way to the shack. "I remember," Meliss replied with a firm nod. It comforted me to know that while she was good at following directions, she also placed great trust in all of us to keep her and Leona safe.

Garett and Roburn joined us without a word as we entered the desolate shack. Aside from a few cobwebs on every corner of the walls, no furniture or sign of previous owners could be found within. The Master looked at the six of us as we entered the shack and gave us nods of acknowledgement.

"Alright, here is how this will work. Thorsen, Thoma, Bernar, Pyle, and I will enter first, while Meliss and Leona stay close behind us. Garett will lead the archers in a superficial attack to draw the Masked One's attention away from the Palace. We'll follow this passage while Roburn and Anwill remain closely behind us to open the Portal Stone once we reach it," the Master said.

"I'm no more than *bait*, Master? Wonderful," Garett said with a sigh. "Just stay out of their range as much as you can, and pick them off as they come," the Master replied. "Will do, Master," Garett nodded and proceeded outside to summon the bow-casters. Thorsen was the first one down the small ladder attached to the open hatch. There was no light inside the tunnel when he reached the bottom, and he could barely see even an arm's length in front of him.

"We need torches," he called out to the others as loudly as he dared. "Here," the Master said, tossing a strange-looking half-faced mask down to him. "What am I supposed to do with this?" Thorsen asked. "Just put it on already," Bernar said playfully. Thorsen shrugged and did as he was told. "I couldn't see shit before, and now I can't see a fucking thing," he said to Bernar.

I knew the feeling all too well and grinned at my brother.

"Just a moment," the Master said as his irises glowed more intensely. *His mana surged* as he waved his hand downward, infusing the wooden mask. I could almost *hear* Thorsen's blinking as the mana began to flow into the mask. "I-I can see everything!" he exclaimed. He let out a small chuckle. "Wish we had these while I was still a Synner," he muttered as the Master ordered the others to do the same.

Neither he, Bernar, nor Pyle needed them, but they helped the others put them on and infused them with mana, getting reactions from my friends similar to Thorsen's. "Hold still," I said, holding Meliss in place as I used the same spell my brother had shown me the night I went to fight the ochelon in the cave.

I *drew just enough mana from the Ethereal* and passed my hands over her mask, getting a sharp gasp of surprise as the mana infused the mask and revealed her surroundings. "Holy shit," she said, cursing for the first time since I'd met her with a disbelieving giggle. "It's great, isn't it?" I asked with a bright smile, to which she nodded rapidly a few times.

"Let's go. We're going to be late, and we don't know what we'll meet down here," Bernar told us. We followed his order and quickly descended into the tunnel, while the others followed in behind us. Thorsen led the way, as he was the largest and most frightening to look upon should any creature get in their way.

Meanwhile, I observed the walls and the fine markings engraved in the stone walls as though time had not noticed them, feeling the mossy floor damp and soft beneath my feet from the humidity.

It feels like I've just walked into the past, I thought idly, running a finger along one of the markings.

The masks provided more than ample sight in the tunnel's darkness, and like the others, Meliss was in awe. "I've never seen anything like it," she said quietly. "This tunnel was one of the sewers of the Arwydus, the ones who resided in these lands many years before the castle was built," Anwill explained in a hushed voice. "Quiet, now. We don't know what lies ahead," the Master whispered, immediately making us *all* take the warning seriously.

Formidable creatures adored being out of reach from the sun's intense rays, and their senses had adapted over the ages accordingly. We went on in utter silence, and the only sounds we heard were those of Meliss and Leona's footfall on the soft, mossy ground.

We went through various passageways for what seemed like forever and an age to reach our destination. Although, in reality, it didn't even take two hours of walking. Suddenly, Thorsen reached a large area ridden with moss hanging from the walls, and a small pool of water in its center. The area was as still as a graveyard, and could have easily been confused for one.

"Anwill, is that what I think it is?" he whispered to Anwill, who stepped forward to investigate. In front of the pair was a large, circular stone with runes engraved in it, and writing only he could understand around its circumference.

He smiled.

"It is, indeed, my enormous friend," he said, lightly patting Thorsen on his shoulder. We soon followed behind them and entered the large area, seeing the stone which had nearly put Anwill in a trance. "Here lies one of the greatest mysteries of old. Folk in my homeland often spoke of such things, though even I am too young to remember them," he continued.

Thorsen looked at him curiously. "How old are you again?" he asked. "Eight hundred and eighty," Anwill replied calmly, making Thorsen visibly shocked to hear as his eyebrows lifted far above his already widened eyes. "I-I must be a *child* in your eyes," he said jokingly. "But you are; an *oversized* child, perhaps, but a child, nonetheless," Anwill replied with a grin.

I wonder what he thinks of Bernar, I thought jokingly.

"Time we got to work, Roburn," Anwill said, gesturing towards his partner. "And you're sure this will work?" he asked skittishly. "I am not certain of anything aside from death," Anwill replied briefly. "Well, that's comforting. Alright, let's get this over with. Just like we practiced," Roburn muttered with a nod as he moved to the elf's side and grabbed his hand.

I closed my eyes and tried to sense the mana they were drawing, and within the heartbeat that followed, I could only *feel* its presence.

"Do you want to see what they're doing?" Bernar asked quietly. I was stunned at his question, to say the least. There was so much more to the realm of mana manipulation that I simply didn't understand, but after having experienced and gained access to the second stage, I wanted more. I *needed* to know more.

"I didn't even know that was *possible*," I said plaintively, trying to hide my evident excitement. "Get into your second stage, and I'll help filter the mana for your augmented vision. If done correctly, you should be able to vaguely see what they're doing in the Ethereal overlapped here in the Real," he said quietly.

I nodded my head and closed my eyes, *drawing my own mana from the Ethereal realm*, before letting him know I was ready. He saw the mana leakage from my eyes beneath my mask and smiled. "You little *monster*," he said lightly before putting his hand on my head. I felt *his* mana surge through my eyes and body to an incredible depiction of what was happening.

I could see Anwill drawing a vast amount of mana, returning a part of his consciousness to infuse the hand that clasped Roburn's. Roburn raised his left hand, and the other that held Anwill's in the Real, completing the connection between them.

Roburn began to forcefully pull on the mana from the Real and send it *back into the Ethereal, forming its own, secondary sphere before him*. Anwill's consciousness began to be forcefully pulled through the channel Roburn created, and he spat himself *out in the Ethereal with Roburn*.

"It worked!" Roburn exclaimed. "Yes, it did, but do not lose focus. We need to activate the stone," Anwill said as *the pair stretched out their arms, pulling vast amounts of mana*.

Anwill condensed the mana to his core, holding it there as compactly as possible. The mana became so bright and dense that it created a mirrored version in the Real. Anwill glanced at Roburn, gave him a nod to sever the connection, and aimed the hyper-dense mana at the large stone.

Bernar immediately undid the spell on my eyes, since it was no longer needed, while I could only watch in awe at Anwill's struggle with the quantity of mana he'd just drawn.

How the hell is he even controlling that much? I thought, feeling my heart begin to race.

"Hera fi Arwydus karuwa," he said through gritted teeth, commanding the mana to do his bidding. The command pulsed out from his core, rapidly enveloping the large runestone in a golden coat of raw mana. The rune in the center began to turn slowly, like it were kicking off the rust and grime of bygone ages.

"Hera fi Arwydus karuwa!" Anwill said again, thrusting another burst of mana into the stone as it spun more quickly in response.

"HERA FI ARWYDUS KARUWA!" he shouted, commanding the mana with as much willpower as he could muster. The spinning rune finally gave in to his command and spun at full speed to the point where the symbol of the rune became one, solid figure.

"You have heard me thrice, O mark of bygone ages. Seethe with my will, and heed my command: *Open*," he said, his voice imbued with mana. A bright burst of mana suddenly exploded from the stone, nearly knocking Roburn off his feet.

Thorsen quickly stepped in and caught him before he fell, avoiding contact with any bare skin that was showing. Roburn's eyes were still glowing as they had been over time, and sweat began to drip from his brow.

"Hold on just a little longer," Thorsen whispered. We all stood around them, observing the largest display of mana any of us, not including the Master, had ever seen. The swirling mana around the stone glowed brightly, illuminating the dark area that we were in, nearly voiding the need for the masks. Suddenly, a single figure appeared and passed through the open portal.

"Anwill?" the figure asked, though the others could not see his face while Anwill desperately struggled to keep the portal open. "I've summoned you to help us face those who would try to destroy this world. I deeply apologize for the abruptness, but I cannot hold this much longer," he said.

The figure slightly tilted his head and stretched his hand outward behind him, holding the portal stable with only one hand and minimal effort. "What, and I cannot stress this enough, *the fuck*?" I quietly said to my brother. "Just wait and see, little brother," Bernar replied, watching Anwill nearly collapse to the floor with exhaustion.

Roburn, on the other hand, remained unconscious in Thorsen's arms. "Make sure he wakes up and gets some food in him. He's going to need it," Anwill said through clenched teeth.

The strange figure's silhouette briefly glanced around the surrounding area, then turned back to face Anwill. "It's been a long time since *anyone* has used this stone. What are you facing, and how many are there?" the figure asked bluntly. "We've surmised there are about ten thousand of all manner of creatures, though our numbers might be off," the Master said.

"If what you say is true, then this situation is not favorable for the ones you have here," the figure said after pausing to consider something no one knew. "It's worse; we believe they're going after the Gwynnleaf," Anwill grunted.

The figure nodded and cast a spell to hold the portal open in his place as he walked back through it. Not a single soul present could even *imagine* how powerful this person was, let alone what other forms of mana manipulation he might know.

The figure reappeared with a small army that filled the space behind him. He closed his hand as the portal shut down behind him. Roburn's eyes finally returned to normal, and he panted heavily in Thorsen's arms. "We've done it," Thorsen said comfortingly. "Thank *fuck*," Roburn coughed.

The area grew dark once more as the figure approached Anwill. His features could be seen through the masks' enhancements, which were similar to Anwill's. His ears held the same, ringed earrings, and his large, green eyes glowed in the dark. His armor was thick, and intricate engravings were set in an unknown metal, as was the gently curved sword at his side.

The figure's cloak nearly reached his ankles, secured by two brooches holding viper-like eyes engraved in amethyst and wrapped in pure silver. "Do not fret, *children of men*, for we mean you no harm," the figure said calmly. The few hundred elves behind him were all clad in the same armor, save for the cape.

Male and female elves composed the army, although due to their fine features, it was difficult to tell which was which. Even their eyes glowed the same yellow as their leader's, though the two by his side stood out, with one having gray eyes and the other a pair of deep scarlet.

"What is your name?" Roburn asked weakly, noticing no one else dared to speak in that moment. "I am called Nenvalur Aralamin of the Arwydus, and I bring with me the aid you and Anwill have sought," the elf replied, gesturing to the ones behind him. "I am at your service," Nenvalur bowed as Thorsen shook his head, trying to wake himself from what he thought to be a dream.

Does he know who Anwill is? That must mean he also *knows who the Master is, but why hasn't he said anything?* I wondered, noticing the one with scarlet eyes stared at me intensely.

I couldn't figure out why he was staring at me, though my only guess was that I looked like someone he either knew or recognized.

Nenvalur nearly stood at Thorsen's height and looked him over. "My, you're a large one, aren't you?" he said, dropping his formal tone a little. No one, not even Anwill, had suspected such a comment from the elf. "I am as my Hjalfarian Blodt has made me," Thorsen said with pride, while Nenvalur grinned. "And such a heritage it is. Honestly, if the ones behind you had your height and strength, there would be no need to summon us," he said playfully.

We all immediately felt more comfortable with him and his presence. Granted, we hadn't spoken to the others he'd brought with him yet, but the friendly display Nenvalur gave us certainly helped quell any nervousness.

"Tell me, how can we help? From what I gather, you said there's a horde, and the Gwynnleaf is at risk?" Nenvalur asked, while Anwill nodded in agreement. "It might very well be, unfortunately," he began. "Leona, the former queen of the land you are in, and the *Master* of Codrean, here, may be more able to give you the details you will need," he continued, struggling to repeat the word *Master* like he had when I first met him, to which Nenvalur seemingly understood his meaning.

He knows. He definitely *knows the Master's real name,* I thought, but as soon as I did so, Nenvalur's eyes snapped to me and he chuckled lightly.

Leona and the Master stepped forward, greeting the elf with a customary bow. "There is no need for that, Your Majesty. I am a simple warrior, not some *king* that requires such formalities to boost his ego," Nenvalur said with a warm smile. He looked around him and only then noticed that nearly everyone wore strange masks. "*Master,* I hope you realize that *this* will not do," he said, shaking his head with a light chuckle.

He motioned to the ones behind him, and a few drew torches, igniting them with mana-flame. The large area soon became bright enough that there was no need for the masks any longer.

"So, what is required of my warriors and me? Support? Security? *Slaughter?*" Nenvalur asked, cutting straight to the point. "All of the above, I suppose," the Master began. "Above us lies a great force of creatures that have invaded the castle. Taking control of it and possibly slaying all who live within it are our top priorities," the Master replied, gesturing upward.

Nenvalur rubbed his clean-shaven chin. "To top it all off, they're probably going after the Gwynnleaf. *Ah,* this is a terrible situation all-round, isn't it?" he asked, sucking wind through his teeth. "Very well, then. Tell me where we must strike, and it will be done," he said with a shrug, indicating that mere monsters were of little nuance to him and his men.

"There is another thing that I believe to be of the utmost importance," Leona began while Nenvalur shifted his gaze to her. "And what might that be, Your Majesty?" he asked. "Unfortunately, the likelihood of there being any survivors, at this point, is *minimal*. However, this castle is home to the source of the Synners' prowess with mana manipulation," Leona said, causing him to raise an eyebrow. "You meant to say *one of the sources,* I presume?" he asked nonchalantly, catching Leona off guard, as was the Master. "I'm sorry?" she blinked as she asked, hoping to confirm what her ears had just heard.

"It is true that a source of great power lies within Coltend, which many of us here were already aware of. Gwynnleaf is the source for *most* Synners on this side of the Continent. However, there are other sources we elves have closely guarded in secret over the ages in which mana has existed," Nenvalur explained as though he were talking to a child.

Thorsen nodded as though it confirmed an old theory of his. "So there *are* other sources. I had always suspected as much, but this news is..." he trailed off. "That is correct, Large One," Nenvalur nodded, noticing the confused look on his face. "Naturally, I cannot tell you much more about them. Simply know that they exist, and that we must preserve the one hidden here," he said nonchalantly.

"Of course, to do so will mean that my men and I require a layout of the castle itself, for as I have said before, it has been a *long time* since *any* of the Arwydus have been here. Well, perhaps not *that* long," Nenvalur said with a wry grin, getting a confused look from everyone who hadn't come with him. "Although things *have changed* quite a lot in the past two millennia," he continued in a rather grim tone.

What the...? I trailed off mentally, trying to process everything he'd just said.

Not a single answer came to mind.

"Here, I hope this will help to refresh your memory," Thorsen approached him and handed him the map he had been entrusted with. "*Ah*, thank you, Large One," Nenvalur said with a smile, which Thorsen awkwardly returned. "It's Thorsen," he said, outstretched his hand while still holding the smile. "Rightly so. A fitting name if I've ever heard one," he stared at the hand awkwardly, but after a nod of confirmation from someone I didn't catch, he shook the hand firmly.

It was probably Anwill, but I can't be sure since I know he hates physical contact, I mentally chuckled as Bernar stifled a laugh.

Nenvalur carefully observed the map, holding every minute detail in his infallible memory. "We need you to attack..." Leona trailed off as he held up a hand. "The ones nearest to the Palace itself, and work our way outwards, giving you a safety bubble around your real target. I understand," Nenvalur finished her sentence with a bright smile.

"R-Rightly so," she stammered with a conceding nod. "Very well, then, but we must move immediately to make it by dawn. Nightfall comes, and even worse things than a simple attack tend to happen in the dark hours of the night," Nenvalur said.

I wonder what he means by that, I thought momentarily.

"The spawning of crying, eating, shitting, *fuck-trophies*, obviously," Nenvalur chirped, making me blink once or twice in surprise.

Did he just read my thoughts? Also, what the fuck? I thought with an internal laugh, standing silently and wondering whether my suspicions were correct.

"I did, young one. I meant what I said in jest, of course, as there are much fouler things than children, though they are rather high on my list, but come; we must move quickly," he said in a much lighter tone than I expected.

Nenvalur's elves, who held the torches, merged with our group, heading through the tunnels for a few kilometers, until we began to feel the rumbling of the hoard above us. I noted that their muffled bellowing could still faintly be heard, even as deep below the castle as we were..

"That sound. It must mean we're inside the castle walls by now," Leona said, hearing the rumbling from above. Thin wisps of dust fell from the ceiling of the tunnel. Nenvalur and Thorsen led the way, while Meliss held my arm tightly. I noticed she had a worried expression, so I silently prodded her to look at me. "What's the matter?" I asked, thinking it was just the sound from above, but her eyes told me a different story almost immediately. "I think we're one man short," she whispered, immediately sending a shiver down my spine.

"What? Who?" I asked quietly. "I can't say for certain, but I've just had a weird feeling since the portal opened," she replied. I didn't dare turn around in case anyone overheard her words, but the thought started to gnaw at my attention span. We went deeper and deeper into the tunnels, making various turns along the way, when we reached a fork in the passageways.

"I believe this is where we split up," the Master held up a hand for us to halt. "Master, need I remind you that dividing an *already divided* force is dangerous in war?" Pyle warned. "Dangerous but *necessary*. We knew it would come to this, and now it has," the Master replied simplistically. Pyle sighed lightly, but nodded his agreement in the torchlight.

"Leona and Meliss, you will accompany Pyle, Bernar, Thoma, Edryd, Batch, and me down the northern passage, while the others will accompany Nenvalur, Thorsen, and the elves to the southern entrance," the Master said.

"It will be an honor to see you fight, Thorsen," I heard Nenvalur say quietly. "Likewise," he replied. "When the battle is over, and should we all survive it, we'll reconvene at the palace, understood?" the Master asked, getting a unified clanging of hands slapping the scabbards of their swords.

"This is it, right? We're doing this?" Meliss asked shakily. My thoughts halted momentarily as I tried to find the right words to say. To be honest, I didn't know *what* to say, other than what I had been trained to do for most of my life.

"Breathe deeply, and draw your blade once we're topside. Stick close to me and the others, and no harm will come to you, got it?" I asked calmly as I could, though I was also beginning to break into a nervous sweat. Meliss nodded and focused on her breathing.

"Time we showed these bastards what we're made of," Batch said to Edryd. "I just hope you know what that is, because it better not be a steaming *pile of shit*," Edryd replied with a grin, which was returned in kind before they continued a quiet, idle conversation that I didn't bother turning around for.

Something's off, I thought, remembering what Meliss had told me.

Bernar walked over to me and put a hand on my shoulder. "I hope you've learned a thing or two, *little shit,*" he said. "So do I, you perennial dingleberry," I retorted, getting a quiet chuckle from Bernar. "That's the best one I've *ever* heard you use as a comeback," he said. "I've been saving it for a special occasion like this," I winked.

"Must you always use derogatory terms between the two of you?" Leona asked, but Bernar merely shrugged his initial response. "He's my little brother and has to be reminded of that fact continuously. *Such is the way of being the older brother,*" he replied as if quoting something from a tome to sound smart.

"Cheeky little..." she trailed off under her breath with a tongue click as she shook her head, but grinned when she turned away from us. Bernar and I winked at each other and looked forward, instantly comforted by her understanding.

"Let's move," the Master called out as loudly as he dared, and no sooner were we off, each to their destinations, and some to their fates.

CHAPTER 22
TRAITOR

The Masked One and his two new servants had prepared as best they could as the sun began to set. "Dakzul," he began, while reviewing a map of Coltend made from violet swirls of mana levitating just above the stone floor.

"You will take the western-facing side of the palace, while Kimzul will watch the northern. I suspect they will attempt a diversion of some sort, so be on your guard for anything that may seem suspicious," he said, pointing to specific areas on the map with a tendril of mana. "I will command creatures to aid you, while I prepare to transport the plants back to Valdis. Any questions?" he asked.

Dakzul shook his head, but Kimzul gazed at the map. He was no strategist and felt something was missing, but said nothing. "Kimzul," the Masked One said, breaking his line of thought. "None, great one," Kimzul quickly answered. "Then go now to your stations and await further instructions," the Masked One said.

He waved his hand, and the two bowed before him and headed to their destinations. The Masked One disintegrated the map he had made and proceeded up the nearby stairs that led to the royal bedroom.

He saw the hand Leona had crushed in her flight still wedged between the door and the frame. It was covered in small, white maggots that bore deeply into the dead flesh.

That must have been interesting to watch. Greedy bastards, he thought.

His eyes glowed intensely, and a blast of violet mana came from his fingertips, splintering the door and twisting the metal hinges. He stepped through the now-empty frame into the room. The large bed was just as Leona had left it on that fateful day; the sheets and red covers were in a wrinkled mound near the center of the bed. The easel in the corner of the bedroom stood as a silent guardian.

If it had eyes, it would have been terrified to see the significant, cloaked figure in the room gazing at it with genuine interest.

The painting on the easel depicted a dense forest with a flowing river running down the center. A fawn drinking from the river gleamed in the small rays of sunlight that seeped through the canopy. He stepped away from the easel and looked out the large windows.

He moved the curtains aside, and before him was a vast field of houses and shacks, with the wall that protected the city itself beyond them. He looked out beyond the wall and toward his dark hall pensively.

"Lord," Kimzul interrupted from the doorway, making him sigh. "What is it?" he asked bluntly. "I know it's not my place to ask, but is something wrong? I don't think this room was one of the locations you mentioned I had to guard," he said shyly. "You're right, it isn't. I just wanted to try to get a better understanding of where her mind is, and what *she* might have told those Synners about this place," the Masked One began bluntly.

"I've spent *centuries* alone, performing a task I was given by some-one *far more powerful* than I, and yet here I stand at the edge of it all, moments before this final leap in progress could, potentially, be stripped away," he continued, stepping away from the window to look at his servant.

"Even though that concept may seem benign to you, or even far out of your realm of understanding, for that matter, it isn't to me. The knowledge I've sought after all these years is right within my grasp, yet these *fools* think they can simply come and take it from me," he said, frustratedly, making Kimzul flinch.

"But lord, a horde is outside to meet them like water on rock. Do you not have faith in them?" Kimzul asked, spreading his arms a little. "I do, but you must remember that those coming here to try to stop us have been training their entire lives for a moment like this. I can't afford to take any chances here, not when I'm so close to achieving my goals, and those of the one who gave me the command to be here," he sighed, glancing out the window again.

"I see, lord," Kimzul nodded. "I'm not sure you do, but I wouldn't expect that from someone of the Church," the mage replied curtly. "I just need to buy enough time to get as much of the Gwynnleaf out of here as possible, and bring it back to Valdis where it will be *safe* from undeserving and unremembered hands," he clenched his fist tightly. "Whose, lord?" Kimzul asked with visible confusion.

"That's for me to know and you to, hopefully, never have to find out. Fate is a fickle, worthless *old hag* who's always challenging those who have sought power with their own hands. Sometimes, however, those challenges of hers require a *challenger*, and in this case, *I am*

that challenger," he said cryptically, leaving Kimzul even more confused than before.

"I'm not sure I follow, lord," he admitted with a shrug. "It's probably for the best, then. Just know that there are powers at work which
drive me to do what I need to do, regardless of how horrible or harsh
it may seem from an outsider's perspective," the Masked One replied.
"Very well, lord. I will trust your judgement," Kimzul bowed.

Just as I want to trust my own. One day, perhaps I just might, the
mage thought, giving his servant a dismissive wave.

He spent the better part of an hour in the royal chamber, noting
the books and tomes kept there. Some were old and covered in dust,
while others appeared to be frequently used. After reading through
a handful of them, he left the royal room and went outside the palace
to find Kimzul, who stood atop the stone wall that guarded the city.

He levitated to his servant's side, the afternoon sun beaming warm
rays onto his mask. "Status," he demanded. "Everything is calm, and
there have been no signs of their approach, lord," Kimzul replied,
gazing off into the distance with the aid of his helmet.

The Masked One looked out in the same direction. "Something
isn't right," he said quietly after a moment's pause, immediately
sending a chill down Kimzul's spine. Off in the distance, a rider
appeared out of the dense forest, coming along the path to the
Northern Gate. The horse's hooves could be heard from a distance
in the silence atop the great wall.

"Lord," Kimzul said urgently, pointing in the rider's direction. "I
see it," the Masked One said before Kimzul could explain what he
saw. The horse snorted heavily under the stress of galloping at such a

high velocity. The cloaked rider pushed the horse as hard as he could, as though he were fleeing from something.

"It's almost as if this was the only one of them who dared to come and fight you, lord," Kimzul scoffed. "Not quite, but let's give this rider a warm welcome, shall we?" the Masked One asked with a tinge of malice. The glow in his eyes intensified as he cast his hands backwards, releasing tendrils of mana down to the great gears that turned to open the massive gates.

The gates opened, and out of it sprinted an ochelon on its fours. It rapidly picked up speed, digging its claws into the dirt beneath it to gain more traction. The rider pressed on, pushing the horse as fast as its legs would carry it. The ochelon saw its prey, and its blackened eyes focused directly on its target, gaining even more speed. Suddenly, the rider lifted the hood of its cloak, and the Masked One looked upon the rider's face.

He made it! I didn't think he would have the audacity to do it after all, he thought.

He raised his hand, and the ochelon abruptly stopped, skidding along the dirt for quite some distance. The rider rode past it, and it followed him back to the gate. Once inside, the rider dismounted his tired horse and led it to a nearby water trough. The Masked One floated down from the walls to greet the newcomer, opening his arms in a welcoming gesture as his cloak fluttered in the wind. "Welcome to the once *impenetrable* Coltend Castle," he said.

"It's an honor to meet you in person, master. I've been waiting for this day for a long time," Irun bowed humbly. "As have I. Your services in Codrean were instrumental in my success here so far, though I will need to know of their most recent movements, as they should be somewhere nearby," the Masked One glanced toward the treeline.

"They have gathered reinforcements from a hidden Synner school in the North, as I'm sure you're already aware. However, instead of taking a conventional approach, they've decided to split into two groups, one below ground and one above," Irun replied, causing his new master to tilt his head in minor confusion. "Strange. They would have sent out ri-..." the Masked One cut himself off as he heard Kimzul call out to him. "They're coming, lord!" he shouted from atop the wall.

There they are, the mage smiled wickedly.

The Masked One levitated himself and Irun to the top of the wall to observe the attackers' approach. They saw a group of horsemen descending the same path Irun had taken a few short minutes before. He cast more violet tendrils to open the gates again, raising his hand to summon glicks and ochelons to fight the riders. The horde left the gates screeching and bellowing as they always did whenever they moved in for a kill, and they watched the riders off in the distance get into their formation.

"They are no match for such a horde, great one," Kimzul said. Irun looked at the tall, armored person towering over him. "Forgive me, master, but who or what the fuck is this *thing*?" he asked, but the Masked One didn't turn to face him; instead, he gazed at the charging creatures. "He is my new servant. Once a member of the Church, he has seen the error of his ways and pledged his service to me, just as you have done from the Synners," he replied.

So, a choir boy gets a fancy suit of armor? That's fair, Irun mentally scoffed in confusion.

The Masked One turned to face him so quickly that it startled Irun. "I hope you know I can hear your thoughts, Irun," he snarled. "I-I apologize, master. I meant no disrespect," Irun stuttered, frozen in place. "I could have decided to let that ochelon kill you, even after all your service to me. You want armor of your own? Here, take it, you little ingrate," the Masked one said.

Irun knew he was angry, but began to feel the cloud of mana enveloping him. The violet mana solidified into the same type of armor as Kimzul's, but it was far less intricate and glorious, leaving more than a few spaces open for a possible attack.

"You already know how to fight, so I don't have to give you as much protection. You ought to thank me for not transmuting you into some sort of *giant prick with legs* and an anus for a mouth," the Masked One growled, causing Irun to swallow dryly. "Thank you, master," he said humbly as the Masked One turned to watch the battle that began to rage in the distance.

Arrows flew through the air at Garret's command and struck their targets with superb accuracy and precision. Irun, too, was observing the battle carefully, but his master seemed oddly satisfied with the result so far. "You said there was a second force coming from below?" he asked.

"Y-Yes, master. There's a passage that begins from far outside the castle and leads directly beneath the city itself. Something of old elvish make, but I didn't stick around long enough to know where it would eventually lead. I needed to get away while I still had the chance to, after all," he said shakily, getting a grunt of understanding from the mage.

"It's a shame I'm only hearing of this right now, Irun Mothac. It seems you may have committed a potentially fatal mistake to our plans," the Masked One sighed. "I-I didn't know until we arrived there, master. If I had, I would have warned you, but by the time I realized what was happening, I knew that was when I had to escape," Irun stammered.

"This is not good news, indeed. There must be countless entrances and exits to this underground passage strewn about the city," the Masked One said grimly, briefly glazing over the city's rooftops. "We must be on our guard for any sign of movement that isn't one of the creatures below. It doesn't seem like they will follow their usual convention of attacking at dawn, so be prepared for a night raid," he continued.

"What do you want me to do when they arrive, master?" he asked after a short pause, watching the battle in the distance, which was coming to an end. "I will send a small portion of the horde to support you when the time comes to fight against your old comrades. Are you prepared to do what's necessary, Irun?" the Masked One asked coldly, but Irun struggled to understand the *true depth* of his master's question.

I've always known that one day it might come to this, he thought.

"I don't have much of a choice, master. I've never really fit in with any of them, or, at least, I don't *think* I ever did. I've always felt more estranged around them than anything else, master," Irun replied, noticing that saying it aloud gave him a small portion of relief.

"That's... not at all what I asked. Does that mean you're willing to fight them? It's a simple *yes* or *no* question," The Masked One said, dumbfounded by the answer. "I-I think I'll be alright, master,"

Irun replied after a few moments of consideration. "I pray you do not hesitate like that when you meet them in battle," the mage said, observing his demeanor and scoffing behind his mask, barely audible to Irun's ears.

"Very well, then. You will be the vanguard of the force that I will send to draw them out of their newfound hiding holes," he said. Irun nodded, then realized it was stupid to do so, since his master wasn't even looking at him.

"Where should I start, master?" he asked. "If what you say about the underground passage is true, and their secondary force is coming from the north, I'd tell you to begin somewhere on the northern side of the palace itself. If you have a better idea of where they might come from, I advise you to take this with you," the Masked One said, pulling a crystal from one of the pouches in his cloak and throwing it over his shoulder for Irun to catch.

He nearly let it drop as it fell from the air, but managed to recover it without any visible damage. "You must go; now," the mage ordered, prompting Irun to leave without another word. He eyeballed the crystal for a moment, realizing he knew nothing about how it should be used. The Masked One also realized it and cast a spell of violet mana into it.

Irun was taken aback by the sudden glow of the crystal and felt the ground beneath his feet begin to rumble. "Do not allow anything to destroy it," the Masked One said cautiously. "If any harm should come to it, the monsters around you may very well turn on you or each other, as is their natural way of doing things," he continued, getting another nod from Irun Irun, still feeling the ground beneath his feet tremble.

The screeching, cackling monsters came en masse towards him. He drew his sword, more out of habit than anything else, at the sight of them. They stopped a few meters away from him, as though awaiting orders. He observed them closely. He had never seen these creatures at such a close range, other than when they attempted to disembowel him.

"Damn glicks," he said quietly, as their jagged teeth and scales flared at the sight of him. He turned his back on them, making his way towards the northern end of the palace with the small horde following closely behind him. The sun was setting on the distant horizon, and they were all now in the shadow of the great wall that had failed to keep the creatures at bay. The houses shook as they passed each one, the smell of the rotting flesh of the people who had lived in them filling the air quickly.

Did I really make the right choice here? I mean, my mother died as a synner, and a damned good one at that. I don't think I've lived up to her reputation, but I'm fucking trying my best, he thought as they went past the derelict houses.

Not much of a choice left but to follow through, I suppose. Gods fucking damn it all, I don't want to die, but I have to go through with this. Mother, have mercy on me when I see you again, he thought, kicking himself for his choice.

He led his small band of grotesque creatures to the general area of the northern gate and waited for those moving between the trees to begin their assault.

And so it begins, he thought.

CHAPTER 23
UNEXPECTED COMPANY

My heartbeat was almost heard throughout the tunnels beneath Coltend as I broke into a nervous sweat.

We knew we had to be close to the exits that the tunnels would eventually lead to. The adrenaline coursing through my veins before the battle began made my hands shake a little, and even though with Meliss at my side, and Bernar just ahead of me, I could sense that I wasn't the only one getting nervous.

I've got to get my shit together. Being a liability now is not something I can afford; neither for me nor Meliss, either, I thought, giving her a reassuring smile as I could manage.

She, too, was a nervous wreck and whispered countless prayers to the gods that the need to fight for her life would not come, but I knew she was nearly in tears.

I put my hand on her shoulder, and she looked at me with no small amount of fear in her eyes. "You alright?" I asked, already knowing the answer. She paused for a moment, then nodded her response. "Other than shaking like I've got an internal earthquake underway, I'm fine," she said quietly in the dimly lit tunnels.

By fine she means fucked up, insecure, needy, and emotional, right? I've been shaking so badly, I hardly noticed her shaking this much, I thought, trying my best to keep my *own* fears under control.

"We're going to be alright," I said as comfortingly as possible, only getting a quick nod before she squeezed her arms around me more tightly. Thorsen was still at the helm of our group, wandering in near darkness, when Nenvalur heard a sound that neither he nor Anwill recognized. "Think we've been noticed?" he asked quietly.

"Nothing's been down here for centuries, it seems. The odds of someone or something wandering down here of their own accord are astronomical," he shook his head, feeling Meliss shudder as soon as he finished. "We should hurry if we wish to maintain the element of surprise," he told Thorsen, who nodded and picked up the pace.

We went on for a few minutes without interruption, except for a few rumblings above us, when Leona pointed at a sign on the wall. "Here, take a look at this. I can't read it, but I recognize it. I believe we are heading in the right direction," she said. Anwill went over to her side and read the barely visible inscription. "Quite an eye you've got there, my lady," he grinned, gesturing for Nenvalur to approach.

"I have been searching for it ever since we entered. When I was younger, I used to sneak into the library to take a gander at the books unsuitable for a queen," she said, returning the grin, causing Anwill to purse his lips while widening his eyes. "Well, I'm glad you did. Nenvalur, I believe she's right," he gestured to the inscription, forcing Nenvalur to lean in and examine it more closely.

"Well, there's something you don't see every day. I'm glad you found it, because now that we're on the right path, we can hurry and reach the battle. My sword is thirsty, and I would be remiss to leave it parched for much longer," Nenvalur chuckled, causing me to raise an eyebrow.

So, you're a nutcase afterall, I thought wryly, knowing he could hear it.

He didn't acknowledge it with anything more than a slight scoff through his nostrils before returning to lead the way with Thorsen and Anwill, but that was enough for me. A few minutes and a few signs later, we came to an open area like the one that held the portal stone, where, near the back, stood a large wooden structure supporting the inner walls.

On the far side of the room was a metallic door with leaf-like designs reaching from the base to the top. However, both Anwill and Nenvalur held up their fists simultaneously, prompting the rest of us to halt.

"This must be the entrance," Anwill said, but Nenvalur observed the detailed workings on the door, using a bit of mana to light up the carvings. It was a beautiful display that shone a dim light in the darkness. "Unless Coltend has such smiths that could craft something like the smiths of my homeland, this has to be it," he said, just as a crumbling sound came from our right.

Nenvalur and the others turned as quickly as a hummingbird and saw the walls begin to move, as large stones and dust kicked up and filled the air. "Sentries!" he called out, drawing his sword immediately. I heard the call and quickly brushed Meliss aside, where Leona took her and maintained a safe distance.

Three gigantic stone figures emerged from their resting places in the walls, crumbling the stones around them. There had been no sign that they were there to begin with, but it was evident that *something* activated them. The Master cast a ball of light high into the air to illuminate our surroundings and reveal the golems for the rest of us.

"*Ah*, I've met these before," Thorsen began, causing me to look at him curiously. "What? When?" I asked, gripping the hilt of my blade tightly, staring straight into the golem's mouth. "I met one along the Rhydian Pass by chance and barely escaped with my life. Three of them will be *nasty* business," he growled, readying his large sword.

"How do you beat them?" I asked quietly. "They can regenerate quickly since they're primarily made of mana, but I'm sure we'll figure something out," he smiled down at me. "Keep the others back to avoid any unnecessary losses," the Master directed, spreading a single arm out as he shouted over his shoulder.

Bernar spread his arms to help the ones behind him remain safe in the tunnel. I could see the sentries still recovering from ages of sleep, one of them even shaking their head to wake themselves from slumber.

While they had no ears, their massive black eyes allowed them to see much more than a normal human could. "They must have woken up because of the mana I used. Inconvenient, but not impossible to overcome. To battle!" the mad elf shouted, charging in directly toward the trio.

The one immediately to his left swung a massive arm covered in moss and other plants that grew within the cave's depths. It struck the ground where he had just stood, blasting rocks and dust into the air. I could have sworn I heard him laughing as he dodged another blow coming from just behind him. "We can't let him do this alone. Even for someone like him, this will not be easy," the Master told Bernar, Thorsen, and Anwill, who immediately followed him into battle.

Thorsen did his best to slash at the nook behind one of their knees to no effect and grunted in frustration. "*Oh*, it's no use slashing at them, Thorsen. We have to find their cores, quickly!" Nenvalur chuckled, dodging yet another blow and infusing his blade with *Recia*. "How the *fuck* do we do that?" Thorsen asked, dashing out of the way of a two-handed slam.

"By attacking them, or pushing them off the side of a cliff, which we don't have," Nenvalur chuckled as he jumped high enough to reach chest height and stabbed his blade into its shoulder. "Damn it," he grunted, pushing off it to get away of another attack that was aimed at where he was going to land.

He must have had multiple encounters with these creatures if he knows so much about them, I thought, watching the Master and Bernar try a similar technique.

The first sentry moved in for a crushing blow aimed at Anwill, who expertly dove out of the way. The blow cast the thin layer of mud where he had once stood into the air, and the ground shook. "Get underneath them, if you can! They don't bend well, so if you just dodge their feet, you might have a better chance at surviving," Nenvalur said after recovering from the first blow from the sentry nearest to him.

Another blow aimed for the Master and Thorsen came in at a sweep, forcing them to jump over the large fist that came for them. "Good thing they're somewhat slow," Thorsen said lightly. "Slow, but still deadly if you don't focus," the Master snapped back.

Anwill circled the sentry nearest to him while watching the others in the area. Another pounding blow shook the ground and made some of the stones from the roof fall to the ground about them, adding a new enemy to the arena. They dodged the falling rocks as best they could, though one hit Anwill in the shoulder, nearly crushing the bone beneath his armor.

"We've got to hurry, or else this entire network will come down on our heads," he shouted as he clutched his shoulder. "I have an idea," the Master said. He moved closer to one of the sentries, grabbing a stone along the way. He threw it at its head, and it instantly swung at him. "Move," he shouted while he and Thorsen dodged the incoming blow, which struck the wall at its side, causing more rubble to fall from the ceiling.

"On me," he said to the others, who came to him, dodging other blows along the way. The sentry nearest to the Master tried to crush them with his enormous, stone foot, and he stepped out of the way. "Cast *Exar* at their heads, make them come this way," he said, already preparing a spell. "Are you insane?" Anwill asked worriedly. "Perhaps, but if we can turn their blows against one another, we might just win this. Let them do the work for us," the Master dodged another stomp.

"That should do it," Nenvalur said, approaching the Master and Thorsen. Anwill came soon after, and the four bunched together. The others and I looked on anxiously and heard some quietly praying for a positive outcome.

Even from where I stood, I could feel the immense amount of mana they drew in preparation for their trickery. "Now!" the Master shouted, and they cast their spells to get the attention of the ones who threatened them. Large bursts of blue mana were emitted from the small group, reaching their targets. However, the sentries replied with their *own* attacks, clasping their hands together and smacking them down towards the ground.

The four of them rolled out of the way of the unified blows, covering themselves in mud. The Master saw his plan had failed miserably, and he sighed when the sentries began to turn on them, more aggravated than before. They struck wildly at the ground beneath them, kicking up a cloud of dust that became difficult to see.

I could tell the four of them weren't having an easy time. Even in the fifth stage, a sentry golem was still quite a challenge to them, since they couldn't simply manipulate the elements the creatures were made of.

Wait a minute. Does it respond to Exar *blasts? I've got an idea,* I thought, rushing out from the entrance to the large room and into the open area before me.

"Thoma, no!" Bernar shouted, trying to grab me by the collar, but I didn't even bother to look back at him. I knew, then and there, that we didn't have time to waste if we wanted to make it to the surface by dawn. "I'll be fine, just keep the others safe!" I shouted over the rumbling to my right, catching the Master's eye.

"Thoma, what are you doing?" he asked after dodging another blow. "I've got an idea, but I'm going to need all of your help for it," I replied, entering my second stage to ensure that whatever I did would work as intended. "Come here, you overgrown *pebble*!" I shouted with my mana-infused voice.

"He knows they don't have ears, right?" Nenvalur muttered, but Anwill could only shrug. My target turned on me with extremely violent intent, forcing me to barely manage to escape the sweeping blow that came much more quickly than anticipated.

"It *turned* to him?" Nenvalur asked, surprised at the response I got from the creature. "It probably has to do with the fact that the second stage of mana manipulation still leaks enough mana to be heard in one's voice. Maybe that's what did it," the Master suggested. "That doesn't explain *shit*! I've never seen a golem move like that before, especially not to someone's voice; mana-infused or not," Nenvalur snarled as he dodged another blow.

Meanwhile, I quickly went beneath the one who attacked me and slid between its legs, casting another *Exar* at the back of its knees to force it to kneel. The Master was visibly shocked by the outrageous idea, but when he saw me climb up the back of it to ride it like a mount, I think he realized what I was doing.

I gripped the stones at the base of its nape, holding on as tightly as possible while its massive arms tried to reach me. "Now you want to ride the damn thing as if it were a giant horse? Fuck me," Anwill shook his head. "I have a plan! Just trust me!" I shouted. Thankfully, the Master had caught onto my plan and was already behind the one nearest to him.

"Nenvalur, take the third and cast an *Exar* behind its knees," the Master shouted. "Understood," the elf replied, not entirely sure what was happening but deciding to trust him anyway. Their golems knelt without much effort, as their control over mana was *much greater* than mine. Still, seeing how quickly they coordinated an absurd attack like this was impressive.

"Now what?" Nenvalur shouted at me as he dodged a swipe of his golem's large fist. "Draw their attention to each other using the same spells as before. They always swing with their right arms first, so we'll have them aim their attacks at the source of the mana, which will be just behind their heads," I returned with a wry grin.

"Forcing *them to* knock each other's heads off. You know you're a few marbles short of a full bag, right?" he laughed. "Well, I trust him, so get ready. Anwill and Thorsen, you're the bait. Draw them to each other!" the Master shouted before giving me a nod of understanding. "I hate being bait," Anwill shook his head, just before he and Thorsen did as requested.

They sent blasts of mana towards the creatures' chests, prompting them to turn and face them as one.

Good, I'm glad that worked. All we have to do is time this correctly, I thought as I felt my golem turn in their direction and begin to move forward.

"Wait for it," I said, watching as the three giant creatures drew nearer. "Thoma!" Thorsen shouted, noticing two were already preparing to crush him with balled fists. "Now!" I shouted, casting an *Exar* blast at the one immediately to my right, while Nenvalur and the Master did the same, as each golem reeled from the blasts momentarily, acquiring new targets in the process.

Each one swung with their right fists exactly as I predicted they would, and targeted the sources of the mana, which, unfortunately, was *us.* The massive fists slammed into the golem's faces as one, crushing the stone into a fine powder as I jumped off my golem's back to avoid getting hit.

Did that work? I know mine's probably dead, but how about the others? I wondered, trying to see the result of the attack through the dust cloud above me.

The sentry I was on began to fall like a large tree towards Anwill and Thorsen, who were observing the coordinated attacks. "Look out!" Anwill shouted, knocking Thorsen out of the way of the falling monsters. The ground trembled and shook violently from the col-lapsing bodies, nearly making me lose my footing.

I noticed the Master and Nenvalur's golems had also fallen, as they walked out from behind the stone corpses. Meanwhile, Anwill and Thorsen recovered quickly and were back on their feet at a moment's notice. "That was too close for comfort. Thank you," Thorsen said, giving the elf a quick pat on the shoulder. The five of us began to laugh heartily at our accomplishments, but it was a short-lived victory.

More stones began to fall due to the rumbling from the golems' attacks, and I noticed a massive chunk coming right for me. I dodged out of the way and shielded my face from the dirt and mud it kicked up, but the open area seemed otherwise structurally sound.

"Well, that was fun! A bit *risky*, but fun nevertheless!" Nenvalur exclaimed with a hearty laugh, while the Master and the others were also visibly pleased that my plan had worked. "I-I just did what I thought would work. After my fight with that pair of ochelons back home, I realized that massive creatures don't see well from behind, *even if* they are sensitive to mana; an observation I wanted to capital-ize on," I replied shyly.

"*Pair* of ochelons? I'm surprised you could even take *one* on for someone your size. What is your name, young one?" he asked with a raised eyebrow. "Thoma Fayren, sir," I replied with a quick bow. However, the look he gave me when I rose was one of unbridled curiosity.

He stared at me blankly for a moment, then looked to the Master and Anwill, exchanging something unspoken. "*Fayren*, right? It's a good name for a Synner of your caliber, and an honor to meet you.

That was an amazing plan, one I'll surely pass on. After that little demonstration, I'm sure you'd fit right in where I live. We could use more Synners like you," Nenvalur gave me a light bow as he grinned.

D-Did that just happen? Wait, where is he even from? I wondered, knowing this elf was *far* stronger than I was.

I did the only logical thing I could think of, and put my hand across my chest and bowed deeply. "Thank you for the compliment, sir," I said. "So *formal*," he spat, then chuckled lightly as he turned to speak with the others.

"You're one ballsy, little shit-head, you know that? You almost up and fucking died on me... *us!*" Bernar said, gesturing to Meliss. "I agree, you almost gave me a heart attack," she said, clutching her chest. "Well, I'm sorry I scared you, but I didn't die. Those sentries took my place," I chuckled, raising my hands placatingly.

Just as I said that, the ground began to shake and the ceiling began to crumble, knocking large chunks of earth loose. "We need to get out of here! Everyone, follow us!" Anwill shouted as the Master tore the large door from the archway they had seen earlier with mana and cast it against the wall. "Move!" he shouted. Everyone rushed into the doorway as the stones fell from above, crushing a handful before even *I* made it out.

Leona, who was just ahead of me, was nearly crushed flat by a large boulder, but Bernar managed to pull her out of the way just in time as Meliss and I dodged a few of our own on our way to the door. The beams that supported the walls caved in behind us, cutting us off from the other passages they had come from.

"Is everyone alright?" the Master asked, shielding his face from the cloud of dust the cave-in caused. A few limbs could be seen crushed beneath the rubble, but we all knew there was nothing to be done, forcing us to realize just how nearly we'd escaped death quickly.

"This is all your fault! Don't you know to stay in your fucking lane?" one of the Synners said, approaching me. I glanced over at the one who had said it, while Roburn stepped between us and put his hand on a woman's shoulders, stopping her in her tracks as he shook his head. "Not worth it, Rosie. There's no way he could have predicted that would happen. If it weren't for him, we still might have gotten crushed by the boulders had that fight dragged on any longer," he said calmly.

Rosie? She's the embodiment of irony with a name like that, I thought as I noticed her glaring at me.

"Even so, does that mean we can all just run off and do whatever we want? What the fuck happened to the chain of command, *huh*? His little stunt put us *all* at risk, regardless of whether it was successful," she spat toward me while Roburn could only shake his head. "She's got a point, you know," he sighed.

"I know she does, but nothing they were doing seemed to be working, and to be entirely honest, I don't think killing the sentries had anything to do with the cave-in. Their bodies were embedded into the walls long before we even arrived, so it's much more likely that our *presence* here in general is what caused it; not just the fight," I explained, but deep down I still couldn't help but feel a sense of guilt for those buried beneath the boulders as I turned away.

"*Tsk.* What the fuck would *you* know?" she muttered with pure rage laced in her tone. Just as she did, a large boulder crumbled from the ceiling and dropped toward her. As soon as I noticed it, I instinctively entered my second stage and cast my *Whip of Doom* to shatter the falling stone, causing bits of gravel and a cloud of dust to rain down on the two in front of me.

"Holy shit. Thanks, Thoma," he said through a light cough as he waved his hand in front of his face, but Rosie stood there silently with a frustrated look. "You don't have to thank me. If I could have done that to all the other boulders that crushed our friends, I would have," I replied, carefully watching Rosie's expression shift from frustration to sadness.

"There wasn't much *any of us* could do except hope to make it out alive," he acknowledged, though I could tell he was wondering why the Master or even Nenvalur hadn't been able to do anything about it with the strange look he had in his eyes.

Wait, why didn't they do anything about it? I wondered, realizing the same thing Roburn had.

Anwill, Nenvalur, the Master, and my brother were all extremely powerful, and yet not even they tried to do anything about it. I surmised that it was a similar case with the golems, since none of them simply used their mana to break them apart.

"You're right. Maybe that cave-in was *meant* to happen, regardless of whether the golems were defeated. I'm sorry I couldn't do more," I said quietly in realization, as Rosie turned her face away from me. "It's alright, Thoma. You still helped them defeat the golems, after all, and I apologize for what she said," he said with a nod. "It's fine, but she might want to learn to live up to her name the next time someone saves her life," I returned the nod, making her wince.

That might have been a bit harsh, I mentally kicked myself before turning to look around and see who was left.

I could see more than a few motionless limbs sticking out from the spaces between the fallen boulders, as blood filled the cracks between them. I gritted my teeth in frustration, knowing there really *wasn't* anything left to do except hope I would see them again in the afterlife. I turned to do a quick headcount and clenched my fist tightly when I realized over a fifth of us were gone.

"Damn it," I hissed as Meliss put a hand on my shoulder. "It could've been worse. If we'd stayed there any longer, we might have *all* been crushed," Bernar muttered as if he knew what I was thinking. It did little to stop my heart from sinking to a depth I didn't know I had in me, and for a few moments, I allowed it to do just that.

We *all* did.

Nenvalur, only having lost one of his own, sent a silent prayer to the gods to guide them safely into the afterlife. The Master surely felt remorse for the ones he had lost, but he knew, just as well as the rest of us, the cost of our sacrifices and how their losses would not be in vain.

"Only one way out now, and I'm sure the ones above us will soon notice the gaping hole in the city, if they haven't already. Let's go," the Master said after allowing us a few moments of silence for the fallen we were forced to leave behind. He cast a new ball of light that led us down the wide passage that would eventually bring us to the castle. Even as we walked, I could hear others sobbing from those who had lost their friends in their flight to escape the rubble, but there was no time to mourn the dead.

We're already on borrowed time as it is, I thought, holding Meliss a little more tightly.

A few minutes passed before we reached the final doorway that would open to the surface. We paused for a moment to ensure everyone had made it. Meliss looked at the others, and the feeling that something was wrong grew as she tugged on my jerkin twice.

"Where's Irun?" she asked quietly, prompting Batch and Ed to glance around briefly. "He was with us when we entered the passage, but he wasn't saying anything. I was too scared to even think about talking to anyone, lest I awake some sort of ancient daemon in here," Edryd replied. "Did he get crushed by the rubble?" I asked. "Can't say for sure. I didn't speak to anyone either, but if he's not with us, chances are he got crushed," Batch replied gloomily.

I never did grow very close to him, but he was still our roommate for more than half our lives. I don't want to believe he's dead, but the alternative isn't much better, either, I thought as my stomach turned.

Meliss must have noticed my expression since she put a hand on my shoulder consolingly. "I'm sorry about your friend," she said, gently rubbing my shoulder, but I could only nod. I had no way of confirming whether he was dead, but that also meant I couldn't confirm he was the traitor, either. Batch's eyes welled with tears as Ed consoled him, but both he and I knew the alternative answer would be much worse than if he'd been killed.

Needless to say, we were both too lost in thought to really feel much else in that moment.

Within the hour, we reached a point where the Master called a halt to lay out the rest of the plan. The door ahead of us reminded me of the one we'd come through to reach this passage after the fight, and I knew that this would be the last few moments of peace before the battle.

"Nenvalur, take your warriors to create distractions and draw the creatures away from the Palace. Kill as many as you can, but don't underestimate these creatures," the Master cautioned as he walked over to the tall elf.

"*Oh*, we'll be alright. Haven't had this good of a fight in what, about *two hundred* years?" he waved his hand dismissively. "I admire your confidence; I just hope it lasts the night," Anwill shook his head, but Nenvalur chuckled and clasped his shoulder firmly. "You're still young and have a lot to learn. We'll be fine," Nenvalur chuckled.

"Anwill's considered *young* to him?" I asked my brother, feeling my jaw drop. "*Ugh*, it's always *something* like that with elves," he shrugged. "I can't imagine what it must be like to be that old," I blinked, realizing there was still so much about the newcomers that I didn't know yet. However, the Master surprised me when I saw a slight grin stretch across his face when he overheard what we said.

"Is everyone ready?" he asked, but no one answered verbally, as we all held the same answer written on our faces. "Let's move," he said to the others, using mana to pull the large metallic door towards us while we drew our swords. I could see Nenvalur's excitement clearly written on his face when he exchanged a glance with Anwill, who scoffed and shook his head at something that wasn't said aloud.

Nenvalur and his group peered out of the small crack the Master had made into the twilight before them. The city was on fire, emitting a bright glow that slowly filled the passage we were in. The smell of smoke began to fill the air, as the sound of the invading creatures reached our ears.

No moon, yet. As unfortunate as it is, at least the fires from within the city will give us just enough light to see, I thought, staring at the orange glow in the sky through the crack.

"Seems to be clear, but we should all have our eyes peeled as best we can in the dark," Nenvalur said cautiously. "Once in position, remember to make a lot of noise to create distractions," the Master said. "Don't worry. We've got that covered," he said with a wink, beginning to pull the door open on his own.

They flowed out of the doorway, and I could hear my heart beating louder than my steps. My palms began sweating, and my breathing grew heavy as the anxiety kicked in. The smell of smoke was thick in the air, and I knew that this battle must have taken more lives than we initially imagined.

Shit, was anyone able to make it out? I wondered, looking out over the flaming city, then shifting my gaze to Leona's tear-filled eyes.

"Go right," Thorsen whispered once we were all out in the open, separating into groups of twenty, with each group finding cover behind the nearest building. The Master, followed by Bernar, Thorsen, Leona, Meliss, and I, alongside a few others from Nenvalur's group, allowed only one of his glowing eyes to show from around the corner of the house we hid behind.

"When I give the signal to Nenvalur, we're going straight to the palace. Thorsen, you know this city like the back of your hand, so I'll leave it to you to lead us there as quickly as possible. Leona, Meliss: you two stick close to me, understood?" he asked hushedly, getting nods of understanding from the rest of us in the dull glow of the burning city.

The Master raised his hand and swung it downward like a black-smith's hammer onto hot steel. Nenvalur and the groups that followed him moved quickly in the darkness to their positions just to the right of us. Thorsen led the way and moved as quietly as his armor would allow, while we trailed closely behind, moving down the alleyways and streets that would lead us through the most direct path to the palace.

We went from cover to cover, house to house, avoiding being seen and ruining our element of surprise. Garett's distraction had clearly worked its magic, since many of the foul creatures seemed to be gathering near the Palace gate in preparation for his eventual arrival. However, the smell of burning buildings, flesh, and death present throughout the city was still more than palpable to all of us.

Suddenly, an uproar came from our left, and we all turned to see what it was. "Horses," the Master whispered, his eyes glowing slightly more than usual. "That must be Garett initiating phase two. We've got to hurry," Thorsen concluded, prompting us to press on as quickly as stealth would allow. When we arrived at the last available cover between us and the Palace entrance, the Master sent a bright ball of light into the sky away from us, signaling Nenvalur to begin his assault.

The creatures surrounding the entrance stared at it curiously, but were soon overwhelmed by Nenvalur's group, along with Batch and Edryd, who charged them with swords drawn. The creatures took a moment to react as if they were confused by what was happening, but knowing they were never very intelligent gave his group an advantage.

Nenvalur's sword sliced into the scales of the first glick, spraying the green, death-smelling blood into the air. "Mae eich enaid yn fy!" he shouted as his sword went deep into the enemy's body, then a few more as if performing a dance worthy of the god of death itself.

The others shouted their war cries, making as much noise as they could. The Master observed the battle for a few moments, ensuring that the creatures around us heard the commotion, and headed towards it. Nenvalur and his group began to sprint down the streets at high speeds, forcing the glicks to give chase and leave the rest of us alone.

Once the Master was sure their plan had worked, he signaled to the rest of us that it was time to move forward into the next stage of the plan. I held Meliss' hand as we went, her palm was feeling just as sweaty as mine, though her breathing was much louder. "We'll make it," I whispered, but she said nothing, not for lack of trying, but simply because she was out of breath.

We quickly reached the palace entrance, where the Master signaled another halt. "We're close, so listen carefully. Thorsen will guard the entrance, while Bernar, Thoma, Meliss, Leona, and I will enter. Ladies, you *must* stay close to Bernar and Thoma at a safe distance away from me, since I will have to face the Masked One alone," he whispered, catching me by surprise.

"We can help you, Master. You don't have to do it alone," I gestured to my brother, but he gave me a pained smile. "I know you can, but I *have to do* this alone. Please, just keep these two safe. I'll explain everything when this is all over," he said, putting a hand on my shoulder as he nodded toward Leona and Meliss.

I could only nod silently, knowing there was no way for me to change his mind. He stood up and motioned for us to move in behind him into the palace.

Where our fates had been woven into a tapestry that none but the Master fully understood at the time.

CHAPTER 24
THE BATTLE FOR COLTEND

When the sounds of battle outside made their way to the Masked One's ears, he immediately felt his frustration boil to its maximum limit. He crushed one of the gigantic skulls in the Great Hall, reducing it to dust in synchrony with his hand.

They're here. I must summon the others, he thought.

He used one of the crystals he kept on him to transmit his commands to all affected creatures. "Return," he commanded, his voice echoing in their minds. Irun, who encountered Garett and his group just outside the palace walls, heard the command in his head when one of the mounted Synners came for him with sword in hand.

Damn it, I can't even tell who it is. They must be using their hoods to avoid being singled out, he thought as he prepared for the strike.

As they rode by, the rider swung down with a grunt of exertion, aiming the blow at his neck. He redirected the blow away from him and got out of the way of the horse at the same time, forcing him into a roll. He quickly rose to his feet and began sprinting toward the palace, constantly glancing over his shoulder to ensure his attacker had stopped their pursuit.

He looked back at the hooded rider and felt his stomach drop when he realized who it was.

Isla? No. Please, it can't be her, he thought through clenched teeth.

He moved much more quickly since his enhancement from the Masked One, but he had only gone a few meters before he heard the hooves approaching him again. He turned to face her, but it was almost too late to do anything about the sword aimed at his head. He rolled out of the way just in time and was quickly back on his feet.

"Fight me, you coward!" she shouted. "You will die if I do," he countered. "Isn't that a risk *anyone* takes when they pick a fight?" she scoffed at his words as she dismounted. She drew the black-hilted sword at her left side and dashed toward him. Irun swept his sword back, in line with his hind leg, waiting for the right time to counter her first blow.

Please, stop! I don't want to do this, he thought, knowing she wouldn't give him much of a choice.

She charged at him with her sword trailing behind her, turning on the ball of her right foot and leaping into the air, sending her into a spinning motion. Her sword struck down at Irun, who quickly raised his sword to glance it off his blade, but she wasn't one to be caught off guard.

She recovered from the parry and swung her sword at Irun's side. He parried and countered with an overhead blow, prompting her to slide beneath the overhand strike off to her left and strike Irun's helmet with the pommel of her sword, removing it. He staggered backward, putting a hand to his face as he recovered.

"Show your face, or are you too much of a coward to do even that?" she asked through clenched teeth, readying her sword for another strike. "I can't," he shook his head, turning his back to her to grab his helmet. "You *dare* show your back to *me*?" she seethed, rushing in for an attack to knock the helmet out of his hands.

The upward cut landed squarely on the helmet, sending it soaring into the air, revealing the look of surprise written on his face. Her eyes widened, forcing herself to take a few steps back as she tried to understand what she was looking at. "I-Irun? What are you doing here? Why are you helping the enemy?" she stammered as tears began to fill her eyes.

"W-We were never meant to meet like *this*, Isla. I'm only here to do what needs to be done," he sighed, feeling the guilt sink like a stone in his gut. "What the *fuck* is that supposed to mean, Irun?" she blinked a few times, wiping away a stray tear from her grimy cheek.

"I-I can't say everything right now. Just know that I never wanted you to see me like... well, *this*," he gestured with his free hand to his entire body, causing her to shake her head. "Then *why* are you *here*? Please, help me understand. M-Maybe I can help you," she pleaded, taking a half-step forward.

"What the hell am I supposed to say? That the Master has been holding us all back? That he's not sharing the *truth* with the rest of us?" he spread his arms as the stone in his gut sank even deeper than before.

Will she know I lied? Irun thought as he swallowed dryly.

She furrowed her brow, though he couldn't tell if it was out of disappointment or anger that caused it. "You really think he's keeping things from us? Irun, please, you're not even a senior yet. *Of course*, there will be a limit on what he can tell you right now. You don't have to do this. You can still walk away," she shook her head in disbelief.

Please. Please, back away now. Please just walk away so I'm not forced to kill you. Please, he thought, hoping those thoughts would be shown through the look he gave her.

The two stared at each other silently as the battle raged around them. Isla darted her eyes between his as if looking for an answer, but found none. For a heartbeat, she closed her eyes and accepted his silence as his answer.

"You know, I've always cared about you, even if I could never fully admit to it," she said, fighting against the lump in her throat. "Isla," he raised his hand to her, but quickly found she was holding up an open palm to stop him from speaking.

"I've never forgotten the kind words you said after my brother died. You were so loving and tender, and I think that was when I knew you had my heart; I just couldn't bring myself to admit it," she shook her head, disappointed in her own foolishness. "I *loved* you, Irun. Even if I never dared to show it, I always have. But this... *new form* of yours, the fact that *you're* the traitor Edryd told me about, and everything that's happened are things I simply cannot accept," she sighed, feeling the tears beginning to stream down her cheeks.

"H-He told you it was me?" he asked shakily. "He came to me, knowing I was probably the only one who could stop you, but I was too late. I can't turn back time to change what you've done, or what I've failed to do, but I *can* stop you here," she said, gripping her hilt tightly. "Isla, please. I don't want to do this," he finally said aloud. "But you've already made your choice, Irun. You've already accepted the power this *dark mage* has given you; leaving me with no choice," she gritted her teeth before dashing in to attack him.

No, please! Irun thought, instinctively raising his sword to block her attack.

Their blades locked as they stared into each other's eyes. Her tears never stopped flowing, but she furrowed her brow and pushed him away, attacking him repeatedly, forcing him to take a defensive stance.

She's not going to stop until I'm dead, is she? Irun asked himself, noticing her attacks becoming sloppier as her rage swelled within her.

"You... *bastard*! You've betrayed us all!" she said, almost as if she were convincing herself of that fact to do what she needed to do. Irun said nothing, silently hoping she would relent and walk away, but when their blades locked again, he could see that she had been successful in convincing herself to kill him.

Suddenly, her eyes opened widely as a pained grunt and a spurt of blood came from her mouth. She looked at him with pure confusion, then down to her abdomen, where she found a dagger buried in her gut. "I-I'm sorry, Isla. I'm..." he couldn't finish his sentence, as she forced his hand to drive the dagger upward, soaking her jerkin in more blood.

"W-Why?" he asked with widened eyes, caressing her head as he gently lowered her to the ground while she gasped for air. "Because I hope you live forever to remember this moment. Welcome to your own, personal *hell*, my love," she said weakly, as tears and blood began to stream down her face, soaking his forearm.

Irun was too stunned for words, knowing there was nothing he could do to change what had happened as he watched the light from her eyes dim, and heard the final burst of air leave her lungs. He gently lowered her head to the ground as he pulled the dagger out of her. Tears welled in his eyes as he gritted his teeth, letting out a roar that caused more than a few glicks to come his way.

Seeing the lifeless corpse before him, they tried their best to get close to eat it, but he severed the heads of each one that came close, glaring angrily at the others as he withdrew the crystal from a pouch on his waist. "Take another step and you'll die like the others," he snarled, causing them to wither away in fear.

He knelt beside her body and brought his lips to her forehead, pushing a few strands of bloodstained hair away from her face before shutting her eyes. He sheathed his dagger and *drew an intense amount of mana*, casting a Pyrus spell around her to prevent any other creatures from trying to consume her.

As he watched the last of her remains float into the air, he heard a unified roar from the creatures on the far side of the castle, letting him know that their defenses had been breached.

I have to get back to the Palace, he thought, shaking away any potential consequences of his failure.

He saw a small group of people off in the distance, also making their way to the palace. He recognized the giant with them and turned away to go down one of the palace's service entrances.

Irun ran into the main hall, where his master awaited his return. "There you are," the Masked One said. "Forgive me, master. I ran into some trouble along the way," Irun said, breathing heavily as he wiped away some of the blood still on his hands.

I'm sorry, Isla, he thought.

"You're not dead yet, which means we still have work to do. You have failed to find where they would come from the tunnels, and as a result, we might have lost the progress we made," the mage continued. "Five hundred synners are hardly a swarm against *ten thousand*, master," Irun spread his arms widely.

"But one Synner does what ten *normal* soldiers would do in half the time, or have you already brain-dumped the training you've had all your life?" the Masked One asked angrily, causing Irun to lower his head and sigh. "We will still win this, master," he said. "*Oh?* Do tell," the Masked One said, making Irun pause momentarily. "If we can just take the damn things from below and be off with them, then we have already won without shedding any more of our own sweat and blood," he explained. "Yes, and your failure to find where they were coming from has put *all our plans* at risk. You will head down with Dakzul and Kimzul to gather what you can. You can *at least* do that much, correct?" the Masked One snarled as Irun froze in fear under the weight of his flaring mana.

"What are you waiting for? A smack upside the skull? *Move,*" he commanded, prompting Irun to bow quickly and dash down the stone stairs to meet with the others. He ran as quickly as he could to catch up to the two, who were already halfway there. "He's really pissed, isn't he?" Dakzul asked in a hushed tone as Irun moved in beside him.

"Well, he's still alive, so I guess he's not *that* angry," Kimzul shrugged, carrying an armful of vases in the opposite direction. "So long as we follow his orders, we should be fine. Let's just get this over with," he continued, suggestively nudging Irun toward the array of vases.

"Wait, what do you mean *we should be fine*?" Irun asked with visible confusion. "*Ah,* well, since we were once servants of the Church of Mideia, the Masked One has given us power in exchange for knowledge of this place, which we happened to find in Mourtis' room," Kimzul replied. "So you *don't* know how to fight. Got it," Irun nodded after his suspicions were confirmed.

"It's not like we've ever *had to*. We were members of the Church, not warriors. It's why he gave us this armor in the first place, because all *we've* done before coming here was *preach to the infidels and pagans*," Dakzul added sardonically. "You mean you spouted a load of bullshit," Irun scoffed, causing Dakzul to tilt his head. "It's not like you Synners aren't blasphemous in your own ways," Dakzul snarled.

"I'm not a Synner anymore, so don't call me that," Irun shook his head sternly. "*Oh*, I'm sure of that. If you were, you wouldn't be *alive* and on *this* side of the battle, would you?" Kimzul asked rhetorically, making Irun click his tongue. They went down the newly-made tunnel to the Plant's location, where the two armored men grabbed armfuls of vases.

"You can use mana, right?" Kimzul asked, trying to steer the conversation into a more amicable tone. "We're taught how to use it from the very beginning, in tandem with sword skills, although I don't think I know of anything that would help me carry anything my arms can't," Irun sighed. "That's mighty helpful," Kimzul muttered sarcastically.

"Grab as many as you can. We're going to have to make a few trips anyway," he continued, patting Irun's shoulder heavily as he observed the seemingly dead plants for a moment. "Why on the Continent would he want a dead source of power?" he asked, gently touching one of the leaves.

"According to *him*, they're not dead, but only meant to *look* like they are," Kimzul replied, as Irun closed his eyes and shook his head.

"If you say so. Come on, let's get this over with," he sighed, reaching down to grab a set of vases and following the others back upstairs.

After gently setting their biddle on the floor, they quickly returned down the stairs to get more, but the Masked One watched the door carefully and expectantly.

I know you're here, so come out already, he thought as he stared at the shattered door.

Meanwhile, far outside the main hall, Edryd, Batch, and a handful of others slaughtered creature after creature. Their swords sang a beautiful tune of death, as the green and blackened blood glazed the cobblestone beneath them. Ed severed another limb from one of the horrid things that came for him, and the green blood flew into the air as the thing writhed on the ground before him, screeching in agony.

He breathed heavily for a moment, gathering information about his surroundings. Nenvalur, Roburn, and Anwill formed a line just ahead of him, carving a path deeper and deeper into the horde, leaving a trail of foul-smelling corpses in their wake.

I wonder how Thoma and the others are doing, he thought as three more glicks began to chase him down.

Edryd cast a fireball at the one in the center, consequently setting the other two alight. They writhed and screamed as their blood boiled, rupturing their skin and making a popping sound as the internal pressure grew too great for their scaly hides.

"*Heh,*" he allowed himself, before charging in alongside Batch, who was just as covered in blood and gore as he was. "How many so far?" Batch asked, severing another set of clawed limbs, sending them soaring through the air. "I've lost count already," he replied, sticking his blade into another's mouth and slicing horizontally through the other side.

Batch severed the head of the one who faced him, and accidentally got some of its blood in his mouth, forcing him to choke and spit the contents. "It tastes *worse* than it smells," he managed to say, desperately fighting to keep whatever was in his stomach where it belonged. "I'm just surprised you're not dead from it," Edryd chuckled, cutting into yet another glick's gullet, nearly severing its head.

"Not yet, but... *hurrok*... I'm pretty sure I swallowed some," Batch returned. Meanwhile, Nenvalur's sword song transformed him into a whirlwind of wet steel, blood, and shouting. He twisted his sword so eloquently and cut so deeply that it made him look like a single, blood-spilling storm. He shouted his war-cry as he went and carved a deep path on his own.

Anwill cast almost as quickly as Nenvalur's blade could strike, scalding one, then another with orbs of flame and spears of lightning. He moved his hands together, keeping a small space between them while compressing a large amount of mana. The hair on his arm stood up as the air surrounding the mana sphere cracked and rumbled. He released the spell, which turned out to be a continuous Kyr spell, chaining lightning between multiple enemies, and charring those affected without so much as a screech.

"There are too many of them!" he shouted to Nenvalur, who was a small distance away, carving his gory path. "Keep fighting no matter what!" he shouted back. Roburn severed limbs from their owners, giving himself a small amount of breathing room, but he was growing worried about Rosie, who fought beside him.

"How are you holding up?" he asked, cutting down another two or three with a single strike. "I'm fine, but there's no end to these bastards! Where the hell are Batch and Edryd?" she asked, ripping her sword from a daemon's neck. "They should be behind us, but we need to regroup. We'll be sitting ducks if we stay separated for too much longer, so let's clear a path for them," he grunted, getting a nod of agreement from her.

The pair cast *Exar* spells to blast a handful of creatures out of their way, clearing a straight-lined path to his two juniors. The small breath of fresh air created by the blast was like a splash of river water to the face. However, it *also* carried the scent of horses, ones he knew were coming to support them.

Garett and the remaining horsemen had come at last, having fought their battle at the Northern Gate from a distance, minimizing their losses as best as possible. He led his horsemen into the horde with their swords drawn. "Leave none alive!" he shouted, pointing his sword toward Roburn's direction. With that burst of courage, Garett and the riders cast, hacked, and infused their remaining arrows to dispel the ones around the small group.

The space between Roburn, Ed, and the other creatures was enlarged, allowing them a moment to rest, even if only for a few seconds.

Garett approached Nenvalur and Anwill, who regrouped as the horsemen did their work behind him. "Gentlemen, my men and I have discovered something as we made our way here," he grinned wryly, prompting Anwill and Nenvalur to glance at him with genuine interest.

"We have spotted several ochelons guarding some massive crystals. They have some of their own, embedded in their skin, but I believe our enemy is using the bigger ones to control the others through mana, as this is not a natural partnership among monsters," he explained. "Please tell me you know where the rest of them are," Anwill stepped forward.

"My scouts informed me earlier that at least twenty, or more, were stationed at the gate. I suspect they were to act as deterrents to any other army that might try to help. Given the direction from which the glicks are coming, they must be somewhere in what remains of the market. We must head there immediately and destroy them if we are to survive this," Garett replied, gesturing toward the market.

Nenvalur came down from the pile of corpses he was standing on and swung his sword quickly to remove the remaining blood. "Let's get going, then. The longer we stay here, the more time it will give whoever's controlling them to regroup their forces," he suggested.

"I'll need a moment to clear my head. It seems I'm not in as good of shape as I used to be," Anwill sighed, but immediately widened his eyes in surprise when Nenvalur handed him a flask of unidentifiable contents. "Here, drink this. It will help with the mental fogginess," he grinned wryly.

Anwill popped the cork and drank the contents, twitching his head and shuddering as he swallowed. "*Ugh*, it tastes like goat piss," he grunted in disgust as Nenvalur patted him on the shoulder, smiling wryly. "I'm just hoping you don't know what that tastes like from personal experience," he said with a chuckle.

"Master Garett, please take point. We'll follow your lead," he said, turning to face the old Synner. "We don't fully know what to expect when we get there, but we'll do what we can to end this," he continued, signaling the rest of his group to gather around.

Though their exhaustion was evident, Roburn, Rosie, Batch, and Ed quickly joined the others. "We'll ride ahead to get a better lay of the market. We'll meet you there," Garett said, spurring his horse after getting a nod of agreement from Nenvalur. "*Oh,* that's great. We *just* got here, and we already have to move?" Batch sighed tiredly. "You'll be fine. Come on, young ones; you're with *me*," Nenvalur grinned maliciously.

How the fuck are we supposed to keep up with him? Ed wondered, shaking his head and beginning to trot behind the others.

They started out at a good pace, as Edryd, Batch, and the others were close behind them. Their footsteps made no sound, but the sheathes and armor rustled lightly as they descended the gentle slope leading to the market. "Look at that, Garett's made us a gorgeous path to follow," Nenvalur said cheerfully, gesturing to the trail of corpses strewn alongside the road.

"That confirms it, you're insane. I don't know how you can fight that hard and long, and still be so cheerful," Anwill shook his head. "When you spend most of your life fighting battle after battle with the creatures, then suddenly come to a halt for a couple of hundred years and end up missing the battle rage, *then* you can call me insane," Nenvalur replied with a chuckle.

No, you're just as crazy as she *is,* Anwill thought, knowing Nenvalur could hear it.

"I wonder if anyone made it out before the invasion," Edryd said remorsefully, gazing down the lifeless streets. The desolated houses and huts along the way gave no signs of human activity, and were as quiet as can be, as the horde's bedlam echoed down the empty streets from a distance. "There's no way to tell right now, young one," Nenvalur said over his shoulder as they continued down the street.

Edryd chewed on the words as he trotted alongside his friend. "Think Thoma and the others have met the enemy, yet?" he asked Batch, but he could only shake his head in response. "I don't know, but I suspect that by now something is going on up there," he replied, prompting Ed to gaze towards the palace, noticing bright shafts of violet, red, and golden light coming from the shattered windows and into the night sky.

Batch noticed Ed wasn't saying anything, and looked off in the same direction, seeing the flashes from the window, and knew Edryd was worried. "Hey, we've got our own shit to deal with. That *lanky fuck* is fine... I think," he said with little confidence. "I hope you're right," Ed replied, doing his best to return his focus to the task at hand.

Good luck, Thoma, he thought with a silent nod.

The war-party trotted on for the next few minutes until Roburn spotted Garett's horse tied to a post. "He's over there," he said, pointing to where he was on top of a roof. "Looks like he's found a decent vantage point," Nenvalur grinned. "He tends to do that before any attack, but let's see what he has to offer," Roburn replied briefly as Nenvalur signaled to the others to move silently toward the master Synner, while Anwill raised his closed fist and held it high in the air to halt the others.

He gestured to Nenvalur, Roburn, Batch, and Edryd to follow him as they crept up to Garett, lying flat on the ground that overlooked the market. "It's about time you got here," he whispered as the small group crept up low to the ground. "See those giant bastards over there?" he whispered, motioning slightly over the ridgeline of the small hill toward a group of ten, monstrous ochelons gathered around a handful of large crystals.

"Those massive crystals must be the ones he mentioned earlier. If I'm right, the smaller crystals are for individual control, while the large ones are for amplifying the controlling spell. We don't even have to *kill* the ochelons themselves, since they might prove useful to us once the crystal is broken. That would save us energy and men in the process," Garett said.

"Master Garett, I think there may be something else there with them," Batch whispered, noticing a vacancy in the group. "*Ah*, yes, that would be the addia," Garett sighed, getting a look of concern from him in return. "Only a few of them are left roaming the world that we *know* of, but it seems this mage was powerful enough to have one under his command. Hopefully, it hasn't picked up our scent, but its invisibility and long tentacles will be a problem if it does," he continued.

"It can make itself *invisible*? Fuck me, that's not even fair," Ed sighed quietly. "It can, but that doesn't mean there aren't ways of making it reveal itself. All you need to do is *burn* its skin; that way, it can't hide itself again," Nenvalur replied lightly, as if doing so were such an easy task.

Maybe Anwill was right; he's insane after all, Ed thought with widened eyes.

"My bow-casters can infuse their arrows to get that done, but the moment we fire, we'll lose the element of surprise," Garett said grimly. "We'll surround them before you launch that attack. If the addia picks up our scent, at least it won't know which direction we're coming from exactly," Nenvalur suggested with a grin, causing Anwill to scoff lightly and shake his head.

"It'll take us a few moments to catch up to you once we do. Until we get there, you're on your own," Garett nodded. "We'll be alright. We'll try to break the crystals in the meantime, while you and your bow-casters get situated for what comes *after* we break them," Anwill chimed in. "Let's get moving then. The longer we wait here, the more likely it is that addia will pick up our scent before we're in position," Nenvalur said, motioning for his group to prepare to move.

The small group retracted itself from the ridgeline and returned to the others who awaited orders. Garett explained his plan to his archers, and they began to move on foot to their vantage points on the roofs of the nearby houses.

Anwill explained the plan to the others, and they began to make their way down the streets, fanning out between the houses as they went. Once all were in position, Anwill spawned a small flame in the palm of his hand and used the glint of his sword to signal Garett that they were primed for action.

He and the others nocked their arrows, *drawing from the Ethereal and directing the flowing mana to the palms of their hands*, where it began to seep into their arrows, making them glow a fiery orange. They drew the strings to their cheeks and tilted their bodies back a little to increase their range.

They had the high ground, but although their bows were power-ful, they needed to ensure their arrows hit their mark. Garett loos-ened his grip on the bowstring, sending the first arrow soaring into the night air, while the others did the same a fraction of a second after. The air flooded past the feathers on the arrows and made them hiss before reaching their target with numerous, squelching *thwacks*.

The arrows struck their invisible mark, and in an instant, the addia was engulfed in mana-flame, revealing itself to its attackers. It writhed and bellowed deeply, swinging its long tentacles at its own body to try and douse the flame that burned it. Anwill immediately sent a large ball of light into the air to illuminate their battlefield. "Now!" he shouted, as he and the others began to charge.

Edryd, Batch, Roburn, Rosie, and Nenvalur were at his side, roaring as they sprinted towards their targets, striking fear into their enemies' hearts. The large group of creatures outside the ring of ochelons messily met their attackers, charging wildly at their armored enemies.

Swords sectioned their enemies, and talons met their marks as the bloodbath ensued, sending all kinds of putrid odors, insides, and blood into the air. Edryd and Batch's strength was beginning to wear thin, but the knowledge that this was one of the most decisive moments of their lives motivated them to continue landing their blows.

Anwill resorted to using his blade instead of spells, though if *anyone* thought he might be out of practice, the carnage he caused told a different story. He and Nenvalur and a handful of others nearby carved a path through the horde as they made their way to the ochelons guarding the crystals.

The uproar caused by the attacking Synners would be remembered for ages. Even after losing more than a few during their first encounter, the power they commanded over the horde was astonishing.

Garett and his men went down the streets to reinforce the ones below them. As they were almost a stone's throw away, one of the side ranks broke, causing glicks to pour out and head for the palace.

"Shit. Take them out!" Garett shouted, drawing his blade as they broke out into a sprint. Within a few moments, they met the enemy where the ranks had broken, sealing the gap with a mountain of severed limbs and lifeless bodies.

Batch and Ed were carving through the monsters, trying desperately to keep up with Nenvalur and Anwill. "Why haven't the ochelons attacked us yet?" Batch shouted over to Edryd. "Maybe they're waiting for us to get closer. Squash us one by one or some weird shit," Ed grunted, cutting the head off another glick.

"That's not happening. Not on my watch," Batch snarled as he cut more quickly than before, carving a path through the horrible creatures. "Batch, don't go in alone!" Edryd shouted desperately.

Damn it, Batch! He's going to get himself fucking killed, he thought, cutting down a handful of creatures to try and make his way over to him.

Nenvalur, Anwill, and Roburn were now completely swarmed by creatures, forming a small circle to fend them off. "We can't hold them much longer! We must break the crystals!" Roburn shouted. Nenvalur caught a glance of Batch and Edryd making their way over to the ochelons.

"Damn it! Those kids are being reckless. Follow me," he shouted. He made himself a trail of severed limbs and writhing bodies as he made his way over to the two boys at twice the speed they were going. Anwill and Roburn followed as closely as they could, but were a bit slower than the master swordsman.

Batch reached the ochelons, though they didn't seem to acknowledge his presence. He staved off a few more glicks who didn't dare to come too close to the looming, stationary giants. "Batch!" Edryd called out a few meters away, but Batch was distracted momentarily, as he tried to figure out what made the ochelons behave the way they were. Their heavy breathing caused their broad, muscular shoulders to rise and fall slowly, but something stirred out of the corner of his vision.

The addia, he realized, as a sinking feeling spawned in his gut.

He turned his attention to the creature, who hadn't noticed him yet since it was too busy tending to its seared hide. It was gurgling mucus in its throat, then using its tentacles to smear it over the burned areas. He watched it closely, as he had never seen such a horrible creature before.

Its large, muscular legs and broad paws made it a formidable enemy, even to the most experienced of Synners. The two tentacles added to the danger, and its large eyes saw everything that would try to flank it. "Damn, you're ugly," Batch growled as the addia gurgled more of the icky goo and opened its eyes to make sure it had enough.

That's when it saw him.

It flared its tentacles and let out a roar that would have ripped Batch's skin off had he been standing any closer. It reared on its hind paws and began to charge him, but he was nearly frozen in fear. The first strike aimed to squash him flat, but he somehow managed to get out of the way of the first flick of the beast's long tentacles. "Batch! Keep moving! Don't try to fight it!" Nenvalur called out from the addia's left side.

Yeah, no kidding, but I think it's too late to run. Time to dance, you slimy piece of shit. Eyes on me, he thought, dodging another swipe of the slimy tentacles.

He saw Nenvalur move out of the corner of his eye and disappear behind the beast. Its retractable claws came out and shone menacingly in the moonlight, sending a slight chill down his spine.

Another blow came for him, but he was too slow to react this time, and the creature struck his side, sending him straight into one of the ochelon's legs. The force of the impact against one of the metal prongs that was used to pull the crystals punctured his leather jerkin, burying itself into his arm and, ultimately, shattering the bone.

"Batch!" Ed called out as he watched it all happen much more slowly than reality allowed, hearing Batch's pained scream in the fear-filled echoes of his mind.

The addia came for Batch at a charge, and picked him up with its tentacles as he grunted in pain. It had grabbed both of his arms, stretching them as far as they would go as they raised him into the air. Edryd had only just made his way to the circle of ochelons and watched his friend being held by the two long tentacles.

"Batch!" Edryd cried out, but it was too late. The tentacles ripped Batch's arms from their sockets, and his body fell to the ground, landing on his neck with a squelching *thud*. He could hear the bones in his neck snapping as the blood pooled beneath his friend.

Tears of anger welled in his eyes as the fire in his belly raged like an unbridled mana flame. "You slimy *fuck*! I'm going to pull those tentacles of yours out through your *ass*!" he shouted as he charged the addia. "Ed, don't do it!" Roburn shouted, but there was little he could do to stop the young Synner from attacking it.

The creature heard his shout and immediately turned on him, whipping Batch's lifeless arms at him. He slid under the limbs, feeling a few warm drops of his friend's blood speckle his face, causing his anger to flare even more. "Fight me fairly, *fuck-face*! How *dare you* use my friend against me like that!" he shouted again, continuing his sprint.

A single tentacle came for him this time, but he was ready for it, leaping over the sweeping attack and swinging his sword downward. It met the slimy flesh, severing the tentacle in two, forcing the creature to reel in pain. It wildly swung another tentacle at him that met the same fate as the first, as he jumped both over Batch's body and the tentacle in one bound. Its steaming blood soaked the floor and body beneath it, making it bellow and screech in pain.

"Doesn't feel good, does it?" he shouted, not caring if the beast could understand him, but it gave him courage. Nenvalur dashed in behind it, hoping to get in close enough to wound its leg, but just as he got in range for a strike, it saw him and flicked its tail toward him. He stepped out of the way and sliced the sharp tip off with a single blow. It screeched and moaned in pain for a moment, and as it did so, he landed a blow to both of its hind legs at the same time, severing the tendons.

The creature's rear fell to the floor with a heavy *thud* as it struggled to keep its other half balanced.

Edryd walked over to it, knowing it still had its claws that could kill him with a single blow. He breathed heavily as his eyes fixed on the addia's that were opened to their widest, glaring back at him. It leaned on one leg and sent a forceful blow aimed at Edryd, but he swung his blade to meet the blow, severing its paw in half.

"This is for Batch!" Edryd screamed, looking directly into its eyes as blood poured from the wound on its paw. Before the addia could even think about trying to strike it with its newfound stump, Edryd spun around and used his momentum to jab his blade under its chin, puncturing its hide and brain. Its glowing eyes twitched for a moment, and blood could be heard gurgling in its throat as it slumped to the ground in a heap.

"*Fuuuuuuuck!*" Edryd shouted with tears in his eyes, ripping the blade out of the creature as violently as he could, and stabbed it again for good measure.

He withdrew his sword that was covered in its warm blood, and walked over to Batch's lifeless body. He fell to his knees in the puddle of blood that had now drenched the stone floor and sobbed as the battle raged on around him.

Glicks and Synners fell around them, though the ochelons were still motionless. He wiped the snot from his nostrils, shutting out everything around him.

"I'm so sorry, Batch. I'm so sorry I couldn't get to you in time to save you. I should have been faster, *stronger*. I..." he trailed off between hiccups, bowing his head and running his fingers over his friend's still-open eyes. His sobbing forced him to lean on the body in support, as tears streamed down his face, as Nenvalur approached him, putting a hand on his shoulder.

"You will see him again in the next life, of this I am certain. I have also lost many of my friends in battle, but I know that I will see them again. Life in our cores can never be *created or destroyed; it can only be transformed*. His core has simply returned to the Ethereal, where he will embrace you once more when the time is right," he said comfortingly to the sobbing boy as Ed tightly gripped Batch's blood-soaked jerkin.

"You've honored him by slaying the beast that took his life, making them even in death," he continued, bowing his head respectfully before helping Ed to his feet. "Now come on; we have a castle to save," he said, patting Ed's shoulder as he wiped away the tears. He gave Nenvalur a nod of understanding, giving Batch one last look before turning away and gripping his sword tightly.

Anwill and Roburn arrived, covered in guts and other entrails, but skidded to a halt when they saw Batch's body drenched in blood. "Holy shit!" Roburn said, shifting his gaze to look at the fallen beast, then back to Batch as he bowed his head. "We'll meet again, my friend," he said quietly, understanding death better than most.

"We need to use mana to either pull these crystals out of their skulls or break the big ones, so I will need the three of you to do that with me," Nenvalur explained, gesturing to the large crystals.

"I think breaking them will be easier than trying to rip the crystals out," Anwill replied before glancing at the young boy's body on the ground, immediately understanding what had happened. "I'm sorry for your loss, young one, but right now, we need your help," he said as he walked over to Ed and put a hand on his shoulder.

"I'll do my best," Ed nodded again, but the tear-stained cheeks told Anwill everything he needed to know. "Good enough for me," Anwill said with a gentle smile. "I can help, too!" Rosie shouted from a distance. She was covered in blood, but seemed to have her wits about her.

"Shit, is that Batch?" she said, gasping lightly when she noticed the body on the ground. "It *was*," Ed replied solemnly without looking behind him. "Damn it. He was a strong Synner, Ed. I'm sorry, but we'll have to mourn him later. I promise we will," she said solemnly, but he gave no other response.

"What do we need to do, Anwill?" she asked, shifting her gaze away before any tears could fall. "We're going to have to crush the crystals as one, but we'll have to make sure not to get in the way of the resulting blasts. Nenvalur, can you take those three over there while we handle the rest?" he asked, getting a nod of confirmation from the large elf.

"Good. Edryd, you're with Roburn. Rosie, you're with me. Let's move," he spread his arm out in a fanning motion. Each pair gathered around their targets and *began to draw as much mana as they could*, pushing the limits of their abilities. "Ready?" Nenvalur called out as massive orbs of mana swirled in his hands. "Now!" he called out, prompting the others to release their spells simultaneously with his.

The five obliterated their targets, though Nenvalur's spell nearly knocked Ed off his feet from the resulting blast. Shards of violet crystals soared through the air, as a burst of mana swelled from each one, and the tendrils of mana that connected them to the creatures flailed loosely before dissipating into the air.

The ochelons that guarded them flinched as they woke from their dazed states. Their large eyes blinked a few times before growing immediately enraged when they noticed the horde of other creatures at their feet. Nenvalur signaled for the others who were still fighting to back away from the titanic beasts since each of their large claws was like a scythe to grass as they cut down dozens of creatures in a single blow.

"It worked! Master Garett was right," Roburn called out, knowing the ochelons were far too angry at whatever was before them to notice him. Their rage unified them, making them one, single force of mass destruction, as their large arms swung down and struck the glicks beneath them, sending more than a few of them flying into the air.

"Retreat to a safe distance!" he shouted, feeling a smile of relief stretch across his face. The order was passed down to any within earshot while the ochelons went to work, slaying every glick they could lay their claws on. The smaller creatures fled as quickly as they could, through the broken gate in hopes of safety from their new, larger enemies, but were met by the ones who remained outside.

Edryd and the others encountered little resistance on their way to regroup with the others, though they made sure not to become targets as they escaped. They gathered at the top of the hill where they'd first met Garett, watching as the remainder of the horde was slaughtered mercilessly by the ochelons.

"By the gods, we've done it! Victory! We have victory!" he shouted, raising his bloodied sword high into the air. The others did the same with a unified roar while watching the large creatures chase and slaughter the horde out of the gate. Ed's eyes widened in disbelief at their brute strength, but he couldn't feel entirely relieved knowing he'd suffered a loss that most didn't even know of.

However, as the battle in the palace raged on, Nenvalur and Anwill glanced at each other knowingly, as they could feel the mana even from where they stood.

It's not over, yet, Anwill thought, gazing toward the source of his discomfort.

CHAPTER 25
WEAVINGS OF FATE

My heart was nearly in my throat as I stared at the entrance to the Palace.

This is it. This is what we've fought so hard for. To those of you who've lost your lives in the cave, your sacrifices will not be in vain, I thought as I swallowed dryly.

"Form a line over there at the top of the steps, and don't let anything get through. Leona and Meliss, you'll have to stay within the hall; you two will guard them," the Master said, gesturing to Bernar and I. "How long do you think you'll need?" Thorsen asked over his shoulder. "As long as you can give me," the Master replied solemnly.

It was strange to hear him use that tone, especially now, but I figured there *had to be* a reason for it. "It's time to go, Thorsen. Lead the way," he said, tapping Thorsen on the shoulder, prompting him to move. We crept behind the stones that held the trees and other such plants in the garden outside the palace. Luckily for us, the architects had placed the ornaments in a perfect line, giving us good concealment as we approached.

Once we reached the base of the steps, the Master signaled Thorsen and the others to form a line. Bernar, Leona, Meliss, and I followed in behind the Master, but as soon as we stepped beyond the threshold of the shattered door, I felt a chill race down my spine.

That must be him, I thought, seeing a prominent masked figure sitting in a glowing, violet throne with a swirling portal behind him.

The Master gestured for us to move off to his right along the wall as he took a deep breath. "No matter what happens, do *not* interfere. Do you understand, Thoma?" he asked me directly. "I do, Master," I gave him a nod he didn't see.

Why is he only telling me *that? Does Bernar already know something I don't?* I wondered, ushering Meliss in the direction he indicated.

I looked around the hall and noticed that its former glory seemed like a distant memory, as the throne, pillars, glass, and long, red carpet were damaged almost beyond recognition. It was clear that whatever had happened there wasn't caused by weapons but by a powerful, rageful spell.

"You have a true taste for destroying other people's beautiful hard work, don't you?" the Master asked as he stepped forward and gestured around him. "I never would have thought a mage as powerful as you would throw a tantrum like a child," he scoffed. "*Tantrum?* I was looking for something," the Masked One said, rising from his violet throne and exuding a powerful aura, causing Leona and Meliss to stumble briefly under its pressure.

If he's that powerful, why the hell is the Master taking him on alone? I wondered, glancing at Bernar, who was observing their approach carefully, as the Master exuded his own golden aura to counteract the mage's.

"Given the state of this place, I'm going to assume you've found *it*," the Master said, watching the mage descend the steps with heavy footfall. Each step he took sent another wave of his aura toward us, and I could even feel my legs beginning to strain against the weight of his aura.

"I have, but if you think I'm going to stand here and tell you *why* I'm taking it, you're mistaken. However, I *do* want to know what you've told the others, since there are many of your Synners outside wreaking havoc on my forces. How many of them will sacrifice their lives for the *truth* you've hidden, *brother*?" the mage asked, shocking me to my core.

Did he just say brother? I wondered as I saw the Master's expression shift into one of pain and confusion.

I could tell that it stung like a wasp for a moment, but his expression immediately shifted into one of uncertainty and fear. "A-Ardrin? Is that *really* you?" he asked, his voice trembling just enough to tell me that his feelings were conflicting. "Alive and in the flesh, Taegin, but I am the Masked One, now," Ardrin replied, spreading his arms.

Holy shit. I don't believe it. That story he told us really was about him, I realized, recalling that night in Taegin's study.

"How is this possible? Where the hell have you been all these years? Do you know how long I spent looking for you?" Taegin asked with a slight amount of anger in his voice. "Well, that doesn't matter now, does it? I'm serving a *higher purpose*, though I'm surprised that *you*, of all people, seem to know nothing about it," Ardrin chuckled maliciously, causing Taegin to draw his sword with gritted teeth.

"What *higher purpose*? I don't think becoming a pawn of the Undergod would be considered a *higher purpose*," Taegin snarled, but Ardrin only shrugged. "I don't have to answer *any* questions you ask, but I will tell you that there are far *worse* things than that, brother,"

Ardrin said as he walked forward. "I *know* that already, but I wish you had come to me with whatever troubles you," Taegin shook his head defeatedly.

"And why would I do that?" Ardrin scoffed. "Because I still care for you, *brother*. I spent *decades* looking for you, only to find you in *his* clutches," Taegin admitted with an unmistakable bitter taste in his mouth as he said the words, causing Ardrin to laugh wickedly. "*Oh*, Taegin. You've always had a bleeding heart, and it makes you *predictable*; a weakness *I* don't share," Ardrin snarled, causing Taegin's aura to flare.

As the two glared at each other momentarily, I leaned in toward my brother. "Did you know?" I asked quietly, hoping he would give me a proper answer. "I've known since I went to train in Caegwen, but I *didn't* know his brother was behind all this," Bernar sighed.

I was dumbfounded. There was still so much I didn't know about the world, let alone my *own family*. Meliss and Leona were still struggling to stay conscious under the combined weight of their auras, prompting Bernar to cast a small golden dome around them when he realized they were suffering. "Anything else you want to surprise me with?" I hissed. "A *lot*, actually, but I'm not the one who should tell you," he nodded in the Master's, rather *Taegin's* direction.

Needless to say, any questions I had at that moment would have to wait, as the two brothers began to flare their mana once more, nearly making me stumble under their combined weight.

Taegin and Ardrin approached each other, then stopped a few paces apart. "You've grown taller, even if it's more than apparent that it was not of natural causes," Taegin said, noting his brother's increased height. "This is the sort of thing you could have had for yourself, had you gone down the same path I did," Ardrin replied with a snarl.

"You mean burning two Synners alive because you were bullied a little bit? That was murder and childish, but I don't think I have to tell you that," Taegin said, but Ardrin shook his head. "That wasn't murder, that was an *eye opener*. I realized that if I wanted to accomplish anything in this world, I would have to throw *everything* and *everyone* away; something *you* evidently struggle with," he replied.

I couldn't see it clearly from where I was, but I don't think I saw Taegin's expression shift when he heard that. "So you decided to side with *him* just to attain your goals? That's ridiculous," he scoffed. "What's ridiculous is that you can't see *beyond* him, even though you already know better," Ardrin replied with a snarl. "Ardrin, please. You know there isn't much we can do about *that*," Taegin sighed and shook his head.

"Spare me the lecture; you know *nothing* of what's happened since I left," Ardrin snarled. "You've sided with the Undergod, brought death and destruction to innocent people, and you're stealing something that does *not* belong to you; I'd say I know enough for now," Taegin growled, spawning a *Kyr* spell in the blink of an eye that he launched at Ardrin.

He deflected it with a speed I couldn't hope to match, causing the bolt of mana to shatter part of the thick stone wall behind him. "You've gotten stronger. Consider me impressed," Ardrin said, briefly staring at his smouldering hand before the charred skin healed. "I'll only ask you one last time, brother: Why are you doing this?" Taegin snarled.

"I see that there is no use convincing you that what *he* has promised me will come to pass," Ardrin shook his head. "And what might that be? Becoming ruler of the Realm? Everlasting life and power?" Taegin asked with a scoff.

"At last, you see *some* potential outcomes, but that's not everything. Like I said before, *many worse* things are happening that I do not have the time to explain," Ardrin said, taking another few steps forward.

"Join me, Taegin. Together we can do what *they've* planned. You know the ways of the Gwynnleaf better than anyone. Just imagine the knowledge we could uncover together!" Ardrin said invitingly, extending a hand to Taegin as he walked forward.

No, he wouldn't accept that... would he? Sacrifice the entire continent and potentially other realms for knowledge? I thought, feeling my heart begin to race.

"There is only so much we can gain from it without angering the gods. You know that just as well as I do," Taegin retorted after a short moment of consideration. "Would you not want to strengthen the Synners by giving them more power? Once the ordeal *he* caused is over, it could become a reality, brother!" Ardrin raised his voice, causing the ground to tremble slightly.

"No, brother, I will not and cannot join you, not after what you've done. You are merely his *pawn*, and once his will is enacted in this realm, he will discard you like he has so many others. He will not give you what you seek, nor what he promised. Instead, he will take everything from you, even your *core*; if you still have one," Taegin said defiantly.

"Then I suppose our paths diverge once again. Mine to glory and god-like power, and yours to your demise," Ardrin replied, shaking his head in frustration, while Taegin lowered his head and sighed deeply.

"I am sorry to see that there is no changing your mind, though I should've known better than to try," he said, readying himself and taking a few steps back. "Then you have chosen *death*? So be it," Ardrin said, taking a few steps back. Taegin drew his sword, and his eyes glowed intensely.

As did his brother's.

In the time it took me to blink, a large spike of mana darted out from across the palace floor, meeting a ward that the Master cast to counter it. Sparks of what looked like lava fell to the floor from the impact, sending a shockwave throughout the hall that nearly knocked me off my feet.

Bernar, realizing the rest of their fight would be like this, brought me beside him and put his hand on my shoulder, giving me some of his mana. "Cast a ward out in front of you to protect them," he nodded toward Leona and Meliss, who looked at us with widened eyes. I did as instructed, entering my second stage to try to keep up, though even with the added mana, my ward was nowhere near as strong as his.

Taegin still couldn't accept his words from earlier, as tears began to well in his eyes. "Ardrin, put an end to this madness! What deal did you make? How can I help you get out of it?" he pleaded. "Have you ever considered that maybe I wanted to bait you out so I could kill you before you became a *threat* to our plans? Perhaps there is *another* reason why I'm here," Ardrin replied, tilting his head and raising his hands slightly.

"You lying *bastard*," Taegin snarled. "*Nah-ah-ah*, you don't get to say that about us. We're twins, after all, so mind your tongue," Ardrin said menacingly. "Then why are you lying to me?" Taegin asked, already knowing the answer to his question.

"You've always known there is only *one* way to stop me when I set my mind to something. If only you knew the true extent of *their* power, you would be standing beside me," Ardrin said, causing Taegin to cast another barrage of spells before dashing in to cut at his brother.

The blow was deflected with a violet mana shield before another spell knocked the Master back a few dozen meters. He landed on his feet, but likely realized there was little hope of dealing a physical blow, prompting him to sheathe his blade and focus on spells.

Ardrin grunted as he cast three fireballs in a single flick of his arm. Taegin dodged the first that would have struck Leona and Meliss were it not for the barrier Bernar and I created. I don't know how Taegin hadn't flinched when blocking the second and third, but it felt like Bernar and I just stopped a bull from charging.

I can't let a single one of those get by me, I thought, sharing the same, determined look as my brother.

We'd always had an unspoken sort of understanding with one another, and we knew that this battle would mostly be about protecting those two behind us. However, our thoughts were cut short, as another set of violet spears barreled down the hall, slamming into the wall again.

Ardrin contorted his hands like claws, and two ghostly hands attempted to strike his brother, who cut at them with his mana-infused sword, forcing them to disappear. The two vanished momentarily, exchanging blow after blow that I could hardly follow along with, even in my second stage.

As I was observing the battle, I saw three figures coming from the stairway on the ground nearest to the Masked One carrying vases, but I barely recognized one of them. I immediately felt rage surging within me as my adrenaline kicked in, and my hands began to shake like a hunter's before a kill.

Irun, the name burned at the forefront of my mind when I recognized who it was.

"They're coming!" Thorsen shouted from behind me as he readied himself to face the small horde of glicks. "Thorsen, hold them off for as long as you can! Meliss, Leona, get somewhere deep inside the castle and stay there. Bernar and I will handle the newcomers," I called out, knowing my brother was still heavily focused on the wall of mana protecting us.

"I don't want to leave you," Meliss said desperately. "You'll be okay so long as Thorsen can hold the line. Leona, please take her somewhere safe," I replied.

She nodded and grabbed Meliss' arm before they scurried off down one of the nearby corners to hide themselves. "*Whoa, whoa, whoa!* We can't just let them go off on their own! What if they run into some monsters we didn't know were in here?" Bernar asked urgently. "If we don't, then the Master will be outmatched, and all of this will have gone to shit," I said quickly, causing him to sigh. "I fucking *hate it* when you're right," he said.

He turned his attention back to the hall and noticed the three newcomers, his eyes stopping on Irun's distorted figure. "Is that who I think it is?" he asked. "The shit-sucking traitor himself. Gods above and below, I had really hoped it wouldn't be him," I replied, my hatred beginning to stir.

Bernar must have felt it immediately because he gave me a concerned look and shook his head. "Well, I'll leave him to you, while I take on the other two," he said with a nod. "I was hoping you would say that," I growled maliciously. "Hey, don't let your emotions make your fighting *sloppy*," my brother cautioned.

"If they allow me to kill the bastard, then I'll let them *devour* me," I said, focusing my attention on my target. "Fine. Let's move," Bernar said before we dashed toward them, veering our attention away from the battle that ensued to our left. "Irun, you slimy *turtle shit*!" I shouted as we approached, hoping he would stop putting whatever Gwynnleaves he had in the portal and overlook Meliss and Leona, who had run off down that side of the hall.

Come on, Irun; I know you heard that, I thought, keeping the two women in my peripheral vision.

Luckily, Irun heard me, lowered his vases to the floor, and turned to face me. "Thoma Fayren, the *Lanky Synner*. I've waited for this moment for a long time," he said with a distorted grin. "You mean *the day you die*, you traitorous fuck? Didn't know you wanted me to tear you from taint to throat so badly," I shouted from across the hall, but he scoffed and shook his head.

"Dakzul, Kimzul. Take care of the larger of the two, leave the lanky one to me," he ordered. The two armored figures said nothing, but made their way towards Bernar. "Heavily armored *pricks* without weapons? This should be interesting," Bernar said, a slight bit of amusement in his voice.

I heard my brother, but said nothing in return since my focus was on my once-called *friend* and the pair of undetected women. I saw Meliss and Leona halt about halfway down the hall, frozen in fear, and likely praying nothing would come after them.

Meanwhile, Thorsen and the others were having it out with the small horde of glicks that attacked them just outside, but during that time, their line hadn't been broken until someone to his right fell to the ground with a large gash in his neck.

"Hold the line, damn it!" I heard him shout, but it was too late, since one of the glicks had managed to slip past the line they'd formed. Bernar and I were too occupied with our enemies to notice initially, but by the time I heard its scales rustling down the vast hallway, Leona and Meliss had gone down, I knew it was too late.

Damn it, I can't get to them in time, I mentally kicked myself.

Thankfully, Meliss still had the dagger Pyle had given her with the armor, and turned to face the creature. "Get behind me," she said, pushing Leona to the side, causing her to stagger and land ass-first on the floor. "What the hell are you doing?" Leona asked. "I'm going to save your life," Meliss replied with a determined look in her eye as she gripped her dagger tightly.

The glick raised its claw just before reaching the young girl, who stepped in when it was at its highest peak, jabbing the blade into the creature's gut. It screeched in pain as she withdrew the dagger, covering her in the foul-smelling blood.

It staggered backwards for a moment, but attempted another at-tack. Meliss responded by jamming the blade into the soft meat just beneath its jaw, piercing its brain. It became limp as blood poured out onto the floor and all over her hands. "*Ugh*, that... *hurngf*... that smells rancid," Meliss said, holding back her puke.

"I can't thank you enough, but we need to keep moving before another one comes," Leona breathed a sigh of relief as she got to her feet. Meliss was still processing what she had just done, staring blankly at the creature's body below her, but responded with a grunt. She had difficulty tearing her eyes off the creature, delaying her turn to sprint to the safety of the royal quarters.

Gods above and below, that could've gone so much worse, I thought, having seen the whole ordeal through my peripheral vision.

Bernar and I formed a line with Taegin, who was deep in battle with his brother, and drew our swords as shockwaves from their battle kicked up dust and debris. My black-hilted sword was practically singing, *yearning* for blood as it left my scabbard. Irun drew his as well, though with the upgrade to his armor, his violet, jagged sword only dully hummed as it was drawn.

The two giants broke out into a run towards Bernar, who got into the Ochs guard. He raised his blade to the height of his right shoulder, with his left hand on the pommel, and tilted the point at a small angle towards the armored men, drawing mana and infusing his blade with *Recia*, igniting the mana that coated his blade.

I let my sword trail behind me just above the ground as Irun and I sprinted toward each other. When we were nearing striking range, I spun on the ball of my left foot and jumped, creating momentum for my attack. He deflected it with a grunt and immediately moved to counter with a strike that nearly slashed my throat. I rolled backward to avoid it and quickly got to my feet just in time to deflect a killing blow that was aimed at my torso, leaving us in a momentary bind.

"You're not using your second stage? Are you trying to say that I'm not worthy of it?" Irun asked through gritted teeth. "Exactly right. The only thing you're worthy of is a swift death, as I have no time to trade words with a witless worm," I said through the bare of my teeth.

"So? Why not use it on me? In your eyes, I'm sure I've done enough to earn it, right?" Irun asked mockingly. "Not yet. Tell me why you did it. Why did you betray us?" I asked through a grunt of exertion. "I began this journey long before you unlocked your second stage. Once I'd heard that you had, it only fueled my jealousy of you, but I have to live up to *someone's* reputation," he snarled as I pushed away and began a barrage of light attacks, hoping it would keep him talking.

He deflected one of my strikes aimed at his throat, but pulled me into another bind. "Your arrogance and lust for power will be your downfall, even if you don't die today," I replied, straining against Irun's pressure on my blade. We pushed away from each other with our blades, but I swung my sword upward from the left, striking Irun's shoulder from beneath the gap that his pauldron failed to protect, forcing him backwards.

"You sneaky little shit! You've never done *that* in training," Irun said, taking a few steps back and harnessing the pain for only a second before I was upon him again.

As I moved in to attack, I felt Taegin draw from the Ethereal and cast a spell simultaneously, creating an extended *Kyr* spell. Ardrin cast one of his own, meeting the spell halfway and creating a sphere of pure mana where they met as I clashed with Irun.

Taegin and his brother struggled to maintain their spells for long, as they were equally matched, eventually causing a blast that kicked up a cloud of dust that blanketed the entire area. "You'll never win this battle, brother! There is nothing you can do to stop me, now!" Ardrin shouted before casting another barrage of spells toward Taegin.

How the hell is he supposed to land a blow? Ardrin has blocked or countered just about everything he's had thrown at him, I thought.

I heard Taegin grunt as he forced the spells upward, ultimately striking the palace ceiling, blasting a hole the size of a giant clean through it. Ardrin momentarily turned his hands at opposing angles and thrust forward with his arms and weight. The resulting motion caused a large orb of violet mana to speed towards Taegin. Taegin countered with a large, golden orb, causing the two spheres to collide halfway and creating a sizable explosion of mana that nearly struck them both.

Meanwhile, Bernar sidestepped and strafed the incoming attacks as much as possible. I soon realized that the two he fought had little or no experience in battle.

If it weren't for their armor, he'd have made quick work of these bastards by now, I thought.

I struck Irun's armored torso, sending him flying backwards to give me some room to breathe while he recovered. I watched Bernar fight the armored giants, but I noticed an expression on his face that made him look like he was almost *calculating* something. Whatever it was, it was both reassuring and horrifying to know that he even *had* that capability.

"Alright *fucksticks*; play time's over," he snarled, but his adversaries laughed with their distorted voices. "Having a hard time getting at us, are you?" one of the giants asked, making Bernar furrow his brow. "*Aw*, look! You made him *angry*," the other replied. "Shut it, Alf," the first one spat.

Alf? That's a human name. Wait, those two aren't daemons? Are they just men in fancy suits of armor? So that's *what he was gauging*, I realized, seeing a slight grin appear on my brother's face.

I was nearly caught by another flurry of Irun's strikes, which I barely managed to dodge. It seemed my brother was also mildly distracted, as he was nearly pommeled by a rapid succession of incoming hammer strikes that cracked the stone beneath where he had just been. Meanwhile, Irun swung almost as quickly as I did, deflecting, parrying, and attacking as quickly as our muscles could manage.

He was never this good when we trained. I might actually have to use the second stage, but I could die if I lose focus for even a split second, I thought.

Another blow came from above, and while I had blocked the majority of the blow, the sharp point managed to cut into my forehead, spilling blood into my right eye.

Shit, I can't see a fucking thing through my right eye. I've got to do something to clean it, I thought as I struggled to deflect the incoming barrage of strikes aimed at my head and torso.

Irun prepared a crushing blow for me, hoping to flatten me against the stone floor, but I quickly stepped out of its way, putting some distance between us. I ended up using the backside of my gauntlet to wipe away some of the blood during the brief pause it gave me.

"Are you even trying to kill me, Thoma? You know, for someone as *blessed* as you are, I expected so much more from you," Irun said mockingly as I caught my breath for a few seconds. I spent the next few moments searing the wound with a bit of mana and holding my sword steady as I did so to show that my guard was not being let down at all.

"*Oh*, you *want* me to try? As you wish," I replied with a wicked grin. He was taken aback as he watched my eyes begin to show signs of entering the second stage. I could see slight amounts of mana leakage from his rapid transformation. It was like there were side effects to having been changed so quickly, and as a result, I noticed weaknesses in his defense and noted them.

I've never seen him like that. That's more like it, I thought as I watched mana race down his spine.

"You know, I'm sorry we never grew close. We might have prevented this whole situation," I said, shaking my head. "What makes you think that *you* could have done anything to stop me?" Irun asked after blowing a raspberry, but I could only sigh in immediate response.

Doesn't look like there's anything I can say that will even begin a real conversation, huh? I thought, leaning forward a little in preparation for what came next.

"I'm only going to warn you of this because I once considered you a *friend*," I began, drawing much more mana from the Ethereal and infusing it into my muscles. "*Friend*? What could you possibly say to me after all these years that I haven't heard already?" Irun asked, preparing to launch an attack aimed at my clavicle.

"*Speed blitz incoming,*" I said maliciously, my voice oozing with an intense amount of mana.

Irun dashed towards me, swinging his sword directly towards the base of my neck, looking to decapitate me in one, clean strike. However, I felt his panic after his sword was left wanting and met nothing but air. I suddenly appeared behind him with a menacing look, the shadow of the night hiding my features, showing only the glow of my eyes and the glint of my sword.

I could tell he was scared by the look on his face when he turned to react to my initial swing, and I'd be lying if I said it didn't make me grin. I began swinging my sword more rapidly than before, leaving Irun minimal time to react. He barely managed to get his jagged blade at a bit of an angle to deflect an incoming blow from above.

"You think your speed will help you?" he asked with false motivation, probably trying to shield himself from the fear that began to creep in, but I didn't reply. I didn't have time to, so I continued berating him with attack after attack.

Meanwhile, I saw Ardrin was growing impatient at his brother's ability to block and counter every spell he tried. He yelled as his mask began to glow, spawning a scarlet claw that extended from his hand. Taegin had only fractions of a second to conjure a mana barrier that was only just able to block it, stopping the claw a few centimeters away from his body.

The two of them struggled for a few moments, but Ardrin began to gain the upper hand, using all his might to push one of the tips of the claws into Taegin's shoulder at the joint, causing him to scream in agony.

Master! Shit, this is bad, I thought for a split second as his cry cut through the sounds of my own battle.

It distracted me from Irun's incoming attack, which sent me flying backwards into the nearby pillar. Taegin seemed to be faltering in his defenses, like something was draining his mana right out of his body. "You cannot defeat me, brother! Surrender, and I will let you live!" Ardrin shouted, forcing the claw in a little more deeply.

Taegin looked tempted to simply let go of it all and give up as his strength waned, but he gritted his teeth and began to forcibly remove the claw from his shoulder as his eyes glowed more intensely than before. "I will never surrender to you, brother, even if it means my *death*," he said with all the strength he could muster.

He used the last of his might to cast the scarlet claw into the ground, nearly severing his arm entirely as it crashed into the stone floor beneath him. Meanwhile, I deflected another set of blows from Irun, who seemed to grow increasingly frustrated with my lack of care for our fight since entering the second stage.

I could only watch as Taegin began falling forward, the blood rushing from his shoulder, far too weak to stand from the blood loss. Ardrin turned away from his younger sibling towards mine and Irun's battle as if he would offer assistance.

Just as Taegin's body hit the floor, Bernar cast an *Exar* blast aimed at his two foes' heads, blowing their helmets clean off their shoulders, causing them to stagger and group together from the forceful blast.

However, they failed to recover in time, as he had already leaped into the air. His airborne strike sliced both of their heads in half with a swift, spinning motion that sent blood high into the air. He landed like a cat jumping off a high shelf, as the fleshy chunks struck the floor beside him.

"You two definitely succeeded in pissing me off," he spat before seeing how the Master's battle was faring, noticing a slight lull in the mana flowing through the air. That was when he noticed Taegin lying on the floor, motionless and in a pool of his own blood. "Taegin!" he shouted as he dashed to his aid, sliding on his knees before turning the body over, noticing the wound.

Meanwhile, Ardrin approached Irun and I with a menacing aura as tendrils of violet mana lurched out from him and wrapped around my core. I couldn't exactly tell what was happening, but it gave Irun enough of an opening to land a pommel strike to the bridge of my nose, causing my eyes to water.

Through the blurriness, I noticed Ardrin's head tilted slightly, making me wonder what the spell he cast on me was even for. Irun dashed in for another strike, but I immediately returned the pommel strike he gave me earlier after deflecting his blade over my shoulder.

"You fucker!" he shouted, swinging aimlessly through teary eyes. Ardrin saw this and sent out another tendril of his dark mana to help him, which leeched my remaining strength.

Irun must have seen it coming, because he began *drawing copious amounts of mana from the Underworld*, landing a crippling strike on my guard, knocking me to the ground.

Damn it, I'm losing consciousness and I don't know why, I thought as I felt my eyes begin to cease their glow.

"Irun, it's time to go. If we don't leave now, all of *this* will be for *nothing*," Ardrin called out just as Irun was about to land a finishing blow on me. However, as he raised his sword, I could have sworn

I saw a hint of either regret or hesitation in his eyes; I couldn't tell which. Whatever it was, it made me sure that he wasn't going to kill me in my weakened state.

He clicked his tongue and turned to leave, and I saw it as an opportunity to get to my feet. He must have known I would, because he quickly turned around and struck me again with his pommel, smashing me in the face and nearly rendering me unconscious. "It seems like you won't have my head today, *Lanky*," he spat a wad of blood near my face.

Damn it, he's going to get away, I noticed through my blurred vision, struggling to get to my feet once more to head after him.

I was on my feet again, but I was bent over like a drunkard and struggling to keep my balance. My blurred vision didn't help much either, but I knew what I had to do. I *drew from the Ethereal* to get back into my second stage, drawing my free hand over my shoulder, then flinging it forward to cast my *Whip of Doom*.

The tendril lashed out and wrapped around his forearm near the height of his elbow, just before I flicked my finger to ignite the mana. I admit I almost chuckled when I saw the chunk of his flesh soaring through the air with a trail of blood following behind it.

Irun screamed in agony as he watched his beloved forearm fly near his face, immediately clutching his new stump tautly as Ardrin seared the wound shut and dragged him towards the swirling, violet portal and threw him inside.

Meanwhile, Bernar was still leaning over Taegin's body, pouring mana into the still-open wound. "Does it look as bad as it feels?" I heard Taegin ask weakly. "It's only a flesh wound," Bernar said as he turned to see that the line outside had kept the creatures at bay.

"Pyle!" he called out, prompting the old Synner to look at Taegin in his arms, bleeding profusely.

Disoriented as I was, I fell to my knees, exhausted from the ordeal and the spell the Masked One had cast on me earlier. "One day, Irun," I mumbled weakly as I watched the pair go through the portal that shut quickly behind them. My eyes were heavier than ever, and I could feel the exhaustion hitting me like a fully loaded wagon.

Can't let him... get... away, I thought briefly before collapsing onto the stone floor as the world around me went dark.

EPILOGUE
AFTERMATH

I opened my eyes only to find myself staring at a ceiling I didn't recognize.

Where the hell am I? Whose bed is this? Why does my face feel like it's been kicked in? I thought as I touched my face.

There was still some minor swelling from the hit I took, but it had mostly subsided. I touched the fractured jawbone that had caused the tissue around it to swell, wincing at the pain, which in turn reopened the cut above my brow.

All fucked up. Excellent, I thought as I looked around the room, trying to gather information on where I was.

Looks like an infirmary, and I'm not alone. Judging by where this would be on the map we looked at, I'm somewhere between the kitchen and the service room, I guess, I thought, noticing the sounds of pained groaning around me.

The room was full of other Synners who were also wounded, but they were either fast asleep or picking at their own wounds. I began to search my own body for unknown wounds as frantically as the pain and lingering effects of the draining spell would allow.

"Calm yourself, will you? You're going to open your wounds if you keep moving like that," a familiar voice said from the doorway.

I lazily carried my line of sight to the voice's origin, and found a pleasant-looking face with a furrowed brow.

"Hullo, *Muluss*," I mumbled, feeling my jaw ache, which made me wince. She stepped over to my bedside, sitting beside me and holding my hand. "Try not to talk, you stubborn bastard," she whispered, putting a hand to my chest. I couldn't smile with my lips, but I did what I could with my eyes.

"The Master would like to see you, if you can stand," she said softly. I closed my eyes and nodded slightly before she helped me up from the bed, swinging my legs lazily over the side. The white, linen sheets and soft pillows seemed to pull me close like they never wanted to let me go. I felt light-headed as I stood, nearly fainting from the rush of blood, but when I glanced down and saw that my clothes had been changed, I blushed.

Instead of my leather jerkin, I was shirtless, but had some linen pants that were loosely tied around my hips. My many cuts and bruises from the battles showed, and the scar on my back from the cave showed in its entirety. "Gods above and below, you're eighteen years old, and you've already been through all that?" she asked, observing wounds both past and present, including the latest addition on the bridge of my nose.

I could barely open my mouth before Meliss put a finger to it. "Sorry, I know I told you not to talk, but these wounds are a bit *excessive*, aren't they?" she asked, to which I could only perform a light shrug that I hoped explained enough. She handed me a shirt, helping me to get it safely around my face and other wounds.

I took a step, but my linen pants decided not to go with me due to their lack of a drawstring. Meliss couldn't help but chuckle a little as she looked down at my waist. "It's kuld," I muttered, trying to tell her it was cold in the room. She lightly patted me on the shoulder with a chagrined smile, letting me stand on my own for a moment as she went over to the nearby chest to grab a large towel.

Better than nothing, I guess, I mentally shrugged, wrapping it around my waist and tucking the corner into the fold at my hip and rolling it over.

I began to walk, but every step I took made my jaw ache more and more. I grunted as I took my first few steps, and then decided it would be best to suck up the pain once and for all. The two of us walked slowly for a few minutes, though it felt like an eternity to me.

Everything hurts. What the hell did I get hit with yesterday? Two days ago? Three? How long has it been? I thought.

My arms were sore, my hips were weak, and my jaw continued its throbbing. We came to a small flight of stairs, and went even more slowly than I had thought possible for humans to walk. "This is *humuliuting*," I mumbled. "Didn't I tell you to keep quiet?" she snapped playfully as I grunted and took another step.

It took us nearly fifteen minutes to make it up the stairs until we finally reached where the Master was being kept. I saw him with a large bandage on his left shoulder, while Pyle sat at his side to keep watch over him. The room still smelled of dried blood, as the used bandages had only recently been removed.

"Welcome back to the land of the living, Thoma. We weren't expecting you to wake up this afternoon, let alone the following day of the battle," Taegin said. "Same to you, *Mustur*," I mumbled as I slowly walked inside. "Gods above, boy, you look like *shit*. Bernar, help your little brother, will you?" Pyle said, noting my swollen face.

Bernar walked over to me, drawing mana to his palm and infusing it into the swollen area. "That's much better, thank you," I said, feeling more relieved than expected. "You really should learn to do this on your own. It's not fully healed yet, but it should allow you to talk a little more freely for now. Speaking of which..." Bernar trailed off.

"I think it would be best if we left them alone," Pyle said, getting up from his seat and glancing at Meliss. "I will return when you summon me, Master. Come, Meliss. I wish to discuss something with you that I think you'll be excited to hear," he continued as he stepped away from Taegin's bedside. "What's this about?" she asked me. "I have absolutely no idea. I just woke up, remember?" I said, putting my hand on Meliss' shoulder. "You'll be fine, so go with him. I'll be here whenever you get done. After all, I'll need help to get back down those damned stairs," I said playfully.

I watched the two leave the room, as Bernar took their place in the doorway and pulled up a chair to sit opposite me.

"Bernar told me what happened to Irun, and I have to say, from the bottom of my heart, I'm sorry to discover he *really was* a traitor. As I understand it, you two weren't very close; even so, it must have been difficult to fight an old friend," Taegin said grimly, but I could only shrug, knowing there was little more I could do at that point.

"He was always a little bratty, but I still considered him a friend. However, I had a hard time controlling my anger when I saw how mutated he was from the dark mana," I muttered, my wound still aching a little. I winced again, and a small drip of blood ran down the side of my face, which I wiped off with the sleeve of my oversized shirt.

"Be that as it may, I wanted to thank both of you for helping me with the others. If you hadn't, I most likely would have died because of my hubris," the Master said humbly. "Which of you two made the call to tag into the fight?" he asked.

"Thoma made the call. I was originally against it, because it would've left Leona and Meliss alone, but he saw something I guess I didn't," Bernar said, jutting his thumb in my direction. "Well, I thank you for making the decision, Thoma. I'm still alive, though it will take some time to fully recover my strength, as the claw that pierced my shoulder nearly severed my arm. I believe he was trying to rip out my core," Taegin sighed.

"Your *core*? What the hell was that claw made of?" I asked with genuine surprise. "It wasn't an ordinary claw of mana. That was the claw from the *Nethersong Mask*, one of the many gifts from the gods all those years ago," Taegin reminded me of our history with the artifacts briefly, as my eyes fell to the side of the bed with a sigh.

"Regardless of the final outcome, you two have fought valiantly in a battle that was *definitely not* in our favor. With that said, I grant you the rank of Adept, Thoma. Although I do apologize that it's taken this long to get you the experience you needed to get there," he said with a small grin that wrinkled the scar on his face.

That's only two away from master, I thought as my eyes widened, and even though it pained me, I bowed from my chair.

"It's about time you got your rank-up. I always knew it would be coming soon," Bernar said, smiling proudly. I allowed myself a small grin out of the corner of the better half of my face. "Thank you, Taegin... I mean, *Master*," I could barely say for the lump in my throat. "*Ah*, so you *did* hear that part of the conversation. There is a lot more to that, but I'll wait for Pyle to heal you completely," Taegin smiled, breathing deeply as he adjusted his position in bed, wincing at the pain.

"However, I did want you to be the first to know that with your new rank, you will aid New Bloods and Juniors for their basic training, since we will require more instructors. Since you're still new to teaching, Bernar and I will handle Senior ranks and above once we return to Codrean, which I hope is soon. The food here is good, but I'm tired of sitting in bed all day," Taegin said playfully.

"There is, of course, one more thing I would like to tell you, but again, we must wait for your jaw to fully heal to have a much deeper conversation than the one we've just had. You will have lots of questions, I imagine," he continued.

I didn't fully understand what he meant by that, so I simply nodded.

"In the meantime, you are free to go where you please. We've won the battle for Coltend, but I am sure it will not be the last for the Continent," Taegin said gravely. "Do you think he will try again soon?" I barely managed to ask, causing him to sigh heavily, like a weight had been put on his chest.

"My brother Ardrin, as you now know him, will most likely have returned to his fortress to rebuild his forces. Since Garett destroyed the crystals that controlled them, the creatures turned on each other, nearly wiping the entire force out in the process. If I'm right, his fortress is in the northern part of Hjalfar, but I have yet to confirm that," he said grimly.

I pondered the words for a few moments, digesting the information given to me.

"In any case, you have your jaw to take care of, so I suggest you go and do that immediately; we still have much to discuss," Taegin said, to which I nodded and rose from my seat. "I'll keep an eye on him until Pyle gets back," Bernar noted as I was leaving the room. Just then, I realized my predicament and the lack of assistance for what I now had to face.

Ah, yes, my arch-nemesis of the day: Stairs. Should I wait for Meliss to come back? No telling how long she'll be gone for, is there? Fuck me, I thought, embracing my demise with a deep, heartfelt sigh.

With every step taken, I could feel my jaw throbbing in response. I found myself praying to all the gods that Pyle would repair the damage Irun had caused with the blow to my face.

After more than a few minutes, I was back on the ground floor. I was still wrapped in my towel, and barefoot on the cold, stone floors of the hallways, I now limped down to find Pyle. I went as quickly as pain would allow me to through the emptied halls and into the main one, where the battle had taken place the previous evening.

That might just be the slowest I've ever moved, I thought as I cast my gaze to the horizon through the destroyed door and saw that it was nearly dusk.

I noticed that the path to the library was now closed and that the throne on mana was gone as well. The shards of the previous thrones still lay about the hall, as if representing days of past glory. I saw a severed hand in a small pool of dried blood near the top of the steps that would have led to the thrones had they still been standing.

I slowly went over to it and picked up the cold, lifeless hand, staring at it for a few moments. My eyes glowed, and I ignited the hand with a directed *Pyrus* spell, turning it to little more than a pile of fine ash.

I dusted my hands and went to the servants' area, where I was sure to find Pyle, and consequently, Meliss.

I came to the wooden door of the room and poked my head through the crack. Meliss was telling him how she had used her previous experience when fleeing the castle to strike down the glick that had come for her and Leona. Pyle was enjoying himself at the tale; he always loved a good story, and he congratulated her on her accomplishment.

"I am curious to see what you might accomplish with a sword in your hand. You might not be as adept as those of us who have done it our entire lives, but you will still learn a vast number of skills," Pyle began as her eyes grew wide.

"Do you mean that? Do you think I could learn sword skills? What about mana? Can I learn that, too?" she asked eagerly. "*Whoa, whoa*. One question at a time. Why do you want to learn so badly?" Pyle gestured, trying to calm her down, making Meliss ponder for a moment, as I listened intently from the doorway.

"Even though I've been a servant all my life, since this incident began, I've had to defend myself twice from both man and monster," she began, looking away as she spoke. "If it weren't for the knife you gave me, I wouldn't be standing here right now. I've learned, very quickly, that I never want to feel that kind of fear or helplessness again," she said, reverting her gaze back to Pyle's glowing eyes.

"You do know that courage is not the absence of fear, right?" Pyle asked. "What do you mean?" Meliss asked, visibly confused. "Being courageous, *brave*, or whatever you want to call it, doesn't mean that you don't *fear* whatever it is in front of you. It simply means that you *accept* the possibility of things going to shit, but you know that you're going to give it your best, regardless of the outcome," he explained.

Meliss took a moment to digest the words and nodded her agreement after toying with the jeweled stubs in her ear lobes. "In that case, I would like to learn to become both courageous and skilled with a sword," she said determinedly.

I knew she would say that, I thought.

"I'm glad to hear that," he began with a light chuckle and a bright smile. "Even though you might still be a little too old for me to train from the very beginning. That's not to say it's *impossible*; only that you'll likely not be as adept as others your age. If you're capable enough, I might be able to begin and still have you graduate with some of the others from Fangsdalr, should you wish to become one of us, that is," he said, prompting her to look down at the ground pensively.

"I've recently put eighteen winters behind me. Is that too old to be trained?" she asked, genuine concern ruling her tone. "It is a little on the older side," Pyle began. "She could always train with us at Codrean," I interjected, making her face light up when she heard my voice more clearly than earlier that day.

"*Ah,* you actually managed to make it down here. I was worried I'd have to send Meliss to carry your ass down the stairs," he jested. "I'm broken, not dead, Master Pyle. The Master sent me here to get my jaw fixed," I muttered. Meliss grabbed me a chair and pulled it up beside her for me. "Thank you," I said quietly with a nod.

"So, you think the Master would let her train with you there at Codrean?" Pyle asked as he poured mana into my jaw. "I think he wouldn't mind, but I'd have to ask and confirm that," I replied, feeling the fracture closing and the swelling dissipating as more mana flowed into my wound. "There, all done," Pyle said, proud of his work. "Gods above and below, that is so much better," I said, moving my jaw around.

"In any case, we might be able to train you as one of our own if you're up for the challenge and the Master agrees to it," I said. Meliss' eyes held both excitement and seriousness that I had never before seen. "If he lets me, I'll do whatever it takes," she stated confidently.

Ah, shit. Leona's going to kill me, isn't she? I mentally chuckled nervously.

"Well, we'll also need to discuss Fangsdalr, since the traitor likely gave away its position," Pyle said solemnly. "I'm sure the Master will be more than willing to accommodate. We've lost many of our own as well, so it wouldn't be too large of a stretch to supplement our forces with yours," I said suggestively. "You might be right, but time will tell," he concluded.

A short silence fell amongst us, each one digesting the information presented here. "*Oh*, fuck! I just realized I haven't seen or heard from anyone else since I woke up. Where are Ed and Batch?" I asked urgently. "Edryd should be just outside the main hall," Pyle began. "The turd survived? *Heh*, I knew he would," I said with a grin, but Pyle and Meliss glanced at each other with knowing looks.

"Wait, what about Batch? Wh-what happened?" I asked, fearing the answer after noticing the pair's exchange. "You should probably go find Edryd. Meliss, take him with you and go find him," Pyle said solemnly. She led me to where Edryd was sitting on a bench in the setting sun's light, while Garret, Roburn, Anwill, and Nenvalur were telling their tales of the monsters they had slain the previous evening.

I greeted them with a wave, and they acknowledged my presence, continuing their conversation. Ed was sitting with his hands folded together, leaning his elbows on his legs, staring off into the distance as he sat silently.

"Hullo, Edryd," I said. Edryd looked up at me in surprise. "I thought you'd be out for a lot longer," he said, but I noticed something was amiss and decided to prod him for the information. "Well, I would have rested longer, but I heard that you were out and bout, so I came to check on you," I shrugged, but his expression soured immediately.

"We won the battle, and managed to turn the fuckers on themselves, but not before the addia tore Batch's arms off in front of me," Edryd said, choking on the last few words. "It was... *effortless* for that addia; killing him, I mean," Edryd struggled to say as the words hit me like a troll's fist.

"Shit. I'm sorry you had to see that, Ed," I said, lowering my head and putting a hand on his shoulder sympathetically. "Batch as a good guy, but he went out the way he always said he would," I continued, but Ed's eyes filled with tears, prompting him to lower his head in a slow nod of agreement.

"I believe we all must see such things at some point. Makes us stronger for whenever it comes around again, I suppose," he said with a shrug, sniffling quietly. "I avenged him by killing the fucker that took his life, but I still wish I could have saved him," he continued, wiping away a stray tear.

"You did what you could, and I don't think *anyone* could have done any better under the circumstances," I said comfortingly, putting my other hand on his shoulder to look at him intently. "You don't know that," he said grimly.

"Perhaps I don't, but what I do know is that death comes for us all sooner or later. All we can do is keep that in mind, and when our times come, we should greet it as though it were an old friend; embracing the harshness of reality, since it's all we can do at the end of the day," I said with a nod, which he returned before wiping a stray tear that streamed down his face.

"I guess you're right, as usual. Thanks," he said as I patted his shoulder, and left him and Roburn to their silent thoughts. I returned to the palace and found Leona in the main hall, picking up a few of the pieces of the smashed thrones.

"I take it they have sentimental value to you," I said quietly as I approached her. "They do. As little as I had liked being the queen of an overweight madman, I still cared deeply for my subjects. I have sent messages out to where, I pray, most of them have escaped before Mourtis closed the city entirely," she sighed heavily.

"Might I ask how many you believe made it out?" I asked, though she shook her head in dejection. "I can't say for sure, but word of the Church's rebellion would have spread about the city within a few minutes, so there's no telling how many survived the attack," she explained.

"I pray that *most* made it out, but after seeing the state of the city, I fear *less than half* made it out alive. We will only know how many within a few days," she continued. I grimaced in solidarity, but handed her a shard with the queen's insignia engraved in the wood. She took it and smiled warmly at me as a token of gratitude.

"I pray that you and your brother will visit me often at the palace. After spending time with you and the others, your sense of humor... well, not only has it rubbed off on me a little, but it would be a *tragedy* to lose friendships like that once you depart," she said, furrowing her brow.

"I *suppose* we could pass by and visit from time to time. It's always nice to have an outsider to talk to about things different from sword maneuvers and spell-casting," I shrugged with a grin.

She chuckled lightly, then bowed gracefully, which I returned. "I suppose I should get back to *formally* addressing you, now that you're back at the palace," I said. Leona waved her hand. "*Oh*, nonsense. So long as there are no official members, you needn't use formal speech with me. We are friends now; something I have longed for since I first became queen of Coltend," she said, making me blush, and bowed again.

"I'd best be off to see the Master now that my jaw has healed. Let us know if you need anything from me or *my brother*," I grinned. "I don't believe I will need anything for now, other than a cup of wine and a warm bed for the night," she said with a knowing smile. "I'll see if I can't have *someone* get you a glass of wine," I said with a wink.

I knew what that entailed, but decided against saying anything before taking my leave.

Meanwhile, Bernar had remained at the Master's side, tending to the wound in Pyle's stead. "I see Pyle has done his work on you," Taegin said, noting my newly scarred, though less swollen face. I grinned. "Indeed, he has. I really should learn how to self-heal. I've noticed a trend in me getting hurt... *a lot*," I said, recalling the past few weeks' adventures.

"Feels like the hands of a *goddess* running over you, doesn't it?" Bernar asked. "Mind is always in the gutter," I said under my breath. "What? You might have different ways of comparing things that touch you, *little turd*, but I prefer to compare mine to women," Bernar said with a grin. "Not all things can be compared to women, Bernar. I thought your mother would have taught you such a thing," Taegin said, immediately making me turn all my attention to him.

"Did you know her? My mother, I mean to say," I asked shyly. Taegin sighed and looked upwards. I know her well. *Too* well, some might say," he replied, making my eyes open widely. A wrinkle began to form in the corner of Bernar's mouth, though I couldn't determine *why*.

"What is she like?" I blurted out, causing him to chuckle lightly. "She is an extraordinary woman, and one of the finest warriors I've ever known. She is as wise as she is beautiful, though I think she takes a bit too much from her great-great-grandfather's side of the family," Taegin began with a shake of his head as I looked at him with utter confusion.

"How do you know so much about her? Did you know her before she abandoned us?" I asked, not bothering to hide my curiosity, and he immediately scowled at me.

"*Abandoned* you? Is that how you remember it, or did your *insolent father,* who hated her and her profession, lie to you?" he snarled, making me flinch. "That obese *sack of shit* only married her because he was forced to do so by his parents to have closer ties to Synners that could protect their farmlands from monsters," he continued with visible frustration.

"What?" I felt my freshly healed jaw drop. "He told you a lie, Thoma, and I suspect many more like it about her. She is the exact opposite of everything he said she was," he said sternly, as though doing so would instantly rid any negative ideas of my mother.

I stared deeply into Taegin's eyes, thinning the gap between the lids of my own. "How *well* do you know her, exactly?" I asked. Taegin raised an eyebrow at Bernar, who shrugged. "Don't look at me; I haven't said anything," he shrugged, upturning his bottom lip and shaking his head.

Taegin closed his eyes and breathed as deeply as the wound in his shoulder would allow him to. "Bernar has known this for quite some time now, but the two, rather *three* of us, decided to keep it from you until we figured you were ready," he began, making me focus all my attention on what he was about to say.

"Thoma, believe me or not, I am your grandfather, and your ancestor was the *Lord of Codrean*, the one who first encountered the gods," Taegin said, as matter-of-factly as he could. "Wait, you're saying that..." I began. "Your mother is, in fact, my *daughter*. Yes," he cut me off with a smile.

My jaw could've split the Continent in two, based on how hard it dropped.

"D-Did I hear that correctly?" I stuttered, taking a moment to gather my thoughts. "You mean to say that not only are we directly related, but that we're the Lord of Codrean's direct descendants?" I asked, only receiving a nod from the Master. "Which also makes Ardrin my *great-uncle*?" I asked again, with the same response. "Damn it, that's, *uh*, that's a lot to take in," I sighed, blinking a few times.

"I have two more questions: What is our *real* last name, and where is our mother?" I asked, wanting to get straight to the point. He looked at Bernar, who could only purse his lips as his reply. "I'm surprised your brother was *this good* at keeping secrets," he said in a slightly playful tone.

"To answer the question about your mother, she's been in Caegwen since you were about five years old. Also, how did you know your last name was a fake?" he asked. "Given our heritage, it would stand to reason that if mother wanted to hide, the first thing she would do is hide her family name, and by default, mine and Bernar's as well. So, what is it?" I asked, noticing Taegin's features twitch.

Whatever ran through his head just now means I just touched a nerve, I thought, watching his expression shift ever-so-slightly.

"Pelantyr," Taegin replied bluntly. "As in *Nexis Pelantyr*? Author of *Dissection*? That's a lot to chew on at once," I said, slumping into the chair to digest the information. "Told you he would handle it well," Bernar said, causing Taegin to push his lips to one side and raise an eyebrow. "*What*? I did, and you know it," Bernar continued, while I was still processing what I'd heard.

"Once we have returned to Codrean, I plan to train you up in your second stage and then send you off to meet her in Caegwen like I did with your brother," Taegin began.

So that's why Bernar knew Anwill so well, I realized.

"What has she been doing in Caegwen all these years? Was it too much to ask for her to visit at least once?" I asked sardonically. Both my brother and Taegin looked at each other, almost as if saying something without words.

"She has been searching for some of the artifacts the gods had given us all those years ago. The night she left Coltend, and the night that I brought you under my wing, she called it her *sacred duty*, but I think she wants to bring back the powers we once held as a family," he chuckled lightly and shook his head.

"However, a few of them have long since gone missing. Where, why, and *which ones* are still unclear, but others were stolen, one of which my brother currently holds in his possession. If I know him, I'm sure he's also searching for the others," Taegin said grimly, making me sigh when I understood the weight of his words.

"I see. Well, if you're already sending me there, I would like to take Anwill up on his offer of learning more about mana manipulation stages," I suggested. "I could let him know, yes, but I feel like *she* might also want to take part in that. However, I'll let you figure that out for yourself," he said, recalling a conversation with Anwill about this topic.

"There are, of course, still a few things I want you to learn before going to Caegwen, so it will be some time before you depart," the Master continued. "Of course, Gran-...Tae-... What the hell do I even call you now?" I asked, genuinely confused. "In front of others, *Master* will suffice. Between the three of us? Call me whatever you want," Taegin smiled, wrinkling the scar on his cheek again.

"I see. Well, *grandpa*, Pyle has something he wants to discuss with you about Meliss and what remains of his Synners, if you're feeling up for it," I said.

It feels weird calling him that, I thought.

"We'll be leaving for Codrean in a few days, perhaps weeks, depending on how much work we need to help with here. We will have plenty of time to talk to him about the next steps," Taegin said.

"Sounds like a plan to me. I'll inform him and try to get some more rest, as I'm still feeling a little queasy from whatever happened during the battle," I replied excitedly. "As we all should. It's been a long few days, though I feel they will only grow more difficult from here on out," he said gravely, as I felt a dry ball of spit scrape down my throat.

"We'll be ready for them when they come," I said with no small amount of bravado, causing Taegin to look at me proudly. "An Adept, indeed. Now, go get some rest," he said. I looked out the window at the back of the room, realizing it had gotten darker since the beginning of the conversation.

"Right. I'll take my leave to be able to process all of this *information*. Goodnight, and I will, *uh*, see you tomorrow," I said awkwardly. "Goodnight, Thoma," he said with a warm smile and a slow nod.

"See you tomorrow, *shit bird*," Bernar said with a grin. "Until tomorrow, you slimy turd-blossom," I shot back. He chuckled, but remained at Taegin's side and returned to his work on the wound, which was not yet fully healed. Just as I was about to exit the room, I halted in the doorway, feeling the shit-eating grin starting to grow rapidly on my face.

"*Oh*, and Bernar," I called out as he turned to face me with a raised eyebrow. "Someone would like a cup of wine brought to them when you are done here," I winked, causing my grandfather to glare at Bernar, who blushed slightly. "Like you didn't know that already," Bernar said sardonically.

Taegin looked at me for an answer, but I could only shrug indifferently before stifling a chuckle as I walked out of the room.

I returned to the infirmary, where Edryd and the others were getting ready to sleep. Meliss approached me with a set of linen sleeping clothes. "Back to square one, I guess. Only this time, you're bringing me clothes, not coming to take them off me to wash them," I said, making her face turn a bright shade of red. "Back to square one," she said with a smile.

"What did the Master say?" she asked, but I knew there was only so much I could tell her then. "Only that I'm going to Caegwen with my brother sometime soon," I said nonchalantly. "Will you at least stay with me awhile in Codrean if the Master allows me to be trained with Master Pyle?" she asked, lowering her head. "Of course I will! He still has things to teach me before I head off, so we'll have a good amount of time to spend together. Besides, I think he'll like having Pyle around at Codrean," I said comfortingly.

"That's all I need to know, then," she smiled, wrapping herself in my arms. I kissed her goodnight and stroked her hair as she fell asleep.

Caegwen, huh? I thought as my mind drifted back to that grassy plane from what felt like forever ago.

And to a new power that I had only scratched the surface of.

AUTHOR'S NOTES

Hello there!

So, you've made it to the end of *Weavings of Fate, huh*? I'll be honest with you, I was really nervous about writing my first novel, let alone publishing it for the entire world to see.

Granted, it's not like I have a huge following or anything, but it's still nerve-wracking nonetheless. Even so, I would like to thank you for reading up until this point, and as a bonus, I'd like to give you, dearest reader, some backstory on how this came about.

Back in 2015, I started out writing a fan fiction for *The Witcher* after having played through *Wild Hunt*. To this day over *a decade later*, it's still one of my favorite games of all time. To honor that, I started writing out characters and an overarching story that I thought would fit the world well.

While I was writing it, an idea struck me: "What if I just took the characters I've already created and made *my own* world, story, lore, and other such stuff rather than trying to make it fit in an already well-established universe?"

That single idea spawned *The Synner Saga*. It took me over a year and a half to build the lore, characters, story , and everything else you'll see in the coming books, should you choose to read them.

There is very little I haven't accounted for in some way or another, and while I'm not trying to *toot my own horn* too much, I *am* proud of where that story has taken me.

In 2017, I finished the second draft and sent it out to close friends and family. Of course, being a first-time author, there were a lot of mistakes and my formatting was trash, but with that in mind, I also knew that I couldn't tell this story without some extra real-world experience. Coincidentally, I'd already signed up to join the military at that time, and knew that if I wanted to present the story in the best way possible, I needed to give myself time to grow, both as a person and professionally. After 5 years, I was out of the military, and decided it was probably time to get back to it, but I'd been through a lot during that time, and knew that it wouldn't be easy to write it as I once had.

A result of that was in the way that Thoma and some of the other characters spoke. Their mannerisms and such were things I'd never really considered until *after* I'd returned to the manuscript. It was almost heartbreaking to see just *how innocent* I was, even though I'd already considered myself *plenty* mature for having gone through a difficult upbringing.

It made me realize the story *wasn't* done yet, and I came to the conclusion that there was more that I needed to do to both improve the story, and give it the attention it deserved. It took another year of editing, changing story beats, and even going so far as shifting the narrative a little right or left to make it fit the ending better. Multiple iterations of the ending of the first book were considered, and I'd finally settled on one that I knew would round it out well.

What you've just read, is the essence of that year. I changed the chapters with Thoma into a first person perspective, and knowing *why* that change was necessary made it that much more satisfying. Granted, I'm just one person doing all of this, so if you happened to spot any mistakes, I sincerely apologize.

All in all, I'm still proud of *Weavings of Fate*, and while it is by no means a *magnum opus*, it does help set up the characters, the world around them, and gives a small look into the potential stakes for them.

As things currently stand, there are a total of 6 planned books, with an ending that was decided from the start. I hate hiatuses as much as the next person, and I wanted to make sure that I got this story out in a timely manner, which is probably why I've been sacrificing my wrist health to get each of these out within a 6-month time frame from each other as of April 24th, 2024. As of writing this, I'm still working on the audiobooks for the series, though I suspect I should be able to get them done when I have enough time (hard to come by, these days).

However, at the end of the day, none of this would have been possible were it not for the support of close friends and family, readers who have given me vital feedback, and those who have *also* tried to tear me down for writing them. My main goal with these books was never financial gain, but instead, *inspiring* at least *one* person to write their own book or story. *Heh*, the day that happens, I'll have gotten pretty much everything I could have wanted from these books.

I know that, for the most part, authors don't usually put notes at the end of their books, but I feel like these few short pages will help to bridge the gap between author and reader, making it feel a bit more personal, a bit more *human*; something we all seem to desperately need in this day and age.

Weeeeell, I guess it's time for me to quit yapping, and guide you on to the next book *The Synner: Echoes in the Snow*. I can only hope that you'll enjoy that one as much as you have this one, and know that there will be an ample amount of faces, both new and old, in the following book (I think I'm at like *80* characters at the time of writing this. *Soooooo*, good luck!). Feel free to reach out on Instagram or some other platform (my username on most platforms is @nooburai), and I'd love to hear your thoughts on *The Synner Saga*.

Stay safe, be kind to one another, and remember that you're never alone. I love you all.

www.ingramcontent.com/pod-product-compliance
Lightning Source LLC
Chambersburg PA
CBHW032250020726
47495CB00001B/47